The Indian Chiefs of Pennsylvania

The
Indian Chiefs
of
Pennsylvania

C. Hale Sipe

SUNBURY
PRESS

Mechanicsburg, PA USA

Published by Sunbury Press, Inc.
Mechanicsburg, Pennsylvania

SUNBURY
PRESS.
www.sunburypress.com

For information about special discounts for bulk purchases, please contact Sunbury Press Orders Dept. at (855) 338-8359 or orders@sunburypress.com.

To request one of our authors for speaking engagements or book signings, please contact Sunbury Press Publicity Dept. at publicity@sunburypress.com.

FIRST SUNBURY PRESS EDITION: April 2022

Cover by Lawrence Knorr.

Publisher's Cataloging-in-Publication Data
Names: Sipe, C. Hale, author.
Title: The Indian Chiefs of Pennsylvania \ C. Hale Sipe.
Description: First trade paperback edition. | Mechanicsburg, PA : Sunbury Press, 2022.
Summary: *The Indian Chiefs of Pennsylvania* is a factual account of the indigenous history of North America's Eastern Frontier and the contributions made by many outstanding chiefs in shaping it.
Identifiers: ISBN 978-1-62006-943-1 (softcover).
Subjects: BIOGRAPHY & AUTOBIOGRAPHY / Cultural, Ethnic & Regional / Indigenous | HISTORY / United States / Colonial Period (1600-1775) | HISTORY / US History / Mid-Atlantic.

Product of the United States of America
0 1 1 2 3 5 8 13 21 34 55

Continue the Enlightenment!

To the Memory of his Sainted Mother,
from Whom he in Inherited a Love
for the History of Pennsylvania,
this Book is Reverently
Dedicated by
The Author

INTRODUCTION

By Dr. George P. Donehoo,
Former State Librarian of Pennsylvania

The early Indian history of Pennsylvania is, in many respects, of more interest and importance in the development of Anglo-Saxon civilization and settlement on the continent, than that of any other section of the United States.

The real importance of this period in the history of Pennsylvania is little realized by students of history, because it has been given but scant attention by historical writers who have dealt with the larger field of the United States.

To a very large extent, the entire Indian "problem" of the Colonies was worked out within the boundaries of Pennsylvania, or by Pennsylvanians outside of these boundaries. The Indian Councils held in New York, Maryland, Virginia, and later in Ohio, were, to a marked degree, dominated by Pennsylvania influence. The most influential Indian diplomats and chiefs, such as Canassatego, Tanacharison, Scarouady, Shikellamy and Peter Chartier, were directly connected with the policy of the Provincial Council, and the influence of such men as William Penn, Richard Peters, Conrad Weiser, George Croghan in the field of Indian Affairs, was almost unbounded. It may be safely said that the entire "Indian problem" of the Colonies, at the most critical period in American history, had to be solved by Pennsylvanians. With the exception of Sir William Johnson, of New York, all of the men who were prominent during this period were Pennsylvanians. It would be possible to carry this influence far beyond the limits of this period in the work and influence of such men as Daniel Boone, Sam Huston, George R. Clark and many others.

From the outbreak of the French and Indian War, in 1755, during the long years of Border Wars and the American Revolution, to the Treaty of Greenville, made by General Anthony Wayne, the "Indian problem" was practically in the hands of Pennsylvanians. The physical reason for this was because Pennsylvania was the Gateway to Ohio, Indiana and the West, as well as to Kentucky and the South. The Ohio river, having its headwaters in Pennsylvania, was the great trail to the Mississippi and to the French possessions in Louisiana. The vast territory through which this great stream flowed was more easily reached from Pennsylvania than from any of the other Colonies, and, notwithstanding the claims of New England historians, this great stream became the highway over which the Pennsylvania influence and not that of New England, reached to the uttermost limits of the Continent, founding new settlements and then moulding the institutions wherever it went.

A knowledge of this early Indian period in the history of Pennsylvania is essential to a right understanding of the history of Ohio, Indiana, Kentucky, Texas, as well as to a comprehensive understanding of the history of the Nation. Nearly all of the early expeditions into the Indian country beyond the Ohio, as well as nearly all of the first companies of settlers in Ohio, Indiana and far distant Texas, were made up of Pennsylvanians. The expeditions of Colonel William Crawford, General Arthur St. Clair, General George R. Clark, General Anthony Wayne and many others of lesser fame were made up chiefly, if not entirely, of Pennsylvanians.

The migration of the Lenape, or Delaware, from the Atlantic to the Susquehanna and then to the Ohio, taking with it the warlike and powerful Shawnee, had a far reaching influence in the development of civilization of the Continent. These two dominant tribes carried after them the great train of Indian traders from Pennsylvania, who roamed as far northward as Detroit and as far westward as the Mississippi. The presence of these traders in the territory claimed by France was the underlying cause of the French and Indian War, which was the first in the series of events resulting in the birth of the United States. With all of these events which were taking place, the migration of the Indians, the Indian trade, the rivalry between France and Great Britain, the building of the French forts, and then the long fight for possession of the Continent, Pennsylvania was directly related.

The period of Border Wars in Pennsylvania is one of the most thrilling and bloody chapters in American history. Pennsylvania suffered more than did any of the other Colonies during this long period stretching from 1755 to 1795. The massacre at Penn's Creek, 1755, marks its actual commencement and the Treaty at Greenville, in 1795, marks its ending. During this period of forty years, Pennsylvania was engaged in an unbroken war with the Indians, and during that time the soil of the Province and then of the State was literally drenched with blood. Years after a new Nation had been born, and after peace had come to the settlements east of the Alleghenies, the settlers on the Ohio were still fighting to hold what they possessed, and it was not until General Anthony Wayne finally conquered the Indians, that peace came to the harried frontiers of Pennsylvania.

The author of this introductory note has long been a student of this vital and romantic period of Pennsylvania history. For many years he has made the period of Indian occupation and the conflict of the Indian with the white man a special field of investigation. He feels that the work, so well done by Mr. Sipe, is a most valuable contribution to the written history of this period. When Mr. Sipe had written a part of his history of "The Indian Chiefs of Pennsylvania", he wrote to the author of this introduction saying that if its publication in book form would in any way interfere with anything which he had in mind, he would stop work. The author replied to this very gracious letter, urging Mr. Sipe to go on with his work and to publish it. After having read the entire manuscript which Mr. Sipe has prepared with infinite care, the writer is glad that he has such a worthy fellow-worker in the field of Indian history of Pennsylvania. His methods have been truly scientific and scholarly, and, as a result the book is accurate and reveals an immense amount of careful research for all of the material used.

The book is a real contribution to the vitally important and thrillingly romantic period of the history of Pennsylvania.

GEORGE P. DONEHOO.

Principal Sources Utilized in the Preparation of this Work

Archives of Pennsylvania.

Colonial Records of Pennsylvania.

Egle's History of Pennsylvania.

Gordon's History of Pennsylvania.

Day's Historical Collections.

Frontier Forts of Pennsylvania.

Pennypacker's Pennsylvania, the Keystone.

Loudon's Indian Narratives.

Rupp's County Histories.

Magazines of the Historical Society of Pennsylvania.

Egle's Notes and Queries.

Miner's History of Wyoming.

Jenkin's Pennsylvania, Colonial and Federal.

Lossing's Field Book of the Revolution.

On the Frontier with Colonel Antes.

Meginness' Otzinachson.

Linn's Annals of Buffalo Valley.

Hassler's Old Westmoreland.

Fisher's Making of Pennsylvania.

McClure's Old Time Notes.

Parkman's Works.

Jones' Juniata Valley.

Hanna's Wilderness Trail.

March's History of Pennsylvania.

Smith's History of Armstrong County.

Veech's Monongahela of Old.

McKnight's Pioneer History of Northwestern Pennsylvania.

Conover's Journal of the Military Expedition of Major-General Sullivan against the Six Nations of New York in 1779.

Craig's The Olden Time.

Darlington's Fort Pitt and Letters from the Frontier.

Darlington's Christopher Gist's Journals.

Hodge's Handbook of American Indians.

Hulbert's Historic Highways of America.

Rupp's Early History of Western Pennsylvania and the West.

Thwaites' Early Western Travels.

Thwaites' Documentary History of Lord Dunmore's War.

Walton's Conrad Weiser and the Indian Policy of Colonial Pennsylvania.

Withers' Chronicles of Border Warfare.

Craig's History of Pittsburgh.

Cort's Henry Bouquet.

Keith's Chronicles of Pennsylvania.

Boucher's History of Westmoreland County.

Albert's History of Westmoreland County.

Donehoo's Pennsylvania—A History.

DeSchweinitz's Life of David Zeisberger.

Espenshade's Pennsylvania Place Names.

Heckewelder's Works.

Mann's Life of Henry Melchior Muhlenberg.

Father Lambing's Works.

Butterfield's Washington-Irvine Correspondence.

Washington's Journal.

Celeron's Journal.

Colden's History of the Five Nations.

Volwiler's George Croghan.

Johnson's Swedish Settlements on the Delaware.

Loskiel's History of the Mission of the United Brethren Among the Indians of North America.

Patterson's History of the Backwoods.

Doddridge's Settlement and Indian Wars of Virginia and Pennsylvania.

Godcharles' Daily Stories of Pennsylvania.

Sawvel's Logan, the Mingo.

And Others.

CONTENTS

CHAPTER I

A View of the Indian Tribes Inhabiting Pennsylvania

WHEN the historic curtain first rises on the region embraced within the bounds of Pennsylvania, we find its remote and awful solitudes inhabited by a number of Indian tribes which it is the purpose of the first two chapters of this book briefly to describe. Here, along the streams and in the mountain valleys of our state, they had lived for generations lives full of romance, of love, of rivalry, of hatred, of tragedy. They roamed the hills and vales; they pursued the deer amid the forests; they paddled their bark canoes along the streams; they built their council-fires on the shore; they warred; they worshipped the Master of Life, and from their dusky bosoms went up many a pure prayer to the Great Spirit. Thus, in the vast solitudes of nature, they had lived from remote ages, never dreaming that from afar would come a stronger race which would plant amid the wilderness the hamlet and the town, and cause cities to rise where the forest waved over the Red Man's home.

Go where we may, in Pennsylvania, we are put in remembrance of the great race that roamed the hills and vales of our state. Their council-fires have long since gone out on the shores of our rivers; they themselves have gone to the "Happy Hunting Ground"; but their names will linger on the mountains and streams of Pennsylvania to the end of time.

> "Ye say they have all pass'd away,
>   That noble race and brave,—
> That their light canoes have vanish'd
>   From off the crested wave;
> That 'mid the forest where they roam'd
>   There rings no hunter's shout:
> But their name is on your waters;
>   Ye may not wash it out.

"Ye say their cone-like cabins,
That cluster'd o'er the vale,
Have disappear'd as wither'd leaves
Before the autumn gale;
But their memory liveth on your hills,
Their baptism on your shore,
Your everlasting rivers speak
Their dialect of yore."

THE DELAWARES OR LENAPE

At the dawn of the historic period of Pennsylvania, we find the basin of the Delaware River inhabited by an Indian tribe called the Delawares, or Lenape. The English called them Delawares from the fact that, upon their arrival in this region, they found the council-fires of this tribe on the banks of the Delaware River. The French called them Loups, "wolves", a term probably first applied to the Mohicans, a kindred tribe, on the Hudson River in New York. However, in their own language, they were called Lenape, or Lenni-Lenape, meaning "real men", or "original men".

The Lenape belonged to the great Algonquin family—by far the greatest Indian family in North America, measured by the extent of territory occupied. This family surrounded on all sides the Iroquoian family, of which we shall hereafter speak, and extended from Labrador westward through Canada to the Rocky Mountains and southward to South Carolina. It also extended westward through the Mississippi Valley to the Rocky Mountains. The most important tribes of this family were the Mohican, Massachuset, Miami, Sac and Fox, Ojibwa, Blackfoot, Illinois, Shawnee, and Lenape; and among the great personages of the Algonquins were King Philip, Pocahontas, Pontiac, Tecumseh, and Tamenend, the last of whom made the historic treaty with William Penn described in Chapter V.

Traditional History of the Lenape

The early traditional history of the Lenape is contained in their national legend, the Walum Olum. According to this sacred tribal history, the Lenape, in long ages past, lived in the vast region west of the Mississippi. For some reason not known, they left their western home, and, after many years of wandering eastward, reached the Namaesi Sipu, or Mississippi, where they fell in with the Mengwe, or Iroquois, who had likewise emigrated from the distant West in search of a new home, and had arrived at this river at a point somewhat higher up. The spies sent forward by the Lenape for the purpose of reconnoitering, had discovered, before the arrival of the main body, that the region east of the Mississippi was inhabited by a powerful nation called the Talligewi, or Alligewi, whose domain reached eastward to the Allegheny Mountains, which together with the beautiful Allegheny River, are named for this ancient race. The Alligewi had many large towns on the rivers of the Mississippi and Ohio valleys, and had built innumerable mounds, fortifications and intrenchments, hundreds of which still remain, and are called the works of the "Mound Builders". Says Schoolcraft: "The banks of the Allegheny were, in ancient times, occupied by an important tribe, now unknown, who preceded the Delawares and Iroquois. They were called Alleghans (Alligewi) by Colden." It is related that the Alligewi were tall and stout, and that there were giants among them.

When the Lenape arrived at the Mississippi, they sent a message to the Alligewi requesting that they be permitted to settle among them. This request was refused, but the Lenape obtained permission to pass through the territory of the Alligewi and seek a settlement farther to the eastward. They accordingly began to cross the Mississippi; but the Alligewi, seeing that their numbers were vastly greater than they had supposed, made a furious attack upon those who had crossed, and threatened the whole tribe with destruction, if they dared to persist in crossing to the eastern side of the river.

Angered by the treachery of the Alligewi and not being prepared for conflict, the Lenape consulted together as to whether they should make a trial of strength, and were convinced that the enemy were too powerful for them. Then the Mengwe, who had hitherto been spectators from a distance, offered to join the Lenape, on condition that, after conquering the Alligewi, they should be entitled to share in the fruits of the conquest.

Having united their forces, the Lenape and the Mengwe declared war against the Alligewi, and started on their onward march eastward across the continent, gradually driving out the Alligewi, who fled down the Mississippi Valley never to return. This conquest lasted many years, during which the Lenape lost great numbers of their best warriors, while the Mengwe would always lag back in the rear leaving them to bear the brunt of battle. At the end, the conquerors divided the possessions of the defeated race; the Mengwe taking the country in the vicinity of the Great Lakes and their tributary streams, and the Lenape taking the land to the south. There has been much conjecture as to who the ancient Alligewi were, some historians believing them to have been the "Mound Builders," but most modern authorities believe them to have been identical with the Cherokees.

For a long period, possibly many centuries, according to the Walum Olum, the Mengwe and Lenape resided peacefully in this country, and increased rapidly in population. Some of their hunters and warriors crossed the Allegheny Mountains, and, arriving at the streams flowing eastward, followed them to the Susquehanna River, and this stream to the ocean. Other enterprising pathfinders penetrated the wilderness to the Delaware River, and exploring still eastward, arrived at the Hudson. Some of these explorers returned to their nation and reported the discoveries they had made, describing the country as abounding in game and the streams as having an abundance of water-fowl and fish, with no enemy to be dreaded.

The Lenape considered these discoveries as fortunate for them, and believed the newly found region to be the country destined for them by the Great Spirit as their permanent abode. Consequently they began to migrate thither, settling on the four great rivers,—the Susquehanna, the Potomac, the Delaware, and the Hudson. The Walum Olum states, however, that not all of the Lenape reached the eastern part of the United States, many of them having remained behind to assist a great body of their people who had not crossed the Mississippi, but had retreated into the interior of the country on the other side, on being informed of the treacherous attack of the Alligewi upon those who had attempted to cross this stream. It is further stated that another part of the Lenape remained near the eastern bank of the Mississippi.

According to this traditional history, therefore, the Lenape nation finally became divided into three separate bodies; the part that had not crossed the Mississippi; the part that remained near the eastern bank of the Mississippi; and the part that settled on the four great eastern rivers above named.

That branch of the Delawares which settled in the eastern part of the country divided into three divisions, or clans,—the Munsee, (later corrupted to Monsey), the Unami, and the Unalachtigo. These were called the Wolf, the Turtle, and the Turkey clans respectively, from their respective animal types of totems. With these creatures which they had adopted as their symbols, they believed themselves connected by a mystic and powerful tie.

The Munsee (Wolf Clan), at the dawn of the historic period, were living in the mountain country, from about the mouth of the Lehigh River northward into New York and New Jersey, embracing the territory between the Blue or Kittatinny Mountains and the sources of the Susquehanna and Delaware rivers. A part of the tribe, also, dwelt on the Susquehanna, and still another part had a village and peach orchard near Nazareth in Northampton County, in the triangle between the Delaware and Lehigh. However, their chief village was Minisink, in Sussex County, New Jersey. The Munsee were the most warlike of the Delawares; they took a prominent part in the Indian wars of Colonial Pennsylvania. Being defrauded out of their lands by the notorious "Walking Purchase" of 1737, which obliged them to move, first to the Susquehanna and then to the Ohio, they became the bitter enemies of the white man, and drenched the frontier settlements with the blood of the pioneers. The Munsee have frequently been considered a separate tribe, inasmuch as they differed greatly from the other clans of the Lenape, and spoke a different dialect.

The Unami (Turtle Clan), "down river people", at the opening of the historic period dwelt on both sides of the Delaware from the mouth of the Lehigh to the line dividing the states of Pennsylvania and Delaware. Their chief village was Shackamaxon, which was probably the capital of the Lenape nation, and it stood on about the site of Germantown, a suburb of Philadelphia. The principal chief of the Unami was the "King" of the united Lenape nation, by immemorial custom presiding at all the councils of the tribe.

The Unalachtigo (Turkey Clan) "people living near the sea," at the opening of the historic period, occupied the land on the lower reach of the Delaware River and Delaware Bay. Their villages were on both sides of the river; and their chief village, or capital of the clan, was Chikoki, on the site of Burlington, New Jersey.

From these three clans, or tribes, comprising the great body of the Delawares, have sprung many others, who, for their own convenience, chose distant parts in which to settle. Among these were the Mahicans, or Mohicans, who by intermarriage became a detached body, and crossing the Hudson River, dwelt in eastern New York and western Connecticut; and the Nanticokes, who had proceeded to the South, and settled in Maryland and Virginia.

It is to be noted, too, that the Delawares, by reason of priority of political rank and of occupying the central home territory from which the kindred tribes had diverged, were assigned special dignity and authority. It is said that forty tribes looked up to them with respect, and that, in the great councils of the Algonquins, they took first place as "grandfathers" of the race, while others were called by them "children", "grandchildren", and "nephews". It is not certain that this precedence of the Delawares had any importance within the period of white settlement, but it no doubt had in the far dim past. And it seems true that the Algonquin tribes refrained from war with one another.

THE IROQUOIS FORM A GREAT CONFEDERATION AND SUBJUGATE THE LENAPE

It will be remembered that, when the Lenape, or Delawares, and the Mengwe, or Iroquois, divided the country of the Alligewi between them, the Mengwe took the part in the vicinity of the Great Lakes and their tributary streams, north of the part taken by the Lenape. The Mengwe later proceeded farther and settled below the Great Lakes and along the St. Lawrence River, so that when the Lenape had moved to the eastern part of the United States, the Mengwe became their northern neighbors. The Mengwe now became jealous of the growing power of the Lenape, and finally assumed dominion over them.

To the Moravian Missionary, Rev. John Heckewelder, who had lived among the Delawares for more than thirty years, they related how this dominion came about. The great chiefs of the Delawares stated to Heckewelder that the Mengwe clandestinely sought to start quarrels between the Lenape and distant tribes, hoping thus to break the might of the Lenape. Each nation had a particular mark on its war clubs, different from that of any other nation. So the Mengwe, having stolen into the Cherokee country and secretly murdered a Cherokee and left beside the victim a war club, such as the Lenape used, the Cherokees naturally concluded that the Lenape committed the murder, and fell suddenly upon them, and a long and bloody war ensued between the two nations. The treachery of the Mengwe having been at length discovered, the Lenape resolved upon the extermination of this deceitful tribe. War was declared against the Mengwe, and carried on with vigor, when the Mengwe, finding that they were no match for the powerful Lenape and their kindred tribes, resolved upon uniting their clans into a confederacy. Up until this time, each tribe of the Mengwe had acted independently of the others, and they had not been inclined to come under any supreme authority. Accordingly, about the year 1570, the Mengwe formed the great confederacy of their five kindred tribes, the Mohawks, the Oneidas, the Onondagas, the Cayugas, and the Senecas, known as the Five (later Six) Nations.

Thus the Delawares claimed that the Iroquois Confederacy was formed for the purpose of preventing the extermination of the Mengwe by the Lenape. Other authorities say that the purpose was to end inter-tribal feud and war among the Mengwe, themselves; to enable the allied tribes to make mutual offense and defense, and to advance their general welfare. Thannawage, it is claimed, was the aged Mohawk chief who first proposed the alliance. Other authorities say that Dekanawida, the Iroquois statesman, prophet and lawgiver, planned and formed the historic confederation; and that he was assisted in this work by his disciple and co-adjutor, Hiawatha, whose name has been immortalized by the poet, Longfellow, in his charming poem. It is to be noted, however, that, while in "Hiawatha", Longfellow gave the English language one of its finest poems; yet, due to his adopting the error of Schoolcraft in applying to Hiawatha the myths and legends relating to the Chippewa deity, Manabozho, this poem does not contain a single fact or fiction relating to the great chieftain of the Iroquois.

The following chiefs, also, assisted in forming the confederacy: Toganawita, representing the Onondagas; Togahayon, representing the Cayugas; and Ganiatario and Satagaruyes, representing the Senecas. This confederacy is known in history as the Five Nations, until the Tuscaroras, a tribe having been expelled from North Carolina and Virginia in 1712 or 1713, and having sought an asylum among the Iroquois of Pennsylvania and New York, were formally admitted to the alliance in 1722, after which time the confederacy is known as the Six Nations. The French gave the Indians of the confederacy the name of Iroquois, while the Delawares continued to call them Mengwe, later corrupted to Mingo. The Mohicans and the Dutch called them Maquas, while Powhatan called them Massawomekes.

But, to resume the story which the Delawares told Heckewelder. They said that, after the forming of the confederacy, very bloody wars were carried on between the Iroquois and themselves in which they were generally successful, and while these wars were in progress, the French landed in Canada and combined against the Iroquois, inasmuch as the Five Nations were not willing that these Europeans should establish themselves in that country. At last the Mengwe, or Iroquois, seeing themselves between two fires, and not seeing any prospect of conquering the Lenape by arms, resorted to a stratagem to secure dominion over them.

The plan was to persuade the Lenape to abstain from the use of arms, and to assume the station of mediators and umpires among their warlike neighbors. In the language of the Indians, the Lenape were to be made "women". As explaining the significance of this expression, the Delawares said that wars among the Indians in those days were never brought to an end, but by the interference of the weaker sex. It was not considered becoming for a warrior to ask for peace. He must fight to the end. "With these dispositions, war would never have ceased among Indians, until the extermination of one or the other party, if the tender and compassionate sex had not come forward, and by their moving speeches, persuaded the enraged combatants to bury their hatchets, and make peace. On these occasions they were very eloquent . . . They would describe the sorrows of widowed wives, and, above all, of bereaved mothers. The pangs of child-birth, they had willingly suffered. They had carefully reared their sons to manhood. Then how cruel it was to see these promising youths fall victims to the rage of war,—to see them slaughtered on the field, or burned at the stake. The thought of such scenes made them curse their own existence and shudder at the thought of bearing children." Speeches like these generally had the desired effect, and the women, by the honorable function of peace-makers, held a very dignified position. Therefore, it would be a magnanimous and honorable act for a powerful nation like the Lenape to assume that station by which they would be the means of saving the Indian race from extinction.

Such, according to Heckewelder, were the arguments used by the artful Iroquois to ensnare the Lenape. Unfortunately the Delawares listened to the voice of their enemies, and consented to become the "woman nation" among the Indians. With elaborate ceremonies, they were installed in their new function. Eloquent speeches were made, accompanied with belts of wampum. The place of the ceremony of "taking the hatchet out of the hand of the Lenape" and of placing them in the situation of "the woman" was at Nordman's Kill, about four miles south of Albany, New York.

The year of the alleged occurrence is unknown, but it is said to have been somewhere between 1609 and 1620. Both the Delawares and the Mohicans told Heckewelder that the Dutch were present at this ceremony and had no inconsiderable part in the intrigue, the Mohicans explaining that it was fear that caused the Dutch of New York to conspire with the Mengwe against the Lenape. It appears that, at the place where the Dutch were then making their settlement, great bodies of warriors would pass and repass, interrupting their undertakings; so that they thought it well to have an alliance with the Iroquois. Furthermore, the Delawares told Heckewelder that, when the English took New York from the Dutch, they stepped into the same alliance with the Iroquois that their predecessors had made.

The Iroquois denied that such an intrigue as related above ever took place. They alleged, on the other hand, that they had conquered the Lenape in battle and had thus compelled them to become "women",—to submit to the greatest humiliation a spirited and warlike nation can suffer. Many historians believe that the Delawares imposed upon the venerable Rev. Heckewelder by inventing a cunning tale in explanation of the humiliation under which they were smarting. Also, President William Henry Harrison, in his "Aborigines of the Ohio Valley", gives the story of the Delawares little credence. He says that the Delawares were too sagacious a race to fall into such a snare as they allege the Iroquois laid for them. Rev. Heckewelder, the staunch friend of the Delawares, calls attention to the fact that, while the Iroquois claim they conquered the Delawares by force of arms and not by stratagem, yet the Iroquois have no tradition among them of the particulars of the conquest.

So much for the story which the Delawares told Heckewelder. Many authorities state, however, that the time of the subjugation of the Delawares was much later than the date given Heckewelder. Some have stated that the Delawares were not made tributaries of the Iroquois until after the coming of William Penn; but the celebrated Delaware chief, King Beaver, told Conrad Weiser at Aughwick on September 4, 1754, that the subjugation took place before Penn's arrival. At the first extended conference between the Pennsylvania Authorities and the Indians, of which a record has been preserved, held at Philadelphia on July 6, 1694, the Delaware chief, Hithquoquean, or Idquoquequoan, advised the Colonial Authorities that he and his associate chiefs had shortly before this time received a message from the Onondagas and Senecas containing the following statement: "You Delaware Indians do nothing but stay at home and boil your pots, and are like women; while we Onondagas and Senecas go ahead and fight the enemy." We, therefore, conclude that it cannot be stated with exactness, just when the subjugation of the Delawares took place; and, inasmuch as there is no record of any conquest after the time of Penn's arrival, it may be that the subjugation took place through fear and intimidation rather than by war.

Whatever may be the facts as to how the Iroquois reduced the Delawares to a state of vassalage—whether by artifice, intimidation, or warfare—the fact remains that about the year 1720, this powerful northern confederacy assumed active dominion over them, forbidding them to make war or sales of lands,—a condition that existed until the time of the French and Indian War. During the summer of 1755, the Delawares declared that they were no longer subjects of the Six Nations, and, at Tioga, in the year 1756, their great chieftain, Teedyuscung, extorted from the chiefs of the Iroquois an acknowledgment of Delaware independence. However, from time to time, after 1756, the Iroquois persisted in claiming the Delawares were their vassals, until shortly before the treaty of Greenville, Darke County, Ohio, in August, 1795, when they formally declared the Delaware nation to be no longer "women", but MEN. This was the famous treaty between the United States Government, represented by General Anthony Wayne, who had defeated the western tribes at the battle of the Fallen Timbers, on August 20 of the preceding year, and the Shawnees, Delawares, Wyandots, Ottawas, Potawattomies, Miamis and smaller tribes, by the terms of which treaty about two-thirds of the present state of Ohio was ceded to the United States. As will be seen later, the subjection of the Delawares to the Six Nations greatly complicated negotiations on the part of the colony of Pennsylvania for the purchase of the lands of the Delawares, inasmuch as the Iroquois' seat of government was in the colony of New York.

WESTWARD MIGRATION OF THE DELAWARES

As early as 1724, Delawares of the Turtle and Turkey clans began, by permission of the Six Nations, to migrate from the region near the Forks of the Susquehanna to the valleys of the Allegheny and Ohio, coming chiefly from the country to the east and southeast of Shamokin (Sunbury). They proceeded up the east side of the West Branch of the Susquehanna as far as Lock

Haven, where they crossed this stream, and ascended the valley of Bald Eagle Creek to a point near where Milesburg, Center County, now stands. From there, they went in a westerly direction along Marsh Creek, over or near Indian Grave Hill, near Snowshoe and Moshanon, Center County, crossing Moshanon Creek; and from there through Morris, Graham, Bradford, and Lawrence townships, Clearfield County, reaching the West Branch of the Susquehanna again at Chinklaclamoose, on the site of the present town of Clearfield, Clearfield County. From this point, they ascended the West Branch of the Susquehanna for a few miles; thence up Anderson's Creek, crossing the divide between this stream and the Mahoning, in Brady Township, Clearfield County; thence down the Mahoning Valley through Punxsutawney, Jefferson County, to a point on the Allegheny River, about ten miles below the mouth of the Mahoning, where they built their first town in the course of their westward migration, which they called Kittanning, —a town famous in the Indian annals of Pennsylvania. Other Delaware towns were soon established in the Allegheny Valley and other places in the western part of the state to which the migration continued until the outbreak of the French and Indian War. The "Walking Purchase" of 1737 caused the westward migration of the Delawares of the Wolf clan. Thus it is seen that the Delawares retraced their steps across Pennsylvania.

DOMAIN OF THE IROQUOIS

When the historic period of Pennsylvania begins, we find the domain of the Five Nations extending from the borders of Vermont to Lake Erie, and from Lake Ontario to the headwaters of the Delaware, Susquehanna, and Allegheny. This territory they called their "long house". The Senecas, who lived on the headwaters of the Allegheny, and many of whose settlements were in Pennsylvania, guarded the western door of the house, the Mohawks, the eastern, and the Cayugas, the southern, or that which opened on the Susquehanna.

The principal village and capital of these "Romans of America", as DeWitt Clinton called them, was called Onondaga, later Onondaga Castle, and was situated from before 1654 to 1681, on Indian Hill, in the present town of Pompey, near Onondaga Lake, in central New York. In 1677 it contained 140 cabins. Afterward it was removed to Butternut Creek, where the castle was burned in 1696, in the war between the Five Nations and the

French. In 1720, it was again removed to Onondaga Creek, a few miles south of Lake Onondaga.

The Smithsonian Institution, in its "Handbook of American Indians", says the following of the Iroquois: "Around the Great Council Fire of the League of the Iroquois at Onondaga, with punctilious observance of the parliamentary proprieties recognized in Indian diplomacyand statescraft, and with a decorum that would add grace to many legislative assemblies of the white man, the federal senators of the Iroquois tribes devised plans, formulated policies, and defined principles of government and political action, which not only strengthened their state and promoted their common welfare, but also deeply affected the contemporary history of the whites in North America. To this body of half-clad federal chieftains were repeatedly made overtures of peace and friendship by two of the most powerful kingdoms of Europe, whose statesmen often awaited with apprehension the decisions of this senate of North American Savages." And Colden in his "History of the Five Nations", says: "The Five Nations are a poor and, generally called barbarious people; and yet a bright and noble genius shines through these black clouds. None of the greatest Roman heroes discovered a greater love to their country, or a greater contempt of death, than these people called barbarians have done, when liberty came in competition . . . . They carried their arms as far southward as Carolina, to the northward of New England, and as far west as the River Mississippi, over a vast country, which extends twelve hundred miles in length, and about six hundred miles in breadth; where they entirely destroyed many nations, of whom there are now no accounts remaining among the English."

So great was the scourge of the Iroquois that, during the closing decades of the seventeenth century and the first two decades of the eighteenth century, the region south of Lake Erie on both sides of the upper Ohio and Allegheny contained practically no Indian population; and the Iroquois looked upon this vast territory as their great hunting ground.

Speaking of the warfare of the Iroquois, DeWitt Clinton said:

"They reduced war to a science, and all their movements were directed by system and policy. They never attacked a hostile country until they had sent out spies to explore and designate its vulnerable points, and when they encamped, they observed the greatest circumspection to guard against spies. Whatever superiority of force they might have, they never neglected the use of stratagem, employing all the crafty wiles of the Carthagenians."

The unwritten law of this great confederation had a power unequaled by any statutes ever recorded in the statute books of the white man. Professor W. W. Clayton, in his excellent work, "The History of Onondaga County, New York," in which county the central seat of the Five Nations was located, gives an instance of the power of this unwritten law. Says Professor Clayton:

"A young man of the Cayugas came to the Onondagas and claimed their hospitality. He lived among them two years, attaching himself to a Mr. Webster who lived for many years among the Onondagas and had a woman of that tribe for a wife. He appeared contented and happy, always foremost in the chase, most active in the dance, and loudest in the song. Mantinoah was his name. One morning he said to his friend, 'I have a vow to perform. My nation and my friends know that Mantinoah will be true. My friend, I wish you to go with me.' Webster consented. After a pleasant journey of a few days, enlivened with fishing and hunting, they came in the afternoon to a place that Mantinoah said was near his village, and where he wished to invoke the Great Spirit. After a repast and after a pipe had been smoked, Mantinoah said: 'Two winters have gone since, in my village, in the fury of anger, I slew my bosom friend and adopted brother. The chief declared me guilty of my brother's blood, and I must die. My execution was deferred for two full years, during which time I was condemned to banishment. I vowed to return. It was then I sought your nation (the Onondagas); it was thus I won your friendship; the nearest in blood to him I slew, according to our customs, is the avenger. The time expires when the sun sinks behind the topmost boughs of the trees. I am ready. My friend, we have had may a cheerful sport together; our joys have been many; our griefs have been few; look not sad now. When you return to the Onondagas, tell them that Mantinoah died like a true brave of the Cayugas; tell them that he trembled not at the approach of death, like the coward pale face, nor shed tears like a woman. My friend, take my belt, my knife, my hunting pouch, my horn, my rifle, as tokens of my friendship. Soon the avenger will come; the Great Spirit calls; Mantinoah fears not death; farewell. Vainly Mr. Webster urged him to escape. A short period of silence, and a yell is heard. Mantinoah responds. The avenger appears and takes the hand of his former friend, now his victim. Mutual salutations follow, with expressions of regret made by the executioner, but none by the doomed. The tomahawk gleams in the air, not a muscle moves nor does the cheek of

Mantinoah blanch; folding his arms on his breast he received the blow. As if by magic, a host appears; the song of death is sung, and the solemn dance or death march is performed. Webster is invited to the village, where he is hospitably entertained, and when ready to return, is accompanied by a party of Cayugas to his home. Thus powerful was the unwritten law of the Iroquois."

The government of the Iroquois gave to the orator, who by his eloquence could sway his hearers, a vast influence; and we find that many men of note appeared among them since they came in contact with the whites, who were well qualified to conduct their negotiations and reflected as much renown on their nation as their bravest warriors. DeWitt Clinton says of the speech of the great Iroquois chief, Garangula, to the French General, De la Barre: "I believe it impossible to find in all the affusions of English or modern oratory a speech more appropriate or convincing. Under the veil of respectful profession, it conveys the most biting irony, and while it abounds with rich and splendid imagery, it contains the most solid reasoning. I place it in the same rank with the celebrated speech of Logan."

In concluding this sketch of the Iroquois Confederation, we add that, for many years after the historic curtain first rises on the domain of Pennsylvania, the Iroquois carried on a relentless warfare with the Catawbas of the South. The Susquehanna River was the highway followed by their war parties on their way to and return from the territory of the Catawbas.

CHAPTER II

A View of the Indian Tribes Inhabiting Pennsylvania

(Continued)

THE SUSQUEHANNAS, MINQUAS, OR CONESTOGAS

HE Susquehannas is the general term applied to the Indians living on both sides of the Susquehanna River and its tributaries, in Pennsylvania, at the beginning of the historic period. Racially and linguistically, they were of Iroquoian stock, but were never taken into the league of the Iroquois, except as subjects. These related tribes were known by various names. Captain John Smith, the Virginia pioneer, who met them while exploring Chesapeake Bay and its tributaries in 1608, called them the "Susquehannocks." The French called them the Andastes, while the Dutch and Swedes called them Minquas. In the latter days of their history as a tribe, they were called the Conestogas.

To Captain John Smith belongs the distinction of being the first white man to see the Indians of Pennsylvania, though he never set foot on Pennsylvania soil; and the Indians, meeting him and his companions, beheld for the first time the race that was coming to drive them from their streams and hunting grounds. These Indians were the Susquehannas. Smith's meeting with them came about in the following manner:

On the 24th day of July, 1608, Smith left Jamestown, Virginia, on a voyage of discovery. He sailed in an open barge of only several tons burden, and had with him only twelve companions. His party entered Chesapeake Bay and the Susquehanna River almost to the Pennsylvania line, returning to Jamestown on the 7th day of September. He states that, in crossing the bay, his party encountered seven or eight canoes full of Iroquois, whom he called Massawomeks, and that, after a parley, they presented the Virginians with venison, bears' flesh, and some bows and arrows, and informed them that they had just been at war with the Tockwoghs, who lived nearby. They exhibited "greene wounds", which they explained to Smith they had received in battle with the Tockwoghs. They left Smith's party in the evening, promising to return in the morning, but never reappeared.

Smith then determined to visit the Tockwoghs, which he did, finding them living near the head of the bay, on the Tockwogh or Sassafras River, in Maryland. He says that he found the Tockwoghs possessed of many hatchets, knives and pieces of brass, which, they explained, they had received from the Susquehannas, a mighty people living farther to the north on the Susquehanna River, and mortal enemies of the Massawomeks, or Iroquois. Smith prevailed with his interpreter to take with him another interpreter from the Tockwoghs, to visit the towns of the Susquehannas, and to persuade them to pay Smith's party a visit. The two interpreters then conveyed Smith's invitation to the Susquehannas, finding their chiefs in one of their principal towns, in what is now Lancaster County, Pennsylvania.

Smith's party remained with the friendly Tockwoghs on the shores of the Sassafras for three or four days, awaiting the return of the two messengers, whom he had sent to the Susquehannas. At the end of that time, in response to Smith's invitation, sixty of the Susquehannas came, and presented themselves before his party. Smith gives the following interesting description of these Indians:

"Such great and well proportioned men are seldom seen, for they seemed like giants to the English, yea, and to their neighbors, yet seemed of an honest and simple disposition. They were with much ado restrained from adoring us as gods. These are the strangest people of all these countries, both in language and attire; for their language it may well become their proportions, sounding from them as a voice in the vault. Their attire is the skins of bears and wolves; some have cossacks made of bears' heads and skins, that a man's head goes through the skin's neck, and the ears of the bear fastened to his shoulders, the nose and teeth hanging down his breast, another bear's face split behind him, and at the end of the nose hung a paw, the half sleeves coming to the elbows were the necks of bears, and the arms through the mouth with paws hanging at their noses. One had the head of a wolfe hanging in a chain for a jewel, his tobacco pipe three quarters of a yard long, prettily carved with a bird, a deer, or some such device at the great end, sufficient to beat out one's brans; with bows, arrows, and clubs, suitable to their greatness. Five of their chief Werowances came aboard us and crossed the bay in the barge. The picture of

the greatest of them is signified in the map. The calf of whose leg
was three-quarters of a yard about, and all the rest of his limbs so
answerable to that proportion that he seemed the goodliest man we
ever beheld. His hair, the one side was long, the other shorn close
with a ridge over his crown like a cock's comb. His arrows were
five quarters long, headed with the splinters of a white christall-
like stone, in form of a heart, an inch broad, an inch and a half
or more long. These he wore in a wolf's skin at his back for his
quiver, his bow in the one hand and his club in the other, as is
described."

Smith goes on to say that these Susquehannas were scarce
known to Powhatan, the great Virginia chief, but that they were a
powerful tribe living in palisaded towns to defend them from the
Massawomeks, or Iroquois, and having six hundred warriors.
During the ceremonies connected with the visit of this band of
Susquehannas, Smith says that they first sang "a most fearful
song," and then, "with a most strange, furious action and a hellish
voice began an oration." When the oration was ended, they decorated Smith with a chain of large white beads, and laid presents
of skins and arrows at his feet, meanwhile stroking their hands
about his neck. They told him about their enemies, the Iroquois,
who, they said, lived beyond the mountains far to the north and
received their hatchets and other weapons from the French in
Canada. They implored Smith to remain with them as their
protector, which, of course, he could not do. "We left them at
Tockwogh," he says, "sorrowing for our departure."

Smith's account of the large stature of the Susquehannas has
been corroborated by subsequent discoveries, when burying
grounds of this tribe, in Lancaster County, were opened and very
large human skeletons found.

The Susquehannas, in the latter part of the seventeenth century, carried on war with the "River Indians", as the Delawares,
or Lenape then living along the Delaware River, were called. The
Susquehannas were friendly with both the Swedes and the Dutch,
and shortly after the Swedes arrived on the Delaware in 1638, they
sold part of their lands to them. The Swedes equipped these
Indians with guns, and trained their warriors in European tactics.
When the Hurons were being worsted by the Iroquois in 1647, the
Susquehannas offered the friendly Hurons military assistance,
"backed by 1300 warriors in a single palisaded town, who had been
trained by Swedish soldiers." They were also friendly with the
colony of Maryland in the early days of its history, selling part of

their lands to the Marylanders, and receiving military supplies from them.

The French explorer, Champlain, says that, in 1615, the Carantouannais, as he calls the Susquehannas, had many villages on the upper part of the Susquehanna, and that their town, Carantouan, alone, could muster more than eight hundred warriors. The exact location of Carantouan has been a matter of much conjecture, but the weight of authority places it on or near the top of Spanish Hill, in Athens Township, Bradford County, Pennsylvania, and within sight of the town of Waverly, New York.

Carantouan has a firm place in the history of Pennsylvania on account of its connection with the Frenchman, Estienne Brule, the first white man, so far as is known, to set foot on Pennsylvania soil, and to behold its Indians on their native heath. The student of history will recall that, in 1615, the French explorer, Champlain, in order to learn more about the region embraced in what is now New York State, joined a war party of Hurons against the Iroquois; and, in August of that year, he and the Hurons proposed to attack a strong town of the Onondaga tribe of the Five Nations, located most likely near the town of Fenner, in Madison County, not far from Lake Oneida, New York. When Champlain was at the village of Cahiague, near the lower end of Lake Simcoe, making preparations for his advance against the Iroquois town, he learned from the Hurons that there was a certain nation of their allies dwelling three days journey beyond the Onondagas; who desired to assist the Hurons in this expedition with five hundred of their warriors. These allies were none other than that portion of the Susquehannas, living along the Susquehanna River, near the boundary between the states of Pennsylvania and New York. Accordingly, Champlain sent his interpreter, Estienne Brule, with twelve Huron companions, to visit Carantouan, the chief town of the Susquehannas in that region, for the purpose of hastening the coming of the five hundred warriors.

Brule and his five hundred allies from Carantouan arrived before the Onondaga fortress too late to be of any assistance to Champlain, who had already made two attacks upon the town, had been wounded twice by the Onondagas, and, despairing of the arrival of the promised assistance of five hundred warriors, had already retreated toward Canada several days before the arrival of Brule and his Indians. Brule then returned with his five hundred warriors to the town of Carantouan.

Brule spent the autumn and winter of 1615 and 1616 in a

tour of exploration into the very heart of Pennsylvania, visiting
the various clans of the Susquehannas and, some authorities say,
the Eries.   He followed the Susquehanna River to its mouth, and
returned to Carantouan.   This intrepid Frenchman thus gained,
by actual observation, a knowledge of a large section of the state
and of its primitive inhabitants almost one hundred years before
any other white man set foot within the same region.

Another town of the Susquehannas was the one, later called
Gahontoto, at the mouth of Wyalusing Creek, Bradford County.
The Moravian missionaries, Bishop Commerhoff and David Zeis-
berger, visited the site of this town in the summer of 1750.   Says
Bishop Cammerhoff:

"On proceeding, we came to a place called Gahontoto by the
Indians.   It is said to be the site of an ancient Indian city, where
a peculiar nation lived.   The inhabitants were neither Delawares
nor Aquanoschioni, (Iroquois) but had a language of their own,
and were called Te-ho-ti-tach-se.   We could still notice a few
traces of this place in the old ruined corn-fields near.   The Five
Nations went to war against them, and finally completely extir-
pated them.   The Cayugas for a time held a number captive, but
the nation and the language are now exterminated and extinct.
The Cayuga told us that these things had taken place before the
Indians had any guns, and still went to war with bows and arrows."

Another of the towns of the Susquehannas is believed to have
been at the mouth of Sugar Creek, in Bradford County, above the
present town of Towanda.   Still another of their towns, this one
fortified, was near the mouth of Octorara Creek, on the east side of
the Susquehanna River, in Maryland, about ten miles south of the
line between Pennsylvania and Maryland.   One of their forts was
in Manor Township, Lancaster County, near the Susquehanna
River, between Turkey Hill and Blue Rock.   Another was on
Wolf Run, near Muncy, Lycoming County.   The location of their
principal fort was long a matter of dispute, and, at one time,
actual warfare, between the heirs of Lord Baltimore and the heirs
of William Penn, for the reason that the southern boundary of
Penn's colony was supposed to be marked by it.   The weight of
authority seems to place its location on the west side of the Susquehanna River, in York County, Pennsylvania, opposite Washington
Borough.

The Iroquois, the mortal enemies of the Susquehannas,
attacked them at one of their principal towns, in either York or
Lancaster County, Pennsylvania, in 1663, sending down the Sus-

quehanna River, in April of that year, an expedition of eight hundred Onondagas, Cayugas, and Senacas. On their arrival, they found the town defended on one side by the river and on the other by tree trunks; it was flanked by two bastions, constructed after the European method, and had also several pieces of artillery. The Iroquois decided not to make an assault, but to attempt to outwit the Susquehannas by a ruse. Twenty-five Iroquois were admitted into the fort, but these were seized, placed on high scaffolds, and burned to death in sight of their comrades. The humiliated Iroquois now returned to their home in New York.

After this defeat of the Iroquois, the war was carried on by small parties, and now and then a Susquehanna was captured and carried to the villages of the Iroquois, and tortured to death. In 1669, the Susquehannas defeated the Cayugas, and offered peace; but their ambassador was put to death, and the war went on. At this time, the Susquehannas had a great chief named Hochitqgete, or Barefoot; and the medicine men of the Iroquois assured the warriors of the confederacy that, if they would make another attack on the Susquehannas, their efforts would be rewarded by the capture of Barefoot and his execution at the stake. So, in the summer of 1672, a band of forty Cayugas descended the Susquehanna in canoes, and twenty Senecas marched overland to attack the enemy in the fields; but a band of sixty Susquehanna boys, none over sixteen, routed the Senecas, killing one and capturing another. The band of youthful warriors then pressed on against the Cayugas, and defeated them, killing eight and wounding fifteen or sixteen more, but losing half of their own gallant band. At this time, it is said, the Susquehannas were so reduced by war and pestilence that their fighting force consisted of only three hundred warriors.

Finally in 1675, according to the Jesuit Relation and Colden in his "History of the Five Nations", the Susquehannas fell before the arms of the Iroquois; but the details of the defeat are sadly lacking. It seems that the Iroquois, about this time, had driven them down upon the tribes of the South who were then allies of the English, and that this involved them in war with Maryland and Virginia. Finding themselves surrounded by enemies on all sides, a portion of the Susquehannas left the land of their forefathers and the beautiful river bearing their name, and took up their abode in the western part of Maryland, near the Piscataways.

In the summer of 1675, a white man was murdered by some Indians, most probably Senecas, on the Virginia side of the Potomac; whereupon, a party of Virginia militia killed fourteen of the Susquehannocks and Doeg Indians in retaliation.   Shortly afterwards several other whites were murdered on both sides of the Potomac.   The colony of Virginia then organized several companies, led by Colonel John Washington, great-grandfather of George Washington, to co-operate with a Maryland force of two hundred and fifty troops, led by Major Thomas Truman.   The Susquehannocks claimed that they were entirely innocent of any of these murders and sent four of their chiefs as an embassy to Major Truman, who were knocked on the head by his soldiers.   This so enraged the Susquehannocks that a long border warfare ensued which was kept up until they became lost to history.

Another portion of the Susquehannocks remained near their old home at Conestoga, Lancaster County, where they were later joined by a third portion which had been taken by the Iroquois to the Oneida country in New York, and there retained until they lost their language, when they were permitted to join their brethren at Conestoga.   Here William Penn and his son, William, visited the Conestogas during his last stay in his province in 1701.   Here, also, the Conestogas lived until the descendants of this remnant of a once powerful tribe were killed in December, 1763, by a band of Scotch-Irish settlers from Donegal and Paxtang,—the last melancholy chapter in the history of the Susquehannas, or Conestogas. Conestoga, for generations the central seat of this tribe in the lower Susquehanna region, was about four miles southwest of Millersville, Lancaster County.   A monument marks the site of this historic Indian town.   It was erected in 1924 by the Lancaster County Historical Society and the Pennsylvania Historical Commission.

THE SHAWNEES

The Shawnees, too, occupied parts of Pennsylvania during the historic period. The name means "Southerners". They were a branch of the Algonquin family, and are believed to have lived in the Ohio Valley in remote ages, and to have built many of the mounds and earthworks found there. Some have attempted to identify them with the Eries of the early Jesuits, the Massawomecks of Smith, and the Andaste, but without success. The traditional history of the Lenape, the Walum Olum, connects them, the Lenape, and Nanticokes as one people, the separation having taken place after the Alligewi, (Cherokees) were driven from the Ohio Valley by the Lenape and the Mengwe (Iroquois) on their onward march eastward across the continent.   Then the Shaw-

nees went south. Their real history begins in 1669-70, when they
were living in two bodies a great distance apart,—one body being
in South Carolina and the other in the Cumberland basin in Tennessee. Between these two bodies were the then friendly Cherokees, who claimed the land vacated by the Shawnees when the
latter subsequently migrated to the North. The Shawnees living
in South Carolina were called Savannahs by the early settlers.

On account, probably, of dissatisfaction with the early settlers,
the Shawnees of South Carolina began a general movement to the
north in 1690, and continued it at intervals for thirty years. The
first reference to this tribe to be found in the Provincial records of
Pennsylvania is probably a deposition made before the Provincial
Council, December 19, 1693, by Polycarpus Rose. In this deposition there is a reference to "strange Indians" called "Shallna-
rooners". These strange Indians appear to have made a temporary stop in Chester County in migrating possibly from Maryland
to the Forks of the Delaware or to Pequea Creek. Many authorities believe these "strange Indians" mentioned in the affidavit of
Polycarpus Rose to have been Shawnees. This is conjecture.

But, leaving the realm of conjecture and entering the realm
of historical truth, we find that the first Shawnees to enter Pennsylvania were a party who settled on the Delaware at Pechoquealin
near the Water Gap, in the summer of 1694, or shortly thereafter.
These came from the Shawnee villages on the lower Ohio. Arnold
Viele, a Dutch trader, from Albany, New York, spent the winter
of 1692-1693 with the Shawnees on the lower Ohio, returning in
the summer of 1694, and bringing with him a number of this tribe
who settled at Pechoquealin. Pechoquealin was a regional name
whose center seems to have been the mouth of Shawnee Run in
Lower Smithfield Township, Monroe County, and which included
the surrounding territory on both sides of the Delaware, above the
Delaware Water Gap. Viele was probably the first white man to
explore the region between the valleys of the Susquehanna and the
Ohio.

About four years later, or in 1697 or 1698, about seventy
families of Shawnees came from Cecil County, Maryland, and
settled on the Susquehanna River, near the Conestoga Indians, in
Lancaster County. Probably at about the same time others
migrated to the Ohio Valley. At the mouth of Pequea Creek,
Lancaster County, the seventy families come from Maryland, built
their village, also called Pequea. Their chief was Wapatha, or
Opessah. They secured permission from the Colonial Govern-

ment to reside near the Conestogas, and the latter became security for their good behavior, under the authority of the Iroquois Confederation. By invitation of the Delawares, a party of seven hundred Shawnees came soon after and settled with the Munsee Clan on the Delaware River, the main body taking up their abode at the mouth of the Lehigh, near Easton, while others went as far south as the mouth of the Schuylkill. Those who had settled on the Delaware afterwards removed to the Wyoming Valley near the present town of Plymouth, Luzerne County, on a broad plain still called Shawnee Flats. This band under Kakowatcheky removed from Pechoquealin to the Wyoming Valley in 1728; and it is probable that they were joined there by those who had settled at Pequea, which was abandoned about 1730.

The Shawnees also had a village on the flats at the mouth of Fishing Creek, near Bloomsburg, and another at Catawissa,—both being in Columbia County. They had other villages in the eastern part of the state on the Swatara, Paxtang, Susquehanna, and Delaware. Several villages were scattered along the west side of the Susquehanna, between the mouth of Yellow Breeches Creek and the Conodoguinet, in Cumberland County. Another of their villages, called Chenastry, was at the mouth of Chillisquaque Creek on the east side of the West Branch of the Susquehanna, in Northumberland County.

The Shawnees from Tennessee migrated to the Ohio Valley, finally collecting along the north bank of the Ohio in Pennsylvania as far north as the mouth of the Monongahela, about the year 1730. Sauconk and Logstown were villages on the Ohio which they established possibly as early as that time. The former was at the mouth of the Beaver, and the latter on the north bank of the Ohio, about eighteen miles below Pittsburgh.

Another clan of Shawnees, called the Sewickleys, Asswikales, Shaweygila, and Hathawekela, came from South Carolina prior to 1730 by way of Old Town, Maryland and Bedford, Pa., and settled in different parts of Southwestern Pennsylvania. Their principal village called Sewickley Town was at the junction of this creek and the Youghiogheny River, in Westmoreland County. They were probably the first Shawnees to settle in Western Pennsylvania.

The Shawnees of the eastern part of Pennsylvania eventually went to the Ohio and Allegheny Valleys. In the report of the Albany congress of 1754, it is found that some of the tribe had moved from the eastern part of the state to the Ohio about thirty years previously; and, in 1734, another Shawnee band consisting of about forty families and described as living on the Allegheny, refused to return to the Susquehanna at the solicitation of the Delawares and Iroquois. During their westward migration, they established villages on the Juniata and Conemaugh. About the year 1755 or 1756, practically all the Shawnees abandoned the Susquehanna and other parts of eastern Pennsylvania, and joined their brethren on the Ohio, where they became allies of the French in the French and Indian War. It should be remembered that, in the early records, the term "Ohio Valley" means both the Ohio and Allegheny valleys. In those times, the present Allegheny River was considered as simply a continuation of the Ohio River.

Wanderings of the Shawnees

There is something mysterious in the wanderings of the Shawnees. As we have seen, their home, in remote times, was in the Ohio Valley; then we later hear of them in the South; and still later they came to Pennsylvania. There is good evidence, however, tending to show that that body of the Shawnees which entered Lancaster County, Pennsylvania, in 1697 or 1698, came originally from as far west as the region of Fort St. Louis, near the town of Utica, LaSalle County, Illinois, leaving that place in 1683 and being accompanied in their wanderings to Maryland by Martin Chartier, a French Canadian, who had spent some eight or nine years among them. At any rate, this band reached Maryland near the mouth of the Susquehanna in 1692, and such is the story they told. They gradually moved up the Susquehanna to Lancaster County, as we have seen, where Chartier became a trader at their village of Pequea, on the east side of the Susquehanna near the mouth of Pequea Creek, and only a few miles from Conestoga, which was on the north side of Conestoga Creek.

The Shawnees who settled at Paxtang, on or near the site of Harrisburg, most likely came from Pequea. Before 1727, many of this tribe from Paxtang and Pequea had settled on the west side of the Susquehanna River at what is now New Cumberland, near the the mouth of Yellow Breeches Creek and as far north as the mouth of the Conodoguinet. These dwellers on the west side of the Susquehanna, about the year 1727, crossed the mountains to the valleys of the Ohio and Allegheny. Some, however, had gone to Big Island (Lock Haven) before going to the Ohio region.

Opessah, the chief of the Shawnees on the lower Susquehanna, did not remove to the Ohio or Allegheny Valley. He remained at Pequea until 1711, when he abandoned both his chieftainship and his tribe, and sought a home among the Delawares of Sassoonan's clan. It is not clear why he abandoned his people. There is a traditionary account that he left because he became enamoured of a Delaware squaw, who refused to leave her own people. Later, in 1722, he removed to what was called Opessah's town on the Potomac, now Old Town, Maryland.

Neither the Pennsylvania Archives nor the Colonial Records show the name of the chief of those Shawnees who settled at Pechoquealin until 1728, when their head man was Kakowatchey. Some of Kakowatchey's clan removed directly to the Ohio before 1732, but a majority seem to have gone only as far as the Wyoming Valley in Luzerne County, where, as we have seen, they took up their abode on the west side of the North Branch of the Susquehanna at a place subsequently known as Shawnee Flats, just below the site of the present town of Plymouth. Their town at this place was called Skehandowana (Iroquois for "Great Flats"), and it remained a town of considerable importance until 1743. Some time after April of that year, Kakowatchey himself, with a number of his followers removed from Skehandowana and settled at Logstown on the Ohio.

After Kakowatchey left Wyoming, Paxinosa became chief of the Shawnees who still remained at that place. He said that he was born "at Ohio", and possibly he was one of the company of Shawnees who accompanied Arnold Viele to the Pechoquealin territory.

A number of the Shawnees at Chenastry, on the West Branch of the Susquehanna, near the mouth of Chillisquaque Creek, went to the valleys of the Ohio and Allegheny prior to the autumn of 1727 to hunt, and no doubt some of them made their permanent homes or took up their abode in this western region, during or prior to the summer of 1727.

But some of the Shawnees went directly from Maryland to the Ohio and Allegheny. Two chiefs of the Potomac Shawnees, Opaketchwa and Opakeita, by name, came from the Ohio Valley to Philadelphia in September, 1732, after they had abandoned their town on the north branch of the Potomac. Governor Gordon asked them why they had gone "so far back into the woods as Allegheny", and they replied that "formerly they had lived at 'Patawmack' [Potomac], where their king died; that, having lost him, they knew not what to do; that they then took their wives and children and went over the mountains (to Allegheny) to live."

THE TUSCARORAS

Another Indian tribe inhabiting portions of Pennsylvania within the historic period was the Tuscaroras. They were of the Iroquoian linguistic group. It will be recalled that this tribe, after being expelled from North Carolina and Virginia, sought an asylum with the Five Nations, and was later, in 1722, admitted formally as an addition to the Iroquois Confederacy, making the Six Nations. The Tuscaroras had suffered greatly in wars with the people of North Carolina and Virginia, before they were expelled in 1712. Their women were debauched by the whites, and both men and women were kidnapped and sold into slavery. Some were brought as far north as Pennsylvania, and sold as slaves. Moreover, the colonists of North Carolina, like the Puritans of New England, did not recognize in the Indian any right to the soil; and so the lands of the Tuscaroras were appropriated without any thought of purchase. They had suffered these and similar wrongs for many years, and, as early as 1710, sent a petition to the Government of Pennsylvania reciting their wrongs and stating that they desired to remove to a more just and friendly government. Governor Charles Gookin and the Provincial Council of Pennsylvania dispatched two commissioners to meet the embassy which brought the petition, at Conestoga, Lancaster County, on June 8, 1710, where they found not only the Tuscarora embassy, but Civility and four other Conestoga chiefs, as well as Opessah, head chief of the Shawnees.

In the presence of these officials, the Tuscarora ambassadors delivered their proposals, which were attested by eight belts of wampum. This petition was a very lucid and condensed statement of the wrongs suffered by the Tuscaroras in their southern home. By the first belt, the aged women and mothers of the tribe besought the friendship of the Christian people and the Indians and Government of Pennsylvania, so that they might bring wood and water without danger. By the second, the children, born and unborn, implored that they might be permitted to play without danger of slavery. By the third, the young men sought the privilege of leaving their towns to pursue the game in the forest for the sustenance of the aged, without fear of death or slavery. By the fourth, the old men sought the privilege of spending their declining days in peace. By the fifth, the entire Tuscarora nation sought a firm and lasting peace with all the blessings attached thereto. By the sixth, the chiefs and sachems sought the establishment of lasting peace with the Government and Indians of Pennsylvania, so that they would be relieved from "those fearful apprehensions which they have these several years felt." By the seventh, the Tuscaroras implored a "cessation from murdering and taking them", so that they might not be in terror upon every rustling of the leaves of the forest by the winds. By the eighth, the entire Tuscarora tribe, being hitherto strangers to the colony of Pennsylvania, implored that the sons of "Brother Onas" might take them by the hand and lead them, so that they might lift up their heads in the wilderness without fear of slavery or death.

This petition, it is seen, was couched in the metaphorical language of the Indian; but its plain meaning proves it to be a statement of a tribe at bay, who, on account of the large numbers of their people killed, kidnapped, or sold into slavery by the settlers of North Carolina, were endeavoring to defend their offspring, friends, and kindred, and were seeking a more friendly dwelling place in the North, within the domain of the just government of Penn, the apostle.

The Provincial Council of Pennsylvania advised the Tuscarora ambassadors that, before they could consent to the Tuscaroras taking up their abode within the bounds of Penn's Province, they should first be required to produce a certificate from the colonial authorities of North Carolina as to their good behavior in that colony. This, of course, the Tuscaroras were unable to do. Then, the Conestoga chiefs, by the advice of their council, determined to send the wampum belts, or petition, of the Tuscaroras to the Five Nations of New York. This was done, and it was the reception of these belts, setting forth the pitiful message of the Tuscaroras, that moved the Five Nations to take steps to shield and protect the Tuscaroras, and eventually receive them, in 1722, as an additional member of the Iroquois Confederation.

In their migration northward, the Tuscaroras did not all leave their ancient southern homes at once. Some sought an asylum among other southern tribes, and lost their identity. However, the major portion came north, and many of them resided for a number of years in Pennsylvania, before going to New York, the seat of the Five Nations. In fact, the Tuscaroras were ninety years in making their exodus from their North Carolina home to more friendly dwelling places in the North.

One body of the Tuscaroras, on their way north, tarried in the Juniata Valley in Juniata County, Pennsylvania, for many years, giving their name to the Tuscarora Mountain. There is evidence of their having been there as late as 1755. Another band settled about two miles west of Tamaqua, in Schuylkill County, where they planted an orchard and lived for a number of years. Also, in May, 1766, a band of Tuscaroras halted at the Moravian mission at Friedensheutten, on the Susquehanna in Wyoming County, and remained there several weeks. Some remained at the mission, and these had planted their crops in 1766, at the mouth of Tuscarora Creek, Wyoming County.

In a word, the residence places of the Tuscaroras in Pennsylvania during their migration to New York, were those localities where their name has been preserved ever since, such as: Tuscarora Mountain dividing Franklin and Perry counties from Huntingdon and Juniata; Tuscarora Path Valley (now Path Valley) in the western part of Franklin County at the eastern base of Tuscarora Mountain; Tuscarora Creek running through the valley between Tuscarora and Shade mountains, which valley forms the greater part of Juniata County; and also the stream called Tuscarora Creek running down through the southeastern part of Bradford County and joining the North Branch of the Susquehanna in the northwestern part of Wyoming County. The Tuscarora Path marks the route followed by the Tuscaroras during their migration to New York and of their subsequent journeyings to and fro between New York and Pennsylvania on the north and Virginia and North Carolina on the south.

THE CONOY, GANAWESE, OR PISCATAWAY

The Conoy, also called the Ganawese and the Piscataway, inhabited parts of Pennsylvania during the historic period. They were an Algonquin tribe, closely related to the Delawares, whom they called "grandfathers", and from whose ancestral stem they no doubt sprang. Heckewelder, an authority on the history of the Delawares and kindred tribes, believed them to be identical with the Kanawha, for whom the chief river of West Virginia is named; and it seems that the names, Conoy and Ganawese, are simply different forms of the name Kanawha, though it is difficult to explain the application of the same name to the Piscataway tribe of Maryland, except on the theory that this tribe once lived on the Kanawha.

As stated formerly, the Conestogas, when defeated by the Iroquois in 1675, invaded the territory of the Piscataways in western Maryland. This, it is believed, caused the northward migra-

tion of the Piscataways. At any rate, they shortly thereafter retired slowly up the Potomac, some entering Pennsylvania about
1698 or 1699, and the rest a few years later. The Iroquois assigned them lands at Conejoholo, also called Connejaghera and Dekanoagah, on the east side of the Susquehanna at the present town of
Washington Borough, Lancaster County. Later they removed
higher up the Susquehanna to what was called Conoy Town, at the
mouth of Conoy Creek, in Lancaster County. Still later they
gradually made their way up the Susquehanna, stopping at Harrisburg, Shamokin (Sunbury), Catawissa, and Wyoming; and in
1765, were living in southern New York. After their arrival in
Pennsylvania, they were generally called Conoy. During their
residence in Pennsylvania, their villages, especially those on the
the lower Susquehanna, were stopping places for war parties of the
Iroquois on their way to and return from attacks upon the
Catawbas in the South; and this fact made considerable trouble for
the Colonial Authorities as well as the Conoy.

THE NANTICOKES

The Nanticokes, also, dwelt within the bounds of Pennsylvania during the historic period. These were an Algonquin tribe,
formerly living on the Nanticoke River on the eastern shore of
Maryland, where Captain John Smith, in 1608, located their principal village called Nanticoke. They were of the same parent
stem as the Delawares. The tenth verse of the fifth song of the
Walum Olum, the sacred tribal history of the Lenape, contains the
statement that "the Nanticokes and the Shawnees went to the
Southlands." It is not clear, however, where the separation of the
Nanticokes from the Lenape took place, but Heckewelder states
that they separated from the Lenape after these had reached the
eastern part of the United States, and that the Nanticokes then
went southward in search of hunting and trapping grounds, they
being great hunters and trappers.

A short time after the settlement of Maryland, they had difficulties with the settlers of that colony. They were formally declared enemies in 1642, and the strife was not ended until a treaty
entered into in 1678. A renewal of hostilities was threatened in
1687, but happily prevented, and peace was once more reaffirmed.
In 1698, and from that time forward as long as they remained
within the bounds of Lord Baltimore's colony, reservations were
set aside for them. At this early day they began a gradual migra-

tion northward, though a small part remained in Maryland. The migration to the North covered many years. On their way they stopped for a time on the Susquehanna as guests of the Conoy; later at the mouth of the Juniata; and still later, in 1748, the greater part of this tribe went up the Susquehanna, halting at various points and finally settling, during the French and Indian War, under the protection of the Iroquois, at Chenango, Chugnut, and Owego, on the east branch of the Susquehanna in southern New York. For a number of years, their principal seat in Pennsylvania was on the east bank of the Susquehanna below the mouth of the Lackawanna, not far from Pittston, Luzerne County.

Many marvelous stories were told concerning this tribe. One was that they were said to have been the inventors of a poisonous substance by which they could destroy a whole settlement at once. They were also accused of being skilled in the art of witchcraft, and, on this account they were greatly feared by the neighboring tribes. Heckewelder states that he knew Indians who firmly believed that the Nanticokes had men among them who, if they wished, could destroy a whole army by merely blowing their breath toward them.

They had the singular custom of removing the bones of their dead from place to place during their migrations, and this they would do even in cases where the dead had not been buried long enough to be reduced to a skeleton. In cases where the dead had not been buried long, they would scrape the flesh from the bones, reinter it, and then take the skeleton with them. Heckewelder relates that between the years 1750 and 1760 he saw several bands of Nanticokes go through the Moravian town of Bethlehem, Pennsylvania, on their migration northward, loaded with the bones of their relatives and friends.

THE TUTELO

The Tutelo were a Siouan tribe, related to the Sioux, of Dakota of the far Northwest. For some time before their entering Pennsylvania soon after 1722, they had been living in North Carolina and Virginia. They were first mentioned by Captain John Smith, of Virginia, in 1609, as occupying the upper waters of the James and Rappahannock, and were described by him as being very barbarous. Their first seat in Pennsylvania was at Shamokin (Sunbury) where they resided under Iroquois protection. At this place, the Rev. David Brainerd found them in 1745. Later they moved up the Susquehanna to Skogari. In 1771, the Tutelo were settled on the east side of Cayuga inlet about three miles from the south end of the lake of that name in New York. How this tribe became so widely separated from the western Sioux still remains unknown.

The Conoy, the Nanticoke, and the Tutelo were not large tribes. In 1763, according to Sir William Johnson, the three tribes numbered about one thousand souls.

As has been stated, the Shawnees, the Conoy, and the Nanticokes, belonged to the Algonquin parent stem; the Tutelo to the Siouan; and the Tuscarora to the Iroquoian. These three groups were widely separated. It is thus seen that, at the time when the English, the Germans, and the Scotch-Irish, and other European races were coming to Pennsylvania, as widely separated races of North American Indians were coming from the South to make their homes in its wilderness and along its streams. Of these incoming tribes, the one to figure most prominently in the history of Pennsylvania was the Shawnee. Following Braddock's defeat, July 9th, 1755, Pennsylvania suffered the bloodiest Indian invasion in American history,—the invasion of the Shawnees and Delawares, brought about in part, by the fact that the Shawnees yielded to French influence.

THE ERIES, WENRO, BLACK MINQUAAS, AND AKANSEA

The Eries, also known as the Erieehronons, were populous sedentary tribe of Iroquoian stock, which, in the seventeenth century, inhabited that part of Pennsylvania extending from Lake Erie to the Allegheny River, possibly as far south as the Ohio River, and eastward to the lands of the Susquehannas. They are also known as the Cat Nation, from the abundance of wild cats and panthers in their territory. Recorded history gives only glimpses of them; but it appears that they had many towns and villages, and that their town, Rique, had, in 1654, between 3,000 and 4,000 combatants, exclusive of women and children.

In the Jesuit Relation of 1653, it is stated that the Eries were forced to proceed farther inland in order to escape their enemies dwelling west of them. Who these enemies were is not positively known. Finally, about 1655 or 1656, they were conquered by the Iroquois. The conquerors entered their palisaded town of Rique, and there "wrought such carnage among the women and children that the blood was knee-deep in places." However, this victory at Rique was dearly bought by the Iroquois, who were compelled to remain in the country of the Eries two months to care for the wounded and bury the dead. The Erie power now being broken, the people were either destroyed, dispersed, or led into captivity. Six hundred Eries, who had surrendered at one time, were taken to the Iroquois country and adopted. There is a tradition that, some years after the defeat of the Eries, a band of their descendants cames from the West, ascended the Allegheny River, and attacked the Senecas, and were slain to a man.

The Wenro, a tribe of Iroquoin stock, also known as the Ahouenrochrhonons, are mentioned in the Jesuit Relation as having dwelt some time prior to 1639, "beyond the Erie", or Cat Nation; and it is probable that their habitat was on the upper territory of the Allegheny, and, part of it at least, within the bounds of the State of Pennsylvania. This tribe, too, fell before the arms of the Iroquois. A notation on Captain John Smith's map of his explorations, says that they traded with the whites on the Delaware River.

They seem to have been allied with the Black Minquaas, which later, according to Herrmann's map of 1670, are placed in the region west of the Allegheny Mountains, and on the Ohio, or "Black Minquaas River". The Jesuit Relation states that both the Wenro and the Black Minquaas traded with the people on the upper Delaware, some going by way of the West Branch of the Susquehanna, down to Sunbury (Shamokin), up to Wyoming, and then across to the Delaware River, near the Water Gap; and others reaching the Delaware by way of the Conemaugh, Juniata, and Susquehanna. The Black Minquaas were so called because "they carried a black badge on their breast." About all that is known of the fate of this tribe is the legend on Herrmann's map, which reads: "A very great river called Black Minquaas River—where formerly those Black Minquaas came over the Susquehanna, as far as the Delaware to trade; but the Sasquhana and the Sinnicus Indians went over and destroyed that very great nation."

A Siouan tribe, the Akansea, in remote times, occupied the upper Ohio Valley, according to many historians, and were driven out by the Iroquois. This stream was called the "River of the Akansea", because this tribe lived upon its shores. When or how long this river valley was their habitat, is not known.

No other rivers in Pennsylvania, or on the continent, have seen more changes in the races of Indians living in their valleys than have the Ohio and the Allegheny,—the dwelling place of the

Alligewi; the Delawares, or Lenape, in the course of their migration eastward; the Akansea; the Shawnees; the Black Minquaas;
the Wenro; the Senecas; then once more the Shawnees and Delawares in their march toward the setting sun before the great tide
of white immigration. What battles and conquests, all untold,
took place in the valleys of these historic streams before the white
man set foot upon their shores! Who would not seek to draw
aside the curtain, which, it seems, must forever hide this unrecord-
ed history from our view?

We have seen that the French explorer, Brule, and the Dutch
explorer, Viele, entered Pennsylvania at the very dawn of the historic period. Perhaps to these should be added the French explorer, LaSalle. It is a moot question, however, among historians whether this gallant Frenchman ever entered the limits of
Pennsylvania, though Parkman lends the weight of his great name
to the contention that he explored the Allegheny Valley.

Having given this survey of the Indian tribes who inhabited
Pennsylvania, we shall now take up the biographies of their outstanding chiefs.* In the course of our narrative will appear many
things that reflect no honor on the whites—the anointed children
of education and civilization. But it is our duty to record the
wrongs committed upon the untutored Red Man, as well as the
wrongs committed by him. History must not hide the truth.
Furthermore, the author has no prejudice against any of the
European races who came in contact with the Indians of Pennsylvania. His ancestors came to the Province in 1693, and the blood
of nearly all these races flows in his veins—English, German, Irish,
Scotch, Scotch-Irish, and French.

---

* See the chapter, "The Red Neighbours" in Charles P. Keith's "Chronicles of
Pennsylvania" for a concise and well written account of the aborigines of Pennsylvania.

CHAPTER III.

Mattahorn and Naaman

HIS chapter is devoted to the two outstanding Delaware chiefs before the arrival of William Penn. Playing a part in the history of the lower Delaware, during its occupancy by the Swedes and the Dutch, the few recorded facts concerning these worthy representatives of the aborigines of Pennsylvania, are as a voice from the distant past.

MATTAHORN

Mattahorn claims our remembrance as one of the few Delaware chiefs distinguishable by name before the arrival of William Penn. We first meet him in April, 1633, when he and several other chiefs sold the land on which Philadelphia stands to Arent Corssen, the Dutch agent, commander of Fort Nassau, on the east bank of the Delaware River, near Gloucester, New Jersey. At that time the Dutch of Manhattan were endeavoring to establish an Indian trade on the South, or Delaware River.

We next meet Mattahorn when the Swedes came to the Delaware. Late in the autumn of 1637, two ships left Sweden carrying a small band of resolute emigrants purposing to establish a Swedish colony in the New World under the patronage of Queen Christina, the daughter of Sweden's most famous king, Gustavus Adolphus, the "Lion of the North". These ships, commanded by Peter Minuit, who had been the Dutch Company's director at Manhattan from 1626 to 1632, arrived on the west bank of the Delaware River in the middle of March, 1638. Charmed by the beauty of the region, the Swedes gave the name of Paradisudden (Paradise Point) to a particularly beautiful spot where they landed temporarily. Passing on up the river, their ships arrived at the Minquas Kill of the Dutch (White Clay and Christina creeks), which enters the Delaware from the west. The ships then sailed up the Minquas Kill some distance, and cast anchor at a place where some Indians had pitched their wigwams.

Peter Minuit then fired a salute of two guns and went ashore with some of his men to reconnoiter and establish connection with the Indians. They also went some distance into the country.

Minuit then returned to his ship. The roar of his cannon had the desired effect; several Indian chiefs made their appearance, and Minuit at once arranged a conference with them for the sale of land. The leader of these chiefs was Mattahorn. Possibly Minuit from his acquaintance with the Dutch trade on the Delaware River during his administration at Manhattan, had some previous knowledge of this chieftain. Minuit and the chiefs had no difficulty in coming to an agreement. He explained to the Indians that he wanted ground on which to build a "house", and other ground on which to plant. For the former he offered a "kettle and other articles", and for the latter, half of the tobacco raised upon it. On the same, or following day, Mattahorn and five other chiefs went aboard one of the ships of the Swedes and sold as much "of the land on all parts and places of the river, up the river, and on both sides, as Minuit requested."

The merchandise specified in the deeds being given to them, the chiefs traced their totem marks on the documents, and Peter Minuit, Mans Kling, and others signed their names below. The extent of this purchase embraced the territory lying below the Minquas Kill to Duck Creek, a distance of forty miles and up the river to the Schuylkill, a distance of twenty-seven miles along the bank of the Delaware, in both cases stretching an indefinite distance to the westward. The purchase being concluded, Minuit with his officers and soldiers went ashore. A pole was then erected with the Coat of Arms of Sweden upon it; "and with the report of cannon, followed by other solemn ceremonies, the land was called New Sweden." This was the first Swedish colony in America.

Mattahorn's next appearance on the stage of history is in 1641 when a third nation, the English, becomes definitely connected with the history of the Delaware. English merchants and planters of New Haven, finding that their colony was poorly situated for trade with the Indians, looked for other places where they could settle and establish trading posts; and some of the principal merchants who had sent ships to the Delaware for some years, and had observed that this territory was sparsely settled and that the Swedish and Dutch forts and trading stations did not control the river, determined, in the autumn of 1640, to extend their activities systematically to the Delaware region. Accordingly, the "Delaware Company" was formed for the purpose of colonizing and trading on the Delaware; and two agents, Lamberton and Turner, with a number of assistants, were sent "to view and purchase part of the Delaware", in the spring of 1641. They were instructed to buy lands from the Indians not yet occupied by any Christian nation. Turner and Lamberton sailed up the Delaware River in April, 1641, held several conferences with Mattahorn on its shores, and on April 19th, purchased from this chieftain certain lands on the Schuylkill, possibly within the limits of Philadelphia.

Mattahorn's name appears, in 1645, in the annals of the Swedes on the Delaware, the only year in which Indian troubles threatened the Swedish colony. The cause of this trouble was the fact that the Dutch at Manhattan adopted a course of "extermination" of the Indians on the lower reaches of the Hudson, and during the years 1644 and 1645, had killed sixteen hundred of the natives at Manhattan and in its neighborhood. They slaughtered all ages and both sexes; and the word of these shocking and unpardonable cruelties spread along the Atlantic Ocean, causing the Indians of the Delaware to feel bitter towards all newcomers. In the spring of 1644, a Swedish woman and her husband, an Englishman, were killed not far from the site of Chester, Pennsylvania,— the first white blood shed in Pennsylvania by the Indians. Governor John Printz of the Swedish colony then assembled his people for the defense of Chester; but the Indian chiefs of that region came to him disowning the act and desiring peace. He then made a treaty of peace with them, distributing presents and restoring friendly relations. During this year there was a great Indian council held, which has been described by Rev. John Campanius, over which Mattahorn presided and in which the destruction of the Swedes was considered. Mattahorn is said to have presented the question for the consideration of the council; but the decision was that the Swedes should not be molested. The warriors said that the Swedes should be considered "good friends", and that the Indians had "no complaint to make of them."

Once more, this time in April, 1648, we meet Mattahorn, when he and the Delaware chief, Sinquees, declared to the Dutch at Fort Nassau that they and others had sold to Corssen, the Dutch agent, in 1633, "the Schuylkill and adjoining lands."

The last time we meet Mattahorn in recorded history is when he appeared, on July 9th, 1651, before a commission presided over by the Dutch Director-General, Peter Stuyvesant, who was then at the mouth of the Schuylkill. Mattahorn was then questioned as to the purchase of lands by the Swedes from him in 1638, and made the following reply: "That when Minuit came to the country with a ship, he lay before the Minquaas Kill, where he, the Sachem, then had a house and lived; that Minuit then presented him with a kettle and other trifles, requesting of him as much land as Minuit could set a house on, and a plantation included between 6 trees, which he, the Sachem, sold him, and Minuit promised him half the tobacco that would grow on the plantation, although it was never given to him. He declared further that neither the Swedes nor any other nation had bought the lands of them as right owners except the patch on which Fort Christina stood, and that all the other houses of the Swedes, built at Tinnecongh, Hingeesingh on the Schuylkill, and at other places were set up there against the will and consent of the Indians, and that neither they, nor any other natives had received anything therefor." On this day, (July 9, 1651), Mattahorn, Pemicka, Ackehon and Sinquees conveyed to Peter Stuyvesant a certain tract named Tamenconch, lying on the west shore of the Delaware, beginning at the west point of the Minquas Kill, extending unto Carasse, "and as far landward as our right extends, to-wit: to the bounds and limits of the Minquas [Susquehanna country]."

It is thus seen that this conveyance to the Dutch included a part, at least, of the lands which the Indians had conveyed to the Swedes in the spring of 1638; but it must be understood that the Indian ownership of the land was very vague and undefined. It was seldom that definite limits were established, and often several chiefs would lay claim to the same land, claiming jurisdiction over any region where they had established their hunting ground, by force or otherwise. Mattahorn assured Stuyvesant that he and his fellow sachems "were great chiefs and proprietors of the lands, both by ownership and consent and appointment of Minquas [Susquehanna] and River Indians." As has already been seen, the term "River Indians" was applied to the Delawares on the river of that name. This conveyance was signed by four Minquas or Susquehanna chiefs as witnesses thereto. It would thus seem that the Delawares on the lower part of the Delaware River were at that time subject to the authority of the Susquehannas. About twenty-five years after this conveyance was made, the Susquehannas were defeated by the Iroquois and the power of their nation forever destroyed. Consequently their sovereignty over the Indians on the Delaware River passed to the Five Nations.

Mattahorn being, in 1633, a chief of such importance as to sell lands of his tribe, was no doubt an elderly man when he made his exit from the stage of history, in 1651.

NAAMAN

Another outstanding Delaware chief, who figured in the history of the lower Delaware before the arrival of William Penn, was Naaman, whose name is preserved in Naaman's Creek, near the Delaware line. About all that is known of him is the fact that he was present on June 17th, 1654, at a great council of the Delawares at Printz Hall, at Tinicum, held for the purpose of renewing the ancient bond of friendship that existed between the Delawares and the Swedes. At this council Naaman praised the virtues of the Swedes. Campanius Holm thus describes this occasion:

"The 17th June, 1654, was gathered together at Printz Hall at Tinicum, ten of the sachemans of the Indian chiefs, and there at that time was spoken to them in the behalf of the great Queen of Sweedland for to renew the old league of friendship that was betwixt them, and that the Sweeds had bought and purchased land of them. They complained that the Sweeds they should have brought in with them much evil, because so many of them since are dead and expired. Then there was given unto them considerable presents and parted amongst them. When they had received the presents they went out, and had a conference amongst them a pretty while, and came in again, and then spoke one of the chiefs, by name Noaman [Naaman], rebuked the rest, and that they had spoken evil of the Sweeds and done them harm, and that they should do so no more, for they were good people. Look, said he, pointing upon the presents, what they have brought us, and they desire our friendship, and then he stroked himself three times down his arm, which was an especial token of friendship. Afterwards he thanked for the presents they had received, which he did in all their behalfs, and said that there should hereafter be observed and kept a more strict friendship amongst them than there hath been hitherto. That, as they had been in Governoeur Printz his time, one body and one heart, (beating and knocking upon his breast), they should henceforward be as one head. For a token waving with both his hands, and made as if he would tye a strong knot; and then he made this comparison, that as the callibash is of growth round without any crack, also they from henceforth hereafter as one body without any separation, and if they heard or understood that any one would do them or any of theirs any harm, we should give them timely notice thereof, and likewise if they heard any mischief plotting against the Christians, they would give them notice thereof, if it was at midnight. And then answer was made unto them, that that would be a true and lasting friendship, if every one would consent to it. Then the great guns were fired, which pleased them exceedingly well, saying, 'Pu-hu-hu! mo ki-rick pickon.' That is, 'Hear! now believe! The great guns are fired.' And then they were treated with wine and brandy. Then stood up another of the Indians and spoke, and admonished all in general that they should keep the league and friendship with the Christians that was made, and in no manner or way violate the same, and do them no manner of injury, not to their hogs or their cattle, and if any one should be found guilty thereof, they should be severely punished, others to an example. They advised that we should settle some Sweeds upon Passaiunck, where then there lived a power of Indians for to observe if they did any mischief, they should be confirmed, the copies of the agreements were then punctually read unto them. But the originals were at Stockholm, and when their names (were read) that had signed, they seemed when they heard it rejoiced, but when anyone's name was read that was dead, they hung their heads down and seemed to be sorrowful. And then there was set upon the floor in the great hall two great kettles, and a great many other vessels with sappan, that is, mush, made of Indian corn or Indian wheat, as groweth there in abundance. But the sachemans they sate by themselves, but the common sort of Indians they fed heartily, and were satisfied. The above mentioned treaty and friendship that then was made betwixt the Sweeds and the Indians, hath been ever since kept and observed, and that the Sweeds have not been by them molested."

In closing this sketch of the two outstanding Delaware chiefs before the arrival of Penn, we call attention to the fact that one of the most notable features in the history of the Swedes on the Delaware, with whom both Mattahorn and Naaman came into intimate contact, is the fact that the Swedes had no war either with the Lenape or Delawares, or their more dangerous neighbors, the Minquas, or Susquehannas. The Swedes even assisted the Susquehannas in their struggle against the might of the Iroquois, furnishing them arms for their warriors after the manner of European soldiers. They were on especially friendly terms with the Delawares, and sought to convert them to the Christian faith.

The principles upon which New Sweden was founded and its benevolent intentions towards the Indians are thus set forth in the letter granting the privileges to the colonists, signed by Chancellor

Axel Oxenstierna of Sweden, dated January 24th, 1640, and directed to the Commandant and inhabitants of Fort Christina, in New Sweden:

"As regards religion, we are willing to permit that, besides the Augsburg Confession, the exercise of the pretended reformed religion may be established and observed in that country, in such manner, however, that those who profess the one or the other religion live in peace, abstaining from every useless dispute, from all scandal and all abuse. The patrons of this colony shall be obliged to support, at all times, as many ministers and schoolmasters as the number of inhabitants shall seem to require, *and to choose, moreover, for this purpose, persons who have at heart the conversion of the pagan inhabitants to Christianity.*"

Carrying out these principles, we find Reverend John Campanius, the Swedish Lutheran clergyman, who accompanied Governor John Printz to New Sweden in 1643, active as a missionary among the Delawares and translating Martin Luther's Catechism into the Delaware tongue,—the first book to be translated into the language of the North American Indians. The petition, "Give us this day our daily bread," Campanius translated, "Give us this day a plentiful supply of venison and corn." Reverend Campanius was the first missionary of the Christian religion to labor among the Indians of Pennsylvania; and the Swedish Lutheran church at Tinicum, which he dedicated on September 4, 1646, and of which he was pastor, "was the first regularly dedicated church building within the limits of Pennsylvania."

If we examine the history of New Sweden from its founding, in 1638, to its overthrow by the Dutch, in 1655, we find many excellencies that stand out in strong contrast with the early history of her neighboring colonies. She had an instructed citizenship. With her, liberty of conscience was a historical fact, and not a mockery, or a myth, as with the "Pilgrim Fathers" of New England. She laid down the principles of liberty of conscience and education of the people, as the foundation of her political structure, before William Penn was born; and she steadfastly adhered to these principles to the end of her separate and independent existence, giving them an impetus that contributed very largely to their adoption as the most cherished and sacred principles in the structure of our American Commonwealth. These "Pilgrim Fathers", who landed on the shores of the Delaware and made the first settlements in Pennsylvania, had far more to do with molding American history than the Pilgrims of New England. "America," says Woodrow Wilson, "did not come out of New England."

Throughout New Sweden's entire history, that other outstanding fact, which has been alluded to, appears,—the preservation of friendly relations with the Indians, in contrast with the
bloody pages in the history of other colonies. Indeed, the just and
kindly treatment of the Delawares by the Swedish colonists had
much to do in causing the friendly reception which these children
of the forest gave William Penn at a later day when, with open
heart and open hand, they welcomed him to the shores of this
Western World.

A Picture of the Delawares in the Day of
Mattahorn and Naaman

On July 28th, 1639, Adriaen van der Donck and others signed
a document describing the Delawares and their manners and customs as they were in the days of Mattahorn and Naaman and when
they first met the Europeans on the Delaware River. This description gives one of the most complete pictures of the Pennsylvania
Indians of this early period, and is as follows:

"The natives are generally well limbed, slender around the
waist, broad shouldered; all having black hair and brown eyes;
they are very nible and swift of pace, well adapted to travel on
foot and to carry heavy burdens; they are dirty and slovenly in
their habits; make light of all sorts of hardships, being by nature
and from youth upwards accustomed thereto. They resemble the
Brazilians in color, or are as tawny as those called Gipsies. Generally, the men have very little or no beard, some even pluck it
out; they use very few words, which they previously well consider.
Naturally they are quite modest, without guile, and inexperienced,
but in their way haughty enough, ready and quick witted to com-
prehend or learn, be it good or bad, whatever they are most inclined to. As soldiers they are far from being honorable, but perfid-
ious and accomplish all their designs by treachery; they also use
many stratagems to deceive their enemies and execute by night
almost all their plans that are in any way hazardous. The thirst
for revenge seems innate in them; they are very pertinacious in
self defence, when they cannot escape, which, under other circumstances, they like to do; they make little of death, when it is inevit-
able, and despise all tortures that can be inflicted on them at the
stake, exhibiting no faintheartedness, but generally singing until
they are dead.

"They also know right well how to cure wounds and hurts, or

inveterate sores and injuries, by means of herbs and roots indigenous to the country, and which are known to them. The clothing as well of men as of women consists of a piece of duffels, or of deerskin, leather, or elk hide around the body, to cover their nakedness. Some have a bearskin of which they make doublets; others again, coats of the skins of raccoons, wild cats, wolves, dogs, squirrels, beavers and the like; and they even have made themselves some of turkey's feathers; now they make use for the most part of duffels cloth which they obtain in trade from the Christians; they make their stockings and shoes of deerskins or elk hides, some even have shoes of corn husks whereof they also make sacks. Their money consists of white and black wampum which they themselves manufacture; their measure and value is the hand of fathom, and if it be corn that is to be measured, 'tis done by the denotas which are bags of their own making. Their ornaments consist of scoring their bodies, or painting them of various colors, sometimes entirely black, when they are in mourning; but mostly the face. They twine both white and black wampum around their heads; formerly they were not wont to cover these, but now they are beginning to wear bonnets or caps, which they purchase from the Christians; they wear wampum in the ears, around the neck and around the waist, and thus in their way are mighty fine. They have also long deers-hair which is dyed red, whereof they make ringlets to encircle the head; and other fine hair of the same color, which hangs around the neck in braids, whereof they are very vain. They frequently smear their skin and hair with all sorts of grease. Almost all of them can swim; they themselves construct the boats they use, which are of two sorts; some of entire trees excavated with fire, axes and adzes; the Christians call these canoes; others, again, called also canoes, are made of bark, and in these they can move very rapidly.

"Traces, and nothing more, of the institution of marriage can be perceived among them. The man and woman unite together without any special ceremony, except that the former, by agreement previously made with the latter, presents her with some wampum or cloth, which he frequently takes back on separating, if this occur any ways soon. Both men and women are excessively unchaste and lacivious, without the least particle of shame; and that is the reason that the men so frequently change their wives and the women their husbands. They have, usually, but one wife; sometimes even two or three, but this mostly obtains among the chiefs. They have also among them different ranks of people, such as noble and ignoble. The men are generally lazy and will not work until they become old and of no consideration; then they make spoons, and wooden bowls, traps, nets, and various other such trifles; in other respects, they do nothing but hunt, fish and go to war.

"The women must perform the remainder of the labor, such as planting corn, cutting and hauling fire wood, cooking, attending to the children, and whatever else has to be done. Their dwellings are constructed of hickory poles set in the ground and bent bow fashion, like arches, and then covered with bark which they peel in quantities for that purpose. Some, but principally the chiefs; houses, have, inside, portraits and pictures somewhat rudely carved. When fishing or hunting, they lie under the blue sky, or little better. They do not remain long in one place, but remove several times a year and repair, according to the season, to wherever food appears to them, beforehand, best and easiest to be obtained.

"They are divided into various tribes and languages. Each tribe usually dwells together, and there is one among them who is chief; but he does not possess much power or distinction except in their dances and in time of war. Some have scarcely any knowledge of God; others very little. Nevertheless they relate very strange fables of the Deity. In general they have a great dread of the Devil, who gives them wonderful trouble; some converse freely on the subject and allow themselves to be strangely imposed upon by him; but their devils they say, will not have anything to do with the Dutch. Scarcely a word is heard here of any ghost or such like. Offerings are sometimes made to them, but with little ceremony. They believe also, in an Immortality of the soul; have likewise, some knowledge of the Sun, Moon, and Stars, many of which they even know how to name; they are passable judges of the weather. There is scarcely any law or justice among them, except sometimes in war matters, and then very little. The next of kin is the avenger; the youngest are the most daring, who mostly do as they like. Their weapons used to be a war club and the bow and arrow, which they know how to use with wonderful skill. Now, those residing near, or trading considerably with the Christians, make use of firelocks and hatchets, which they obtain in barter. They are excessively fond of guns; spare no expense on them, and are so expert with them that, in this respect they excel many Christians.

"Their fare, or food, is poor and gross, for they drink water, having no other beverage; they eat the flesh of all sorts of game that the country supplies, even badgers, dogs, eagles, and similar trash, which Christians in no way regard; these they cook and use uncleaned and undressed. Moreover, all sorts of fish likewise, snakes, frogs, and such like, which they usually cook with the offals and entrails. They know, also, how to preserve fish and meat for the winter in order then to cook them with Indian meal. They make their bread, but of very indifferent quality, of maize, which they also cook whole, or broken in wooden mortars. The women likewise perform this labor and make a pap or porridge, called by some Sapsis, by others, Duundare, which is their daily food. They mix this, also, thoroughly with little beans, of different colors, raised by themselves; this is esteemed by them rather as a dainty, than as a daily dish."

CHAPTER IV

Tamanend

AMANEND, (Tammany, etc.) was the head chief of the Unami or Turtle Clan of Delawares from before 1683 until 1697 and, perhaps later. He is referred to in the Colonial Records of Pennsylvania as "King" of the Delawares. As was seen in Chapter I, the head chief of the Turtle Clan always presided at the councils of the three clans composing the Delaware Nation. Tamanend lived and hunted along the Neshaminy Creek in what is now Bucks County. His name signifies "the affable". The town of Tamanend, in Schuylkill County, is named for this noted chieftain.

Tamanend is thus described by the Moravian missionary, Rev. John Heckewelder, who, as was stated in the first chapter of this book, was the staunch friend of the Delawares, and had lived among them in all the intimacy of friends and companions for more than thirty years:

"The name of Tamanend is held in the highest veneration by all the Indians. Of all the chiefs and great men which the Lenape nation ever had, he stands foremost on the list. But, although many fabulous stories are circulated about him among the whites, but little of his real history is known. The misfortunes which have befallen some of the most beloved and esteemed personages among the Indians since the Europeans came among them, prevent the survivors from indulging in the pleasure of recalling to mind the memory of their virtues. No white man who regards their feeling, will introduce such subjects in conversation with them. All we know, therefore, of Tamanend is that he was an ancient Delaware chief who never had an equal. He was, in the highest degree, endowed with wisdom, virtue, prudence, charity, affability, meekness, hospitality; in short with every good and noble qualification that a human being may possess. He was supposed to have had intercourse with the great and good Spirit; for he was a stranger to everything that is bad. The fame of this great man extended even among the whites, who fabricated numerous legends concerning him, which I never heard, however, from the mouth of an Indian, and, therefore, believe to be fabulous. In the Revolutionary War, his enthusiastic admirers dubbed him a saint and he was established under the name of Saint Tammany, the Patron Saint of America. His name was inserted in some calendars and his festival celebrated on the first day of May in every year."

Heckewelder then describes the celebrations in honor of Saint Tammany. They were conducted along Indian lines, and included the smoking of the calumet and Indian dances in the open air. "Tammany Societies" in the early part of our history as a nation, were organized in several American cities.

William Penn Purchases Land From Tamanend

William Penn did not set foot upon the soil of his Province until the 29th day of October, 1682; but, after maturing his plans for the new colony during the summer of 1681, he appointed his cousin, William Markham, to be his deputy governor. Markham left England in the spring of 1682, and arrived at New York about the middle of June of that year. He then proceeded to Upland, or Chester, Pennsylvania, and, no doubt, presented his credentials to the justices and announced to them and the settlers that once more a change of government had been decreed.

William Penn decided to follow the advice of the Bishop of London and the example of the Swedes, and purchase from the Indians inhabiting his Province whatever lands, within the bounds of the same, might from time to time, become occupied by his colonists. The first Indian deed of record was a purchase of lands in Bucks County, made by Deputy Governor Markham for William Penn, dated the 15th day of July, 1682; and though Tamanend was not of the grantors therein, we mention it in this connection on account of its historical importance. The native grantors were fourteen Delaware chiefs or "sachemakers", bearing the following names: Idquahon, Ieanottowe, Idquoquequon, Sahoppe for himself and Okonikon, Merkekowon, Orecton for Nannacussey, Shaurwawghon, Swanpisse, Nahoosey, Tomakhickon, Westkekitt and Tohawsis.

Markham paid the Indians for this purchase: 350 fathoms of wampum, 20 fathoms of "stroudwaters", 20 white blankets, 20 guns, 20 coats, 40 shirts, 40 pairs of stockings, 40 hose, 40 axes, 2 barrels of powder, 60 fathoms of "duffields", 20 kettles, 200 bars of lead, 200 knives, 200 small glasses, 12 pairs of shoes, 40 copper boxes, 40 tobacco tongs, 2 small barrels of pipes; 40 pairs of scissors, 40 combs, 20 pounds of red lead, 100 awls, two handfuls of fish hooks, two handfuls of needles, 40 pounds of shot, 10 bundles of beads, 10 small saws, 12 drawing knives, 2 ankers of tobacco, 2 ankers of rum, 2 ankers of cider, 2 ankers of beer, and 300 guilders in money,—a formidable list, indeed, and all very acceptable to the Indians.

However, on June 23rd, 1683, William Penn, at a meeting with Tamanend and a number of other Delaware chiefs at Shakamaxon, within the limits of Philadelphia, purchased four different tracts of land from the Indians. The first deed was from Tamanend, who made "his mark" to the same, being a snake coiled. This deed conveyed all of Tamanend's lands "lying betwixt the Pemmapecka [Pennypack] and Nessaminehs [Neshaminy] Creeks, and all along Nessaminehs Creek." The consideration was "so many guns, shoes, stockings, looking glasses, blankets, and other goods as the said William Penn shall please to give."

On the same date, (June 23, 1683), William Penn purchased a second tract of land from Tamanend, the deed being signed by Tamanend and Metamequan. It conveyed all the grantors' lands "lying betwixt and about Pemmapecka and Nessaminehs Creeks, and all along Nessaminehs Creek." The consideration was "so much wampum and other goods as he, the said William Penn, shall be pleased to give unto us." However, there is a receipt attached to this deed for the following articles: 5 pairs of stockings, 20 bars of lead, 10 tobacco boxes, 6 coats, 2 guns, 8 shirts, 2 kettles, 12 awls, 5 hats, 25 pounds of powder, 1 peck of pipes, 38 yards of "duffields", 16 knives, 100 needles, 10 glasses, 5 caps, 15 combs, 5 hoes, 9 gimlets, 20 fish hooks, 10 tobacco tongs, 10 pairs of scissors, 7 half-gills, 6 axes, 2 blankets, 4 handfuls of bells, 4 yards of "stroudswaters" and 20 handfuls of wampum.

Also, on the 5th day of July, 1697, "King Taminy [Tamanend], and Weheeland, my Brother and Weheequeckhon alias Andrew, who is to be king after my death, Yaqueekhon alias Nicholas, and Quenameckquid alias Charles, my Sons", granted to William Penn, who was then in England, all the lands "between the Creek called Pemmapeck [Pennypack] and the Creek called Neshaminy, in the said province extending in length from the River Delaware so far as a horse can travel in two summer dayes, and to carry its breadth according as the several courses of the said two Creeks will admit, and when the said Creeks do so branch that the main branches or bodies thereof cannot be discovered, then the Tract of Land hereby granted, shall stretch forth upon a direct course on each side and so carry on the full breadth to the extent of the length thereof."

It is to be noted that in the list of articles which Penn gave in exchange for the various tracts of land purchased from Tamanend and his associate chiefs, no brandy or other strong liquor appeared. It will be recalled that in Markham's purchase in Bucks County on the 15th of July, 1682, he gave the contracting sachems, rum, cider and beer as part of the purchase price. Penn, however, was more scrupulous than his deputy governor, doubtless having realized more strongly than Markham, the injury done the Indians by liquor. Indeed, in the "Great Law" which Penn drew up shortly after his arrival, there was a provision for punishing any person by fine of five pounds who should "presume to sell or exchange any rum or brandy or any strong liquors at any time to any Indian, within this province." Later the Indians found their appetite for strong liquor to be so strong that they agreed, if the colonists would sell them liquor, to submit to punishment by the civil magistrates "the same as white persons."

Penn's Treaty with Tamanend

Penn's memorable treaty with Tamanend and other Delaware chiefs, under the great elm at Shakamaxon, within the limits of Philadelphia, is full of romantic interest. Unarmed, clad in his sombre Quaker garb, he addressed the Indians assembled there, uttering the following words, which will be admired throughout the ages: "We meet on the broad pathway of good faith and good-will; no advantage shall be taken on either side, but all shall be openness and love. We are the same as if one man's body was to be divided into two parts; we are of one flesh and one blood." The reply of Tamanend, is equally noble: "We will live in love with William Penn and his children as long as the creeks and rivers run, and while the sun, moon, and stars endure."

No authentic record has been preserved of the "Great Treaty", made familiar by Benjamin West's painting and Voltaire's allusion to it "as the only treaty never sworn to and never broken;" and there has been a lack of agreement among historians as to the time when it took place. Many authorities claim that the time was in the November days, shortly after Penn arrived in his Province. "Under the shelter of the forest," says Bancroft, "now leafless by the frosts of autumn, Penn proclaimed to the men of the Algonquin race, from both banks of the Delaware, from the borders of the Schuylkill, and, it may have been, even from the Susquehanna, the same simple message of peace and love which George Fox had professed before Cromwell, and Mary Fisher had borne to the Grand Turk."

Other authorities, in recent times, fix the time of the treaty as on the 23rd day of June, 1683, when Penn, as has been seen, purchased the four tracts of land from Tamanend and his associates; in other words, that the purchase of land and the "Great Treaty" took place at the same time and at the same place. Moreover, a study of West's painting of the treaty scene shows the trees to be in full foliage, thus not suggesting a late autumn or winter day, as contended by Bancroft, but rather a day in the leafy month of June. Even if we should not grant the purchase of the four tracts of land from Tamanend and others on the 23rd of June, 1683, the distinction of being the "Great Treaty", it was most certainly *a treaty* of great importance and entitled to a prominent place in the Indian history of Pennsylvania and the Nation.

Says Jenkins, in his "Pennsylvania, Colonial and Federal": "In the years following 1683, far down into the next century, the Indians preserved the tradition of an agreement of peace made with Penn, and it was many times recalled in the meetings held with him and his successors. Some of these allusions are very definite. In 1715, for example, an important delegation of the Lenape chiefs came to Philadelphia to visit the Governor. Sassoonan— afterward called Allummapees, and for many years the principal chief of his people—was at the head, and Opessah, a Shawnee chief, accompanied him. There was 'great ceremony', says the Council record, over the 'opening of the calumet'. Rattles were shaken, and songs were chanted. Then Sassoonan spoke, offering the calumet to Governor Gookin, who in his speech spoke of 'that firm Peace that was settled between William Penn, the founder and chief governor of this country, at his first coming into it', to which Sassoonan replied that they had come 'to renew the former bond of friendship; that William Penn had at his first coming made a clear and open road all the way to the Indians, and they desired the same might be kept open and that all obstructions might be removed', etc. In 1720, Governor Keith, writing to the Iroquois chiefs of New York, said: 'When Governor Penn first settled this country he made it his first care to cultivate a strict alliance and friendship with all the Indians, and condescended so far as to purchase his lands from them.' And in March, 1722, the Colonial Authorities, sending a message to the Senecas, said: 'William Penn made a firm peace and league with the Indians in these parts near forty years ago, which league has often been repeated and never broken.' '' In fact, the "Great Treaty" was never broken until the Penn's Creek Massacre of October 16, 1755.

Unhappily, then, historians are not able to agree in stating the exact date of the "Great Treaty" under the historic elm on the banks of the Delaware,—a treaty that occupies a high and glorious place in the Indian history and traditions of Pennsylvania and the Nation. Though the historian labors in vain to establish the date, the *fact* of the treaty remains as inspiring to us of the present day as it was to the historians, painters, and poets of the past.

On August 16th, 1683, William Penn wrote a long letter to the Free Society of Traders, in which he describes a council that he had with the Indians,—possibly the "Great Treaty":

"I have had occasion to be in council with them (the Indians) upon treaties for land, and to adjust the terms of trade. Their order is thus: The King sits in the middle of an half moon, and hath his council, the old and wise, on each hand; behind them or at a little distance, sit the younger fry in the same figure. . . . When the purchase was agreed, great promises passed between us of kindness and good neighborhood, and that the Indians and English must live in love as long as the sun and moon give light; which done, another made a speech to the Indians in the name of all the Sachamakers or Kings, first to tell them what was done; next to charge and command them to love the Christians, and particularly live in peace with me, and the people under my Government; that many Governors had been on the River, but that no Governor had come himself to live and stay here before; and having now such an one that treated them well, they should never do him or his any wrong. At every sentence of which they shouted and said Amen in their way."

Last Days of Tamanend

Tamanend's last appearance in recorded history was when he, his brother and sons, conveyed the lands to William Penn on July 5th, 1697. But three years prior thereto, or on July 6th, 1694, he appeared at a council at Philadelphia, a number of other Delaware chiefs accompanying the venerable sachem. At this council, he thus expressed his friendly feelings for the colonists, in a speech addressed to Lieutenant-Governor Markham: "We and the Christians of this river [Delaware] have always had a free roadway to one another, and although sometimes a tree has fallen across the road, yet we have still removed it again, and kept the path clean; and we design to continue the old friendship that has been between us and you."

Tamanend died before July, 1701, but the date of his death is not known. All that is mortal of this great and good chieftain reposes in the soil of the beautiful valley of the Neshaminy,—the region which he and his associate chiefs conveyed to "Miquon", or "Brother Onas", as the Indians affectionately called William Penn. His grave is believed to be in "Tammany Burial Ground", near Chalfonte, Bucks County.

CHAPTER V.

Opessah and His Son, Loyparcowah

OPESSAH

S we have seen, in Chapter II, Opessah, or Wopaththa, was the chief of the band of Shawnees, consisting of seventy families, who came from Cecil County, Maryland, and settled at Pequea, Lancaster County, Pennsylvania, about the year 1697 or 1698. No doubt his name was pronounced "Opeththa", as the Shawnee language did not contain the sibilant.

William Penn's Treaty with Opessah and Other Indians of the Susquehanna Region

William Penn returned to Pennsylvania in December, 1699, after an absence of fifteen years; and he remained in his Province until the autumn of 1701, when he left finally, arriving in England about the middle of December of that year. During his second sojourn in Pennsylvania, he made his home in his commodious Manor House, at Pennsbury, in Falls Township, Bucks County, about twenty miles from Philadelphia. The erection of the mansion had been started during his absence and was completed by him after his return. Here he received many visits from different Indian chiefs, a room in the mansion having been set apart for Indian conferences.

During Penn's second sojourn in his Province, he endeavored to obtain additional legislation placing restrictions on the intercourse with the Indians, in order to protect them from the arts of the whites and the ravages of the rum traffic. He also endeavored to have the natives instructed in the doctrines of Christianity. In order to improve the temporal condition of the natives, he held frequent conferences at his manor house with various sachems; and frequently visited them in their forest homes, participating in their festivals. When they visited him at Pennsbury, it is said that he joined with them in their sports and games, ate hominy, venison, and roasted acorns with them, and matched them in strength and agility. It is recorded that nineteen Indian treaties were concluded and conferences held at Pennsbury.

After the close of King William's war, the governor of New York made a treaty of peace with the Five Nations; and at William Penn's suggestion it was extended to the other English colonies. On April 23rd, 1701, Penn entered into "Articles of Agreement", or a treaty, at Philadelphia, with the Susquehannas, Minquas, or Conestogas, the Shawnees, the Ganawese, Conoys, or Piscataways, the latter then dwelling on the northern bank of the Potomac, and the Five Nations. In this treaty the Susquehannas were represented by Connodaghtoh, their "king", and three chiefs of the same; the Shawnees were represented by Opessah, or Wopaththa, their "King", and two other chiefs; the Conoys, Ganawese, or Piscataways, were represented by four of their chiefs; and the Five Nations were represented by Ahoakassongh, "brother to the emperor or great king of the Onondagas."

We are now ready to state the provisions of the treaty. After first reciting the good understanding that had prevailed between William Penn and his lieutenants, on the one hand, and the various Indian nations inhabiting his Province, on the other hand, since his first arrival in Pennsylvania, and expressing that there should be forever a firm and lasting peace between Penn and his successors and the various Indian chiefs of his Province, the treaty provided as follows:

First. That the said "kings and chiefs" and the various Indians under their authority should, at no time, hurt, injure or defraud any inhabitants of the Colony of Penn; and that Penn and his successors should not suffer any injury to be done the Indians by any of his colonists.

Second. That the Indians should, at all times, behave themselves in a sober manner according to the laws of the Colony where they lived near or among the Christian Inhabitants thereof; and that they should have the full and free privileges and immunities of the laws of the Colony of Penn in the same manner as the whites, and acknowledge the authority of the crown of England in the Province.

Third. That none of the Indians should, at any time, aid, assist or abet any other nation, whether of Indians or others, that would at any time not be in amity with the king of England.

Fourth. That, if at any time, the Indians should hear from evil-minded persons or sowers of sedition any unkind reports of the English, representing that the English had evil designs against the Indians, in such case the Indians should send notice thereof to Penn or his successors, and not give credence to such reports until fully satisfied concerning the truth of the same. Penn agreed that he and his successors should at all times act in the same manner toward the Indians.

Fifth. That the Indians should not suffer any strange nations of Indians to settle on the farther side of the Susquehanna or about the Potomac, except those that were already seated there, nor bring any other Indians into any part of the Province without the permission of Penn or his successors.

Sixth. Penn, for the purpose of correcting abuses that were too frequently connected with the fur trade with the Indians, agreed on the part of himself and his successors, that no one should be permitted to trade with the Indians without first securing a license under the Governor's hand and seal; and the Indians agreed, on their part, not to permit any person whatsoever to buy or sell, or have any trade with them, without first having a license so to do.

Seventh. The Indians agreed not to sell or dispose of any of their skins or furs to any person whatsoever outside of the Province; and Penn bound himself and his successors to furnish the Indians with all kinds of necessary goods for their use, at reasonable rates.

Eighth. The Conoys, Ganawese, or Piscataways, should have leave of Penn and his successors to settle on any part of the Potomac River within the bounds of Penn's Province. (At this time, the vexed question as to the boundary line between Pennsylvania and Maryland was unsettled).

Ninth. The Susquehannas, or Conestogas, as a part of these articles of agreement, absolutely ratified and confirmed the sale of lands lying near and about the Susquehanna, formerly conveyed to William Penn, by deed of Governor Dongan of New York, and later confirmed by the deed of the Conestogas, dated the 13th day of September, in the year 1700, to both of which conveyances reference will be made in Chapter VI. The Susquehannas also agreed to be, at all times, ready further to confirm and make good the said sale, according to the tenor of the same, and that they would be answerable to Penn and his successors for the good behavior of the Conoys or Ganawese, and for their performing of their several agreements which were a part of this treaty.

Tenth.   In the last item of the agreement, Penn promised, for himself and his successors, that they would, at all times, show themselves true friends and brothers to all of the Indians by assisting them with the best of their "advices, directions and counsel", and would, in all things just and reasonable, befriend them; and the chiefs promised, for themselves and their successors, to behave themselves according to the tenor of the agreement, and to submit to the laws of the Province in the same manner as "the English and other Chrstians therein do."   The agreement was then concluded by the exchange of skins and furs, on the part of the Indians, and goods and merchandise, on the part of Penn.

At about the time of making this historic treaty of peace with the Indians on the Susquehanna, William Penn had journied into the interior of his Province, and conferred with the Conestogas at Conestoga, their principal town, in Lancaster County, the Conestogas being responsible for the good behavior of the Shawnees in their vicinity, as was pointed out in Chapter II.   Penn wrote to James Logan, in June, 1701, of his visit to the Conestoga region, as follows: "We were entertained right nobly at the Indian King's palace at Conestoga."   At that time, Penn intended the founding of a "great city" in the Conestoga region, on the Susquehanna.

At the time of this treaty, most of the Conoy were living on the north bank of the Potomac, though some had already entered Pennsylvania as early as 1698 or 1699, as stated in Chapter II. Some years after the treaty, or in the summer of 1705, the Delaware chief, Manangy, living on the Schuylkill, interviewed Governor John Evans, at Philadelphia, explaining that the Conoy, "settled in this Province near the head of the Potomac, being now reduced by sickness to a small number, and desirous to quit their present habitation where they settled about five years ago with the Proprietor's consent, the Conestoga Indians then becoming guarantees of a treaty of friendship, made between them, and showing a belt of wampum they had sent to the Schuylkill Indians to engage their friendship and consent that they might settle amongst them near Tulpehocken, request of the Governor that they may be permitted to settle in the said place."   The Governor then permitted the Conoy to settle in the valley of the Tulpehocken, Manangy and his band on the Schuylkill guaranteeing their good behavior.

Governor Evans Holds Councils with Opessah

On the sixth and seventh of June, 1706, a council was held at Philadelphia between Governor John Evans and "the chiefs of the Conestogas, Shawnees, and Ganawese, or Conoys", concerning pub-

lic affairs relating to these tribes. Indian Harry, of the Conestogas, was the interpreter. In the minutes of the council, the
Colonial Records do not specifically state that Opessah was present,
but, being the head of the Shawnees at Pequea, there is no doubt
that he attended the council. This council opened with Secretary
James Logan's account of his journey to the Conestogas and Conoy
during the preceding October and the treaty which was then held
with the Conoy at their town (Connejaghera, Conejoholo, Dekanoagah) near the site of Washington Borough, Lancaster County,
by the terms of which treaty, the Conoy were assured that they
would be safe in Penn's Province. The Conoy explained to James
Logan, at the time of his visit, that they had had much trouble
with the Virginians, and, considering it not safe to dwell in their
old abode on the Potomac, had come within the bounds of Pennsylvania, where they hoped to dwell in peace.

During this council at Philadelphia, Andaggy-Junguagh, chief
of the Conestogas, laid before Governor Evans a very large belt of
wampum, which he said was a pledge of peace formerly delivered
by the Onondagas to the Nanticokes when the Onondagas had subjugated this tribe. He explained that the Nanticokes, being lately
under some apprehension of danger from the Five Nations, some
of them had, in the spring of 1706, come to the region of the Conestogas, and had brought this belt with them, as well as another belt,
which, the chief explained, he left at his village in Lancaster
County. He further advised the Governor that the Five Nations,
of whom the Onondagas, as has been seen, were a member, were
presently expected to send deputies to receive the tribute of the Nanticokes; that he had brought this belt to Philadelphia in order that
the Colonial Authorities might be able to show it to any of the
Five Nations, who might come to Philadelphia, as evidence to
them that peace had been made. The Provincial Council, after
considering the matter, concluded to keep the belt according to the
proposal of the Conestogas; and the Conestogas promised to retain the other belt at their chief town, to be shown to the Five
Nations, if any of their deputies should come to Conestoga.

The remaining time of the council was taken up by explaining
to the chiefs of these three nations the laws which had been recently enacted regulating the intercourse between the Province and
these Indians. Evans explained to the chiefs that a law had recently been enacted providing that no person should trade with
them but such as should first have a license from the Governor
under his hand and seal. The chiefs requested the Governor that

only two traders be licensed, but Evans explained that the fewer the number of traders the more likely it would be that the Indians would be imposed upon. They then desired of the Governor that he would not permit the traders to go beyond their towns and meet the Indians returning from hunting, explaining that it had been the traders' custom to meet the Indians returning from their hunt, when they were loaded with furs and peltries, make them drunk, and get all of the fruits of their hunt before they returned to their wives and families. The Governor agreed to this proposal and told the chiefs that their people should have no dealings with the traders, except at their own villages, and that he would instruct the traders not to go any farther into the Susquehanna region than the principal Indian towns, and to do no trading whatever, except in those places. Liberal presents were then given the chiefs, and the council adjourned.

At a meeting of the Provincial Council on the 31st of August, 1706, it was decided that Governor Evans should visit Conestoga and the region round about it, for the purpose of further strengthening the bond of friendship between the Indians and the Colony. The Governor accordingly journeyed to this region early in September, where he was well received by the Conestogas, Shawnees and Conoys; but his visit was the cause of much scandal on account of his actions while there.

The French, as early as 1707, had their emissaries among the Conestogas under the guise of traders, miners or colonists, in an effort to draw them away from their allegiance to the English. Likewise, the colony of Maryland was pushing her pioneers over the boundary, in an effort to forestall the claims of William Penn by actual settlement.

In the month of June, 1707, Governor Evans, accompanied by Colonel John French, William Tonge, and several other Friends, and four servants, made a journey among the Susquehanna Indians, upon receiving a message from the Conestogas that the Nanticokes, who now had been tributaries of the Five Nations for twenty-seven years, intended journeying to the Onondagas in New York. He visited the following places: Pequea, Dekonoagah, Conestoga, and Paxtang, near Harrisburg.

At Pequea, the Governor and his party were received by the Shawnees with a discharge of firearms, and a conference was held, on June 30th, with Opessah, in which the chief told the Governor that he and his people were "happy to live in a country at peace, and not as in those parts where we formerly lived, for, then, upon returning from hunting, we found our town surprised, and our women and children taken prisoners by our enemies." While the Governor was at Pequea, several Shawnees from the South came to settle there, and were permitted to do so by Opessah, with the Governor's consent.

At Dekonoagah, the Governor was present at a meeting of the Shawnees, Conoys, and Nanticokes from seven of the surrounding towns. After having satisfied himself that the Nanticokes were a well meaning people, the Governor guaranteed them the protection of the Colony of Pennsylvania.

The Governor, having received information at Pequea that a Frenchman, named Nicole, was holding forth among the Indians at Paxtang, about whom he had received many complaints, and having advised the chief at Paxtang of his intention to seize this French trader, captured Nicole, after much difficulty, and, having mounted him on a horse with his legs tied, conveyed him through Tulpehocken and Manatawney, to Philadelphia, and lodged him in jail.

In Chapter II, a detailed account was given of the conference at Conestoga, on June 8th, 1710, between the two commissioners of Governor Evans (John French and Henry Worley) and Opessah, Civility, and the Tuscarora commissioners, to which conference reference is made at this point.

Opessah continued as chief of the Shawnees on the lower Susquehanna, with his principal seat at Pequea, until 1711. Then he voluntarily abandoned both his chieftainship and his tribe, and made his home among the Delawares to the northward, whose chief was Sassoonan, or Allummappees. Three principal chiefs of the Conestogas appeared before Governor Charles Gookin and the Provincial Council, at Philadelphia, on October first, 1714, and advised them that Opessah, "the late King of their neighbors and friends, the Shawnees," had left his people about three years previously, and, though often urged to return, refused to do so. The Shawnees at Pequea then elected a new king, named Cakundawanna, who accompanied the delegation of Conestoga chiefs and was presented to the Council. On June 14, 1715, Opessah, with Sassoonan, chief of the Delawares, attended the conference with Governor Gookin, mentioned in Chapter IV.

It is probable that Opessah sought an asylum among the Delawares through fear that the Five Nations or the English would hold him responsible for the murder of Francis de la Tore and several other white bond-servants of the trader, John Hans Steelman, by some young Shawnees, in 1710. Another account, this one traditionary, ascribes his desertion to the fact that he fell in love with a Delaware squaw who refused to leave her people.

A few years later, (1722) Opessah settled at Old (Shawnee) Town, on the Potomac, in Maryland, a town frequently called Opessah's Town by the Marylanders, as late as 1725. It is probable that he was the chief referred to by the Potomac Shawnee chiefs from the Ohio, Opakethwa and Opakeita, when they told Governor Gordon, upon their visit to Philadelphia, in September, 1732, that "formerly they lived at Patowmack, where their king died; that, having lost him, they knew not what to do; that they took their wives and children and went over the mountains, [to the Ohio and Allegheny valleys] to live."

LOYPARCOWAH

Loyparcowah was a son of Opessah. His name appears several places in the Colonial Records in the following form: "Loyparcowah, Opessah's Son." The Shawnee chief, Neucheconneh, "Deputy King", seems to have acted as vice-regent during the young manhood of this heir of the famous Shawnee chief, who came with his people to Pequea, Lancaster County, in 1697, or thereabouts.

Loyparcowah was one of the Shawnees who left the Susquehanna Valley and crossed the mountains to the valley of the Allegheny. The year in which he did this is not known, but it is likely that he was among those of his tribe who went west from Paxtang and New Cumberland about 1727—the first Shawnees to follow the Delawares to the valleys of the Ohio and Allegheny.

Loyparcowah Opposes Rum Traffic

Reference has been made to the fact that the Shawnees were highly displeased on account of the constant supply of rum brought to them by the traders in violation of the laws of the Colony. Their wise men recognized that it was the curse of the Red Man, causing his physical, mental, and moral deterioration. Protests were made by the leaders of this tribe time and again to the effect that the Colony failed to enforce the laws against the rum traffic. In fact, one of the main reasons why the Shawnees migrated to the western part of Pennsylvania was their desire to escape the ruinous effects of strong liquor. But the trader with his rum followed them into the forests of their western homes.

Then the Shawnee on the Conemaugh, Kiskiminetas, and Allegheny took steps, in 1738, to restrain this pernicious traffic. On March 20th of that year, three of their chiefs in this region, namely: "Loyporcowah (Opessah's Son), Newcheconneh (Deputy King), and Coycacolenne, or Coracolenne (Chief Counsellor)", wrote a letter to Thomas Penn and James Logan, Secretary of the Provincial Council, in which they acknowledged the receipt of a present from Penn and Logan of powder, lead, and tobacco, delivered to them by the trader, George Miranda; in which they say they have a good understanding with the French, the Five Nations, the Ottawas, and all the French Indians; that the tract of land reserved for them by the Proprietory Government on the west side of the Susquehanna does not suit them at present; and that they desire to remain in the region of the Allegheny and Kiskiminetas, make a strong town there, and keep their warriors from making war upon other nations at a distance. They then add:

"After we heard your letter read, and all our people being gathered together, we held a council together, to leave off drinking for the space of four years. . . . There was not many of our traders at home at the time of our council, but our friends, Peter Chartier and George Miranda; but the proposal of stopping the rum and all strong liquors was made to the rest in the winter, and they were all willing. As soon as it was concluded of, all the rum that was in the towns was staved and spilled, belonging both to Indians and white people, which in quantity consisted of about forty gallons, that was thrown in the street; and we have appointed four men to stave all the rum or strong liquors that is brought to the towns hereafter, either by Indians or white men, during the four years." A pledge signed by ninety-eight Shawnees and the two traders above named accompanied this letter, agreeing that all rum should be destroyed, and four men appointed in every town to see that no strong liquor should be brought into the Shawnee towns for the term of four years.

Previous to this action on the part of Loyparcowah and other chiefs of the Shawnees, the Delawares at Kittanning made complaints concerning the rum traffic. In 1732, the trader, Edmund Cartlidge, wrote the Governor from Kittanning that the chiefs there made reflections on the Government for permitting such large quantities of rum to be carried to the Allegheny and sold to the Indians at that place, contrary to law. Also, in 1733, the Shawnee chiefs in the Allegheny region wrote the Governor requesting that he send them an order permitting them "to break in pieces all kegs of rum so brought yearly and monthly by some new upstart of a trader without a license, who comes amongst us and brings nothing but rum, no powder, nor lead, nor clothing, but takes away with him those skins which the old licensed traders, who bring us everything necessary, ought to have in return for their goods sold us some years since." Also in 1734, the Shawnee chiefs at Allegheny wrote the Governor and requested that none of the licensed traders be allowed to bring them more than thirty gallons of rum twice in a year, except Peter Chartier, who "trades further than ye rest."

Loyparcowah later descended the Allegheny and Ohio, probably remaining for some time at Chartier's Old Town, on or near the site of Tarentum, Allegheny County, and at Logstown, near the site of Economy, in the same county. In 1752, we find him at the Lower Shawnee Town, at mouth of the Scioto. On February 8th, of this year, he joined with three other Shawnee chiefs of the Lower Shawnee Town, in a letter to Governor James Hamilton of Pennsylvania, informing the Governor that "all the nations settled on this River Ohio and on this side of the Lakes are in friendship and live as one people; but the French trouble us much; they threaten to cut us off, and have killed thirty of our brothers, the Twightwees (Miamis); and we now acquaint you that we intend to strike the French."

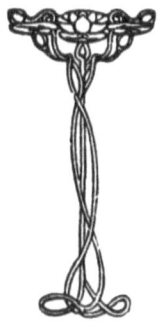

CHAPTER VI

Oretyagh, Ocowellos and Captain Civility

ORETYAGH

RETYAGH claims our remembrance as one of the chiefs of the Conestogas to come into touch with William Penn. He attended the council at Philadelphia, on July 6th, 1694, mentioned at the close of Chapter IV. This is his first appearance in recorded history.

Oretyagh Sells Susquehanna Land to William Penn

Oretyagh next appears as one of the grantors of lands on the Susquehanna to William Penn, the history of which transaction is as follows:

By deed, dated September 10th, 1683, the Conestoga chief, Kekelappan, granted to Penn "that half of all my lands betwixt Susquehanna and Delaware, which lieth on ye Susquehanna side." In this same deed he promises to sell Penn in the following spring, upon his return from hunting, the other half of his lands. Also, on October 18th, 1683, the Conestoga chieftain, Machaloha, who claimed to exercise authority over the Indians "on the Delaware River, Chesepeake Bay and up to ye falls of ye Susquehanna River", conveyed to Penn his right in his land.

With reference to the deeds of Kekelappan and Machaloha, Penn seems to have thought it advisable to get the consent of the Five Nations to his possession of the lands in the interior of the country in the region of the Susquehanna. He had no doubt learned of the defeat of the Susquehannas at their fort, in either Lancaster or York County, at the hands of the Five Nations, or Irquois, in 1675. Accordingly, he sent two agents to confer with the Irquois chiefs in New York, in the summer of 1683, with reference to these lands; and in July of that year, he wrote acting Governor Brockholls of New York, commending to his favor these agents sent to treat with the Iroquois "about some Susquehanna land on ye back of us, where I intend a colony forthwith."

On August 25th, 1683, a new Governor, Thomas Dongan, reached New York, displacing Brockholls. He remained Governor of the colony until August, 1688. Immediately upon his arrival, he heard of the negotiations of Penn's agents; and both he and the Albany justices feared that Penn would plant a strong settlement on the Susquehanna, and thus get the profitable fur trade of the Five Nations of New York. The Susquehanna River afforded a splendid highway from the central part of the Five Nations' territory right to the settlement which Dongan feared Penn would found on the lower part of that river. Dongan called "an extraordinary meeting" of the justices on September 7th. When they assembled, they had with them several chiefs of the Iroquois, among them being two Cayugas and "a Susquehanna." The justices closely questioned the chiefs concerning the "situation of the Susquehanna River" as to its geographical and trade relations with the settlements of the colony of New York, especially that of Albany. The chiefs replied that it was "one day's journey" from the Mohawk castles to the lake where the Susquehanna rises; that it was one and one-half days' journey overland from Oneida "to the kill which falls into the Susquehanna River", and one day from there to the river itself; that it was but a half day's journey overland and one day by water from Onondaga to the Susquehanna River; that it was but one and one-half days' journey by land and water from Cayuga to the Susquehanna River; and that it was three days' journey overland and two by water from the "four castles" of the Senecas to the Susquehanna River, and then only five days' journey by water to the Susquehanna castles. The chiefs explained that all this journey was "very easy, they conveying their packs in canoes."

It was but natural that the chiefs should inquire as to the reason for such detailed questioning. They inquired why the justices wanted all this information and pointedly asked whether the white men were coming to the Susquehanna. The justices asked them in turn how that would suit them, and the chiefs frankly replied "very well"; that it would be much easier and nearer for trade than Albany offered, "insomuch as they must bring everything thither on their backs." This candid statement of the chiefs was very alarming to the justices, and they immediately wrote Dongan urging that he find "an expedient for preventing" Penn's acquisition of a Susquehanna Indian title. On September 18th, Dongan advised the justices that he considered it "very convenient and necessary to putt a stopp to all proceedings in Mr. Penn's affairs with the Indians until his bounds and limits be adjusted"; and he instructed them "to suffer no manner of proceedings in that business" until they should receive further advice from him.

The justices, therefore, prevailed with the chiefs to advise the agents of Penn that they had no right to sell the Susquehanna lands, having promised them to "Corlaer"—the generic name for the New York governors—on some previous occasion, and to decline to proceed with the negotiations. Then Dongan, in order to get the matter in his own hands, procured from some of the sachems a deed of the lands to himself. Then he wrote Penn, on the 10th of October, advising him of the purchase, and again, on the 22nd of October, saying that it had been further confirmed by the Iroquois, but that he and Penn would not "fall out" over the matter.

Thus the matter stood until the 13th day of January, 1696, on which date Dongan executed a lease and release to William Penn of "all that tract of land lying upon, on both sides, the river commonly called or known by the name of Susquehanna River, and the lands adjacent, beginning at the mountains or head of the said river, and running as far as and into the bay of Chesapeake." The territory conveyed is further described as being the same "which the said Thomas Dongan lately purchased of or had given him by the Sinneca Susquehanna Indians."

This deed gave Penn whatever title to the Susquehanna Dongan had procured in 1683 from the Iroquois as over lords of the Susquehanna clans. But, in order to get indisputable title to these Susquehanna lands, Penn, after he returned to his Province early in December, 1699, from his fifteen years absence in England, made and concluded, on the 13th day of September, 1700, a treaty with Oretyagh, or Widaagh, and Andaggy-Junkquagh, "Kings or Sachems of the Susquehannagh Indians, and of the river under that name, and lands lying on both sides thereof", by the terms of which these chiefs granted to him all the rights they possessed on the Susquehanna, and ratified and confirmed unto him "ye bargain and sale of ye said lands, made unto Col. Thomas Dongan, now Earl Limerick, and formerly Governor of New York." This sale was further confirmed in the "Articles of Agreement" which Penn concluded with the Susquehanna or Conestoga Indians, at Philadelphia, on April 23, 1701, which agreement was related in Chapter V.

Oretyagh Bids Farewell to William Penn

Shortly before embarking for England, in the autumn of 1701, William Penn assembled a large company of the Delawares at his manor house at Pennsbury to review and confirm the covenants of peace and good will, which he had formerly made with them. The meeting was held in the great hall of the manor house. The sachems assured him that they had never broken a covenant "made with their hearts and not with their heads." After the business of the conference had been transacted, Penn made them many presents of coats and other articles, and then the Indians retired into the courtyard of the mansion to complete their ceremonies.

Likewise, Oretyagh, with a number of the sachems of the Conestogas and Shawnees, came to Philadelphia shortly before Penn's final departure for England, to take leave of their beloved "Brother Onas." At this conference, which was held on October 7th, 1701, Penn informed the chiefs that it was likely the last interview that he would ever have with them; that he had ever loved and been kind to them and ever would continue so to be, not through political designs or for a selfish interest, but out of real affection. He desired them, in his absence to cultivate friendship with those whom he would leave in authority, so that the bond of friendship already formed might grow the stronger throughout the passing years. He also informed them that the Assembly was at that time enacting a law, according to their desire, to prevent their being abused by the selling of rum among them, with which Oretyagh, in the name of the rest, expressed great satisfaction, and desired that the law might speedily and effectually be put into execution. Oretyagh said that his people had long suffered from the ravages of the rum traffic, and that he now hoped for redress, believing that they would have no reason for complaint of this matter in the future.

Penn early saw the degradation which the Indians' unquenchable thirst for strong drink wrought among them, and he did all in his power to remedy this matter. He said that it made his heart sick to note the deterioration of character and the degradation which the strong liquor and vices of the white man wrought among the Indians during his short stay in the Province.

Finally, at this leavetaking, Penn requested the Indians that, if any of his colonists should ever transgress the law and agreement, which he and his governor had entered into with them, they should at once inform the government of his Province, so that the offenders might be prosecuted. This they promised to observe faithfully, and that, if any rum were brought among them, they would not buy it, but send the person who brought it back with it again. Then, informing the chiefs that he had charged the members of his Council that they should, in all respects, be kind and just to the Indians in every manner as he had been, and making them presents, he bade them adieu never to meet them again.

Well would it have been for the Colony of Pennsylvania, if Penn's successors had always emulated his example in dealing with the Indians—if his successors had been imbued with his kindly spirit, and had treated the natives with justice. He died on the 30th of July, 1718, at Ruscombe, near Tywford, in Buckinghamshire, England, at the age of seventy-four; and when his great heart was cold and still in death, the Red Man of the Pennsylvania forests lost his truest friend. During Penn's life there were no serious troubles between his colony and the Indian, and no actual warfare, as we shall see, for some years thereafter; but, less than a generation after this great apostle of the rights of man was gathered to his fathers, the Delawares, who had welcomed him so kindly, and the Shawnees, rose in revolt, after a long series of wrongs, and spread terror, devastation, and death throughout the Pennsylvania settlements.

Says Dr. George P. Donehoo: "The memory of William Penn lingered in the wigwams of the Susquehanna and the Ohio until the last red man of this generation had passed away; and then the tradition of him was handed down to the generations which followed until today, when it still lingers, like a peaceful benediction, among the Delaware and Shawnee on the sweeping plains of Oklahoma."

Oretyagh made a later protest against the abuses of the rum traffic by the Pennsylvania traders. In May, 1704, according to the Colonial Records: "Oretyagh, the chief now of Conestoga, requested him [Nicole Godin, a trader] to complain to the Governor [John Evans] of the great quantities of rum continually brought to their town, insomuch that they (the Conestogas) are ruined by it, having nothing left, but have laid out all, even their clothes for rum, and may now, when threatened with war, be surprised by their enemies, when besides themselves with drink, and so utterly be destroyed." With this protest against the detestable traffic, which, even at this early day, was bringing ruin upon the Pennsylvania Indians, we close this sketch of Oretyagh, the friend of William Penn.

OCOWELLOS

Perhaps the first reference to the Shawnee chief, Ocowellos, is in the account of the conference which Governor William Keith of Pennsylvania held with the Shawnees, Conestogas, Conoy, and other Indians at Conestoga, in July, 1717, at which time and place he asked them to explain their connection with an attack made by the Senecas upon the Catawbas, then under the protection of Virginia. The Shawnee chief advised the Governor that six Shawnees had accompanied the war party of Senecas who made the attack, but that these six were from a Shawnee settlement much higher up the Susquehanna. At any rate, Ocowellos is referred to as "King of the Upper Shawnees" in the minutes of a council held at Philadelphia, May 20th, 1723, when an address from him to the Provincial Council was read in which he mentioned past visits to the Governor of Canada, and another which he then contemplated making. Most authorities believe that his seat was then near the mouth of Chillisquaque Creek, on the east bank of the West Branch of the Susquehanna, in Northumberland County.

Ocowellos removed from the Susquehanna to the valley of the Conemaugh prior to 1731, possibly several years earlier. On October 29th, 1731, Jonas Davenport, an Indian trader, made an affidavit for the Provincial Council, in which he said: "On Connumach [Conemaugh] Creek, there are three Shawnee towns; 45 families; 200 men; Chief Okowela [Ocowellos], suspected to be a favorer of the French interest."

The three Conemaugh towns, over which Ocowellos ruled in 1731 and later, can not be definitely located. They were probably the following: Keckenpaulin's Old Town, at the mouth of the Loyalhanna, in Westmoreland County; Black Legs Town, at the mouth of Black Legs Creek, in Indiana County; and Conemaugh Old Town on the site of Johnstown, Cambria County.

From the few glimpses of Ocowellos that we get in the Colonial Records, it is seen that he was one of the Shawnee chiefs who early yielded to French influence.

CAPTAIN CIVILITY

Captain Civility, or Civility, was a chief of the Conestogas, descendants of the ancient Susquehannas. As "Chief of the Conestogas", he is mentioned in the Colonial Records from 1710 to 1736. He was present at the conference at Conestoga, June 8th, 1710, between the Pennsylvania commissioners, John French and Henry Worley, and the deputies of the Tuscaroras, when this tribe sought permission to settle within the bounds of Penn's Colony, an account of which conference was given in Chapter II.

He seems to have had varying degrees of authority. For instance, in the minutes of the conference at Conestoga, above referred to, he is mentioned as "the Senneques' [Conestogas'] King", and on July 23rd, 1712, as a "War Captain and Chief"; in June, 1713, he is mentioned as "the young Indian called Civility, now one of their [the Conestogas] chiefs; in June, 1715, he and Satayoght, or Satayriote, are called "the chiefs of the Conestogas"; while, July 30th, 1716, Satayriote is called chief, and Civility the "Captain", of the Conestogas. In June, 1718, he attended a conference at Philadelphia, in the minutes of which he is called "the present chief or captain of the Conestogas."

In this conference, Civility informed Governor Keith that the Conestogas had chosen, Oneshanayan, to be their new king. He also attended a conference at Philadelphia, in July, 1720, and soon thereafter seems to have become the ruling chief of the Conestogas; though in the minutes of a conference held at Conestoga, May 26th, 1728, between Governor Gordon and the Conestogas, Shawnees, and Conoy, (which will be described in Chapter VIII) he, Tawenna, Ganyataronga, and Tanniatchiaro are mentioned as "chiefs of the Conestogoe Indians." In October, 1728, he wrote Governor Gordon acquainting him with the fact that several of the Delawares, Shawnees, and Conoy had come to Conestoga and brought many skins with them as a present for the Governor; "that they purposed to fulfill their promise of coming to Philadelphia this fall, but that the death of his, Civility's, child had so much afflicted him that he could not come with them, and therefore they had all resolved to defer their visit until spring, at which time they would surely come to the Governor of Philadelphia."

In 1729, he wrote Governor Gordon concerning the killing and capture of nine Shawnees near the Potomac by the "Southern Indians" [Catawbas]; and, on May 26th of that year, he was the chief speaker of the Conestogas at a conference held at Philadelphia between Governor Gordon and the Conestogas, Shawnees, and Conoy, in which he complained very bitterly of the baneful effects of the carrying of so much rum to the Indians. The last mention of Civility, in the Colonial Records, is in the minutes of a conference held at Philadelphia, on October 14th, 1736, between Thomas Penn and eighteen Iroquois chiefs, whose speaker informed Penn and the Provincial Council; "That if Civility at Connestogoe should attempt to make a sale of any lands to us, or any of our neighbors, they must let us know that he hath no power to do so, and if he does any thing of the kind, they, the Indians, will utterly disown him."

Troubles Between the Northern and the Southern Indians

But Civility claims our remembrance chiefly on account of his conferences with the Colonial Authorities during the troubles between the Northern and the Southern Indians in the years following the migration of the Tuscaroras from Carolina and Virginia to the territory of the Five Nations in New York. As was pointed out in Chapter II, they began this migration in 1712 or 1713, and were formally admitted, in 1722, as a constituent part of the Iroquois Confederation. However, while the Tuscaroras were still living in their southern home, they were the bitter enemies of the Catawbas, and their hatred did not abate upon their removing to New York.

Almost every summer after 1713, roving bands of the Tuscaroras and other members of the Five Nations, followed the mountain valleys through Pennsylvania to the South, on their way to attack the Catawbas and Cherokees; and many Conestogas joined these war parties. Some destruction was done by these bands within the Province of Pennsylvania, but presently the Colonial Authorities adopted the method of having the farmers, whose crops were injured, place their bill in the hands of the nearest justice of the peace, who would, in turn, forward it to the Provincial Council; and, at the next conference with the Indians, the Council would deduct the amount of the bill from the present given to the Indians at that conference. This method made Pennsylvania practically free from ravages wrought by these bands. The colony of Virginia, however, did not fare so well, and both lives and property were destroyed by these bands of warriors from the North.

These war parties of the Iroquois frequently made Conestoga their stopping place on their way to and return from the territory of the Catawbas and Cherokees, and many a captive Catawba and Cherokee was tortured to death at Conestoga. Finally a treaty of peace was made between the Conestogas and Catawbas, on August 31st, 1715, but this did not put a stop to the expeditions of the Iroquois against the Southern Indians.

In June, 1717, Governor William Keith received a message from Civility and several other chiefs of the Conestoga region, desiring him to visit them without delay to consult about affairs of great importance. The Governor, accordingly, journeyed to Conestoga, in July, where he met the chiefs of the Conestogas, Delawares, Shawnees, and Conoys, and inquired of them the cause of their alarm. He ascertained that about two months previously a young Delaware, son of a chief, had been killed on one of the branches of the Potomac by a party of Virginians accompanied by some Indians. These latter were no doubt Catawbas, who, at that time, were at peace with Virginia. At this meeting at Conestoga, Governor Keith brought to the attention of the Indians that many complaints had been made by the inhabitants of Virginia concerning the destruction caused by the war parties of the Iroquois against the Catawbas; and he reminded them of the fact that, although divided into different colonies, the English were one people; that to injure or make war upon one body of them was to make war upon all, and that the Indians, therefore, must never molest or trouble any of the English colonists, nor make war upon any Indians who were in friendship with, or under the protection of, the English.

At this conference, Keith stressed the fact that recently a band of Senecas had attacked some Catawbas near Fort Christian, in the colony of Virginia, killing six and capturing a woman; and he called upon the Indians of the Conestoga region to explain their connection with this insult to Virginia. The Shawnee chief told the Governor that six young men of this tribe had accompanied the party of Senecas who made the attack upon the Catawbas, but explained that none of the six were present at the time and place of this conference, "their settlements being much higher up the Susquehanna River." The chief further stated that the six Shawnees declared, upon their return, that they had nothing to do with the attack upon the Catawbas.

Governor Keith closed the conference with the following stipulations, quoted from the minutes of the conference:

"1st. That he expected their strict observance of all former contracts of friendship made between them and the Government of Pennsylvania.

"2dly. That they must never molest or disturb any of the English Governments, nor make war upon any Indians whatsoever who are in friendship with and under the protection of the English.

"3dly. That, in all cases of suspicion or danger, they must advise and consult with this Government before they undertook or determined any thing.

"4thly. That, if through accident any mischief of any sort should happen to be done by the Indians to the English, or by the English to them, then both parties should meet with hearty intention of good will to obtain an acknowledgment of the mistake, as well as to give or receive reasonable satisfaction.

"5thly. That, upon these terms and conditions, the Governor did, in the name of their great and good friend, William Penn, take them and their people under the same protection, and in the same friendship with this Government, as William Penn himself had formerly done, or could do now if he was here present.

"And the Governor hereupon did promise, on his part, to encourage them in peace, and to nourish and support them like a true friend and brother.

"To all which the several chiefs and their great men presently assented, it being agreed, that, in testimony thereof, they should rise up and take the Governor by the hand, which accordingly they did with all possible marks of friendship in their countenance and behaviour."

But the trouble between them did not end with the foregoing conference at Conestoga. In 1719, great difficulties arose concerning the hunting grounds of the Northern and the Southern Indians. The Iroquois sent out many war parties, which stopped at Conestoga on their way south, and were joined by many of the Conestogas. These raids into the Shenandoah Valley brought many white settlers of Virginia and the Carolinas into hostility to the Iroquois; for these Colonies were then on friendly terms with the Catawbas and Cherokees, against whom the raids were directed. In fact, a general uprising of the settlers of Virginia and the Carolinas was imminent. The Iroquois conducted their warfare on the Southern Indians with great brutality, torturing many captives to death at Conestoga and villages on the Susquehanna.

On receiving a letter from Civility and other chiefs at Conestoga advising that some of their Indians had been killed by the Southern Indians, Governor Keith sent Colonel John French to Conestoga, where a council was held on June 28th, 1719, with Civility and Queen Canatowa of the Conestogas, "Wightomina, King of the Delawares, Sevana, King of the Shawnees", who succeeded Opessah at Pequea, and "Winninchack, King of the Canawages" [Conoys]. In the name of Governor Keith, Colonel French made the following demands of Civility and the other chiefs: That they should not receive the war parties of the Tuscaroras, or any other tribes of the Five Nations, if coming to their towns on their way to or return from the South; and that they would have to answer to the Colonial Authorities, if any prisoner were tortured by them. It appeared, however, that the warriors of the Five Nations, on their way southward, practically forced the young men of the Conestogas, Shawnees, and Conoy to accompany them. As the conquerors of these tribes, the Iroquois demanded their allegiance and help. The chiefs promised faithfully to obey the commands of Governor Keith, but the war went on.

James Logan, Secretary of the Provincial Council, on June 27, 1720, held a conference at Conestoga with Civility and chiefs of the Shawnees, Delawares, and Conoy, in an attempt to persuade these Indians from making raids into Virginia. Not long before, ten Iroquois and two Shawnees had been killed by the Southern Indians about one hundred and sixty miles from Conestoga. At this conference, Logan learned that the Pequea Shawnees could not be restrained from assisting the Iroquois, inasmuch as since the departure of Opessah, no one could control them. True, the Conestogas were answerable for the behavior of these Shawnees, but Civility advised Logan that he "had only the name without any authority, and could do nothing." Moreover, it was difficult for Logan to impress upon the minds of these Indians the fact that the English of Virginia and Maryland were not at war with the English of Pennsylvania. They could not see why the Indians in friendship with Pennsylvania should not go to war against the Virginians, just as the Iroquois went to war against the Indians of Virginia and the Carolinas.

At the close of the conference, Captain Civility told Logan privately that the Five Nations, especially the Cayugas, were much dissatisfied because of the large settlements the English were making on the Susquehanna, and that the Iroquois claimed a property right in those lands. As to the Iroquois' claim to a property right in the Susquehanna lands, Logan told Civility that the Indians well knew that the Iroquois had long before conveyed those lands to the Governor of New York, and that William Penn had purchased this right, as was pointed out in Chapter VI. Civility acknowledged this fact.

Realizing the awful consequences of a general war between the Iroquois and their allies, on the one side, and the Southern Indians on the other, involving the settlers of the South, Governor Keith, in the spring of 1721, visited Governor Spotswood of Virginia with whom he framed an agreement, by the terms of which the tributary Indians of Virginia would not, in the future, pass the Potomac nor "the high ridge of mountains extending along the back of Virginia; provided that the Indians to the northward of the Potomac and to the westward of those mountains" would observe the same limits.

Governor Keith, accompanied by seventy armed horsemen, visited Conestoga on July 5th, 1721, where he conferred, at Civility's lodge, not only with the Conestogas but also with four deputies of the Five Nations, who had recently arrived there, telling the spokesman of the Five Nations, Ghesoant, that, "whereas the English from a very small beginning had now become a great people in the Western World, far exceeding the number of all the Indians, which increase was the fruit of peace among themselves, the Indians continued to make war upon one another and were destroying one another, as if it was their purpose that none of them should be left alive." He called attention to the suffering that their wars caused to the women and children at home, and, in various ways, tried to mollify their warlike passions, but stated that, if they were determined to continue warfare, they must, in journeying to and from the South, take another path lying farther to the west, and not pass through the settled parts of the Province. The result of the conference was the ratifying by the Conestogas and Five Nations of the agreement arranged by Governor Keith and Governor Spotswood as to the limits of the hunting grounds of the Virginia and the Pennsylvania Indians. Keith closed the conference by giving Ghesoant a gold coronation medal of George, the First, which he asked him to take as a token of friendship to the greatest chief of the Five Nations, Kannygoodk. Thus, happily, the immediate danger of a general Indian uprising was averted.

This was the most important Indian treaty ever held at Conestoga. Later, troubles came on apace between the Iroquois and the Southern Indians, but the Iroquois abandoned the Susquehanna route to the South, taking the Warrior's Path, which crossed the Potomac at Old Town (Opessah's Town), and, still later, when white settlers occupied the valley along Warrior Ridge, a trail farther westward, crossing the counties of Westmoreland and Fayette.

While there was now a lull in the trouble between the Northern and the Southern Indians, the fears of the Province were further awakened by a quarrel between two brothers, John and Edmund Cartilidge, and a Seneca Indian, near Conestoga, in which the latter was cruelly murdered early in 1721. The Colonial Authorities well knew the Indians' love for revenge, and they apprehended severe retaliation. A rigid inquiry was made into the matter, and an inquest was ordered to be held on the body, though the same had been buried for more than two months. The Cartilidge brothers were seized and put in jail in Philadelphia, awaiting trial under the laws of the Colony. Messengers were sent by the Colonial Authorities to the Five Nations, advising them that the Provincial Council deplored the incident, and, in order to prevent a repetition of such unfortunate occurrences, had prohibited the sale of rum and other strong drink to the Indians by re-enacting the former law on this matter, with additional penalties.

Treaty at Albany

In this sketch of Civility, we call attention to the Albany Treaty of 1722, definitely ending, for a time, the troubles between the Iroquois and the Catawbas, in which troubles he had a prominent part. The Iroquois, in the summer of 1722, invited Governor Keith to meet them with the Governors of Virginia, New York, and New England, in a great council at Albany, New York, in which all matters between the Indians and these colonies could be taken up. In extending the investigation, they explained that their king was an old man, and could not make a journey to Philadelphia. The council was accordingly held at Albany, on the 10th day of September, 1722, in which the Five Nations acknowledged that Penn's Governors had always observed the treaties that Penn had entered into with the Indians, surrendered all claim to their lands on the Susquehanna concerning which the Cayugas had made claim, and with great magnanimity pardoned the offense of the Cartilidge brothers in having murdered the Seneca Indian. Governor Keith had explained to them that the brothers were now out on bail awaiting trial. The reply of the great "king" of the Five Nations, pardoning the Cartilidge brothers, shows the better qualities of the Indians' nature. It is thus recorded in Volume III of the Colonial Records of Pennsylvania: "The great King of the Five Nations is sorry for the death of the Indian that was killed, for he was of his own flesh and blood; he believes the Governor [Keith] is also sorry; but, now that it is done, there is no help for it, and he desires that Cartilidge may not be put to death, nor that the Governor should be angry and spare him for some time, and put him to death afterwards; one life is enough to be lost; there should not two die."

At this treaty, Governor Spotswood, or Virginia, secured the assent of the Tuscaroras and other members of the Five Nations to a proposed boundary within the limits of which the Indians of Virginia should be safe, as follows: That the various tribes tributary to the colony of Virginia should not, without having a passport from the Governor, on any pretense whatsoever, cross to the northern side of the Potomac or to the west side of the Allegheny Mountains; in case they should do so without such passport, it should be lawful for the Indians to the northward to put such Southern Indians to death. Also that the Five Nations and the Shawnees, should not, without having a passport, cross to the southern side of the Potomac River or to the eastward of the Allegheny Mountains; that, in case any of these Northern Indians should pass beyond these boundaries, they should be put to death or sold into slavery.

At the close of the treaty, "the speaker of the Five Nations holding up the Coronet, they [the Iroquois] gave six shouts, five for the Five Nations, and one for a Castle of the Tuscaroras, lately seated between Oneyde [Oneida] and Onondage [Onondaga]", indicating that the Tuscaroras were, at that time, an integral part of the Confederation of the Iroquois, thus making the Six Nations.

First Reference to the Ohio and Allegheny

In closing this sketch of Civility, we call attention to the fact that he attended a council held in Philadelphia on July 3rd to 5th, 1727, at which the Indians requested that "none of the traders be allowed to carry any rum to the remoter parts where James LeTorte trades, (that is Allegheny on the branches of the Ohio)." This is the first mention in the Colonial Records of Pennsylvania of the region on the Ohio and Allegheny, and shows that, at this early date, the Indian traders from Conestoga had established trading posts in the valleys of the Ohio and Allegheny. In the minutes of this conference, also, we find reference to "a fort" (no doubt trading house) which the French had already built in the valley of the Allegheny. He also attended the conference held at Conestoga May 26th, 1728, between Governor Gordon and the chiefs of the Conestogas, Shawnees, Conoy, and Delawares, with reference to the Indian troubles of that year, as related in the chapter on Kakowatcheky (Chapter VIII).

CHAPTER VII

Sassoonan or Allumapees

The Line of Succession From Tamanend

ASSOONAN, or Allumapees, was head chief of the Turtle Clan of Delawares from a date prior to June 14th, 1715, until his death in the autumn of 1747. By some very high authorities, it is claimed that he was a son of the great Tamanend and, as a little boy, was with his father at the "Great Treaty". These authorities make Sassoonan identical with "Weheequeckhon, alias Andrew", who as stated in Chapter IV, joined with his father, Tamanend, his two brothers, and his uncle, in conveying to William Penn, on the fifth day of July, 1697, certain lands between the Pennypack and Neshaminy creeks, and whom Tamanend describes in the deed, as, "my son who is to be king after my death."

As stated in Chapter IV, Tamanend died probably before 1701; for, at council held at Philadelphia on July 26th of that year, his name is not mentioned in the list of Delaware chiefs at that time. Who succeeded Tamanend in the kingship of the Turtle Clan of Delawares is not known, though some authorities think that Owechela was his successor, and identify him with Weheelan, Tamanend's brother, one of the grantors in the deed of July 5th, 1697, suggesting that he may have acted as vice-regent during the minority of Weheequeckhon, alias Andrew. Plausibility is given to the claim that Owechela succeeded Tamanend by the fact that a·chief named Owhala, or Ochale, (a name very similar to Owechela, if he was not actually this same chief) is called "King of the Delawares" in the Maryland Council Records of 1698 and 1700. Says Charles A. Hanna:

"Whether or not Owechela was the ruling chief of the Delawares from 1701 to 1709, the name of a new chief appears on the records of the latter year. This was Skalitchy, who with Owechela, Passakassy, and Sassoonan, attended the conference at Philadelphia in July, 1709."

The conference to which Mr. Hanna refers was held on the 26th of July, and, in the minutes thereof, Sassoonan's place of residence is set forth as being "at Peshtang [Paxtang] above Conestoga." But Skalitchy also attended a conference between the Indians and Governor Charles Gookin and the Provincial Council, held on May 19th, 1712, at the house of Edward Farmar, at White Marsh, in what is now Montgomery County, in which he took the most prominent part. Sassoonan, too, was present at the conference.

We pause in the narration of the successors to Tamanend's kingship to call attention to the fact that the conference at the house of Edward Farmar deserves our attention on account of the light it throws on the subjugation of the Delawares by the Five Nations. Governor Gookin and the Provincial Council had been summoned to Farmar's house to meet Skalitchy, Sassoonan and twelve other Delaware chiefs, who desired to confer with the Governor and Council before setting out on a journey to the Five Nations. At the conference, Skalitchy addressed the Governor as follows: "Many years ago, being made tributaries to the Mingoes, or Five Nations, and being now about to visit them, they [the Delaware chiefs] thought fit first to wait on the Governor and Council; to lay before them the collection they had made of their tribute to offer; and to have a conference with the Governor upon it."

They then spread out on the floor thirty-two belts of wampum having figures and designs wrought therein by their women, and a long pipe having a stone head and a cane shaft with feathers attached and arranged to resemble wings. They called this pipe the Calumet, and said that it had been given to them by the Five Nations at the time of their subjugation, to be kept and shown to other nations, among whom they might go, as a token of their subjection to the Iroquois. One of the wampum belts, they said, "was sent by one, who at the time of their agreement or submission, was an infant and orphan, the son of a considerable man amongst them." Skalitchy explained that twenty-four of these wampum belts were sent by women, because "the paying of tribute becomes none but women and children." Hanna suggests that the receipt by the Council of the Five Nations of so many tribute wampum belts from the women of the Delawares at this time and, no doubt, at times earlier and later, probably "did much to confirm the tradition among the Five Nations that the Delaware Indians were but a nation of women."

Skalitchy's name does not appear again in the Colonial Records until the conference held at Philadelphia on June 14th, 1715, which was the conference with Governor Gookin and the Provincial

Council mentioned in Chapter IV, in the minutes of which Sassoonan is reported as saying, among other things, "that their [the Delawares'] late king, Skalitchy, desired of them that they would take care to keep a perfect peace with ye English." Sassoonan was the head of the Delaware delegation at this conference, and his statement, just quoted, fixes the date af Skalitchy's death and Sassoonan's succession to the kingship of the Delawares as between the conference of May 19th, 1712, and the conference of June 14th, 1715.

As we have seen, there had been many conferences between the Colonial Authorities, on the one hand, and the Delawares, Shawnees, Conestogas, and Conoy on the other, during the intervening years; but the conference of June 14th, 1715, is entitled to more than passing notice, for the reason that Sassoonan referred particularly to the "Great Treaty", which Penn made with the Delawares in the early days of the history of the Province. The conference was simply for the purpose of renewing the ancient bond of friendship. In the minutes of this conference, we read the following:

"Then Sassoonan rose and spoke to the Governor and said that the calumet, the bond of peace, which they had carried to all the nations round, they had now brought hither; that it was a sure bond and seal of peace amongst them and between them and us, and desired, by holding up their hands, that the God of Heaven might be witness to it, and that there might be a firm peace between them and us forever. . . . . That they desired the peace that had been made should be so firm, that they and we should join hand in hand so firmly that nothing, even the greatest tree, should be able to divide them asunder."

The minutes of this council contain the statement that, "We [the Governor and Council] doubted not but they [the Indians] think themselves and their children, from generation to generation, obliged to keep inviolably those firm treaties of peace which had been made."

Sassoonan's Deed of Release

In the autumn of 1718, Sassoonan and several other chiefs of the Delawares came to Philadelphia, claiming that they had not been paid for their lands. Then, James Logan, secretary of the Provincial Council, produced to them, in the presence of the Council, a number of deeds, and convinced Sassoonan and his brother chiefs that they were mistaken in their contention. Accordingly, Sassoonan and six other chiefs executed a release on the 17th day of September, 1718, by the terms of which they acknowledged that their ancestors had conveyed to William Penn, in fee, all the land and had been paid for the same. By the same instrument these Indians released all the land "between the Delaware and the Susquehanna from Duck Creek [in Delaware] to the mountains [the South Mountain] on this side of Lechay [by the Lehigh River]."

At the time of executing this deed of release, Sassoonan was still living at Paxtang, and adjacent parts; but it is probable that shortly thereafter he took up his abode at Shamokin (Sunbury), which became his home for the remainder of his life. The Delawares, who, as pointed out in Chapter I, migrated from the vicinity of Shamokin to the Allegheny in 1724, were of Sassoonan's clan.

Sassoonan Clears Members of Turtle Clan From Blame for Murder of Thomas Wright

At a meeting of the Provincial Council, on September 27th, 1727, Secretary James Logan, advised the Council that, on the day before, he received a letter from John Wright, justice of the peace, giving an account of the murder of one, Thomas Wright, who was killed, on the eleventh day of that month, by some Indians at Snaketown, forty miles above Conestoga, possibly above the mouth of Swatara Creek, in Dauphin County. Enclosed with the letter were the depositions of John Wilkins, Esther Burt, and Mary Wright, and the inquisition held on the dead body.

The affair took place at the trading house of John Burt, an Indian trader at Snaketown. The unfortunate Thomas Wright and some Indians were drinking with Burt near the house, when a dispute arose between one of the Indians and Wright; whereupon, Burt urged Wright to knock the Indian down. Wright then laid hold of the Indian, and Burt struck him (the Indian) several blows with his fist. Wright and Burt then retired into the trading house, and the Indians followed. Wright endeavored to pacify them, but Burt called for his gun, and continued to provoke them more and more in a way too revolting and disgusting to be told in the language of decency. Wright fled to the hen-house to hide himself, whither the Indians pursued him, and the next morning he was found there dead. The inquisition on his body set forth that he came to his death by several blows on his head, neck, and temples.

The Colonial Authorities were much disturbed by this, the first murder of a white man by the Indians after William Penn first arrived in his Province, forty-five years before. They were of the opinion that John Burt was to blame for the unhappy incident, on account of his provoking the Indians to such a high degree. The record of the incident, as set forth in Volume III of the Colonial Records, states that although Burt was a licensed trader, yet "it was scarce possible to find a man in the whole Government more unfit for it." A warrant was issued for his arrest, but he escaped, and was next heard of at the Forks of the Ohio.

The Indians were Delawares of the Munsee or Wolf Clan as was ascertained in June, 1728, when Sassoonan, his nephew, Opekasset, and a number of other chiefs, including the great Shikellamy, the vice-gerent of the Six Nations, who had recently been sent to Shamokin (Sunbury) by the Six Nations to rule over the Shawnees and Delawares on the Susquehanna, met Governor Patrick Gordon at Philadelphia, where a great council was held on the 4th and 5th of that month. Sassoonan being asked by Governor Gordon about the death of Thomas Wright, replied: "That it [the murder] was not done by any of their people; that it was done by some of the Menysinck [Minisink] Indians; that the Menysincks live at the Forks of the Susquehannah, above Meehayomy [Wyoming], and that their king's name is Kindassowa." The "Forks of the Sasquehannah" may refer to the forks of the Tioga, or Chemung, and the Susquehanna near Athens, Bradford County; or it may refer to the junction of the Lackawanna and the Susquehanna in Luzerne County. At any rate, wherever the Indians lived that killed Thomas Wright, they never were brought to account.

Sassoonan and the Tulpyhocken Lands

At this same conference, (June 4th and 5th, 1728,) Sassoonan complained that the Palatines (immigrants from Germany) were settling on the lands in the valley of the Tulpyhocken, in Berks and Lebanon counties, which, as he claimed, had not been purchased from the Indians. These particular Palatines had first settled in the Schoharie Valley in New York, where they endured much suffering. When Governor William Keith, of Pennsylvania, attended the Albany conference in September, 1727, the hardships of these Palatines were related to him; whereupon his interest and sympathy were aroused, and he offered them a home in Pennsylvania. Then, in the autumn of 1727, about fifty families of these

Germans, under the leadership of the father of the famous Conrad Weiser, the Indian interpreter of the Colony of Pennsylvania, cut a road from the Schoharie Valley through the wilderness to the headwaters of the Susquehanna. They then descended this river to the mouth of Swatara Creek, in Dauphin County. Ascending this stream and crossing the divide between the Susquehanna and the Schuylkill, they entered the fertile and charming valley of the Tulpyhocken. They had scarcely erected their rude cabins and commenced to plant their little patches of corn in the clearings in the wilderness, when the Indians of the neighborhood informed them that this land had never been purchased by the Pennsylvania Government. The Indians were much surprised that these settlers should be permitted to take up their abode on unpurchased land. "Surely," said they, "if Brother Onos were living, such things would never happen."

At this conference, Sassoonan said that he could not have believed that these lands were settled upon, if he had not gone there and seen the settlements with his own eyes. In the minutes of the conference, we read: "He (Sassoonan) said he was grown old and was troubled to see the Christians settle on lands that the Indians had never been paid for; they had settled on his lands for which he had never received anything. That he is now an old man, and must soon die; that his children may wonder to see all their father's lands gone from them without his receiving anything for them; that the Christians now make their settlements very near them (the Indians); and they shall have no place of their own left to live on; that this may occasion a difference between their children and us, and he would willingly prevent any misunderstanding that may happen."

Governor Gordon suggested to Sassoonan that possibly the lands in dispute had been included in some of the other purchases; but Sassoonan and his brother chiefs replied that no lands had ever been sold northwest of the Blue Ridge, then called the Lehigh Hills. This conference did not succeed in settling the matter of these settlements in the Tulpyhocken Valley. The matter dragged along until 1732, when Sassoonan, Elalapis, Ohopamen, Pesqueetamen, Mayemoe, Partridge, and Tepakoasset, on behalf of themselves and all other Indians having a right in the lands, in consideration of 20 brass kettles, 20 fine guns, 50 tomahawks, 60 pairs of scissors, 24 looking glasses, 20 gallons of rum, and various other articles so acceptable to the Indians, conveyed unto John Penn, Thomas Penn, and Richard Penn, proprietors of the Province, all those lands "situate, lying and being on the River Schuylkill and the branches thereof, between the mountains called Lechaig (Lehigh) to the south, and the hills or mountains, called Keekachtanemin, on the north, and between the branches of the Delaware River on the east, and the waters falling into the Susquehanna River on the west,"—a grant which embraced the valley of the Tulpyhocken.

Sassoonan attended another conference at Philadelphia in the year 1728. This was a conference with Governor Gordon and the Provincial Council, on October 10th of that year, in which the old chief expressed his pleasure on the settlement of the troubles in that year with Kakowatcheky's Clan of Shawnees at Pechoquealin, an account of which is given in Chapter VIII. In the minutes of the conference of October 10th, are found these sentiments of Sassoonan: "He tells the Governor that he hopes all the differences between them and us will be buried deep and covered from sight; that, when our and their children, in after times, observe the great friendship that has been between us, it may rejoice and gladden their hearts. And he now hopes . . . . that their children may afterwards say: 'This is the place where our fathers and our brethren (meaning the Christians) ended and composed all their differences.' "

A Threatened Uprising

Sassoonan's name appears another time in the Colonial Records for the year 1728. In April of that year, James LeTort, a trader, who was then living in the Indian town of Chenastry, located on the West Branch of the Susquehanna, at the mouth of Chillisquaque Creek, not far above the present town of Sunbury, informed Governor Gordon that he had intended, in the autumn of 1727, taking a journey as far as the Miami Indians, who were then living on the Wabash River, to trade with them; but, on consulting with Madam Montour, then living at Chenastry, but who had lived among the Miamis and had a sister married to one of that nation, and also with Manawkyhickon, a celebrated chief of the Munsee Clan of Delawares in the region of Chenastry, he learned from these persons that the Delawares who were hunting on the Allegheny and Ohio, had been called home. Upon further inquiry he learned that Manawkyhickon was a near relative of Wequela, who had been hanged in New Jersey in 1727, and that Manawkyhickon, resenting the death of his relative had "sent a black belt to the Five Nations, and that the Five Nations sent the same to the Miamis with a message desiring to know if they would lift up their axes and join with them against the Christians; to which they agreed." LeTort advised that he inquired of Sassoonan whether he knew anything concerning the matters which had been brought to LeTort's attention by Madam Montour, and found Sassoonan entirely ignorant of them. The information which LeTort brought to the Colonial Authorities caused considerable uneasiness, and the Council ordered that presents be sent to Sassoonan, Madam Montour, and Manawkyhickon, and that messages be sent to them desiring them to report any new developments in regard to this rumor, which proved to be unfounded.

Governor Gordon Writes Sassoonan as to Robbing of Traders

Anthony Sadowsky, John Maddox, and John Fisher, traders on the Allegheny, made a complaint to Governor Gordon, on August 8th, 1730, stating that, in June, 1729, they had been robbed of one hundred pounds worth of goods, by the Indians on the Allegheny; and they asked that a demand for satisfaction be sent through "Allumappees [Sassoonan] at Shackachtan [Shamokin, now Sunbury] and Great Hill, at Allegheny." The Governor then wrote a letter concerning the matter to Sassoonan and Opekasset, at Shamokin, and Mechouquatchough, or Great Hill, at Kittanning. However, Maddox stated two years later that he was still without satisfaction for his stolen goods.

Sassoonan Kills Shackatawlin

At a meeting of the Provincial Council held in August, 1731, the frequent complaints made by the Indians on account of the large quantities of rum being carried to them by the traders, were taken up. The Council's attention was called to the fact that the pernicious liquor traffic had recently caused a very unhappy incident in the family of Sassoonan. In a fit of drunkenness, he had killed his nephew, (some authorities say his cousin) Shackatawlin, at their dwelling place at Shamokin, now Sunbury. Sassoonan's grief over the unhappy incident was so great that it almost cost him his life.

Asked at this conference whether he desired an entire stop put to the sending of rum to the Indians, Sassoonan replied, on August 13th, as follows:

"That the Indians do not desire that rum should be entirely

stopped and that none at all should be brought to them; they would have some but not much, and desire none may be brought but by sober good men, who will take a dram with them to refresh them and not so much as to hurt them. The Governor knows there are ill people amongst the Christians as well as amongst them; that what mischief is done he believes is mostly owing to rum, and it should be prevented.

"He desires that no Christian should carry any rum to Shamokin where he lives, to sell; when they want any, they will send for it themselves; they would not be wholly deprived of it, but they would not have it brought by the Christians.

"He desires four men may be allowed to carry some rum to Allegheny, to refresh the Indians when they return from hunting, and that none else be permitted to carry any. They also desire that some rum may be lodged at Tulpyhockin and Pextan, to be sold to them, that their women may not have too long a way to fetch it."

Sassoonan Requests Shawnees to Return to the Susquehanna Valley

Reference has been made in former chapters to the fact that the Shawnees began a migration from the Susquehanna Valley to the valleys of the Ohio and Allegheny as early as 1727. A few years later, the Colonial Authorities of Pennsylvania took measures to induce the Allegheny Shawnees to return to a point nearer the Pennsylvania settlements, fearing that they would be drawn into an allegiance with the French, who, at that time, had their emissaries in the Allegheny Valley. These efforts on the part of Pennsylvania will be more fully discussed in the chapters on Shikellamy. But in order to show the part Sassoonan took in the efforts to induce the Shawnees to return, we point out that, at a conference held at Philadelphia, on October 15th, 1734, the Senaca chief, Hetaquantagechty, who accompanied Shikellamy and Conrad Weiser to this meeting, advised Governor Gordon and the Provincial Council: "That he has understood that when the Shawnees were desired to leave Allegheny, they sent a belt of wampum to the Delaware Indians, with a message intimating to them that, as they, the Shawnees, were to seek out a new country for themselves, they should be glad to have the Delawares with them. That Sassoonan, the Delaware chief, had forbid any of his people to go with the Shawnees, and had desired that these last mentioned Indians should rather return to Susquehannah." Hetaquantagechty said that he was afraid that, if the Shawnees went to the "French Country", the Delawares would follow them. Later developments proved the correctness of the Seneca chief's opinion.

A Friendly Visit

Sassoonan appeared at Philadelphia at a conference held with the Provincial Council on August 20th, 1736. Several other Delaware chiefs, a Cayuga chief and a Tuscarora chief, accompanied him. Sassoonan stated that "they were not come on any particular business, or to treat of anything of importance, but only to pay a friendly visit to their brethren, whose welfare they think themselves obliged to inquire after, as they and the Indians are one people. That when they came from home, they expected to have seen here their good friends, the Proprietor, the Governor, and the Council all together, but when they had come so far on their journey as George Boone's, they learned that one of their good friends, the Governor [Governor Patrick Gordon, who died in August, 1736,] was dead; this news made them sorrowful, but they are comforted in meeting their other friends, who, they hope, will still continue in their regards towards the Indians and their care and concern for preserving the same friendship that has hitherto subsisted between us and them."

Sassoonan was then asked whether or not the deputies of the Six Nations were on their way to Philadelphia to attend the treaty of September, 1736, an account of which treaty will be given in the chapter on Shikellamy (Chapter X). Sassoonan answered that "he knew nothing particularly of them, that he has been in expectation of seeing them for each of these three years past, but he understands they have been detained by nations that come to treat with them." These deputies finally arrived at Philadelphia on August 27th, 1736.

Nearing End of Old Regime

After William Penn returned to England, it was the custom for the old men of the Delawares to visit Philadelphia each autumn to "brighten the chain of friendship" by presenting the Governor and Provincial Council with skins and furs, and receiving presents in return. On such a mission Sassoonan, "with divers of their ancient men", conferred with Governor George Thomas and the Provincial Council, on October 3rd, 1738. Governor Thomas had arrived in the Province only a few months before. In the minutes of this conference, we find that Sassoonan said: "That, when he was at home at his own house, he heard his brother, the Governor, was arrived in this country, and thereupon he resolved to come to Philadelphia to visit him, and now he was glad to see him; that his brother, the Proprietor, told him he should come once a year to visit him." And, further, we read: "Then laying down four strings more of wampum, he [Sassoonan] said that there had always subsisted a perfect friendship and good understanding between the Indians and this Government, and it is his desire and hope that it will ever continue, and grow stronger and stronger, and that it will never be in the power of any to interrupt or break it. . . . . Then presenting three small bundles of deer skins in the hair, he said he had brought a few skins to the Governor; they were but a trifle and of little value, but he had no more, and desired the Governor's acceptance of them to make him gloves."

Still further we read in the minutes of this conference: "It is considered that the Old man (Sassoonan) being now become very weak, and the other Old people with him, as well as himself, poor and necessitous, the value of thirty pounds should be returned to them in Goods proper for them, which it was agreed should consist of Six Strowd Matchcoats, Twelve Dussells, Twelve Blankets, six hatts, Four shirts, Fifty Pounds of Powder and as much lead, a Dozen of knives, a Gross of Pipes with Tobacco, and also that they should be supplied with some necessary Provisions for their Journey home."

J. S. Walton, in his "Conrad Weiser and the Indian Policy of Colonial Pennsylvania", gives the following comment on this visit of the aged Sassoonan: "This was almost the last of the old regime in Indian affairs. A younger set of men were coming into power among the Delawares, and they were susceptible to the influence of the Shawnees."

Final Conferences of Sassoonan

On August 1st to 6th, 1740, Conrad Weiser served as interpreter at a conference held in the Friends' Meeting House, Philadelphia, between Governor Thomas and a party of eastern and western Delawares and a group of Iroquois. At this conference, Sassoonan represented the Delawares and Shikellamy the Iroquois. The Delawares from the Allegheny, under Captain Hill from Kittanning and Shannopin from Shannopin's Town, (on the east bank of the Allegheny within the present limits of Pittsburgh) fresh from French overtures, complained that the traders were charging them too much for goods, and that the whites were killing and driving away their game. "Your young men," said they, "have killed so many deer, beavers, bears, and game of all sorts that we can hardly find any for ourselves." They also desired that their guns and axes should be mended free. They were given presents to the value of one hundred fifty pounds, a more valuable gift than usually besowed upon the Delawares, and it is very likely that the giving of it aroused jealousy among the eastern Delawares. They were told that the Colony could not fix the price of traders' goods. As for the killing of game by the whites, they were told that this was done by unlicensed traders, and that, if the Indians would not patronize such, it would prevent their coming among the Indians and killing their game.

At this conference, Captain Hill and Shannopin told the Governor that about six years prior to that time, two children of the Delawares were taken prisoner and carried away by the Catawbas, and that they were advised that these children were still living among the Catawbas. These chiefs then asked the Governor to make inquiry of the Governor of Virginia concerning the captives; whereupon Governor Thomas promised to write the Governor of Virginia in the matter.

Sassoonan also attended the great conference or treaty with the Six Nations, at Philadelphia, in July, 1742, though he took little part in the proceedings. This treaty will be described in the Chapter on Shikellamy (Chapter X).

On February 4th, 1743, Sassoonan attended an important conference at Shamokin between Conrad Weiser and Shikellamy, as well as other chiefs of the Six Nations, Delawares, and Shawnees. Fresh troubles had recently broken out between the Catawbas and other Indians of Virginia, on the one hand, and the Iroquois and their tributary tribes on the other, which threatened the peace, not only of Pennsylvania and Virginia, but of all the English Colonies. The Iroquois were determined to chastize the Catawbas for recent injuries, and it was feared that they would involve Pennsylvania by demanding that the Colony should furnish provisions for their warriors passing through the Colony on their way to the country of the Catawbas.

Upon hearing of the fresh trouble between the Northern and the Southern Indians, Weiser was sent by Governor Thomas to meet the chiefs at Shamokin. It is not too much to say that the fate of the future nation was at stake when Weiser started for this

conference. The Governor, upon receiving his report, sent him
again to Shamokin, where, on April 9th, he held another conference with Shikeallamy, Sassoonan, and others, relative to the same
matters taken up in the conference of February 4th At the conference of April 9th, Sassoonan sent a message to Governor
Thomas upholding him in his efforts to make peace between the
Northern and the Southern Indians. He (Sassoonan) said that, as
he "lives in the midway between the one and the other, and as both
pass through the place of his residence, a state of war would be
very disagreeable to him."

When the Governor and the Provincial Council received
Weiser's report of his conference on a second trip to Shamokin,
they resolved that he should at once go to the great council of the
Six Nations at Onondaga, to deliver a generous present sent by
Virginia, and arrange for the time and place of making a treaty.
Weiser, then, in July, 1743, went to Onondaga accompanied by
Shikellamy, and delivered the present of Virginia. After several
days of ceremony and speech making, Weiser arranged for a treaty
to take place at Lancaster, Pennsylvania, the following year between the Six Nations, Pennsylvania, Maryland, and Virginia.
Weiser thus prevented a war between Virginia and the Six Nations, which would eventually have involved the other colonies.

Last Days of Sassoonan

Sassoonan was now nearing the end of his earthly career. He
was visited at his home at Shamokin (Sunbury) by the Moravian
Bishop Spangenberg, in May, 1745, as the Bishop and Conrad
Weiser were on their way to the Great Council of the Six Nations,
at Onondaga. Of this visit, Bishop Spangenberg wrote: "We
also visited Allumapees, the hereditary king of the [Delaware]
Indians. His sister's sons are either dead or worthless; hence it is
not known on whom the kingdom will descend. He is very old,
almost blind, and very poor; but withal has still power over and is
beloved by his people; and he is a friend of the English." The
sister's sons to whom Bishop Spangenberg refers were possibly
Nettawatwees, or New Comer, who, among others, joined with
Sassoonan, in 1718, in the deed of release to William Penn, and
Kelappana, both of whom removed to Ohio, and were living at
New Comer's Town at the time of the expedition of Colonel
Bouquet, in 1764.

Again, on June 20th, 1747, Conrad Weiser wrote from his home near Womelsdorf, Berks County:

"Olumpies [Sassoonan] would have resigned his crown before now; but as he had the keeping of the public treasure (that is to say, the Council Bag), consisting of belts of wampum, for which he buys liquor, and has been drunk for these two or three years, almost constantly, and it is thought he won't die as long as there is a single wampum left in the bag, Sapapitten is the most fittest person to be his successor." Rum, the curse of the Red Man, was wearing the old chief's life away. About two months later, Weiser again wrote: "I understand Olumpies is dead, but I can not say I am sure of it." Finally, on October 15th, Weiser wrote: "Olumpies is dead. Lapaghpitton is allowed to be the fittest to succeed him, but he declines."

Thus, at Shamokin, on the banks of the beautiful Susquehanna, in the autumnal days of 1747, this aged chief, who had done so much to preserve the friendship that William Penn established with the Indians, yielded up his soul to the Great Spirit. Great changes in the relations between the Delawares and the Colony had taken place during the span of his life, and still greater changes were destined to come. In life's morning and noontide, he beheld the Delawares contented and happy in the bond of affection between them and "Onas"; yet, before the night had come, his dim eyes saw on the horizon the gathering clouds of the storm that, in the autumn of 1755, broke with fury upon the land of his birth.

We close this sketch of Sassoonan with the statement that, upon his death most of the Delawares moved to the Allegheny and the Ohio, living at Kittanning, Logstown, Sauconk, and Kuskuskies. As we have already seen, the town of Kittanning had been established by the Delawares possibly as early as 1724; and Logstown and Sauconk by the Shawnees possibly as early as 1730, the latter town being at the mouth of the Beaver. Kuskuskies, or Kuskuskie, was a regional name for a territory whose center was at or near the present site of New Castle, Lawrence County. Some authorities claim that the region extended westward into Butler county. This was a very important Indian settlement consisting of three or four towns of the Mingoes, or Iroquois, located along the Beaver, Mahoning, and Shenango Rivers, and Neshannock and Slippery Rock Creeks, and established some time prior to 1742.

CHAPTER VIII

Kakowatcheky, Peter Chartier
Kishacoquillas and Neucheconneh

KAKOWATCHEKY

AKOWATCHEKY, chief of the Shawnees at Pechoquealin, near the Delaware Water Gap, is believed to have been the leader of the band of this tribe that accompanied Arnold Viele to Pechoquealin from the Shawnee villages on the lower Ohio, in 1794. At any rate, he was chief of the Pechoquealin as early as 1709; for, in the minutes of a meeting of the Provincial Council of New Jersey, on May 30th of this year, he is referred to as one of the sachems of the Shawhena (Shawnee) Indians then with the Maninsincks (Munsee, or Wolf Clan of Delawares).

Kakowatcheky's name does not appear in the Colonial Records of Pennsylvania until 1728, in connection with the following Indian troubles:

On May 6, 1728, Governor Gordon advised the Provincial Council that he had recently received a letter from John Wright, a trader, at Conestoga, stating that two Conestogas had been murdered by several of the Shawnees in that neighborhood, and that the Conestogas seemed to be preparing to declare war on the Shawnees, in retaliation. The Governor also advised the Council, at this time, that he had received a petition signed by a great number of the settlers in the back parts of Lancaster County, setting forth that they were under great apprehension of being attacked by the Indians, and that many families had left their homes through fear of an Indian uprising. Wright further informed the Governor, in his letter, that the Shawnees had brought the Shawnee murderers as far as Peter Chartier's house, at which place the party engaged in much drinking, and, through the connivance of Chartier, the two Shawnee murderers escaped. It is not surprising that Chartier let the murderers escape, as he himself was a half blood Shawnee. He was at that time trading at Pequea Creek. His action so incensed the Conestogas that they threatened to destroy all the Shawnees in that region.

Almost at the same time that the murder of the Conestogas

occurred, the settlers along the valley of the Schuylkill became much alarmed for their safety from another quarter. Kako-watcheky, who was the head of the Shawnees living at Pecho-quealin, in what is now lower Smithfield Township, Monroe County, claimed that he had learned that the Flatheads, or Catawbas, from North Carolina, had entered Pennsylvania with the intention of striking the Indians along the Susquehanna; and he, accordingly, led eleven warriors to ascertain the truth of this rumor, who, when they came into the neighborhood of the Durham Iron Works, near Manatawny, in the northern part of Bucks County, their provisions failed, and they forced the settlers to give them food and drink. The settlers did not know these Indians, and believing the chief of the band to be a Spanish Indian, they were in great terror; families fled from their plantations and women and children suffered greatly from exposure, as the weather was raw and cold. There seems to be little doubt that Kakowatcheky was leading this band to Paxtang to assist the Shawnees of that place, who had been threatened by the Conestogas on account of the above mentioned murder of the two Conestogas.

A band of about twenty settlers took up arms and approached the invaders, sending two of their number to treat with the chief, who, instead of receiving them civilly, brandished his sword, and commanded his men to fire, which they did, and wounded two of the settlers. The settlers thereupon returned the fire, upon which the chief fell, but afterwards got up and ran into the woods, leaving his gun behind him. The identity of this Indian band was not known until May 20th, when two traders from Pechoquealin, John Smith and Nicholas Schonhoven, came to Governor Gordon and delivered to him a message from Kakowatcheky, explaining the unfortunate affair, sending his regrets, and asking the Governor for the return of the gun which he dropped when wounded. The Governor, then, accompanied by many citizens of Philadelphia, went to the troubled district, and personally pleaded with those settlers who had left their plantations to return. He found them so excited that they seemed ready to kill Indians of both sexes, but finally succeeded in pacifying them.

The Governor was about ready to return home when he received the melancholy news from Samuel Nut that an Indian man and two women were cruelly murdered, on May 20th, at Cucussea, then in Chester County, by John and Walter Winters, without any provocation whatever, and two Indian girls badly wounded; upon which a hue was immediately issued in an effort to apprehend the murderers. It appeared from investigation that, on the day of this murder, an Indian man, two women, and two girls, appeared at John Roberts' house, and that their neighbors noticing this, rallied to their defense, shot the man and one of the women, beat out the brains of the other woman, and wounded the girls, their excuse being that the Indian had put an arrow into his bow, and that they, having heard reports that some settlers had been killed by Indians, believed that the settlers might lawfully kill any Indian they could find.

The murderers were apprehended and placed in jail at Chester, for trial. A message was then sent to Sassoonan, Opekasset, and Manawkyhickon, acquainting them with the unhappy affair and requesting them to come to Conestoga, where a treaty would be held with Chief Civility and the other Indians at that place. The Provincial Council being apprehensive that this barbarous murder would stir up the Indians to take revenge on the settlers, a commission was appointed to get the inhabitants together and put them in a state to defend themselves. This commission consisted of John Pawling, Marcus Hulings, and Mordecai Lincoln, an ancestor of Abraham Lincoln, whose home was about ten miles south of the present town of Reading. Having sent Kakowatcheky the gun he had dropped, as well as the tomahawks dropped by his eleven warriors when they fled from the band of twenty settlers, as related above, together with a request that he warn the Indians under his authority to be more careful in the future, the Governor, accompanied by thirty residents of Philadelphia, met the Indians at a council at Conestoga on the 26th of May, where he conferred with Civility and other Conestoga, Shawnee, Conoy, and Delaware chiefs, made them many presents, and promised to punish the two murderers, if found guilty. John and Walter Winters were subsequently tried, found guilty, and hanged for the murder of the Indian man and two women.

Kakowatcheky Leaves Pechoquealin

As said in Chapter II, some of Kakowatcheky's clan left Pechoquealin before 1732, and went to the valley of the Ohio. Kakowatcheky himself, with the majority of his clan left Pechoquealin in the latter part of 1728, and went to the Wyoming Valley, settling on the Susquehanna, just below the town of Plymouth, Luzerne County. Here he was living in 1732, when some chiefs of the Six Nations on their way to attend a conference at Philadelphia, in August of that year, told him "that he should not look to Ohio, but turn his face to us." Evidently at that time, he contemplated joining his brethren on the Ohio and Allegheny.

Kakowatcheky at Treaty of 1739

The Colonial Authorities of Pennsylvania, realizing that the Shawnees were rapidly being won over by the French, induced Kakowatcheky, of Wyoming, Kishacoquillas of the Juniata, and Neucheconneh and Tamenebuck, of the Allegheny, and other Shawnee chiefs, whose settlements were scattered from Wyoming and Great Island (Lock Haven) to the Allegheny, to come to a conference, or treaty, at Philadelphia on July 27th to August 1st, 1739. At this conference the Conestoga and Shawnee agreement with William Penn, dated April 23rd, 1701, was brought to the attention of the chiefs; and they were told that the Colonial Authorities thought it proper to remind them of this solemn engagement which their ancestors had entered into with Penn, inasmuch as the said Authorities knew that the emissaries of the French were endeavoring to prevail upon the Shawnees to renounce their agreement with the Colony. In other words, the Governor and Provincial Council put the plain question of the Shawnees' loyalty to past agreements with Pennsylvania. The chiefs desired that their reply be postponed until the following day, explaining that "it was their custom to speak or transact business of importance only whilst the sun was rising, and not when it was declining." "In the morning, they showed that all past agreements had been kept by them quite as faithfully as by the white men. And since Pennsylvania had, about a year previously, promised to issue an order forbidding the sale of any more rum among them, they had sent one of their young men to the French, as an agent to induce them 'for all time, to put a stop to the sale of rum, brandy, and wine'." The result of the conference was that the Shawnees, with the full understanding that the rum traffic was to be stopped, promised not to join any other nation, and confirmed the old Conestoga and Shawnee agreement or treaty of April 23rd, 1701.

At this treaty, the Shawnee chief, Neucheconneh, repudiated the letter of March 20, 1738, which he, Loyparcowah, and Coycacolenne had sent the Governor advising him, among other things, that the Shawnees on the Kiskiminetas, Allegheny and Ohio had "a good understanding with the French." No doubt it was on account of this particular statement that Neucheconneh now repudiated the letter. He explained that it was written by "two white men", evidently the half-breed, Peter Chartier, and George Miranda, when all "were merry over a cup of good liquor."

Kakowatcheky Removes to the Ohio

Kakowatcheky did not obey the command that the representatives of the Six Nations gave him in August, 1732, "that he should not look to Ohio." He, with most of his clan, removed from Wyoming, in 1743, to Logstown, on the right bank of the Ohio, about eighteen miles below Pittsburgh. Possibly he founded Logstown, though some authorities claim, as pointed out in Chapter II, that this town was founded by Shawnees from Tennessee, possibly as early as 1730. Here he was living in the summer of 1744, when many Shawnees, under Peter Chartier, deserted to the French, which desertion will be described later in this chapter. However, Kakowatcheky remained true to the English, and was commended by the Colonial Authorities. On April 20th, 1747, he joined with Scarouady, Neucheconneh, Tanacharison and others, in writing a letter from "Aleggainey" to the Governor of Pennsylvania, in behalf of the Twightwees or Miamis of the Ohio Valley.

He was living at Logstown in the summer of 1748, when he, Neucheconneh, Tanacharison, Scarouady, and several other chiefs met in council and sent a message through the Delawares and Six Nations to the Colony of Pennsylvania, apologizing for the desertion of Peter Chartier and his band. Here, also, this aged sachem was met by George Croghan when the latter held a council with the Indians of Logstown on April 28th, 1748. Croghan had been sent by the Colony of Pennsylvania to advise the Ohio and Allegheny Indians that Conrad Weiser would come later in that year to make a treaty with them in behalf of the Colony, and to distribute generous presents. Weiser arrived at Logstown in September of that year as the head of what is generally called the first embassy ever sent by the Colony of Pennsylvania to the Indians of the Ohio and Allegheny, although it would be more nearly correct to say that Croghan's mission in the preceding April was the first. Weiser met Kakowatcheky at his conference in September, and his journal, under date of September 10th, contains the following reference to the sachem:

"This day I made a present to the old Shawnee chief, Kakowatcheky, of a strand, a blanket, a match-coat, a shirt, a pair of stockings, and a large twist of tobacco, and told him that the President and Council of Philadelphia remembered their love to him as to their old and true friend, and would clothe his body once more, and wished he might wear them out, so as to give them an opportunity to clothe him again.   There was a great many Indians present, two of which were the Big Hominy and the Pride, those that went off with Chartier, but protested his proceedings against our traders.   Kakowatcheky returned thanks, and some of the Six Nations did the same, and expressed their satisfaction to see a true man taken notice of, although he was now grown childish."

Kakowatcheky took no other part in Weiser's conferences at Logstown than that just mentioned.   In passing, we call attention to the fact that this embassy to the Shawnees, Senecas, and other Indians on the Ohio was eminently successful.   It left Pennsylvania in possession of the Indian trade from Logstown to the Mississippi and from the Ohio to the Great Lakes.   Moreover, its success was most gratifying to all the frontier settlers.   Not only Pennsylvania, but Maryland and Virginia were active in following up the advantage thus gained.   A number of Maryland and Virginia traders pushed into the Ohio region, and presently the Ohio Land Company, formed by leading men of Virginia and Maryland, among whom were George Washington's half-brothers, Lawrence and Augustine, sought to secure the Forks of the Ohio.

Last Days of Kakowatcheky

Once more, at Logstown on the Ohio, we meet this venerable chieftain, who, no doubt, was born in the valley of the beautiful river where he now is spending his latter years. On May 18th, 1751, George Croghan, the "King of the Traders", and Andrew Montour, visited Logstown bringing the Colony's present to the Ohio Indians, which they had promised on their former visit to this town in November, 1750.   Croghan and Montour were welcomed by a great number of Delawares and Shawnees "in a very complacent manner in their way, by firing guns and hoisting the English colors."   Among the sachems who welcomed them were the Seneca chief, Canayachrera, or Broken Kettle, who came to Logstown with a delegation from the Kuskuskies region, whose center was on or near the site of New Castle, Lawrence County.

On May 21st, Croghan visited the aged Kakowatcheky, writing in his journal under this date:

"I paid Kakowatcheky, the old Shawnee King, a visit, as he was rendered incapable of attending the Council by his great age, and let him know that his brother, the Governor of Pennsylvania, was glad to hear that he was still alive and retained his senses, and had ordered me to clothe him and to acquaint him that he had not forgot his strict attachment to the English interest. I gave him a strowd shirt, a match-coat, and a pair of stockings, for which he gave the Governor a great many thanks."

At this time, the English and the French were each doing everything possible to win the friendship and allegiance of the Indians of the Ohio and Allegheny. Each claimed the territory drained by these streams, the French basing their claim on the discoveries and explorations of La Salle and the heroic Jesuit missionaries,—true Knights of the Cross, to whom anyone who correctly writes the early history of the region between the Allegheny Mountains and the Mississippi must needs pay a high tribute of esteem. And at this conference at Logstown, Croghan met Joncaire, the French Indian agent, but succeeded in outwitting him in diplomacy, and the chiefs ordered the French from their lands, and reasserted their friendship for the English—a friendship which was broken four years later. The speaker of the Six Nations thus addressed Joncaire:

"How comes it that you have broken the general peace? Is it not three years since you, as well as our brother, the English, told us that there was a peace between the English and French, and how comes it that you have taken our brothers as your prisoners on our lands? Is it not our land (stamping on the ground, and putting his finger to Joncaire's nose)? What right has Onontio (the Governor of Canada) to our lands? I desire that you may go home directly off our lands, and tell Onontio to send us word immediately what was his reason for using our brothers so, or what he means by such proceedings that we may know what to do, for I can assure Onontio that we, the Six Nations, will not take such usage. You hear what I say, and that is the sentiments of all our Six Nations; tell it to Onontio that that is what the Six Nations said to you . . . . . . Our brothers [the English] are the people we will trade with and not you."

While there is no doubt about the loyalty of the Ohio Indians to the Pennsylvania Government at the time of Croghan's visit to Logstown (May, 1751); yet it is fair to assume that he exaggerated his translation of the speech which the Iroquois chief delivered to Joncaire, in that he alleged that the speaker told Joncaire that the Council of the Six Nations had determined to trade only with the English. The Onondaga Council had made no such decision.

For years it had endeavored to play an even game with the French and the English, preferring to be courted by both France and England.

While at Logstown, on the occasion just described, Croghan learned from Tanacharison and Scarouady that the Great Council of the Six Nations had agreed, since Celeron's expedition down the Allegheny and Ohio in the summer of 1749, that the English be permitted to build a trading house at the Forks of the Ohio; and, in open Council with Croghan, the chiefs at Logstown "requested that the Governor of Pennsylvania would immediately build a strong house [fort] . . . . . . for the protection of themselves and the English traders", where Pittsburgh now stands.

In June, 1752, Virginia and the Ohio Land Company made a treaty at Logstown with the Delawares, Shawnees, and Senecas of the Ohio Valley, by the terms of which Virginia secured permission to erect a few forts and make a few settlements west of the Allegheny Mountains. Colonel James Patton, one of the Virginia Commissioners at this treaty, makes the following reference to Kakowatcheky in his journal, under date of June 11th:

"The Commissioners, addressing themselves to the Shawnees, acquainted them that they understood that their chief, Kakowatcheky, who had been a good friend to the English, was lying bed-rid, and that, to show the regard they had for his past services, they took this opportunity to acknowledge it by presenting him with a suit of Indian clothing."

The year of Kakowatcheky's death is not known, but it was probably in 1755, as that is the last year in which his name appears in the Colonial Records. If he was the chief who led the Shawnees from the lower Ohio Valley to Pechoquealin, in 1694, his chieftainship must have extended over a period of sixty years.

PETER CHARTIER

Peter Chartier was the only son of Martin Chartier, who accompanied the Shawnees, under Opessah, to Pequea, Lancaster County, in 1697 or 1698, and his mother was a Shawnee squaw. The father was a Frenchman, who had lived among this band of Shawnees for many years prior to their entering Pennsylvania, and accompanied them in their wanderings. He set up a trading house at Pequea a few years after the Shawnees took up their abode there. At least, he traded at Pequea as early as 1707. Some years later, he removed his trading post to Dekanoagah, which we have seen was located on or near the present site of Washington Borough, Lancaster County. Here he died in 1718.

Peter Chartier is said to have followed his father's example by marrying a Shawnee squaw. In 1718, he secured a warrant for three hundred acres of land "where his father is settled, on Susquehanna river." For some years he traded with the Shawnees who had left Pequea and settled near the site of Washington Borough and at Paxtang. Later he traded with those members of this tribe who had settled on the west side of the Susquehanna, at the mouth of Shawnee (now Yellow Breeches) Creek, on the site of the present town of New Cumberland, Cumberland County. We have already seen how he, in 1728, aided in the escape of the Shawnees who had murdered the two Conestogas. Still later, he is said to have removed to the valley of the Conococheague. About 1730, he commenced trading with the Shawnees on the Conemaugh, and Kiskiminetas, and a little later, on the Allegheny.

Manor of Conodoguinet

On November 19th, 1731, Peter Chartier was informed by John Wright, Tobias Hendricks, and Samuel Blunston of the survey of the tract called the "Manor of Conodoguinet", a tract of land on the west side of the Susquehanna between Conodoguinet and Yellow Breeches creeks, set aside for the Shawnees, in an effort to induce those of that tribe who had gone to the Ohio and Allegheny, to return to the Susquehanna. Chartier conveyed this information to the Shawnees on the Ohio and Allegheny, but they refused to return.

Neucheconneh's Letter

Chartier was a witness to a letter which Neucheconneh and several other Shawnee chiefs on the Allegheny wrote Governor Gordon, in June, 1732, in response to a message which the Governor sent them in December of the preceding year. In their letter they explained why the Shawnees had removed from the Susquehanna. Said they:

"About nine years ago, the Five Nations told us at Shallyschohking, [Chillisquaque, a Shawnee town at the mouth of the creek of the same name in Northumberland County] we did not do well to settle there; for there was a great noise in the Great House [at Onondaga], and that in three years' time all should know what they [the Five Nations] had to say as far as there was any settlements or the sun set.

"About ye expiration of three years aforesaid, the Five Nations came and said, 'Our land is going to be taken from us. Come, brothers, assist us. Let us fall upon and fight with the English.' We answered them, 'No; we came here for peace, and have leave to settle here; and we are in league with them, and cannot break it.'

"About a year after, they, ye Five Nations, told the Delawares and us, 'Since you have not hearkened to us nor regarded what we have said, now we will put petticoats on you, and look upon you as women for the future, and not as men. Therefore, you Shawanese, look back toward Ohio, the place from whence you came; and return thitherward; for now we shall take pity on the English, and let them have all this land.'

"And further said, 'Now, since you are become women, I'll take Peahohquelloman [Pechoquealin], and put it on Meheahoming [Wyoming]; and I'll take Meheahoming and put it on Ohioh; and Ohioh I'll put on Woabach; [Wabash] and that shall be the warriors' road for the future.

"One reason of our leaving our former settlements and coming here is, several negro slaves used to run away and come amongst us; and we thought ye English would blame us for it.

"The Delaware Indians some time ago bid us depart, for they was dry, and wanted to drink ye land away. Whereupon, we told them, 'Since some of you are gone to Ohioh, we will go there also. We hope you will not drink that away, too.''

At about the time of the above letter, the Shawnees in the Allegheny had received a report from John Kelly, a trader, that the Six Nations were ready to destroy them and drive out the French, if the English Governor would say the word. This report greatly agitated the Western Shawnees, and they would have declared war on the English traders at once, if Peter Chartier and some French agents had not persuaded them that the information was false.

Chartier Acts as Interpreter

On September 30th and October 5th, 1732, Opakethwa and Opakeita, two Shawnee chiefs from the Allegheny attended a conference at Philadelphia, with Thomas Penn, Governor Gordon and the Provincial Council, Peter Chartier, Edmund Cartilidge and John Wray being the interpreters. This is the conference, referred to in Chapter V, in which they explained that they had formerly lived on the Potomac, but their "king" having died, they knew not what to do, and "went over the mountains [meaning to the Allegheny] to live." The Proprietor urged them to return to lands which the Colony had set apart for them on the west side of the Susquehanna near Paxtang (Harrisburg), and they replied "that their young men had gone over the mountains to hunt where they might have more game, that when that was over they would return and see the land." They were also told that the traders might cease carrying goods as far as the Allegheny, and that the French could not supply them with as valuable goods, or at as cheap a price as the English traders could; "to which they answered that they were sensible of this, but they had horses of their own, and could bring their skins to the trader, or to this town (Philadelphia), if there were occasion." It was clear that the Shawnees who had gone to the Allegheny had no intention of returning nearer the English settlements.

With Chartier and the two chiefs, was Quassenung, son of the old Shawnee King, Kakowatcheky. On October 7th, Quassenung was taken ill with small-pox, and was nursed by Opakethwa, speaker for the Shawnees at the conference. In the minutes of the conference, we read: "Quassenung recovered from the small-pox, but Opakethwa, who tended him, was taken most violently with the same distemper, and dying on the 26th, was next day handsomely buried. Quassenung was seized with violent pains, and languished until the sixteenth of January. He then died, and was likewise the next day buried in a handsome manner."

Chartier's principal seat on the Allegheny was a town which he, and, no doubt, the Shawnee chief, Neucheconneh, founded about 1734, called Chartier's Town, or Chartier's Old Town, also Neucheconneh's Town, and located near the site of Tarentum, Allegheny County. Here he lived until his desertion to the French, in 1744. Other Shawnee villages west of the Alleghenies, at this time, besides those on the Juniata, Conemaugh, Kiskiminetas, and Allegheny, were Logstown and Sauconk on the Ohio, the latter being at the mouth of the Beaver; Asswikales, or "Sewickley Town", on the Youghiogheny, at the mouth of Big Sewickley Creek, in Westmoreland County; and "James Le Tort's Town", where Shelocta, Indiana County, now stands, the present town of Shelocta bearing the name of a Shawnee chief. The Shawnees at Asswikales are described in a letter of James Le Tort to Governor Gordon, October 29, 1731, as "about fifty families lately from South Carolina to Potowmack, and from thence thither."

Murder of Sagohandechty

The Asswikales Shawnees, also called the Hathawekela, before coming to Pennsylvania, were known to the early settlers of South Carolina, as the Savannas.   On September 10th, 1735, Hetquantagechty, a Seneca chief, and Shikellamy, the vice-gerent of the Six Nations, attended a meeting of the Provincial Council at Philadelphia, and gave the Council a report concerning the mission which the Six Nations had sent to the Ohio and Allegheny in a vain attempt to have the Shawnees of that place return to the Susquehanna.   At this conference Hetaquantagechty informed the Council that a great chief of the Iroquois, named Sagohandechty, who lived on the Allegheny, probably at Kittanning, went with the other chiefs of the Six Nations in 1734 to prevail upon the Shawnees to return.   Sagohandechty pressed the Shawnees so closely to return that they took a great dislike to him, and some months after the other chiefs had returned, the Shawnees cruelly murdered him. Hetquantagetchty said that this murder had been committed by the Asswikales, who then fled southward, and as he supposed had returned "to the place from whence they first came, which is below Carolina." Hetaquantagechty described them as "one tribe of those Shawnees who had never behaved themselves as they ought." The Asswikales were probably the first Shawnees to settle in Western Pennsylvania within historic times, coming by way of Old Town, Maryland, to Bedford, and then westward.   Sewickley Creek, in Westmoreland County, Sewickley Town, at the mouth of that creek, and another placed called Sewickley Old Town, which some authorities locate on the Allegheny River some miles below Chartier's Old Town, were named for them.

Peter Chartier Deserts to the French

At a meeting of the Provincial Council held April 25, 1745, Governor Thomas laid before the Council a deposition made by James Cunningham, a servant of Peter Chartier, to the effect that Chartier had accepted a military commission under the French, and was going to Canada.   Later, at a meeting of the Pennsylvania Assembly, held July 23, 1745, a petition from James Dinnen (Dunning) and Peter Tostee, two Indian traders from the Allegheny Valley, was presented and read, setting forth that, as Dunning and Tostee were returning up the Allegheny River, in canoes, on the 18th of April, 1745, from a trading trip, with a considerable quantity of furs and skins, "Peter Chartier, late an

Indian trader, with about 400 Shawne Indians, armed with guns, pistols, and cutlasses, suddenly took them prisoners, having, as he said, a captain's commission from the King of France; and plundered them of all their effects, to the value of sixteen hundred pounds; by which they are become entirely ruined, and utterly uncapable to pay their debts, or carry on any further trade."

The actual date of Charter's desertion is unknown, but it was likely some time during the summer of 1744.

Chartier and Chief Neucheconneh headed this band of Shawnees. They had fled from Chartier's Old Town, and started down the Allegheny and Ohio, when they met and robbed Dunning and Tostee. At Logstown, they made an unsuccessful attempt to have Kakowatcheky join them. They proceeded on down the Ohio to the mouth of the Scioto, at which place another Shawnee settlement had been made possibly a decade before, and known for many years afterwards as the Lower Shawnee Town. From the Lower Shawnee Town, Chartier and his Shawnees proceeded southward along the Catawba Trail, and established a town about twelve miles east of the site of the present town of Winchester, Kentucky. Their object was to be nearer the French settlements on the Mississippi.

Shortly after Chartier led his Shawnees from the Allegheny, there were many rumors that the Shawnees intended making raids upon the frontiers of Pennsylvania, Maryland, and Virginia. At a meeting of the Provincial Council at Philadelphia on December 17th, 1745, Governor Thomas laid before the board a letter he had just received from the Governor of New York advising him that Major Swartwoutz, a dweller in the Minisink region, had recently written the Governor that he (Swartwoutz) had received intelligence from two Indians at different times within a month to the effect that "the French and French Indians living at a town or fort on a branch of the River Mississippi have made a large house full of snow shoes, in order so soon as the snow shall fall, to attack Albany, Sopus, and the back parts of Jersey and Pennsylvania." Governor Thomas said that, although he was not apt to give credit to rumors of this kind, since they were often found false, yet, considering the fact that the French had recently plundered the inhabitants near Saratoga, New York, carrying off seventy as prisoners and burning their houses, barns and mills, and considering the further fact that Peter Chartier was now with the French, it was not improbable that something would be attempted upon the inhabitants of the back parts of Pennsylvania likewise. Hence the Governor dispatched a messenger with circular letters to the officers of the militia in Lancaster County, directing them to be on their guard and to make the best preparations they could for defense, at the same time cautioning them not to "do any injury to the Indians in amity with us, or to molest them in their hunting." He likewise sent directions to Conrad Weiser "to employ some of the Delaware Indians at Shamokin (Sunbury) as scouts to watch the enemy's motions, and to engage the whole body of Indians there to harrass them in their march, in case they should attempt anything against us, and afterwards to join our remote inhabitants for their mutual defense." However, Chartier and his Shawnees did no mischief in Pennsylvania, except the plundering of the traders, Dunning and Tostee.

Chartier's Shawnees Ask to Be Forgiven

Some time after the desertion of Peter Chartier, a number of his Shawnees returned, among whom were Neucheconneh and his band. In 1747, the Onondaga Council placed the Oneida chief, Scarouady, in charge of Shawnee affairs, with his central seat at Logstown. Shortly thereafter, Neucheconneh, with Kakowatcheky, at that time king of the Shawnees at Logstown, who had withstood the solicitations of Chartier, and whom the reader has followed in his migration from the eastern part of Pennsylvania to the Ohio Valley, applied submissively to Scarouady then living on the Ohio, to intercede for them with the Colonial Authorities of Pennsylvania. At a meeting on July 21st, 1748, at Lancaster, Pennsylvania, with the commissioners appointed by the Colony to hold a conference with the Six Nations, Twightwees, and other Indians, Conrad Weiser, having received the following apology of the Shawnees from Scarouady, who was too badly injured from a fall to attend the conference, delivered it to the commissioners, as follows:
"We, the Shawnees, have been misled, and have carried on a private correspondence with the French without letting you [the Delawares and Six Nations] or our brethren, the English, know of it. We traveled secretly through the bushes to Canada, and the French promised us great things, but we find ourselves deceived. We are sorry we had anything to do with them. We now find that we could not see, although the sun did shine. We earnestly desire that you would intercede with our brethren, the English, for us who are left at Ohio, that we may be permitted to be restored to

the chain of friendship, and be looked upon as heretofore the same flesh with them." Scarouady reported to Weiser that the foregoing apology had first been addressed to the Six Nations and Delawares dwelling on the Ohio and Allegheny, by Neucheconneh, Kakowatcheky, Sonatziowannah, and Sequeheton, after these Shawnee chieftains had met in council.

Conrad Weiser was consulted as to the sincerity of the apology of the Shawnees. It does not appear what Weiser said on this occasion, but it is well known that he was always outspoken in his contempt for the Shawnees, and doubtless his influence shaped the course of the commissioners at Lancaster, who severely reprimanded the Shawnees for their conduct. Addressing the Six Nations, from the Ohio, the commissioners said through Weiser, the interpreter:

"Your intercession for the Shawnees puts us under difficulties. It is at least two years since the Governor of Pennsylvania wrote Kakowatcheky a letter, wherein he condescended out of regard to him and a few other Shawnees who preserved their fidelity, to offer those who broke the chain, a pardon, on their submission, on their return to the towns they had deserted, and on their coming down to Philadelphia to evidence in person the sincerity of their repentence. They should have immediately complied with, and they would have readily been admitted into favor, but as they did not, what can be said of them? . . . . Take this string of wampum and therewith chastize Neucheconneh and his party in such terms as will be a proper severity with them. . . . . Then tell the delinquent Shawnees that we will forget what is past, and expect a more punctual regard to their engagements hereafter. 'Tis but justice to distinguish the good from the bad; Kakowatcheky and his friends, who had virtue enough to resist the many fine promises made by the emissaries of the French, will ever be remembered with gratitude, and challenge our best services."

Then Taming Buck (Tamenebuck), one of the Shawnee chiefs, who had been in Chartier's band, and later returned, replied to the above reprimand as follows: "We, the Shawnees, sensible of our ungrateful returns for the many favors we have been all along receiving from our brethren, the English, ever since we first made the chain of friendship, came along the road with our eyes looking down to the earth, and have not taken them from thence until this morning, when you were pleased to chasitze us and then pardon us. We have been a foolish people, and acted wrong, though the sun shone bright, and showed us very clearly what was our duty. We are sorry for what we have done, and promise better behavior for the future. We produce to you a certificate of the renewal of our friendship in the year 1739, by the Proprietor and Governor. Be pleased to sign it afresh, that it may appear to the world we are now admitted into your friendship, and all former crimes are buried and entirely forgot."

The request of Taming Buck was rejected. The commissioners refused to sign the certificate, and the Shawnees were told that it was enough for them to know that they were forgiven on condition of future good behavior, and that when that condition was performed, it would be time enough for them to apply for such testimonials. It is not known whether Weiser advised this course or not, but it is certain that he could have prevented it, and induced the Colonial Authorities to make a valuable peace with the Shawnees now when they were so submissive and humble. Other tribes received presents at this Lancaster conference, but the Shawnees only had their guns mended. They went away in disgrace, brooding over such treatment.

Peter Chartier figured no more in Pennsylvania history after he deserted to the French in 1744. Two creeks in Pennsylvania bear his name—Chartier's Run, in Westmoreland County, emptying into the Allegheny not far from Chartier's Old Town (Tarentum), and Chartier's Creek, in Washington and Allegheny counties, emptying into the Ohio at McKees Rocks, once known as Chartiers, from the fact that he had a trading post near this place.

KISHACOQUILLAS

Kishacoquillas was one of the Shawnee chiefs who never waivered in friendship for the English. The first glimpse we get of him in the Colonial Records is in the year 1731, when he was living with his clan of twenty families at Ohesson,—later called Kishacoquillas' Town, located at the mouth of Kishacoquillas Creek, named for him, on the Juniata River, near Lewistown, Mifflin County. With Kakowatcheky, Neucheconneh, and Taming Buck, and other Shawnee chiefs, he attended the conference held at Philadelphia on July 27th to August 1st, 1739, which has been mentioned earlier in this chapter.

Kishacoquillas was well advanced in years when the first settlers entered the valley of the beautiful mountain stream bearing his name. With one of these, Arthur Buchanan, he was on especially friendly terms, and had his wigwam near Buchanan's cabin.

Some of Kishacoquillas' followers are said to have warned Buchanan and his sons of the expected attack on Fort Granville, near Lewistown, July 30th, 1756, enabling them and their families to escape to Carlisle.

He died in the summer of 1754. His sons notified Governor Morris of his death through John Shikellamy, son of the great vice-gerent of the Six Nations. As Kishacoquillas had always been a good friend of the Colony and well respected, the Governor sent a present to his sons, and a letter of condolence in which he said:

"I heartily condole with you on the loss of your aged father, and mingle my tears with yours, which, however. I would now have you wipe away with the handkerchiefs herewith sent. As a testimony of the love that the Proprietaries and this Government retain for the family of Kishacoquillas, you will be pleased to accept of the present which is delivered to John Shikellamy for your use. May the Great Spirit confer on you health and every other blessing. Continue your affection for the English and the good people of this Province, and you will always find them grateful."

NEUCHECONNEH

As pointed out in Chapter V, the Shawnee chief, Neucheconneh, very probably acted as vice-regent during the youth of Loyparcowah, the son of Opessah. As stated, also, in Chapter V, Neucheconneh joined with Loyparcowah and Coycacolenne, on March 20th, 1738, in sending a letter from the Allegheny to Thomas Penn and Secretary James Logan, advising of their desire to remain on the Allegheny, and of the steps they had taken against the rum traffic. He was no doubt then residing at Neucheconneh's Town, or Chartier's Old Town, on the Allegheny, near Tarentum, which, as we have seen, in the present chapter, he and Peter Chartier founded in 1734. In the present chapter, we have also seen that Neucheconneh joined with several other Shawnee chiefs on the Allegheny, in June, 1732, in a letter to Governor Gordon, explaining why the Shawnees had removed from the Susquehanna; that he, with Kakowatcheky, Kishacoquillas, and Tamenebuck, attended the conference at Philadelphia, on July 27th to August 1st, 1739, where he repudiated the letter of March 20th, 1738; that, in 1744, he, with Peter Chartier, left Chartier's Old Town, and deserted to the French; that he afterwards returned to Logstown; and that, in 1748, he asked the Colony that he be forgiven for his having, for a time, deserted to the French.

On May 1st, 1734, Neucheconneh and several other Shawnee chiefs dictated a letter to Governor Gordon and the Provincial

Council, regarding the character of the traders who came among them at Allegheny. This letter, which was probably written by Jonah Davenport, and which was witnessed by James Le Tort, Larey Lowrey, and Peter Chartier, was as follows:

"Edward Kenny, Jacob Pyatt, Timy. Fitzpatrick, Wm. Dewlap, and Jno. Kelly of Donegal, come trading with us without license; which is a hindrance to ye licensed Traders.

"Charles Poke and Thos. Hill are very pernicious; for they have abused us; and we gave them a fathom of white wampum, desiring them by that token to acquaint you how they had served us.

"And at a drinking bout, Henry Bayley, Oliver Wallis, and Jno. Young, took one of our old men, and after having tied him, abused him very much. Jas. Denning was among them, and abused us likewise. Such people, we think, are not proper to deal with us.

"Jno. Kelly of Paxtang has made a great disturbance by raising false reports among us; and Timy. Fitzpatrick, Thos. Moren, and Jno. Palmer quarrel often with us; therefore, we desire those four men may be kept particularly from us.

"Jonas Davenport, Laz. Lowrey, Jas. Le Tort, Fras. Stevens, Jas. Patterson, Ed. Cartilidge, we desire, may have license to come and trade with us; as also, Peter Cheartier, who we reckon one of us; and he is welcome to come as long as he pleases.

"Likewise, we beg at our Council, that no Trader above mentioned may be allowed to bring more than thirty gallons of rum, twice in a year, and no more; for by that means, we shall be capable of paying our debts and making our creditors easy; which we cannot do otherwise. And that every Trader may be obliged to bring his rum in ye cabin where he lives, directly, and not to hide any in ye woods; but for P. Cheartier to bring what quantity he pleases; for he trades further yn. ye rest. And that every Trader bring his license with him.

"And for our parts, if we see any other Traders than those we desire amongst us, we will stave their cags, [kegs] and seize their goods, likewise.

"We also beg, every Trader may be obliged to bring good powder.

"And, if we are indebted to any of those we desire may not be admitted to trade with us, if they will come without goods or rum, if we have it by us, we will pay them their due.

"We also hope no hired man will have liberty to bring any rum with him."

Other letters and messages of Neucheconneh were:

(1)   A letter from the Allegheny to Secretary James Logan, dated April 9th, 1738, advising that three Indians "of the nation called Maychepese, living near the French", had passed through the Shawnee Town (Chartier's Old Town) having three scalps of white persons killed by them in Virginia.   Says Neucheconneh: "We thought it proper to acquaint you by the first opportunity who they were that killed our brothers . . . . to prevent any suspicion; when inquiry is made, it will prevent enmity between us and our brothers."   He signed this letter, as "King" of the Allegheny Shawnees.

(2)   On April 9th, 1743, at a council at Shamokin (Sunbury), a message sent by him from the Allegheny, was delivered to Conrad Weiser for transmission to Governor Thomas, as follows: "Brother, the Governor of Pennsylvania:

"I live upon this River of Ohio [Allegheny] harmless like a child.   I can do nothing.   I am but weak, and I don't so much as intend mischief.   I have nothing to say, and do; therefore, send these strings of wampum to Kakowatcheky, the chief man again. He will answer your message, as he is the older and greater man."

In explanation of this message, we state that, early in 1743, it was feared that the Shawnees on the Allegheny might attack the English traders.   Conrad Weiser was accordingly sent to Shamokin, where, on February 4th, he held a council with Shikellamy, Sassoonan and other chiefs of the Delawares, Shawnees, and Six Nations, which conference was mentioned in Chapter VII, and gave the Shawnee chief, Big Hominy, some belts of wampum to "send to the Great Island [Lock Haven], and Allegheny, in favor of the traders."   Weiser returned to Shamokin on April 9th, when Neucheconneh's answer was received, as above set forth.   Kakowatcheky was then at Wyoming, but, as is seen in the present chapter, he removed from that place to Logstown that same year, 1743.

(3)   On April 20th, 1747, he joined with Kakowatcheky, Tanacharison, Scarouady, Tamenebuck, and several others, in a letter to Governor Thomas, requesting friendly relations on the part of the Colony with the Miamis, with whom the Shawnees had entered into a treaty.

There are two other letters which Neucheconneh had a part in sending.   The one is a letter from the "Chiefs of the Shawnees at Allegheny" which James Logan laid before the Provincial

Council on August 10th, 1737, which was, in substance, that they were strongly solicited by the French, who were supplying them with some powder and lead to fight the Southern Indians; that they (the Allegheny Shawnees) were so far away that they could go no farther without falling into the hands of their enemies or going over to the French; and that, if they should return to the Susquehanna, as the Colony had often insisted, they must starve, as there was little game there. The letter ended with a request that the Colony furnish them with arms and ammunition to defend themselves against their enemies The other is a message from "Nuckegunnah, King of the Shawnees living at Allegheny", dated August 4th, 1738, and sent to the Governor of Virginia, advising that, the Catawbas had made an attack upon them, killing several and taking others prisoners; and that this attack had happened after the Shawnees had refrained from sending war parties against the Catawbas upon learning that the Governor of Virginia was endeavoring to make peace between the Catawbas and the Northern Indians.

Another reference to this famous chief, who ended his days in the valley of the Ohio, is when Captain William Trent and Andrew Montour found him near the mouth of the Miami, on August 4th, 1752. Trent and Andrew Montour had attended the Virginia treaty at Logstown in June, and from there had gone down the Ohio past the Lower Shawnee Town with a present for the Miamis. His last appearance in history is when he attended the Carlisle treaty of October, 1753.

In closing this chapter, we call attention to the fact that Chartier's Town, founded by Peter Chartier and Neucheconneh, and the scene of their principal activities until they led the Shawnees from that place down the Ohio to the French, in 1744, figured little in the Indian history of Pennsylvania after that event. When Celeron came down the Allegheny and Ohio in the summer of 1749, burying leaden plates at the mouths of the tributary streams, proclaiming that the region drained by the "Beautiful River" belonged to France, his detachment stopped at Chartier's Town, on August 6th, where he found six English traders, with fifty horses and one hundred and fifty bales of furs, who were returning from there to Philadelphia. He ordered them to withdraw from this territory claimed then by France, and sent with them a letter to the Governor of Pennsylvania warning him to forbid the traders of the Colony to come into the valleys of the Ohio and Allegheny.

CHAPTER IX

Shikellamy

HIKELLAMY (Shikellimmy, Shikillimus, Swateny, etc.), who has been mentioned several times thus far, holds a high place in the Indian annals of Pennsylvania. His name literally means, "He causes it to be light, or day-light"; or "He enlightens us." Hence he has frequently been call-ed "Our Enlightener." He was an Oneida chieftain, though he claimed he was born a Cayuga and was adopted by the Oneidas. It has also been said that he was a Frenchman, born in Montreal and taken captive, when a child two years old by the Oneidas, by whom he was reared.

Shikellamy was the great exponent of the policy of the Six Nations, and was sent by the Great Council at Onondaga to the Forks of the Susquehanna, then called Shamokin, (Sunbury, Penn-sylvania), in 1727 or 1728, to conserve the interests of the Six Nations in the Susquehanna Valley, and to keep a watchful eye on the tributary Shawnees, Delawares, and other Indians in that region. The exact date of his coming to the Forks of the Susque-hanna as the over-lord of the Shawnees, Delawares, and others is not known, but it is clear it was prior to June, 1728; for in that month, he, Sassoonan, and several other chiefs of the Delawares and Shawnees attended a conference with Governor Gordon and the Provincial Council at Philadelphia, with reference to the troubles between the Shawnees of Pechoquealin and the settlers, as related in Chapter VIII.

The first definite reference in the Colonial Records to Shikel-lamy's vice-gerency is in the minutes of a meeting of the Provincial Council held on September 1, 1728. This conference after discus-sing the endeavors of Manawkyhickon to set the Miamis and the Five Nations at variance with the English, as related in Chapter VII, was informed by Governor Gordon that two Indian traders from the region of Pechoquealin had advised him that the Shaw-nees of that place during the month of August had received a message from the Susquehanna, which caused them to remove to the Wyoming Valley, leaving their corn standing—the removal of Kakowatcheky's Clan as related in Chapter VIII. The Council then decided to send a message to Kakowatcheky asking why he had left Pechoquealin and "to acquaint Shikellima [Shikellamy] that, as he is appointed, as it is said, by the Five Nations to preside over the Shawnees, it is expected that he will give a good account of them."

The importance of Shikellamy's office as the over-lord or vice-gerent of the Six Nations over the Indians of the Susquehanna is seen from the fact that, after the Iroquois subjugated the Susquehannas, or Conestogas, in 1675 or 1676, they assigned the valley of this river as a hunting ground for the Shawnees, Delawares, Conoy, Nanticokes, Tutelo, and Conestogas. Moreover, Shikellamy's coming to the Forks of the Susquehanna, probably marks the date of the complete subjugation of the Delawares by the Iroquois.

Shikellamy was a man of dignity, sobriety, and prudence, and a great friend of the whites, especially the Moravian Missionaries, by whom he was converted to Christianity near the close of his life. He was not baptized by the Moravians, because he had been baptized many years before by a Jesuit priest in Canada. In the execution of his trust, he conducted many important conferences and treaties between the Government of Pennsylvania and the Council of the Six Nations. In 1745, he was promoted to the full vice-gerency of all the tributary tribes in the Susquehanna region.

Shamokin

Before proceeding further, attention is called to the fact that the term "Shamokin" was a regional name applied to the territory at and around the Forks of the Susquehanna with its center at the present town of Sunbury, Northumberland County, where the *town* of "Shamokin" was located on the level ground south of the mouth of the North Branch of the Susquehanna. The term "Shamokin" is Delaware and probably another form of the word "Shackamaxon". The Iroquois name "Chenasky", or "Chenastry" (now generally called Otzinachse, or Otzinachson) was given at least to the northern part of the Shamokin region.

The town of Shamokin (Sunbury) and the surrounding country were strategically located. It was in this region that the Catawba War Trail leading from the central seat of the Six Nations, through the valleys of Lycoming Creek and the West Branch, intersected with the trail leading from Wyoming to the Allegheny Valley; and it was no doubt the strategic location of the Shamokin region that caused Shikellamy to select it as his seat, when he was sent by the Great Council of the Six Nations as vice-gerent over he Indians of the Susquehanna Valley. In fact, from 1728 and possibly prior thereto, until 1737 or 1738, he resided at the intersection of the Catawba and Wyoming trails, in a village called Shikellamy's Town located on the West Branch of the Susquehanna, in Northumberland County, opposite the mouth of Sinking Run, or Shikellamy's Run, about half a mile below the present town of Milton. Here Conrad Weiser found him, as will presently be seen, when going to Onondaga in 1737. About 1738, Shikellamy removed to Shamokin proper, the Shamokin of Pennsylvania history (Sunbury), where he resided until his death. Here, also, it will be recalled, resided the great sachem of the Turkey Clan of Delawares, Sassoonan, from about the latter part of 1718 until his death in 1747.

Shikellamy Delivers Ultimatum on the Rum Traffic

While Shikellamy on October 10th, 1728, attended the conference with Governor Gordon and the Provincial Council, mentioned in Chapter VII, which resulted in a settlement of the troubles in that year with Kakowatcheky's Clan of Shawnees at Pechoquealin, his first great act after coming into the vice-gerency of the Iroquois over the Indians of the Susquehanna, was to deliver an ultimatum to the Colonial Authorities of Pennsylvania, in 1731, to the effect that, unless the liquor trade should be better regulated with regard to its sale to the Indians under his jurisdiction, friendly relations between the Colony of Pennsylvania and the powerful Six Nations would cease.

Shikellamy Sent to Onondaga to Arrange a Treaty

As has been seen in former chapters, the abuses of the liquor traffic among the Shawnees were among the causes which forced a large number of this tribe to migrate from the Susquehanna to the Ohio and Allegheny valleys several years prior to 1730, when French emissaries seized upon this opportunity to alienate the Shawneees from the English interest. Therefore, Governor Gordon at a council held at Philadelphia on August 16th, 1731, decided to adopt the suggestion of Secretary James Logan that a treaty be arranged with the Six Nations "to renew and maintain the same good-will and friendship for the Five Nations which the Honorable William Penn always expressed to them in his lifetime", and to prevail upon the Six Nations to assist in holding the Shawnees in

their allegiance to the English. Accordingly, at this same conference, it was decided to send Shikellamy, "a trusty, good man
and a great lover of the English" to Onondaga, the capital of the
Six Nations, to invite them to send deputies to Philadelphia to
arrange a treaty.

In keeping with Pennsylvania's efforts to retain the friendship
of the Shawnees on the Allegheny, Governor Gordon sent them a
message in December, 1731, reminding them of the benefits they
had received from William Penn and his successors, while they
lived in the eastern part of the Province, to which message
Neucheconneh and other Shawnee chiefs on the Allegheny, replied
in their letter to the Governor, of June, 1732, giving the reasons
why they had removed from the Susquehanna, which letter was
quoted in Chapter VIII.

Shikellamy returned to Philadelphia from his journey to
Onondaga, on December 10th, 1731, accompanied by a Cayuga
chief named Cehachquely, and Conrad Weiser and John Scull as
interpreters. He reported that the Six Nations were very much
pleased to hear from the Governor of Pennsylvania, but that, as
winter was now coming on and their chiefs were too old to make
such a fatiguing journey in the winter time, they would come to
Philadelphia in the spring to meet the Governor.

Conrad Weiser

On his way to meet the Governor at this time, Shikellamy
stopped at the home of Conrad Weiser, near Womelsdorf, in the
present county of Berks, took him along to Philadelphia and introduced him to Governor Gordon as "an adopted son of the Mohawk
Nation"; and as this conference (December 10, 1731,) is Weiser's
first connection with the Indian affairs of Pennsylvania, it will be
well to pause long enough, at this point, to give a short sketch of
the history of this noted man of the frontier, who later had so
much to do with bringing about the ascendency of the Anglo-
Saxon in the Western World.

This sturdy German was born at Afsteadt, in Herrenberg,
near Wurtemberg, Germany, in 1696. At the age of thirteen, he
accompanied his father to America, and, for several years, assisted
him in making tar and raising hemp on Livingston Manor, New
York. The Weiser family spent the winter of 1713 and 1714 with
several of the Iroquois at Schenectady, New York, where Conrad
doubtless secured his first lessons in the Iroquois tongue. In the

spring of 1714, he accompanied his father to the Schoharie Valley, where they endured much hardship in company with the other Palatines in that valley. When he was seventeen years old, young Weiser went to live with Quagnant, a prominent Iroquois chief, who, taking a great fancy to Conrad, requested the father that the young man might dwell with him for a time. He remained with the Iroquois chief for eight months, learning the Iroquois language and customs thoroughly, and was adopted by them.

In 1729, Conrad Weiser and his young wife followed the elder Weiser into the Tulpyhocken Valley, Pennsylvania, where, as has been related, a number of Palatines from the Schoharie Valley had settled, under the leadership of Conrad Weiser, Sr. The young couple built their home about one mile east of Womelsdorf, Berks County, where Weiser continued to reside until a few years before his death, when he removed to Reading. It is said that while on a hunting trip he met the great Iroquois chief, Shikellamy, the vicegerent of the Six Nations, who was well pleased with Weiser on account of his being able to speak the Iroquois tongue, and they became fast friends.

While visiting his old home near Womelsdorf, he died July 13, 1760, much lamented by the Colony of Pennsylvania as well as by the Indians. Said a great Iroquois chieftain, commenting on the death of Weiser: "We are at a loss, and sit in darkness."

If all white men had been as just to the Indians as was this sturdy German, the history of the advance of civilization in America undoubtedly would not contain so many bloody chapters. Conrad Weiser's home is still standing, and in the orchard above the house, rests all that is mortal of this distinguished frontiersman; while beside him are the graves of several Indian chiefs. Having loved him in life, they wished to repose beside him in death. A beautiful monument has been erected to his memory in Womelsdorf, having thereon the words which George Washington uttered concerning him, while standing at his grave, in 1793: "Posterity Will Not Forget His Services."

Conrad Weiser was the progenitor of one of the most noted families of Pennsylvania. His daughter, Anna, became the wife of Henry Melchoir Muhlenberg, founder of the Lutheran Church in America, was the mother of Frederick A. Muhlenberg and General John Peter Gabriel Muhlenberg. Frederick A. Muhlenberg became a distinguished Lutheran clergyman and later was elected to the Legislature of Pennsylvania. He was also chosen President of the Pennsylvania Convention, in 1787, which ratified the Constitution of the United States. From 1789 to 1797, he served in the Congress of the United States, and was speaker of the First and Third Congresses.

John Peter Gabriel Muhlenberg also became a distinguished Lutheran clergyman, and, at the outbreak of the Revolutionary War, was pastor of the German Lutheran congregation at Woodstock, Virginia. While serving this parish, he became well known to George Washington, and was selected to command the Eighth Virginia Regiment. His farewell sermon, preached to his congregation in January, 1776, is memorable in the annals of America. On the appointed day, an immense congregation greeted him. Clad in his clerical gown, he preached a burning sermon on the duty of the hour, at the close of which he made the statement: "There is a time to pray and a time to fight; now is the time to fight." The benediction pronounced amidst a deathlike silence, he threw aside his gown, revealing himself clad in the full uniform of a Continental officer, and ordered the drums to beat for recruits. With the noble men who there gathered around him by the hundreds, he started on his undying career as a soldier.

He endured the rigors of the terrible winter at Valley Forge, and fought valiantly at Germantown, Monmouth, and Stony Point. He was the leader of the American final assault at Yorktown, when the American arms finally triumphed.

He was promoted to Major General, and, after the close of the Revolution, removed from Virginia to Pennsylvania, where he was elected a member of the Supreme Executive Council of the state. He was a member of the First, Third, and Sixth Congresses, and was elected United States Senator in 1801, but resigned this post to receive the appointment by President Jefferson as Supervisor of Internal Revenue for Pennsylvania. At the time of his death in July, 1802, he was collector of the port of Philadelphia. His statue is placed in the rotunda of the Capitol at Washington, with that of Robert Fulton, the two representing the State of Pennsylvania. This statue shows him throwing aside his clerical robe and revealing the uniform of a Continental officer.

The Treaty of 1732

The Six Nations, no doubt mistrusting the motives of the English, failed to send deputies to Philadelphia in the spring of 1732, as they had promised Shikellamy. In the meantime, traders in the valleys of the Ohio and Allegheny reported that the French were rapidly gaining the friendship of the Shawnees in the Ohio Valley; that these Indians complained bitterly about the great quantities of rum brought to them by the English traders; and that they would have declared war against the English, on this account, save for the influence of Peter Chartier. The Shawnees said, furthermore, that it had been only five years since the Six Nations themselves had endeavored to persuade the Ohio Indians to declare war on the English. In view of these facts, there was much anxiety on the part of the Provincial Council of Pennsylvania, over the failure of the deputies of the Six Nations to make their appearance in Philadelphia in the spring of 1732.

Finally, on August 18th, 1732, the deputies of the Six Nations arrived, consisting of a number of Oneida, Cayuga, and Onondaga chiefs, among whom was the celebrated Shikellamy. A few days' time being given the chiefs in which to refresh themselves after their long and toilsome journey, the famous treaty of August 23rd to September 2nd, 1732, was entered into between the Six Nations and the Colony of Pennsylvania.

We have stated that Secretary James Logan suggested this treaty; but Logan's knowledge of the influence and importance of the Six Nations and their power over the Shawnees, Delawares and other tributary tribes, was gotten from Conrad Weiser. Not until the coming of Weiser did the Colony fully realize the importance of this powerful confederation.

The deputies of the Six Nations, who arrived in Philadelphia some days before the opening of the conference, as we have seen, were chiefs of only the Oneida, Cayuga, and Onondaga tribes; but they claimed that they were authorized to speak for the other members of the Iroquois Confederation. In the early stages of the conference, complaints were made, possibly by members of the Assembly, against the private nature of the council; and Conrad Weiser, the interpreter, was selected to interview the Iroquois deputies to learn their pleasure in the matter. The chiefs replied that they were content to continue in secret session, but were willing to deal in a more public manner, if such was desired. Thomas Penn, son of the founder of the Colony, having lately arrived in Philadelphia, spoke for the Province. He called the attention of the chiefs to the policy which his father had pursued in dealing with the Indians, and assured them that he came to the Province with a desire and design to follow in the footsteps of his parent. He then asked the Iroquois deputies how their Confederation stood toward the French, their former enemies. He inquired how the French behaved toward the Six Nations, and how all the other nations of Indians to the northward or the westward were affected toward the Iroquois.

The Iroquois deputies replied through their speaker, Hetaquantagechty, that they had no great faith in the governor of Canada, or the French, who had deceived them. "The Six Nations", said they, "are not afraid of the French. They are always willing to go and hear what they have to propose. Peace had been made with the French. A tree had been planted big enough to shelter them both. Under this tree, a hole had been dug, and the hatchets had been buried therein. Nevertheless, the chiefs of the Six Nations thought that the French charged too much for their goods, and, for this reason, they recommended their people to trade with the English, who would sell cheaper than the French." The deputies confided to the Governor that, when representatives of the Six Nations were at Montreal, in 1727, the governor of Canada told them that he intended to make war upon Corlear (the term applied to the governors of New York), and that he desired the Six Nations to remain neutral. On this occasion, one of the chiefs answered, saying: "Onontejo [the Indian name for the governor of Canada], you are very proud. You are not wise to make war with Corlear, and to propose neutrality to us. Corlear is our brother; he came to us when he was very little and a child. We suckled him at our breasts; we have nursed him and taken care of him till he is grown up to be a man. He is our brother and of the same blood. He and we have but one ear to hear with, one eye to see with, and one mouth to speak with. We will not forsake him nor see any man make war upon him without assisting. We shall join him, and, if we fight with you, we may have our own father, Onontejo, to bury in the ground. We would not have you force us to this, but be wise and live in peace."

The Iroquois deputies were told, through Conrad Weiser, that the Shawnees who were settled to the southward, being made uneasy by their neighbors, had come up to Conestoga about thirty-five years before, and desired leave of the Conestoga Indians located at that place, to settle in the neighborhood; that the Conestogas applied to the Government of Pennsylvania that the Shawnees might be permitted to settle there, and that they would become answerable for their good behavior; that William Penn, shortly after the arrival of the Shawnees, agreed to their settlement, and the Shawnees thereupon came under the protection of the Pennsylvania Colony; that, from that time, greater numbers of the Shawnee Indians followed, settling upon the Susquehanna and the Delaware. The deputies were further told that the Colony of Pennsylvania had held several treaties with the Shawnees, treating them from their first coming as "our own Indians", but that some of their young men, four or five years previously, being afraid of the Six Nations, had removed to the Allegheny Valley, and put themselves under the protection of the French, who had received them as children; that the Colony had sent a message asking them to return, and to encourage them, had laid out a large tract of land on the west side of the Susquehanna near Paxtang, and desired, by all means, that they would return to that place.

The Iroquois answered that they never had intended to harm the Shawnees, and that, as they were coming on their way to Philadelphia, they had spoken with Kakowatcheky, their (the Shawnees') old chief, then at Wyoming, and told him that he should not "look to Ohio, but turn his face to us." They had met Sassoonan, too, the old chief of the Delawares, then at Shamokin, and told him that the Delawares, too, should not settle in the Ohio and Allegheny valleys, upon which Sassoonan had sent messengers to the Delawares lately gone to the Ohio and Allegheny valleys, requiring them to return. It will be remembered that, in the times of which we are writing, and for a long period thereafter, the Allegheny River was considered simply as a continuation of the Ohio, and was generally called the Ohio.

The deputies were then told that, as they were the chiefs of all the northern Indians in the Province, and the Shawnees had been under their protection, they should oblige them to return nearer the Pennsylvania settlements; whereupon the chiefs asked if the Six Nations should do this themselves, or join with the Authorities of Pennsylvania. They were told that it was the desire of the Pennsylvania Colony that the Six Nations should join with the Colonial Authorities in efforts to have the Shawnees return.

The representatives of the Six Nations told the Governor that they believed that they could bring the Shawnees back, if Pennsylvania would prohibit her traders from going to the Allegheny Valley, explaining that, as long as the Shawnees were supplied at that place with such goods as they needed, they would be more unwilling to remove. It was finally agreed that Pennsylvania would remove such traders, and that the Six Nations would see that the French traders in the Ohio region were also removed.

The main purpose of this treaty was to secure the aid of the

Six Nations in efforts to bring the Shawnees from the Allegheny Valley; but it contained other provisions, notably the one obligating the Six Nations to "forbid all their warriors, who are often too unruly, to come amongst or near the English settlements, and especially that they never, on any account, rob, hurt, or molest any English subjects whatsoever, either to the Southward or elsewhere."

The Iroquois delegation having requested that, in their future dealings with Pennsylvania, Conrad Weiser should continue to be the interpreter, this request was granted, and the conference came to an end by the giving of many presents to the deputies, among which were six japanned and gilt guns, which were to be delivered one to each chief of the Six Nations. These guns were the gift of Thomas Penn, which he had brought with him from England for this purpose.

Shikellamy at Conference June, 1733

Shikellamy's next appearance before the Provincial Council was at a conference held at Philadelphia with Governor Gordon on June 18, 1733. Three matters were taken up at this conference. The first was a report which Shikellamy gave the Governor of the news of a plot on the part of the whites to take up arms against the Indians. Shikellamy said that he had received this news from "an Indian who lives in his neighborhood, named Katarioniecha (Peter Quebec), who is married to one Margaret, a daughter of Mrs. Montour." The second was a complaint on the part of Shikellamy that "since the Indian traders were prohibited to bring rum among the Indians, Cheaver, beyond all others, has brought in very large quantities, and gives out that he will not regard the orders of the Government on this head; that his behavior is such as gives just apprehension some mischiefs may happen if he is not called away from these parts; that formerly an order was given to the Indians to stave rum brought among them, but Cheaver threatens any Indians that shall offer to touch his; that it is to be feared he may either kill an Indian or some Indian him; that Cheaver intends this summer to go to Allegheny, contrary to what was agreed upon between this Government and the Six Nations last fall [at the treaty of 1732]." The third was a letter which Sassoonan had sent to John Harris asking him to desist from making a plantation at the mouth of the Juniata where Harris had built a house and cleared some fields.

Shikellamy Tells of Efforts of Six Nations to
Have Shawnees Return to the Susquehanna

The Six Nations were faithful to their promise, in the treaty of 1732, to induce the Shawnees in the Allegheny Valley to take up their adobe in the valley of the Susquehanna; and they used every means short of war in efforts to accomplish this result. On September 10th, 1735, Shikellamy and Hetaquantagechty, with three other Iroquois chiefs, reported at a meeting of the Provincial Council, that, in accordance with the treaty of 1732, the Six Nations had sent some of their chief men to the valley of the Allegheny, who met the Shawnees and urged them to return to the valley of the Susquehanna, assuring them that the Six Nations would protect them, but that the Shawnees had utterly refused to leave their western home, which, they said, was more commodious than was their home on the Susquehanna. This was the same conference referred to in Chapter VIII, in which Shikellamy and Hetaquantagechty advised the Governor of the murder of Sagohandechty by the Asswikales clan of Shawnees.

But before giving the Provincial Council this definite information as to the refusal of the Shawnees to return, Shikellamy had made two other visits to Philadelphia after the treaty of 1732, as follows:

On August 15th, 1733, Shikellamy and Hetaquantagechty, a Seneca chief, coming to Philadelphia, as messengers from the Six Nations, accompanied by Conrad Weiser from the latter's home in the Tulpehocken Valley, and advised the Provincial Council that, owing to a pestilence among the Six Nations, they could not send a delegation to consult with the Governor this year concerning the matters mentioned in the treaty of August, 1732. Hetaquantagechty stated that, before he left home, a great meeting of the Iroquois chiefs was appointed at Onondaga.

Also, on October 15th, 1734, Hetaquantagechty, accompanied by Shikellamy and Conrad Weiser, appeared before the Provincial Council at Philadelphia, and advised that the Six Nations, being delayed in waiting for a message from the Conoys at Conoy Town, near the mouth of the creek of the same name in Lancaster County, advising them that they had been wrongly accused of having killed two people in Virginia, could not send a deputation to Philadelphia this year to confer with the Governor and Council concerning the carrying out of the promises the Iroquois had made in the treaty of 1732. He stated, however, that the Six Nations had sent messengers to the Shawnees on the Allegheny, desiring them to return to the Susquehanna, who answered that they would remove farther north and nearer the French; whereupon some chiefs of the Six Nations went to confer with the Shawnees; and that he did not know what happened at their meetings with them.

What happened was the refusal of the western Shawnees to comply with the demand of the Iroquois that they return to the Susquehanna, and the murder of Sagahandechty by the Asswikales band of Shawnees, as was related in Chapter VIII. These facts were brought to the attention of the Provincial Council by Shikellamy and Hetaquandechty at the conference of September 10th, 1735. The Six Nations, said Shikellamy, greatly resented this barbarous and inhuman act, and thought it ought not to pass unrevenged, but they were willing to receive the advice of the Provincial Council on the matter. Shikellamy also suggested that, as that particular clan of Shawnees had fled southward, it would perhaps be well to write the Governor of Virginia, acquainting him with what they had already done and what mischief they might still do.

John and Thomas Penn replied, urging them to keep the peace at all hazards. They said they had learned that this particular band of Shawnees had entered the Allegheny Valley only a few years before they so cruelly murdered the Iroquois chieftain, coming from the South, and were practically strangers. The Penns, dissuading, further argued that since the murderers fled to the South, no one knowing exactly where, it would be better to let the matter drop. They said that the traders need not be withdrawn from the Allegheny. Then they presented the chief "six handkerchiefs to wipe and dry away [the]tears."

CHAPTER X

Shikellamy

(Continued)

THE TREATY OF 1736

T the instigation of Shikellamy and Conrad Weiser, the Colonial Authorities of Pennsylvania were very anxious to have the treaty of August, 1732, confirmed by deputies representing all the members of the Iroquois Confederation, and Conrad Weiser was directed to employ his influence with Shikellamy to the end that these two mediators between the Colony of Pennsylvania and Great Council of the Six Nations might bring about a conference that would represent every member of that great Confederation. The summers came and went, and still the promised visit of the Iroquois was deferred. Finally, at a conference of Delaware and Conestoga chiefs, among whom were Sassoonan, representing the Delawares, and Civility, representing the Conestogas, held at Philadelphia on August 20, 1736, an appeal was made to them to explain why the Iroquois did not send deputies to Philadelphia, as they had promised. Sassoonan said that he knew nothing particularly of the Iroquois; that he had been in expectation to see them for three years past, but understood that they had been detained by nations that came to treat with them. He further stated that he expected that they would be on hand the next spring. The Provincial Council made a very liberal present to the Delawares and Conestogas on the occasion of this conference, accompanying it with the special request that they make an effort to ascertain from the Six Nations why they had not sent their deputies as they promised the preceding year, or at least to send a message stating the reasons for their delay.

This present to the Delawares had the desired effect, and in less than six weeks thereafter, Conrad Weiser sent word to the Provincial Council from his home near Womelsdorf, in the Tulpehocken Valley, that he had received intelligence that one hundred chiefs, representing all members of the Iroquois Confederation, had arrived at Shamokin (Sunbury) on their way to Philadelphia. On the 27th of September, Weiser arrived at Philadelphia, accompanied by this delegation of one hundred Iroquois. At this time, smallpox was raging in Philadelphia, on account of which Weiser took the Indians to James Logan's mansion at Stenton, a few miles from the city (now in the Twenty-second Ward, Philadelphia), and invited the provincial officers and proprietors out to meet them. The Indians were greatly pleased with Weiser's care for their health, and the esteem in which they held him increased by this act of solicitation on his part. The Iroquois had told the Colonial Authorities at the treaty of 1732 that Weiser and Shikellamy were the proper persons "to go between the Six Nations and this government." They said that their bodies were to be equally divided between "the Sons of Onas and the Red Men, half to the Indian and half to the white man." Weiser, said they, was faithful, honest, good, and true; that he had spoken their words for them, and not his own.

The Iroquois delegation, by far the largest that ever appeared at Philadelphia at a treaty, was entertained for three nights at Stenton. The sessions of the different conferences connected with the making of this treaty lasted until the 25th of October. They were held in the great meeting house at Fifth and Arch Streets. The Iroquois deputies reported that, following the suggestion of the Provincial Council at the treaty of 1732, they had strengthened their confederation by entering into firm leagues of friendship and alliance with other nations around them, to-wit: Onichkaryagoes, Sissaghees, Troumurtihagas, Attawantenies, Twechtwese, and Oachtaumghs. All these tribes, said the deputies, had promised to acknowledge the Iroquois as their elder brother and to act in concert with them.

The Iroquois deputies made the request that the Pennsylvania traders be removed from the Ohio and Allegheny country, but the Provincial Council politely refused this request, arguing that its Indians there could not live without being supplied with goods, and that, if the Pennsylvania traders did not supply them with goods, others from Maryland and Virginia would. The Iroquois also asked that no strong drink be sold at Allegheny by the traders. This petition was evaded. James Logan, President of the Council, upon which the administration of the government devolved since the death of Governor Gordon, on August 5th, 1736, rebuked the Indians for not controlling their appetite for rum. "All of us here," said he, "and all you see of any credit in this place, can every day have as much rum of their own to drink as they please, and yet scarce one of us will take a dram, at least not one man will, on any account, be drunk, no, not if he were hired to it with great sums of money."

But the most important part of this treaty was the execution and delivery of two deeds by the Iroquois to the Proprietaries of the Province of Pennsylvania—a momentous transaction brought about by that astute Iroquois statesman, Shikellamy, assisted by Conrad Weiser.

Deed of Susquehanna Lands

The first was a deed to all the lands on both sides of the Susquehanna, extending as far east as the heads of the streams running into the Susquehanna, as far west "as the setting of the sun" (afterwards interpreted by the Indians to mean as far as the crest of the Allegheny Mountains), as far south as the mouth of the Susquehanna, and as far north as the Blue, Kittatiny, or Endless Mountains. As related in Chapter VI, William Penn, in order to get undisputed title to the lands he had purchased from the Susquehanna or Conestoga Indians, thought it advisable to get the consent of the (then) Five Nations; and, on January 13th, 1696, he purchased these same Susquehanna lands from Governor Thomas Dongan of New York, who had gotten his title from the Iroquois. Penn, thus recognized a feudal lordship of the Susquehanna lands in the Iroquois; and his deed to the same from Dongan was "confirmed" by the treaty with the Susquehannas, or Conestogas, at Philadelphia, on April 23, 1701. The Six Nations, however, contended that they had deeded the Susquehanna lands to Dongan simply in trust and did not release any control over or rights in the same. At the time of this treaty of 1736, the Colonial Authorities of Pennsylvania were impressed by Conrad Weiser with the power and influence of the Six Nations, and, accordingly, did not dispute with their deputies when they claimed indemnity for all the Susquehanna lands south and east of the Blue Mountains.

The consideration of the deed for these lands, dated October 11th, 1736, was 500 pounds of powder, 600 pounds of lead, 45 guns, 100 blankets, 200 yards of cloth, 100 shirts, 40 hats, 40 pairs of shoes and buckles, 40 pairs of stockings, 100 hatchets, 500 knives, 100 hoes, 100 tobacco tongs, 100 scissors, 500 awls, 120 combs, 2000 needles, 1000 flints, 20 looking glasses, 2 pounds of vermillion, 100 tin pots, 25 gallons of rum, 200 pounds of tobacco, 1000 pipes, and 24 dozens of garters. That part of these goods which represented the consideration for the lands on the east side of the Susquehanna, was delivered, but that which represented the consideration for the lands on the west side of the river, was, at the Indians' desire, retained, and was finally delivered in 1742.

Deed of Delaware Lands

On October 25th, just two weeks after the signing of the deed of the Susquehanna lands, when most of the influential deputies of the Iroquois had left Philadelphia, and after those who remained had been drinking heavily, another deed was drawn up embracing all the Six Nations' claim to lands within Pennsylvania "beginning eastward on the River Delaware, as far northward as the ridge or chain of Endless Mountains as they cross ye country of Pennsylvania, from eastward to the West." This deed established a precedent for an Iroquois claim to all the lands owned by the Delaware Indians, and was the cause, as we shall see, of greatly embittering the Delawares.

Effects of Sale of Delaware Lands By Iroquois

It is clear that, while William Penn recognized the claim of the Six Nations to the lands of the Susquehannas or Conestogas, yet he never recognized any claim on the part of the Six Nations to the lands of the Delawares; and, prior to this treaty of 1736, it cannot be found that the Iroquois themselves ever made any claim to the lands of the Delawares, although of course, they had exercised an overlordship over them, "declaring them women and forbidding them to make war." It is very probable that, at the time of making the Iroquois deed for the Delaware lands, no one realized what the outcome of such a deed would be. It was an indirect way of denying to the Delaware Indians all title to their lands. The Iroquois had promised that in the future they would never sell any land within the limits of Pennsylvania to anyone except Penn's heirs, and, probably, the chief purpose in securing this deed was to place this promise of the Six Nations permanently in writing.

Shikellamy and Weiser Cause Change in the Indian Policy of Colonial Pennsylvania

This action in purchasing the Delaware lands from the Iroquois marked a great change in the Indian policy of Pennsylvania —a change brought about by Shikellamy and Conrad Weiser. Weiser interpreted the deed to the Iroquois, and they were evidently aware that they had gained a most important point; that, henceforth, the Colony of Pennsylvania would be a sponsor for their claims on the Delaware River; and that all the ancient disputes with the Delawares in this matter were settled. Furthermore, by this action, the Colony of Pennsylvania had taken sides in the age-long quarrel between the Iroquois on the one hand and the Delawares on the other. William Penn had refused to take sides in any Indian differences, but his sons were more bent on personal profit than on public justice and public security.

From the date of this purchase, it was no longer possible for the Colony of Pennsylvania to treat the Delawares as formerly. The Six Nations had been recognized as the favorite people and the Delawares, the affectionate friends of William Penn, as underlings. The Delawares had already been offended through the long delay in purchasing from them the Tulpehocken lands, which had been settled many years before the Colony got an Indian title for the same. Now, in purchasing their lands from the Iroquois, the Colony started that long series of events with the Delawares, which resulted in the bloodiest invasion in colonial history—an invasion which drenched Pennsylvania in blood from 1755 to 1764; but at the same time, while thus bringing upon herself a Delaware and Shawnee war, she escaped a Six Nation war, which no doubt would have been much more serious in its consequences.

Sale of Susquehanna Lands Involves Maryland and Virginia

"Since Pennsylvania had paid the Six Nations for their Susquehanna claims south of the Blue Mountains, the shrewd Iroquois became aware that neither Maryland nor Virginia had ever paid them for lands to the southward which lay within the western borders of those States. They stated that their claims to this region were based upon the conquests of their fathers. They now insisted that Pennsylvania should assist them in securing this land from Virginia and Maryland. The Governor, who was evidently following the advice of Conrad Weiser, put the Indians off until he could secure better information about these claims." (J. S. Walton's "Conrad Weiser and the Indian Policy of Colonial Pennsylvania").

This matter dragged along until the Lancaster treaty of 1744, when Maryland and Virginia formally purchased the Iroquois lands in their dominions.

Sale of Susquehanna Lands Offends Shawnees

"The growing discontent among the Shawnese seized upon the recent Iroquois land sale as another source of their dissatisfaction. When these Shawanese heard of the treaty of 1736, one hundred and thirty of their leaders sent a belt to the French, saying, 'Our land has been sold from under our feet; may we come and live with you?' The French not only readily consented, but offered to come and meet them with provisions. This information came from the Mohawks, who received no share from the recent Iroquois land sale. In the treaty of 1736, the Six Nations had promised to send all the Shawnees back from the Ohio, and compel them to live on the Susquehanna lands, where forty-five years before they had asked permission to live. The Iroquois found this a difficult thing to do, especially since the Mohawks received nothing from the late treaty. The Shawanese, moreover, were learning valuable lessons in diplomacy from the Iroquois and the French. In August, 1737, a message and a belt came to Philadelphia from the Shawanese on the Ohio, saying that the French had always been their friends, that each year they gave them powder, lead and tobacco, that these presents enabled them to hold their own against their Indian enemies in the South. Now if they should go back to their Susquehanna lands, as the leading men in Pennsylvania, and the Iroquois chiefs desired, they must starve, and lay themselves open to their enemies. With genuine shrewdness the Shawnees declared that they had no desire to join the French, and if the Pennsylvania authorities would send them a present as compensation for the land they had lost, they could keep back their enemies, and avoid falling into the hands of the French.

"The Pennsylvania Council, after 1736, always consulted Conrad Weiser on all Indian affairs. Weiser had little or no respect for a Shawnees Indian. The Council, while it realized that the Shawnees had no legal claims on the Susquehanna land, from a white man's standpoint in reference to land tenure, inclined to take Weiser's advice, and believed that it would be establishing a dangerous precedent to recognize Shawnees claims when they were but sojourners in the country. The Indians had a quite different conception of land tenure, and the Shawnees held that occupancy did, in time, become possession. Therefore, when they received a present of ten pounds from the Province, and an invitation to a treaty, they swallowed their chagrin, and found solace in the sympathy of the French. This paltry present was the beginning of a series of misunderstandings with these tribes which finally led to their total alienation from the English cause."—(J. S. Walton's "Conrad Weiser and the Indian Policy of Colonial Pennsylvania").

The two deeds gotten from the Iroquois at the treaty of 1732 embraced the counties of York, Adams, and Cumberland, that part of Franklin, Dauphin, and Lebanon southeast of the Blue or Kittatiny Mountains, and that part of Berks, Lehigh, and Northampton not already possessed.

Shikellamy and Weiser's Terrible Journey to Onondaga in Effort on Part of Virginia to Make Peace Between the Iroquois and the Catawbas

Shortly after the treaty of 1736, Virginia's difficulties with the Iroquois, on account of the damage done by their war parties against the Catawbas and other southern tribes, became so acute that Governor Gooch of Virginia decided that the only solution of the problem was to arrange a peace between the Six Nations and the Catawbas and their allied tribes. Gooch succeeded, in the autumn of 1736, in securing the consent of one of the southern tribes to make peace, and, finally, later in the winter, the entire Southern Confederacy of Indians agreed to send deputies the next spring to Williamsburg, the capital of Virginia, to meet similar deputies from the Iroquois. Governor Gooch then decided to secure an armistice between the two great confederations and to persuade the Iroquois to send deputies to Williamsburg. In his effort to accomplish these things, he appealed to the Colonial Authorities of Pennsylvania, as a result of which, Conrad Weiser was selected to proceed to the Great Council of the Six Nations at Ondaga, New York, to arrange an armistice and, if possible, to secure the promise of the Six Nations to send their deputies to Virginia.

It was now mid-winter (1737), and the snow lay several feet deep on the mountains of Pennsylvania and New York; yet it was very important that Weiser should arrive at the Great Council of the Six Nations before the opening of spring, as, at that time, war parties of Iroquois would already be on their way to Virginia. He started on his journey on the 27th of February, 1737, accompanied by a white man, named Stoffel Stump. They rode on horseback to Shikellamy's Town, where they found the Indians on the verge of starvation, and were unable to get the horses across the Susquehanna. Finally, after a day's delay an Indian succeeded in taking Weiser and Stump over the river in a canoe. At Shikellamy's Town, Weiser and Stump were joined by Shikellamy and two other Indians, who acted as guides; and they set forth, on foot, on their journey through the trackless and snow clad forest to Onondaga. They followed the north bank of the West Branch of the Susquehanna, called "Otzinachson" by the Indians, and proceeded to the mouth of Loyalsock Creek, in Lycoming County, where they found Madam Montour at her village called Ostonwacken, near the mouth of the Loyalsock, and near the present site of Montoursville. Weiser and his companions were almost starved. At first Madam Montour told Weiser that she had no food; but, when the Indians had withdrawn from her cabin, she raised a board from the floor and fed him bountifully from a supply which she had concealed.

Bidding Madam Montour good-bye, the little party of four left the West Branch of the Susquehanna, and followed what the Indians called the "Lost, or Bewildered Stream." This was a dismal region. Said Weiser: "The woods was so thick that for a mile at a time we could not find a place the size of a hand where the sunshine would penetrate, even on the clearest day." In one valley, probably Loyalsock Creek, they encountered such storms that the Indians believed that an evil spirit, called Otkon, ruled in that place. They were now traveling northward through Lycoming and Sullivan counties.

On March 25th Shikellamy almost met his death on this terrible journey. Weiser describes the incident as follows:

"After we had gone óne hundred and fifty miles on our journey, we came to a narrow valley, about half a mile broad, and thirty miles long, both sides of which were encompassed by high mountains, on which the snow lay about three feet deep; in it ran a stream of water also three feet deep. The stream was so crooked that it kept a continual winding from one side of the valley to the other. In order to avoid wading so often through the water, we endeavored to pass along the slope of the mountain—the snow now being three feet deep, and so hard frozen on the top that we walked upon it, but were obliged to make holes into the snow with our hatchets, that we would not slide down the mountain, and thus we crept on. It happened that the old Indian's [Shikellamy's] foot slipped, and the root of the tree by which he held breaking, he slid down the mountain, as from the roof of a house; but happily he was stopped in his fall, by the string which fastened his pack, hitching on the stump of a small tree. The two Indians could not go to his aid, but our Dutch fellow traveler did; yet not without visible danger of life. I also could not put a foot forward, till I was helped; after this we took the first opportunity to descend into the valley, which was not till after we had labored hard for half an hour with hands and feet. Having observed a tree lying directly off from where the Indian fell, when we were got into the valley again, went back about one hundred paces, where we saw that, if the Indian had slipped four or five paces farther, he would have fallen over a rock one hundred feet perpendicular, upon craggy pieces of rocks below. The Indian was astonished, and turned quite pale; then with outstretched arms, and great earnestness, he spoke these words: 'I thank the Great Lord and Governor of this World, in that He had mercy upon me, and has been willing that I should live longer.'"

On the 28th of March, their food supply became exhausted, but they hoped to reach the North Branch of the Susquehanna before night, expecting to find there an abundant supply of provisions. Near the middle of the forenoon, they came to Sugar Creek, Bradford County, and were detained a considerable time in an effort to cross the same. Finally, reaching the North Branch of the Susquehanna, several miles above the site of Towanda, Bradford County, instead of finding an abundant food supply as they had hoped, they found the Indians at that place on the verge of starvation. All the able bodied men were searching for game, and the old men, squaws, and children had been living for weeks upon maple juice and sugar. The only food offered Weiser's party at this place was a weak soup made of corn meal and ashes, but Weiser was unable to partake of any of it, giving his portion "to the bony little children who crowded around with tears on their stolid faces." However, later in the evening he succeeded in buying about a pound of corn bread.

Weiser had been at this place about twelve years before, and, at that time, found an abundance of game. He asked the old men why game had become so scarce; whereupon, they replied that the Great Spirit had resolved to destroy all the Indians. One old, gray-haired chief told Weiser that he recently had a vision of the Great Spirit of whom he inquired why game was so scarce, and received the following reply: "Your inquiry after the cause why game has become so scarce, I will tell you. You kill it for the sake of the skins, which you give for strong liquor and drown your senses, and kill one another, and carry on dreadful debauchery. Therefore, I have driven the wild animals out of the country, for they are mine. If you will do good, and cease from your sins, I will bring them back; if not, I will destroy you from off the earth."

Proceeding on their way, Weiser's party, on the 8th of April,

reached the "Great Water Shed", dividing the basin of the Susquehanna from that of the Hudson on the east, the Mississippi on
the west, and the St. Lawrence on the north. The forest seemed
endless, and a fresh snow of about twenty inches had recently
fallen. They were still three days' journey from Onondaga. At
this time, the spirit of the resolute Weiser was almost broken.
"I went to one side," said he, "and sat down under a tree, Intending to give up the ghost there, to attain which end, I hoped the
cold of the night then approaching would assist me. My companions soon missed me, and the Indians came back and found me
sitting there. I would not go any further, but said to them in one
word: 'Here I will die;' they were silent a while; at last the old
man [Shikellamy] began: 'My dear companion, take courage;
thou hast until now encouraged us; wilt thou now give up entirely?
Just think that the bad days are better than the good ones, and
when we suffer much, we do not sin, and sin is driven out of us by
suffering. But the good days cause men to sin, and God cannot
be merciful; but on the other hand, when it goes badly with us,
God takes pity on us.' I was, therefore, ashamed and stood up
and journeyed on as well as I could."

They crossed the "Water Shed" the following day, and on the
next, having traveled forty miles, they reached the Onondaga
Council. Weiser gives no report of the conference and negotiations which he there had with the Six Nations. He gives only the
results. The Six Nations consented to an armistice, but refused
to send deputies to Williamsburg, claiming that it was too far to
travel. They suggested that, if the Southern Indians wished to
meet the Iroquois, they should come to Albany.

It is thus seen that Weiser failed to accomplish everything
desired, but the armistice which he secured saved Virginia from an
Iroquois invasion that spring. Upon making a report to the Provincial Council, the Governor immediately advised the Governor of
Virginia of the results of Weiser's mission; whereupon, Governor
Gooch at once sent deputies to the Cherokees and Catawbas.
However, while these deputies were in session, a band of Iroquois
warriors, possibly in ignorance of the decision of the Onondaga
Council, attacked a hunting party of Cherokees, killing three of
them; and this deed so angered the Southern Indians that they
declared all further peace negotiations to be at an end. Once
more Virginia appealed to the Colonial Authorities of Pennsylvania,
and the matter was turned over to Weiser to secure a lasting peace,
if possible, between the Six Nations and the Southern Indians.
This question did not come up again for several years, and history

is silent as to whether Conrad Weiser, in the interim, did anything or not.

The next mention of Shikellamy, in the Colonial Records, is his presence at the conference with Thomas Penn, Governor Thomas, and the Provincial Council, August 1st to 6th, 1740, being accompanied by Sassoonan from Shamokin, Captain Hill from Kittanning, and Shannopin from Shannopin's Town, which conference was described in Chapter VII, and needs no further reference at this point.

The Treaty of 1742

Shikellamy attended the conference or treaty held in Philadelphia in July, 1742, called for the purpose of paying the Six Nations for that part of the land purchased from them in the treaty of 1736 which lay west of the Susquehanna River. It will be recalled that, at the time of the Treaty of 1736, the Six Nations accepted pay for that portion of their lands lying east of the Susquehanna, and desired that the purchase price of that part lying west of the Susquehanna should be paid at a future date. The deputies of the Six Nations were expected to arrive in Philadelphia in May, 1742, but it was not until June 30th that the deputies, representing all tribes of the Confederation, except the Senecas and the Mohawks, arrived at Philadelphia, empowered to receive the pay for the lands west of the Susquehanna. The Senecas were not present at this treaty, because of a great famine among them; nor were the Mohawks, because they were not considered to have any claims upon the Susquehanna lands. The sessions of the treaty began on July 2nd. The three remaining nations of the Iroquois confederacy, early in the conference, received the goods in payment of that part of the Susquehanna lands lying west of the Susquehanna River, comprising the counties of York, Cumberland, Adams, and most of Franklin.

Soon after the goods in payment of the Susquehanna lands were divided, the Iroquois deputies expressed their dissatisfaction with the amount, although admitting that it was as agreed upon. They said they felt sure that, if the sons of William Penn, who were then in England, were present, they would agree to giving a large amount out of pity for the Indians on account of their poverty and wretchedness. Through their chief speaker, Canassatego, an Onondago chieftain, they begged Governor Thomas, inasmuch as he had the keys to the Proprietors' chest, to open the same and take out a little more for them. Governor Thomas replied that the Proprietors had gone to England and taken the keys with them; whereupon, the Indians, as an additional reason for their request, called attention to the increasing value of the lands sold, and also to the fact that the whites were daily settling on Indian lands that had not been sold. They called attention to the fact that, at the last treaty with the Colony, the Iroquois had complained about the whites settling on unsold lands, and that the Governor, at that time, agreed to remedy this wrong.

Said Canassatego: "Land is everlasting, and the few things we receive for it are soon worn out and gone; for the future, we will sell no lands but when Brother Onas [meaning the sons of William Penn] is in the country, and we will know beforehand the quality of goods we are to receive. Besides, we are not well used with respect to the lands still unsold by us. Your people daily settle on these lands and spoil our hunting. We must insist on your removing them, as you know they have no right to the northward of the Kittochtinny Hills [Kittatinny, or Blue Mountains]. In particular, we renew our complaints against some people who are settled at Juniata, a branch of the Susquehanna, and all along the banks of that river as far as Mahaniay, and desire that they be forthwith made to go off the land, for they do great damage to our cousins, the Delawares."

Canassatego further called attention to the fact that Maryland and Virginia had not paid the Iroquois for lands within their bounds upon which the whites were settling, and that, at the treaty of 1736, the Governor of Pennsylvania had promised to use his influence with Maryland and Virginia in their behalf in regard to this matter. "This affair," said Canassatego, "was recommended to you by our chiefs at our last treaty and you then, at our earnest desire, promised to write a letter to that person who has authority over those people, and to procure us an answer. As we have never heard from you on this head, we want to know what you have done in it. If you have not done anything, we now renew our request, and desire you will inform the person whose people are seated on our lands that that country [western Maryland and Virginia] belongs to us by right of conquest, we having bought it with our blood, and taken it from our enemies in fair war." Canassatego threatened that, if Maryland and Virginia did not pay for these lands, the Iroquois would enforce payment in their own way.

Governor Thomas replied that he had ordered the magistrates of Lancaster County to drive off the squatters from the Juniata lands, and was not aware that any had stayed. The Indians interrupted, and said that the persons who had been sent to remove the squatters, did not do their duty; that, instead of removing them from the Juniata lands, they were in league with the squatters, and had made large surveys for themselves. The earnest arguments of Canassatego had the desired effect. The Provincial Council decided to add to the value of the goods a present of three hundred pounds.

The Governor advised Canassatego that, shortly after the treaty of 1736, James Logan, President of the Council, had written the Governor of Maryland about the lands, but received no reply. Now the Governor promised to intercede with Maryland and Virginia, and, if possible, to secure payment for the lands of the Iroquois upon which the whites of those colonies were settling. He also renewed his promise to remove the squatters from the Juniata Valley.

At this treaty of July, 1742, Canassatego, the principal speaker of the Iroquois deputation, ordered the Delawares of the Munsee Clan to remove from the territory of the "Walking Purchase" of 1737. This will be discussed in the chapter on the Munsee Delaware chief, Nutimus (Chapter XII).

More Troubles Between the Iroquois and Virginia

Hardly had the Iroquois deputies to the treaty of 1742 returned home when a war party of Iroquois started southward, afterwards claiming to have gone against their old enemies, the Catawbas. Coming down the Susquehanna River in canoes to John Harris' Ferry, the first important white settlement on their route, they secured from a magistrate of Lancaster County a pass for their safe passage through the inhabited parts of Pennsylvania. With this pass, they proceeded across the country in a southwestern direction toward the Shenandoah Valley, traveling without molesting anyone until they reached Virginia, where they had a severe engagement with a party of settlers, and several lives were lost on each side. They then retreated hastily to New York.

The first word that the Colonial Authorities of Pennsylvania had of this fresh trouble between the Iroquois and the Colony of Virginia was received on January 24th, 1743, from Thomas McKee, a trader then living on the Susquehanna at Big Island, (Lock Haven). McKee made a deposition on January 24th, stating as follows: "Being concerned in the Indian trade, he has a store settled at an Indian town on the South Branch Sasquehanna River, near an Island called the Big Island, inhabited by the Shawna [Shawnee] Indians; and that on the 12th or 13th of this instant,

January, about seven o'clock in the morning, the Indians of the Town came to this Deponent's store, and told him they had heard the Dead Halloa, and were much surprised at it. And soon after, the same halloa, as from the Big Island, was repeated in the hearing of this Deponent. Whereupon, he, with a servant of his, took a canoe and went over to the Island, and in his passage, heard the Indians belonging to the Town call over to those on the Island, and ask them what was the matter. To which they answered, that the white men had killed some of their men. And on this Deponent coming to them on the Island, he saluted them according to the usual way, saying, 'How do you do, my friends?' At which they shook their heads, and made no answer; but went over to the Shawnas' town. And this Deponent further saith, that there were ten in number of those Indians, and that they belonged to the Five Nations; and on their coming to town, immediately a council was called; and this Deponent attended at the Council House, and was admitted."

At this council, the leader of the band of the Iroquois who had made the expedition to Virginia informed the Shawnees of the misfortune that had befallen his band. The leader's speech was delivered in the Iroquois language, and interpreted to McKee in Shawnee. Whereupon, McKee addressed the council, and reminded them that none of the disorders of which the Indians complained had happened in Pennsylvania. One of the Shawnees made the remark that the white people were all of one color and, in case of war, would stand together. Another Shawnee asked the warriors if they had met any of McKee's men, who had been sent to the Juniata on a trading expedition. "They could not have met them," said a third warrior, "for if they had, they would have cut them off."

McKee adds in his affidavit: "On hearing these discourses, he [McKee] rose up, and called out an old Shawna, with whom he was best acquainted, and took him to his store; made him a present of two or three twists of tobacco, and desired him to press to the Indians in Council their treaty of peace with Pennsylvania, and the ill consequences of breaking it in cutting him off, as he apprehended he had great reason to fear they intended. That some short time after, the same Indian called this Deponent from his store, and told him that he had offered in Council what he had requested, and it was approved, though it seemed disagreeable to some of the Shawnees. And in a short time after, this Deponent [McKee] was informed by a white woman, who had been taken prisoner by the Indians in their Carolina wars, that it was left to the Shawnees to deal with him as they pleased; and that they were gone to hold a council concerning him at some distance from the town; and that if he did not make his escape, he would certainly be cut off. Upon which last information, together with some observations he had made of their behavior, he thought it not safe to trust his life in their hands, and notwithstanding a considerable quantity of goods which he had carried up there to trade, he determined to withdraw, and leave his effects among them; and accordingly communicated his designs to his man; and they came off privately, traveling by night and day through the uninhabited parts of the country, till they apprehended themselves to be out of danger, being out three days and three nights."

Shikellamy and Weiser Go to Onondaga to Arrange for Treaty

The foregoing matters caused the Provincial Council to send Conrad Weiser to Shamokin, where on February 4th and April 9th, 1743, he held the conferences with Shikellamy, Sassoonan, and Great Hominy, chief of the Shawnees, mentioned in Chapter VII. At the first of these conferences, Weiser, learning that Shikellamy's cousin had been killed in the recent skirmish in Virginia, presented the old chief with "two Strowds" to wpie away his tears. He also sent a present to Kakowatcheky, then head of the Shawnees at Wyoming, with a message asking him, "as he lived about half way between Philadelphia and the Six Nations, to take care of the chain of friendship betwixt the Six Nations and Pennsylvania." A grand-son of Shikellamy, who was present at the skirmish, gave Weiser a full account of the expedition, and of the fight, in which it appeared that the whites were the aggressors. At this conference, Shikellamy ordered the Shawnees to return the goods they had stolen from the trader, Thomas McKee.

Weiser returned to Philadelphia, and made a report of his conference with Shikellamy, but, before he returned, Governor Thomas had received a letter from Governor Gooch of Virginia, offering to accept the mediation of Governor Thomas in the matter. Weiser was then sent again to Shamokin, where he met Shikellamy in council on April 9th, and told him of the desire of the Governor of Virginia to come to an agreement with the Iroquois in this matter.

At this council, (April 9th), Weiser learned that the Indians who had been sent to Onondaga as deputies on behalf of the Virginia affair had returned, among whom were Shikellamy's son and Sachsidowa, a Tuscarora chief. They brought word that the Iroquois were willing to meet the Governor of Virginia at a council at the mouth of the Conodoguinet, opposite Harrisburg, the next spring, and, in the meantime, had ordered their warriors not to make expeditions into Virginia. Shikellamy told Weiser that the Six Nations could not meet Virginia in Council "with a hatchet stuck in their head; the Governor of Virginia must wash off the blood first, and take the hatchet out of their head, and dress the wound, (according to the custom that he who struck first must do it), and the Council of the Six Nations will speak to him and be reconciled to him, and bury that affair in the ground that it never may be seen nor heard of any more so long as the world stands." "But if the Virginians would not come to do that," said Shikellamy, "he [Shikellamy] believed there would be war." Shikellamy further told Weiser that, if war with Virginia should come, the Six Nations would not disturb the people of Pennsylvania, but their warriors would go directly to Virginia from Big Island (Lock Haven).

Shikellamy, Sachsidowa, several other chiefs, and Conrad Weiser brought this information to Philadelphia, laying it before the Provincial Council on April 22nd and 23rd. They also brought with them the message of Sassoonan commending Governor Thomas in his efforts as mediator, mentioned in Chapter VII. The Indian delegation was entertained free, and the Governor gave to Shikellamy a present of ten pounds; to Shikellamy's two sons, six pounds; and to Sachsidowa, five pounds.

When Virginia received the report, she lost no time in coming to terms, and a present of one hundred pounds' value was placed by her in the hands of Governor Thomas for the Iroquois. Governor Gooch of Virginia writing Governor Thomas, in May, said: "We request that you will be pleased to send your honest Interpreter [Weiser] once more to the Indian chiefs, and if possible, prevail with them to accept through your hands a present of one hundred pounds sterling value, in such goods as you may think proper, as a token of our sincere disposition to preserve peace and friendship with them, and as an earnest that we will not fail to send commissions next spring, at a time and place that shall be agreed upon, to treat with them." Thus did Virginia prepare to "take the hatchet out of the head" of the Iroquois, put there by her settlers in the unfortunate skirmish, and to "wash away the blood, and dress the wound."

The Provincial Council then sent Weiser and Shikellamy to

the Great Council of the Iroquois at Onondaga to arrange for the time and place of meeting, and to deliver Virginia's present. They arrived at Onondaga late in July where Taconte, the "Black Prince" of the Onondagas expressed great satisfaction at Weiser's arrival. Said he: "You never come without good news from our brethren in Philadelphia." "I smiled," says Weiser, "and told him it was enough to kill a man to come such a long and bad road over hills, rocks, old trees, and rivers, and to fight through a cloud of vermin, and all kinds of poisoned worms and creeping things, besides being loaded with a disagreeable message, at which they laughed." The Great Council of the Six Nations, after several days of oratory and imposing ceremonies, accepted the offer of Governor Thomas of Pennsylvania and Governor Gooch of Virginia for a confernce or treay at Harris Ferry (Harrisburg) the next spring. Later, on account of the inconvenience of meeting at Harrisburg, it was decided to hold the treaty at Lancaster, a small town then sixteen years old.

At Onondaga, the Iroquois chief, Zillawallie, gave the cause of the war between the Six Nations and the Catawbas. Addressing Weiser, he said; "We are engaged in a great war with the Catawbas, which will last to the end of the world; for they molest us, and speak contemptuously of us, which our warriors will not bear, and they will soon go to war against them again. It will be in vain for us to dissuade them from it."

On this mission to Onondaga, Conrad Weiser prevented a war between Virginia and the Six Nations—a war which would eventually have involved the other colonies.

Before describing the Lancaster Treaty, we call attention to the fact that, scarcely had the treaty of 1742 been concluded, when the Colonial Authorities of Pennsylvania were asked by the Governor of Maryland for advice and assistance in that Colony's trouble with the Six Nations. It appeared that, in the early part of the summer of 1742, some Nanticokes in Maryland were imprisoned, and that their friends, the Shawnees and Senecas, threatened to make trouble unless they were released. Governor Thomas of Pennsylvania engaged Conrad Weiser to accompany the Maryland messenger to the region of the Six Nations, as interpreter, for the purpose of inviting the Six Nations to a treaty to be held at Harris' Ferry (Harrisburg) in the spring of 1743. It does not appear that the Iroquois did any more than simply deliberate on this matter; but Maryland's advances at least had the virtue of opening negotiations at the Great Council of the Six Nations on the part of that Colony.

CHAPTER XI

Shikellamy

(Continued)

THE LANCASTER TREATY OF 1744

N FRIDAY, June 22nd, 1744, the long expected delegation of the Six Nations arrived at Lancaster for the purpose of entering into a treaty with Pennsylvania, Maryland, and Virginia. The delegation consisted of two hundred and forty-two, and was headed by Canassatego. There were many squaws and children mounted on horseback. Arriving in front of the Court House, the leaders of the delegation saluted the commissioners from Pennsylvania, Maryland, and Virginia, with a song. This was an invitation to the whites to renew former treaties and to make good the one now proposed.

Maryland Purchases Land from Iroquois

When the Maryland commissioners came to the Lancaster treaty, they had no intention whatever of recognizing any Iroquois claims to lands within the bounds of their province, basing their position upon the following facts: (1) Maryland had bought from the Minquas, or Susquehannas, in 1652, all their claims on both sides of the Chesapeake Bay as far north as the mouth of the Susquehanna River. (2) The Minquas, aided by troops from Maryland, had, in 1663, defeated eight hundred Senecas and Cayugas from the Iroquois Confederation.

But the Iroquois never abandoned their war on the Minquas until they overwhelmingly defeated this tribe in 1675, when they were reduced by famine and Maryland had withdrawn her alliance. Now, in view of their conquest of the Minquas, the Six Nations claimed a right to the Susquehanna lands to the head of Chesapeake Bay.

The Maryland commissioners receded from their position. The release for the Maryland lands was signed, on Monday, July 2nd, at George Sanderson's Inn, instead of at the Court House. Conrad Weiser signed in behalf of the absent member of the Iroquois Confederation, (Mohawk), both with his Indian name of Tarach-a-wa-gon, and that of Weiser. By his dexterous management, the lands released were so described as not to give Maryland a title to lands claimed by Pennsylvania, the boundary dispute between Maryland and Pennsylvania being at the time still pending. The release was for all "lands lying two miles above the uppermost forks of Patowmack or Cohongoruton River, near which Thomas Cresap has his hunting or trading cabin, [at Old Town fourteen miles east of Cumberland, Maryland,] by a line north to the bounds of Pennsylvania. But, in case such limits shall not include every settlement or inhabitant of Maryland, then such other lines and courses from the said two miles above the forks to the outermost inhabitants or settlements, as shall include every settlement and inhabitant in Maryland, and from thence by a north line to the bounds of Pennsylvania, shall be the limits. And, further, if any people already have or shall settle beyond the lands now described and bounded, they shall enjoy the same free from any disturbance of us in any manner whatsoever, and we do and shall accept these people for our Brethren, and as such will always treat them." Thus was the purchase happily effected.

However, Shikellamy refused to sign the deed of the Maryland lands, being determined not to recognize that Maryland had any land claims north of the disputed boundary line between herself and Pennsylvania.

Virginia Purchases Land from Iroquois

The Virginia commissioners had their negotiations with the Iroquois deputies in progress at the same time as Maryland. They found the Iroquois very determined not to yield any part of their claim to the Virginia lands. Said Tachanoontia, an Onondaga chieftain: "We have the right of conquest—a right too dearly purchased, and which cost us too much blood to give up without any reason at all." Finally, after much oratory, the Six Nations released all their land claims in Virginia for a consideration of two hundred pounds in goods and two hundred pounds in gold, with a written promise to be given additional remuneration as the settlements increased to the westward; and the Virginia commissioners guaranteed the Indians an open road to the Catawba country, promising that the people of Virginia would do their part if the Iroquois would perform theirs. The Iroquois understood this to mean that the Virginians would feed their war parties, if they (the Iroquois) would not shoot the farmers' cattle, chickens, etc., when passing to and from the Catawba country.

"When the treaty was over, the Indians believed that they had established land claims in Virginia, that the open road was guaranteed, that their warrors were to be fed while passing through the state, and that they had sold land only to the head-waters of the streams feeding the Ohio River. The Virginians, on the other hand, believed that they had extinguished all Iroquois land claims forever within the charter limits of their colony." The western bounds of the Virginia purchase were set forth as "the setting sun", leading Virginia to believe that the purchase included the Ohio Valley, but the Iroquois afterwards explained that by "the setting sun" was meant the crest of the Allegheny Mountains. It was after the treaty that large tracts of land were granted the Ohio Company; and it was not until the year 1768 that the Six Nations, by the treaty of Fort Stanwix, New York, relinquished all their rights to the region on the east and south side of the Ohio, from the Cherokee River, in Tennessee, to Kittanning, Pennsylvania.

Pennsylvania, the Peacemaker

In the Lancaster Treaty, Pennsylvania was the mediator and peacemaker, inducing Maryland and Virginia to lay aside their opposition to Iroquois land claims, and settle in such a manner as to secure the friendship of the Six Nations. Thus the French were thwarted, and the English frontier from New England to the Carolinas was protected. Pennsylvania also confirmed her former treaties with the Iroquois.

But while Pennsylvania was acting as peacemaker, she had trouble of her own to adjust with the Iroquois deputies. On April 9th, 1744, John (Jack) Armstrong, a trader on his way to the Allegheny, and his two servants, James Smith and Woodward Arnold, were murdered at Jacks Narrows (named for "Jack" Armstrong), on the Juniata, in Huntingdon County, by a Delaware Indian named Musemeelin. It appeared that Musemeelin owed Armstrong some skins, and Armstrong seized a horse and rifle belonging to the Indian in lieu of the skins. Later Musemeelin met Armstrong near the Juniata and paid him all his indebtedness except twenty shillings, and demanded his horse, but Armstrong refused to give the animal up until the entire debt was paid. Shortly after this, Armstrong and his servants passed the cabin of Musemeelin on their way to the Allegheny, and Musemeelin's wife demanded the horse, but by this time Armstrong had sold it to James Berry. Musemeelin was away on a hunting trip at the time his wife made the demand on Armstrong, and, when he returned, she told him about it. This angered him and he determined on revenge. Taking two young Indians with him, Musemeelin went to the camp of Armstrong, shot Smith who was there alone and Arnold whom they found returning to camp, and, meeting Armstrong, who was sitting on an old log, he demanded his horse. Armstrong replied: "He will come by and by." "I want him now", said Musemeelin. "You shall have him. Come to the fire and let us smoke and talk together," said Armstrong. As they proceeded, Musemeelin shot and tomahawked him.

The matter was placed by Governor Thomas in the hands of Shikellamy at Shamokin, who caused the murderers to be apprehended, and, after a hearing, ordered two of them to be sent to the Lancaster jail to await trial. Conrad Weiser was the bearer of the Governor's message to Shikellamy and Sassoonan. While Shikellamy's sons were conveying the prisoners to Lancaster, the friends of Musemeelin, who was related to some important Delaware chiefs, induced Shikellamy's sons to allow Musemeelin to escape. The other Indian was locked in jail.

At the Lancaster treaty, Governor Thomas demanded of the Iroquois that they command their subjects, the Delawares, to surrender Musemeelin to the Provincial Authorities, and the Indians were invited to Lancaster to witness the trial. The Iroquois deputies replied that the Provincial Authorities should not be too much concerned; that three Indians had been killed at different times on the Ohio by the whites, and the Iroquois had never mentioned anything concerning them to the Colony. However, they stated that they had severely reproved the Delawares, and would see that the goods which the murderers had stolen from Armstrong be restored to his relatives, and Musemeelin be returned for trial, but not as a prisoner. Later, on August 21st, 1744, Shikellamy brought the two prisoners to the Provincial Authorities at Philadelphia. Musemeelin was not convicted. He returned to his wigwam.

Importance of the Lancaster Treaty

No Delawares, the friends of William Penn, were present at the Lancaster Treaty, the Iroquois having forbidden them to attend.

It is difficult to overstate the importance of the Lancaster Treaty—in many respects the most important Indian Council ever held in Pennsylvania up to this time. War between England and

France, King George's War, was then raging. At the opening of
this conflict, the question uppermost in the minds, not only of the
Governors of Pennsylvania, Maryland, and Virginia, but of all the
colonies, was, "What will be the attitude of the powerful Six
Nations?" The successful settling of the disputed land claims of
the Iroquois in Maryland and Virginia, by this treaty, through the
mediation of Pennsylvania, with Weiser as mentor, had much to
do with making possible the success of Weiser's future negotiations
with the Onondaga Council, negotiations that resulted in the neutrality of the Iroquois during King George's War. Had not the
Iroquois deputies, at the Treaty of Lancaster, promised to inform
the Governor of Pennsylvania as to the movements of the French?
Had this great Confederation sided with the French, the English
colonies would have been swept into the sea.

Disquieting Reports

The Six Nations faithfully kept their promise, made to Pennsylvania at the treaty of Lancaster, to advise the Colony of the
movements of the French. In September following the treaty,
Conrad Weiser had gone to Shamokin, with eight young Germans,
and built Shikellamy a house "49½ feet long, 17½ feet wide, and
covered with shingles." While engaged in this work, he received
some disquieting news from the aged sachem. Weiser wrote
Secretary James Logan, concerning it, on September 29th, 1744, as
follows: "Shikellamy informed me that the Governor of Canada
hath sent an embassy to Onondaga, to lament over the death of
Tocanuwarogon, a chief of the Onondagas, who died last spring
(in whose house I used to lodge), and to let the Council of the Six
Nations know that the French had made war against the English,
whom they would soon beat, and as they, the Six Nations, loved
their brethren, the English, their father, Onontio, [the generic name
for the Governors of Canada] desired them to take no offense nor
be on either side concerned, but stand neutral, and they should be
supplied by the French with powder, lead, and other commodities,
at their several trading houses, as usual, as cheap as before, and as
the English had run away from Oswego, cowards as they were,
Onontio would take the house [fort] of Oswego to himself, as his
people are the oldest settlers in the Northern countrys, and would
supply his children, all the Indians, with all sorts of goods very
cheap."
Shikellamy further told Weiser that the Council of the Six

Nations had resolved to notify the Governor of Canada that they did not approve of his "intention to take the House at Oswego to himself, which could not be done without bloodshed." They insinuated that the French were cowardly to attack the English "in their backs." Said Shikellamy: "They [the Six Nations] would therefore advise him [the Governor of Canada] to act more honorably, as becometh a warrior, and go around by sea, and face the English."

The Catawbas Willing to Make Peace

In the latter part of 1744, the news of Peter Chartier's desertion reached the Colonial Authorities of Pennsylvania and Virginia, and it was believed that the Catawbas were the instigators of Chartier's action. Fearing that, not only the Catawbas, but the whole Muskokee Confederation would join the French, Virginia and Carolina renewed their efforts to bring about a peace between the Catawbas and Iroquois; and Governor Gooch of Virginia wrote Governor Thomas of Pennsylvania in November of that year advising that the Catawbas were willing to make peace, and requesting that Conrad Weiser get in touch with the Six Nations in the matter.

Shikellamy and Weiser Once More Journey
to Onondaga

Governor Thomas made the recommendation to the Assembly that Conrad Weiser should be sent to the Great Council of the Six Nations at Onondaga to ascertain if it were possible to bring about peace between the Catawbas and Iroquois. To make a journey at this time when King George's War was raging and French intrigue working among the Indians, was fraught with much danger; besides, it looked as if the attempt to work out a peace would not be successful, inasmuch as the Six Nations declared at the Lancaster treaty of 1744 that the war between them and the Catawbas must go on "to the end of the world." Conrad Weiser was the one white man in the colonies courageous enough to undertake the journey.

Weiser realized that Shikellamy was the key to the door of the Six Nations. Late in 1744, Weiser had sent his son, Sammy, to Virginia to collect a debt for him. While in Virginia, Sammy Weiser met a band of Iroquois returning from an expedition against the Catawbas, who told him that "Unhappy Jake", one of Shikellamy's sons, had been killed in a fight with the Catawbas. Weiser feared that this unhappy incident would so harden the heart of Shikellamy that it would be useless to attempt to work out a peace between the Iroquois and the Catawbas. He then suggested to the Colonial Authorities, in a letter written on January 2nd, 1745, that it would be the part of policy to give old Shikellamy a present "to wipe away his tears", explaining that "it is customary with the Indians that, let what will happen, the chiefs or people in trust with them, don't stir to do any service or business to the public when they are in mourning, till they have in a manner a new commission as before said in being fetched out of mourning and invested with new courage and dispositions."

Weiser accordingly set out for Shamokin taking with him a present for Shikellamy purchased by the Colony, consisting of three match-coats and half a dozen silk handkerchiefs. Realizing the importance of Shikellamy's position Weiser had always made it a point to pay the old chief every attention. Three years before this time he had recommended the Moravian missionaries to build a free blacksmith shop at Shamokin, and we have already seen how he built a house for Shikellamy in the latter's declining years.

Finally, on the 19th of May, 1745, Weiser in company with Shikellamy, Shikellamy's son, Andrew Montour (son of Madam Montour), Bishop Spangenberg, of the Moravian Church, and two other Moravian missionaries, set out from Shamokin for Onondaga, at which place they arrived on the 6th day of June. At Tioga, a messenger had been sent ahead to apprise the Iroquois of their coming.

Representatives of all the members of the Iroquois Confederation, except the Mohawks, assembled in great numbers to hear what Weiser and Shikellamy had to say. There was a great stir among the Six Nations inasmuch as they were arranging to meet at Oswego and go to Canada to hold a treaty with the French Governor. Indeed, they would have started a day before Weiser's arrival, if his messenger had not appeared. Weiser asked the Great Council of the Iroquois whether they believed that their going to Canada to meet the French Governor would comport with the promises which they had made at the Lancaster treaty the year before. The sachems replied that they knew perfectly well what they were doing. Said they: "The French Governor of Canada will try to gain upon us. . . . . The French are known to be a crafty people. but it will be in vain for him, as we have already agreed what to say to him and will not go from it." Weiser and Shikellamy then delivered the message of the Catawbas suggesting Williamsburg, Virginia, as the place of meeting of the deputies from the opposing tribes. Weiser made the best apology he could for the past conduct of the Catawbas, and urged the Iroquois to send deputies for the sake of the Governors of Virginia and Pennsylvania, if for no other reason. After a few minutes delay the Black Prince of the Onondagas, the speaker of the Iroquois, replied that no council fire had ever been kindled at Williamsburg, but that the Iroquois would be willing to send deputies to Philadelphia. However, the Black Prince further advised that the deputies could not be sent that summer, but that they would be sent during the summer of 1746.

At this point we call attention to the fact that, at the Albany Treaty, held in October, 1745, between the Six Nations and New York, Connecticut, Massachusetts, and Pennsylvania, the matter of the Catawba war again came up, but was not pressed. On that occasion, Canassatego explained to Thomas Laurence, John Kinsey, and Isaac Norris, the Commissioners from Pennsylvania, that the chiefs of the Six Nations were not able to restrain their young warriors from making raids into the Catawba country until peace was declared. The Great Council of the Six Nations had all it could do, at that time, to preserve neutrality in the struggle between the French and English, known as King George's War.

Shikellamy and Weiser found the Great Council at Onondaga very much incensed at the conduct of Peter Chartier, in deserting to the French and leading a band of Shawnees down the Ohio. They asked why Pennsylvania did not declare war against him at once.

When the Council was over, the Black Prince invited Shikellamy and Weiser's party and all the chiefs of the Onondagas to a great dinner. All the company went directly to the house of the Black Prince and partook of hominy, dried venison, and fish, after which they were "served with a dram round." While they were feasting, Weiser ascertained that many of the Iroquois were in favor of a war with the Shawnees and peace with the Catawbas. He also learned, in a confidential conversation with one of the old sachems, that the Six Nations believed it to be to their best interests to maintain strict neutrality in the war beween the English and the French. This chief said that the Iroquois would not join with either nation unless compelled to it for their own preservation; that, hitherto, from their situation and alliance, they had been courted by both the French and the English, but should either party prevail so far as to drive the other out of the country, the Iroquois would not be considered by the victorious nation.

Presents would no longer be made to them, and, in the end, they would be obliged to submit to such laws as the conquerors should think fit to impose on them.

At this point, we call attention to the fact that, while there was a strong English party among the Mohawks, and a strong French party among the Senecas, the great Confederation of the Iroquois remained neutral throughout King George's War. Had the Confederation sided with the French in this conflict, there is little doubt that the career of the Anglo-Saxon on the North American Continent would have been put to an end. There is little doubt, also, that, if Shikellamy and Conrad Weiser had not brought the Iroquois Confederation into such friendly relations with the English in bringing about the treaties of 1732, 1736, 1742, and 1744, the Iroquois would have taken the part of the French in King George's War.

The reason why Bishop Spangenberg and the other Moravian missionaries accompanied Shikellamy and Weiser on this journey, was that the Moravians at that time had a project on foot to transfer their mission at Shekomeko, New York, to the Wyoming Valley, on the North Branch of the Susquehanna, in Pennsylvania; and this necessitated negotiations with the Great Council at Onondaga to whose dependencies Wyoming belonged. Count Zinzindorf had held a conference with the great Iroquois chieftain, Canassatego, at Weiser's home near Womelsdorf, in August, 1742, when the Iroquois deputies were returning from the treaty of 1742, at which conference the Moravians were given permission by the Iroquois to establish their missions in Pennsylvania. Now the Onondaga Council replied to the request of Bishop Spangenberg that they were glad to renew their contract with Count Zinzindorf and the Moravians, and they gave their consent to the proposed Moravian settlement at Wyoming.

The Moravians founded the town of Bethlehem in December, 1741, which has ever since been the central seat of the Moravian Church in America. Later, they established a mission at Friedensheutten, near Bethlehem, another called Friedensheutten, (Tents of peace), the Indian town of Wyalusing, Bradford County, another at Gnadenhuetten (Tents of grace), near Weissport, in Carbon County, another at Shamokin, the great Indian capital, and another at Wyoming, Luzerne County. They also established missions in the western part of the state. These were at and in the vicinity of the Munsee Delaware town of Goschgoschunk, near Tionesta, Forest County, and Friedenstadt (City of peace) on the Beaver, in Lawrence County. In 1772, the Moravian missionaries,

John Etwein and John Roth, conducted the congregation from Wyalusing to Friedenstadt on the Beaver. The efforts of the Moravian Church to convert the Delawares and other Indians of Pennsylvania to the Christian faith is one of the most delightful chapters in the history of the Commonwealth.

Incidents of Shikellamy's Journey Home

De Schweinitz, in his "Life of David Zeisberger", relates the following incidents of Shikellamy's journey home:

"After a stay of twelve days, the visitors began their homeward journey. At the first village they separated. Conrad Weiser and Andrew Montour took a circuitous trail; Spangenberg, Zeisberger, Shebosh, and Shikellamy and his son followed that which had brought them to Onondaga. The experiences of this latter party were even more trying than when they had come that way the first time. Not only had they to contend with the same horrors of the swamps, but a succession of rainstorms occurred that made traveling almost unendurable; and, the greatest calamity of all, their provisions failed. They braved these hardships for eight days until they reached Ostonwacken almost exhausted, hearts full of hope. A bitter disappointment awaited them. There was not a morsel of food to be had in the village, and not even a fire burning in a single lodge. Riding on in garments wringing-wet and barely alleviating the worst pangs of hunger with a few fishes which they had got in the Susquehanna, they lay down on the bank of the river at noon of the 7th of July utterly overcome. They could go no farther. It was an hour to try their souls. A handful of rice constituted the remnant of their provisions. Faint and silent, the Bishop and his young companions waited to see what God would do; while Shikellamy and his son, with the stoicism of their race, resigned themselves to their fate. Presently an aged Indian emerged from the forest, sat down among them, opened his package, and gave them a smoked turkey. While they proceeded, he joined their party, camped with them at night, and produced several pieces of delicious venison. They could not but recognize in this meeting a direct interposition of their Heavenly Father. The next day they reached Shamokin, where a trader supplied their wants.

"On their way to this town they came upon a rattlesnake nest, amid the hills of the Susquehanna. At first but a few of the reptiles were visible, basking in the sun. No sooner, however, did they kill these than the whole neighborhood seemed to be alive with them, and a rattling began which was frightful. Snakes crawled out of holes, from crevices in the rocks, and between loose stones, or darted from thickets, and lifted up their heads above patches of fern, until there was a multitude in motion. They completely surrounded the travelers, who hastened from the spot. It was a place where the reptiles had gathered in autumn and lain torpid, coiled together in heaps during the winter. From Shamokin, Spangenberg and his associates hastened to Bethlehem."

Shikellamy Opposes Weiser's Ohio Journey

While Shikellamy conferred with Weiser at Chamber's Mill, near Harrisburg, in the summer of 1747, concerning the dishonesty of a number of the traders, his next important action was to oppose Conrad Weiser's journey to the Ohio, in the summer of 1748, as the agent of the Colony of Pennsylvania in making a treaty at Logstown with the Ohio tribes. Shikellamy insisted that no present should be sent by the Colony to the Western Indians, inasmuch as they had not actually gone to war against the French, and could not do so without the permission of the Six Nations, their overlords. When Weiser asked the old chief to accompany him to the Ohio, Shikellamy stated that Weiser's attendance as interpreter would be necessary at the Great Council of the Six Nations in the spring of 1748, for the purpose of deciding upon a successor to Sassoonan. Shikellamy's opposition, while unsuccessful, postponed Weiser's journey for a time.

Last Days of Shikellamy

In the summer of 1747, Shikellamy's health began to fail. In July of that year, Weiser, in a report to the Provincial Council of a journey to Shamokin, says:

"I was surprised to see Shikellamy in such a miserable condition as ever my eyes beheld; he was hardly able to stretch forth his hand to bid me welcome; in the same condition was his wife, his three sons not quite so bad but very poorly, also one of his daughters and two or three of his grandchildren all had the fever; there was three buried out of the family a few days before . . . . . Next morning I administered the medicine to Shikellamy and one of his sons, under the direction of Dr. Grome, which had a very good effect on both. Next morning I gave the same medicine to two more (who would not venture at first); it had the same effect, and the four persons thought themselves as good as recovered, but above all Shikellamy was able to walk about with me with a stick in his hand before I left Shamokin. He, (Shikellamy), is extremely poor; in his sickness the horses have eaten all his corn; his clothes he gave to the Indian doctor to cure him and his family, but all in vain; he has nobody to hunt for him, and I cannot see how the poor old man can live. He has been a true servant to the Government and may perhaps still be, if he lives to be well again. As the winter is coming on again, I think it would not be amiss to send him a few blankets or match-coats and a little powder and lead. If the Government would be pleased to do it, and you could send it up soon, I would send my sons with it to Shamokin before the cold weather comes." The Council then resolved that a present of goods to the value of sixteen pounds be made to Shikellamy, and that it be sent to Weiser at his home near Womelsdorf with a request to dispatch it immediately by one of his sons to the aged sachem.

Death of Shikellamy

On the 6th day of December, of the eventful year of 1748, occurred the death of Shikellamy, the most picturesque and historic Indian character who ever lived in Pennsylvania. As we have seen, his residence was at Sunbury, and Conrad Weiser, in the later years of the old chief's life, had built him a substantial house which rested upon pillars for safety, and in which he always shut himself up when any drunken frolic was going on in the village. He had been taken ill in Philadelphia, but so far recovered that he had visited his old friend, Conrad Weiser, at his home near Womelsdorf, in April, 1748, and was able to complete his journey to Shamokin. Upon his return to Shamokin, he was again taken ill, and in June the Provincial Council was advised that he he was so ill that he might lose his eyesight; but he recovered sufficiently to make a trip to Bethlehem early in December. On his return from that place, he became so ill that he reached home only by the assistance of the Moravian missionary, Bishop Zeisberger. His daughter and the good bishop were with him during his last illness and last hours. Bishop Zeisberger and Henry Frye made the old chief a coffin, and the Indians painted the body in their gayest colors, bedecked it with his choicest ornaments, and placed with it the old chief's weapons according to the Indian custom. Then, after Christian burial services conducted by Bishop Zeisberger,

Shikellamy was buried in the Indian burying ground of his people in the present town of Sunbury.

The Moravian missionary, Watteville, visited Shamokin in October, 1748, where he was warmly welcomed by Shikellamy. We quote the following from De Schweinitz's "Life of David Zeisberger", giving an account of Watteville's visit and the last days of Shikellamy:

"Watteville's visit made a deep impression upon this sachem. Zeisberger had sent him a costly gift (a silver knife, fork and spoon, together with an ivory drinking cup, heavily mounted with silver), and an affectionate message entreating him to remember the Gospel, which he heard from his lips, and to turn to Christ. Watteville urged the subject with all the glowing warmth of his own love, Zeisberger interpreting his words into the Mohawk language. The heart of the old chief was touched; and several weeks after the departure of the party, he [Shikellamy] arrived at Bethlehem, in order to hear more of Christ. He was daily instructed in the plan of salvation, until he experienced the power of divine grace and could make a profession of personal faith. He had been baptized by a Jesuit father in Canada many years before this. Laying aside a manitou, last relic of his idolatry, he took his way rejoicing to his forest home. At Tulpehocken, however, he fell ill, and had barely strength to reach Shamokin. There he stretched himself on his mat, and never rose again. Zeisberger, who had returned to his post while Watteville and Cammerhoff had gone to Bethlehem, faithfully ministered to his body and soul. He died on the 6th of December, conscious to the last, but unable to speak, a bright smile illuminating his countenance."

Shikellamy left to mourn him his three sons and a daughter. We have already seen how another son, Unhappy Jake, was killed in the war with the Catawbas. The three sons who survived were: (1) Taghneghdoarus, also known as John Shikellamy, who succeeded his honored and distinguished father in authority, but never gained the confidence with which the father was held by both the Indians and the whites; (2) Taghahjute, or Sayughdowa, better known in history as Logan, Chief of the Mingoes, having been given the name of James Logan by Shikellamy, in honor of the distinguished secretary of the Provincial Council; (3) John Petty. His daughter was the widow of Cajadies, known as the "best hunter among all the Indians", who died in November, 1747. After the death of Shikellamy, Shamokin (Sunbury) rapidly declined as a center of Indian affairs, as his son who succeeded him was not able to restrain the Indians under his authority.

Among the tributes which have been paid to this great chieftain are the following: "He was a trustly, good man, and a great lover of the English", said Governor Hamilton, of the Colony of Pennsylvania. Said Count Zinzindorf, Moravian missionary, who, like all the prominent leaders of the Moravian Church, had been kindly received by Shikellamy: "He was truly an excellent and good man, possessed of many noble qualities of mind, that would do honor to many white men, laying claims to refinement and intelligence. He was possessed of great dignity, sobriety and prudence, and was particularly noted for his extreme kindness to the inhabitants with whom he came in contact." Also, the Moravian historian, Loskiel, says of him: "Being the first magistrate, and the head chief of all the Iroquois Indians living on the banks of the Susquehanna, as far as Onondaga, he thought it incumbent upon himself to be very circumspect in his dealings with the white people. He assisted the Missionaries in building, and defended them against the insults of the drunken Indians; being himself never addicted to drinking, because, as he expressed it, he never wished to become a fool."

The dust of this astute Iroquois statesman reposes at Sunbury on the banks of his long loved Susquehanna; and, as one stands near his grave and looks at the high and rocky river hill on the opposite side of the river, he beholds a strange arrangement of the rocks on the mountainside, resembling the countenance of an Indian warrior, and known locally as "Shikellamy's Profile." Thus, his face carved by nature's hand in the imperishable rock, gazes on the region where "Our Enlightener" had his home for so many years.

CHAPTER XII

Nutimus and Manawkyhickon

NUTIMUS

UTIMUS was a chief of the Munsee Clan of Delawares residing near the Forks of the Delaware. He has a firm place in the Indian history of Pennsylvania on account of his connection with the "Walking Purchase" of 1737, which we shall now describe.

The Walking Purchase

While the Six Nations at the treaty held at Philadelphia in October, 1736, described in Chapter X, went on record in declaring that the Delaware nation had no lands to sell, yet the Colonial Authorities of Pennsylvania depended for quiet enjoyment upon the old deeds from the Delawares to William Penn and his heirs, mentioned in an earlier chapter. In 1734, Thomas Penn, son of the founder of the Colony, claimed to have found a copy of a certain deed from the Delaware chiefs, Mayhkeerickkishsho, Taughhoughsey, and Sayhoppy, to his father, dated August 30, 1686, calling for a dimension "as far as a man can go in a day and a half", and thence to the Delaware River and down the courses of the same. The original of this deed, Thomas Penn claimed, had been lost for many years. The alleged description set forth in the original deed was as follows:

"All those lands lying and being in the province of Pennsylvania, beginning upon a line formerly laid out from a corner spruce tree, by the river Delaware, and from thence running along the ledge or the foot of the mountains west northwest (west southwest) to a corner white oak marked with the letter P. standing by the Indian path that leadeth to an Indian town called Playwiskey, and from thence extending westward to Neshaminy creek, from which said line, the said tract or tracts thereby granted doth extend itself back into the woods, as far as a man can go in one day and a half, and bounded on the westerly side with the creek called Neshaminy, or the most westerly branch thereof, and from thence by a line to the utmost extent of said creek one day and a half's journey to the aforesaid river Delaware, and thence down the several courses of the said river to the first mentioned spruce tree."

The dimension set forth in the foregoing alleged deed was never "walked" in the lifetime of William Penn. Thomas Penn and the other Colonial Authorities were anxious that the lands described in the alleged deed should be measured without further delay. Some of the Delawares did not wish the line measured, but, on August 25, 1737, the more influential chiefs of the Munsee Clan, among whom were "King Nutimus" and Manawkyhickon, entered into a treaty with Thomas Penn by the terms of which they agreed that the land should be measured by a walk according to the provisions of the deed. This agreement of August 25th was virtually a deed of release of the lands claimed to have been granted by the deed of August 30, 1686. We shall now see how well Thomas Penn and his associates were prepared for the "walk" and how it was accomplished:

The 19th day of September, 1737, was the day appointed for the "walk." It was agreed that the starting point should be a chestnut tree standing a little above the present site of Wrightstown, Bucks County. Timothy Smith, the sheriff of Bucks County, and Benjamin Eastburn, the surveyor-general, supervised the so-called walk. The persons employed by the Colonial Authorities to perform the walk, after the Proprietaries had advertised for the most expert walkers in the Province, were athletes famous for their abilities as fast walkers; and, as an inducement for their making this walk a supreme test of their abilities, a compensation of five pounds in money and 500 acres of land was offered the one who could go the longest distance in the allotted time. Their names were Edward Marshall, a native of Bucks County, a noted chain carrier, hunter and backwoodsman; James Yates, a native of the same county, a tall and agile man, with much speed of foot; and Solomon Jennings, also a man of remarkable physique. These men had been hunted out by the Proprietaries' agents as the fastest backwoodsmen in the Province, and as a preliminary measure, they had been taken over the ground before, spending some nine days, during which their route was marked off by blazing the trees and clearing away the brush.

At sunrise on the day appointed, these three athletes, accompanied by a number of Indians and some white persons, some of whom carried refreshments for them, started from the chestnut tree above Wrightstown; and, at first, they walked moderately, but before long they set such a pace that the Indians frequently called upon them to walk and not run. The remonstrance of the Indians producing no effect, most of them left in anger and disgust, asserting that they were basely cheated. By previous arrangement, a number of white people were collected about twenty miles from the starting point, to see the "walkers" pass. Yates was much in the lead, and was accompanied by several persons on horseback; next came Jennings, but out of sight; and lastly, Marshall, proceeding in an apparently careless manner, eating a biscuit and swinging a hatchet from hand to hand, evidently to balance the motion of his body. The above mentioned body of whites bet strongly in favor of Yates. Jennings and two of the Indians who accompanied him were exhausted before the end of the first day, and were unable to keep up with the other two. Jennings never thereafter recovered his health. However, Yates and Marshall kept on, and, at sunset, had arrived at the north side of the Blue Mountains.

At sunrise of the next day, Yates and Marshall started again, but, when crossing a stream at the foot of the mountain, Yates fell into the water, and Marshall turned back and supported him until some of the attendants came up, and then continued on his way alone. Yates was stricken with blindness and lived only three days. At noon Marshall threw himself full length upon the ground and grasped a sapling which stood'on a spur of the Second or Broad Mountain, near Mauch Chunk, Carbon County, which was then declared to mark the distance that a man could travel on foot in a day and a half—estimated to be about sixty-five miles from the starting point. Thus, one man out of three covered this distance, and lived.

An Eye-Witness Describes the "Walk"

The following account of the walk is given by an eye-witness, Thomas Furniss:

"At the time of the walk I was a dweller at Newtown, and a near neighbor to James Yeates. My situation gave him an easy opportunity of acquainting me with the time of setting out, as it did me of hearing the different sentiments of the neighborhood concerning the walk; some alleging it was to be made by the river, others that it was to be gone upon a straight line from somewhere in Wrightstown, opposite to a spruce-tree on the river's bank, said to be a boundary to a former purchase.

"When the walkers started I was a little behind, but was informed they proceeded from a chestnut tree near the turning out of the road from Durham road to John Chapman's; and, being on horseback, overtook them before they reached Buckingham, and kept company for some distance beyond the Blue Mountains, though not quite to the end of the journey. Two Indians attended, whom I considered as deputies appointed by the Delaware Nation, to see the walk honestly performed. One of them repeatedly expressed his dissatisfaction therewith. The first day of the walk, before we reached Durham Cr., where we dined in the meadows of one Wilson, an Indian trader, the Indian said the walk was to have been made up the river, and complaining of the unfitness of his shoe-packs for traveling, said he expected Thomas Penn would have made him a present of some shoes. After this, some of us that had horses, walked, and let the Indians ride by turns; yet in the afternoon of the same day, and some hours before sunset, the Indians left us, having often called to Marshall that afternoon, and forbid him to run. At parting they appeared dissatisfied, and said they would go no further with us; for as they saw the walkers would pass all the good land, they did not care how far or where we went to. It was said we traveled twelve hours the first day, and it being in the latter end of Sept., or beginning of Oct., to complete the time were obliged to walk in the twilight. Timothy Smith, then sheriff of Bucks, held his watch for some minutes before we stopped, and the walkers having a piece of rising ground to ascend, he called out to them, telling the minutes behind, and bid them pull up, which they did so briskly, that immediately upon his saying the time was out, Marshall clasped his arms about a sapling to support himself. Thereupon, the sheriff asking him what was the matter, he said he was almost gone, and that, if he had proceeded a few poles further, he must have fallen. We lodged in the woods that night, and heard the shouting of the Indians at a cantico, which they were said to hold that evening, in a town hard by.

"Next morning the Indians were sent to, to know if they would accompany us any further; but they declined it, although I believe some of them came to us before we started, and drank a dram in the company, and then straggled off about their hunting, or some other amusement. In our return we came through this Indian town or plantation, Timothy Smith and myself riding forty yards, more or less, before the company; and as we approached within about 150 paces of the town, the woods being open, we saw an Indian take a gun in his hand, and advancing towards us some distance, placed himself behind a log that laid by our way.

Timothy observing his motions, and being somewhat surprised, as I apprehended, looked at me, and asked what I thought that Indian meant. I said I hoped no harm, and that I thought it best to keep on; which the Indian seeing, he arose and walked before us to the settlement. I think Smith was surprised, as I well remember I was, through a consciousness that the Indians were dissatisfied with the walk—a thing the whole company seemed to be sensible of, and upon the way, in our return home, frequently expressed themselves to that purpose. And indeed, the unfairness practiced in the walk, both in regard to the way where, and the manner how it was performed, and the dissatisfaction of the Indians concerning it, were the common subjects of conversation in our neighborhood, for some considerable time after it was done. When the walk was performed, I was a young man in the prime of life. The novelty of the thing inclined me to be a spectator, and as I had been brought up most of my time in Burlington, the whole transaction to me was a series of occurrences almost entirely new; and which, therefore, I apprehend, made the more strong and lasting impression on my memory."

Course of the Line From the End of the "Walk" to the Delaware

In the agreement with Thomas Penn to have the bounds of the alleged deed made by a walk, the Delawares believed that as far as a man could go in a day and a half would not extend beyond the Lehigh Hills, or about thirty miles from the place of beginning; but the crafty and unprincipled Colonial Authorities had laid their plans to extend the walk to such a point as to include the land in the Forks of the Delaware and also farther up that river, it being their desire to obtain, if possible, the possession of that desirable tract of land along the Delaware River above the Blue Mountains, called the "Minisink Lands." Having, as we have seen, reached a point more than thirty miles farther to the northwestward than the Delawares had anticipated, the Colonial Authorities now proceeded to draw a line from the end of the walk to the Delaware River. The alleged deed did not describe the course that the line should take from the end of the walk to the river; but any fair-minded person would assume that it should follow the shortest distance between these two places. However, the agent of the Proprietaries, instead of running the line by the nearest course to the Delaware, ran it northeastward across the country so as to strike the river near the mouth of the Lackawaxen, which flows into the Delaware River in the northern part of Pike County. The extent of this line was sixty-six miles. The territory as thus measured was in the shape of a great triangle whose base was the Delaware River and whose apex was the end of the walk, and included the northern part of Bucks, almost all of Northampton, and a portion of Pike, Carbon, and Monroe counties. This fraudulent measurement thus took in all the Minisink Lands and many thousand acres more than if the line had been run by the nearest course from the end of the walk to the Delaware.

King Nutimus and His Clan Refuse to Remove From Lands of the Walking Purchase

When the settlers began to move upon the lands covered by the Walking Purchase of 1737, which they did soon after the "walk" was made, King Nutimus and several of the other Delaware chiefs who had signed the treaty or deed of release of 1737, were not willing to quit the lands or to permit the new settlers to remain in quiet possession. Indeed, they remonstrated freely and declared their intention to remain in possession, even if they should have to use force of arms.

In the spring of 1741, a message was sent by the Colonial Authorities to the Six Nations, requesting them to come down and force the Delawares of the Munsee Clan to quit these lands. The Six Nations complied and sent their deputies to Philadelphia, where this and other matters were taken up in the treaty of July, 1742, which treaty was discussed in Chapter X. At this treaty, Governor Thomas called the attention of Canassatego, the speaker of the Iroquois delegation, to the fact that a number of the Delaware Indians, residing on the Minisink lands above the mouth of the Lehigh River, had refused to surrender peaceful possession of the territory secured to the Colony by the Walking Purchase. However, the Governor did not tell Canassatego that, when John and Thomas Penn were persuading the Delawares to confirm the deeds covered by the Walking Purchase, they had promised these Indians that the said papers "would not cause the removal of any Indians then living on the Minisink Lands." These Delawares had requested that they be permitted to remain on their settlements, though within the bounds of the Walking Purchase, without being molested, and their request was granted. Later, on August 24, 1737, just the day before the Delaware chiefs signed the deed, or treaty, confirming the alleged deed of August 30, 1786, the assurances given the Delawares by John and Thomas Penn were repeated and confirmed at a meeting of the Provincial Council at Philadelphia.

Canassatego, unaware of the assurances given the Delawares, replied as follows:

"You informed us of the misbehavior of our cousins, the Delawares, with respect to their continuing to claim and refusing to remove from some land on the River Delaware, notwithstanding their ancestors had sold it by deed under their hands and seals to the Proprietors for a valuable consideration, upwards of fifty years ago, and notwithstanding that they themselves had about five years ago, after a long and full examination, ratified that deed of their ancestors, and given a fresh one under their hands and seals; and then you requested us to remove them, enforcing your request with a string of wampum. Afterwards you laid on the table, by Conrad Weiser, our own letters, some of our cousins' letters, and the several writings to prove the charge against our cousins, with a draught of the land in dispute. We now tell you that we have perused all these several papers. We see with our own eyes that they [the Delawares] have been a very unruly people, and are altogether in the wrong in their dealings with you. We have concluded to remove them, and oblige them to go over the River Delaware, and to quit all claim to any lands on this side for the future, since they have received pay for them, and it has gone through their guts long ago. To confirm to you that we will see your request executed, we lay down this string of wampum in return for yours."

Canassatego Commands Delawares to Remove
From Bounds of Walking Purchase

Attending the treaty were some Delawares from the Sunbury region, headed by Sassoonan, and a delegation from the Forks of the Delaware, headed by Nutimus. As soon as Canassatego finished the foregoing speech, taking a belt of wampum in his hand, he turned to the Delawares, and delivered the following humiliating address:

"COUSINS:—Let this belt of wampum serve to chastise you; you ought to be taken by the hair of the head and shaked severely till you recover your senses and become sober; you don't know what ground you are standing on, or what you are doing. Our Brother

Onas' case is very just and plain, and his intentions to preserve friendship; on the other hand your cause is bad; your head far from being upright, you are maliciously bent to break the chain of friendship with our Brother Onas. We have seen with our eyes a deed signed by nine of your ancestors above fifty years ago for this very land, and a release signed not many years since by some of yourselves and chiefs now living to the number of fifteen or upwards.

"But how came you to take upon you to sell land at all? We conquered you; we made women of you; you know you are women, and can no more sell land than women. Nor is it fit that you should have the power of selling land, since you would abuse it. This land that you claim is gone through your guts. You have been furnished with clothes and meat and drink by the goods paid you for it, and now you want it again like children, as you are. But what makes you sell land in the dark? Did you ever tell us that you had sold this land? Did we ever receive any part, even the value of a pipe shank for it?

"You have told us a blind story that you sent a messenger to inform us of the sale, but he never came amongst us, nor we never heard anything about it. This is acting in the dark, and very different from the conduct which our Six Nations observe in their sales of land. On such occasions, they give public notice and invite all the Indians of their united nations, but we find that you are none of our blood. You act a dishonest part, not only in this, but in other matters. Your ears are ever open to slanderous reports about our brethren . . . . . And for all these reasons we charge you to remove instantly; we don't give you liberty to think about it. You are women; take the advice of a wise man, and remove immediately. You may return to the other side of the Delaware, where you came from, but we don't know whether, considering how you have demeaned yourselves, you will be permitted to live there, or whether you have not swallowed that land down your throats, as well as the land on this side. We, therefore, assign you two places to go,—either to Wyoming or Shamokin. You may go to either of these places, and then we shall have you more under our eye, and shall see how you behave. Don't deliberate, but remove away, and take this belt of wampum."

Canassatego spoke with the air of a conqueror and one having authority; and both the manner of the delivery of his speech and the manner in which it was received by the trembling Delawares, would indicate that the Six Nations must have been right in their contention that they gained the ascendency over the Delawares, not by artifice, as the Delawares told Heckewelder, but by force of arms, some authorities asserting that, when the Iroquois conquered the Susquehannas in 1675, this conquest carried with it the subjugation of the Delawares, inasmuch as the Susquehannas were overlords of the Delawares. "When this terrible sentence was ended", says Watson, "it is said that the unfeeling political philosopher [Canassatego] walked forward, and, taking strong hold of the long hair of King Nutimus, of the Delawares, led him to the door and forcibly sent him out of the room, and stood there while all the trembling inferiors followed him. He then walked back to his place like another Cato, and calmly proceeded to another subject as if nothing happened. The poor fellows [Nutimus and his company], in great and silent grief, went directly home, collected their families and goods, and, burning their cabins to signify they were never to return, marched reluctantly to their new homes."

The Delawares Remove From Bounds
of Walking Purchase

Shortly after the treaty of 1742, the Delawares of the Munsee Clan left the bounds of the "Walking Purchase" and the beautiful river bearing their name, and began their march toward the setting sun. The greater part of them, under Nutimus settled on the site of Wilkes-Barre, opposite Wyoming Town, and at "Niskebeckon", on the left bank of the North Branch of the Susquehanna, not far from the mouth of Nescopeck Creek, in Luzerne County. The town which they established near the mouth of Nescopeck Creek was called "Nutimy's Town." Others went to the region around Sunbury; and others took up their abode on the Juniata, near Lewistown, Mifflin County. Later all went to the valleys of the Ohio and Allegheny with their wrongs rankling in their bosoms.

The Walking Purchase was the subject of much discussion between the Quaker and Proprietary parties as being one of the chief causes of the alienation of the Delawares and of their taking up arms against the Colony during the French and Indian War, until the charge of "fraud" was withdrawn and the Delawares were reconciled through the influence of the Moravian Missionary, Christian Frederick Post, at the treaty at Easton, in the summer of 1758, described in Chapter XXII. Says Dr. George P. Donehoo, in his recent great work, "Pennsylvania—A History": "It matters little whether the Delaware were influenced by the Quakers to complain of the 'fraud', or whether they themselves felt that they had been cheated, the fact still remains that the 'Walking Purchase' directly and indirectly, led to the gravest of consequences, so far as the warlike Munsee Clan of the Delaware was concerned."

The Sad Case of Captain John and Titami

In connection with the removal of the Delawares from the territory within the bounds of the Walking Purchase, is the case of Captain John and Titami, two worthy old Delaware chiefs who had always been warm friends of the white man. In November, 1742, they petitioned Governor Thomas, setting forth that they had embraced Christianity, and desired to live where they were, near the English. The Governor sent for them, and they appeared before the Provincial Council. Captain John did not own any ground, but advised the Governor that, if permitted to live among the English, he would buy some. Titami owned three hundred acres of land, granted him by the Proprietors; and he said he simply wanted to spend his few remaining years on his own plantation in peace with everybody. The Governor ordered that Canassatego's speech be read to these old men, refused their petition, and told them they would have to secure the consent of the Six Nations. To compel these aged chiefs to ask permission of the Iroquois was too much for Delaware pride. They sadly left their homes, and went farther into the forests. Their white friends never knew why the old men left their former homes. They were never heard of again by the whites.

Indian Hannah

In this connection, we state that a small number of the Delawares remained within the borders of Bucks County until the outbreak of the Revolution. In 1775, Isaac Still, a prominent Delaware, collected forty of his tribe and led them to the Wabash, as he said, "far away from war and rum." Also, at the outbreak of the Revolution a family of four Delawares dwelt in wigwams in Marlborough Township, Chester County. Later, three of these died, and the remaining one, known as Indian Hannah, took up her abode near the Brandywine. In the summer time, she traveled through the countryside, selling willow baskets of her own make, and visiting persons who would receive her kindly. When old age came upon her, she removed from her wigwam and dwelt among friendly families. Though she had been associated with the whites for many years, yet she retained her Indian character to the last. She had a proud, haughty spirit, and did not condescend to associate with the lower order of whites. Her kindred dead, and all the companions of her race gone, she was desolate and often spoke of the wrongs and misfortunes of the Indian race. She died in 1803 at the great age of almost one hundred years.

Nutimus Joins in Sale of Lands Between Susquehanna and Delaware

On July 1, 1749, a number of Seneca, Onondaga, Tutelo, Nanticoke, and Conoy chiefs came to Philadelphia to interview Governor Hamilton, with reference to the settlements which the white people were making "on the other side of the Blue Mountains." This delegation had gone first to Wyoming, the place appointed for the gathering of the deputies of the various tribes, had waited there a month for the other deputies, and then decided to go on to Philadelphia. Governor Hamilton advised the chiefs that the Province had been doing everything in its power to prevent persons from settling on lands not purchased from the Indians. Immediately after the conference the Governor issued a proclamation, which was distributed throughout the Province, and posted upon trees in the Juniata and Path valleys, and other places where settlers had built their homes beyond the Blue Mountains, ordering all such settlers to remove from these lands by the 1st of November.

The delegation of chiefs had left Philadelphia but a short time when Governor Hamilton received word from Conrad Weiser that the other Indian deputies, who had failed to join the previous delegation at Wyoming, were at Shamokin (Sunbury) on their way to Philadelphia. The Governor then sent word to Weiser, urging him to divert this new delegation from coming to the city. Weiser did all in his power to carry out the Governor's orders, but the Indians soon let him see that they were determined to go on to Philadelphia, at which place they arrived on the 16th of August, numbering two hundred and eighty, and led by Canassatego, the speaker at the former treaties at Lancaster and Philadelphia.

Canassatego was the speaker of the Indian delegation at the conferences which were then held with the Governor and Provincial Council. When advised of the efforts that Pennsylvania had made to prevent her people from settling on unpurchased land, Canassatego excused the Government for this, saying: "White people are no more obedient to you than our young Indians are to us."

He thus also excused the war parties of young Iroquois who went against the Catawbas. Canassatego further offered to remedy the situation by saying that the Iroquois were "willing to give up the Land on the East side of Sasquehannah from the Blue Hills, or Chambers' Mill to where Thomas McGee [McKee], the Indian trader, lives, and leave it to you to assign the worth of them." This great Iroquois statesman complained especially of the settlements on the branches of the Juniata, saying that these were the hunting grounds of the Nanticokes and other Indians under the jurisdiction of the Iroquois. He told the Governor that, when the Nanticokes had trouble with Maryland, where they formerly lived, they had been removed by the Six Nations and placed at the mouth of the Juniata, and that there were three settlements of the tribe still remaining in Maryland. These latter, he explained, wished to join their relatives in Pennsylvania, but that Maryland would not permit them to do so, "where they make slaves of them and sell their Children for Money." He then asked the Governor to intercede with the Governor of Maryland to the end that the Nanticokes in Maryland might be permitted to join their brethren on the Juniata. Explaining why the proposed treaty with the Catawbas had not taken place, Canassatego said that King George's War breaking out had prevented them from getting together, "and now we say we neither offer nor reject Peace." He also let it be known that he did not believe that the Catawbas were sincere in their offers of peace.

Governor Hamilton then took up with Canassatego the proposed sale of lands, and, after much discussion, the Six Nations' deputies sold to the Colony of Pennsylvania a vast tract of land between the Susquehanna and the Delaware, including all or parts of the present counties of Dauphin, Northumberland, Lebanon, Schuylkill, Columbia, Carbon, Luzerne, Monroe, Pike, and Wayne. This is known in Pennsylvania history as the "Purchase of 1749", the deed having been signed on the 22nd of August of that year. Nutimus joined in the deed as chief of the Delawares at Nutimus' Town, at the mouth of Nescopeck Creek, Luzerne County. Also, Paxinosa, then residing at Wyoming, and the leading chief of the Shawnees of Eastern Pennsylvania, joined in this deed.

Last Days of Nutimus

Nutimus attended the great Easton conference of July, 1757, an account of which is given in Chapter XXII. Soon thereafter, he disappears from history.

MANAWKYHICKON

Manawkyhickon was a chief of the Munsee or Wolf Clan of Delawares. We have seen, in the present Chapter, that he joined with Nutimus in the agreement and deed of release of August 25, 1737. We met him also in Chapter VII, in connection with the threatened uprising of the Five Nations and the Miamis, in 1727 and 1728, where he, resenting the hanging of his near relative, Wequeala, was alleged to have "sent a black belt to the Five Nations", who, in turn, sent it to the Miamis, with the request that the latter join them in attacking the English, "to which they agreed." This relative, Wequeala, who was hanged at Perth Amboy, New Jersey, June 30th, 1727, for the murder of Captain John Leonard of that town, is believed by some authorities to have been Owechela, or Weheelan, Tamanend's brother, who, as stated in Chapter IV, joined with Tamanend and others in the deed of July 5th, 1697, and, as stated in Chapter VII, probably acted as vice-regent during the minority of Tamanend's son, Weheequeckhon, alias Andrew. This is speculation, however.

We also met Manawkyhickon, in Chapter VIII, in connection with the fight between the settlers and Kakowatcheky's band of Shawnees from Pechoquealin and the murder of the Indian man and two women at Cucussea, in Chester County. At a meeting of the Provincial Council, on June 3rd, 1728, in reference to the above mentioned troubles, Governor Gordon informed the Council that he had received a message from Manawkyhickon to the effect: "That he believed the Governor knew nothing of the fight between the Shawnees and white people, and desires that the back inhabitants may be cautioned not to be so ready to attack the Indians as they were at that time; that he very well remembers the League between William Penn and the Indians, and hopes that the Governor may be careful thereof."

At that time, Manawkyhickon was living at "Catawasse", a town of the Conoy and Delaware Indians at the mouth of Catawissa Creek, on the North Branch of the Susquehanna, on or near the site of the present town of Catawissa, Columbia County; and at Chenastry, at the mouth of Chillisquaque Creek, on the West Branch of the Susquehanna, in Northumberland County. But for some years prior to this time, the habitat of himself and his band of Munsees was Muncy Creek and the Muncy Hills in the southern part of Lycoming County.

At a conference held at Philadelphia on August 6th, 1740, between the Colonial Authorities, Sassoonan, Shikellamy and other chiefs, Manawkyhickon was referred to as "the King of the Minisincks." This conference took up the matter of the grievous wounding of a white man, Henry Webb, on the Minisink lands, by a Mohican tributary to the Six Nations, named Awamameak, whom the Mohicans refused to surrender when the Governor of Pennsylvania demanded the person of the offender.   Manawkyhickon, as "King of the Minisincks" wrote the "King" of the Mohicans, who lived near Esopus, New York, to deliver the offender up.   Webb recovered from his injury, and the matter of delivering the offending Mohican was dropped.

When Manawkyhickon died is not known, but in 1756 many of the Delawares of the Munsee Clan who had formerly been under him were living at Tioga (now Athens, Bradford County, Pennsylvania), and chose the great Teedyuscung as their "king".   An account of Teedyuscung will be found in Chapters XXI and XXII.

CHAPTER XIII

Tanacharison, the Half King

ANACHARISON (Scruniyatha, Seruniyattha, Tanngris-hon) was an Oneida chief, sent by the Great Council of the Six Nations, about 1747, as vice-gerent of the Iroquois over the Delawares, Mohicans, and others in the Ohio Valley. He was born about 1700. His residence was at or in the vicinity of Logstown, according to most authorities, though others say it was at Sauconk, at the mouth of the Beaver River, about fifteen miles below Logstown. The first mention of Tanacharison in recorded history is when he, Neucheconneh, Kakowatcheky, Scarouady, and others wrote a letter from "Aleggainey", on April 20th, 1747, to the Governor of Pennsylvania, on behalf of the Twightwees, or Miamis of the Ohio Valley. He was called the Half King, because, like Shikellamy, he was simply the representative of the Iroquois Confederation.

Tanacharison was living at Logstown when Conrad Weiser came to that place in September, 1748, and entered into a treaty with the various tribes in that region, on the part of the Colony of Pennsylvania, as mentioned in Chapter VIII. He promised Weiser that he would keep Pennsylvania posted as to the movements of the French in the valleys of the Ohio and Allegheny. "Let us", said he, "keep up true correspondence, and always hear of one another." His protestation of friendship for the English was sincere. He remained faithful to the English interest to the end of his life.

No doubt he met George Croghan when the latter was at Logstown in April, 1748, to tell the Indians of the Ohio that Conrad Weiser was coming with the Pennsylvania present. It is likely, too, that he was at Logstown when Celeron stopped there on his way down the Allegheny and Ohio in the summer of 1749. At least, he was there when George Croghan arrived at that place a few days after Celeron's departure and succeeded in counteracting the influence of this French emissary. At this time, he and Scarouady deeded Croghan a large tract of land at the Forks of the Ohio. No doubt he again met George Croghan when the latter was at Logstown, in November, 1750, with Andrew Montour, in an effort to counteract the intrigues of the French. Once more, in May, 1751, he met Croghan and Montour when they visited this important Indian town, bringing the present from the Colony of Pennsylvania, which they had promised on their visit in the preceding November. It may be that Tanacharison met Christopher Gist, the agent of the Ohio Company, when the latter was at Logstown on November 25th and 26th, 1750, though Gist says in his journal that the Indians were nearly all out hunting at that time.

Tanacharison at Virginia Treaty at Logstown

As we have seen, Pennsylvania was following up the advantages gained by Croghan's and Weiser's embassy to Logstown in 1748. In the meantime the Colony of Virginia had not relinquished its claim to the Ohio Valley. In June, 1752, the commissioners of Virginia, Joshua Fry, L. Lomax, and James Patton, held a treaty with the Delawares, Shawnees, and Mingoes of the Ohio Valley, at Logstown. Christopher Gist, the agent of the Ohio Company, George Groghan, and Andrew Montour were present, the latter acting as interpreter. The Great Council of the Six Nations declined to send deputies to attend the treaty. Said they: "It is not our custom to meet to treat of affairs in the woods and weeds. If the Governor of Virginia wants to speak with us, and deliver us a present from our father [the king], we will meet him at Albany, where we expect the Governor of New York will be present."

The object of the treaty was to obtain from the Indians a confirmation of the Lancaster Treaty of 1744, by the terms of which Virginia claimed that the Iroquois had ceded their right to all lands in the Colony of Virginia. The task of the Virginia commissioners was not an easy one for the reason that the Pennsylvania traders had prejudiced the Indians against Virginia. However, the commissioners secured permission to erect two forts and to make some settlements. Tanacharison, who was present and took a prominent part in the negotiations, advised that his brothers of Virginia should build "a strong house" at the mouth of the Monongahela to resist the designs of the French. As related in Chapter VIII, a similar request had been made to the Governor of Pennsylvania by the chiefs at Logstown when George Crogan was at that place in May, 1751.

The Virginians laid claim to all the lands of the Ohio Valley by virtue of the purchase made at the treaty of Lancaster, in 1744, in which the western limit of the Iroquois sale was set forth as the "setting sun". Conrad Weiser had advised the Governor of Pennsylvania that the Six Nations never contemplated such sale, explaining that by the "setting sun" was meant the crest of the Allegheny Mountains, the divide between streams flowing to the Atlantic Ocean on the East and the Mississippi River on the West. At this Logstown treaty one of the Iroquois chiefs told the Virginia commissioners that they were mistaken in their claims. The chiefs agreed with the commissioners not to molest any settlements that might be made on the southeast side of the Ohio. At the treaty, two old chiefs, through an interpreter, said to Mr. Gist: "The French claim all on one side of the river [the Ohio], and the English all on the other side. Where does the Indian land lie?" This question Gist found hard to answer.

Tanacharison Appoints Shingas Chief of the Delawares

During the proceedings of the Virginia treaty Tanacharison, as representative of the Six Nations, bestowed the sachemship of the Delawares upon Shingas, an account of whom is given in Chapter XIX. The Journal of the Commissioners' proceedings makes note of this fact, under date of June 11th, as follows:

"Afterwards the Half King [Tanacharison] spoke to the Delawares: 'Nephews, you received a speech last year from your brother, the Governor of Pennsylvania and from us, desiring you to choose one of your wisest Councillors, and present him to us for a King. As you have not done it, we let you know it is our right to give you a King, whom you must look upon as your chief, and with whom all public business must be transacted between you and your brethren, the English.' On which the Half King placed a laced hat on the head of the Beaver, who stood proxy for his brother, Shingas, and presented him with a rich jacket and a suit of English clothes, which had been delivered to the Half King by the Commissioners for that purpose."

Murder of Old Britain

At this time the great chief of the Miamis, or Twightwees, was a sachem whom the French called La Demoiselle (the Young Lady), for what reason it is difficult to conjecture, and whom the English called Old Britain, on account of his steadfast friendship for them. His village stood near the confluence of Loramie Creek with the Miami. When Celeron made his expedition down the Ohio in 1749, he endeavored to draw Old Britain into a French alliance, but without success. Three years later, when Celeron was commander of the French fort of Detroit, the Governor of Canada resolved that the British power in the valley of the Miami should be overthrown. Accordingly, on June 21, 1752, over two hundred Ottawa and Chippewa Indians, under the leadership of a French officer, named Charles Langlade, who had married an Indian squaw, attacked Old Britain's town when nearly all the warriors were absent on a hunting expedition. Those who remained were taken by surprise. Before Old Britain and the five English traders who were with him in the village could get safely within the fort, the enemy were in their midst. One of the traders was stabbed and his heart eaten by his savage captors, as they said, "to increase their courage." Thirteen of Old Britain's warriors were killed and scalped, and he was killed, boiled, and eaten.

The Miamis sent a message to the Governor of Pennsylvania discribing this tragic affair, which was laid before the Governor and Provincial Council later in the summer. Said the message: "We still hold our integrity with our brothers, the English, and are willing to die for them, and will never give up this treatment, although we saw our great Piankashaw King, which commonly was called Old Britain by us, taken, killed, and eaten within a hundred yards of the fort before our faces. We now look upon ourselves as lost people, fearing that our brothers will leave us; but before we will be subject to the French, or call them our fathers, we will perish here." Later, as we shall see, the Governor made a present of condolence to the Miamis on account of this unhappy event.

Tanacharison and Croghan Hold Conference

In May, 1753, Sir William Johnson of New York, sent Governor Hamilton of Pennsylvania the intelligence that a large French expedition was headed for the Ohio for the purpose of erecting forts and expelling the English. Hamilton at once sent messengers to the governors of Maryland and Virginia and the traders on the Ohio, advising them of the message he had received from Johnson. Before this message was received, George Croghan's cousin and partner, William Trent, had written Governor Hamilton that the French attacks on traders near Lake Erie and along the great Miami had caused Croghan to return to his trading house on the

Allegheny near the mouth of Pine Creek, about six miles above the mouth of the Monongahela, with some Indians and white refugees with him.

On May 7, 1753, while these refugees were gathered at Croghan's Pine Creek storehouse, a message was received from the Pennsylvania trader, John Frazer, sent down from Venango, (Franklin) stating that the French were coming with eight brass cannon, ammunition and stores. Croghan and his associates were thrown into consternation. On the following day, two Iroquois runners from the Great Council House at Onondaga brought similar news; and on May 12th, Governor Hamilton's warning to the Allegheny and Ohio traders arrived. The entire party looked to Croghan as leader. A conference was at once held at Pine Creek with Tanacharison and Scarouady. After much deliberation these sachems decided "that they would receive the French as friends, or as enemies, depending upon their attitude, but that the English would be safe as long as they themselves were safe. Croghan's partners, Teafee and Calendar, with the two messengers that had been sent out by Hamilton returned to Philadelphia on May 30th to report in person." Governor Hamilton at once laid these reports before the Assembly which, on May 31st, made an appropriation of two hundred pounds for condolence presents to the Twightwees, and six hundred pounds for the "Necessities of Life" (guns and ammunition), for the other tribes on the Ohio.

Tanacharison Appeals to Virginia

For more than three months, Governor Hamilton held this money, and then apologized to the Pennsylvania Assembly for not having sent a portion of it as a present to the Miamis, explaining that there was danger of the present being stolen by the French while being transported to the Ohio Valley. In the meantime, on June 23rd, Tanacharison and Scarouady wrote Governor Dinwiddie of Virginia, from Logstown stating:

"We send you this by our brother, Mr. Thomas Burney [a blacksmith living at Logstown] to acquaint you that we, your brethren, together with the head men of the Six Nations, the Twightwees [Miamis], Shawnees, and Delawares, were coming down to pay you a visit, but were prevented by the arrival here of four men, two Mingoes and two Delawares, who informed us that there were three hundred Frenchmen and ten Connewangeroonas within two days journey of this place, and we do not know how soon they may come upon us. Therefore, our request is, that you would send out a number of your people, our brethren, to meet us at the Forks of Mohongiale [the Monongahela], and see what is the reason of their coming."

It is thus seen that since no reply came from the Colonial Authorities at Philadelphia, the Ohio Indians turned to Virginia, which colony had promised them arms and ammunition. They then sent a delegation of about one hundred deputies to Winchester, Virginia, in September, 1753, to arrange for aid and supplies at a treaty then and there held between Virginia, in the interest of the Ohio Company, and the Six Nations and their tributary tribes in the Ohio Valley,—the Delawares, Shawnees, Twightwees, or Miàmis, and Wyandots. Tanacharison and Scarouady headed this delegation. Early in 1753, Andrew Montour, at the instance of Governor Dinwiddie of Virginia, had visited the Great Council at Onondaga, to invite the Six Nations to hold this treaty, and he (Montour) was the interpreter at the treaty. George Croghan was present to aid William Fairfax, the commissioner of Virginia. At the Winchester treaty Tanacharison and Scarouady withdrew the consent that they had given at the Virginia treaty at Logstown in the summer of 1742, to any settlements west of the Allegheny Mountains, but they decided that a "strong house" might be built in the vicinity of Logstown in which to store goods. Virginia, on the other hand, promised to supply the Indians with ammunition to defend themselves against the French.

Indian Conference at Carlisle

While attending the Winchester treaty, the Indians heard of the appropriation which had been voted by the Pennsylvania Assembly; and thereupon, although no invitation had been received by them, they sent a portion of their deputies to Carlisle, Pennsylvania, to ascertain whether the report were true. This delegation consisted of a number of the important chiefs of the Six Nations, Delawares, Shawnees, Twightwees, or Miamis, and the Owendats, or Wyandots. Governor Hamilton sent Conrad Weiser, Richard Peters, Isaac Norris, and Benjamin Franklin to Carlisle to meet these deputies, October 1st to 4th, 1753. George Croghan was present to give advice. These commissioners had gone to Carlisle without presents, and they had Conrad Weiser interview one of the chiefs to ascertain if it were not possible to go through the forms of condolence on the promise to pay when

---

Author's note on second paragraph, page 184

Scaróuady led the Indian delegation to Winchester, Tanacharison being then on journey to forbid French advance. These chiefs had recently conferred with Capt. Trent, at Logstown, relative to French encroachments. Virginia's Logstown treaty was June, 1752. Date 1742 is typographical error.

the goods should arrive later. The chief replied that his people could and would not do any public business while the blood of their tribe remained upon their garments, and that "nothing would wash it unless the presents intended to cover the graves of the departed were actually spread upon the ground before them."

Tanacharison Forbids French to Advance

While the commissioners and Indians were awaiting for the goods to arrive, Conrad Weiser learned from Scarouady that, when the Ohio Indians received the messages in May, 1753, advising them of the threatened French invasion, they at once sent a warning to the French, who were then at Niagara, forbidding them to proceed further toward the Ohio Valley. This notice not deterring the French, the Indians then held a conference at Logstown, and sent a second notice to the French when they were approaching the headwaters of French Creek, as follows:

"Your children on Ohio are alarmed to hear of your coming so far this way. We at first heard that you came to destroy us. Our women left off planting, and our warriors prepared for war. We have since heard that you came to visit us as friends without design to hurt us, but then we wondered you came with so strong a body. If you have had any cause of complaint, you might have spoken to Onas or Corlear [meaning the Governors of Pennsylvania and New York], and not come to disturb us here. We have a Fire at Logstown, where are the Delawares and Shawnees and Brother Onas; you might have sent deputies there and said openely what you came about, if you had thought amiss of the English being there, and we invite you to do it now before you proceed any further."

The French replied to this notice, stating that they would not come to the council fire at Logstown; that they meant no harm to the Indians; that they were sent by command of the king of France, and that they were under orders to build four forts,—one at Venango, one at the Forks of the Ohio, one at Logstown, and another on Beaver Creek. The Ohio Indians then held another conference, and sent a third notice to the French, as follows: "We forbid you to come any farther. Turn back to the place from whence you came."

Tanacharison was the bearer of this third notice to the French, and very likely, of the other two. Before the conference at Carlisle ended, it was learned that Tanacharison had just returned to

Logstown from delivering the third notice; that he had been received in a very contemptuous manner by the French; and that, upon his return, had shed tears, and actually warned the English traders not to pass the Ohio.

Tanacharison's notice given the French was equivalent to a declaration of war. Conrad Weiser was consulted as to what was best to be done, and he urged that the entire appropriation which the Pennsylvania Assembly had made on May 31st be expended at once. Said he: "Only by a generous donation could we expect to hold the friendship of those Indians."

The goods were then brought, the forms of condolence properly observed, and then the conference was resumed. After expressing their thanks for the goods and their deep affection for the English, the Indians called attention to the fact that Virginia desired leave to build a fort on the Ohio, which, coming to the ears of the Governor of Canada, was, as the Indians supposed, the cause why the French were determined to invade the Ohio country. The Indians then requested that no Pennsylvania and Virginia settlements be made at present west of the Allegheny Mountains, and that all trade in the Ohio Valley be confined to three posts,— Logstown, the mouth of the Monongahela, and the mouth of the Kanawha; that the prices be reasonable; and that future conferences be held at Croghan's house at Aughwick. In order to keep trade and friendship open with Pennsylvania, the Indians urged that George Croghan and someone else to be chosen by the Governor of Pennsylvania, be stationed at George Croghan's trading house at Aughwick, or Aughwick Old Town, now the site of Shirleysburg, Huntington County, to whom goods and supplies for the Western Indians could be sent, and who should guide and control Indian affairs. Croghan had recently settled at Aughwick when he was forced by impending bankruptcy to leave the Cumberland Valley.

At the close of the Carlisle treaty, Tanacharison returned to the Ohio, and, on October 27th, joined with Scarouady in writing the Governors of Pennsylvania and Virginia urging that they join with the Indians of the Ohio and Allegheny in an effort to prevent the occupation of the valleys of these streams by the French. This letter was written from Shanoppin's Town.

Tanacharison Accompanies Washington on Mission to the French

On October 31st, 1753, Major George Washington, then a youth of twenty-one years, was commissioned by Governor Robert Dinwiddie of Virginia, to deliver the Governor's message to St. Pierre, commandant of the French forts on the headwaters of the Allegheny River, in Northwestern Pennsylvania, protesting against the encroachments of the French on territory claimed by the English. On the same day that Washington received his commission he set forth from Williamsburg, the capital of Virginia, on his journey of more than five hundred miles through the wilderness. The next day, he arrived at Fredericksburg, where he engaged Jacob VanBraam, a Dutchman, who had been his old fencing master, to act as French interpreter. He and VanBraam then proceeded to Alexandria, where they procured supplies. From there they went to Winchester, where they got baggage, horses, etc.

Leaving Winchester, they traveled to Will's Creek (Cumberland, Maryland), where they arrived on November 14th. Here Washington hired Christopher Gist, as Washington expressed it "to pilot us out", and also procured the services of four others, namely: Barnaby Curran and John McGuire, Indian traders; and Henry Stewart and William Jenkins, servants.

Leaving Will's Creek on November 15th, the party proceeded over the Nemacolin Indian Trail to Turtle Creek, near Braddock, Pennsylvania, where they met John Frazer, the English trader, who, as has already been seen, was driven away from Venango by the French. At Frazer's, they sent their baggage down the Monongahela by canoes to the Forks of the Ohio, while Washington and Gist rode to Shannopin's Town on the east bank of the Allegheny a few miles above the mouth of the Monongahela. From there, they proceeded to the mouth of the Monongahela where they met their baggage. They then called on the Delaware chief, King Shingas, at his town on the north and south banks of the Ohio about two miles below the mouth of the Monongahela. The principal part of this village was on the south bank of the Ohio near the mouth of Chartier's Creek and the present town of McKees Rocks; and Washington mentions in his journal that the Ohio Company intended to build a fort at that place. Shingas accompanied Washington's party to Logstown, where they arrived on the evening of November 24th.

Upon his arrival at Logstown, Washington learned that

Tanacharison was absent at his hunting cabin on the Beaver, some fifteen miles distant. He therefore called upon Monacatootha, or Scarouady, and informed him by John Davidson, his Indian interpreter, that he was sent as a messenger to the French general, and was ordered to call upon all the sachems of the Six Nations to acquaint them with it. Monacatootha sent a messenger to Tanacharison early on the morning of the 25th.

Washington's Journal, under date of November 25th, describes his meeting with Tanacharison at Logstown:

"About three o'clock this evening the Half King [Tanacharison] came to town. I went up and invited him with Davidson, privately, to my tent; and desired him to relate some of the particulars of his journey to the French commandant, and of his reception there; also, to give me an account of the ways and distance. He told me that the nearest and levelest way was now impassable, by reason of many large miry savannas; that we must be obliged to go by Venango, and should not get to the near fort in less than five or six nights sleep, good traveling. When he went to the fort, he said, he was received in a very stern manner by the late commander, who asked him very abruptly, what he had come about, and to declare his business." Tanacharison then said that he delivered to the French commander the third notice to advance no further, as related earlier in this chapter, and that the commander disregarded it.

Washington's Journal further says, under date of November 25th:

"The Half King told me he had inquired of the general after two Englishmen, who were made prisoners, and received this answer:

" 'Child, you think it a very great hardship that I made prisoners of those two people at Venango. Don't you concern yourself with it; we took and carried them to Canada, to get intelligence of what the English were doing in Virginia.'

"He informed me that they had built two forts, one on Lake Erie, and another on French Creek, near a small lake, about fifteen miles asunder, [apart] and a large wagon road between. They are both built after the same model, but different in size; that on the lake the largest. He gave me a plan of them of his own drawing."

Under date of November 26th, Washington's Journal says:

"We met in councl at the long house about nine o'clock, where I spoke to them as follows:

" 'Brothers, I have called you together in council, by order of your brother the governor of Virginia to acquaint you that I am sent with all possible despatch, to visit and deliver a letter to the French commandant of very great importance to your brothers, the English; and I dare say to you, their friends and allies.

" 'I was desired, brothers, by your brother, the governor, to call upon you, the sachems of the nations, to inform you of it, and to ask your advice and assistance to proceed the nearest and best road to the French. You see, brothers, I have gotten thus far on my journey.

" 'His honour likewise desired me to apply to you for some of your young men to conduct and provide provisions for us on our way; and be a safeguard against those French Indians who have taken up the hatchet against us. I have spoken thus particularly to you, brothers, because his honour our governor treats you as good friends and allies, and holds you in great esteem. To confirm what I have said, I give you this string of wampum.'

"After they had considered for some time on the above discourse, the Half King got up and spoke:

" 'Now, my brother, in regard to what my brother, the governor, had desired of me, I return you this answer:

" 'I rely upon you as a brother ought to do; as you say we are brothers, and one people. We shall put heart in hand and speak to our fathers, the French, concerning the speech they made to me; and you may depend that we will endeavor to be your guard.

" 'Brother, as you have asked my advice, I hope you will be ruled by it, and stay until I can provide a company to go with you. The French speech belt is not here; I have it to go for to my hunting cabin. Likewise, the people whom I have ordered in are not yet come, and can not until the third night from this; until which time, brother, I must beg you to stay.

" 'I intend to send the guard of Mingos, Shannoahs, [Shawnees], and Delawares, that our brothers may see the love and loyalty we bear them.'

"As I had orders to make all possible despatch, and waiting here was very contrary to my inclination, I thanked him in the most suitable manner I could; and told him [Tanacharison] that my business required the greatest expedition, and would not admit of that delay. He was not well pleased that I should offer to go before the time he had appointed, and told me that he could not consent to our going without a guard, for fear some accident should

befall us and draw a reflection upon him. 'Besides,' said he, 'this is
a matter of no small moment, and must not be entered into without due consideration; for I intend to deliver up the French speech
belt, and make the Shannoahs and Delawares do the same.' And
accordingly he gave orders to King Shingiss, who was present, to
attend on Wednesday night with the wampum; and two men of
their nation to be in readiness to set out with us next morning.
As I found it was impossible to get off without affronting them in
the most egregious manner, I consented to stay."

Washington's Journal continues:

"November 27th. Runners were despatched very early for
the Shannoah [Shawnee] chiefs. The Half King set out himself
to fetch the French speech belt from his hunting cabin.

"Nov. 28th. He returned this evening, and came with
Monakatoocha and two other sachems to my tent; and begged as
they had complied with his honour the governor's request, in providing men, &c to know on what business we were going to the
French. This was a question I had all along expected and had
provided as satisfactory answers to as I could; which allayed their
curiosity a little.

"Nov. 29th. The Half King and Monakatoocha came very
early and begged me to stay one day more; for notwithstanding
they had used all the diligence in their power, the Shannoah chiefs
had not brought the wampum they ordered, but would certainly
be in tonight; if not, they would delay me no longer, but would
send it after us as soon as they arrived. When I found them so
pressing in their request, and knew that returning of wampum was
the abolishing of agreements, and giving this up was shaking off all
dependence upon the French, I consented to stay, as I believed an
offence, offered at this crisis, might be attended with greater ill
consequence than another day's delay. They also informed me
that Shingas could not get in his men; and was prevented from
coming himself by his wife's sickness; (I believe, by fear of the
French) but that the wampum of that nation was lodged with
Kustalogo, one of their chiefs, at Venango.

"In the evening, late, they came again, and acquainted me that
the Shannoahs were not yet arrived, but that it should not retard
the prosecution of our journey. He delivered in my hearing the
speech that was to be made to the French by Jeskakake, one of
their old chiefs, which was giving up the belt the late commandant
had asked for and repeating nearly the same speech he himself had
done before.

"He also delivered a string of wampum to this chief, which was sent by King Shingiss, to be given to Kustalogo, with orders to repair to the French, and deliver up the wampum.

"He likewise gave a very large string of black and white wampum, which was to be sent up immediately to the Six Nations, if the French refused to quit the land at this warning; which was the third and last time, and was the right of this Jeskakake to deliver.

"Nov. 30th. Last night, the great men assembled at their council house, to consult further about this journey, and who were to go; the result of which was, that only three of their chiefs, with one of their best hunters, should be our convoy. The reason they gave for not sending more, after what had been proposed at council the 26th, was, that a greater number might give the French suspicions of some bad design, and cause them to be treated rudely; but I rather think they could not get their hunters in.

"We set out about nine o'clock with the Half King, Jeskakake, White Thunder, and the Hunter [Guyasuta]; and traveled on the road to Venango, where we arrived the fourth of December, without anything remarkable happening but a continued series of bad weather.

"This is an old Indian town, situated at the mouth of French Creek, on Ohio [Allegheny], and lies near north about sixty miles from the Loggstown, but more than seventy the way we were obliged to go."

At Venango, Washington learned that he would have to proceed to Le Boeuf (Waterford, Erie County) to deliver his message. His Journal continues:

"Dec. 5th. Rained excessively all day, which prevented our traveling. Captain Joncaire [the French commandant at Venango], sent for the Half King, as he had just heard that he came with me. He affected to be much concerned that I did not make free to bring them in before. I excused it in the best manner of which I was capable, and told him I did not think their company agreeable, as I had heard him say a good deal in dispraise of Indians in general; but another motive prevented me from bringing them into his company; I knew that he was an interpreter, and a person of very great influence among the Indians, and had lately used all possible means to draw them over to his interest; therefore, I was desirous of giving him no opportunity that could be avoided.

"When they came in, there was great pleasure expressed at seeing them. He wondered how they could be so near without coming to visit him, made several trifling presents, and applied liquor so fast that they were soon rendered incapable of the business they came about, notwithstanding the caution which was given.

"Dec. 6th. The Half King came to my tent, quite sober, and insisted very much that I should stay and hear what he had to say to the French. I fain would have prevented him from speaking anything until he came to the commandant, but could not prevail. He told me that at this place a council fire was kindled, where all their business with these people was to be transacted, and that the management of the Indian affairs was left solely to Monsieur Joncaire. As I was desirous of knowing the issue of this, I agreed to stay; but sent our horses a little way up French Creek, to raft over and encamp; which I knew would make it near night.

"About ten o'clock, they met in council. The King [Tanacharison] spoke much the same as he had before done to the general, and offered the French speech belt which had before been demanded, with the marks of four towns on it, which Monsieur Joncaire refused to receive, but desired him to carry it to the fort [Fort Le Boeuf, now Waterford, Erie County,] to the commander.

"Dec. 7th. Monsieur LaForce, Commissary of the French stores, and three other soldiers, came over to accompany us up. We found it extremely difficult to get the Indians off today, as every stratagem had been used to prevent their going up with me. I had last night left John Davidson (the Indian interpreter) whom I brought with me from town, and strictly charged him not to be out of their company, as I could not get them over to my tent; for they had some business with Kustologa, chiefly to know why he did not deliver up the French speech belt which he had in keeping; but I was obliged to send Mr. Gist over today to fetch them, which he did with great persuasion.

"At twelve o'clock, we set out for the fort [Le Boeuf], and were prevented from arriving there until the eleventh day by excessive rains, snows, and bad traveling through many mires and swamps; these we were obliged to pass to avoid crossing the creek, which was impossible, either by fording or rafting, the water was so high and rapid.

"We passed over much good land since we left Venango, and through several extensive and very rich meadows, one of which, I believe, was nearly four miles in length, and considerably wide in some places.

Dec. 12th. I prepared early to wait upon the commander, and was received, and conducted to him by the second officer in com-

mand. I acquainted him with my business and offered my commission and letter; both of which he desired me to keep until the
arrival of Monsieur Reparti, captain at the next fort, who was sent
for and expected every hour.

"This commander is a knight of the military order of St.
Louis, and named Legardeur de St. Pierre. He is an elderly
gentleman, and has much the air of a soldier. He was sent over to
take the command, immediately upon the death of the late general,
and arrived here about seven days before me.

"At two o'clock, the gentleman who was sent for arrived,
when I offered the letter, &c. again, which they received, and adjourned into a private apartment for the captain to translate, who
understood a little English. After he had done it, the commander
desired I would walk in and bring my interpreter to peruse and
correct it; which I did.

"Dec. 14th. As the snow increased very fast, and our horses
daily became weaker, I sent them off unloaded, under the care of
Barnaby Currin and two others, to make all convenient despatch
to Venango, and there to wait our arrival, if there was a prospect
of the river's freezing; if not, then to continue down to Shanapin's
town, at the Forks of Ohio, and there to wait until we came to
cross the Allegheny; intending myself to go down by water, as I
had the offer of a canoe or two. This evening, I received an
answer to his honour the governor's letter, from the commandant.

"Dec. 15th. The commandant ordered a plentiful store of
liquor, provisions, &c. to be put on board our canoes, and appeared
to be extremely complaisant, though he was exerting every artifice
which he could invent to set our Indians at variance with us, to
prevent their going until after our departure; presents, rewards,
and everything which could be suggested by him or his officers. I
can not say that ever in my life I suffered so much anxiety as I
did in this affair. I saw that every stratagem, which the most
fruitful brain could invent, was practised to win the Half King to
their interest; and that leaving him there was giving them the
opportunity they aimed at. I went to the Half King and pressed
him in the strongest terms to go; he told me that the commandant
would not discharge him until the morning. I then went to the
commandant, and desired him to do their business, and complained
of ill treatment; for keeping them, as they were part of my company, was detaining me. This he promised not to do, but to forward my journey as much as he could. He protested he did not
keep them, but was ignorant of the cause of their stay; though I
soon found it out. He had promised them a present of guns, &c.

if they would wait until the morning. As I was very much pressed by the Indians to wait this day for them, I consented, on a promise that nothing should hinder them in the morning.

"16th. The French were not slack in their inventions to keep the Indians this day, also. But as they were obliged, according to promise, to give the present, they then endeavored to try the power of liquor, which I doubt not would have prevailed at any other time than this; but I urged and insisted with the King [Tanacharison] so closely upon his word, that he refrained, and set off with us as he had engaged.

"We had a tedious and very fatiguing passage down the creek. Several times we had like to have been staved against rocks; and many times were obliged all hands to get out and remain in the water half an hour or more, getting over the shoals. At one place, the ice had lodged, and made it impassable by water; we were, therefore, obliged to carry our canoe across the neck of land, a quarter of a mile over. We did not reach Venango until the 22d, where we met with our horses.

"Dec. 23d. When I got things ready to set off, I sent for the Half King, to know whether he intended to go with us, or by water. He told me that White Thunder had hurt himself much, and was sick, and unable to walk; therefore he was obliged to carry him down in a canoe. As I found he intended to stay here a day or two, and knew that Monsieur Joncaire would employ every scheme to set him against the English, as he had before done, I told him I hoped he would guard against his flattery, and let no fine speeches influence him in their favour. He desired I might not be concerned, for he knew the French too well for any thing to engage him in their favour; and that though he could not go down with us. he yet would endeavour to meet at the Forks with Joseph Campbell, to deliver a speech for me to carry to his honour, the governor. He told me he would order the Young Hunter to attend us, and get provisions, &c. if wanted.

"Our horses were now so weak and feeble, and the baggage so heavy, (as we were obliged to provide all the necessaries which the journey would require) that we doubted much their performing it. Therefore, myself and others, except the drivers, who were obliged to ride, gave up our horses for packs, to assist along with the baggage. I put myself in an Indian walking dress, and continued with them three days, until I found there was no probability of their getting home in any reasonable time. The horses became less able to travel every day; the cold increased very fast; and the roads were becoming much worse by a deep snow, continually freezing; therefore, as I was uneasy to get back, to make report of my proceedings to his honour, the governor, I determined to prosecute my journey, the nearest way through the woods, on foot.

"Accordingly, I left Mr. Vanbraam in charge of our baggage, with money and directions to provide necessaries from place to place for themselves and horses, and to make the most convenient despatch in traveling.

"I took my necessary papers, pulled off my clothes, and tied myself up in a match coat. Then with gun in hand, and pack on my back, in which were my papers and provisions, I set out with Mr. Gist, fitted in the same manner, on Wednesday, the 26th."

History does not say how Tanacharison and the other members of the party whom Washington and Gist left behind when they set out on foot, reached Logstown. Nor shall we follow Washington further on his return trip. Every school child is familiar with the fact that he was shot at by a hostile Indian near Murdering Town, not far from Evans City, Butler County, on the afternoon of December 27th, as he and Gist were on their way back to Virginia, and that he was almost drowned in the icy waters of the Allegheny within the present limits of Pittsburgh.

A Personal Statement

At this point, the author asks that the reader indulge him in making the statement that he traces his love for the history of Pennsylvania to the story of the attack on Washington by the hostile Indian on that December evening of 1753, told him under the following circumstances: On the farm on which he was reared in Armstrong County, the ancestral home of his paternal forebearers since 1795, is a high hill, commanding a majestic sweep of the horizon in all directions. To the eastward, the blue outline of the Chestnut Ridge can be seen, on a clear day, almost fifty miles away, while to the westward, are the undulating hills of Butler County. One of his earliest recollections is that of his accompanying his revered mother to this hilltop on summer evenings and, with her, watching the sun set in floods of gorgeous and golden beauty behind the western hills. On those occasions she told him that the western region, where the sun was setting, was Butler County, and that it was in this county where George Washington was shot at by a hostile Indian in the dead of winter and in the depth of the forest. The author shall always cherish the recollection of those summer evenings, when, as a child in company with his mother in the grace and beauty of her young womanhood, he watched those golden sunsets bathe the Butler County hills in glory, and in his fancy, pictured the region of the sunset as an enchanted land, inhabited by the ghosts and shadows of the past and hallowed by the footsteps of Washington.

Nemacolin

We have stated earlier in this chapter that Washington and Gist followed the Nemacolin Indian Trail from Cumberland, Maryland, to the Forks of the Ohio. This trail was named for the Delaware chief, Nemacolin, who in 1752, was employed, with others, by Colonel Thomas Cresap and Christopher Gist, acting for the Ohio Company, in blazing the most direct route between Cumberland and the mouth of Redstone Creek (Brownsville, Fayette County), on the Monongahela River. This trail followed the route of Christopher Gist's second journey from Cumberland to the Forks of the Ohio, in November, 1751. It was much shorter than the path which the Virginia traders had used from a date as early as 1740, in traveling from the Potomac to the Ohio. It was the same course followed by Washington's army on its unsuccessful march against Fort Duquesne in the summer of 1754, described in Chapter XIV, and also, in part, the same followed by Braddock's army in the summer of 1755.

Nemacolin's residence at the time of blazing this trail was at the mouth of Dunlap's Creek, also, in early times, called Nemacolin's Creek, in Fayette County. How long Nemacolin resided at this place is unknown. In 1785, General Richard Butler, in company with Colonel James Monroe, (afterwards President Monroe), made an expedition down the Ohio to treat with the Miamis. In General Butler's journal of this expedition, he speaks of an island called Nemacolin's, between the mouths of the Little Kanawha and Hocking, no doubt a subsequent dwelling place of Nemacolin.

Nemacolin was the son of the Delaware chief, Checochinican, or Specokkenecan, who dwelt on Brandywine Creek about 1716, and removed to the Susquehanna before June 16, 1718, as on that date he accompanied Captain Civility and other chiefs of the Conestogas, Shawnees, and Delawares of the Susquehanna, to Philadelphia, and complained to Governor Keith "that they have reason to think the authority of this Government is not duly observed, for that notwithstanding all our former agreements that rum should not be brought amongst them, it is still carried in great quantities." Checochinican added "that the young men about

Paxtan [Paxtang] had been lately so generally debauched with rum carried amongst them by strangers, that they now want all manner of clothing and necessaries to go a hunting; wherefore, they wish it would be so ordered that no rum should be brought amongst them by any except the traders who furnish them with all other necessaries."

In the Pennsylvania Archives, (Vol. I, page 239), is a letter from Checochinican to Governor Patrick Gordon, dated June 24, 1729, in which he says that, when the Indians sold their lands on the Brandywine to William Penn, they reserved a part on the head of the creek, by a written instrument which later was lost. Checochinican complains that settlers are crowding the Indians out, and hopes that the Governor "will be pleased to take care and protect us."This is his last appearance in history.

Another Delaware chief living in Southwestern Pennsylvania at the time of the blazing of Nemacolin's Trail, was Catfish. He had his cabin where Washington, the county seat of Washington County, now stands.

Tanacharison Asks Pennsylvania to Build Fort on the Ohio

In January, 1754, Gorge Croghan and Andrew Montour were sent to Logstown by Governor Hamilton of Pennsylvania, to ascertain from Tanacharison and Scarouady a full account of the activities of the French in the valleys of the Allegheny and Ohio, the attitude of the Western Indians, and what assistance in the way of arms and ammunition Virginia had given these Indians. Croghan and Montour found some French soldiers at Logstown and most of the Indians drunk. John Patten, a trader, who accompanied Croghan and Montour, was captured by the French, but Tanacharson caused his release. The Pennsylvania emissaries remained at Logstown until February 2nd. They found the Indians determined to resist the French. A few days before they left, Tanacharison, Scarouady, and Shingas addressed a speech to Governor Hamilton in which they said: "We now request that our brother, the Governor of Virginia, may build a strong house at the Forks of the Mohongialo [Monongahela], and send some of our young brethren, the warriors, to live in it. And we expect our brother of Pennsylvania will build another house somewhere on the river, where he shall think proper, where whatever assistance he will think proper to send us may be kept for us, as our enemies are just at hand, and we do not know what day they may come upon us."

CHAPTER XIV

Tanacharison, the Half King

(Continued)

Tanacharison Sees French Commit First
Overt Act of War

ARLY in 1754, Virginia decided to fortify the Forks of the Ohio (Pittsburgh). She sent Captain William Trent to this place with a company of men to erect a fort. Trent arrived on February 17, 1754, and immediately began the erection of a fort, called Fort Trent.

After the work was well started, Captain Trent returned to Will's Creek (Cumberland, Maryland), to secure supplies, leaving a young commissioned officer, an ensign, named Edward Ward, who was a half-brother of George Croghan, in command. The Indian trader, John Frazer, was among Ward's forces, having the commission of lieutenant. The French were promptly warned of the arrival of Trent's forces, and with the opening of spring, marshalled their forces to the number of about one thousand, including French-Canadians and Indians of various tribes, with eighteen pieces of cannon, in all a flotilla of about sixty battaux and three hundred canoes, and descended the Allegheny from LeBoueff and Venango. The French forces arrived at the Forks of the Ohio on the evening of the 17th of April, under command of Captain Contrecoeur. Planting his artillery, Contrecoeur sent Chevalier Le Mercier, Captain of the Artillery of Canada, with a summons to Ensign Ward, demanding immediate surrender. This was the first overt act of war on the part of the French, in the conflict known as the French and Indian War.

Ward thus found himself surrounded by a force of one thousand French and Indians with the fort still uncompleted.

The Half King, Tanacharison, was present, and advised Ensign Ward to reply to the demand of Contrecoeur that he was not an officer of rank to answer the demand, and to request a delay until he could send for his superior in command. Contrecoeur, however, refused to parley; whereupon, Ward, having less than forty men, and, therefore, being utterly unable to resist the opposing force, prudently surrendered the half-finished stockade without further hesitation.

Contrecoeur, upon the surrender of Ward, treated him with the utmost politeness, invited him to sup with him, and wished him a pleasant journey back to Virginia. The French commander permitted him to withdraw his men, and take his tools with him; and on the next morning, he started on his return to Virginia going up the Monongahela to the mouth of Redstone Creek (Brownsville, Fayette County), where the Ohio Company had a stockade, erected by Trent on his way to the Ohio Valley. George Croghan, about the time Trent began erecting the fort at the Forks of the Ohio, had contracted with the Ohio Company to furnish provisions for Trent's forces, valued at five hundred pounds, from the back parts of Pennsylvania; and half of these were on their way to the Ohio when Contrecoeur captured the fort.

The French then took possession of the half-finished fort, completed it early in June, and named it Fort Duquesne, in honor of Marquis DuQuesne, then the Governor General of Canada.

Tanacharison with Washington in Virginia's Campaign of 1754

While Captain Trent was pushing on toward the Forks of the Ohio in the early part of 1754, Colonel Joshua Fry, with George Washington second in command, was raising additional troops in Virginia to garrison the fort Trent was to build. Soon Washington, under the rank of Lieutenant-Colonel, hastened to Will's Creek (Cumberland, Maryland), to push forward the preparations to reinforce the fort at the Forks of the Ohio, when the news of its capture was brought to him in the latter part of April, 1754. A council of war was then called in which it was agreed that it would be impossible to march to the French fort without reinforcements, but that an advance should be made to the mouth of Redstone Creek, where a fortification should be made and reinforcements awaited.

Washington was not yet joined by Colonel Fry, and had only one hundred fifty men under his command. On the 25th of April, he sent a detachment of sixty men to open the road, which detachment was joined by the main body on May 1st. By the 9th of May, he reached a place called the Little Meadows. Learning from Indian scouts, which had been sent him by his ally, Tanacharison, that the French were rapidly marching toward him, Washington hastened to take a position in a place called the Great Meadows along the national pike, in Fayette County. "I hurried to this place," says Washington, "as a convenient spot. We have, with nature's assistance, made a good entrenchment, and by clearing the bushes out of these meadows, prepared a charming field for an encounter."

Christopher Gist visited Washington's camp at the Great Meadows early in the morning of May 27th, coming from his plantation at Mount Braddock, thirteen miles distant, and reporting that on May 26th, M. La Force, with fifty soldiers had been at his plantation the day before, and that on his way to Washington's camp, he had seen the tracks of the same party only five miles from the encampment at the Great Meadows. Tanacharison, with a number of his warriors was but six miles from the Great Meadows, and a little after eight o'clock on the night of the same day, May 27th, he sent Washington intelligence that he had seen the tracks of Frenchmen, and had traced them to an obscure retreat. Washington feared that this might be a stratagem of the French for attacking his camp, and so, placing his ammunition in a place of safety and leaving a strong guard to protect it, he set out before ten o'clock with forty men, and reached Tanacharison's camp a little before sunrise, marching through a heavy rain, a night of intense darkness and the obstacles offered by an almost impenetrable forest. In a letter to Governor Dinwiddie, he says: "We were frequently tumbled over one another, and often so lost that fifteen or twenty minutes' search would not find the path again."

Tanacharison Helps Washington Fight First Battle of His Career

At early dawn (May 28th), Washington held a council with Tanacharison at the latter's camp, which was near a spring, now known as Washington's Spring, about two miles north of the Summit on the old national pike, near Uniontown; and it was agreed at this council to unite in an attack upon the French, Washington's forces to be on the right and Tanacharison's warriors on the left. The French were soon traced to an almost inaccessible rocky glen in the Allegheny Mountains, about three miles north of the Summit. The forces of Washington and Tanacharison advanced until they came so near as to be discovered by the French, who instantly ran to their arms. The firing continued on both sides for about fifteen minutes, when the French were defeated with the loss of their whole party, ten of whom, including their commander, M. de Jumonville, were killed, one wounded, and twenty-one taken prisoners. Of the prisoners, the two most important were an officer named Drouillon, and the redoubtable LaForce. The prisoners were marched to the Great Meadows, and from there sent over the mountains to Virginia. Of Washington's party, only one was killed, and two or three were wounded. Tanacharison's warriors sustained no loss, as the fire of the French was aimed exclusively at Washington and his soldiers. It is said that Washington fired the first shot in this skirmish, the opening conflict of the French and Indian War. Jumonville was buried where he fell, and a tablet marks the spot where his remains lie. The scene of this encounter, the first battle of Washington's illustrious career, is almost as wild and primitive as it was on that fateful morning of the 28th day of May, 1754.

At a council held at Philadelphia on December 19th, 1754, between Governor Morris of Pennsylvania, and Scarouady, Jagrea, a Mohawk, and Aroas, a Seneca, the said Scarouady gave the following account of events leading up to the fight with Jumonville and the part that the Indian allies took in the same:

"This belt [holding up a belt of wampum] was sent by the Governor of Virginia and delivered by Captain Trent. You see in it the representation of an hatchet. It was an invitation to us to join with and assist our brethren to repel the French from the Ohio. At the time it was given, there were but four or five of us, and we were all that knew any thing about the matter; when we got it, we put it into a private pocket on the inside of our garment. It lay next to our breasts.

"As we were on the road going to Council with our brethren, a company of French, in number thirty-one, overtook us and desired us to go and council with them; and when we refused, they pulled us by the arm and almost stripped the chain of covenant from off it, but still I would suffer none to go with them. We thought to have got before them, but they passed us; and when we saw they endeavored to break the chain of friendship, I pulled this belt out of my pocket and looked at it and saw there this hatchet, and then went and told Colonel Washington of these thirty-one French Men, and we and a few of our brothers fought with them. Ten were killed, and twenty-one were taken alive whom we delivered to Colonel Washington, telling him that we had blooded the edge of his hatchet a little."

John Davidson, the Indian trader, acted as interpreter, at the above council. He was in the action, and gave Governor Morris the following account of it:

"There were but eight Indians, who did most of the execution that was done. Colonel Washington and the Half King [Tanacharison] differed much in judgment, and on the Colonel's refusing to take his advice, the English and Indians separated. After which the Indians discovered the French in an hollow and hid themselves, lying on their bellies behind a hill; afterwards they discovered Colonel Washington on the opposite side of the hollow in the gray of the morning, and when the English fired, which they did in great confusion, the Indians came out of their cover and closed with the French and killed them with their tomahawks, on which the French surrendered."

In writing to his brother, John Augustine, Washington, referring to the engagement with Jumonville, said:

"I have heard the bullets whistle, and believe me, there is something charming in the sound."

This remark was reported later to George the Second, King of England, who commented: "He would not say so if he had been used to hearing many."

Washington Gives Tanacharison an English Name

Two days after the death of Jumonville, Colonel Fry died at the camp at Will's Creek on his way to join the army, and the chief command now devolved upon Colonel Washington. Washington immediately commenced enlarging the intrenchment at the Great Meadows, and erecting palisades, anticipating an attack from the French. The palisaded fort at the Great Meadows having been completed, Washington's forces were augmented to three hundred by the arrival from Will's Creek of the forces which had been under Colonel Fry. With these was the surgeon of the regiment, Dr. James Craik, a Scotchman by birth, who was destined to be a faithful friend of Washington's throughout the remainder of his life, and was present at his bedside, when he closed his eyes in death within the hallowed walls of his beloved Mount Vernon.

On the 9th of June, Washington's early instructor, Adjutant Muse, accompanied by Andrew Montour, now Provincial Captain, arrived at the Great Meadows. Adjutant, now Major Muse, brought with him a belt of wampum, and a speech from Governor Dinwiddie to Tanacharison, with medals and presents for the Indians under his command. Says Washington Irving in his classic "Life of Washington": "They were distributed with that grand ceremonial so dear to the Red Man. The chiefs assembled, painted and decorated in all their savage finery. Washington wore a medal sent to him by the Governor for such occasions. The wampum and speech having been delivered, he advanced, and, with all due solemnity, decorated the chiefs and the warriors with the medals, which they were to wear in remembrance of their father, the King of England." Among the warriors thus decorated, was Canachquasy, the son of old Queen Alliquippa, who, with her son, had arrived at the Great Meadows on June 1st. Upon his decoration Canachquasy was given the English name of Lord Fairfax. Tanacharison was given the English name of Dinwiddie on this occasion, and returned the compliment by giving Washington the Indian name of Connotaucarius.

On the 10th day of June, Washington wrote Governor Dinwiddie from the camp at the Great Meadows, concerning the decoration of Canachquasy, as follows:

"Queen Alliquippa desired that her son, who was really a great warrior, might be taken into Council, as she was declining and unfit for business; and that he should have an English name given him. I therefore called the Indians together by the advice of the Half-King, presented one of the medals, and desired him to wear it in remembrance of his great father, the King of England; and called him by the name of Colonel Fairfax, which he was told signified 'the First in Council.' This gave him great pleasure."

At the end of the ceremonies of giving English names to Tanacharison and Canachquasy, Washington read the morning service. Dr. James Craik, who was present, said, in a letter home, that the Indians "believed he was making magic."

Washington Advances to Gist's Plantation

On the 10th of June, there was great agitation in the camp over the report that a party of ninety Frenchmen were approaching, which report was later found to be incorrect. On the same day, Captain Mackay of the Royal Army, in command of an independent company of one hundred riflemen from South Carolina, arrived at the Great Meadows, increasing Washington's forces to about four hundred men. Leaving one company under Captain Mackay to guard the fort, Washington pushed on over the Laurel Hill as far as Christopher Gist's plantation at Mount Braddock, near Connellsville, Fayette County. So difficult was the passage over Laurel Hill that it took approximately two weeks for Washington's forces to reach Gist's plantation from Great Meadows, a distance of thirteen miles. Washington's Indian allies refused to accompany him as far as Gist's plantation, and returned to the Great Meadows. The trouble was that Washington and Tanacharison could not agree as to the method of conducting the campaign. On the 27th of June, Washington had sent a party of seventy men under Captain Lewis to clear a road from Gist's plantation to the mouth of the Redstone (Brownsville), and another party under Captain Polson was, on the same day, sent ahead to reconnoiter.

While these movements of Washington's forces were taking place, a force of five hundred French and some Indians, afterwards augmented to about four hundred, left Fort Duquesne on the 28th of June to attack Washington, the French being commanded by M. DeVilliers, a half brother of Jumonville, who it is said, sought the command from Contrecoeur as a special favor that he might avenge his half-brother's "assassination". This force went up the Monongahela in large canoes, and on the 30th of June, reached the mouth of Redstone, and encamped on the rising ground about half a mile from the stockade, which, it will be recalled, Captain Trent had erected during the preceding winter as a storehouse for the Ohio Company. M. DeVilliers described it as "a sort of fort built of logs, one upon another, well notched in, about thirty feet long and twenty feet wide."

While at the mouth of the Redstone, M. DeVilliers learned that Washington's forces were entrenching themselves at Gist's plantation. He thereupon disencumbered himself of all his heavy stores, and leaving a sergeant and a few men to guard the boats, pushed on in the night, cheered by the hope that he was about to capture the forces of Washington. Arriving at Gist's plantation in the early morning of July 2nd, he saw the intrenchments which Washington had there begun to erect, at once invested them, and fired a general volley. No response came from the intrenchments; for the prey had escaped. M. DeVilliers was then about to retrace his steps, when a deserter, coming from the Great Meadows, disclosed to him the whereabouts and the half-famished condition of Washington's forces. Having made a prisoner of the deserter with a promise to reward or hang him after proving his story true or untrue, M. DeVilliers continued the pursuit. While he is pursuing Washington, we will relate how the latter's forces escaped capture.

At Gist's plantation, on June 28th, Washington held a council of war, upon receipt of intelligence that the French in large numbers, accompanied by many Indians, were marching against him. At this council, it was resolved to send a message to Captain Mackay, who was then at the Great Meadows, desiring him to join Washington at once, and also to call in Captain Lewis and Captain Polson, who, as we have seen, had been sent forward to cut the road from Gist's to Redstone, and to reconnoiter. Captain Mackay and his company arrived on the evening of the 28th, and the foraging parties on the morning of the 29th, when a second council of war was held, and it was decided to retreat as speedily as possible.

Washington Surrenders at Fort Necessity

The troops, with great difficulty, succeeded in reaching the Great Meadows. Here they halted on July 1st. The suffering among Washington's forces was great. For eight days they had no bread, and had taken little of any other food. It was not the intention of Washington at first to halt at this place, but his men had become so fatigued from great labor and hunger that they could draw the swivels no further. Here, then, it was resolved to make a stand. Trees were felled, and a log breastwork was raised at the fort, in order to strengthen it in the best manner that the circumstances would permit. Washington now named the stockade "Fort Necessity" from the circumstances attending its erection. At this critical juncture, many of Washington's Indian allies, under Tanacharison, deserted him, being disheartened at the scant preparations of defense against the superior force, and offended at being subject to military command.

Early on the morning of July 3rd an alarm was received from a sentinel, who had been wounded by the enemy, and, at nine o'clock, word was received that the whole body of the French and Indian allies amounting, as some authorities say, to nine hundred men, was only four miles off. Before noon, distant firing was heard, and the enemy reached a woods about a third of a mile from the fort. Washington had drawn his men up on the open and level ground outside the trenches, and waited for the attack, which he thought would be as soon as the enemy emerged from the woods; and he ordered his troops to reserve their fire until they should be near enough to do execution. The French did not incline to leave the woods and to attack the fort by assault. Washington then drew his men back within the trenches, and gave them orders to fire at their discretion, as suitable opportunities might present themselves. The enemy remained on the side of the rising ground next

to the fort, and were sheltered by the trees.   They kept up a brisk
fire of musketry, but never appeared in open view.   In the meantime, rain was falling in torrents, the trenches were filled with
water, and many of the arms of Washington's men were out of
order.   Until eight o'clock at night—the rain falling without intermission—both parties kept up a desultory fire, the action having
started at about eleven o'clock in the morning.   By that time, the
French had killed all the horses and cattle at the fort.

At eight o'clock at night, the French requested a parley, but
Washington, suspecting this to be a feint to procure the admission
of an officer into the fort to discover his condition, declined.   They.
repeated their request with the additional request that an officer
might be sent to them, they guaranteeing his safety.   Washington
then sent Captain Jacob Van Braam, the only person under his
command who understood the French language, with the exception
of Chevalier de Peyrouny, an Ensign in the Virginia regiment, who
was dangerously wounded.   Van Braam returned and brought with
him from D. DeVilliers, the French commander, the proposed
articles of capitulation.   Villiers was a half-brother of the ill-
fated Jumonville.   Owing to the overpowering number of the
enemy, Washington decided to come to terms.   After a notification
of the proposed articles, he consented to leave the fort the next
morning, July 4, 1754, but was to leave it with the honors of war,
and with the understanding that he should surrender nothing but
the artillery.

French Accuse Washington of Having
Assassinated Jumonville

Considerable dissatisfaction was expressed with regard to
several of the article of capitulation when they were made public.
One of these was an article, by consenting to which Washington
virtually admitted that Jumonville had been "assassinated" in the
action of May 28th.   Another was an article, by consenting to
which, Washington virtually admitted the validity of the French
claim to the Ohio Valley.   M. DeVilliers, the commandant of the
French forces, in his account of the marcn from Fort Duquesne
and the affair at the Great Meadows said, "We made the English
consent to sign that they had assassinated my brother in his camp."
A copy of the capitulation was subsequently laid before the House
of Burgesses of Virginia, with explanations.   The conduct of
Washington and his officers was properly appreciated, and they re-

ceived a vote of thanks for their gallant defense of their country. However, from this vote of thanks, two officers were excepted— Major Muse, who was charged with cowardice, and Captain Jacob VanBraam, who was accused of treachery in purposely misinterpreting the articles of capitulation. The truth is that Washington had been greatly deceived by VanBraam, either through ignorance or design. An officer of his regiment, who was present at the reading and signing of the articles of capitulation, wrote a letter to a friend, in which he discusses the true intent and meaning of the articles and of their bungling translation by VanBraam, as follows:

"When Mr. VanBraam returned with the French proposals, we were obliged to take the sense of them from his mouth; it rained so hard that he could not give us a written translation of them; we could scarcely keep the candle lighted to read them by; and every officer there is ready to declare that there was no such word as 'assassination' mentioned. The terms expressed were 'the death of Jumonville.' If it had been mentioned, we would by all means have had it altered, as the French, during the course of the interview, seemed very condescending and desirous to bring things to a conclusion; and, upon our insisting, altered the articles relating to the stores and ammunition, which they wanted to detain; and that of the cannon, which they agreed to have 'destroyed', instead of 'reserved for their use.'

"Another article, which appears to our disadvantage, is that whereby we oblige ourselves not to attempt an establishment beyond the mountains. This was translated to us, not 'to attempt' buildings or 'improvements on the lands of his most Christian Majesty.' This we never intended, as we denied he had any there, and therefore thought it needless to dispute this point.

"The last article, which relates to the hostages, is quite different from the translation of it given to us. • It is metioned 'for the security of the performance of this treaty', as well as for the return of the prisoners. There was never such an intention on our side, or mention of it made on theirs, by our interpreter. Thus, by the evil intention or negligence of VanBraam, our conduct is scrutinized by a busy world, fond of criticizing the proceedings of others, without considering circumstances, or giving just attention to reasons which might be offered to obviate their censures."

"VanBraam was a Dutchman, and had but an imperfect knowledge of either the French or English language. How far his ignorance should be taken as an apology for his blunders, is uncertain. Although he had proved himself a good officer, yet there were other circumstances, which brought his fidelity in question. Governor Dinwiddie, in giving an account of this affair to Lord Albermarle says: 'In the capitulation they made use of the word 'assassination', but Washington, not understanding French, was deceived by the interpreter, who was a paltroon, and though an officer with us, they say he has joined the French."

Also, Washington expressed himself on Van Braam's translation, as follows:

"That we were willfully or ignorantly deceived by our interpreter in regard to the word 'assassination', I do aver and will to my dying moment; so will every officer who was present. The interpreter was a Dutchman little acquainted with the English tongue, and therefore might not advert to the tone and meaning of the word in English; but whatever his motives were for so doing, certain it is he called it the 'death' or the 'loss' of the Sieur Jumonville. So we received and so we understood it until, to our great surprise and mortification, we found it otherwise in a literal translation."

Washington Marches Out With Honors of War

On the morning of July 4th, Washington and his forces marched out of Fort Necessity with the honors of war, taking with them their regimental colors, but leaving behind a large flag, too cumberous to be transported. His forces set out for Will's Creek, but had scarcely left the Great Meadows when they encountered one hundred Indian allies of the French, who, in defiance of the terms of capitulation, began plundering the baggage, and committing other irregularities. Seeing that the French did not or could not prevent their Indian allies, Washington's men destroyed their powder and other stores, including even their private baggage, to prevent its falling into the hands of the Indians. M. DeVilliers sent a detachment to take possession of the fort as soon as Washington's forces defiled therefrom. Washington's regiment left twelve dead on the ground, and the number left by Captain Mackay's company is not known. DeVillier said that the number of dead excited his pity.

Thus ended the affair at the Great Meadows, Washington's first and last surrender, the location of which is along the National Pike, in Fayette County, a few miles east of the Summit. On reaching Will's Creek, where his half-famished troops found ample provisions in the military magazine, he hastened with Captain

Mackay, to Governor Dinwiddie, at Williamsburg, whom they particularly informed of the events of their expedition. Washington
soon thereafter resigned his commission, and retired to private life
at Mount Vernon. His first act, after relinquishing his command,
was to visit his mother, inquire into the state of her affairs, and
look after the welfare of his younger brother and his sister, Betty.
He continued his residence at Mount Vernon until the following
year, when he again entered the service of Virginia in the army of
General Braddock.

Tanacharison Complains of Washington

After the defeat of Washington at the Great Meadows, Tanacharison and Scarouady, with some of their followers, "came down
to the back parts of Virginia", and then with Seneca George and
about three hundred Mingos (Iroquois), retreated to George Croghan's trading post at Aughwick, now Shirleysburg, Huntingdon
County. At about the same time, many Shawnees, Delawares, and
an inconsiderable number of renegades of the Seneca tribe of the
Six Nations, joined the French. Tanacharison and Scarouady
after retreating to Aughwick, sent out messages to assemble the
friendly Delawares and Shawnees at that place, and asked the
Colony of Pennsylvania to support their women and children while
the warriors fought on the side of the English, whom they expected
speedily to take decisive steps against the French. In response to
these messages, great swarms of excited Indians came to Aughwick,
clamoring for food, and were fed at the expense of the Colony
throughout the fall and winter.

Angered by the charge of the Virginians that the friendly
Indians were treacherous and secretly aided the French in this campaign, Tanacharison expressed himself as dissatisfied with the conduct of Colonel Washington. In August, 1754, the old chief came
to John Harris' Ferry (Harrisburg) to meet Conrad Weiser and
accompany him to Aughwick. "On the way," says Weiser, "Tanacharison complained very much of the behavior of Colonel Washington, (though in a very moderate way, saying the Colonel was a
good-natured man, but had no experience); that he took upon him
to command the Indians as his slaves, and would have them every
day upon the Out Scout, and attack the Enemy by themselves, and
that he would by no means take advice from the Indians; that he
lay at one place from one full moon to another, and made no fortifications at all but that little thing upon the meadow, where he

thought the French would come up to him in open field; that had he taken the Half King's advice and made such fortifications as the Half King advised him to make, he would certainly have beat the French off; that the French had acted as great cowards and the English as fools in that engagement; that he [the Half King] had carried off his wife and children; so did other Indians before the battle begun, because Colonel Washington would never listen to them, but was always driving them on to fight by his directions."

Tanacharison and Scarouady Protest
Albany Purchase

In order to combine the efforts of the colonies in their resistance of the encroachments of the French, a conference was ordered by the British Ministry, at Albany, New York, which was held in June and July, 1754, to which the Six Nations were invited. They came, and peace was established with them. Governor Hamilton of Pennsylvania, unable to be present, commissioned John Penn and Richard Peters of the Provincial Council, and Isaac Norris and Benjamin Franklin of the Assembly, to attend the Council in his stead. At this conference, a plan was proposed for a political union, and adopted on the 4th of July. It was subsequently submitted to the Home Government and the Provincial Assemblies. The British Government condemned it, according to Franklin, on account of its being too democratic; and the various Provincial Assemblies objected to it as containing too much power of the king, Pennsylvania negativing the same without discussion.

Although the Albany Conference, therefore, was not satisfactory in all its results, the Pennsylvania commissioners secured a great addition to the Province of Pennsylvania, to which the Indian title was not extinct. The deed, which was signed by chiefs of the Six Nations on July 6, 1754, conveyed to Pennsylvania all the land extending on the west side of the Susquehanna River from the Blue Mountains to a mile above the mouth of Kayarondinhagh (Penn's) Creek; thence northwest by west to the western boundary of the Province; thence along the western boundary to the southern boundary; thence along the southern boundary to the Blue Mountains; and thence along the Blue Mountains to the place of beginning.

George Croghan was in charge of distributing provisions and supplies to the friendly Indians, who had assembled at Aughwick after Washington's surrender at Fort Necessity. The bills which he was sending the Colonial Authorities for feeding these Indians having grown rather large, Croghan was suspicioned as not being reliable, and finally there were hints that he was in league with the French. The Pennsylvania Assembly then cut down his bills, and he decided to leave Aughwick. Conrad Weiser was then directed by the Colonial Authorities to go to Aughwick, and make a report on Croghan. He reached this place on August 31st, 1754, being accompanied by Tanacharison from Harris' Ferry, as we have already seen.

Weiser found that Croghan was entirely worthy of being trusted. He also found that the inhabitants of Cumberland County caused much trouble in selling so much strong liquor to the Indians assembled at Aughwick. In the conferences which he held with Tanacharison, Scarouady, King Beaver, and various other chiefs, he completely won old Tanacharison and his people back to the English cause after their anger at Washington and the Virginians. Moreover, at these conferences, Weiser learned that the Shawnees and Delawares had formed an alliance; that the French had offered them presents, either to join them or to remain neutral, and that to these proposals, the Delawares made no reply, but at once sent their deputies to Aughwick for the purpose, as Weiser thought, of learning the attitude of the English.

Near the close of the conference, Tanacharison and Scarouady pressed Weiser to tell them what transpired at the Albany Treaty; and he then told them all about the purchase of the vast tract west of the Susquehanna. "They seemed not to be very well pleased," says Weiser, "because the Six Nations had sold such a large tract." Weiser then explained that the purchase was made in order to frustrate land schemes of the Connecticut interests, and of the French on the Ohio. This appeared to satisfy them, though they resented not receiving a part of the consideration. For a time they were content, not knowing that the purchase included most of the lands on the West Branch of the Susquehanna. The Shawnee and Delaware deputies then went back to the Ohio into danger and temptations, and to learn from the French that their vast hunting grounds on the West Branch of the Susquehanna had been sold to the Province of Pennsylvania at the Albany Treaty.

No wonder that Tanacharison and Scarouady complained to Weiser. The Albany purchase was a very powerful factor in alienating, not only the Delawares, but the other Indians, from Pennsylvania. The Shawnees and Delawares of the Munsee Clan (Monseys) in the valleys of the Susquehanna, Juniata, Allegheny, and Ohio, thus found their lands "sold from under their feet" which the Six Nations had guaranteed to them, so they claimed, on their migration to these valleys. It was provided in the contract of sale of these lands that half of the purchase price should be paid upon delivery of the deed, and the remainder was not to be paid until the settlers had actually crossed the Allegheny Mountains, and taken up their abode in the purchased territory. The Indians declared in July, 1755, that they would not receive the second installment, but the Mohawk chief, Hendricks, persuaded them to stand by the deed. After Braddock was defeated on July 9, 1755, the entire body of dissatisfied Indians on the Albany Purchase took bitter vengeance on Pennsylvania. After three years of bloodshed, outrage and murder, Conrad Weiser persuaded the Proprietaries of Pennsylvania to deed back to the Indians that part of the Albany purchase which lay west of the Allegheny Mountains. This was done at the treaty at Easton, in October, 1758, which treaty will be discussed in Chapter XXII.

Death of Tanacharison

After the series of conferences with Conrad Weiser at Aughwick, in September, 1754, Tanacharison returned to the trading house of John Harris, at Harris' Ferry, where he became dangerously ill; and a conjuror, or "medicineman", was summoned to make inquiry into the cause and nature of his malady. The "medicineman" gave it as his opinion that the French had bewitched Tanacharison, in revenge for the great blow he had struck them in the affair of Jumonville; for the Indians gave him the whole credit of that success, Tanacharison having made it clear that it was he who killed Jumonville, in revenge of the French, who, as he declared, had killed, boiled, and eaten his father. Furthermore, Tanacharison had sent around the French scalps taken at that action, as trophies. All the friends of the old chieftain concurred in the opinion of the "medicineman", and when Tanacharison died at the house of John Harris, on October 4, 1754, there was great lamentation among the Indians, mingled with threats of immediate vengeance. Thus was this noted sachem gathered to his fathers in the "Happy Hunting Ground", at a time when his services and influence among the Western Indians were greatly needed by the English.

CHAPTER XV

Scarouady

CAROUADY (Monacatuatha, Monacatoocha, etc.) was an Oneida chieftain who was sent by the Great Council of the Six Nations to the Ohio Valley, about 1747, as vice-gerent over the Shawnees of that region. He was an elderly man at that time, but lived long enough to take a prominent part, on the side of the English, in the stirring events of King George's War and the French and Indian War. Upon his coming to the Ohio Valley, he took up his residence at Logstown.

The first mention of Scarouady in the recorded history of Pennsylvania is when he, Kakowatcheky, Neucheconneh, Tanacharison and others wrote a letter from "Aleggainey", on April 20th, 1747, to the Governor of Pennsylvania on behalf of the Twightwees, or Miamis, of the Ohio Valley, a letter which has already been mentioned in Chapters VIII and XIII.

In November of this year, he accompanied Canachquasy and a delegation of ten Mingo warriors from the Kuskuskies region to Philadelphia, when Canachquasy informed the Provincial Council that, while it was true that the Onondaga Council had taken a stand for neutrality in King George's War, yet the young men of that part of the Iroquois in the Ohio Valley, under his command, had determined to take up arms against the French,—information that caused Pennsylvania to send George Croghan and Conrad Weiser on their embassies to Logstown, Croghan in April, 1748, and Weiser, in September of that year, as related in Chapters VIII and XIII. In the minutes of this Council (November 13th, 1747), Scarouady is described as old and infirm and as having commended himself to "James Logan's and the Council's Charity." He advised the Council that he had visited Philadelphia many years before.

Conrad Weiser accompanied Scarouady, Canachquasy, and their delegation on their homeward journey as far as John Harris' Ferry (Harrisburg), where the old chief complained bitterly to Weiser concerning the abuses of the rum traffic among the Western Indians. Then Weiser wrote the Provincial Council, on November 28th, characterizing the abuses of the rum traffic among the

Indians as "an abomination before God and man." On the way, the party stopped at Weiser's home, near Womelsdorf, where "Scarouady told Shikellamy very privately that Peter Chartier and his company had accepted the French hatchet, but kept it in their bosom till they would see what interest they could make in favor of the French."

But it is in connection with the return to Logstown and other parts of the upper Ohio Valley of a portion of Peter Chartier's band of Shawnees that Scarouady's name comes into prominence in the annals of Pennsylvania. Indeed, it was owing to the subtle influence of Scarouady that a large number of Chartier's disaffected Shawnees were induced to desert Chartier and come back under dominion of the Six Nations. As stated in Chapter VIII, the Shawnee chiefs, Kakowatcheky and Neucheconneh applied very submissively to Scarouady, in 1748, to itercede with the Colonial Authorities for those members of Chartier's band who had returned; and Scarouady's apology for them was laid before the Pennsylvania Commissioners at Lancaster, on July 21st, of that year, as also related in Chapter VIII.

Treaty with the Miamis, or Twightwees

This conference at Lancaster deserves additional mention for the reason that the Colony of Pennsylvania then and there entered into a treaty with the Twightwees, or Miamis. These Indians became deeply interested in the English when Croghan carried the information to Logstown in April, 1748, that Weiser was coming later in the year with a substantial present from the Province to the western tribes.

Their fur market with the French was very poor, and they had heard of the profitable conferences of the Six Nations with Pennsylvania. Accordingly, they sent word to the Colonial Authorities that their deputies were coming eastward with the hope of holding a conference with the Colony of Pennsylvania, at Lancaster. Weiser urged that a delegation be sent to meet them and conduct them to Lancaster.

In June, 1748, Weiser presented Andrew Montour, the son of Madam Montour, to the Provincial Council as a person "who might be of service to the Colony as Indian interpreter and messenger." Andrew Montour was a prominent man among the Delawares, and well fitted to serve as interpreter. In introducing Montour, Weiser said that "he had found him faithful, knowing and prudent." During the previous winter Weiser had sent Montour to the Indians on the Ohio and Lake Erie "to observe what passed among the Indians."

Montour was directed to meet the deputies of the Twightwees and, if possible, persuade them to come to Philadelphia instead of Lancaster. When he met the Ohio Indians, however, he found it impossible to persuade them to come to Philadelphia, because they feared that the city was "sickly". The Council, therefore, decided to appoint four commissioners to meet these Indians at Lancaster at the treaty of July, 1748. At this conference, Montour was the interpreter of the Twightwees, Conrad Weiser of the Six Nations, and Scarouady was to have been the speaker of the Ohio Indians, but was unable to speak on this occasion on account of being disabled by a fall. Therefore, Andrew Montour became the speaker for all the Western Indians.

After making an appeal on the part of the Shawnees who had accompanied Chartier down the Ohio, the Twightwee chief took a piece of chalk and drew on the court house floor a map of the Ohio, Mississippi, and Wabash. He represented that on the Wabash and another stream called the Hatchet, the Twightwees had twenty towns in which they had more than one thousand fighting men. After the Pennsylvania commissioners and the Twightwees had smoked the pipe of peace together, a treaty of peace was formally drawn up with the Twightwees, on condition that they would have no communication with the French. An exchange of presents then took place. Pennsylvania gave these Indians goods to the value of one hundred eighty-nine pounds, and the Twightwees gave the Pennsylvania commissioners many beaver and deer skins.

Before the Twightwees departed, they were told by the Pennsylvania commissioners that there was a prospect of peace between England and France, to which important statement the Indians made no answer. The Pennsylvania authorities greatly appreciated the value of this newly formed relation with the Twightwees, inasmuch as such an alliance tended to enlarge the Indian trade, and would seriously interrupt communication of the French in Quebec with their settlements on the Mississippi River, for the reason that the towns of the Twightwees lay on the route followed by the French in traveling between their Quebec and Mississippi settlements.

Scarouady at Logstown Conferences

Scarouady took part in the following conferences at Logstown:

1st. The conference which George Croghan held with the Indians of that place in April, 1748, advising them that Conrad Weiser was coming later in the year with a generous present from the Province of Pennsylvania.

2nd. The conferences which Conrad Weiser held with the Indians at Logstown in September, 1748, when he delivered the present above referred to, and allied them with Pennsylvania.

3rd. The conference which Celeron held with the Indians of Logstown in August, 1749, while on his way down the Ohio, burying leaden plates at the mouths of tributary streams, proclaiming that the region drained by the "Beautiful River" belonged to France.

4th. The conference which George Croghan held with the Indians at Logstown a few days after Celeron's departure, when he succeeded in counteracting the influence of the Frenchman. At about this time, he and Tanacharison deeded Croghan a large tract of land near the Forks of the Ohio, as mentioned in Chapter XIII.

5th. The conference which George Croghan and Andrew Montour had with the Indians at Logstown on November 15, 1750, in an effort to counteract the intrigues of the French, and in which they promised that a present for the Indians would be brought to that place the next spring from the Colony of Pennsylvania.

6th. The conference which Christopher Gist, the agent of the Ohio Company, had with the Indians at Logstown on November 25 and 26, 1750, though, as stated in Chapter XIII, Gist said in his journal that nearly all of the Indians were out hunting at that time.

7th. The treaty which the Commissioners from Virginia held with the Indians at Logstown in June, 1752, which was described in Chapter XIII.

8th. Scarouady also attended the conference which Croghan and Montour had with the Indians at Logstown in May, 1751, when they delivered the present from the Colony of Pennsylvania, which they had promised on their visit to this place in the preceding November. This conference was mentioned in Chapter XIII.

It was pointed out, in Chapter XIII, that Scarouady was present at the council held at George Croghan's trading house at the mouth of Pine Creek on May 12, 1753, at which he and Tanacharison, on learning that the French were descending the Allegheny River, decided "that they would receive the French as friends, or as enemies, depending on their attitude, but that the English would be safe as long as they themselves were safe." Scarouady's next important act was to join with Tanacharison in writing a letter, on June 23d, 1753, to Governor Dinwiddie of Virginia, appealing to this colony for help to resist the French. This letter was mentioned in Chapter XIII; and, as stated in that chapter, Scarouady was one of the deputies of the western tribes at the treaty at Winchester, in September, 1753.

Scarouady at Carlisle Treaty

The treaty at Carlisle, in October, 1753, was described in Chapter XIII. . At this point, we call attention to the fact that Scarouady took a prominent part in this treaty, and was one of the principal speakers. His most important speech was a bitter complaint against the abuses of the rum traffic among the Indians of the Ohio Valley by the unlicensed traders. Said he:

"The rum ruins us. We never understood the trade was to be for whiskey and flour. We desire it may be forbidden, no more sold in the Indian country, but that if the Indians will have any, they may go among the inhabitants and deal with them for it. When whiskey traders come, they bring thirty or forty kegs and put them down before us and make us drink, and get all the skins that should go to pay the debts we have contracted for goods bought of the fair traders, and by this means we not only ruin ourselves, but them too. These wicked whiskey sellers, when they have once got the Indians in liquor, make them sell the very clothes from their backs. In short, if this practice be continued, we must inevitably be ruined. We most earnestly, therefore, beseech you to remedy it."

The Pennsylvania commissioners expressed their sympathy for these complaints of the Indians, and promised to lay them before Governor Hamilton. Then the Indians went to their forest homes, pleased with their presents and the promises, but the Colonial Authorities did not recall the traders. Neither was the rum traffic stopped, in spite of the Indians' most solemn protestations. In the meantime, the great French and Indian War was coming apace.

After the Carlisle Treaty, Scarouady returned to the Ohio, where he joined with Tanacharison, an Shannopin's Town, on October 27th, in writing letters to the Governors of Virginia and

Pennsylvania, urging that they join with the Indians of the Ohio and Allegheny in resisting the occupation of the valleys of those streams by the French.

Scarouady Meets Washington

Scarouady's next appearance in the history of Pennsylvania was when George Washington met him at Logstown, in November, 1753, when Washington was on his way to the commandant of the French forts on the headwaters of the Allegheny, bearing the message of Governor Dinwiddie of Virginia. This meeting was described in Chapter XIII, and needs no further reference at this point. Also, in January, 1754, he held council with George Croghan and Andrew Montour, at Logstown, and joined with Tanacharison and Shingas in sending a request to Governor Hamilton to build a fort on the Ohio, as stated at the end of Chapter XIII.

Scarouady in Washington's Campaign of 1754

In Chapter XIV, we found Scarouady assisting Washington in his unsuccessful campaign of 1754. This campaign marked the end of Scarouady's residence at Logstown. On June 26th, while Washington's forces were in the neighborhood of Gist's plantation (Mount Braddock), Washington made the following note in his journal: "An Indian arrived bringing news that Monacatoocha [Scarouady] had burned his village, Logstown, and was gone by water to Redstone [Brownsville, Fayette County], and might be expected there in two days." This was the end of "Old Logstown". The French, however, rebuilt the village before March, 1755, for the Shawnees who remained in the vicinity.

Scarouady Succeeds Tanacharison as Half King

In Chapter XIV, we saw that Scarouady, after the defeat of Washington at the Great Meadows, retreated with Tanacharison and the Indians remaining loyal to the English, to Aughwick, where the Indians were provisioned throughout the fall and winter at the expense of Pennsylvania. He took a prominent part in the conferences with Conrad Weiser at this place in September, 1754, in which, it will be remembered, he protested against the Albany purchase. Upon the death of Tanacharison (October 4th, 1754), Scarouady succeeded him, not only in the direction of Indian affairs at Aughwick, but as Half King generally.

Scarouady Goes to Onondaga Council in English Interest

We saw, in Chapter XIV, how Scarouady, at a Council in Philadelphia, on December 19th, 1754, gave Governor Morris an account of the skirmish in which Jumonville was killed. He was then on his way to the Great Council of the Six Nations, at Onondaga, as the representative of Pennsylvania, Virginia, and the Western Indians, to ask the Onondaga Council to send deputies to Winchester, Virginia, the next spring, to confer on matters of common interest. The old chief's heart was set on war against the French. He remained in Philadelphia until Christmas day, and, before leaving, was given a message by Governor Morris to deliver to the Onondaga Council, protesting against the sale of the Wyoming lands to Connecticut. This sale had been very irregularly made by the Mohawks at the time of the great Albany Conference of June and July, 1754; although the Great Council of the Six Nations had declared, at this conference, that they would not sell the Wyoming lands to either Pennsylvania or Connecticut, but would reserve them as a hunting ground and for the residence of such Indians as cared to remove from the French and settle there, and had appointed Shikellamy's son, John, in charge of this territory.

Scarouady Returns from His Mission

Scarouady returned to Philadelphia in March, 1755, from his journey to the Six Nations. At a meeting of the Provincial Council held on March 31st, he gave a report of his mission. He had gone no farther than to the Oneidas, who told him that the Onondagas were not well disposed at that time toward the English. He had held council with the representatives of the Oneidas, Mohawks, Tuscaroras, and Nanticokes, who desired him, in the name of the Six Nations, to deliver to them what he had to say, assuring him that it would be as good and effectual as if delivered at the Great Council House at Onondaga. Scarouady said to the Provincial Council:

"I asked how the French came to set down on the Ohio. Is it by the advice of the counsellors or is it by the orders of the warriors of the Six Nations? I hāve it in charge from the Indians with whom I live at the Ohio, to make this my first question and not to proceed farther till I am informed of this fact. nor shall I say a word more till you give me your answer. On which the chiefs withdrew to council and then returned and spoke as follows:

" 'Brother: Our four nations are no ways concerned in the

settlement of the French on the Ohio, nor is it with our advice or well-liking. Our fathers, the Mohawks, when they first heard of the French going to the Ohio, sent a message with a large belt to the other nations, wherein they set forth that this proceeding of the French was extremely disagreeable to them and desired that it might be obstructed and that none of the Nations would suffer it, but do all in their power to prevent any settlement of the French in those parts. This message came first to our castles and was readily agreed to, and then we sent it forward to Onondaga where it has remained ever since; for the Onondagas said they approved of what the French were doing, that it was good and would do no hurt to the Indians, and by this means stopped the belt so that it went no further.'

"I then delivered Assaragoa's [Virginia's] belt, inviting the chiefs of the Six Nations to a Council at Winchester, and along with it and tyed to it, the large belt that was given me jointly by the Governments of Maryland and Pennsylvania, desiring them to agree to the Governor of Virginia's proposal, and assuring them, if they would come to Virginia, they would give them the meeting there. These invitations they received very gladly, and said they would lay them before the Great Council that was to meet in a little time at Onondaga, and did not doubt but that they should prevail with the Six Nations to comply with the invitation, and that great numbers would go; but then, as there were several old people, they could not take upon them to say that they could be got to come as far as Winchester, but would rather choose Conodogiunet [near Harrisburg], on Sasquehannah: but I said there were no conveniences there, and that this was but a little way from John Harris' Ferry where a large company might be accommodated, and I believe they will readily come there.

"The next thing I have to communicate to you is a message from these four nations to their brethren, the Shawnees, and their cousins, the Delawares. They desire them to consider themselves as under the protection of the Six Nations, and that they are well affected towards them. They bid them be quiet, easy, and still, nor be disturbed at what is going on, nor meddle at all on any side till they see or hear from them, and that it will not be long before they shall see one another and hold conversation together. In the meantime, as the English were their brethren and their cause was much favored by the Indians, they desired them to have their eyes and ears towards the Six Nations and their brethren, the English, as they had hitherto done, and not to look towards the French."

Closing his address to the Provincial Council, Scarouady gave the following good advice, not only to Pennsylvania but Virginia and Maryland as well:

"You think you prefectly well understand the management of Indian affairs, but I must tell you that it is not so, and that the French are more politick than you. They never employ an Indian on any business but they give him fine clothes, besides other presents, and this makes the Indians their hearty friends and do anything for them. If they invite the Indians to Quebec, they all return with laced clothes on, and boast of the generous treatment of the French Governor.

"Now, Brethren, some of the Six Nations are going to Canada, and some say a great number are coming to Virginia. Let me advise you, as you have time enough, to open those large pieces of goods that your city is full of, and cut them up into fine clothes, and have them ready against the treaty at Virginia, for you may depend upon it those who go to Canada will be finely clothed, and if your Indians, at their return, do not appear finer than they, they will be laughed at and made ashamed.

"Further, Brethren:

"I have brought with me three or four warriors, Mohawks and Oneidas; they are in King George's service; they are valiant men and faithful friends; I have a particular duty for them to do, of great consequence to the general cause. These you will be pleased to take notice of and give them clothes, that they may perform their business cheerfully, and leave your city well pleased."

A few days later Governor Shirley and Governor Delancey came to Philadelphia on their way to Annapolis, Maryland, to meet General Braddock, Governor Dinwiddie, and Governor Sharp. Scarouady was presented to the visiting governors, and made many complaints that the Indians whom he had brought with him from the country of Six Nations to serve in the operations against the French, were "naked", and that he would be ashamed to take them with him to Aughwick in so miserable condition. He pointed out that, if they should be permitted "to go so bare to Aughwick," it would prejudice the Indians there very much against the people of Pennsylvania.

The proposed treaty at Winchester, Virginia, in the spring of 1755 did not take place. General Braddock had his army on the march toward Fort Duquesne early in the spring. On April 23rd, Governor Morris of Pennsylvania, wrote George Croghan at Aughwick advising:

"Let the Indians know that there is no meeting of Governors at Winchester, but that as the General is on his march, all true friends of the English are desired not to proceed to Winchester, but to repair to the army, and distinguish themselves agreeable to their repeated professions."

Scarouady in Braddock's Campaign

Scarouady took an important part in the fateful campaign of General Edward Braddock against Fort Duquesne, in the summer of 1755. We shall not give the details of this campaign, more or less familiar to all students of Pennsylvania history. All of Braddock's forces were finally collected at Will's Creek, (Cumberland, Maryland), on the 19th day of May, at which place he remained until the 10th of June, before setting out for Pennsylvania.

In the latter part of May, George Croghan reached Braddock's camp at Will's Creek with about fifty warriors whom he had brought from Aughwick. Among the chiefs assembled to assist Braddock were: Scarouady, White Thunder, the keeper of the speech-belts, and Silver Heels, so called, probably, from being swift of foot. Braddock had expected not only a large delegation of the Indians from the Ohio Valley, but also a number of Cherokees and Catawbas, whom Governor Dinwiddie of Virginia, had given him reason to expect. He was therefore disappointed in the number of his Indian allies. Scarouady addressed the assembled chiefs and urged them to take up the English cause with vigor.

Washington Irving's "Life of Washington" contains the following interesting paragraphs concerning the assembling of Scarouady and his warriors at Will's Creek:

"Notwithstanding his secret contempt for the Indians, Braddock, agreeably to his instructions, treated them with great ceremony. A grand council was held in his tent, at Fort Cumberland, where all his officers attended. The chiefs, and all the warriors, came painted and decorated for war. They were received with military honors, the guards resting on their firearms. The general made them a speech through his interpreter, expressing the grief of their father, the great King of England, at the death of the Half King, Tanacharison, and made them presents to console them. They in return promised their aid as guides and scouts, and declared eternal enemity to the French, following the declaration with the war song, 'making a terrible noise.'

"The general, to regale and astonish them, ordered all the artillery to be fired, 'the drums and fifes playing and beating the point of war'; the fete ended by their feasting in their own camp on a bullock which the general had given them, following up their repast by dancing the war dance round a fire, to the sound of their uncouth drums and rattles, 'making night hideous', by howls and yellings.

"For a time all went well. The Indians had their separate camp, where they passed half the night singing, dancing, and howling. The British were amused by their strange ceremonies, their savage antics, and savage decorations. The Indians, on the other hand, loitered by day about the English camp, fiercely painted and arrayed, gazing with silent admiration at the parade of the troops, their marchings and evolutions; and delighted with the horse-races, with which the young officers recreated themselves.

"Unluckily the warriors had brought their families with them to Will's Creek, and the women were even fonder than the men of loitering about the British camp. They were not destitute of attractions; for the young squaws resemble the gypsies, having seductive forms, small hands and feet, and soft voices. Among those who visited the camp was one who no doubt passed for an Indian princess. She was the daughter of the sachem, White Thunder, and bore the dazzling name of Bright Lightning. The charms of these wild-wood beauties were soon acknowledged. 'The squaws,' writes Secretary Peters, 'bring in money plenty; the officers are scandalously fond of them.'

"The jealousy of the warriors was aroused; some of them became furious. To prevent discord, the squaws were forbidden to come into the British camp. This did not prevent their being sought elsewhere. It was ultimately found necessary, for the sake of quiet, to send Bright Lightning, with all the other women and children, back to Aughwick. White Thunder, and several of the warriors, accompanied them for their protection.

"As to the Delaware chiefs, they returned to the Ohio, promising the general they would collect their warriors together, and meet him on his march. They never kept their word. 'These people are villians, and always side with the strongest,' says a shrewd journalist of the expedition.

"Either from disgust thus caused, or from being actually dismissed, the warriors began to disappear from the camp. It is said that Colonel Innes, who was to remain in command at Fort Cumberland, advised the dismissal of all but a few to serve as guides; certain it is, before Braddock recommended his march, none remained to accompany him but Scarouady and eight of his warriors."

Scarouady Captured

On the 19th of June, when Braddock's first division, with whom the Indian allies were marching as an advanced party, was near or within the limits of Somerset County, Pennsylvania, and not far from the Maryland line, Scarouady and his son being at a small distance from the line of march, were surrounded and taken by some French and Indians. The son escaped and brought the intelligence to the warriors, who hastened to rescue or avenge the aged chief, but found him tied to a tree. The French had been disposed to kill him; but the Indians with them declared that they would abandon the French should they do so, thus showing some tie of friendship or kindred with Scarouady, who then rejoined Braddock's forces unharmed.

Scarouady's Son Killed

On the 6th of July, three or four soldiers, loitering in the rear of Braddock's forces, were killed and scalped by the Indian allies of the French, and several of the grenadiers set off to take revenge. These came upon a party of the Indians who held up boughs and grounded their arms as the sign of amity. Either Braddock's grenadiers did not perceive this sign, or else misunderstood it. At any rate, they fired upon the Indians and one of them fell, who proved to be the son of Scarouady. The grenadiers brought the body of the young warrior to camp. Braddock then sent for Scarouady and the other Indians, and condoled with them on the lamentable occurrence, making them the customary presents to wipe away their tears. He also caused the young man to be buried with the honors of war, and at his request the officers attended the funeral and fired a volley over the grave. The camp that night, located about two miles southeast of Irwin, Westmoreland County, was given the name of Camp Monacatoocha, in honor of Scarouady. Says Irving:

"These soldier-like tributes of respect to the deceased and sympathy with the survivors, soothed the feelings and gratified the pride of the father, and attached him more firmly to the service. We are glad to record an anecdote so contrary to the general contempt for the Indians with which Braddock stands charged. It speaks well for the real kindness of his heart."

What part Scarouady played in the remaining part of Braddock's march, or in the disastrous battle with the French and
Indians at the site of the present town of Braddock, Allegheny
County, on the afternoon of July 9th, is clouded in obscurity.
The story of Braddock's defeat has often been told and needs
no further reference at this place, except to point out that Braddock was not ambushed, as many historians have stated.   It is
true that Beaujeu, the French commander, had planned an ambush,
and picked a place for it on the evening of July 8th.   In the meantime, Braddock had crossed the Monongahela, and started up the
slopes of the field of encounter, before the French and Indians had
reached the place which they had selected for ambushing him.
The French account of the battle, after giving the plans of
Beaujeu's detachment, says that he had orders to lie in ambush at
a favorable spot which had been reconnoitered the previous evening; that the detachment, before it could reach the place selected
for ambush, found itself in the presence of Braddock's army; that
Beaujeu, finding his plan of ambush had failed, decided on an
attack; and that he made this attack with so much vigor as to
astonish Braddock's forces.   Surely, if the French and Indians
had been lying in ambush, Braddock's scouts would have found
them.
    Beaujeu fell early in the action, and the command of the
French and Indians then devolved upon M. Dumas, who with
great presence of mind rallied the Indians when they had begun to
waver upon the death of Beaujeu.   They were terrified at the
sound of the English cannon.   Dumas then ordered his officers to
lead the Indians to the wings and attack Braddock's forces in the
flank, while he, with the French troops, would maintain a position
in front.   This order was promptly obeyed, resulting in the overwhelming and inglorious defeat of Braddock's army.
    Washington saved the army from total destruction.   Two
horses were shot under him, and four balls passed through his
clothing.   An Indian chief and his braves, after firing at him
many times, concluded that he was protected by the Great Spirit.
In 1770, when Washington, in company with Dr. Craik and
William Crawford, made a journey down the Ohio River to examine lands given the Virginia soldiers, he met this chief, who,
hearing that Washington was coming down the Ohio Valley, made
a long journey to see the man at whom he and his warriors fired
so often in the battle on the Monongahela fifteen years before.
    At the time of the battle Colonel Dunbar, who followed in the

rear of Braddock's army with his division, artillery, and heavy stores, had reached a point in the Allegheny Mountains not far from the place where Jumonville was killed in the first skirmish of the French and Indian War, and near the former Soldiers' Orphans' Home at Jumonville. Here he encamped. Here also the survivors of Braddock's defeat joined him on the 11th. Everything in the camp was in the greatest confusion. Some of his forces had deserted upon hearing the reports of the battle, and "the rest", says Orme, "seemed to have forgot all discipline." Destroying and burying most of his ammunition, Dunbar then began his disgraceful retreat. General Braddock, who had been carried with the retreating troops, died at the Orchard Camp near the Great Meadows on the 13th.

Colonel James Smith's Account of Happenings at Fort Duquesne on the Day of Braddock's Defeat

In May, 1755, the Colony of Pennsylvania began cutting a wagon road from Fort Loudon to join Braddock's road at Turkey Foot. James (later Colonel) Smith, then a young man eighteen years of age, was one of the force of three hundred men engaged in this work. At a point four or five miles above Bedford, he was captured by the Indians and carried to Fort Duquesne, where he was a prisoner at the time of Braddock's defeat. He gives the following description of the happenings at the fort on the day of the battle:

"Shortly after this, on the 9th day of July, 1755, in the morning, I heard a great stir in the fort. As I could then walk with a staff in my hand, I went out of the door, which was just by the wall of the fort, and stood upon the wall and viewed the Indians in a huddle before the gate, where were barrels of powder, bullets, flints, &c., and every one taking what suited; I saw the Indians also march off in rank entire—likewise the French Canadians, and some regulars. After viewing the Indians and French in different positions, I computed them to be about four hundred, and wondered that they attempted to go out against Braddock with so small a party. I was then in high hopes that I would soon see them fly before the British troops, and that General Braddock would take the fort and rescue me.

"I remained anxious to know the advent of this day; and, in the afternoon, I again observed a great noise and commotion in the fort, and though at that time I could not understand French, yet I found that it was the voice of joy and triumph, and feared that they had received what I called bad news.

"I had observed some of the old country soldiers speak Dutch [German]; as I spoke Dutch, I went to one of them, and asked him, what was the news? He told me that a runner had just arrived, who said that Braddock would certainly be defeated; that the Indians and French had surrounded him, and were concealed behind trees and in gullies, and kept a constant fire upon the English, and that they saw the English falling in heaps, and if they did not take the river, which was the only gap, and make their escape, there would not be one man left alive before sundown. Some time after this, I heard a number of scalp halloos, and saw a company of Indians and French coming in. I observed they had a great many bloody scalps, grenadiers' caps, British canteens, bayonets, &c., with them. They brought the news that Braddock was defeated. After that, another company came in, which appeared to be about one hundred, and chiefly Indians, and it seemed to me that almost every one of this company was carrying scalps; after this, came another company with a number of wagon horses, and also a great many scalps. Those that were coming in, and those that had arrived, kept a constant firing of small arms, and also the great guns in the fort, which were accompanied with the most hideous shouts and yells from all quarters; so that it appeared to me as if the infernal regions had broke loose.

"About sundown I beheld a small party coming in with about a dozen prisoners, stripped naked, with their hands tied behind their backs, and part of their bodies blackened,—these prisoners they burned to death on the bank of the Allegheny river opposite the fort. I stood on the fort wall until I beheld them begin to burn one of these men; they had him tied to a stake, and kept touching him with fire-brands, red-hot irons, &c., and he screaming in the most doleful manner,—the Indians in the meantime yelling like infernal spirits. As this scene appeared too shocking for me to behold, I retired to my lodgings both sore and sorry.

"When I came into my lodgings, I saw Russel's Seven Sermons, which they had brought from the field of battle, which a Frenchman made a present of to me. From the best information I could receive, there were only seven Indians and four French killed in this battle, and five hundred British lay dead on the field, besides what were killed in the river on their retreat. The morning after the battle, I saw Braddock's artillery brought into the fort; the same day I also saw several Indians in British officers' dress, with sash, half moons, laced hats, &c., which the British then wore."

Smith was a native of Franklin County, Pennsylvania. He remained in captivity among the Indians at Fort Duquesne, Mahoning, and Muskingum. He was adopted by his captors. During his captivity among the Indians, he was carried from place to place, spending most of his time at Mahoning and Muskingum. In about 1759, he accompanied his Indian relatives to Montreal, where he managed to secrete himself on board a French ship. He was again taken prisoner and confined for four months, but was finally exchanged and reached his home in 1760, to find the sweetheart of his boyhood married, and all his friends and relatives supposing him dead. He became a very prominent man on the Pennsylvania frontier, and during the Revolution, was a captain on the Pennsylvania line, being promoted, in 1778, to the rank of colonel. In 1788, he removed to Kentucky, where he at once took a prominent part in public affairs, serving in the early Kentucky conventions and in the legislature. He died in Washington County, Kentucky, in 1812, leaving behind him as a legacy to historians a very valuable account of his Indian captivity.

In the autumn following Braddock's inglorious defeat, the Delawares and Shawnees began their bloody invasion of Eastern Pennsylvania. However, there were few, if any, of these tribes fighting on the side of the French during the Braddock campaign. The Indians fighting on the side of the French in this campaign were mostly from the region of the Great Lakes. The Delawares and Shawnees were simply waiting to see which side would be victorious.

In closing this sketch of Scarouady's part in Braddock's campaign, it may be interesting to state the route followed by Braddock's army after entering Pennsylvania.

On June 19th the army reached Bear Camp, which was almost directly on the Pennsylvania and Maryland line, about three miles southeast of Addison, Somerset County. By the 23rd of June, it had reached Squaw Fort, situated a short distance southeast of Somerfield, Somerset County. On June 24th, the army passed over the Great Crossing of the Youghiogheny and encamped three or four miles east of the Great Meadows, the site of Fort Necessity, where Washington surrendered the year before. On June 25th, the army marched over the very spot where Braddock was buried a fortnight later, and encamped at the Orchard Camp, where he died on the night of July 13th. Both the Orchard Camp and the place of Braddock's burial are not far from the Summit on the National Pike, in Fayette County. On June 26th, the army encamped at Rock Fort Camp, not far from Washington's Spring, where, as stated in Chapter XIV, Tanacharison was encamped with his warriors when he and Washington set out to make the attack on Jumonville. On June 27th, the army reached Gist's Plantation, the present Mount Braddock, in Fayette County. On June 28th, the army reached Stewart's Crossing on the Youghiogheny, at Connellsville, Fayette County, where it encamped on the western side of this stream. The army remained in camp all day during the 29th, crossing the river on the 30th and encamping on the flats above the river at the mouth of Mount's Creek, Fayette County. On July 1st, the army encamped at what is known as the Camp at the Great Swamp, the location of which was near the old Iron Bridge, southeast of Mount Pleasant, Westmoreland County, and near the headwaters of Jacob's and Mount's creeks. On July 2nd, the army encamped at Jacob's Cabin, making a march of about six miles. This "cabin" belonged to the famous Delaware chief, Captain Jacobs, whose biography is given in Chapter XVIII. On July 3rd, the army passed near Mount Pleasant, and encamped at the headwaters of Sewickley Creek, about five miles southeast of Madison, Westmoreland County. The camp at this place was called Salt Lick Camp. On July 4th, the army encamped at Thicketty-Run (Sewickley Creek), about a mile west of Madison. From this camp two Indians were sent forward as scouts, as was also Christopher Gist. All three returned on the 6th, the Indians bringing the scalp of a French officer they had killed near Fort Duquesne. On July 6th, the army reached Camp Monacatoocha, located as we have seen in this chapter, not far from Irwin, Westmoreland County. Here Braddock abandoned his plan to approach Fort Duquesne by the ridge route or Nemacolin's Trail, in order to avoid the Narrows of Turtle Creek; and turning sharply westward, the army followed the valley of Long Run at or near Stewartsville, and encamped on the night of July 8th, about two miles from the Monongahela and an equal distance from the mouth of the Youghiogheny, near McKeesport, Allegheny County. This was the last camp of the army before the fatal encounter. Here George Washington, who had been left at the Little Crossing, near Grantsville, Maryland, on June 19th, on account of illness, rejoined the army on the morning of July 9th.

Scarouady's Opinion of Braddock

On August 15, 1755, Scarouady and six other chiefs who had fought with the English at Braddock's defeat, appeared before the Provincial Council at Philadelphia, received the thanks of the Council, and were given rewards for their fidelity. At a council held on August 22nd, Scarouady informed Governor Morris why most of the Indians with Braddock's army had left him before he reached the battlefield. Said he: "It is now well known to you how unhappily we have been defeated by the French near Monongahela. We must now let you know that it was the pride and ignorance of that great general [Braddock] that came from England. He is now dead; but he was a bad man when he was alive; he looked upon us as dogs; would never hear anything that was said to him. We often endeavored to advise him, and to tell him of the danger he was in with his soldiers; but he never appeared pleased with us, and that was the reason a great many of our warriors left him, and would not be under his command. We would advise you not to give up the point; though we have in a manner been chastised from above. But let us unite our strength. You are very numerous, and all the English Governors along your seashore can raise men enough. Don't let those that come from over the great sea be concerned any more. They are unfit to fight in the woods. Let us go ourselves, we that came out of this ground. We may be assured to conquer the French. The Delawares and Nanticokes have told me that the French never asked them to go on the late expedition against Braddock; one word of yours will bring the Delawares to join you. I am going to the Nanticokes, and shall pass by the Delawares, and any message you have to send or answer you have to give to them I will deliver to them."

Scarouady insisted that, if the Governor did not avail himself of this opportunity to engage these Indians as allies, they would go over to the French. He endeavored to impress upon the Governor and Provincial Council that it was impossible to remain neutral and live in the woods. Moreover, he claimed to have great influence among, not only the Indians on the Susquehanna, but also the Western Indians and the Wyandots in Ohio.

Governor Morris was at a loss to know how to reply to Scarouady's request that the Delawares be asked to take up arms against the French. The King of England had not yet declared war, and so the Governor did not feel at liberty to employ the Delawares in warlike measures. In his embarrassment he turned to Conrad Weiser, who advised him to give Scarouady a general answer thanking him for his advice and soliciting the lasting friendship of the old chief and his followers, begging them in the meantime to await until the decision of the Great Council of the Six Nations could be learned.

After holding conferences with the Governor on August 18th and 22nd, Scarouady went by way of Harris' Ferry (Harrisburg) to Shamokin (Sunbury) to hunt and await developments, from which place he sent a message to Governor Morris on September 11th, advising him that the Six Nations had sent a black belt of wampum to the Delawares and Shawnees, ordering them "to lay aside their petticoats, and clap nothing on but a breech-clout"; to come with speed to their assistance in the war against the French; and that he [Scarouady] was assembling a force of Indians to go against the French among whom were John, James-Logan, and John-Petty, the three sons of Shikellamy. The Seneca chief, the Belt, was Scarouady's authority as to the message of the Six Nations, but it is not known to what extent the Belt's information was true.

In the meantime, Conrad Weiser had gone to Harris' Ferry, where, early in September, he distributed a wagonload of flour and other supplies among the friendly Indians. Scarouady's wife was one of the recipients of this bounty. She informed Weiser that, shortly after Braddock's defeat, she had aroused her brothers, Moses and Esras, to go to the Ohio and bring her some French scalps in revenge for Braddock's death.

CHAPTER XVI

Scarouady
(Continued)

Penn's Creek Massacre

IT is the autumn of 1755. By this time nearly all the Delawares and Shawnees have gone over to the French. The bitter fruitage of the Walking Purchase of 1737 and the Albany Purchase of 1754 is about to be gathered. The Delawares and Shawnees are about to let loose the dogs of war on defenseless Pennsylvania.

On the 16th of October of this year, occurred the first Indian outrage in Pennsylvania after Braddock's defeat. This was an attack upon the German settlers near the mouth of Penn's Creek, which flows into the Susquehanna at Selinsgrove, in Snyder County. It is known in history as the "Penn's Creek Massacre." It was the first actual break of the treaty of peace which Penn had entered into with Tamanend shortly after his arrival in the Province; and it is significant that the massacre took place almost on the line of the Albany Purchase of 1754, which so angered the Delawares. The Indians killed, scalped and carried away all the men, women and children, amounting to about twenty-five in number, and wounded one man, who fortunately made his escape, and carried the word to George Gabriel's, at the mouth of Penn's Creek. The company who went out to bury the dead found the corpses of thirteen men and elderly women and one child two weeks old. One of the leaders of the Indians on this occasion was Keckenepaulin, a Delaware chief, who lived near Jenner's Cross Roads, in Somerset County. His name has been applied, as stated in Chapter VI, to the Shawnee town at the mouth of the Loyalhanna, possibly due to the fact that he resided there for a time. The prisoners were taken to Kittanning, among them being Barbara Leininger and Marie LeRoy (Mary King).

Only two days after the Penn's Creek Massacre, or on October 18th, another occurred only a short distance to the eastward, at the mouth of Mahanoy Creek, about five miles south of Sunbury, where twenty-five inhabitants were killed or carried into captivity and every building of the settlement was burned. This massacre differed from that of October 16th in that none escaped the massacre of the 18th, whereas one escaped the massacre of the 16th.

Scarouady Warns Settlers

On the 23rd of October, John Harris, Thomas Forster, Captain McKee, and Adam Terence went to Penn's Creek with a force of forty men to bury the dead of the massacre of October 16th. When they arrived, they found that this had already been done. They then decided to return immediately to the settlements at Paxtang (Harrisburg), but were urged by John Shikellamy, son of the vice-gerent of the Six Nations, and the Belt, a Seneca chief, to go to Shamokin (Sunbury), in order to ascertain the feelings of the Indians at that place, which they did. They stayed at Shamokin during the night of the 24th, and heard much in the talk of the Delawares at that place to alarm them. Scarouady was present, and advised the party to follow the eastern side of the river on their return. They left on the morning of the 25th, but fearing an ambush on the east side of the river they marched down the western bank; and when they reached the mouth of Penn's Creek, they were fired upon by a large number of Delawares hidden in the bushes.

John Harris describes this attack as follows:

"We were attacked by about twenty or thirty Indians, received their fire, and about fifteen of our men and myself took to the trees and attacked the villians, killed four of them on the spot, and lost but three men, retreating about half a mile through the woods and crossing the Susquehanna, one of which was shot from off an horse riding behind myself through the river. My horse before was wounded, and falling in the river, I was obliged to quit and swim part of the way. Four or five of our men were drowned crossing the river." Harris further says that the Belt became enraged when he heard of this attack, and gathered up a party of thirty friendly Indians, and pursued the enemy.

The same day that the attack was made on John Harris and his force, or probably on the next day, the Indians crossed the Susquehanna and killed many people from Thomas McKee's to Hunter's Mill. Conrad Weiser gave an account of the massacre in a letter written at eleven o'clock on the night of October 26th from his home near Womelsdorf, to James Reed at Reading.

John Harris further advised in the above letter, which was written from Paxtang on the 28th of October: "The Indians are all assembling themselves at Shamokin to counsel; a large body of them were there four days ago. I cannot learn their intentions, but it seems Andrew Montour and Scarouady are to bring down the news from them. There is not a sufficient number of them to oppose the enemy; and perhaps they will all join the enemy against us. There is no dependence on Indians, and we are in imminent danger.

"I got information from Andrew Montour and others that there is a body of French with fifteen hundred Indians coming upon us,—Picks, Ottawas, Orandox, Delawares. Shawnees, and a number of the Six Nations,—and are not many days march from this Province and Virginia, which are appointed to be attacked. At the same time, some of the Shawnee Indians seem friendly, and others appear like enemies. Montour knew many days ago of the Indians being on their march against us before he informed; for which I said as much to him as I thought prudent, considering the place I was in."

Massacres in Fulton and Perry Counties

On October 31st the Delaware chief, Shingas, began incursions into Fulton County which lasted for several days. Nearly all of the settlers of the Great Cove and Little Cove were murdered or taken captive, and their houses and barns were burned. The same was true of the settlements at McDowell's Mill and Conococheague. Most of the prisoners were taken to Kittanning where many of them were burned to death.

Shortly after the incursion into Fulton County, occurred the murder of the Woolcomber family, Quakers, in Perry County, thus described in "Loudon's Narratives":

"The next I remember of was in 1755, the Woolcombers family on Shearman's Creek; the whole of the inhabitants of the valley was gathered at Robinson's, but Woolcomber would not leave home, he said it was the Irish [Scotch-Irish] who were killing one another; these peaceable people, the Indians would not hurt any person. Being at home and at dinner, the Indians came in, and the Quaker asked them to come and eat dinner; an Indian announced that he did not come to eat, but for scalps; the son, a boy of fourteen or fifteen years of age when he heard the Indian say so, repaired to a back door, and as he went out he looked back, and saw the Indian strike the tomahawk into his father's head. The boy then ran over the creek, which was near the house, and heard the screams of his mother, sisters and brother. The boy came to our Fort [Robinson] and gave us the alarm; about forty went to where the murder was done and buried the dead."

Cause of Indian Alienation Investigated

The news of these various massacres was laid before the Provincial Assembly by Governor Morris; whereupon the Assembly answered with a request to the Governor to inform the House "if he knew of any injury which the Delawares and Shawnees had received to alienate their affections, and whether he knew the part taken by the Six Nations in relation to this incursion."

Robert Strettell, Joseph Turner, and Thomas Cadwalader, were appointed a committee to inspect all "minutes of Council and other books and papers" relating to Pennsylvania's transactions with the Delawares and Shawnees from the beginning of the Colony. The committee made an elaborate report, which was approved and sent to the House on November 22nd, setting forth the findings of the committee that "the conduct of the Proprietaries and this Government has been always uniformly just, fair, and generous towards these Indians."

Scarouady Threatens to Go to the French

While the terrible things related above were happening, Scarouady was exerting his utmost influence on behalf of the English. On November 1st, he was at Harris' Ferry where he delivered a message to John Harris, who forwarded it to the Governor, advising, among other things, that "about twelve days ago the Delawares sent for Andrew Montour to go to Big Island [Lock Haven], on which he [Scarouady] and Montour with three more Indians went up immediately, and found there about six of the Delawares and four Shawnees, who informed them that they had received a hatchet from the French, on purpose to kill what game they could meet with, and to be used against the English if they proved saucy."

On November 8th, Scarouady and Montour appeared before the Provincial Council, and gave additional details of their trip to Big Island. Scarouady said that two Delawares from the Ohio appeared at the meeting at Big Island and spoke as follows: "We, the Delawares of Ohio, do proclaim war against the English. We have been their friends many years, but now have taken up the hatchet against them, and will never make it up with them whilst there is an English man alive.

"When Washington was defeated, we, the Delawares, were blamed as the cause of it. We will now kill. We will not be blamed without a cause. We make up three parties of Delawares. One party will go against Carlisle; one down the Susquehanna; and . . . . . another party will go against Tulpehocken to Conrad Weiser. And we shall be followed by a thousand French and Indians, Ottawas, Twightwees, Shawnees, and Delawares."

It will be noted that the Delawares gave their being blamed for Washington's defeat at the Great Meadows, in the summer of 1754, as the cause of their having taken up arms against Pennsylvania. Later they told the Shawnee chief, Paxinosa, of Wyoming, that the cause of their hostility was the Walking Purchase of 1737 and the Albany Purchase of 1754; and the great Delaware chief, Teedyuscung, stoutly insisted that it was these wrongs upon the Delawares that caused these friends of William Penn to take up arms against the Colony he founded.

On the afternoon of the same day, November 8th, Scarouady appeared before the Governor, his Council, and the Provincial Assembly, and told them of the journey which he had recently made in the interest of the English, up the North Branch of the Susquehanna "as far as the Nanticokes live." He stated that he had told the Nanticokes and other Indians on the Susquehanna that the defeat of General Braddock had brought about a great turn of affairs; that it was a great blow, but that the English had strength enough to recover from it. He further said that there were three hundred friendly Indians on the Susquehanna. (Delawares and Nanticokes) "who were all hearty in the English interest." For these he desired the Colony's assistance with arms and ammunition. He insisted that they should be given the hatchet, and that a fort should be built for the protection of their old men, women, and children. They had told him, he said, that whichever party, the French or English, would seek their assistance first, would be first assisted; and that he "should go to Philadelphia and apply immediately to the Government and obtain explicit answer from them whether they would fight or no." These Indians "waited with impatience to know the success of his application."

Then the old chief threw down his belts of wampum upon the table before the members of the Assembly and said: "I must deal plainly with you, and tell you if you will not fight with us, we will go somewhere else. We never can nor ever will put up the affront. If we cannot be safe where we are, we will go somewhere else for protection and take care of ourselves. We have no more to say, but will first receive your answer to this, and as the times are too dangerous to admit of our staying long here, we therefore entreat you will use all the dispatch possible that we may not be detained." It is possible that Scarouady meant that he and his followers would go to one of the other colonies, but he was understood as meaning that, unless the Pennsylvania Authorities acted promptly, he and his followers would go over to the French.

Governor Morris then said to the Provincial Assembly: "You have heard what the Indians have said. Without your aid, I can not make a proper answer to what they now propose and expect of us." The Assembly replied that, as Captain General, the Governor had full authority to raise men, and that "the Bill now in his hands granting Sixty Thousand Pounds will enable him to pay the expenses." This was a bill just passed by the Assembly, granting this sum for the defense of the Colony, to be raised by a tax on estates. The Governor opposed the bill on the ground that the Proprietary estates should not be taxed. He then explained to Scarouady how his controversy with the Assembly stood, and that he did not know what to do. Scarouady was amazed and said that Pennsylvania's failure to comply with his (Scarouady's) request in behalf of his three hundred friendly Indians would mean their going over to the French. However, he still offered his own services and counseled the Governor not to be cast down, but to keep cool.

After long consultations between Scarouady and Conrad Weiser, it was determined that Scarouady could render an important service to the Colony by visiting the Six Nations and Sir William Johnson, and, after gaining what intelligence he could on his way to New York, as to the actions of the Indians on the Susquehanna, by laying before the Great Confederation such intelligence as well as the recent conduct of the Delawares.

Scarouady Sent on Mission to Six Nations

Scarouady's decided stand had a good effect on the Governor and Council. On November 14th, the old chief and Andrew Montour were sent by the Governor on a mission to the Six Nations. They were instructed to convey the condolence of Pennsylvania to the Six Nations on the death of several of their warriors who had joined General Shirley and General Johnson and had fallen in battle with the French, and to advise the Six Nations how the Delawares had, in a most cruel manner, fallen upon and murdered so many of the inhabitants of Pennsylvania. In a word, Scarouady was to give the Six Nations a complete account of the terrible invasion of the Delawares and Shawnees and to ascertain whether or not this invasion was made with the knowledge, consent, or order of the Six Nations, and whether the Six Nations would chastise the Delawares.

Massacres in Berks County

Berks County, the home of Conrad Weiser, suffered terribly during this dreadful autumn. On November 14th, as six settlers were on their way to Dietrick Six's plantation, near what is now the village of Millersburg, they were fired upon by a party of Indians. Hurrying toward a watch-house, about half a mile distant, they were ambushed before reaching the same, and three of them killed and scalped. A settler named Ury, however, succeeded in shootng one of the Indians throught the heart, and his body was dragged off by the other savages. The Indians then divided into two parties. The one party, lying in ambush near the watch-house, waylaid some settlers who were fleeing toward that place, and killed three of them.

The next night some savages crept up to the home of Thomas Bower, on Swatara Creek, and pushing their guns through a window of the house, killed a cobbler who was repairing a shoe. They set fire to the house before being driven off. The Bower family, having sought refuge through the night at the home of a neighbor, named Daniel Snyder, and returning to their home in the morning, saw four savages running away and having with them the scalps of three children, two of whom were still alive. They also found the dead body of a woman with a two week's old child under her body, but unharmed.

Scarouady in Danger From Settlers

Conrad Weiser returned home from Philadelphia on November 17th, accompanied by Scarouady and Andrew Montour on their way to the Six Nations. He found the Berks County settlers in a state of great excitement, on account of the Indian outrages. The settlers of Berks County knew that he had frequently accompanied delegations of friendly Indians to Philadelphia. To many of the settlers whose homes and barns were destroyed and whose dear ones were murdered or carried into captivity, all Indians looked alike. Consequently, many of the settlers were now suspicious of Weiser, and believed that he was protecting Indians who did not deserve it. Consequently, also, he had now great difficulty in conducting Scarouady and Montour towards the Susquehanna. Said he, in a letter to Governor Morris on November 19th: "I made all the haste with the Indians [Scarouady and Montour] I could, and gave them a letter to Thomas McKee, to furnish them with necessaries for their journey. Scarouady had no creature to ride on. I gave him one. Before I could get done with the Indians, three or four men came from Benjamin Spikers to warn the Indians not to go that way for the people were so enraged against all the Indians and would kill them without distinction. I went with them. So did the gentlemen before named. When we came near Benjamin Spikers, I saw about 400 or 500 men, and there was loud noise. I rode before, and in riding along the road and armed men on both sides of the road, I heard some say: 'Why must we be killed by the Indians, and not kill them? Why are our hands so tied?' I got the Indians into the house with much ado, where I treated them with a small dram, and so parted in love and friendship. Captain Diefenback undertook to conduct them, with five of our men, to the Susquehanna."

Weiser in Danger

Continuing the above letter, Weiser says:
"After this, a sort of a counsel of war was held by the officers present, the before named, and other Freeholders.

"It was agreed that 150 men should be raised immediately to serve as out scouts, and as Guards at Certain Places under the Kittitany Hills for 40 days. That those so raised to have 2 Shillings a Day & 2 Pounds of Bread, 2 Pounds of Beaff and a jill of rum, and Powder and lead. Arms they must find themselves.

"This Scheme was signed by a good many Freeholders, and read to the people. They cried out that so much for an Indian scalp would they have, be they friends or enemies, from the Governor. I told them I had no such power from the Governor nor Assembly. They began some to curse the Governor; some the Assembly; called me a traitor of the country, who held with the Indians, and must have known this murder beforehand. I sat in the house by a lowe window; some of my friends came to pull me away from it, telling me some of the people threatened to shoot me.

"I offered to go out to the people and either pasefy them or make the King's Proclamation. But those in the house with me would not let me go out. The cry was, The Land was betrayed and sold. The common people from Lancaster [now Lebanon County] were the worst. The wages they said was a Trifle and some Body pocketed the Rest, and they would resent it. Some Body had put it in their head that I had it in my power to give them as much as I pleased. I was in danger of being shot to death.

"In the meantime, a great smoke arose under Tulpenhacon Mountain, with the news following that the Indians had committed a murder on Mill Creek (a false alarm) and set fire to a barn; most of the people ran, and those that had horses rode off without any order or regulation. I then took my horse and went home, where I intend to stay and defend my own house as long as I can. The people of Tulpenhacon all fled; till about 6 or 7 miles from me some few remains. Another such attack will lay all the country waste on the west side of Schuylkill."

Moravians Massacred

Scarouady was hardly started on his journey to the Six Nations when the tomahawk and scalping knife of the Delawares became stained anew with the blood of the settlers of Eastern Pennsylania. On November 24th, the Moravian missionaries at Gnadenhuetten, Carbon County, were cruelly murdered by a band of twelve warriors of the Munsee Clan of Delawares, led by Jachebus, chief of the Assinnissink, a Munsee town in Steuben County, New York. The bodies of the dead were placed in a grave. A monument marks the spot where the dust of these victims of savage cruelty reposes, a short distance from Lehighton, and bears the following inscription:

"To the memory of Gottlieb and Joanna Anders, with their child, Christiana; Martin and Susanna Nitschnann; Anna Catherine Senseman; John Gattermeyer; George Fabricius, clerk; George Schweigert; John Frederick Lesly; and Martin Presser; who lived here at Gnadenhuetten unto the Lord, and lost their lives in a surprise from Indian warriors, November 24, 1755. Precious in the sight of the Lord is the death of his saints.—Psalm 96 CXVI 15".

Attack on Hoeth and Broadhead Families

On December 10th and 11th, occurred the attack on the Hoeth and Broadhead families. The Hoeth family lived on Poco-Poco Creek, afterwards known as Hoeth's Creek, and now generally

known as Big Creek, a tributary of the Lehigh above Weissport.
This family was almost exterminated.

After committing the outrages on the Hoeths, the same
band proceeded to the Broadheads, who lived near the mouth of
Broadhead Creek, not far from the site of Stroudsburg, Monroe
County. In the attack on the Broadhead family, they met with
determined resistance, and were finally obliged to retire. All the
members of the Broadhead family were noted for their bravery.
Among the sons was the famous Colonel, later General Broadhead,
of the Revolutionary War.

Also on New Year's Day, 1756, a guard of forty militia, who
had been sent to erect a fort near the Moravian town of Gnadenhuetten, above mentioned, were attacked by hostile Delawares, and
the greater number of them killed. The Indians on the same day
laid waste the country between Gnadenhuetten and Nazareth,
Northampton County, killing many settlers and burning farm
houses and barns.

Assembly and Governor Dispute While Settlers Die

Indeed, from the Penn's Creek massacre until well into the
year of 1756, terror reigned throughout the Pennsylvania settlements. It is a sad fact that while the Indians were thus burning
and scalping on the frontier, the Assembly and Governor, instead
of putting the Colony in a state of defense, spent their time in disputes as to whether or not the Proprietary estates should be taxed
to raise money to defend the Province,—a disgusting chapter in the
history of Pennsylvania. The smoke of burning farm houses
darkened the heavens; the soil of the forest farms of the German
and Scotch-Irish settlers was drenched with their blood; the
tomahawk of the savage dashed out the brains of the aged and the
infant; hundreds were carried into captivity, many of whom were
tortured to death by fire at Kittanning and other Indian towns in
the valleys of the Allegheny and the Ohio to which they were
taken—all of these dreadful things were taking place as the disputes between the Governor and the Assembly continued.

Says Egle, in his "History of Pennsylvania": "The cold in-
difference of the Assembly at such a crisis awoke the deepest indignation throughout the Province. Public meetings were held in
various parts of Lancaster and in the frontier counties, at which it
was resolved that they would repair to Philadelphia and compel
the Provincial authorities to pass proper laws to defend the country
and oppose the enemy. In addition, the dead bodies of some of
the murdered and mangled were sent to that city and hauled about

the streets, with placards announcing that these were the victims of the Quaker policy of non-resistance. A large and threatening mob surrounded the house of Assembly, placed the dead bodies in the doorway, and demanded immediate relief for the people of the frontiers. Such indeed were the desperate measures resorted to for self defense."

Finally, on November 26th, the very day that the news reached Philadelphia of the slaughter of the Moravian missionaries at Gnadenhuetten, "An Act For Granting 60,000 pounds to the King's Use" was passed, after the Proprietaries had made a grant of 5,000 pounds in lieu of the tax on the Proprietary estates.

Benjamin Franklin Begins Erection of Chain of Forts

Pennsylvania then began erecting a chain of forts and block-houses to guard the frontier. These forts extended along the Kittatinny or Blue Mountains from the Delaware River to the Maryland line, and the cost of erection was eighty-five thousand pounds. They guarded the important mountain passes, were garrisoned by from twenty-five to seventy-five men in pay of the Province, and stood almost equi-distant, so as to be a haven of refuge for the settlers when they fled from their farms to escape the tomahawk and scalping knife. The Moravians at Bethlehem cheerfully fortified their town and took up arms in self-defense. Benjamin Franklin and James Hamilton were directed to go to the Forks of the Delaware and raise troops in order to carry the plan into execution. On December 29th, 1755, they arrived at Easton, and appointed William Parsons major of the troops to be raised in the county of Northampton. In the meantime, Captain Hays had been ordered to New Gnadenhuetten, the scene of the massacre of the Moravian missionaries on November 24th, with his militia from the Irish settlement in the county. The attack on these militia on New Year's Day, 1756, has been narrated. Finally, the Assembly requested Franklin's appearance, and, responding to this call, he turned his command over to Colonel William Clapham.

This chain of forts began with Fort Dupui, erected on the property of the Hugenot settler, Samuel Dupui, in the present town of Shawnee, on the Delaware River, in Monroe County. Next came Fort Hamilton, on the site of the present town of Stroudsburg, in Monroe County. Fort Penn was also erected in the eastern part of this town. These three forts were in the heart of the territory of the Munsee Clan of Delawares. Next was Fort

Norris, about a mile southeast of Kresgeville, Monroe County; and fifteen miles west was Fort Allen where Weissport, Carbon County now stands. Then came Fort Franklin in Albany Township, Berks County; and nineteen miles west was, Fort Lebanon, also known at Fort William, not far from the present town of Auburn, in Schuylkill County. Then came Fort Henry at Dietrick Six's, near Millersburg, Berks County. This post is sometimes called "Busse's Fort" from its commanding officer, also the "Fort at Dietrick Six's". Fort Lebanon and Fort Henry were twenty-two miles apart, and midway between them was the small post, Fort Northkill. Next came Fort Swatara, located in the vicinity of Swatara Gap, or Tolihaio Gap; then Fort Hunter, on the east bank of the Susquehanna River at the mouth of Fishing Creek, six miles north of Harrisburg; then Fort Halifax at the mouth of Armstrong Creek, half a mile above the present town of Halifax, on the east bank of the Susquehanna, in Dauphin County. While there were numerous block-houses, these posts were the principal forts east of the Susquehanna.

Crossing the Susquehanna, we find Fort Patterson in the Tuscarora Valley at Mexico, Juniata County; Fort Granville, near Lewistown, Mifflin County; Fort Shirley, at Shirleysburg, Huntingdon County; Fort Lyttleton at Sugar Cabins, in the northeastern part of Fulton County; Fort McDowell, where McDowell's Mill, Franklin County, now stands; Fort Loudoun, about a mile distant from the town of Loudoun, Franklin County; and Fort Lowther, at Carlisle, Cumberland County. Like the forts east of the Susquehanna, these forts were supplemented with block-houses in the vicinity. The erection of the entire chain of forts was completed in 1756.

Regina Hartman, the German Captive

As an example of the tragedies which the invasion of the Delawares brought upon the settlers of Eastern Pennsylvania, at the time of which we are writing, we deem it not inappropriate to insert, at this place, the account of the capture of Regina Hartman. The story of her capture, captivity among the Indians, and release has been told in many works dealing with the early history of Pennsylvania; and we quote as it is related in the "Frontier Forts of Pennsylvania":

"The Rev. Henry Melchior Muhlenberg [a son-in-law of Conrad Weiser] relates in the 'Hallische Nachrichten,' p. 1029, a touching incident, which has been frequently told, but is so 'apropos' to this record that it should not be omitted. It was of the widow of John Hartman who called at his house in February, 1765, who had been a member of one of Rev. Kurtz's [a Lutheran pastor in Berks County] congregations. She and her husband had emigrated to this country from Reutlingen, Wurtemberg, and settled on the frontiers of Lebanon County. The Indians fell upon them in October, 1755, killed her husband, one of the sons, and carried off two small daughters into captivity, whilst she and the other son were absent. On her return she found the home in ashes, and her family either dead or lost to her, whereupon she fled to the interior settlements at Tulpehocken and remained there.

"The sequel to this occurrence is exceedingly interesting. The two girls were taken away. It was never known what became of Barbara, the elder, but Regina, with another little girl two years old, were given to an old Indian woman, who treated them very harshly. In the absence of her son, who supplied them with food, she drove the children into the woods to gather herbs and roots to eat, and, when they failed to get enough, beat them cruelly. So they lived until Regina was about nineteen years old and the other girl eleven. Her mother was a good Christian woman, and had taught her daughters their prayers, together with many texts from the Scriptures, and their beautiful German hymns, much of which clung to her memory during all these years of captivity.

"At last, in the providence of God, Colonel Bouquet brought the Indians under subjection in 1764, [at the end of Pontiac's War] and obliged them to give up their captives   More than four hundred of these unfortunate beings were gathered together at Carlisle; amongst them the two girls, and notices were sent all over the country for those who had lost friends and relatives, of that fact.   Parents and husbands came, in some instances, hundreds of miles, in the hope of recovering those they had lost, the widow being one of the number. There were many joyful scenes, but more sad ones. So many changes had taken place, that, in many instances, recognition seemed impossible. This was the case with the widow. She went up and down the long line, but, in the young women who stood before her, dressed in Indian costume, she failed to recognize the little girls she had lost. As she stood, gazing and weeping, Colonel Bouquet compassionately suggested that she do something which might recall the past to her children. She could think of nothing but a hymn which was formerly a favorite with the little ones:

'Allein, und doch nicht ganz allein,
Bin ich in meiner Einsamkeit.'

[The English translation of the first stanza of this hymn is as
follows:
'Alone, yet not alone am I,
Though in this solitude so drear;
I feel my Saviour always nigh,
He comes the very hour to cheer;
I am with Him, and He with me,
E'en here alone I cannot be.']

"She commenced singing, in German, but had barely completed two lines, when poor Regina rushed from the crowd, began to
sing also and threw her arms around her mother. They both wept
for joy and the Colonel gave the daughter up to her mother. But
the other girl had no parents, they having probably been murdered.
She clung to Regina and begged to be taken home with her. Poor
as was the widow she could not resist the appeal and the three departed together."

The Murder of Frederick Reichelsdorfer's Daughters

"The Frontier Forts of Pennsylvania" contains, also, the following account of one of the saddest tragedies of the autumn of
1755:
"The Rev. Henry Melchior Muhlenberg, D. D., in the Hallische Nachrichten, tells the soul-stirring story of Frederick Reich-
elsdorfer, whose two grown daughters had attended a course of instruction, under him, in the Catechism, and been solemnly admitted by confirmation to the communion of the Ev. Lutheran
Church, in New Hanover, Montgomery County.
"This man afterwards went with his family some distance into
the interior, to a tract of land which he had purchased in Albany
township, Berks County (see under Fort Everett also). When
the war with the Indians broke out, he removed his family to his
former residence, and occasionally returned to his farm, to attend
to his grain and cattle. On one occasion he went, accompanied by
his two daughters, to spend a few days there, and bring away some
wheat. On Friday evening, after the wagon had been loaded, and
everything was ready for their return on the morrow, his daughters
complained that they felt anxious and dejected, and were impressed
with the idea that they were soon to die. They requested their
father to unite with them in singing the familiar German funeral
hymn,

'Wer weiss wie nahe meine Ende?'
[Who knows how near my end may be?]

after which they commended themselves to God in prayer, and retired to rest.

"The light of the succeeding morn beamed upon them, and all
was yet well. Whilst the daughters were attending to the dairy,
cheered with the joyful hope of soon greeting their friends, and being out of danger, the father went to the field for the horses, to prepare for their departure home. As he was passing through the
field, he suddenly saw two Indians, armed with rifles, tomahawks
and scalping knives, making towards him at full speed. The sight
so terrified him that he lost all self command, and stood motionless
and silent. When they were about twenty yards from him, he
suddenly, and with all his strength, exclaimed 'Lord Jesus, living
and dying, I am thine!' Scarcely had the Indians heard the words
'Lord Jesus' (which they probably knew as the white man's name
of the Great Spirit), when they stopped short, and uttered a
hideous yell.

"The man ran with almost supernatural strength into the
dense forest, and by taking a serpentine course, the Indians lost
sight of him, and relinquished the pursuit. He hastened to an adjoining farm, where two German families resided, for assistance,
but on approaching near it, he heard the dying groans of the
families, who were falling beneath the murderous tomahawks of
some other Indians.

"Having providentially not been observed by them, he hastened back to learn the fate of his daughters. But, alas! on arriving within sight, he found his home and barn enveloped with
flames. Finding that the Indians had possession here too, he hastened to another adjoining farm for help. Returning, armed with
several men, he found the house reduced to ashes and the Indians
gone. His eldest daughter had been almost entirely burnt up, a
few remains only of her body being found. And, awful to relate,
the younger daughter though the scalp had been cut from her head,
and her body horribly mangled from head to foot with the tomahawk, was yet living. 'The poor worm,' says Muhlenberg, 'was
able to state all the circumstances of the dreadful scene.' After
having done so she requested her father to stoop down to her that
she might give him a parting kiss, and then go to her dear Saviour;
and after she had impressed her dying lips upon his cheek, she
yielded her spirit into the hands of that Redeemer, who, though

His judgments are often unsearchable, and His ways past finding out, has nevertheless said, 'I am the resurrection and the life; if any man believe in me, though he die yet shall he live.' "

Murder of the Kobel Family

On November 24th, 1755, Conrad Weiser wrote Governor Morris concerning the murder of the Kobel family, as follows:

"I cannot forbear to acquaint your Honor of a certain Circumstance of the late unhappy Affair: One .... Kobel, with his wife and eight children, the eldest about fourteen Years and the youngest fourteen Days, was flying before the Enemy, he carrying one, and his wife and a Boy another of the Children, when they were fired upon by two Indians very nigh, but hit only the Man upon his Breast, though not Dangerously. They, the Indians, then came with their Tomahawks, knocked the woman down, but not dead. They intended to kill the Man, but his Gun (though out of order so that he could not fire) kept them off. The Woman recovered so farr, and seated herself upon a Stump, with her Babe in her Arms, and gave it Suck, and the Indians driving the children together, and spoke to them in High Dutch, 'Be still; we won't hurt you.' Then they struck a Hatchet into the woman's Head, and she fell upon her Face with her Babe under her, and the Indian trod on her neck and tore off the scalp. The children then run; four of them were scalped, among which was a Girl of Eleven Years of Age, who related the whole Story; of the Scalped, two are alive and like to do well. The Rest of the Children ran into the Bushes and the Indians after them, but our People coming near to them, and hallowed and made noise; the Indians Ran, and the Rest of the Children were saved. They ran within a Yard by a Woman that lay behind an Old Log, with two Children; there was about Seven or Eight of the Enemy."

Scarouady Returns From Mission to the Six Nations

As stated earlier in this chapter, Scarouady and Andrew Montour had been sent by the Governor of Pennsylvania as messengers to the Six Nations, late in 1755. They returned to Philadelphia from this mission on March 21, 1756, and on the 27th of that month, they appeared before the Provincial Council, and made a report of their journey. They had gone by way of Tulpehocken and Thomas McKee's trading post to Shamokin; and from there through Laugpaughpitton's Town and Nescopeck to Wyoming

(Plymouth, Luzerne County). At Wyoming they found a large number of Delawares, some Shawnees, Mohicans, and members of the Six Nations. They next came to Asserughney, a Delaware Town, twelve miles above Wyoming, on the north side of the Lackawanna River at its mouth. Their next stop was at Chink-annig (Tunkhannock), twenty miles farther up the Susquehanna, where they found the great Delaware chief, Teeduscung, with some Delawares and Nanticokes. Their next stop was at Diahogo (Tioga), a town composed of Mohicans and Delawares of the Munsee Clan, located where Athens, Bradford County, now stands, at which place they found ninety men. About twenty-five miles beyond, they came to the deserted town of Owegy. Leaving this place they arrived at Chugnut, about twenty miles distant. About five miles above Chugnut, was the town of Otseningo, where they found thirty cabins and about sixty warriors of the Nanticokes, Conoys, and Onondagas. Fourteen miles beyond this place they came to Oneoquagque, where they sent a message to the Governor of Pennsylvania, written by Rev. Gideon Hawley. From there they proceeded to Teyonnoderre and Teyoneandakt, and next to Caniyeke, the Lower Mohawk Town, located about two miles from Fort Johnson, and about forty miles from Albany, New York. At Fort Johnson, they held a conference in February, 1756, with Sir William Johnson and the chiefs of the Six Nations, who expressed great resentment over the action of the hostile Delawares.

This was a very dangerous journey for Scarouady and Montour. While they were at Wyoming, their lives were threatened by a party of eighty Delaware warriors, who came soon after their arrival. While Scarouady was consulting with the oldest chief in the evening, the rest cried out of doors: "Let us kill the rogue; we will hear of no mediator, much less of a master; hold your tongue, and be gone, or you shall live no longer. We will do what we please." Said Scarouady: "All the way from Wyoming to Diahogo, a day never passed without meeting some warriors, six, eight, or ten in a party; and twenty under command of Cut Finger Pete, going after the eighty warriors which we saw at Wyoming. . . . . . . All the way we met parties of Delawares going to join the eighty warriors there."

Scarouady reported that, at Wyoming he and Montour found John Shikellamy, son of the great vice-gerent of the Six Nations, with the hostile Delawares. They took him aside, and upbraided him severely for his ingratitude to Pennsylvania, "which had ever

been extremely kind to his father when alive." Then John
Shikellamy explained that he was with the enemies of the Colony,
because he could not help it, as they had threatend to kill him if
he did not join them.

Scarouady again appeared before the Provincial Council on
April 3rd and gave additional details of his journey. Said he:
"You desired us in your instructions to inquire the particular reasons assigned by the Delawares and Shawnees for their acting in
the manner they do against this Province. I have done it and all
I could get from the Indians is that they heard them say their
brethren, the English, had accused them very falsely of joining
with the French after Colonel Washington's defeat, and if they
would charge them when they were innocent, they could do no
more if they were guilty; this turned them against their brethren
and now indeed the English have good reason for any charge they
may make against them, for they are heartily their enemies."

As to the attitude of the Six Nations, Scarouady reported:
"The Six Nations in their reply expressed great resentment of the
Delawares; they threatened to shake them by the head, saying they
were drunk and out of their senses and would not consider the
consequences of their ill behavior and assured them that, if they
did not perform what they had promised they should be severely
chastized." At this meeting of the Provincial Council and at
others held early in April, Scarouady expressed himself as favoring
a declaration of war by Pennsylvania against the Delawares, and
ventured the opinion that the Six Nations would approve of such
action.

Pennsylvania Declares War Against the Delawares

As a result of the foregoing conferences with Scarouady, Governor Morris and the Provincial Council on April 14, 1756, made a
formal declaration of war against the Delawares, and offered rewards for Indians' scalps, as follows:

"For every male Indian enemy above twelve years old, who
shall be taken prisoner and delivered at any fort, garrisoned by the
troops in pay of this Province, or at any of the county towns to
the keepers of the common jail there, the sum of 150 Spanish dollars or pieces of eight; for the scalp of every male enemy above
the age of twelve years, produced to evidence of their being killed
the sum of 130 pieces of eight; for every female Indian taken
prisoner and brought in as aforesaid, and for every male Indian
prisoner under the age of twelve years, taken and brought in as

aforesaid, 130 pieces of eight; for the scalp of every Indian woman, produced as evidence of their being killed, the sum of fifty pieces of eight, and for every English subject that has been killed and carried from this Province into captivity that shall be recovered and brought in and delivered at the City of Philadelphia, to the Governor of this Province, the sum of 130 pieces of eight, but nothing for their scalps; and that there shall be paid to every officer or soldier as are or shall be in the pay of the Province who shall redeem and deliver any English subject carried into captivity as aforesaid, or shall take, bring in and produce any enemy prisoner, or scalp as aforesaid, one-half of the said several and respective premiums and bounties."

The Scalp Act had the effect of causing hundreds of brave warriors of the Delawares and Shawnees who were up to that time undecided, to take up arms against the Colony. "A mighty shout arose which shook the very mountains, and all the Delawares and Shawnees, except a few old sachems, danced the war dance."

James Logan, a prominent Quaker member of the Provincial Council, and former Secretary of the same, opposed the declaration of war, though he was a strict advocate of defensive warfare. Conrad Weiser was in favor of the declaration of war, but strongly opposed to offering rewards for scalps. He said that the Colony might offer rewards for Indian prisoners, but that a bounty for scalps would certainly tend to aggravate existing affairs. He argued that anyone could bring in these scalps, and there was no means of distinguishing the scalps of friendly Indians. "Indeed," says Walton, "this was the core of the whole difficulty. Scalps of friendly Indians were taken, and the peace negotiations with the Eastern Indians frustrated."

Scarouady Favors Peace

The declaration of war against the Delawares was very distasteful to the Quaker members of the Provincial Assembly. They believed that the entire Indian policy of the Colony had been reversed by such declaration and that the Delawares and Shawnees would not have taken up arms against the Colony without a grievance. Furthermore, they believed that adequate efforts had not been made towards reconciliation before war was declared. Therefore, when some friendly Indians were in Philadelphia a few days after the declaration of war, Israel Pemberton waited upon the Governor on behalf of numerous members of the Society of

Friends, and asked the Governor's permission to invite the Indians
to dine with a committee of Quakers, to the end that the Indian
grievances might be ascertained and additional efforts made to
bring about peace. The Quakers offered to bear all expenses, to
conduct the negotiations as a private matter, and do nothing without the approval of the Governor. The Governor granted permission on condition that Conrad Weiser should be informed of
everything said to the Indians by the Quakers and everything said
to the Quakers by the Indians. Pemberton then set forth at a dinner the well known peace principles of the Society of Friends.
The Indians, especially Scarouady, their speaker, were greatly
pleased. The old chief declared that the Six Nations would join
eagerly in a project for establishing peace.

Following the dinner, Weiser and Pemberton had a long conference with Scarouady, in which it was decided to send messengers to the Six Nations "setting forth their conferences with the
Quakers, their religious principles and their characters, and the
influence they had as well with the Government as a people, their
desiring to bring about a peace, and their offer to become mediators between them and the Government; that he [Scarouady] and
the other Six Nations had heard what they said with pleasure and
desired that they would hearken to it, cease their hostilities and
accept this mediation, and lest they (the Delawares and Shawnees)
might be afraid that they had done too much mischief and taken
too many lives, even more than could be possibly forgiven, he
assured them that these peaceable people would, notwithstanding
this, obtain their pardon if they would immitaely desist, send
the English prisoners to some place, and deliver them up to the
Governor, and request peace of him and forgiveness for what was
passed."

Pemberton and Weiser laid the report of the conference before
the Governor, who called the Provincial Council together and submitted four questions:

1st. Whether it were proper to permit the Society of Friends
to act as mediators. 2nd. Whether or not a peace should be proposed on conditions of forgiveness and return of prisoners taken.
3rd. Whether or not such a message would obstruct the establishing of a fort which the Colony contemplated building at Shamokin.
4th. Whether or not it would be better to invite such friendly
Indians as Paxinosa, chief of the Shawnees of Wyoming, to come
near the settlements and be out of danger.

The Provincial Council being opposed to the Government's

assuming any responsibility, advised the Governor to leave the matter entirely with the Quakers. Scarouady, Captain New Castle, and several other friendly Indians agreed to carry the peace message among the hostile Delawares and the Six Nations. They were instructed to ask the Six Nations to solicit the influence of Sir William Johnson, of New York, in persuading the Colony of Pennsylvania to recall the declaration of war and the act providing a bounty for scalps.

Weiser advised the Governor that the declaration of war should stand, believing that it would influence the Delawares to ask for peace. He believed further that the Six Nations would agree to this, and called the attention of both the Governor and the Provincial Council to the fact that Scarouady as the representative of the Six Nations was not offended at the "Scalp Act."

The Delaware chiefs, Captain New Castle, Jonathan, and Andrew Montour were very eager for peace and offered to risk their lives in carrying the overtures of the Governor. However, while the Delawares had virtually thrown off the yoke of Iroquois bondage, yet the hatred of these three Delaware chiefs for their former masters was so strong that they positively declared that they would do nothing for Scarouady and the Six Nations. The Governor then decided to have no professional connection with the matter, but the day following his decision, he received a letter from Sir William Johnson, of New York, criticizing Pennsylvania's declaration of war and the Scalp Bounty Act. Governor Morris then changed his mind once more, and decided that he would send the peace message in his own name. The messengers then went forth among the Delawares and the Shawnees of the Susquehanna.

Scarouady also went to the territory of the Six Nations, carrying the Governor's peace message to Sir William Johnson, attending many conferences and making speeches in an effort to bring about peace. One of these was delivered at a meeting at Fort Johnson, New York, on May 10, 1756, between Sir William Johnson and a number of Oneida chiefs. Another was delivered on July 1, 1756, at the conference of the Six Nations with Sir William Johnson in behalf of the Shawnees and Delawares. Another was made at the German Flats, New York, on August 26, 1756, when Sir William Johnson spoke to the two parties of Indians, one under the command of Scarouady and Montour and another under command of Thomas, an Oghquaga chief. On this occasion Johnson asked the two bands of Indians to go to the Oneida Carrying Place to meet the army of General Webb. He

said that he would send Croghan with them to this place. Scarouady and Montour promised to accompany Croghan, but delayed
their departure from day to day. In the meantime General Webb
having destroyd his forts and abandoned the Carrying Place, returned to the German Flats. The proposed expedition under
Croghan therefore did not start.

Final Conferences of Scarouady

While Scarouady was in New York exerting all the powers of
his eloquence in behalf of peace, the French and Indian War went
on in Pennsylvania. A line of forts with intervening block houses
was erected along the base of the Blue Mountains from Easton to
the Maryland line; but the savages broke through this line of
fortifications and continued their work of blood and death on the
frontier. On April 4, 1756, they burned McCord's Fort on the
Conococheague, in Franklin County, and the entire garrison of
twenty-seven was killed or captured. On August 1, 1756, they
burned Fort Granville, near Lewistown, Mifflin County, and captured the entire garrison after killing Lieutenant Edward Armstrong, the commander. The Indian forces were Delawares under
command of Captain Jacobs of Kittanning. The prisoners were
carried to that place where some of them were tortured to death,
among these being John Turner, who had opened the gates at Fort
Granville to the enemy. Lieutenant Armstrong's brother, Colonel
John Armstrong, then raised a force of three hundred soldiers from
Cumberland County, marched over the Allegheny Mountains, and
on September 8th, burned the great Delaware town of Kittanning,
which had been the starting point for so many expeditions that
spread terror and death on the frontier. An account of the destruction of Kittanning will be given more fully in Chapter XVIII.
    Scarouady returned to Pennsylvania and held a conference
with George Croghan and one hundred and sixty Indians, chiefly
chiefs from the Six Nations, at Harris' Ferry, on April 1st and 2nd,
1757. He then accompanied them to Lancaster, where they remained until the end of the month and where additional conferences were held in the hope of establishing permanent peace.
Many of the chiefs died of smallpox while at Lancaster.
    On April 26, 1757, Scarouady, with a party of Mohawk war-
riors, set forth for Fort Augusta which had been erected at
Shamokin, to reconnoiter the wilderness in that vicinity, and then
to proceed toward the Ohio on a scouting expedition. Scarouady

proposed this expedition, stating that he was very apprehensive that the French would make an attempt against Fort Augusta; and so he believed it well to reconnoiter the country between that place and the Ohio, and if he found any French in the region, he would return and give notice to the commander of the fort.

The Colonial Records are not clear as to whether Scarouady actually went to the region of the Ohio and Allegheny, but on May 9th, Croghan reported that "three of the messengers I sent to the Ohio, returned." They had gone to Venango (Franklin) and other points in the western region. They reported that they were advised by the Indians of Venango, Kuskuskies, and those who had formerly lived at Kittanning, that the French were determined to make another trial against the English, but that they could not tell where they intended to strike next.

Death of Scarouady

The date of Scarouady's death is not known, but it was prior to August 26th, 1758, on which day several Mohawks came to Philadelphia from the territory of the Six Nations, bringing with them Scarouady's wife and all her children. She presented Governor Denny with "her husband's Calumet Pipe, and desired that he and the Indians might smoke it together; she intended to have gone into the Cherokee country, but had altered her mind, and would stay here with her children." Probably the old chief lost his life in one of Johnson's expeditions in New York.

It is with sincere regret that we take leave of Scarouady, an admirable character, a forceful orator, the leading speaker at many important conferences, the wise counselor, the strong enemy of the French, the firm friend of the English. Far past the prime of life when he first appears upon the scene, his aged shoulders bore a mighty burden to the end of his eventful career.

CHAPTER XVII.

Queen Allaquippa, Canachquasy
and Paxinosa

NTERRUPTING, for a moment, the recital of the atrocities and battles of the French and Indian War, we devote
this chapter to the biographies of three great Indian personages who were loyal to Pennsylvania before and during this bloody conflict.

QUEEN ALLAQUIPPA

Queen Allaquippa (Aliquippa), for whom the town of Aliquippa, in Beaver County, is named, and near which she is said to
have at one time lived, is generally spoken of as a Seneca, though
some authorities say that it is probable that she was a Mohawk.
The weight of authority, however, is in favor of the contention
that she was a Seneca. Conrad Weiser says that she belonged to
this tribe. If she were a Mohawk, Weiser certainly would have
known it, as he himself was an adopted son of the Mohawk nation.
By many authorities Queen Allaquippa is said to have been
the mother of Canachquasy, the account of whom is given later in
this chapter, and that she and her husband visited William Penn
at New Castle, Delaware, shortly before he sailed for England the
last time, in the autumn of 1701. There is no doubt that the parents of Canachquasy, whoever they were, went with their child to
New Castle to bid farewell to the founder of the Colony; and if
Queen Allaquippa were the mother of Canachquasy, the bidding of
farewell to William Penn is her first appearance in history.

Distinguished Personages Visit Queen Allaquippa

When Conrad Weiser made his journey to the Ohio in the
summer of 1748, in order to enter into a treaty on behalf of Pennsylvania with the western tribes, at Logstown, as mentioned in
Chapter VIII, Queen Allaquippa was living at a village on the
north bank of the Allegheny, a short distance above the mouth of
the Monongahela. Weiser makes mention of his visit in a note in
his journal, under date of August 27th, as follows: "Set off again

in the morning early. Rainy weather. We dined at a Seneca town where an old Seneca woman [Queen Allaquippa] reigns with great authority. We dined at her house and they all used us very well."

Weiser reached Logstown on the evening of that same day (August 27th), at which place he made George Groghan's trading house his headquarters until he left for the settlements, on September 19th, in the meantime having visited Sauconk, at the mouth of the Beaver, and gotten in touch with the Indians of Kuskuskies, who were to receive part of the Pennsylvania present. Before leaving Logstown, he made another notation in his journal concerning Queen Allaquippa, as follows:

"The old Sinicker Queen from above, already mentioned, came to inform me some time ago that she had sent a string of wampum of three fathoms to Philadelphia by James Dunnings, to desire her brethren would send her up a cask of powder and some small shot to enable her to send out the Indian boys to kill turkeys and other fowls for her, whilst the men were gone to war against the French, that they may not be starved. I told her I had heard nothing of her message, but if she had told me of it before I had parted with all the powder and lead, I could have let her have some, and promised I would make inquiry; perhaps her messenger had lost it on the way to Philadelphia. I gave her a shirt, a Dutch wooden pipe and some tobacco. She seemed to have taken a little affront because I took not sufficient notice of her in coming down. I told her she acted very imprudently not to let me know by some of her friends who she was, as she knew very well I could not know by myself. She was satisfied, and went away with a deal of kind expressions."

When Celeron led his expedition down the Allegheny and Ohio in the summer of 1749, he found her living as nearly as can be determined at Shannopin's Town, on the east bank of the Allegheny, a few miles above the mouth of the Monongahela and within the present limits of Pittsburgh, though some assert that her residence was at McKees Rocks. He noted in his journal under date of August 7th as follows: "I re-embarked and visited the village which is called the Written Rock. The Iroquois inhabit this place, and it is an old woman of this nation who governs it. She regards herself as sovereign. She is entirely devoted to the English."

When Messrs. Patten, Fry and Lomax, the Commissioners of Virginia, who entered into a treaty with the Western Indians at

Logstown in 1752, as referred to in former chapters, were on their way to Logstown, they called on this old Indian Queen at Allaquippa's Town, located on the south bank of the Ohio below the mouth of Chartier's Creek, where she was living at that time. The journal of the Commissioners under date of May 30, 1752, describes their visit as follows:

"The goods being put on board four large canoes lashed together [at Shannopin's Town], the Commissioners and others went on board also, to go down the river with colors flying. When they came opposite the Delaware town, they were saluted by the discharge of firearms, both from the town and opposite shore where Queen Allaquippa lives; and the compliment was returned from the canoes. The company then went on shore to wait on the Queen, who welcomed them, and presented them with a string of wampum, to clear their way to Logstown. She presented them also with a fine dish of fish to carry with them, and had some victuals set, which they all ate of. The Commissioners then presented the Queen with a brass kettel, tobacco and some other trifles and took their leave."

When Washington made his journey to the French forts in the latter part of 1753, Queen Allaquippa was living at the present site of McKeesport, Allegheny County. When he and Christopher Gist reached Frazer's cabin at the mouth of Turtle Creek late in December, he learned from Frazer that Queen Allaquippa was offended by his failure to call on her on his way from Virginia to LeBouef. He then determined to visit her on his way back. He makes the following notation in his journal without giving a specific date, but from the context it is clear that it was some time between December 28th and the last day of the year: "As we intended to take horse here [at Frazer's], and it required some time to find them, I went up about three miles to the mouth of the Youghiogheny to visit Queen Alliquippa, who had expressed great concern that we passed her in going to the fort. I made her a present of a match-coat and a bottle of rum, which latter was thought much the better present of the two."

As has been seen in Chapter XIV, Queen Allaquippa was at the Great Meadows during Washington's campaign in the summer of 1754, and no doubt witnessed the conferring of the name of Colonel Fairfax upon Canachquasy by Washington at that place on the 10th day of June.

After Washington's surrender at Fort Necessity, July 4th, 1754, Queen Allaquippa went to Aughwick with the other Indians of the Ohio still friendly to Pennsylvania. Here she died some time prior to December 23rd, 1754, as, on that date, George Croghan, then in charge of Indian affairs at Aughwick, wrote the Colonial Authorities: "Alequeapy, ye old quine, is dead."

CANACHQUASY (CAPTAIN NEW CASTLE)

As stated earlier in this chapter, it is probable that Canachquasy was the son of Queen Allaquippa. But whether he was her son or not, there is no doubt, as will be seen later, that, when a child, he accompanied his parents to New Castle, Delaware, in the autumn of 1701, when they went to that place to bid farewell to William Penn. His first appearance in Colonial history after attaining manhood was when he led a band of ten Mingo (Iroquois) warriors from Kuskuskies to Philadelphia in November, 1747, and brought the Provincial Council the first authentic news of the operations of the French in that quarter. In his speech delivered to the Provincial Council on November 13th, he advised the Governor that, although the Onondaga Council had taken a stand for neutrality during King George's War, which was then raging, yet the young warriors of the Iroquois in the Kuskuskies region had determined to take up arms against the French. The gist of his speech was given in the first part of Chapter XV. After apprising the Provincial Authorities of the attitude of the young Iroquois under his command, he asked for assistance by way of arms and ammunition from the Colony. "The French," said he, "have hard heads, and we have nothing strong enough to break them. We have only little sticks and hickories and such things that will do little or no service against the hard heads of the French."

Canachquasy was then told that a present had been prepared for them and the Cuyahogas. He then thanked the Council on behalf of his own delegation and the Cuyahogas, who, he said were of their own flesh and blood, and were pleased for the regard shown to them. The Council then purchased two hundred pounds worth of goods, a present for these Indans, and sent them as far as Harris' Ferry, where they were held until the following spring. Additions thereto were made so as to bring the total value up to about one thousand pounds. George Croghan was sent to Logstown the next spring, with a portion of these goods, to advise the Indians of that place and of Kuskuskies that Conrad Weiser would bring the balance later in the year. This Weiser did, as has

already been seen, in the summer of 1748, when as agent of Pennsylvania, he entered into a treaty at Logstown with the Western
Indians. Therefore, it is seen that Canachquasy's visit to the
Provincial Council in November, 1747, was the means of the
Colony's getting information which led to its sending Croghan
and later Weiser the following year on the first embassy on the
part of Pennsylvania to the Indians of the valleys of the Ohio
and Allegheny.

Canachquasy spent the winter of 1747-48 with the Nanticokes
at their village at the mouth of the Juniata. Just where he resided
from this time until Washington's campaign in the summer of
1754 is uncertain; but it is probable that, during a large part of
this period, his residence was at Kuskuskies or in that vicinity.

Canachquasy Given Name of New Castle

Canachquasy was the recipient of two English names. We
have already seen, in Chapter XIV, that he was given the name of
Lord Fairfax by Washington at the camp at the Great Meadows,
on June 10, 1754. Later, he attended Weiser's conferences at
Aughwick, in September, 1754. Likewise, we saw, in Chapter XV,
that he was one of the chiefs who fought on the side of the English
in Braddock's campaign in 1755, and that, at a meeting of the
Provincial Council on August 15th of that year, he was thanked
by the Council and rewarded for his fidelity. He was also present
at a meeting of the Provincial Council on August 22, 1755, when
Scarouady complained of the obstinacy of General Braddock. At
this meeting, Canachquasy was given the name of New Castle.
In the minutes of the Council, on this occasion, we read:

"The Governor [Governor Morris] addressing himself to
Kanuksusy [Canachquasy], the son of old Allaguipas, whose
mother was now alive and living near Ray's Town, desired
him to hearken for he was going to give him an English name,
then spoke as follows: 'In token of our affection for your parents
and in expectation of you being a useful man in these perilous
times, I do, in the most solemn manner, adopt you by the name of
New Castle, and order you to be called hereafter by that name,
which I have given to you, because, in 1701, I am informed that
your parents presented you to the late Mr. William Penn at New
Castle.' "

In this connection, we call attention to the fact that the minutes of the meeting of the Provincial Council above quoted (Col-

onial Records, Vol. VI, pages 588 and 589), refer to Canachquasy as "the son of old Allaguipas, whose mother was now alive and living near Ray's Town." That eminent authority on the Indian history of Pennsylvania, Dr. George P. Donehoo, points out that, inasmuch as George Croghan wrote from Aughwick, on December 23d, 1754, that "Alaqueapy, ye old quine, is dead," the "old Allaguipas," mentioned in the minutes of the Council of August 22nd, 1755, was not the mother of Canachquasy, but evidently an Indian chief, the father of Canachquasy, having a name similar, in sound, to that of Queen Allaquippa.

Canachquasy at Carlisle Council

An important Indian Council was held at Carlisle from January 13th to 16th, 1756, which was attended by Governor Morris, Richard Peters, William Logan, Joseph Fox, Conrad Weiser, George Croghan, and the following Indians: Canachquasy, The Belt, Aroas (Silver Heels), Jagrea, Seneca George, and others.

This Council had reference to Indian affairs on the Ohio and Allegheny at that time. Croghan reported that he had sent a friendly Indian, Delaware Jo, to the Ohio to get intelligence as to the situation there. Delaware Jo had gone to Kittanning, where the Delaware chief, Beaver, brother of Shingas, told him that the Six Nations had given the war hatchet to the Delawares and Shawnees. From Kittanning, Delaware Jo had gone to Logstown, where he was told the same thing by the Shawnees of that place. Furthermore, Delaware Jo had found some members of the Six Nations living in the Delaware towns on the Ohio and Allegheny, who always accompanied them in their war parties against the Pennsylvania settlements.

James Hamilton told the members of the conference how he had sent Aroas in the preceding November among the Indians of the Susquehanna to gain information, and that Aroas had learned from his uncle, who lived between Nescopeck and Wyoming, that the Delawares and Shawnees on the Ohio were persuaded by the French to strike the English, and had "put the hatchet into the hands of the Susquehanna Indians." After Croghan had listened to these accounts, he gave it as his opinion that the hostile Delawares and Shawnees were acting by the advice and approval of the Six Nations.

The Belt reviewed the events on the Ohio from the time of its first occupation by the French until the attacks upon Pennsylvania by the Delawares and Shawnees. He said that the French had entered into a secret treaty with the Delawares and Shawnees of the Ohio, who were in alliance with the Six Nations and were occupying the valleys of the Ohio and Allegheny by permission of the Six Nations, by the terms of which the Delawares and Shawnees permitted the French occupation and agreed to assist the French against the English.

Therefore, the thing uppermost in the mind of Canachquasy and his associates at the Carlisle Council was how to win back to the English interest the hostile Shawnees and Delawares, especially since it appeared, on the surface at least, that the Six Nations countenanced their hostility. But it must be remembered that those members of the Six Nations, living on the Ohio and Allegheny, at that time, and to whom Delaware Jo referred, were not true representatives of the Great Confederation of the Six Nations. They were a mongrel population, a mixture of all the Iroquoian stock on the outskirts of the territory of the Senecas. This mongrel population of the Ohio and Allegheny valleys was known as "Mingoes," and was really beyond the jurisdiction of the Six Nations.

Canachquasy Attends Other Conferences

Canachquasy attended a conference at Harris' Ferry on January 31, 1756, between Conrad Weiser, representing the Colony of Pennsylvania, and the friendly Indians of the Susquehanna. There was great danger, at this time, that the Pennsylvania settlers would not distinguish between good Indians and bad Indians; and Weiser's mission was for the purpose of retaining the friendship of the few that had not taken up arms against the Colony. In his report of this conference, written at his home at Womelsdorf on February 4th, and laid before the Governor on February 10th, he said:

"I had a good deal of trouble to quiet their minds (if I did at all). Satacarkoyies and New Castle went to Michael Taef's that night [January 31st], and New Castle got in the night light-headed. He looked upon every person as an enemy, and did persuade Satacarkoyies to run away with him. He himself made off privately next morning, and had not been heard of when I left John Harris', which was on the second instant on the afternoon. . . . . . . I sent word about it to the people to take care of the said

New Castle if he should be seen anywhere; he had no arms with him. I think it highly necessary that the said Indians should be taken care of deeper within the Inhabitants; for should they suffer by our foolish people, we should lose all confidence and honor with the rest of the Indians."

On February 24th, Canachquasy attended a Council at Philadelphia. It seems that, shortly after his disappearance from the council held by Weiser at Harris' Ferry, on January 31st, he returned to that place. At any rate, he accompanied the delegation from Harris' Ferry which attended the conference at Philadelphia on the 24th of February.

Canachquasy also attended the councils at Philadelphia mentioned in Chapter XVI, held between the Colonial Authorities and the friendly Indians prior to and following the declaration of war against the Delawares, following which he offered, with Jonathan, and Andrew Montour, to carry the Governor's peace proposals among the Delawares.

Peace Missions of Canachquasy

Shortly after Pennsylvania's declaraton of war against the Delawares, Canachquasy carried the Governor's proposals of peace to these Indians. He spent four days at Wyoming, and then went on to Tioga, an important town of the Six Nations, Nanticokes, and Munsee Clan of Delawares, situated on the site of Athens, Bradford County. It was the southern gateway to the country of the Iroquois, and all the great war paths and hunting trails from the South and Southwest centered there. He held conferences with the Indians of this place and the surrounding towns, and made known to them the Governor's message. These Indians agreed to lay aside the hatchet and enter into negotiations for peace; but they cautioned Canachquasy not to charge them with anything that may have been done by the Delawares of the Ohio and Allegheny valleys under the influence of the French.

Canachquasy then returned to Philadelphia early in June, and laid his report before the Governor and Provincial Council. The Governor and Council, upon hearing the favorable report, drafted a proclamation for a suspension of hostilities with the enemy Indians of the Susquehanna Valley for a period of thirty days, and desired that a conference with them for the purpose of making peace, should be held at the earliest possible date.

Canachquasy then left once more for Tioga, bearing the Governor's message, advising the Susquehanna Indians that the

Colony would agree to a truce of thirty days and that, as one of the conditions of making peace, the prisoners taken on both sides should be delivered up. Shortly after he left, messengers were sent to him by the Governor carrying a few additional instructions, which were delivered to him at Bethlehem. In the meantime, Sir William Johnson, of New York, was holding a peace conference with the Six Nations at Otseningo, at which the assembled sachems of the Iroquois decided that the Delawares were acting like drunken men, and sent deputies to order them to become sober and cease their warfare against the English. This conference was composed of only a portion of the Iroquois, and the Delawares replied very haughtily saying that they were no longer women but men. "We are determined," said they, "to cut off all the English except those that make their escape from us in ships."

After a dangerous journey over the mountains and through the wilderness, Canachquasy reached Tioga, held conferences with the great Delaware chieftain, Teedyuscung, and persuaded him to bury the hatchet,—a most remarkable victory.

Canachquasy then returned to Philadelphia in the middle of July, 1756, and laid before the Governor and Provincial Council the results of his second mission to Tioga. Addressing the Governor and Council he said:

"As I have been entrusted by you with matters of highest concern, I now declare to you that I have used all the ability I am master of in the management of them, and that with the greatest cheerfulness. I tell you in general, matters look well. I shall not go into particulars. Teedyuscung will do this at a public meeting, which he expects will be soon. The times are dangerous. The swords are drawn and glittering all around you; numbers of enemies in your borders. I beseech you, therefore, not to give any delay to this important affair; we hear the council fire is to be kindled; come to a conclusion immediately; let us not wait a moment, lest what has been done should prove ineffectual. The times are very precarious; not a moment is to be lost without the utmost danger to the good cause we are engaged in. The Delaware King [Teedyuscung] wants to hear from your own mouth a confirmation of the assurances of peace and good will given him by me in your name; he comes well disposed to make you the same declarations. The Forks [Easton] is believed to be the place of meeting. What need of any altercation? Let it be. Tarry not, but hasten to meet him."

Arrangements were then completed for a conference with the hostile Delawares at Easton, and Conrad Weiser was ordered to concentrate his soldiers in the vicinity of that place and to furnish a guard for the Governor, who, with his Council, reached Easton on the 24th of July. Nothing of any moment could be done until the 27th of that month, inasmuch as Weiser had not arrived. Teedyuscung, on opening the conference, insisted on having his own interpreter. This request was granted, and the treaty was formally opened on July 28th. Teedyuscung claimed to have been appointed King over all the Clans of Delawares and to have been authorized by the Six Nations to negotiate for peace. The details of the treaty will be set forth more fully in the account of Teedyuscung, Chapter XXI. At this point, however, we call attention to the fact that Canachquasy's advice and activities during the treaty were very valuable; that the treaty resulted in a temporary peace, and that Canachquasy and Teedyuscung were to go back among the Delawares and give the "Big Peace Halloo." At the end of the conferences, Teedyuscung lingered at Fort Allen, which had been erected where the town of Weissport, Carbon County, now stands. At this place, Teedyuscung's inordinate appetite for rum, the curse of the Red Man, was taken advantage of, and he remained intoxicated for a considerable time. Canachquasy then went away in disgust.

The Pennsylvania Authorities were apprehensive that Teedyuscung was not sincere in the peace proposals that he had made at the treaty at Easton. Besides, a number of Indians on the border insinuated that the Easton treaty was but a ruse to gain time; and that Teedyuscung was a traitor working in the interest of the French. Finally, the Governor, becoming suspicious of Teedyuscung's long delay at Fort Allen, sent Canachquasy secretly to New York to learn from the Six Nations whether or not they had deputized Teedyuscung to represent them in public treaties. Canachquasy returned to Philadelphia in October with the report that the Six Nations denied Teedyuscung's authority. At a meeting of the Provincial Council on the 24th of that month, he said:

"I have but in part executed my commission, not having opportunity of having done it so fully as I wished. I met with Canyase, one of the principal counsellors of the Six Nations, a Mohawk chief, who has a regard for Pennsylvania. . . . . . I related to this chief very particularly the manner in which Teedyuscung spoke of himself and his commission and authority from the Six Nations at the treaty at Easton. I gave him a true notion of all he said on this head and how often he repeated it to the Governor, and then asked whether he knew anything of this matter.

Canyase said he did; Teedyuscung did not speak the truth when he told the Governor he had a regular authority from the Six Nations to treat with Onas. Canyase then proceeded and said: 'Teedyuscung on behalf of the Delawares did apply to me as chief of the Six Nations. He and I had long discourses together and in these conversations, I told him that the Delawares were women and always treated as such by the Six Nations.' "

Death of Canachquasy

While attending the Easton treaty, Canachquasy had a presentiment of impending death,—a presentiment soon to be fulfilled, the account of which is thus given in Volume II of the Pennsylvania Archives, Series 1, under date of July 27, 1756:

"Mr. Weiser coming to Town, the Governor proposed to open the conferences, but on his saying he was a stranger to Teedyuscung and it would take up some time, at least a day, to be rightly informed of his temper and expectations, it was deferred till tomorrow. Captain New Castle (Canachquasy) came to the Governor, much in liquor, tho' otherwise a very sober man, and requested a Council might be called, saying he had something of a particular nature to communicate . . . . . . with which being obliged, he acquainted the Governor that the Delawares had bewitched him and he should die soon; the Governor would have rallied it off, but he grew more serious and desired this information might be committed to writing and inserted in the minutes of Council, and sent to the Six Nations; that if any harm came to him, they might know to whom to impute it, and not charge others with it. Teedyuscung, he declared, had warned him in a friendly manner, that he would not live long, having overheard two Delawares say they would put an end to his life by witchcraft. And whilst he was speaking, Teedyuscung mistrusting what New Castle was upon, bolted into the room, fell into a violent passion with New Castle, who he supposed had been telling the Governor foolish words, and desired he might not be regarded in anything he should say on such a foolish subject, exclaiming, 'He bewitched!' The Governor was too wise to hearken to such silly stories, and then left the room in as abrupt a manner as he had entered it. After he was gone, the Governor endeavored to show New Castle that he was in no danger, but he made no impression. New Castle still urging that information might be taken down, and, in case of his death, be communicated in a special message to the Six Nations, which was promised; and he then withdrew, to appearance, more composed."

Shortly after Canachquasy's appearance before the Provincial Council on October 24, 1756, he contracted small-pox, at Philadelphia, and before the middle of November, this great peace apostle among the Indians was no more. Canachquasy's devotion to the cause of the English commands our great admiration and respect. He said that he would die for the sons of Onas. In the following chapter (Chapter XVIII), we shall see some of the terrible atrocities, committed by the Delawares, while this firm friend of Pennsylvania was wroking for peace.

PAXINOSA (PAXNOUS, PAXIHOS)

Paxinosa was a noted chief of the Shawnees. His first appearance in history is among the Shawnees at Pechoquealin, near the Delaware Water Gap, and it is probable that he was one of the band of this tribe which Arnold Viele conducted to that region from the lower Ohio Valley, in 1794, as set forth in Chapter II. He removed from the Pechoquealin and Minisink region, and took up his abode just below Plymouth, Luzerne County, among the other Shawnees who had removed from Pechoquealin to that place. The date of his removal from Pechoquealin, however, is not known. As stated in Chapter VIII, Kakowatcheky, who had been chief of the Shawnees at Wyoming, removed to the Ohio Valley in 1743. A few years later, Paxinosa succeeded him as chief of the Shawnees at Wyoming.

Paxinosa Joins in Sale of Lands Between
Susquehanna and Delaware Rivers

As stated in Chapter XII, the Six Nations, on August 22nd, 1749, sold to the Colony of Pennsylvania, a vast tract of land between the Susquehanna and the Delaware, including all or parts of the present counties of Dauphin, Northumberland, Lebanon, Schuylkill, Columbia, Carbon, Luzerne, Monroe, Pike and Wayne. Paxinosa, as chief of the Shawnees at Wyoming, joined in the sale of these lands. The sale was made at Philadelphia.

Paxinosa Befriends Moravians

In the summer of 1754, when most of the Shawnees and Delawares of the valleys of the Ohio and Allegheny began to waver in their allegiance to the English, attempts were made to induce the Christian Delawares at Gnadenhuetten to remove from that place and come nearer the dissatisfied Indians. Paxinosa was one of the chiefs who endeavored to induce the Christian Delawares of Gnadenhuetten to move. At first, he was not friendly toward the Moravian missionaries, but later his wife, for whom he had great affection and to whom he had been married almost forty years, was converted to the Christian faith by the gentle Moravians and baptized by Bishop Spangenberg, with Paxinosa's concent. A deep impression of the truths of the Christian religion was thus made upon the heart of the old chief, causing him to change his attitude toward the Moravians and their converts.

At the time of the Penn's Creek Massacre and the attack upon John Harris and his band, the Moravian missionary, Keifer, was residing at Shamokin and exposed to imminent danger. Paxinosa, who was then at Shamokin, sent two of his sons who rescued the missionary and conducted him safely to Gnadenhuetten.

In the summer of 1757, he greatly befriended the Moravians. A' report had been circulated among the hostile Delawares and Shawnees that the Moravian missionaries at Bethlehem were killing the Indian converts there, and sending their heads in bags to Philadelphia. This report greatly excited the Delawares and Shawnees, and they gathered a force of two hundred warriors for the purpose of destroying the Moravians. Paxinosa and Teedyuscung pacified the enraged Delawares and Shawnees, and persuaded them to desist from their design.

Paxinosa Loyally Supports the English

Paxinosa attended the conference which Scarouady held with the Indians at Wyoming on the latter's journey as the messenger of Pennsylvania to the Six Nations, described in Chapter XVI. On this occasion, he spoke boldly in favor of the English, but was silenced by the Delawares, who threatened to knock him on the head if he said anything more. He was also present at the conference which Canachquasy held with the Indians of Tioga, when the latter visited that place as the peace messenger of Pennsylvania shortly after the declaration of war against the Delawares in the spring of 1756. Shortly before this time, he and the Shawnees under his command at their town on the Shawnee Flats, now Plymouth, Luzerne County, had removed, through compulsion of the hostile Delawares, to Tioga. He sat for days meditating on the waywardness of his people in taking up arms against the sons of "Brother Onas."

Paxinosa Removes to the Ohio

In April, 1757, Paxinosa was living at Osteningo, now Binghampton, New York; and, in August of that year, he attended the third conference with Teedyuscung at Easton, more particularly described in Chapter XXII. In the early part of May, 1758, he was met by Benjamin, a Mohican Indian, of Bethlehem, near Tioga, with his entire family. He told Benjamin that he had heard that the English had very bad designs against the Indians, and that he therefore was going with his family to the Ohio "where he was born." Benjamin tried to persuade him not to go, but without avail. Paxinosa had heard that his hated enemies, the Cherokees, had been sent for by the English to destroy all the Indians on the Susquehanna. As a matter of fact, there were a few Cherokees and Catawbas at that time joining the expedition of General Forbes against Fort Duquesne. Not only the recently pacified Eastern Delawares, but also the Iroquois, were becoming aroused because of the presence of their hated enemies in Forbes' expedition. Paxinosa told Benjamin that he had recently been asked to attend a great council at Onondaga, at which it would be determined whether the Iroquois would side with the English or the French, but, as he had already resolved to move to the Ohio, he would not attend the council at Onondaga. The old chief then went back to the land of his birth.

Final Conferences of Paxinosa

On the 29th of June, 1760, General Monckton arrived at Fort Pitt for the purpose of taking possession of the posts on the Allegheny, as well as those along the frontier to Detroit, at the close of the French and Indian War. On August 12th of that year, Monckton held a great conference at Fort Pitt, with the chiefs of the Six Nations, Miamis, Delawares, Ottawas, Wyandots, and Shawnees. General Monckton advised the assembled chiefs that he had come to take possession of the western region; that he did not intend to drive the Indians from their lands, nor to take their lands from them, but he desired to establish once more peaceful relations between the western tribes and the British Government. Paxinosa attended this conference.

Not long thereafter, he ended his days on the Scioto Plains in Ohio.

CHAPTER XVIII

Captain Jacobs

APTAIN JACOBS was one of the Delaware chiefs who took up arms against Pennsylvania shortly after Braddock's defeat. He had at one time resided near Lewistown, where he sold lands to Colonel Buchanan, who gave him the name of Captain Jacobs, because of his close resemblance to a burly German in Cumberland County. Later he resided at "Jacob's Cabin," not far from Mount Pleasant, Westmoreland County. His principal residence was at the famous Indian town of Kittanning, Armstrong County, which, as we have seen in an earlier chapter, was the first town established by the Delawares on their migration into the Allegheny Valley with the consent of the Iroquois Confederation. From this town, he and that other noted chief, Shingas, led many an expedition against the frontier settlements. For a time, in the autumn of 1755, they made their headquarters at Nescopeck, in Luzerne County, and at that place, also, planned many a bloody expedition.

Captain Jacobs Captures Fort Granville

Reference was made, in Chapter XVI, to the capture of Fort Granville, near Lewistown, Mifflin County, by Captain Jacobs, on August 1, 1756. We quote the following account of this event from the "Frontier Forts of Pennsylvania":

"The attack upon Fort Granville was made in harvest time of the year 1756. The Fort at this time was commanded by Lieut. Armstrong, a brother of Colonel Armstrong, who destroyed Kittanning. The Indians, who had been lurking about this fort for some time, and knowing that Armstrong's men were few in number, sixty of them appeared, July 22nd, before the fort, and challenged the garrison to a fight; but this was declined by the commander in consequence of the weakness of his force. The Indians fired at and wounded one man, who had been a short way from it, yet he got in safe; after which they divided themselves into small parties, one of which attacked the plantation of one Baskins, near the Juniata, whom they murdered, burnt his house and carried off his wife and children. Another made Hugh Carroll and his family prisoners.

"On the 30th of July, 1756, Capt. Edward Ward, the commandant of Granville, marched from the fort with a detachment
of men from the garrison, destined for Tuscarora Valley, where
they were needed as guard to the settlers while they were engaged
in harvesting their grain. The party under Capt. Ward embraced
the greater part of the defenders of the fort, under command of
Lieut. Edward Armstrong. Soon after the departure of Capt.
Ward's detachment, the fort was surrounded by the hostile force of
French and Indians, who immediately made an attack, which they
continued in their skulking, Indian manner through the afternoon
and following night, but without being able to inflict much damage
on the whites. Finally, after many hours had been spent in their
unsuccessful attacks, the Indians availed themselves of the protection afforded by a deep ravine, up which they passed from the
river bank to within twelve or fifteen yards of the fort, and from
that secure position, succeeded in setting fire to the logs and burning out a large hole, through which they fired on the defenders,
killing the commanding officer, Lieut. Armstrong, and one private
soldier and wounding three others.

"They then demanded the surrender of the fort and garrison,
promising to spare their lives if the demand was acceded to.
Upon this, a man named John Turner, previously a resident in the
Buffalo valley, opened the gates and the besiegers at once entered
and took possession, capturing as prisoners twenty-two men, three
women and a number of children. The fort was burned by the
chief, Jacobs, by order of the French officer in command, and the
savages then departed, driving before them their prisoners, heavily
burdened with the plunder taken from the fort and the settlers'
houses, which they had robbed and burned. On their arrival at
the Indian rendezvous at Kittanning, all the prisoners were cruelly
treated, and Turner, the man who had opened the gate at the fort
to the savages, suffered the cruel death by burning at the stake,
enduring the most horrible torment that could be inflicted upon
him for a period of three hours, during which time red hot gun
barrels were forced through parts of his body, his scalp torn from
his head and burning splinters were stuck in his flesh, until at last
an Indian boy was held up for the purpose who sunk a hatchet
in the brain of the victim and so released him from this cruel torture."

Captain Jacobs Killed at the Destruction of Kittanning

Kittanning, in addition to being the center from which Captain Jacobs and Shingas sent their expeditions against the frontier settlements, was the place for the detention of English prisoners. George Croghan reported at the Carlisle Council of January 13, 1756, that he had sent the friendly Indian, Delaware Jo, in December, 1755, to the Ohio for intelligence; and that this friendly Indian had visited Kittanning, where he found more than one hundred English prisoners taken from various parts of Pennsylvania and Virginia. In order, therefore, to break up this harboring place of the Delawares, an expedition was authorized by the representatives of Governor Morris and the Provincial Council, to be conducted by Lieutenant-Colonel John Armstrong, of the Second Battalion of the Pennsylvania Regiment. Colonel Armstrong was a brother of the ill-fated Lieutenant Edward Armstrong, who was killed by Jacobs in the attacks on Fort Granville.

The capture of Fort Granville greatly elated Captain Jacobs. He said: "I can take any fort that will catch fire, and I will make peace with the English when they teach me to make gun powder."

The following description of Colonel Armstrong's march over the mountains to Kittanning and the destruction of that place is quoted from Egle's "History of Pennsylvania":

"On the 20th of August, 1756, William Denny arrived in the Province, superseding Governor Morris. He was hailed with joy by the Assembly, who flattered themselves that, with a change of government, there would be a change of measures. Upon making known the Proprietary instructions, to which he stated he was compelled to adhere, all friendly feeling was at an end, and there was a renewal of the old discord.

"Before Governor Morris was superseded, he concerted with Colonel John Armstrong an expedition against the Indian town of Kittanning, on the Allegheny, the stronghold of Captain Jacobs and Shingas, the most active Indian chiefs, and from whence they distributed their war parties along the frontier. On the arrival of Governor Denny, Morris communicated the plan of his enterprise to him and his Council.

"Colonel Armstrong marched from Fort Shirley [Shirleysburg, Huntingdon County], on the 30th of August, with three hundred men, having with him, besides other officers, Captains Hamilton, Mercer, Ward, and Potter. On the 2nd of September, he joined an advance party at the Beaver dams, near Frankstown. On the 7th, in the evening, within six miles of Kittanning, the scouts discovered a fire in the road, and around it, as they reported, three, or at most, four Indians. It was deemed prudent not to attack this party; but lest some of them should escape and alarm the town, Lieutenant Hogg and twelve men were left to watch them, with orders to fall upon them at day-break. The main body, making a circuit, proceeded to the village. Guided by the whooping of the Indians at a dance, the army approached the place by the river, about one hundred perches below the town, at three o'clock in the morning, near a cornfield, in which a number of the enemy were lodged, out of their cabins, on account of the heat of the weather. As soon as the dawn of day made the town visible, the troops attacked it through the cornfield, killing several of the enemy. Captain Jacobs, their principal chief, sounded the war-whoop, and defended his house bravely through loop-holes in the logs; and the Indians generally refused quarter, which was offered them, declaring that they were men, and would not be prisoners.

"Colonel Armstrong, who had received a musket ball in his shoulder, ordered their houses to be set on fire over their heads. Again the Indians were required to surrender, and again refused, one of them declaring that he did not care for death, as he could kill four or five before he died, and as the heat approached, some of them began to sing. Others burst from their houses, and attempted to reach the river, but were instantly shot down. Captain Jacobs, in getting out of a window, was shot, as also a squaw, and a lad called the king's son. The Indians had a number of small arms in their houses, loaded, which went off in quick succession as the fire came to them; and quantities of gunpowder, which were stored in every house, blew up from time to time, throwing some of the bodies of the enemy a great height in the air. A party of Indians on the opposite side of the river fired on the troops, and were seen to cross the river at a distance, as if to surround them; but they contented themselves with collecting some horses which were near the town to carry off their wounded, and then retreated without attempting to take from the cornfield those who were killed there in the beginning of the action. Several of the enemy were killed in the river as they attempted to escape by fording it, and between thirty and forty, in the whole, were destroyed.

"Eleven English prisoners were released, who informed that, besides the powder, of which the Indians boasted they had enough for ten years' war with the English, there was a great quantity of goods burned, which the French had presented to them but ten days before; that two batteaux of French Indians were to join Captain Jacobs to make an attack upon Fort Shirley, and that twenty-four warriors had set out before them on the preceding evening. These proved to be the party discovered around the fire, as the troops approached Kittanning. Pursuant to his orders, and relying upon the report made by the scouts, Lieutenant Hogg had attacked them, and killed three at the first fire. He, however, found them too strong for his force, and having lost some of his best men, the others fled, leaving him wounded, overlooked by the enemy in their pursuit of the fugitives. He was saved by the army on their return. [He afterwards died of his wounds]. Captain, afterwards General, Mercer was wounded in the action at Kittanning, but was carried off safely by his men.

"The corporation of Philadelphia, on occasion of this victory, on the 5th of January following, addressed a complimentary letter to Colonel Armstrong, thanking him and his officers for their gallant conduct, and presented him with a piece of plate. A medal was also struck, having for device an officer followed by two soldiers, the officer pointing to a soldier shooting from behind a tree, and an Indian postrate before him; in the background Indian houses in flames. Legend: Kittanning, destroyed by Colonel Armstrong, September the 8th, 1756. Reverse device: The arms of the corporation. Legend: The gift of the corporation of Philadelphia.

"The destruction of the town of Kittanning, and the Indian families there, was a severe stroke on the savages. Hitherto the English had not assailed them in their towns, and they fancied that they would not venture to approach them. But now, though urged by an unquenchable thirst of vengeance to retaliate the blow they had received, they dreaded that, in their absence on war parties, their wigwams might be reduced to ashes. Such of them as belonged to Kittanning, and had escaped the carnage, refused to settle again on the east of Fort Duquesne, and resolved to place that fortress and the French garrison between them and the English."

Many blankets were afterwards found on the ground where Lieutenant Hogg and his party were defeated. Hence the battlefield has ever since borne the name of "Blanket Hill." It is in Kittanning Township, Armstrong County.

The English prisoners recovered from the Indians at the destruction of Kittanning were:

Ann McCord, wife of John McCord, and Martha Thorn, a child seven years of age, both captured at Fort McCord, on April 1st, 1756; Barbara Hicks, captured at Conolloways; Catherine Smith, a German child captured near Shamokin; Margaret Hood, captured near the mouth of the Conococheague, Maryland; Thomas Girty, captured at Fort Granville; Sarah Kelly, captured near Winchester, Virginia; a woman, a boy, and two little girls, who were with Captain Mercer and Ensign Scott, and had not reached Fort Littleton when Colonel Armstrong made his report.

It will be recalled that among the prisoners captured by the Delawares at the Penn's Creek Massacre of October 16th, 1755, were Barbara Leininger and Marie LeRoy (Mary King). They were carried to Kittanning and were there when Colonel Armstrong made the attack; but in order to prevent their being rescued by Armstrong's forces, they were taken ten miles westward into the wilderness, and thence to Fort Duquesne, where they stayed for two months. They were then taken to Sauconk, at the mouth of the Beaver; and in the spring of 1757, they were carried to Kuskuskies, where they remained until the Indians of that place learned during the next summer that General Forbes was marching on Fort Duquesne. They were then taken to the Muskingum, where they made their escape on March 16, 1759, and reached Fort Pitt on the 31st of that month.

SOME OTHER EVENTS OF THE TERRIBLE YEAR 1756

Massacre at Fort Allen

Reference was made, in Chapter XVI, to the massacre of a number of militia at Fort Allen (Weissport, Carbon County) on New Year's Day, 1756. The Governor had ordered the soldiers to this place to protect the property of those Delawares who had been converted to the Christan religion by the Moravians and to defend the country in general. A temporary stockade had been built, and, on this day, while the soldiers were amusing themselves skating on the Lehigh River, they saw two Indians farther up the stream. They gave chase, but the Indians proved to be decoys, and skillfully maneuvered to draw the soldiers into an ambush. After proceeding some distance, a band of Indians rushed out behind the soldiers, cutting off their retreat, and massacreing almost all. The Indians then fired the stockade and surrounding houses and mills of the Moravians.

On the same day, the Delaware chief, Teedyuscung led a band of about thirty Indians into lower Smithfield Township, Monroe County, destroying the plantation of Henry Hess, killing Nicholas Colman and a laborer named Gotlieb, and capturing Peter Hess and young Henry Hess, son of Peter Hess and nephew of Henry Hess, the owner of the plantation. This attack took place about nine o'clock in the morning. Teedyuscung's band then went over the Blue Mountains and overtook five Indians with two prisoners, Leonard and William Weeser, and a little later killed Peter Hess in the presence of his son.

In a few days the Indians over-ran the country from Fort Allen as far as Nazareth, burning plantations, and killing and scalping settlers. During this same month, the Delawares entered Moore Township, Northampton County, burning the buildings of Christian Miller, Henry Shopp, Henry Diehl, Peter Doll, Nicholas Scholl, and Nicholas Heil, and killing one of Heil's children and John Bauman. The body of Bauman was found two weeks later, and buried in the Moravian cemetery at Nazareth.

Massacre Near Schupp's Mill

On January 15th, some refugees at Bethlehem went out into the country to look after their farms and cattle, among them being Christian Boemper. The party and some friendly Indians who escorted them, were ambushed by hostile Delawares near Schupp's Mill, and all were killed except one named Adam Hold, who was so severely wounded that it was necessary later to amputate his arm. Those killed were Christian Boemper, Felty Hold, Michael Hold, Laurence Knuckel, and four privates of Captain Trump's Company then stationed at Fort Hamilton (Stroudsburg).

At about the same time, a German, named Muhlhisen while breaking flax on the farm of Philip Bossert, in Lower Smithfield Township, Monroe County, was fatally wounded by an unseen Indian. One of Bosserts's sons, hearing the report of the Indian's rifle, ran out of the house and was killed. Then old Philip Bossert, the owner of the farm, appeared on the scene, wounded one of the Indians, and was himself wounded badly. Neighbors then arrived upon the scene, and the Indians retreated.

Massacre of Settlers in the Juniata Valley

On January 27th, a party of Indians from Shamokin made an incursion into the Juniata Valley, attacked the house of Hugh

Mitcheltree, near Thompsontown, Juniata County, killing Mrs. Mitcheltree and a young man named Edward Nicholas, Mr. Mitcheltree being then absent at Carlisle. This same party of savages then went up the Juniata River to the house of Edward Nicholas, Sr., where they killed Nicholas and his wife, and captured Joseph Thomas, Catherine Nicholas, John Wilcox, and the wife and two children of James Armstrong. While these atrocities were being committed, an Indian named John Cotties, who had failed in his effort to be chosen captain of the party, took with him a young warrior and went to Sherman's Creek, where the two killed William Sheridan and his entire family, thirteen in all. Proceeding down the creek to the home of two old men and an elderly woman named French, they took the lives of these aged people. Cotties made the boast afterwards that he and his young companion had taken more scalps than all the others of the party. It will be noted that these massacres took place within the bounds of the purchase of 1754, which so angered the Delawares and Shawnees.

Capture of John and Richard Coxe and John Craig

In February, 1756, occurred the capture of John Coxe, his brother Richard, and John Craig, thus described in the "Frontier Forts of Pennsylvania":

"At a council, held at Philadelphia, Tuesday, September 6th, 1756, the statement of John Coxe, a son of the widow Coxe, was made, the substance of which is: He, his brother Richard, and John Craig were taken in the beginning of February of that year by nine Delaware Indians from a plantation two miles from Mc-Dowell's mill, [Franklin County], which was between the east and west branches of the Cononocheague Creek, about 20 miles west of the present site of Shippensburg, in what is now Franklin County, and brought to Kittanning on the Ohio. On his way hither he met Shingas with a party of 30 men, and afterward Capt. Jacobs and 15 men, whose design was to destroy the settlements on Cononcocheague. When he arrived at Kittanning, he saw here about 100 fighting men of the Delaware tribe, with their families, and about 50 English prisoners, consisting of men, women and children. During his stay here, Shingas' and Jacobs' parties returned, the one with nine scalps and ten prisoners, the other with several scalps and five prisoners. Another company of 18 came from Diahogo with 17 scalps on a pole, which they took to Fort Duquesne to obtain their reward. The warriors held a council, which, with their war dances, continued a week, when Capt. Jacobs left with 48 men, intending as Coxe was told, to fall upon the inhabitants at Paxtang. He heard the Indians frequently say that they intended to kill all the white folks, except a few, with whom they would afterwards make peace. They made an example of Paul Broadley, who, with their usual cruelty, they beat for half an hour with clubs and tomahawks, and then, having fastened him to a post, cropped his ears close to his head, and chopped off his fingers, calling all the prisoners to witness the horrible scene."

Additional details of the incursion during which the Coxe boys and John Craig were captured are given in Egle's "History of Pennsylvania", as follows:

"In February, 1756, a party of Indians made marauding incursions into Peters Township. They were discovered on Sunday evening, by one Alexander, near the house of Thomas Barr. He was pursued by the savages, but escaped and alarmed the fort at McDowell's mill. Early on Monday morning a party of fourteen men of Captain Croghan's company, who were at the mill, and about twelve other young men, set off to watch the motion of the Indians. Near Barr's house they fell in with fifty, and sent back for a reinforcement from the fort. The young lads proceeded by a circuit to take the enemy in the rear, whilst the soldiers did attack them in front. But the impetuosity of the soldiers defeated their plan. Scarce had they got within gunshot, they fired upon the Indians, who were standing around the fire, and killed several of them at the first discharge. The Indians returned fire, killed one of the soldiers, and compelled the rest to retreat. The party of young men, hearing the report of firearms, hastened up; finding the Indians on the ground which the soldiers had occupied, fired upon the Indians with effect; but concluding the soldiers had fled, or were slain, they also retreated. One of their number, Barr's son, was wounded, would have fallen by the tomahawk of an Indian, had not the savage been killed by a shot from Armstrong, who saw him running upon the lad. Soon after soldiers and young men being joined by a reinforcement from the mill, again sought the enemy, who, eluding the pursuit, crossed the creek near William Clark's, and attempted to surprise the fort; but their design was discovered by two Dutch lads, coming from foddering their master's cattle. One of the lads was killed, but the other reached the fort, which was immediately surrounded by the Indians, who, from a thicket, fired many shots at the men in the garrison, who appeared above the wall, and returned the fire as often as they obtained sight of the enemy. At this time, two men crossing to the mill, fell into the middle of the assailants, but made their escape to the fort, though fired at three times. The party at Barr's house now came up, and drove the Indians through the thicket. In their retreat they met five men from Mr. Hoop's, riding to the mill; they killed one of these and wounded another severely. The sergeant at the fort having lost two of his men, declined to follow the enemy until his commander, Mr. Crawford, who was at Hoop's, should return, and the snow falling thick, the Indians had time to burn Mr. Barr's house, and in it consumed their dead. On the morning of the 2nd of March, Mr. Crawford, with fifty men, went in quest of the enemy, but was unsuccessful in his search."

Attack on Andrew Lycans and John Rewalt

On March 7th, Andrew Lycans and John Rewalt, settlers in the Wiconisco, or Lykens Valley in Dauphin County, went out early in the morning to feed their cattle when they were fired upon by savages. Hastening into the house, they prepared to defend themselves. The Indians concealed themselves behind a pig-pen some distance from the dwelling. Lycans' son, John, John Rewalt, and Ludwig Shutt, a neighbor, upon creeping out of the house, in an effort to discover the whereabouts of the Indians, were fired upon and each one wounded, Shutt very dangerously. At this point Andrew Lycans discovered an Indian named Joshua James and two white men running away from their hiding place near the pig-pen. The elder Lycans then fired, killing the Indian; and he and his party then sought safety in flight, but were closely pursued by at least twenty of the Indians. John Lycans and John Rewalt, although badly wounded, made their escape with the aid of a negro servant, leaving Andrew Lycans, Ludwig Shutt, and a boy to engage the Indians. The Indians then rushed upon these and, as one of their number, named Bill Davis, was in the act of striking the boy with his tomahawk, he was shot dead by Shutt, while Andrew Lycans killed another and wounded a third. Andrew Lycans also recognized two others of the band, namely, Tom Hickman and Tom Hays, members of the Delaware tribe. The Indians then momentarily ceased their pursuit, and Lycans, Shutt, and the boy, weak from the loss of blood, sat down on a log to rest, believing that they were no longer in imminent danger. Later, Lycans managed to lead his party to a place of concealment and then over the mountain into Hanover Township, where they were given assistance by settlers. Andrew Lycans, however, died from his wounds and terrible exposure. His name has been given to the charming valley of the Wiconisco.

Attack on Zeislof and Kluck Families

On March 24th, some settlers with ten wagons went to Albany, Berks County, for the purpose of bringing a family with their effects to a point near Reading. As they were returning, they were fired upon by a number of Indians on both sides of the road. The wagoners, leaving the wagons, ran into the woods, and the horses, frightened at the terrible yelling of the Indians, ran off. The Indians on this occasion, killed George Zeislof and his wife, a boy aged twenty, another aged twelve, and a girl aged fourteen. Another girl of the party was shot through the neck and mouth, and scalped, but made her escape.

On the same day the Indians burned the home of Peter Kluck, about fourteen miles from Reading, and killed the entire family. While the Kluck home was burning, the Indians assaulted the house of a settler named Lindenman nearby, in which there were two men and a woman, all of whom ran upstairs, where the woman was killed by a bullet which penetrated the roof. The men then ran out of the house. Lindenman was shot through the neck. In spite of his wound, Lindenman succeeded in shooting one of the Indians.

At about the same time a boy named John Schoep, who lived in this neighborhood, was captured and taken seven miles beyond the Blue Mountains where, according to the statement of Schoep, the Indians kindled a fire, tied him to a tree, took off his shoes, and put moccasins on his feet. They then prepared themselves some mush, but gave him none. After supper they took young Schoep and another boy between them, and proceeded over the second mountain. During the second night of his captivity, when the Indians were asleep, young Schoep made his escape, and returned home.

During the raid in which the above outrages occurred, the Indians killed the wife of Baltser Neytong, and captured his son aged eight. And in November, the Indians entered this region, and carried off the wife and three children of Adam Burns, the youngest child being only four weeks old. They also killed a man named Stonebrook, and captured a girl in this raid.

Shingas Captures Fort McCord

On April 1st, 1756, Shingas attacked and burned Fort Mc-Cord, a private fort located several miles northwest of Fort Loudon, Franklin County, and all the inmates, twenty-seven in number, were either killed or carried into captivity. At the time of the capture of the fort, Dr. Jamison was killed near that place; and at about the same time, a number of persons, employed by William Mitchell to harvest his crops, were likewise killed or captured in the field while at work. After the destruction of the fort, Shingas' band was pursued by three parties of settlers. The third party overtook them at Sidling Hill, where a brisk engagement took place for two hours, but Shingas being reinforced, the settlers retreated. Hance Hamilton, in a letter written to Captain Potter, dated Fort Lyttleton, April 4th, 1756, at eight o'clock in the evening, describes this engagement:

"These come to inform you of the melancholy news of what occurred between the Indians, that have taken many captives from McCord's Fort and a party of men under the command of Captain Alexander Culbertson and nineteen of our men, the whole amounting to about fifty, with the captives, and had a sore engagement, many of both parties killed and many wounded, the number unknown. Those wounded want a surgeon, and those killed require your assistance as soon as possible, to bury them. We have sent an express to Fort Shirley for Doctor Mercer, supposing Doctor Jamison is killed or mortally wounded in the expedition. He being not returned, therefore, desire you will send an express, immediately, for Doctor Prentic to Carlisle; we imagining Doctor Mercer cannot leave the fort under the circumstances the fort is under."

Likewise, Robert Robinson thus describes the attack on McCord's Fort and the pursuit of the savages:

"In the year 1756 a party of Indians came out of the Conococheague to a garrison named McCord's Fort, where they killed some and took a number prisoners. They then took their course near to Fort Lyttleton. Captain Hamilton being stationed there with a company, hearing of their route at McCord's Fort, marched with his company of men, having an Indian with him who was under pay. The Indians had McCord's wife with them; they cut off Mr. James Blair's head and threw it into Mrs. McCord's lap, saying that it was her husband's head; but she knew it to be Blair's."

As related earlier in this chapter, Mrs. McCord was taken to

Kittanning, where she was recaptured by Colonel Armstrong when he destroyed that Indian town on September 8, 1756.

An appropriate monument now marks the site of Fort Mc-Cord.

Attack on Wuench and Dieppel Families

On June 8th, a band of Indians crept up on Felix Wuench as he was ploughing on his farm near Swatara Gap, and shot him through the breast. The poor man cried lamentably and started to run, defending himself with a whip; but the Indians overtook him, tomahawked and scalped him. His wife, hearing his cries and the report of the guns, ran out of the house, but was captured with one of her own and two of her sister's children. A servant boy who saw this atrocity ran to a neighbor named George Miess, who, though he had a crippled leg, ran directly after the Indians and made such a noise as to scare them off.

On June 24th, Indians attacked the home of Lawrence Dieppel, in Bethel Township, Berks County, carrying off two of the children, one of whom they later killed and scalped.

Attack on Bingham's Fort

On June 12th occurred the attack on Bingham's Fort, located in the Tuscarawa Valley, in Tuscarawa Township, Juniata County. The Delaware chief, King Beaver, was the leader of the Indians on this occasion. On that day, as John Gray and Francis Innis were returning from Carlisle, where they had gone for salt, Gray's horse scared at a bear, threw him off, and ran away. While he was catching his horse and gathering up his pack of salt, Innis pressed on rapidly toward the fort, where his wife and three children, George Woods, Mrs. John Gray and her little daughter, Jane, and others, were carried off by King Beaver of the Turkey Tribe of Delawares. The Pennsylvania Gazette gave the following account of the capture of this fort: "George Woods, Nathaniel Bingham, Robert Taylor, his wife and children, and John Mc-Donell, were missing. Some of these it was supposed were burnt as a number of bones were found. Susan Jiles was found dead and scalped; Alexander McAlister and wife, James Adams, Jane Cochran and two children were missed. McAlister's house had been burned, and a number of cattle and horses had been driven off."

All the prisoners taken at Bingham's Fort were marched to Kittanning and from there to Fort Duquesne, where they were parceled out and adopted by the Indians. George Woods, one of the prisoners, was a very remarkable man. The French commander gave him to an old Indian named John Hutson, who removed him to his own wigwam. Woods later purchased his own ransom, and returned to the settlements. He was a surveyor, and followed this business in the counties of Juniata, Bedford, and Allegheny. When Pittsburgh was laid out, in 1765, he assisted in this work, and one of its principal streets, Wood Street, is named after him.

Capture of John McCullough

On July 26th the Indians entered the valley of the Conococheague, in Franklin County, killing Joseph Martin, and taking captive two brothers, John and James McCullough. James McCullough, the father of these boys, had only a few years before removed from Delaware into what is now Montgomery Township, Franklin County. At the time of this Indian incursion, the McCullough family were residing temporarily in a cabin three miles from their home, and the parents and their daughter, Mary, on the day of the capture, went home to pull flax. A neighbor, named John Allen, who had business at Fort Loudon, accompanied them to their home, and promised to return that way in the evening, and accompany them back to their cabin. However, he did not keep his promise, and returned by a circuitous route. When he reached the McCullough cabin on his return, he told John and James to hide, that Indians were near and that he supposed they had killed Mr. and Mrs. McCullough. John was but eight years old, and James but five at the time. They alarmed their neighbors, but none would volunteer to go to the McCullough home to warn Mr. and Mrs. McCollough, being too much interested in making preparations to hurry to the fort a mile distant for safety.

Then the boys determined to warn their parents themselves. Leaving their little sister, Elizabeth, aged two, asleep in bed, they proceeded to a point where they could see the McCullough home, and began to shout. When they had reached a point about sixty yards from the house, five Indians and a Frenchman, who had been secreted in the thicket, rushed upon them and took them captive. The parents were not captured, inasmuch as the father, hearing the boys shout, had left his work and thus the Indians missed him, and they failed to notice the mother and Mary at work in the field.

John and James were taken to Fort Duquesne. From this place James was carried to Canada, and all trace of him became

lost. John was taken to Kittanning, Kuskuskies, and the Muskingum, was adopted by the Delawares, and remained among them
for nine years until liberated by Colonel Bouquet in the autumn
of 1764. At one time his father came to Venango (Franklin) to
liberate him, but the boy had been so long among the Indians that
he preferred the Indian life to returning with his father, and succeeded in eluding him. After his liberation by Colonel Bouquet,
he returned to the community from which he had been taken nine
years before, and lived there nearly sixty years. He wrote a most
interesting account of his captivity, which sheds much light on the
manners and customs of the Delawares at that time.

During the same month (July), Hugh Robinson was captured
and his mother killed at Robinson's Fort, in Perry County. Hugh,
after being carried to the western part of the state, made his escape.
Also, during this same month a number of Indians appeared near
Fort Robinson, killed the daughter of Robert Miller, the wife of
James Wilson, and a Mrs. Gibson, and captured Hugh Gibson and
Betty Henry.

Also, during July, Samuel Miles and Lieutenant Atlee were
ambushed by three Indians near a spring about half a mile from
Fort Augusta, at Sunbury. A soldier named Bullock, who had
come to the spring for a drink, was killed. Miles and Atlee made
their escape. A rescuing party came out from the fort, and found
the soldier scalped, with his blood trickling into the spring, giving
its waters a crimson hue. The spring was ever afterwards called
the Bloody Spring.

Massacre Near Brown's Fort

On August 6th, a soldier named Jacob Ellis, of Brown's Fort,
about two miles north of Grantville, Dauphin County, desired to
cut some wheat on his farm a few miles from the fort, and, accordingly, took with him a squad of about ten soldiers as a guard. At
about ten o'clock a band of Indians crept up on the reapers, shot
the corporal dead, and wounded another of the soldiers. A little
after this attack, a soldier named Brown was found missing, and
the next morning his body was found near the harvest field. On
October 12th, the Indians made an incursion into this same neighborhood, killing Noah Frederick who was ploughing his field, and
capturing three children that were with him. A little later, Peter
Stample and Frederick Henley were killed in the same neighborhood.

Conococheague Valley Again Invaded

On August 27th, another incursion was made into the beautiful valley of the Conococheague, resulting in the slaying of thirty-nine settlers near the mouth of this stream. Also, early in November, some soldiers of the garrison at Fort McDowell, in the western part of Franklin County, where McDowell's Mill now stands, were ambushed, Privates James McDonald, William McDonald, Bartholomew McCafferty, and Andrew McQuoid being killed and scalped, and Captain James Corkin and Private William Cornwall carried into captivity. At the same time, the following settlers in the neighborhood were killed: John Culbertson, Samuel Perry, Hugh Kerrel, John Woods and his mother-in-law, and Elizabeth Archer; also four children of John Archer, and two boys named Sam Neily and James Boyd, were carried into captivity.

Attack on the Boyer Family

Sometime during the summer of 1756, though authorities differ as to the exact date, occurred the attack on the Boyer family, who lived in the vicinity of Fort Lehigh, at Lehigh Gap. The "Frontier Forts of Pennsylvania" thus describes this event:

"His [Boyer's] place was about 1½ miles east of the Fort, on land now owned by Josiah Arner, James Ziegenfuss and George Kunkle. With the other farmers he had gathered his family into the blockhouse for protection. One day, however, with his son Frederick, then thirteen years old, and the other children, he went home to attend to the crops. Mr. Boyer was ploughing and Fred was hoeing, whilst the rest of the children were in the house or playing near by. Without any warning they were surprised by the appearance of Indians. Mr. Boyer, seeing them, called to Fred to run, and himself endeavored to reach the house. Finding he could not do so, he ran towards the creek, and was shot through the head as he reached the farther side. Fred, who had escaped to the wheat field, was captured and brought back. The Indians, having scalped the father in his presence, took the horses from the plough, his sisters and himself, and started for Stone Hill, in the rear of the house. There they were joined by another party of Indians and marched northward to Canada. On the march the sisters were separated from their brother and never afterwards heard from. Frederick was a prisoner with the French and Indians in Canada for five years, and was then sent to Philadelphia. Of Mrs. Boyer, who remained in the blockhouse, nothing further is known. After reaching Philadelphia, Frederick made his way to Lehigh Gap, and took possession of the farm. Shortly after he married a daughter of Conrad Mehrkem, with whom he had four sons and four daughters. He died October 31, 1832, aged 89 years."

Expedition Against Great Island and Other Indian Strongholds

During the summer of 1756, Fort Augusta was built and garrisoned at Sunbury. The Delawares and Shawnees in the valley of the West Branch of the Susquehanna were committing so many atrocities that Colonel William Clapham, commander of the fort, sent an expedition against the Indian towns on the Juniata, Chincklamoose (Clearfield, Clearfield County), Great Island (Lock Haven, Clinton County), and other places on both branches of the Susquehanna. During October, Colonel Clapham received the intelligence that the Indians at Great Island were making incursions against the settlements. He then directed Captain John Hambright, of Lancaster, to lead a company of thirty-eight men, and destroy that Indian stronghold. There is no doubt that Captain Hambright carried out his instructions, but, unhappily, no records giving the details of his expedition are to be found. In this connection, we state that Colonel Clapham was one of the most conspicious figures on the frontier. In the early spring of 1763, he removed with his family to Sewickley Creek, where the town of West Newton, Westmoreland County, now stands. Here he and his entire family were cruelly murdered on the afternoon of May 8, 1763, by The Wolf, Kekuscung, and two other Indians, one of whom was called Butler.

Attack on a Friendly Delaware

This chapter has been devoted largely to a recital of atrocities committed by the Indians during the French and Indian War, —atrocities that make our flesh creep and cause chills to run down our pulses. Yet this history would be incomplete and unfair if we neglected to say that the white men were not always fair and honorable, on their part. The following instance of an attack on a friendly Delaware who had been converted to Christianity by the Moravian missionaries was reported to Governor Denny by Timothy Horsefield, in a letter dated November 29th, 1756:

"I beg leave to mention to your Honour, that a few Days Since as one of our Indians was in the Woods a Small distance from Bethlehem, with his Gun, hoping to meet with a Deer, on his return home he met with two men, who (as he Informs) he Saluted by taking off his Hat; he had not gone far before he heard a gun fired, and the Bullet whistled near him, which terefied him very much, and running thro' the thick Bushes, his gun lock Catched fast, and went off; he dropt it, his Hat, Blanket, &c., and came home much frightened. The Indians came to me complaining of this Treatment, Saying they fled from amongst the Murthering Indians, and come here to Bethlehem, and Adresst his Honour the Late Governor, and put themselves under His protection, which the Governor Answered to their Satisfaction, Desireing them to Sit Still amongst the Brethren, which they said they had done, and given offence to none. I told them I would do all in my Power to prevent such Treatment for the future, and that I would write to the Governor and inform him of it, and that they might be Assured the Governor would use proper measures to prevent any mischief happening. I thought at first to write a few Advertisements to warn wicked People for the future how they Behave to the Indians, for if one or more of them should be kill'd in such a manner, I fear it would be of very bad consequence; but I have since considered it is by no means proper for me to advertise, for as the Late Governor's proclamation is Expired, the first Proclamation of War against the Indians I conceive is still in force. I thought it my Duty to Inform your Honor of this Affair, and Doubt not you will take the matter into your wise Consideration."

CHAPTER XIX

Shingas, King Beaver and Pisquetomen

SHINGAS

HINGAS (Chingas, Shingiss, etc.) was a noted chief of the Turkey Clan of Delawares, a brother of King Beaver and Pisquetomen. By many authorities he is believed to have been a nephew of the great Sassoonan. He was a very cruel warrior. Heckewelder says of him: "Were his war exploits all on record, they would form an interesting document, though a shocking one. Conococheague, Big Cove, Sherman's Valley, and other settlements along the frontier, felt his strong arm sufficiently that he was a bloody warrior, cruel his treatment, relentless his fury. His person was small, but in point of courage and activity, savage prowess, he was said to have never been exceeded by anyone."

Shingas Made King of the Delawares

Shingas did not come into the kingship of the Delawares until 1752, on which date, at the Virginia treaty at Logstown, he was made head chief of the Delawares by Tanacharison as representative of the Six Nations. The Journal of the Virginia Commissioners to this treaty, under date of June 11th, describes his coronation as follows: "Afterwards the Half King [Tanacharison] spoke to the Delawares: 'Nephews, you received a speech last year from your brother, the Governor of Pennsylvania and from us, desiring you to choose one of the wisest councellors, and present him to us for a King. As you have not done it, we let you know it is our right to give you a King, and we think proper to give you Shingas for your King, whom you must look upon as your head chief, and with whom all public business must be transacted between you and your brethren, the English. On which the Half King put a laced hat on the head of The Beaver, who stood proxy for his brother, Shingas, and presented him with a rich jacket and a suit of English clothes, which had been delivered to the Half King by the Commissioners for that purpose.' "

Attention is called to the fact that, while Shingas is called "King" of the Delawares, it is hardly likely that either he or his brother, Beaver, who upon his death or abdication, became "King" could have been the leading chief of this tribe as they belonged to the Turkey Clan. According to immemorial custom the "King" of the three Delaware Clans had to be a member of the Turtle Clan, as were Tamanend and Sassoonan.

As has been seen in earlier chapters, a treaty between Pennsylvania and the Delawares, Shawnees and other Indians of the valleys of the Ohio and Allegheny, was held at Carlisle in October, 1753. Shingas was present at this treaty, as was also his brother, Pisquomen, representing the Delawares.

Washington Meets Shingas

When George Washington made his journey to the French forts in November, 1753, he found Shingas living where the town of McKees Rocks, Allegheny County, now stands. We read the following in Washington's Journal: "About two miles from this [the Forks of the Ohio], on the Southeast side of the River at a place where the Ohio Company intended to erect a fort, lives Shingas, King of the Delawares. We called upon him to invite him to council at the Logs Town. Shingas attended us to the Logs Town, where we arrived between sun setting and dark on the 25th day after I left Williamsburg."

Shingas took part in the conferences which Washington held with the Indians of Logstown before setting forth from that place to Venango and Le Boueff.

Croghan and Montour Meet Shingas at Logstown

When George Croghan and Andrew Montour were at Logstown in January and February, 1754, Shingas was one of the chiefs with whom they had conferences. On this occasion, Shingas joined with Scarouady, Delaware George, and several other chiefs on the Ohio, in requesting that the Governor of Virginia might build a "strong house" at the Forks of the Ohio and that the Governor of Pennsylvania might build "another house" somewhere on the Ohio. Just before these Pennsylvania messengers left Logstown (February 2nd), Shingas delivered to them the following speech:

"Brother Onas: I am glad to hear all our people here are of one mind. It is true I live on the river side, which is the French road, and I assure you by these strings of wampum [gave them

strings of wampum] that I will neither go down or up, but will remove nearer to my brethren, the English, where I can keep our
women and children safe from the enemy."

This promise Shingas did not keep, but deserted to the French.
We have seen, in Chapter XVIII, that, at Kittanning, on the Allegheny, and at Nescopeck, on the North Branch of the Susquehanna, he and Captain Jacobs planned many bloody expeditions
which they made against the frontier settlements after Braddock's
defeat.   He spent much of his time, during the French and Indian
War, inciting the Indians of Kittanning, Kuskuskies, Logstown, and
Sauconk against the English.   The latter town, at the mouth of
the Beaver, is sometimes called Shingas' Old Town.

Shingas Ravages the Frontier

As stated in Chapter XVI, on October 31st, 1755, Shingas began incursions into Fulton County, which lasted for several days,
and were the beginning of those incursions which made his name
"a terror to the frontier settlements of Pennsylvania."   The following letters describe these initial incursions:

Adam Hoops wrote Governor Morris from Conococheague
November 3rd:

"I am sorry I have to trouble you with this melancholy and
disagreeable news, for on Saturday I received an express from
Peters Township that the inhabitants of the Great Cove were all
murdered or taken captive, and their houses and barns all in
flames.   Some few fled, upon notice brought them by a certain
Patrick Burns, a captive, that made his escape that very morning
before this sad tragedy was done.

"Upon this information, John Potter, Esq., and self, sent express through our neighborhood, which induced many of them to
meet with us at John McDowell's Mill, where I with many others
had the unhappy prospect to see the smoke of two houses that were
set on fire by the Indians, viz, Matthew Patton's and Mescheck
James', where their cattle were shot down, the horses standing
bleeding with Indian arrows in them, but the Indians fled.

"The Rev. Mr. Steel, John Potter, Esq., and several others
with us, to the number of about an hundred, went in quest of the
Indians, with all the expedition imaginable, but to no success.
These Indians have likewise taken two women capitves, belonging
to said township.   I very much fear the Path Valley has under-
gone the same fate.

"We, to be sure, are in as bad circumstances as ever any poor Christians were in, for the cries of the widowers, widows, fatherless and motherless children, with many others, for their relations, are enough to pierce the hardest of hearts; likewise it's a very sorrowful spectacle to see those that escaped with their lives with not a mouthful to eat, or bed to lie on, or clothes to cover their nakedness, or keep them warm, but all they had consumed into ashes.

"These deplorable circumstances cry aloud for your Honour's most wise consideration, that you would take cognizance of and grant what shall seem most meet, for it is really very shocking, it must be, for the husband to see the wife of his bosom, her head cut off, and the children's blood drank like water by these bloody and cruel savages as we are informed has been the fate of many."

On the same day, John Potter, Sheriff of Cumberland County, wrote Richard Peters:

"Sir: This comes ye melancholy account of the ruin of the Great Cove, which is reduced to ashes, and numbers of the inhabitants murdered and taken captives on Saturday last about three of the clock in the afternoon. I received intelligence in conjunction with Mr. Adam Hoopes, and sent immediately and appointed our neighbors to meet at McDowell's. On Sunday morning, I was not there six minutes till we observed, about a mile and half distant, one, Matthew Patton's house and barn in flames, on which we sat off with about forty men, tho' there was at least one hundred and sixty there. Our old officers hid themselves for (ought as I know) to save their scalps until afternoon when danger was over; we went to Patton's with a seeming resolution and courage but found no Indians there, on which we advanced to a rising ground, where we immediately discovered another house and barn on fire belonging to Mesach James, about one mile up the creek from Thomas Bar's; we set off directly for that place, but they had gone up the creek to another plantation left by one widow Jordan the day before, but had unhappily gone back that morning with a young woman, daughter to one William Clark, for some milk for childer, were both taken captives but neither house nor barn hurt. I have heard of no more burnt in that valley yet, which makes me believe they have gone off for some time, but I much fear they will return before we are prepared for them, for it was three of the clock in the afternoon before a recruit came of about sixty men. Then we held council whether to pursue up the valley all night or return to McDowell's, the former of which I and Mr. Hoop and some others plead for, but could not obtain without putting it to votes, which done, we were out voted by a considerable number, upon which I and my company was left by them that night and came home, for I will not guard a man that will not fight when called in so eminent manner, for there was not six of these men that would consent to go in pursuit of the Indians.

"I am much afraid that Juniata, Tuscaroro, and Sherman's Valley hath suffered. There is two-thirds of the inhabitants of this valley who hath already fled, leaving their plantations, and, without speedy succor be granted, I am of opinion this county will be lead dissolute without inhabitant. Last night I had a family of upwards of an hundred of women and children who fled for succor. You cannot form no just idea of the distressed and distracted condition of our inhabitants unless your eyes seen and your ears heard their crys. I am of opinion it is not in the power of our representatives to meet in assembly at this time. If our Assembly will give us any additional supply of arms and ammunition, the latter of which is most wanted, I could wish it were put into the hands of such persons as would go out upon scouts after the Indians rather than for the supply of forts."

Benjamin Chambers, on November 2nd, wrote the following "to the inhabitants of the lower part of the County of Cumberland":

"If you intend to go to the assistance of your neighbours, you need wait any longer for the certainty of the news. The Great Cove is destroyed; James Campbell left this company last night and went to the fort at Mr. Steel's meeting house, and there saw some of the inhabitants of the Great Cove, who gave this account that, as they came over the hill, they saw their houses in flames. The messenger says that there is but 100, and that they divided into two parts. The one part to go against the Cove and the other against the Conolloways, and that there are no French among them. They are Delawares and Shawnees. The part that came against the Cove are under the command of Shingas, the Delaware King; the people of the Cove that came off saw several men lying dead; they heard the murder shout and the firing of guns, and saw the Indians going into the houses that they had come out of before they left sight of the Cove. I have sent express to Marsh Creek at the same time that I send this, so I expect there will be a good company from there this day, and as there is but 100 of the enemy, I think it is in our power (if God permit) to put them to flight, if you turn out well from your parts. I understand that the west settlement is designed to go if they can get any assistance to repel them."

Likewise, John Armstrong wrote Governor Morris from Carlisle, on November 2nd:

"At four o'clock this afternoon by expresses from Conegochego, we are informed that yesterday about 100 Indians were seen in the Great Cove. Among whom was Shingas, the Delaware King; that immediately after the discovery, as many as had notice fled, and looking back from an high hill, they beheld their houses on fire, heard several guns fired and the last shrieks of their dying neighbours; 'tis said the enemy divided and one part moved towards Canallowais. Mr. Hamilton was here with 60 men from York County when the express came, and is to march early tomorrow to the upper part of the county. We have sent out expresses everywhere, and intend to collect the forces of this lower part, expecting the enemy every moment at Sherman's Valley, if not nearer hand. I'm of opinion that no other means than a chain of block houses along or near the south side of the Kittatinny Mountain, from Susquehannah to the temporary line, can secure the lives and properties even of the old inhabitants of this county, the new settlement being all fled except Sherman's Valley, whom (if God do not preserve) we fear will suffer very soon."

Sherman's Valley and numerous other frontier settlements were desolated by this scourge of the frontier. Finally, Governor Denny, in 1756, set a price of two hundred pounds upon Shingas' head, but unhappily he was not killed or captured.

Capture of the Martin and Knox Families

Among the outrages committed by Shingas during the above incursion into Fulton County, was the capture of the family of John Martin, a settler in the Big Cove. On Saturday morning, November 1, 1755, Mrs. Martin learned that Indians were in the neighborhood, and, thereupon, sent her son, Hugh, aged seventeen, to their neighbor, Captain Stewart, requesting him to come and take her family with his to the block-house, as her husband, John Martin, had gone to Philadelphia for supplies for the family, and had not returned. When Hugh came in sight of his home on his way back from Captain Stewart's, whose house was burned, he saw the Indians capture his mother; his sister, Mary, aged nineteen; his sister, Martha, aged twelve; his sister, Janet, aged two; his brother, James, aged ten; and his brother, William, aged eight.

Hugh hid where a fallen tree lay on the bank of Cove Creek not far from the Martin house, which the Indians now burned to the ground.

After the Indians left, Hugh started toward Philadelphia to meet his father. All that day he found nothing but desolation, and in the evening, he came to a stable with some hay in it. Here he lay until morning. During the night something jumped on him, which proved to be a dog. In the morning he found some fresh eggs in the stable, which he ate. When he was ready to leave, a large colt came to the stable. Making a halter of rope, he mounted the colt and rode on his way. In the afternoon, he met some men who had gathered to pursue the Indians, among them being the owner of the colt, who was much surprised to find it so easily managed, as it was considered unruly. It is not known when Hugh met his father, but, at any rate, they returned and rebuilt the house.

Mrs. Martin and her children were taken to the Indian town of Kittanning. A warrior wished to marry Mary, which made the squaws jealous and they beat her dreadfully, so much so that her health rapidly declined, and one morning she was found on her knees dead in the wigwam. An Indian squaw claimed little Janet, and tied her to a rope fastened to a post. While she was thus confined, a French trader named Baubee came to the child, and she reached out her arms and called him father. He then took her in his arms, and the Indian woman who claimed her sold her to the trader for a blanket, who carried her to Quebec intending to adopt her. Later, Mrs. Martin was bought by the French, and also taken to Quebec, not knowing her child was there. Still later, Mrs. Martin bought her own freedom, and one day she found little Janet on the streets of Quebec. Janet was well dressed and had all appearances of being well cared for, but did not recognize the mother. Mrs. Martin followed Janet to the home of the French family who had her, identified her by some mark, and the family reluctantly gave up the child to the mother, who paid them what they had paid the Indians for her.

Mrs. Martin then sailed with Janet to Liverpool, England, from which place she took ship to Philadelphia, and joined her husband.

The boys, James and William, and the daughter, Martha, were taken to the Tuscarawas and Musknigum, in the state of Ohio. After Mrs. Martin and Janet returned to their home in the Big Cove, Mr. Martin, upon the close of the French and Indian War, endeavored to recover his child from the Indians. Traveling on horseback to the Ligonier Valley, he found an encampment of Indians, and tried to make arrangements with them for the return of his children, when they claimed to have raised his family and wanted pay. Being unable to pay them, he said something about not having employed them to raise his family; thereupon, they became angry, and he made his escape as fast as he could, being chased by two Indians on horseback to a point on the Allegheny Mountain, where the sound of the bells of the Indian horses ceased.

Mr. Martin eventually recovered his children when ten Shawnee chiefs, with about fifty of their warriors, together with a large body of Delawares, delivered to George Croghan, then deputy agent of Sir William Johnson, at Fort Pitt, on May 9th, 1765, the remainder of their prisoners that had not been delivered to Colonel Henry Bouquet when the latter made his expedition to the Muskingum, in the autumn of 1764, for the purpose of recovering the prisoners taken by the Indians during the French and Indian and the Pontiac-Guyasuta Wars,—just nine years and six months after their capture. Martha could read when captured, but during her captivity, she had forgotten this art. William and James, during their captivity, assisted the squaws in raising vegetables, caring for the children and old people, and grew up as Indians, in contrast to their brother, Hugh, who had escaped capture and became a man of considerable influence on the Pennsylvania frontier. Before being taken to the Muskingum, Martha, James, and William spent some time with their Indian captors on Big Sewickley Creek, in Westmoreland County. The boys became attached to the locality, and after their return, they patented two tracts of land in that vicinity, and lived there most of their lives.

Janet Martin, in 1774, married John Jamison. She has many descendants in Western Pennsylvania, especially in Westmoreland County, among them being the well-known Robert S. Jamison family, of Greensburg.

During the same incursion, occurred the capture of the Knox family, who lived some distance from the Big Cove. On Sunday morning, November 2nd, 1755, while the family were engaged in morning worship, they were alarmed by the barking of their dogs. Then, two men of their acquaintance, who had come to the Knox home on Saturday evening for the purpose of attending religious services the next day, went to the door. They were immediately shot down by the Indians, and the rest of the family taken prisoners. After the Indians returned to the town from which they had come, no doubt Kittanning, each warrior who had lost a brother in the incursion was given a prisoner to kill. As there were not enough men to go around, little Jane Knox was given to one of the warriors as his victim. Placing her at the root of a tree, this savage commenced throwing his tomahawk close to her head, exclaiming that his brother, who was killed, was a warrior, and that the other Indians had given him only a squaw to kill. Jane expected that every moment would be her last. Presently, an Indian squaw came running and claimed Jane as her child, thus saving her life. She later returned to the settlements, and became the wife of Hugh Martin, mentioned above. Later Hugh Martin was one of the commissioners who located the first court house in Greensburg.

Shingas Burns Fort McCord

In the spring of 1756, Shingas again scourged the Pennsylvania frontier. His principal act in the incursions of this spring was the capture and burning of Fort McCord, in Franklin County, on April 1st. This atrocity was described in Chapter XVIII, and needs no further reference here.

Post Meets Shingas on Peace Mission
To Western Indians

When the Moravian missionary, Christian Frederick Post, as the agent of Pennsylvania, made his two journeys to the Ohio and Allegheny in the summer of 1758, he met and conferred with Shingas. During this summer Shingas was located most of the time at Kuskuskies, Logstown, and Sauconk, but shortly prior thereto had been residing, for a time, on the Muskingum in Ohio. The object of Post's mission was to make peace with the Western Indians. The neutrality of the Delawares on the Susquehanna had already been secured by treaties with Teedyuscung, an account of which will be given in the chapters on Teedyuscung (Chapters XXI and XXII), and now the problem was to secure the neutrality of the Delawares and Shawnees of the valleys of the Ohio and Allegheny.

It is doubtful whether any more suitable person could have been found in all the colonies for carrying the peace proposal to the Western Delawares than Christian Frederick Post. Born in Germany, he came to America and labored as a Moravian missionary among the Delawares. For a time he was located at Wyoming.

The Delawares loved and trusted him. For years he had lived among them in all the intimacy of friends and companions. His first wife was Rachael, an Indian convert, whom he married in 1743, and who died at the Moravian mission at Bethlehem in 1747 In 1749, he chose as his second wife, Agnes, a dusky daughter of the Delawares, who was baptized by Bishop Cammerhof March 5, 1749, and who died at Bethlehem in 1751. So that the Delawares, in dealing with Post, looked upon him as of their own flesh and blood.

At Kuskuskies, on the 18th day of August, Shingas, Delaware George, and King Beaver advised Post that before they could enter into a treaty of peace with Pennsylvania, it would be necessary for them to get in touch with the tribes living as far as beyond the Lakes, but that they would work steadfastly to this end.

Some of Post's conferences on this first mission to the Ohio were held under the very guns of Fort Duquesne. On the 24th of August his party arrived on the bank of the Allegheny River directly opposite the fort, where King Beaver introduced the missionary to a number of Indians, all of whom were glad to hear his message of peace, except an old, deaf Onondaga, who objected strongly to both Post's message and his presence. At the same place, on August 25th, Post was told "not to stir from the fire, that the French had offered a great reward for my [Post's] scalp, and that several parties were out for that purpose." "Accordingly," says Post, "I stuck constantly as close to the fire as if I had been charmed there." At a council held here on the 26th, the intrepid missionary gave his message of peace. There were present altogether three hundred French and Indians. That aftrnoon, the French in council at the fort, demanded that Post be delivered to them, but their Indian allies objected. In fact the French were anxious to kill him, and had bribed one of his Indian companions named Daniel "to leave me there."

Says Dr. Donehoo: "It is a marvel that Post ever returned from this mission at the site of Fort Duquesne, from which place no Englishman had returned alive since Braddock's defeat, except a few prisoners who had escaped. Post was in a hostile country, with a large reward offered for his scalp, and there were many Indians about him who were not entirely friendly, and one of his own companions had been bribed to kill him—yet he came through it all. On the night of 26th of August the Indians who had taken Post to Fort Duquesne realized it was no longer safe for him to remain there, so before daybreak on the 27th, Post left with a party of six Indians taking a different trail than the ones over which they had come. The main body of Indians remained behind to know whether the French would make any attempt to take him by force. . . . . . . They [Post and his party] reached Sauconk that night, where they were gladly received."

A Significant Question

Post notes in the journal of his first mission to the Ohio, under date of August 28th, the following in regard to Shingas and Daniel:

"We set out from Sauconk in company with twenty for Kuskuskies. On the road Shingas addressed himself to me and asked if I did not think that, if he came to the English, they would hang him, as they had offered a great reward for his head. He spoke in a very soft and easy manner. I told him that was a great while ago; it was all forgotten and wiped away; that the English would receive him very kindly. Then Daniel interrupted me and said to Shingas: "Don't believe him; he tells nothing but idle lying stories. Wherefore did the English hire one thousand two hundred Indians to kill us?' I protested it was false; he said: 'G—d d—n you for a fool; did you not see the woman lying in the road that was killed by the Indians that the English hired?' I said: 'Brother, do consider how many thousand Indians the French have hired to kill the English and how many they have killed along the frontier.' Then Daniel said: '*D—n you. Why do not you and the French fight on the sea? You come here only to cheat the poor Indians and take their land from them.*' Then Shingas told him to be still, for he did not know what he said. We arrived at Kuskuskies before night, and I informed Pisquetomen of Daniel's behavior, at which he appeared sorry."

Shingas Kind to Prisoners

Also, under date of August 29th, Post notes again in his journal:

"I dined with Shingas. He told me, though the English had set a great price on his head, he never thought to revenge himself, but was always very kind to any prisoners that were brought him; and that he assured the Governor he would do all in his power to bring about an established peace, and wished he could be certain of the English being in earnest."

We state in this connection that Heckewelder testifies that

Shingas, though a terrible warrior in battle, was never known to treat prisoners cruelly. "One day," says Heckewelder, "in the summer of 1762, while passing with him near by where two prisoners of his, boys about twelve years of age, were amusing themselves with his own boys, as the chief observed that my attention was arrested by them, he asked me at what I was looking. Telling him in reply that I was looking at his prisoners, he said: 'When I first took them, they were such; but now they and my children eat their food from the same bowl, or dish.' Which was equivalent to saying that they were, in all respects, on an equal footing with his own children, or alike dear to him." Shingas was, at that time, living on the Muskingum.

The Indians' Point of View

On September 1st, at Kuskuskies, Shingas, King Beaver, Delaware George, and Pisquetomen unburdened their hearts, and frankly told Post the cause of their hostility to the English during the French and Indian War. Their statements, also, revealed the real reason why, after the close of this conflict, they again took up arms against the English in Pontiac's War, which, in 1763, drenched the frontier with the blood of the pioneers. Post reports the truly patriotic speeches of these great chiefs, as follows:

"Brother, we have thought a great deal since God has brought you to us; and this is a matter of great consequence, which we cannot readily answer; we think on it, and will answer you as soon as we can. Our feast hinders us; all our young men, women and children are glad to see you; before you came, they all agreed together to go and join the French; but since they have seen you, they all draw back; *though we have great reason to believe you intend to drive us away, and settle the country; or else, why do you come to fight in the land that God has given us?*"

"I said, we did not intend to take the land from them; but only to drive the French away. *They said, they knew better;* for that they were informed so by our greatest traders; and some Justices of the Peace had told them the same, and the French, said they, tell us much the same thing,—'that the English intend to destroy us, and take our lands; but the land is ours, and not theirs; therefore, we say, if you will be at peace with us, we will send the French home. It is you that have begun the war, and it is necessary that you hold fast, and be not discouraged, in the work of peace. We love you more than you love us; for when we take any prisoners from you, we treat them as our own children.   We are poor, and yet we clothe them as well as we can, though you see our children are as naked as at the first.   By this you may see that our hearts are better than yours.   It is plain that you white people are the cause of this war; *why do not you and the French fight in the old country, and on the sea?   Why do you come to fight on our land?   This makes every body believe you want to take the land from us by force, and settle it.'*

"I told them, 'Brothers, as for my part, I have not one foot of land, nor do I desire to have any; and if I had any land, I had rather give it to you, than take any from you.   Yes, brothers, if I die, you will get a little more land from me; for I shall then no longer walk on that ground, which God has made.   We told you that you should keep nothing in your heart, but bring it before the council fire, and before the Governor, and his council; they will readily hear you; and I promise you, what they answer they will stand to.   I further read to you what agreements they made about Wyoming, and they stand to them.'

"They said, 'Brother, your heart is good; you speak always sincerely; but we know there are always a great number of people that want to get rich; they never have enough; look, we do not want to be rich, and take away that which others have.   God has given you the tame creatures; we do not want to take them from you.   God has given to us the deer, and other wild creatures, which we must feed on; and we rejoice in that which springs out of the ground, and thank God for it.   Look now, my brother, the white people think we have no brains in our heads; but that they are great and big, and that makes them make war with us; we are but a little handful to what you are; but remember, when you look for a wild turkey you cannot always find it, it is so little it hides itself under the bushes; and when you hunt for a rattlesnake, you cannot find it; and perhaps it will bite you before you see it.   However, since you are so great and big, and we so little, do you use your greatness and strength in completing this work of peace.   This is the first time that we saw or heard of you, since the war begun, and we have great reason to think about it, since such a great body of you comes into our lands.   It is told us, that you and the French contrived the war to waste the Indians between you; and that you and the French intended to divide the land between you; this was told us by the chief of the Indian traders; and they said further, brothers, this is the last time we shall come among you; for the French and the English intend to kill all the Indians, and then divide the land among themselves.'

"Then they addressed themselves to me, and said: 'Brother, I suppose you know something about it; or has the Governor stopped your mouth, that you cannot tell us?'

"Then I said: 'Brothers, I am very sorry to see you so jealous. I am your own flesh and blood, and sooner than I would tell you any story that would be of hurt to you, or your children, I would suffer death; and if I did not know that it was the desire of the Governor, that we should renew our old brotherly love and friendship, that subsisted between our grandfathers, I would not have undertaken this journey. I do assure you of mine and the people's honesty. If the French had not been here, the English would not have come; and consider, brothers, whether, in such a case, we can always sit still.'

"Then they said: 'It is a thousand pities we did not know this sooner; if we had, it would have been peace long before now.'

"Sept. 2nd.—I bade Shingas to make haste and dispatch me, and once more desired to know of them, if it was possible for them to guide me to the General. [General Forbes, who was then marching against Fort Duquesne]. Of all which they told me they would consider; and Shingas gave me his hand, and said, 'Brother, the next time you come, I will return with you to Philadelphia, and will do all in my power to prevent any body's coming to hurt the English more.'

"6th.—Pisquetumen, Tom Hickman and Shingas told me, 'Brother, it is good that you have stayed so long with us; we love to see you, and wish to see you here longer; but since you are so desirous to go, you may set off tomorrow; Pisquetumen has brought you here, and he may carry you home again; you have seen us, and we have talked a great deal together, which we have not done for a long time before. Now, Brother, we love you, but cannot help wondering why the English and French do not make up with one another, and tell one another not to fight on our land.'

"King Beaver and Shingas spoke to Pisquetumen. 'Brother, you told us that the Governor of Philadelphia and Teedyuscung took this man [Post] out of their bosoms, and put him into your bosom, that you should bring him here; and you have brought him here to us; and we have seen and heard him; and now we give him into your bosom, to bring him to the same place again, before the Governor; but do not let him quite loose; we shall rejoice when we shall see him here again.' They desired me to speak to the Governor, in their behalf, as follows:

" 'Brother, we beg you to remember our oldest brother, Pis-quetumen, and furnish him with good clothes, and reward him well for his trouble; for we shall look upon him when he comes back.'"

While at Kuskuskies, on this first peace mission to the Western Indians, Post received from Shingas, King Beaver, Delaware George, Pisquetomen, John Hickman, Killbuck, Keckenapaulin, and eight other chiefs, a "speech belt" of eight rows, by which the western tribes agreed to the peace with the English. The accept-ance of this belt by the Governor of Pennsylvania would make peace effective with these Indians. Pisquetomen and John Hick-man delivered the belt at the Grand Council at Easton, in October, 1758.

On Post's second journey to the Ohio (Autumn of 1758), he again met Shingas and held council with him at Kuskuskies, Sau-conk, and Logstown, finding him anxious to make peace with the English on behalf of the Western Indians. Before Post left for Eastern Pennsylvania, the French had abandoned and set fire to Fort Duquesne, November 24th. The next day the advance troops of the army of General John Forbes took possession of its smould-ering ruins, and this "Gateway of the West", which had cost Pennsylvania and the English great sacrifies of blood and treasure to possess, was named Pittsburgh, in honor of William Pitt. Had not Shingas and his associate chiefs, welcomed the peace message of the gentle Moravian missionary, who can tell how different would have been the result? Would the Anglo-Saxon today have the ascendancy in the Western World? Would America be speak-ing French today? Logstown and Sauconk were filled with war-riors, and in the villages in the valleys of the Tuscarawas and Muskingum were hundreds of others. One word from Shingas or King Beaver, and they would have arisen in savage wrath. But that word was not spoken, because Post, whom they loved and in whom they had confidence, held them silent and kept them from assisting the French, as the army of General Forbes marched over the mountains and through the wilderness to dislodge the French from the beautiful and fertile valleys of the Ohio and Allegheny, and to end the French and Indian War in Pennsylvania.

Shingas at Fort Pitt

On July 5th, 1759, a council was held, at the newly erected Fort Pitt, between George Croghan, Captain William Trent, and Captain Thomas McKee, on the one hand, and the representatives of the Six Nations, Delawares, Shawnees, and Wyandots. This was the first large gathering of Indians at Fort Pitt. Andrew Montour was the interpreter, while Colonel Hugh Mercer and the garrison were also present. The Delawares were represented by Shingas, King Beaver, Delaware George, Killbuck, and The Pipe; and the Six Nations by Guyasuta. Croghan informed the assembled chiefs of the terms of the Treaty of Easton. These were confirmed, and the Indians promised to return the captives held in their villages.

On August 12th, 1760, General Monckton held a conference at Fort Pitt with the Western Indians, for the purpose of assuring them that the English had no design of taking the Indians' lands. In the first part of September, Shingas and Andrew Montour went to Presque Isle (Erie) to join Croghan and Major Robert Rogers in leading an expedition to take possession of Detroit and other western posts surrendered by the French.

Shingas Attends Lancaster Treaty of 1762

After the erection of Fort Pitt in 1759 Shingas retired to Kuskuskies, and later to the Muskingum and the Tuscarawas.

Early in February, 1762, Governor James Hamilton received a letter from Shingas and King Beaver, through their faithful friend, Christian Frederick Post, advising the Governor that they desired to hold a treaty with him in the following spring.

The Colonial Authorities had made many efforts after Post's mission to the Western Indians in 1758, to induce Shingas and King Beaver to come to Philadelphia for a conference. Shingas had declined to come, fearing that the English would retaliate upon him for the terrible atrocities that he had committed upon the frontier settlements during the French and Indian War. Now, however, that peace was secure and the Indian raids upon the border had stopped, Shingas wanted to meet the Governor in conference.

In March, the Governor sent a reply to Shingas and Beaver through Post, inviting these two chiefs to come to Lancaster to hold a conference at that place, inasmuch as smallpox was raging in Philadelphia. Post was appointed as the guide and escort, not only for the two chiefs and their delegation of Indians, but also for the captives which were to be returned by the Indians from the villages on the Muskingum and Tuscarawas, as well as the villages on the Beaver and Ohio. Post immediately went to the villages of Shingas and Beaver on the Tuscarawas, and began preparations for their return on the 25th of June. He was beset with many troubles. He had difficulty in getting Shingas and Beaver to return with him and also in keeping the captives from running away and returning to the Indian villages. Dr. George P. Donehoo, in "Pennsylvania A History" thus comments upon the reluctance of the white captives to return to the settlements:

"One of the most remarkable facts in the relation of the English with the Indians during this entire period is that these captives, whose parents or husbands or wives had been most cruelly killed and scalped by Indians, had to be guarded and oftentimes fettered in order to keep them from running back to the captivity from which they had been released. One explanation of this most peculiar condition has been attempted by some writers, who have dealt with the topic, saying that the captives were men and women of the lower sort, and had not been accustomed to anything different from that which had been their condition in the villages of their Indian masters. But this is an absolutely false statement. Some of them had been taken from the best class of frontier families. The great majority of them, as shown by their names, belonged to the hardy, religious Scotch-Irish families along the frontiers of Pennsylvania and Virginia, which furnished the leading men and women of the Colonial period. The only explanation is to be found in the statements made by the captives and by the Indians, that these adopted relations were treated with the utmost kindness and respect by their captors."

When Post, Shingas, Beaver, the other Indians, and the white captives reached Fort Pitt, Post held a conference with King Beaver in which this chief advised him that the Indians had already delivered seventy-four prisoners at that fort. After many difficulties, Post, Shingas, Beaver, the other Indians, and the remaining captives reached Lancaster, on August 8th, where the great conference began on the 12th of that month. Further details of this conference are given in Chapter XXII, but in this connection, we state that the principal matters discussed were the return of the prisoners and the claim on the part of the Delawares that they had been defrauded out of their lands by the Pennsylvania authorities. The conference was closed by giving the Indian delegation many presents.

Shingas in Pontiac's War

After a few year's of peace between Pennsylvania and the Indians, Pontiac's War, which opened in May, 1763, desolated the frontier. On the opening of this war, Shingas was living on the Tuscarawas, and Fort Pitt was commanded by Captain Simon Ecuyer. On May 31st, Captain Ecuyer received the following account from Shingas and King Beaver, which they had delivered to Thomas Calhoun, a trader at Tuscarawas, at eleven o'clock, on the night of May 27, 1763:

"Brother, King Beaver, with Shingas, Windohala, Wingenum, Daniel, and William Anderson, out of regard to you and the friendship that formerly subsisted between our grandfathers and the English, which has been lately renewed by us, we come to inform you of the news we had heard, which you may depend upon as true. All the English that were at Detroit were killed ten days ago; not one left alive. At Sandusky, all the white people there were killed five days ago, nineteen in number, except the officer, who is a prisoner, and one boy who made his escape, whom we have not heard of. At the mouth of the Mamee River, Hugh Crawford with one boy was taken prisoner and six men killed. At the Salt Licks [on the Mahoning in Ohio], five days ago, five white men were killed. We received the account this day. We have seen a number of tracks on the road between this and Sandusky, not far off, which we are sure is a party come to cut you and your people off; but as we have sent a man to watch their motions, request you may think of nothing you have here, but make the best of your way to some place of safety; as we would not desire to see you killed in our town. Be careful to avoid the road, and every part where Indians resort. Brother, what goods and other effects you have here, you need not be uneasy about them. We assure you that they will take care to keep them safe for six months. Perhaps by that time we may see you, or send you word what you may expect of us."

As set forth in Chapter XXIII, Shingas took part in the siege of Fort Pitt, in July, 1763. On July 26th, he and Turtle Heart, held a parley with Captain Ecuyer, the commandant, under a flag of truce, and requested him to withdraw the troops from that place. Soon after this Shingas disappears from history. What became of him or when he died is not known, though some authorities have endeavored to identify him with Buckongehelas, a Delaware chief, who was living in Ohio as late as 1800. Some have suggested, too, that Shingas commanded the Indians at the battle of Bushy Run, Westmoreland County, on August 6th, 1763, but this is very improbable, as both he and King Beaver were not in entire sympathy with Pontiac's uprising. It is much more likely that Guyasuta, an account of whom is given in Chapter XXIII, commanded the Indians at this battle.

KING BEAVER

King Beaver, or Tamaque, a chief of the Turkey Clan of Delawares, was, as has been seen in this chapter, a brother of Shingas and Pisquetomen, and possibly a nephew of the great Sassoonan. Upon the death or abdication of Shingas, he succeeded to the kingship of the Delaware tribe.

King Beaver's first important appearance in history is when George Croghan and Andrew Montour were at Logstown, in May, 1751, delivering the present of Pennsylvania to the tribes of the Ohio and Allegheny. On this occasion, King Beaver requested that Pennsylvania would build a "strong house on the River Ohio, so that in case of war with the French, the Indians of the Ohio Valley might have a place of security."

On this occasion, too, he replied to a suggestion that the Delawares should comply with the promise that they had made the Governor of Pennsylvania, three years before to choose a new chief to succeed Sassoonan, who, as we have seen, died in the autumn of 1747. King Beaver said that, inasmuch as all the wise men of the Delawares were not gathered together, it would take considerable time to select a man competent to rule over them, but that as soon as possible they would make a selection, which he trusted would be satisfactory, not only to the English, but also to the Six Nations.

He was also present at the treaty which the Virginia commissioners held with the Western Indians at Logstown, in June, 1752. On this occasion he stood proxy for his brother, Shingas, when Tanacharison as the representative of the Six Nations crowned Shingas King of the Delawares, as was seen earlier in this chapter.

King Beaver at Aughwick Conferences

As was related in the latter part of Chapter XIV, King Beaver attended the conferences with Conrad Weiser, George Croghan, Tanacharison, and Scarouady, held at Aughwick in September,

1754. It will be recalled that upon Washington's defeat at the Great Meadows in the early part of July of that year, the friendly Indians assembled at Aughwick, where supplies were distributed to them by George Croghan, and that Weiser was sent to Aughwick to investigate the manner in which Croghan was distributing the supplies, and make a report thereon to the Pennsylvania Authorities.

Tanacharison and Scarouady were the principal Indian speakers at these conferences; but King Beaver, as the representative of the Delawares, also took part. A speech which he made at Aughwick on this occasion sheds some light on the time of the subjugation of the Delawares by the Iroquois.

Said he: "I must now go into the depth and put you in mind of old histories and our first acquaintance with you when William Penn first appeared in his ship on our lands. We looked in his face and judged him to be our brother and gave him a fast hold to tie his ship to; and we told him that a powerful people called the Five Nations had placed us here and established a fair and lasting friendship with us, and that he, the said William Penn, and his people shall be welcome to be one of us, and in the same union, to which he and his people agreed; and we then erected an everlasting friendship with William Penn and his people, and we on our side, so well as you, and observed as much as possible to this day. We desire you will look upon us in the same light, and let that treaty of friendship, made by our forefathers on both sides, subsist and be in force from generation to generation."

King Beaver in the French and Indian War

There are very few records of the activities of King Beaver during the French and Indian War; but there is no doubt that he assisted in many an incursion against the Pennsylvania frontier. Egle in his "History of Pennsylvania" states that it was King Beaver who led the band of Delawares who captured Bingham's Fort in the Tuscarora Valley in Juniata County, on June 12, 1756, an account of which was given in Chapter XVIII. We have already seen, in this chapter, the important part that he played in the peace missions of Christian Frederick Post to the Western Indians in the summer and autumn of 1758.

King Beaver was the principal speaker at the great council held at Fort Pitt on July 5, 1759, referred to earlier in this chapter, which gathered the fruits of Post's mission of the preceding year.

He was also present at the great Indian conference with General Monckton at Fort Pitt on August 12, 1760, held for the purpose of assuring the Western Indians that the English had no design of taking their lands upon the close of the French and Indian War. In the spring of 1761 he sent White Eyes, (also known as Grey-Eyes) and Wingemund to meet Governor Hamilton in council at Philadelphia and to advise him that a number of chiefs of the Western Indians proposed coming to Philadelphia to cement the bond of peace established between them and the Colony at the close of the French and Indian War.

As we have seen in the present chapter, in 1762 King Beaver, Shingas, and a number of other chiefs from the Mukingum, Tuscarawas, and Ohio, accompanied Christian Frederick Post to the great conference which was held at Lancaster in August of that year, where they delivered up the white captives which had been taken during the French and Indian War, and held in various villages on the Muskingum and Tuscarawas. His speech at this conference, that he knew nothing of the basis of the charge which Teedyuscung made as to the fraudulent character of the Walking Purchase, had no doubt much to do with Teedyuscung's finally agreeing to withdraw the charge of fraud.

On the outbreak of Pontiac's War, in May, 1763, King Beaver was one of the chiefs who, as related earlier in this chapter, warned Thomas Calhoun, a trader at Tuscarawas, to flee toward the eastern settlements. What part, if any, he took in Pontiac's uprising is not definitely known, though both he and Shingas had warned the English that a war would result if they remained on the Ohio. From all the data that can be found, we are justified in assuming that King Beaver was not in hearty sympathy with Pontiac's aims and purposes, at least at the beginning of the uprising. When Colonel Bouquet led his expedition to the Muskingum and Tuscarawas in the summer and autumn of 1764, King Beaver was one of the principal Delaware chiefs in that region, and Colonel Bouquet compelled him and the other chiefs of the western tribes to surrender the prisoners which had been taken in Pontiac's War.

King Beaver's next appearance in the history of Pennsylvania is when he, with New Comer, Wingenund, Custaloga, Guyasuta, White-Eyes, Captain Pipe, and other chiefs of the western tribes, attended the great conference which opened at Fort Pitt, on May 10th, 1765, held for the purpose of resuming trade relations between Pennsylvania and these Indians after the close of Pontiac's

War.   Andrew Montour, it will be remembered, was the interpreter on this occasion.

King Beaver also attended the great council at Fort Pitt April 26th to May 9th, 1768, held between Pennsylvania, the western tribes, and Six Nations, for the purpose of adjusting the difficulties growing out of the fact that settlements were being established in the valleys of the Youghiogheny and Monongahela, on territory not purchased from the Indians.   Over one thousand Indians attended this council, which led to the great purchase at Fort Stanwix (Rome, New York), on November 5th of this year, more particularly described in Chapter XX.

King Beaver had various residences during that part of his life spent in Western Pennsylvania—Logstown, Sauconk, and Kuskuskies.   The Beaver River bears his name.   As early as 1756, he established the town of Tuscarawas on the river of the same name in Ohio, a town which was later known as King Beaver's Town. Here he died in 1771, admonishing his people to accept Christianity.   In the latter years of his life, he had come under the influence of the Moravians, and invited them to establish missions among the Delawares of Ohio.   Upon his death, Captain Johnny, or Straight Arm, succeeded to the kingship of the Turtle Clan of Delawares, but White Eyes, an account of whom is given in Chapter XXV, was the actual ruler.

PISQUETOMEN

As we have seen also, in this chapter, Pisquetomen, a chief of the Turkey Clan of Delawares, was a brother of Shingas and King Beaver, and possibly a nephew of Sassoonan.   His first important appearance in Pennsylvania history is when he, Sassoonan, and other Delaware chiefs conveyed to the Penns, in September, 1732, "all the land along the Schuylkill between the Lechay Hills and Kittochtinny Hills, from the Branches of the Delaware to the Branches of the Susquehanna."   He was also one of the chiefs who attended the great conference at Carlisle in October, 1753, mentioned in former chapters.

We have seen in this chapter the important part that Pisquetomen played in Post's mission to the Western Indians in the summer and autumn of 1758.   It is on account of these services that this chief especially claims our remembrance.

We close this sketch of these three distinguished brothers by calling attention to the statement which King Beaver and Shingas made to Pisquetomen at Kuskuskies just before Post left for the East upon the completion of his first mission to the Western Indians:

"Brother, you told us that the Governor of Pennsylvania and Teedyuscung took this man [Post] out of their bosoms and put him into your bosoms, that you should bring him here; and you have brought him to us; and we have seen and heard him; and now we give him into your bosom, to bring him to the same place again before the Governor."

CHAPTER XX

Madam Montour and Her Son, Andrew Montour

MADAM MONTOUR

MADAM MONTOUR was the first of a family whose name is closely connected with the Indian annals of Pennsylvania. There is much doubt as to her birth. She claimed to be the daughter of an Indian woman, probably a Huron, and one of the governors of Canada. Whether this is true or not, about 1664, a Frenchman, Montour by name, settled in Canada, where he married an Indian woman by whom he became the father of a son and two daughters. The son grew up among the Indians, who were, at that time, allies of the French. In 1685, while in the service of the French, he was wounded in a fight with two Mohawks on Lake Champlain. Later, he deserted the French, and, in 1709, he was killed while inducing twelve of the western tribes to support the English.

So much for the son of the nobleman, Montour. One of the daughters married a Miami Indian, and became lost to history. The other daughter, the noted Madam Montour, was born prior to 1684. When a child of ten years, she was captured by the Iroquois, and adopted, probably by the Seneca tribe, for, upon reaching womanhood, she married a Seneca, named Roland Montour, according to the "Hand Book of American Indians," by whom she had the following children: Andrew, Robert, Louis, and Margaret. Upon the death of her Seneca husband, she married the noted Oneida chief, Carondowanen, or "Big Tree", who later took the name of Robert Hunter, in honor of the Governor of New York. He was killed, about the year 1729, in North Carolina, in the war between the Iroquois and the Catawbas.

Madam Montour's first appearance as an official interpreter was at the Albany Treaty, in August, 1711. Her first appearance as an official interpreter in Pennsylvania was at a conference held in Philadelphia, July 3rd to 5th, 1727, between the Provincial Council and chiefs of the Six Nations, mostly Cayugas, in which the chiefs requested that no English settlements be made up the Susquehanna farther than Paxtang (Harrisburg), explaining that this territory was on the road by which the Six Nations went to war against the Catawbas, and that they feared that misfortunes would befall their warlike activities, if their warriors were furnished with rum by the settlers along the route. She became a noted interpreter, and was uniformly friendly to the Colony of Pennsylvania. Her sons, too, were loyal to the Colony, and Andrew, received large grants of donation lands lying along Chillisquaque Creek, in Northumberland County, and on the Loyalsock, where Montoursville, Lycoming County, is situated. A creek, a river, a town, a county, and a mountain range—all in Pennsylvania—are named for her, or members of her family. She lived for many years at the village of Ostonwackin, sometimes called Frenchtown, at the mouth of Loyalsock Creek, in Lycoming County.

She was living at Ostonwackin when she and her son, Andrew, welcomed Count Zinzindorf, the Moravian missionary, upon his visit to that place, in 1742. Upon hearing the Count preach the Gospel and relate the history of the Saviour's life upon earth, she burst into a flood of tears, as the almost forgotten truths flashed upon her mind. It was learned that she believed that Bethlehem, the birthplace of Christ, was situated in France, and that it was the English who crucified Him,—a perversion of the truth that it is believed, she had heard in her youth from French teachers among the Indians. It is thought that she died in 1752 at the home of her son, Andrew.

Madam Montour and two of her daughters attended the Lancaster Treaty of June and July, 1744. One daughter, known as French Margaret, was the wife of Keteriondia, alias Peter Quebec, and lived near Sunbury prior and subsequent to 1733. Another daughter was one of the converts at the Moravian Mission, at New Salem, Ohio, April 14th, 1791. This daughter spoke English, French, and six Indian languages. A granddaughter was Catherine, of Catherine's Town, near the head of Seneca Lake, New York, destroyed by General Sullivan, on September 3rd, 1779. Catherine was a daughter of French Margaret. Esther Montour, known as Queen Esther, "the fiend of Wyoming," was a granddaughter of Madam Montour and a daughter of French Margaret.

It is claimed that Madam Montour was a lady of education, of genteel manners, and handsome of face and form. It is said, too, that, on her various trips to Philadelphia as interpreter at Indian conferences, she was entertained by ladies of the best society. But, inasmuch as she was twice married to an Indian warrior, it is probable that her education and refinement have been overstated. Some have made the claim that she had no Indian blood, and that, for some unknown reason, she preferred the life and dress of the Indian. Near the end of her life, she became blind, but had sufficient bodily vigor to go on horseback from Logstown to Venango in two days, a distance of about seventy miles, her son, Andrew, leading the horse. She and this son are among the most picturesque characters in the Indian history of Pennsylvania.

ANDREW MONTOUR

Andrew Montour, whose Indian name was Sattelihu, was the oldest and most noted of the children of Madam Montour. We have met Andrew many times thus far in these sketches, but we devote the remainder of this chapter to additional information concerning this interesting character.

The first glimpse that we get of the "Half Indian", as Montour is frequently called, is when Count Zinzindorf, the Moravian missionary, visited Ostonwackin in September of 1742. Zinzindorf writes of his meeting with Montour as follows:

"On September 30, 1742, as we were not far from Ostonwackin, Conrad Weiser rode to the village. He soon returned in company with Andrew, Madam Montour's oldest son. Andrew's cast of countenance is decidedly European, and had his face not been encircled with a broad band of paint applied with bear's fat, we would certainly have taken him for one. He wore a brown broadcloth coat, a scarlet damasken lapel waistcoat, breeches, over which his shirt hung, a black cordovan neckerchief decked with silver bangles, shoes and stockings, and a hat. His ears were hung with pendants of brass and other wires plaited together, like the handle of a basket. He was very cordial; but on addressing him in French, he, to my surprise, replied in English."

Montour's Activities Prior to Braddock's Campaign

Andrew Montour's first important appearance in Colonial history was in February, 1743, at a conference held at Shikellamy's house, in Shamokin, between Conrad Weiser and the Indians of that place. At this conference Montour acted as interpreter for the Delawares. In 1744, he was captain of a party of warriors of the Six Nations, who marched against the Catawbas of Carolina. On this expedition, he fell sick on his way to the James River in Virginia, and was obliged to return to Shamokin.

In May, 1745, as has already been seen, he accompanied

Shikellamy, Conrad Weiser, and Bishop Spangenberg on their mission to the Onondago Council, in an effort to induce the Six Nations to make peace with the Catawbas. In June, 1748, Conrad Weiser introduced him to the President and Provincial Council of Pennsylvania, and informed them that he had employed Montour in various matters of importance and found him faithful and prudent; "that he [Weiser] had, for his own private information, as Andrew lives among the Six Nations between the branches of Ohio and Lake Erie, sent a message to him in the winter, desiring him to observe what passed among those Indians on the return of Scarouady, and come down to his home in the spring, which he did." The Council then voted Montour a reward for his trouble, and employed him to meet a deputation of Shawnee chiefs from the Allegheny then on their way to Philadelphia. He then assisted as interpreter at the conference held with these chiefs and others of the Six Nations and Miamis (Twightwees) at Lancaster in July, 1748, as was related in Chapter XIII. In August, 1748, he accompanied Weiser on his mission to Logstown. In May, 1750, he came from the Allegheny Valley, possibly Kuskuskies, and took part in the conference held at George Croghan's house at Pennsboro, Cumberland County, with some chiefs of the Six Nations and Conestogas.

Montour's next appearance in the history of Pennsylvania is when he accompanied George Croghan to Logstown in November, 1750, as was also related in Chapter XV, where they succeeded in counteracting, in a measure, the intrigues of the French, and promised the Indians of that place that a present from the Colony of Pennsylvania would be brought for them the following spring. After leaving Logstown, Montour and Croghan proceeded by way of the Lower Shawnee Town, at the mouth of the Sioto, to the Miami village of Pickawillany in the lower Ohio Valley, on a mission to strengthen the alliance between the English and Ohio Indians. They returned in the spring of 1751, and were sent in May of that year to carry the present to the Indians at Logstown, which had been promised on their visit to that place in the preceding November. As stated in Chapter VII., Montour and Croghan, by means of the Pennsylvania present, were able to make quite a favorable impression upon the Indians of Logstown in favor of the English on this occasion, and some French, who were present, were virtually ordered away by a speech which a certain speaker of the Six Nations delivered to the French Indian agent, Joncaire.

Montour and Croghan returned to Pennsboro early in June.

In a letter which George Croghan wrote the Governor on June 10th, enclosing a journal of his and Montour's transactions at Logstown, he said: "Mr. Montour has exerted himself very much on this occasion, and as he is not only very capable of doing the business, but looked on amongst all the Indians as one of their chiefs, I hope your Honor will think him worth notice, as he has employed all his time in the business of this Government."

Montour then returned to the Ohio some time in the summer or autumn of 1751, where he remained until near the beginning of the year 1752. His next act of importance was to act as interpreter at the Virginia treaty at Logstown, in June, 1752. In April of that year, he had received a grant of one hundred forty-three acres of land lying on what is still called Montour's Run, near its junction with Sherman's Creek, in Perry County; and on the same day that he received the grant, he requested of Governor Hamilton permission to interpret for the Governor of Virginia at the Logstown Treaty. The Virginians were so well pleased with his services that they allowed him thirty pistoles, and offered to give him a tract of one thousand acres if he would remove to Virginia and settle within the grant of the Ohio Company. At this treaty Montour was addressed by the Six Nations as one of their counsellors.

Early in 1753 we find Montour visiting the Great Council of the Six Nations at Onondaga, at the instance of Governor Dinwiddie, to invite the Iroquois to hold a treaty with Virginia at Winchester. In August of that year, he stopped at John Frazer's trading post near Braddock, Allegheny County, on his way back to Virginia with a number of chiefs of the Six Nations, Picks, Shawnees, Wyandots, and Delawares. Captain William Trent accompanied the party and spent some time in viewing the ground near the Forks of the Ohio, on which the Ohio Company contemplated erecting a fort. As we have already seen, Virginia made a treaty with the Iroquois chiefs at Winchester in September of that year. Andrew Montour was the interpreter on the occasion, as has been seen in former chapters.

The Indians who had attended the Winchester Treaty in September held a treaty with the Pennsylvania Commissioners at Carlisle in October. Andrew Montour also attended this treaty. Toward the close of the conference, Scarouady presented a large belt of wampum to Montour, addressing the Pennsylvania commissioners as follows: "Since we are now here together, with a great deal of pleasure, I must acquaint you that we have set a horn on Andrew Montour's head; and that you may believe what he says to be true between the Six Nations and you, they have made him one of their counsellors and a great man among them, and they love him dearly."

At the close of the Carlisle conference, Montour went to his home on Sherman's Creek, where he remained until early in November. He was then joined, at that place, by his brother, Louis, bringing two messages from the Indians of the Ohio, one for the Governor of Pennsylvania, and the other for Governor Dinwiddie of Virginia. These messages were sent by Tanacharison and Scarouady from Old Town, which Louis Monour explained was Shannopin's Town, on October 27th. Andrew then sent messengers to carry the Virginia message to its destination, and Louis brought the other to Governor Hamilton. These messages, which have been referred to in Chapters XIII and XV, contained the urgent request that Pennsylvania and Virginia join with the Indians on the Ohio in prohibiting the French from occupying the valleys of those streams.

Governor Hamilton replied to Tanacharison and Scarouady's letter on November 20th, advising that he would communicate with the Governor of Virginia in an effort to carry out their wishes. The Governor's letter was sent to Andrew Montour and George Croghan to be taken by them to the Ohio. On January 13, 1754, Croghan reached Shannopin's Town, at which place he was overtaken by Montour, and they proceeded to Logstown the next day, where, as stated at the end of Chapter XIII, they held council with Tanacharison and Scarouady, who requested both Pennsylvania and Virginia to build forts on the Ohio. Montour then left for Philadelphia, leaving Croghan at Logstown to interpret for Captain William Trent, who had "just come out with the Virginia goods and has brought a quantity of tools and workmen to begin a fort."

On February 20th, 1754, Montour was closely examined by the Governor and Assembly as to the location of Shannopin's Town, Logstown, and Venango. Montour proved that these towns were all within the limits of the Province of Pennsylvania; but the Assembly decided that the encroachments of the French on the Ohio and Allegheny did not concern Pennsylvania any more than Virginia. Montour then returned to his home on Sherman's Creek, at which place he wrote to Secretary Richard Peters, on May 16th, advising that the Indians of the Ohio did not look upon their friendship with Virginia as sufficient to engage them in war with the French, and urged Pennsylvania to send assistance to these Indians at once, as if they were to be retained in the interest of

Pennsylvania. "I have delayed my journey to the Ohio," said he, "and waited with great impatience for advices from Philadelphia, but have not yet received any. I am now obliged to go to Colonel Washingon, who has sent for me many days, to go with him to meet the Half-King [Tanacharison], Monacatooth [Scarouady], and others, that are coming to meet the Virginia Commissioners, and, as they think, some from Pennsylvania."

Before the above letter was written, Governor Dinwiddie had given Montour a captain's commission "to head a select company of friendly Indians, as scouts, for our small army." Montour, however, did not organize a company of Indians, as he had been instructed, but raised a company of traders and woodsmen, who had been driven from the valley of the Ohio on the approach of the French. His company consisted of eighteen men, and with these, he and Croghan joined Washington at the Great Meadows on the 9th of June. Montour and his forces assisted Washington in the battle of Fort Necessity, on July 3rd and 4th, where two of his men, Daniel Lafferty and Henry O'Brien, were taken prisoners.

On August 31st, Montour met Weiser at Harris' Ferry and accompanied him and Tanacharison to Aughwick, where, as has been seen in Chapter XIV, Weiser held conferences with Croghan, Tanacharison, and Scarouady, in September. On the way to Aughwick, Montour became intoxicated several times, and abused Governor Hamilton for not paying him for is trouble and expenses. Weiser reprimanded him when sober, and he begged Weiser's pardon and desired him not to mention the matter to the Governor. "I left him drunk at Aughwick," said Weiser; "on one leg he had a stocking and no shoe; on the other, a shoe and no stocking. From six of the clock till past nine, I begged him to go with me, but to no purpose. He swore terrible when he saw me mount my horse." On Weiser's way home Montour met him at Carlisle, having arrived there the day before. He again begged Weiser's pardon, and left for Virginia.

Montour either remained in Maryland or Virginia until the middle of December, or else returned there before that time, inasmuch as Governor Sharp mentions his being at Wills Creek (Cumberland, Md.,) on December 10th. He then came back to his home in Sherman's Valley.

We next hear of him in the spring of 1755, when he and George Croghan joined Braddock's army at Fort Cumberland with about fifty warriors. After Braddock's army began to advance on Fort Duquesne, many of the Indian allies under Montour and Croghan deserted, or were dismissed by Braddock; and when the army reached the Little Meadows, near Grantsville, Maryland, there were but seven in the company. Both Montour and Croghan continued with Braddock and took part in the terrible defeat at the mouth of Turtle Creek, on the Monongahela, on July 9th. We have already seen how the seven faithful Indians were thanked by the Provincial Council, in August, 1755, for the assistance which they rendered in Braddock's campaign.

Montour's Activities in the French and Indian War

Montour and Scarouady, after leaving Philadelphia, in August, 1755, went to Shamokin, from which place Scarouady sent a message to the Governor, on September 11th, advising that the Six Nations had ordered the Delawares at Shamokin to take up arms against the French.

The next glimpse we get of Montour is when he met John Harris at Shamokin, on the night of October 24th, in full war paint, and he and Scarouady advised Harris' party to keep on the east side of the Susquehanna on their return to Paxtang. It will be recalled that, as stated in Chapter XVI, John Harris had led a party to bury the dead of the Penn's Creek Massacre of October 16th, but finding that they were already buried, had come to Shamokin to ascertain the sentiments of the Indians at that place. During the month of October, Montour and Scarouady, as was also seen in Chapter XVI, attended the Indian council at Big Island (Lock Haven), where they found six Delawares and four Shawnees, who informed them that they had received a hatchet from the French to be used against the English "if they proved saucy."

Montour and Scarouady then went to Philadelphia, where, on November 8th, they gave the Governor the details of their trip to Big Island. In the middle of November, Montour and Scarouady left Philadelphia on a trip up the North Branch of the Susquehanna to Onondaga, on a mission from Pennsylvania to the chiefs of the Six Nations. The details of this trip have already been given in Chapter XVI, and need not be stated at this point. We have also seen, in Chapter XVI, that Montour and Scarouady returned to Philadelphia in March, 1756, from their mission to the Six Nations, and held conferences with the Governor and Provincial Council, which resulted in Pennsylvania's declaring war against the Delawares, April 14, 1756.

We saw in Chapter XVI that shortly after Pennsylvania's declaration of war against the Delawares, Scarouady went to the territory of the Six Nations, carrying Pennsylvania's peace message. He was accompanied on this mission by Montour, who, before leaving Philadelphia, put his children under the Governor's care, "as well the three that are here, to be independent of the mother, as a boy twelve years old, that he had by a former wife, a Delaware granddaughter of Allompis [Sassoonan]".

Montour acted as interpreter at the conference at Fort Johnson, on May 10, 1756, between Sir William Johnson, Scarouady, and a number of other Oneida chiefs.   In June, he acted as interpreter at the camp on Lake Onondaga; and on July 25th, at Fort Johnson, he was appointed Captain of the Indian allies of Sir William Johnson.   On September 10th, he appears once more as interpreter at Fort Johnson, and on the 20th of that month, he marched with Sir William Johnson to the relief of the army besieged at Fort Edward.   He was ordered back, however, by General Webb, and reached Fort Johnson on the 2nd of November, where on the 17th to the 23rd of that month, he acted as interpreter at a conference with a number of chiefs and warriors of the Six Nations.

We find Montour at Fort Johnson once more, on June 13, 1757, attending a conference in which it was brought out that he had been sent during the preceding winter by Sir William Johnson to Onondaga Castle, to let the Six Nations know that he "expected that they should use the hatchet against the French." Another conference was held at Fort Johnson, on September 12, 1757, at which Montour offered five chiefs of the Mohawks and Senecas and four deputies of the Cherokees, the calumet of peace.

On November 12th, 1757, the French burned the settlement at the German Flats, in the Mohawk Valley; whereupon General Johnson sent Montour and Croghan to the Oneida Castle to learn why the Oneidas had not given the English notice of the approach of the French.   They met the leading Oneida chiefs at Fort Herkimer, on November 30th, who advised them and also some German officers present, that the Oneidas had sent a warning to the settlers at the German Flats more than two weeks before, and that the settlers had paid no attention to it.

It is not clear as just how long Montour remained in the service of Sir William Johnson; but it is likely that he took part in the attack on Fort Ticonderoga and witnessed the terrible slaughter of the English troops under General Abercombie.   Montour then returned to Pennsylvania, and with George Croghan, took part in the Great Council at Easton in October, 1758, between the Governors of Pennsylvania and New Jersey, on the one hand, and the chiefs of the Six Nations, Delawares, Nanticokes, Tutelos, and other tribes on the other hand.   He acted as the interpreter of the

Delawares and Six Nations at this Council, but in the minutes of the same, his name is erroneously set forth as Henry Montour.

At the close of the treaty, Montour and Croghan at once went to the Ohio. As has been seen in Chapter XIX, the French burned Fort Duquesne on November 24th, and General Forbes' army occupied its site the next day. Two days later (November 27th), Montour and Croghan crossed the Allegheny, and reached Logstown on November 28th. On the 29th they reached Sauconk, at the mouth of the Beaver, where they were joined by some Delawares from Kuskuskies, accompanied by Christian Frederick Post. Here they conferred with Post, Shingas, and King Beaver, respecting the message that General Forbes had sent to these Indians. On December 2nd they returned to Logstown, and on the 3rd, reached Killbuck, or Smoky Island, opposite Pittsburgh. On the 4th, they crossed the river to Fort Pitt and held a conference with Colonel John Armstrong and Colonel Henry Bouquet.

Montour and Croghan then returned to Philadelphia, where the former was interpreter at a conference on February 8th and 9th, 1759, between General Forbes and some Indians from Buccaloons, an Indian town in Warren County. On February 20th, Montour reported to the Governor that these Indians were dissatisfied with the answer that they had received from General Forbes, and desired that he should return with them to the Allegheny, but that he had told them that he was an officer subject to General Forbes and could not go without his written consent. These Indians wished to learn fully the intentions of the English after driving the French from the Ohio and Allegheny.

Montour's Activities From the Close of the French and Indian War to the Outbreak of the Pontiac-Guyasuta War

In May, 1759, Montour was sent by Croghan to collect all the Indians he could for the purpose of meeting the latter in council at Fort Pitt; and on July 5th to 11th the conference took place there between Croghan as Sir William Johnson's deputy, Col. Hugh Mercer, and Captain William Trent, and the chiefs of the Six Nations, Delawares, Shawnees and Wyandots, at which conference Montour acted as interpreter. The chiefs were advised of the terms of the Treaty of Easton, and promised to return the prisoners taken during the French and Indian War. On October 24, 1759, he acted as interpreter at a conference at Fort Pitt between General Stanwix and the Western Indians. Still another conference with these Indians was held at the same place, by General Monckton, on August 12, 1760, at which Montour acted as interpreter.

Montour then accompanied Shingas to Presque Isle (Erie) to join the expedition which Major Robert Rodgers and George Croghan were leading to Detroit to take possession of the western posts, which had been surrendered by the French. On November 4th, 1760, Rodger's expedition left Presque Isle, consisting of a flotilla of nineteen whale boats and batteaux and a shore party of forty-two rangers, as well as twenty Indians of the Six Nations, Shawnees, and Delawares, under the command of Montour. Detroit surrendered on November 29th, and on December 8th, Major Rodgers and Montour set off with a party of Indians to take possession of Mackinaw. After proceeding about ninety miles, the Indians declared that it was impossible to proceed further without snow-shoes, and returned to Detroit.

Montour's next important work was to act as interpreter at a conference held at Philadelphia, on May 22, 1761, between the Governor and a number of Indians from the Allegheny. In the summer and autumn of this year, he accompanied Sir William Johnson to Detroit, narrowly escaping death by drowning, when his boat overturned on Lake Erie. On December 22nd of this year, he received a grant of two hundred acres of land in Sakson's Cove, between Kishacoquillas Creek and the Juniata River. He also acted as interpreter at the great conference at Lancaster on August 23, 1762, between the Provincial Authorities and King Beaver, Shingas, and other chiefs of the western tribes, who accompanied Christian Frederick Post to that place, as related in Chapter XIX.

Montour's Activities in Pontiac's War

Pontiac's War began in May, 1763. On the 5th of this month, Sir William Johnson directed Montour to proceed to Chillisquaque, on the West Branch of the Susquehanna, to endeavor to allay the fears of the Indians of that vicinity concerning their lands and to co-operate with Thomas McKee, the assistant deputy Indian Agent. In July, John Harris wrote Colonel Bouquet, at Carlisle, that Montour had arrived at Paxtang from a tour of the villages of the upper Susquehanna, where he found the Indians "inveterate and inclined for war", and that he, (Harris), would have Montour go to Carlisle and give this information to Colonel Bouquet personally. Soon thereafter Colonel Bouquet wrote Governor Hamilton from Carlisle that Montour reported that at the time of his leaving, neither he nor Johnson knew anything of Pontiac's uprising. Montour, on July 23rd, was at Fort

Augusta (Sunbury) on his way up the Kest Branch of the Susquehanna, returning on August 7th with the news of the attack on
Fort Pitt and Fort Ligonier.

Montour's next important act was to deliver, on December 19,
1763, to the newly arrived Governor, John Penn, an address of
welcome from the Conestoga Indians, of Conestoga, Lancaster
County. The unfortunate Conestogas had sent this address just a
few days before this massacre, on December 14th, by the Paxtang
boys.

Early in 1764, Sir William Johnson sent Montour with a
force of nearly two hundred Tuscaroras, Oneidas, and a few
rangers, against the Delawares on the upper Susquehanna, to punish them for their hostility against the settlers. On their way to
Kanestio, (a Delaware village in Steuben County, New York,) they
encountered a force of Delawares going against the English settlements, and captured twenty-nine of them. These prisoners,
among whom was Captain Bull, son of the famous Teedyuscung,
were sent by way of Fort Stanwix (Rome, New York), to Johnson
Hall; and later Captain Bull and thirteen of his associates were
sent to New York, and confined in jail. On April 7th, Montour
wrote from Tioga concerning the success of his expedition, stating
that the Delawares had fled before his arrival at Kanestio, but
that, with one hundred and forty warriors, he had destroyed three
large Delaware towns, all the outlying villages, and one hundred
and thirty scattered Delaware houses, together with horses and
cattle. The houses were well built of square logs, with good
chimneys, and many had four fire places.

Later Activities of Montour

We hear little of Montour for the next three years. Part of this
time, he assisted Sir William Johnson in New York, and part was
spent in Pennsylvania. By many it is thought that he accompanied George Croghan and his party from Fort Pitt to New
Orleans in the summer and autumn of 1766. On May 19, 1767,
he received a large grant of land on the head of Penn's Creek, above
the Great Spring. Montour's next appearance in history is when
he attended the council at Fort Pitt, April 26th and May 9th, 1768,
between George Croghan, Deputy Agent of Indian affairs, John
Allen, and Joseph Shippen, Commissioners of Pennsylvania, and
eleven hundred and three chiefs and warriors of the Six Nations,
Delawares, Munsees, Shawnees, Mohicans, and Wyandots. He
acted as interpreter on this occasion. The matters taken up at
this conference or treaty were the difficulties growing out of the

fact that the whites were settling on lands west of the Allegheny
Mountains that had not been purchased from the Indians. It led
to the purchase at Fort Stanwix, in October, 1768, to be mentioned
presently.

Atrocious Murder of Indians By Frederick Stump

Shortly before the treaty at Fort Pitt, above mentioned, great
consternation was caused throughout Pennsylvania and great fear
of Indian outrages following the atrocious murders committed by
Frederick Stump. On Sunday morning, January 10, 1768, six
Indians, namely, White Mingo, Cornelius, John Campbell, Jones,
and two squaws, came to Stump's cabin on Stump's Run, near
Middleburg, Snyder County, in a drunken condition. Stump and
his servant, John Ironcutter, after endeavoring without success to
persuade them to leave, killed them all, dragging their bodies to
the creek, where they cut a hole in the ice, and pushed them into
the stream. Then fearing that the news of these murders might be
carried to other Indians in the vicinity, Stump went the next day
to their cabin fourteen miles up the creek, where he found a squaw,
two girls, and a child, killed them all and threw their bodies into
the cabin and burned it. One of the bodies which he had pushed
through the hole in the ice on the preceding day, floated down Middle Creek to the Susquehanna, and then down this stream, finally
lodging against the shore opposite Harrisburg, just below the location of the present bridge on Market Street of that city.

Several Indians who had escaped the murderous wrath of
Stump, chased him toward Fort Augusta, at Sunbury. Stump did
not enter this fort, but ran to a house occupied by two women,
whose protection he implored, alleging that he was pursued by
Indians. The women did not believe his story, but he begged very
piteously. They then hid him between two beds. His pursuers
were only a moment behind him. To their questioning, the women replied that they knew nothing of Stump. Before the Indians
left the house of the two women, they seized a cat, pulled out its
hair, and tore it to pieces, thus illustrating what they would have
done with Stump, had they found him.

Shortly after the atrocious murder committed by Stump, the
Delaware chief, Newahleeka, residing at the Great Island (Lock
Haven), sent a message to Governor John Penn, advising that the
Delawares and other Indians at the Great Island were much dis-
pleased on account of the fact that five white men had lately been
seen marking trees and surveying land in that region not yet pur-

chased from the Indians. This message was delivered by a Dela-ware named Billy Champion. Governor Penn then took occasion to send a message to Newahleeka, advising him that the Province had offered two hundred pounds as a reward for the capture of Stump. Said Penn: "Brother, I consider this matter in no other light than as the act of a wicked, rash man, and I hope you will also consider it in the same way. . . . . . There are among you and us some wild, rash, hot-headed people who commit actions of this sort." Then Shawnee Ben, a chief of the Shawnees at Great Island, sent word to Captain William Patterson: "As it was the Evil Spirit who caused Stump to commit this bad action, I blame none of my brothers, the English, but him."

Stump and Ironcutter were apprehended and lodged in jail at Carlisle on Saturday evening, March 23rd. On the following Fri-day, a company of settlers from Sherman's Valley, where he had lived, marched to Carlisle, surrounded the jail, entered it with drawn pistols, and released the murderers. After their rescue, they both returned to the neighborhood of their shocking crime, where they found their presence very disagreeable to the inhabitants. They then left the neighborhood. They were never again arrested for their crime. Both went to Virginia, where Stump died at an ad-vanced age.

Penns Make Last Purchase at Fort Stanwix

Montour was also one of the interpreters at the Great Con-gress with the Indians at Fort Stanwix (Rome, New York), in October, 1768, in which the Six Nations conveyed to the Proprie-taries of Pennsylvania all the land, within the boundaries of the Province, extending from the New York line on the Susquehanna River, past Towanda and Tyadahgon Creeks, up the West Branch of the Susquehanna, over to Kittanning, and thence down the south side of the Allegheny and the Ohio to the mouth of the Ten-nessee River.

By this purchase, for a consideration of ten thousand pounds, the Proprietaries acquired the present counties of Green, Washing-ton, Fayette, Somerset, Westmoreland, Cambria, Susquehanna, Sullivan, and Wyoming, and parts of Beaver, Allegheny, Arm-strong, Indiana, Clearfield, Center, Clinton, Lycoming, Bradford, Lackawanna, Wayne, Luzerne, Columbia, Montour, Union, Pike, and Snyder. The date of executing and delivering the deed was November 5, 1768. This was the last purchase made by the Penns.

During the year 1769, Montour was granted a tract of three hundred acres situated on the south side of the Ohio River opposite Montour's Island, about nine miles below the mouth of the Monongahela. This is the last definite reference that we have to this distinguished and picturesque character, except that, on September 7, 1771, Richard Brown made an affidavit in which he mentioned that a certain Andrew McConnell had recently seen and talked with Montour at Fort Pitt concerning the murder of two Indians by a white man. His death occurred some time prior to 1775. Some claim that he ended his days at the home of his niece, who was the wife of White Mingo, a Six Nation's chief, who lived near the mouth of Pine Creek on the Allegheny, five or six miles above the mouth of the Monongahela, from 1759 to 1777. Others believe that he died on Montour's Island in the Ohio River

GEORGE CROGAN

We have met George Crogan, the "King of Traders," frequently in these sketches. At this point, it will be well to devote a few paragraphs to this influential man of the frontier. His name was one of the most conspicuous in the western annals in connection with Indian affairs at the time of which we are writing, and for many years thereafter. Bore in Ireland and educated at Dublin, he came to America somewhere between the years 1740 and 1744. He engaged in the Indian trade and appears to have been first licensed as an Indian trader in Pennsylvania, in 1744. In 1746, he was located in Silver Spring Township, in the present county of Cumberland, a few miles west of Harris' Ferry, now Harrisburg. During the same year, he was made a counsellor of the Six Nations at Onondaga, according to his sworn statement; and in March, 1749, he was appointed by the Governor and Council of Pennsylvania one of the justices of the peace in Common Pleas for Lancaster County.

As early as the years 1746 and 1747, he had gone as far as the southwestern border of Lake Erie in his trading expeditions. In 1748, he had a trading house at Logstown, which was made the headquarters of Weiser upon his visit to the Indians of that place, in the month of September, 1748. He had also branch trading establishments at the principal Indian towns in the valleys of the Ohio and Allegheny, one being on the northwestern side of the Allegheny River, at the mouth of Pine Creek, five or six miles above the forks of the Ohio. From this base of operations and from Logstown, trading routes "spread out like the sticks of a fan." One of these routes went up the Allegheny past Venango, (Franklin), where Crogan had a trading house and competed with John

Frazer, another Pennsylvania trader, who for some years, had traded at this place, maintaining both a trading house and a gunsmith shop.

Croghan's abilities and influence among the Indians soon attracted the attention of Conrad Weiser, who, in 1747, recommended him to the Council of Pennsylvania, and, in this way, he entered the public service of the Colony. We have already seen the part he played in Washington's campaign of 1754. The outbreak of the French and Indian War ruined his prosperous trading business, and brought him to the verge of bankruptcy. To add to his financial troubles, the Irish traders, because most of them were Roman Catholics, fell under suspicion of acting as spies for the French, and Croghan was unjustly suspicioned by many in authority. He was granted a captain's commission to command the Indian allies during Braddock's campaign. He resigned his office early in the year 1756, and retired from the Pennsylvania service, going to New York where his distant relative, Sir William Johnson, chose him deputy Indian agent, and appointed him to manage the Susquehanna and Allegheny tribes. From this time forward, he was engaged in important dealings with the Western Indians, and had much to do in swaying them to the British interest and making possible the success of Forbes in 1758. In 1763, he went to England on private business, and was shipwrecked upon the coast of France. Upon his return to America in 1765, he was dispatched to Illinois, going by way of the Ohio River, and was taken prisoner near the mouth of the Wabash, and carried to the Indian towns upon that river. Here he not only secured his own release, but conducted negotiations putting an end to Pontiac's War. He also took part in the Great Treaty of Fort Stanwix (Rome, New York), in 1768, and, as a reward, was given a grant of land in Cherry Valley, New York. Shortly prior to this, however, he had purchased a tract on the Allegheny, about four miles above the mouth of the Monongahela, where he entertained George Washington in 1770. When the Revolutionary War came on, it seems he embarked in the patriotic cause, and later was an object of suspicion; and, in 1778, Pennsylvania proclaimed him a public enemy, and his place as Indian agent was conferred upon Colonel George Morgan. He continued, however, to reside in Pennsylvania—the scene of his early activities and the Colony which he rendered such signal service—and died at Passayunk on August 31, 1782. His funeral was conducted at the Episcopal Church of St. Peter's in Philadelphia, but the place of his burial remains unknown.

CHAPTER XXI

Teedyuscung

EEDYUSCUNG was one of the famous, able chiefs of the Delawares. He was the son of the Delaware chief, Captain John Harris, of the Turtle Clan, and was born at Trenton, New Jersey, about 1705. The early part of his life is clouded in obscurity; but, when he was about fifty years of age, he was chosen chief of the Delawares on the Susquehanna, and from that time until his tragic death on April 16th, 1763, he was one of the chief figures in the Indian history of Pennsylvania.

He was one of the founders, if not the actual founder, of the Delaware town of Wyoming, in 1742 or 1743. He came under the influence of the Moravian missionaries, and was baptized by them as Brother Gideon. Honest John was also a name applied to him by the Moravians and others. Later he became an apostate, and endeavored to induce the Christian Delawares of Gnadenhuetten to remove to Wyoming, actually succeeding in gaining a party of seventy of the converts, who left Gnadenhuetten, April 24th, 1754, and took up their abode at Wyoming.

In April, 1755, he attended a conference with the Provincial Authorities at Philadelphia, assuring them of his friendship for the English. At that time, he was still living at Wyoming. His friendship for the English and Pennsylvania did not continue long after the conference of April, 1755. When the Delawares and Shawnees took up arms against Pennsylvania following Braddock's defeat, Teedyuscung, at Nescopeck with Shingas and other leaders of the hostile Indians, planned many a bloody expedition against the frontiers of Eastern Pennsylvania. In Chapter XVIII, we saw that, on New Year's Day, 1756, he led a band of twenty-five hostile Delawares into Lower Smithfield Township, Monroe County, attacking the plantation of Henry Hess, killing several persons and capturing several others.

In March, 1756, he and the Delawares under him left the town of Wyoming and removed to Tioga (now Athens, Bradford County), followed at about the same time by the Shawnees from their town where Plymouth, Luzerne County, now stands, under the leadership of Paxinosa. After the death of Shikellamy, in

1749, some of the Shamokin Delawares had settled at Tioga, and upon Teedyuscung's removal to that place, they and the Delawares of the Munsee Clan chose him "King of the Delawares". He was at that time busily engaged in forming an alliance between the three clans of Delawares and the Shawnees, Nanticokes, and Mohicans of Northwestern Pennsylvania.

Teedyuscung Agrees to Enter Into Peace Negotiations

As was stated in Chapter XVI, Scarouady and Andrew Montour were sent by the Governor of Pennsylvania, in November, 1755, on a mission to the Six Nations, going as far as Fort Johnson, New York, where, in February, 1756, they held council with the Iroquois chiefs. On their way up the Susquehanna Valley, they found Teedyuscung with a number of Delawares and Nanticokes at the Indian town of Chinkanning, now Tunkhannock, Wyoming County, shortly before taking up his residence at Tioga. We have also seen, in Chapter XVII, that Canachquasy, shortly after Pennsylvana's declaration of war against the Delawares, in April, 1756, carried the Governor's peace message to the Indians at Tioga, at which place he held conference with Teedyuscung. We saw also, in the same chapter, that Canachquasy returned from this mission early in June, and laid before the Governor and Provincial Council the favorable report that the Delawares, Nanticokes, and Shawnees under Teedyuscung, were willing to enter into negotiations for peace. Likewise it was seen, in the same chapter, that the Governor then drafted a proclamation for a suspension of hostilities against the Indians in the Susquehanna Valley, for a period of thirty days, and sent Canachquasy once more to Tioga with this information, where he held a number of conferences with Teedyuscung, persuaded this renowned warrior to lay aside the hatchet, and returned to Philadelphia in July, where he laid before the Provincial Council the result of his second mission to Tioga.

Teedyuscung at Easton Treaty of July, 1756, Declares Delawares are No Longer Slaves of the Six Nations

Immediately upon Canachquasy's return to Philadelphia from his second mission to Tioga, arrangements were made for a conference with Teedyuscung at Easton, which place Governor Morris with the Provincial Council, reached on July 24, 1756. The conference formally opened on July 28th, Conrad Weiser in the mean-

time having posted his troops in the vicinity of Easton. Teedyuscung's insistent request that he have his own interpreter was granted. He and the fourteen other chiefs accompanying him were formally welcomed by Governor Morris. Teedyuscung made the
following reply:

"Last spring you sent me a string [of wampum], and as soon
as I heard the good words you sent, I was glad, and as you told us,
we believed it came from your hearts. So we felt it in our hearts
and received what you said with joy. The first messages you sent
me came in the spring; they touched my heart; they gave me
abundance of joy. You have kindled a council fire at Easton.
I have been here several days smoking my pipe in patience, waiting to hear your good words. Abundant confusion has of late
years been rife among the Indians, because of their loose ways of
doing business. False leaders have deceived the people. It has
bred quarrels and heart-burnings among my people.

"The Delaware is no longer the slave of the Six Nations. I,
Teedyuscung, have been appointed King over the Five United
Nations and representative of the Five Iroquois Nations. What
I do here will be approved by all. This is a good day; whoever
will make peace, let him lay hold of this belt, and the nations
around shall see and know it. I desire to conduct myself accord-
ing to your words, which I will perform to the utmost of my power.
I wish the same good that possessed the good old man, William
Penn, who was the friend to the Indian, may inspire the people of
this Province at this time."

In the conferences that followed, the Governor insisted that, as
a condition for peace, Teedyuscung and the Indians under his command should return all the prisoners that they had captured since
taking up arms against the Colony. But, inasmuch as only a small
delegation of chiefs had accompanied Teedyuscung to Easton, it
was desired that he and Canachquasy should go back among the
Indians, give the "Big Peace Halloo", and gather their followers
together for a larger peace conference that would be more representative of the Indians, and to be held in the near future.

The Governor then gave Teedyuscung a present, informing
him that a part of it "was given by the people called Quakers, who
are descendants of those who first came over to this country with
your old friend, William Penn, as a particular testimony of their
regard and affection for the Indians, and their earnest desire to
promote the good work of peace, in which we are now engaged."

What Caused Teedyuscung to Declare That
the Delawares Were No Longer Women?

We saw in, Chapter XVII, that, at the council held at Otseningo (Binghampton, New York), in the spring of 1756, the Delawares broke away from the Iroquois and declared: "We are men
and are determined not to be ruled any longer by you as women;
and we are determined to cut off all the English except those that
make their escape from us in ships." Teedyuscung, therefore, at
the Easton conference, simply was the spokesman expressing the
determination of the Delawares to remain free from the domination
of the Iroquois; and he also made the statement that the Iroquois
had authorized him as their spokesman at this conference.

What were the causes of Teedyuscung's assertion that the
Delawares were no longer women but men? Many answers have
been given to this question. The Quakers endeavored to make the
Delawares ascribe their bold stand against their conquerors, the
Iroquois, and the taking up of arms against the Colony, to the
Walking Purchase of 1737, in which they had undoubtedly been
overreached; and as we shall see, Teedyuscung bitterly complained
of this notorious purchase.

Others, including George Croghan, were of the opinion that it
was because the Quaker Assembly, of 1751, had refused to build a
"strong-house" at the Forks of the Ohio, when the Delawares and
Shawnees of the Ohio Valley were still united in the English interest, and, as we have seen in former chapters, had repeatedly asked
that a fort be built in that region.

The Governor of Pennsylvania said that it was because, when
Scarouady appeared before the Governor and Assembly on
November 8, 1755, and implored that Pennsylvania give the hatchet to the Shawnees and Delawares on the Susquehanna, then
faithful in the English interest and anxious to take up arms against
the French, the Assembly did not permit Governor Morris to give
these Indians the hatchet and join them against the French, the
consequence being that the Delawares and Shawnees of the Susquehanna became greatly dissatisfied and went over to the French.

The great English statesman, Edmund Burke, said that it was
because it was "an error to have placed so great a part of the Government in hands of men who hold principles directly opposite to
its end and design; as a peaceable industrious people the Quakers
cannot be too much cherished; but surely they cannot themselves
complain that, when by their opinions they make themselves sheep,

they should not be entrusted with office, since they have not the nature of dogs."

Benjamin Franklin said it was because "these public quarrels were at the bottom owing to the Proprietaries, our hereditary Governors, who, when any expense was to be incurred for the defense of their Province, with increditable meanness, instructed their deputies to pass no act for levying the necessary taxes, unless their vast estates were in the same act expressly excused."

No doubt all of the reasons, enumerated above, contributed to the remarkable change in the character of the Delawares, as did also the Albany purchase of 1754, which, as we have seen in Chapter XIV, caused the Delawares and Shawnees of the West Branch of the Susquehanna and of the valleys of the Ohio and Allegheny to complain bitterly that their lands had been sold from under their feet.

Then, the Delawares received a message purporting to come from the Six Nations that their petticoats should be shortened to reach only to their knees, and that they should again receive the hatchet to defend themselves; but this was no doubt a message from the Senecas and not from the whole Iroquois Confederation.

Teedyuscung Boastful

Teedyuscung was very boastful at this Easton conference of July, 1756, conceiving himself to be a great man, and pompously asserting that he appeared in the name of ten nations, meaning the six clans of the Iroquois and the four tribes on the Susquehanna. The Moravian missionary, Zeisberger, attended the conference, and, during the six days of negotiations, moved among the Indian delegation pleading that they accept Christianity; but Teedyuscung had no ear for this message.

After Teedyuscung was given a present by the Governor, at the Easton conference, he and his followers were given a grand entertainment with which he was greatly pleased, and declared frequently that he would go forth, and do all in his power for peace. After the entertainment, when some of the Quakers, who attended the conference, came to bid him farewell, "he parted with them in a very affectionate manner." He plead strongly for peace, insisting that he and his people on the Susquehanna were not responsible for the actions of the Indians on the Ohio.

The peace belt, which he had brought to the conference and to which he urged that the white people hold fast, was then produced.

It contained "a square in the middle, meaning the lands of the Indians, and at one end the figure of a man, indicating the English, and at the other end another, meaning the French." Teedyuscung said that the Iroquois told the Delawares that both the English and the French coveted their lands, and urged the Delawares to join the Iroquois in defending against both the English and the French. Governor Morris was suspicious of this statement, called together his Council, and secretly consulted with Conrad Weiser as to whether it would be proper to keep the belt. Weiser said that he doubted the statement of Teedyuscung and sought advice from New Castle (Canachquasy), who told him that the Six Nations had sent the belt to the Delawares, who, in turn, sent it to the Governor of Pennsylvania. Canachquasy advised that Teedyuscung be liberally supplied with wampum, if peace was expected to be brought about. Weiser seconded this advice, and called attention to the fact that the French gave great quantities of wampum to their Indians, and that the English would have to outbid the French in the length of wampum belts. A messenger was then sent to the Moravian mission at Bethlehem to bring material for making a belt to be given Teedyuscung, and the Indian women converts were called in and set to work making the belts. The belt that was to be given to Teedyuscung was to be a fathom long and sixteen beads wide, in the center of which was to be the figure of a man, typifying the Governor of Pennsylvania, and on each side five other figures typifying the ten nations, which Teedyuscung claimed to represent.

While the Indian women were making the belts, Teedyuscung became very angry. He supposed that the Governor had invited Indian women into his councils. Said he: "Why do you council in the dark? Why do you consult with women? Why do you not talk in the light?" The Governor replied: "My councils are set on a hill; I have no secrets. The Governor never sits in swamps, but speaks his mind openly. The squaws are here making belts, not holding council." This answer appeased the anger of the great chief.

Before the end of the conference, the Governor, holding the two belts in his hands and addressing Teedyuscung and Canachquasy, declared them to be messengers of peace for the Province of Pennsylvania, to go among the hostile tribes on the Susquehanna in an effort to persuade them to desert the French and unite with the English. Giving each of these peace messengers an armload of wampum, the Governor bade them Godspeed on the important mission undertaken by these two chiefs,—a mission fraught with much difficulty and danger, as the secret emissaries of the French were using every device to thwart their designs.

As was related in Chapter XVII, Teedyuscung and Canachquasy, after the conference, started to give the "Big Peace Halloo" among the hostile tribes, but Teedyuscung remained for a time at Fort Allen, where he secured liquor and remained intoxicated for a considerable time. Lieutenant Miller was in charge of the fort at this time, and Teedyuscung brought sixteen deer skins which he said he was going to present to the Governor "to make him a pair of gloves." Lieutenant Miller insisted that one skin was enough to make the Governor a pair of gloves, and after supplying Teedyuscung liberally with rum, he secured from him the entire sixteen deer skins for only three pounds. The sale was made while the chief was intoxicated, and afterwards he remained at the fort demanding more rum, which Miller supplied, Canachquasy in the meantime having gone away in disgust.

On August 21st, Teedyuscung and his retinue went to Bethlehem, where his wife, Elizabeth, and her three children desired to remain while the "King" went on an expedition to the Minisinks, for the purpose of putting a stop to some depredations which they were committing in New Jersey. Returning from this expedition, he went to Wyoming, where he sent word to Major Parsons at Easton requesting that his wife and children be sent to join him. Upon Parson's making known the King's desire, the wife determined to stay at Bethlehem. He then made frequent visits to this place, much to the annoyance of the Moravian missionaries.

When the Provincial Authorities learned of the cause of Teedyuscung's detention at Fort Allen, Lieutenant Miller was discharged, and Teedyuscung went to Wyoming, thence up the North Branch of the Susquehanna, persuading the Indians to lay down their arms, and to send deputies to a second conference to be held at Easton, in October. However, in the meantime, the Governor, becoming suspicious of the chief's long delay at Fort Allen and being influenced, no doubt by the statements of many Indians on the border that Teedyuscung was not sincere in his peace professions, that he was a traitor, and that the Easton conference was but a ruse to gain time, sent Canachquasy secretly to New York to ascertain from the Six Nations whether or not they had deputized Teedyuscung to represent them in important treaties. Canachquasy returned with the report that the Six Nations denied Teedyuscung's authority, as was related more fully in Chapter XVII.

Obstacles in the Way of Peace

J. S. Walton, in his "Conrad Weiser and the Indian Policy of Colonial Pennsylvania", thus sets forth the obstacles which confronted Pennsylvania in her efforts to make peace with the hostile Delawares:

"The prospects of peace were growing more and more embarrassing. England, now that war was declared with France (April, 1756) sent Lord Loudon to America to take charge. Indian affairs were placed under the control of two men, Sir William Johnson for the northern, and Mr. Atkins for the southern colonies. Loudon's policy was to secure as many Indians as possible for allies, and with them strike the French. To this end Mr. Atkins secured the alliance of the Cherokee and other southern tribes. These were immediately added to the armies of Virginia and Western Pennsylvania. This act stirred the Northern Indians. The Iroquois and the Delawares declared that they could never fight on the same side with the despised Cherokees. This southern alliance meant northern revolt, and threatened to crush the peace negotiations at Easton. At this critical juncture, Lord Loudon, whose ignorance of the problem before him was equalled only by his contempt for provincialism, ordered the Governor of Pennsylvania to have nothing whatever to do with Indian affairs. Sir William Johnson, only, should control these things. Moreover, all efforts towards peace were advantages given to the enemy. Johnhon, however was inclined towards peace, but he seriously complicated affairs in Pennsylvania by appointing George Croghan his sole deputy in the Province. Croghan and Weiser had quite different views upon Indian affairs. The Indians were quick to notice these changes. Jonathan, an old Mohawk chief, in conversation with Conrad Weiser said: 'Is it true that you are become a fallen tree, that you must no more engage in Indian affairs, neither as counsellor nor interpreter? What is the reason? Weiser replied, 'It is all too true. The King of Great Britain has appointed Warruychyockon [Col. William Johnson] to be manager of all Indian affairs that concern treaties of friendship, war, etc. And that accordingly the Great General (Lord Loudon) that came over the Great Waters, had in the name of the King ordered the Government of Pennsylvania to desist from holding treaties with the Indians, and the Government of Pennsylvania will obey the King's command, and consequently I, as the Government's servant, have nothing more to do with Indian affairs.' Jonathan and his companion replied in concert, 'Ha! Ha!' meaning 'Oh ,sad.' The two Indians then whispered together a few minutes, during which Weiser politely withdrew into another room. When he returned Jonathan said, 'Comrade, I hear you have engaged on another bottom. You are made a captain of warriors and laid aside council affairs and turned soldier.'

"To this Weiser replied with some spirit, setting forth his reasons for self-defense, the bloody outrages of the Indians, the reception of the first peace messengers. 'You know,' said Weiser, 'that their lives were threatened. You know the insolent answer which came back that caused us to declare war. I was at Easton working for peace and if I had my wish there would be no war at all. . . . . . So, comrade, do not charge me with such a thing as that.' The Indians thanked Weiser for the explanation and went away satisfied. But at the same time Weiser was shorn of his power among the Indians. Making him commander of the Provincial forces robbed Pennsylvania of her most powerful advocate at the council fires of the Indians."

Teedyuscung at the Second Easton Conference

In August, 1756, Governor Morris was superseded by Governor William Denny. Governor Denny endeavored to have Teedyuscung attend a conference in Philadelphia, in an effort to continue the peace work begun at the Easton Conference of July of that year. Teedyuscung sent the following reply by Conrad Weiser to Governor Denny's invitation: "Brother, you remember very well that in time of darkness and danger, I came in here at your invitation. At Easton, we kindled a small council fire. . . . If you should put out this little fire, our enemies will call it only a jack lantern, kindled on purpose to deceive those who approach it. Brother, I think it by no means advisable to put out this little fire, but rather to put more sticks upon it, and I desire that you will come to it [at Easton] as soon as possible, bringing your old and wise men along with you, and we shall be very glad to see you here."

Upon Teedyuscung's refusal to go to Philadelphia, Governor Denny decided to meet the chief at Easton, where the second great conference with him and the Indians under his command opened on November 8, 1756. "The Governor marched from his lodgings to the place of conference, guarded by a party of Royal Americans on the front and on the flanks, and a detachment of Colonel

Weiser's provincial's in subdivisions in the rear, with colors flying, drums beating, and music playing, which order was always observed in going to the place of conference." Says Dr. George P. Donehoo, in his "Pennsylvania—A History":

"Teedyuscung opened the council with a speech and with all of the usual formalities of an Indian council. This Indian chief, called a 'King', was a most gifted orator and talented diplomat. His one most bitter enemy was his own vice of drunkenness which led to all of his troubles and to his death. The one marvel about him was that when he had been on a drunken spree all night and kept so by his enemies, he would appear the next day with a clear head, fully fit to deal with all of the complex problems which arose. His foes among the Indians and among the English kept him filled with rum in the hope that he could be rendered so drunk that he could not attend to his business. He would sleep out all night, under a shed, anywhere, in a drunken stupor, and appear the next day with a clear head and an eloquent tongue to 'fight for peace, at any price.' In his opening address, in referring to the tales which had been told about him he says: 'Many idle reports are spread by foolish and busy people; I agree with you that on both sides they ought to be no more regarded than the chirping of birds in the woods.' What great orator today could express himself more perfectly and beautifully?"

In his opening address, Teedyuscung gave the following additional assurances of his desire to make peace with Pennsylvania:

"I remember well the leagues and covenants of our forefathers. We are but children in comparison with them. What William Penn said to the Indians is fresh in our minds and memory, and I believe it is in yours. The Indians and Governor Penn agreed well together; this we all remember, and it is not a small matter that would then have separated us, and now you fill the same station he did in this Province; it is in your power to act the same part. I am sorry for what our foolish people have done. I have gone among my people pleading for peace. If it cost me my life, I would do it."

Teedyuscung Charges That Delawares Were Defrauded Out of Their Lands

Governor Denny in his reply to Teedyuscung's speech, asked him why the Delawares had gone to war against the English. Teedyuscung in his reply stated that great injustice had been done the Delawares in various land purchases. The Governor then asked him to be specific in his statements and point out what land sales, in his opinion, had been unjust. Then Teedyuscung stamped his foot upon the ground and made the following heated reply:

"I have not far to go for an instance; this very ground that is under me [striking it with his foot] was my land and inheritance, and is taken from me by fraud. When I say this ground, I mean all the land lying between Tohiccon Creek and Wyoming, on the River Susquehannah. I have not only been served so in this Government, but the same thing has been done to me as to several tracts in New Jersey over the River. When I have sold lands fairly, I look upon them to be really sold. A bargain is a bargain. Tho' I have sometimes had nothing for the lands I have sold but broken pipes or such triffles, yet when I have sold them, tho' for such triffles, I look upon the bargain to be good. Yet I think that I should not be ill used on this account by those very people who have had such an advantage in their purchases, nor be called a fool for it. Indians are not such fools as to bear this in their minds."

Governor Denny then asked him if he (Teedyuscung) had ever been dealt with in such a manner, and the chief replied:

"Yes, I have been served so in this Province; all the land extending from Tohiccon, over the great mountain, to Wyoming, has been taken from me by fraud; for when I agreed to sell the land to the old Proprietary, by the course of the River, the young Proprietaries came and got it run by a straight course by the compass, and by that means took in double the quantity intended to be sold. . . . . I did not intend to speak thus, but I have done it at this time, at your request; not that I desire now you should purchase these lands, but that you should look into your own hearts, and consider what is right, and that do."

It is thus seen that Teedyuscung referred directly to the notorious Walking Purchase of 1737. Governor Denny then consulted Richard Peters and Conrad Weiser about the transactions complained of. Peters said that Teedyuscung's charges should be considered, inasmuch as they had been made before; but Weiser advised that none of the 'Indians attending Teedyuscung at this second Easton conference had ever owned any of the lands in question; that if any were living who had at one time owned the lands, they had long since removed to the valleys of the Ohio and Allegheny. Weiser further told the Governor that the land in question had been bought by the Proprietaries when John and Thomas

Penn were in the Colony; that a line was soon after run by Indians and surveyors; and that, when a number of the chiefs of the Delawares complained about the Walking Purchase afterwards, the deeds were produced and the names of the grantors attached to them examined at the council held in Philadelphia, in 1742, at which council, after a long hearing, Canassatego as the speaker of the Six Nations declared that the deeds were correct, and ordered the Delawares to remove from the bounds of the purchase.

The Governor then advised Teedyuscung that the deeds to which he referred were in Philadelphia; that he would examine them upon his return to the city, and if any injustice had been done the Delawares, he would see that they should receive full satisfaction. Some days later, however, Governor Denny denied that any injustice had been done the Delawares by the Walking Purchase, but offered a very handsome present to make satisfaction for the injuries which they complained of. This present Teedyuscung refused to receive; and the matter was then placed in charge of an investigating committee.

It was then decided that a general peace should be proclaimed, provided that the white prisoners were delivered up, and that the declaration of war and Scalp Act should not apply to any Indians who would promise to lay down their arms.

Teedyuscung then made the following promise in regard to the delivery of the captives:

"I will use my utmost endeavors to bring you down your prisoners. I have to request you that you would give liberty to all persons and friends to search into these matters; as we are all children of the Most High, we should endeavor to assist and make use of one another, and not only so, but from what I have heard, I believe there is a future state besides this flesh. Now I endeavour to act upon both these principles, and will, according to what I have promised, if the Great Spirit spare my life, come next spring with as great a force of Indians as I can get to your satisfaction."

At the close of the conference, Teedyuscung's delegation was given a present to the value of four hundred pounds, the Governor advising that the larger part of it was from the Quakers. Teedyuscung in his reply urged that the work of peace be continued. Said he:

"Hear me with patience; I am going to use a comparison in order to represent to you better what we ought to do.

"When you choose a spot of ground for planting, you first prepare the ground, then you put the seed into the earth; but if you don't take pains afterwards, you will not obtain fruit. To instance, in the Indian corn, which is mine, I, as is customary, put seven grains in one hill, yet without further care it will come to nothing, tho' the ground be good; tho' at the beginning I take prudent steps, yet if I neglect it afterwards, tho' it may grow up to stalks and leaves, and there may be the appearance of ears, there will be only leaves and cobs. In like manner in the present business, tho' we have begun well, yet if we hereafter use not prudent means, we shall not have success answerable to our expectations. God that is above hath furnished us both with powers and abilities. As for my own part, I must confess to my shame I have not made such improvements of the power given me as I ought; but as I look on you to be more highly favored from above than I am, I would desire you that we would join our endeavours to promote the good work, and that the cause of our uneasiness, begun in the times of our forefathers, may be removed; and if you look into your hearts, and act according to the abilities given you, you will know the grounds of our uneasiness in some measure from what I said before in the comparison of the fire; tho' I was but a boy, yet I would according to my abilities bring a few chips; so with regard to the corn; I can do but little; you may a great deal; therefore, let all of us, men, women, and children, assist in pulling up the weeds, that nothing may hinder the corn from growing to perfection. When this is done, tho' we may not live to enjoy the fruit ourselves, yet we should remember our children may live and enjoy the good fruit, and it is our duty to act for their good."

The second conference at Easton closed on November 17th. In the minutes of this great council, we read: "Teedyuscung showed great pleasure in his countenance, and took a kind leave of the Governor and all present."

Teedyuscung's Activities After the Second Easton Conference

Conrad Weiser accompanied Teedyuscung and the Indian delegation to Fort Allen at the close of the conference, reaching that place after dark. The old chief's wife was at that time among the Moravians at Bethlehem, and the next morning she declared that she would not live with Teedyuscung any longer on account of his drunkenness. Teedyuscung then took all the children away from her but one. Whereupon Weiser, induced by the Moravians, urged his influence in persuading the wife to live once more with her husband. In this task Weiser succeeded, and he and the Indian delegation left Bethlehem for Fort Allen. At Hessey's Inn at Bethlehem, the Indian delegation had dined on cider and beef, and a ten gallon keg of rum had been sent along for them to drink after they had gotten beyond Fort Allen. However, when the party came near the fort, some Indians came to meet Teedyuscung, to receive their share of the presents which had been given at the Easton conference, constantly importuning that the chief treat them with rum. In spite of all that Weiser could do, five gallons of rum were consumed by them before they reached the fort; and then Teedyuscung demanded that the remaining five gallons be given him to have a frolic with the Indians. After much importuning, Weiser surrendered the keg, on condition that the Indians stay away from the fort while engaged in their frolic, to which terms Teedyuscung agreed.

"I ordered a soldier to carry it [the rum] down to the fire," said Weiser. "About the middle of the night he [Teedyuscung] came back and desired to be let in and it was found that he was alone; orders were given to let him in, because his wife and children were in the fort; he behaved well. After awhile we were alarmed by one of the drunken Indians that offered to climb over the stocaddoes. I got on the platform and looked out the porthole and saw the Indian and told him to be gone, else the sentry should fire upon him. He ran off as fast as he could and cried, 'damn you all, I value you not;' but as he got out of sight immediately we heard no more of it."

After the rum was consumed, Teedyuscung parted with tears in his eyes, desiring Weiser "to stand a friend to the Indians and give good advice, till everything that was desired was brought about." "Though he is a drunkard and a very irregular man," wrote Weiser, "yet he is a man that can think well and I believe him to be sincere in what he says."

Teedyuscung then went out among the Delawares and other Indians of the Susquehanna Valley, to hunt up the white captives and to work for peace. By this time, as we say in Chapter XVII, his great collaborator in the work of peace, Canachquasy, was no more. Teedyuscung continued pleading for peace. The charge that he had made concerning the Walking Purchase caused considerable civil strife in the Colony. The Governor had promised that the chief's charges would be investigated, and the Quakers were determined that the committee in charge of the investigation should not shirk their duty.

The Lancaster Treaty of May, 1757

At about this time, Sir William Johnson, who, as we have seen, had been put in charge of Indian affairs in the colonies, appointed George Croghan as his deputy in charge of Indian affairs in Pennsylvania. Following Croghan's desire, a treaty with a large number of the Susquehanna Indians was held at Lancaster during May, 1757. Teedyuscung, however, did not attend, being still among the Indians, working for peace. It was the desire of Johnson and Croghan that all friendly Indians should take up the hatchet in the English cause; but Teedyuscung opposed this, and contended that the friendly Indians should be asked no more than to remain neutral. While the delegation of chiefs were waiting near Lancaster for Teedyuscung, Governor Denny received orders from Lord Loudon not to take part in Indian treaties, and to forbid the Quakers from attending such treaties or contributing thereto in any manner. The Governor then declined to take part in the Lancaster treaty.

Says Walton: "Letters and petitions now poured in upon the Governor. William Masters and Joseph Galaway, of Lancaster, voiced the sentiment of that vicinity in a letter urging the Governor to come to Lancaster immediately, and use every possible means to ascertain the truth or falsity of Teedyuscung's charges. 'The Indians now present have plainly intimated that they are acquainted with the true cause of our Indian war.' The Friendly Society for the Promotion of Peace Among the Indians asked permission of the Governor to examine the minutes of the Provincial Council and the Proprietaries' deeds, in order to 'assist the Proprietaries in proving their innocence of Teedyuscung's charges.' The Governor positively refused to show them any papers. The Commissioners in charge of Indian affairs were also refused the same request. The Governor then lost his temper and charged the Quakers of Pennsylvania with meddling in affairs which did not concern them. The Assembly then sent a message to the Governor, denying that the people of the Province ever interfered with his majesty's prerogative of making peace and war. . . . . Their known duty and loyalty to his majestiy, notwithstanding the pains taken to misrepresent their actions, forbids such an attempt. It is now clear by the inquiries made by your Honor, that the cause of the present Indian incursions in this Province, and the dreadful calamities many of the inhabitants have suffered, have arisen in a great measure from the exorbitant and unreasonable purchases made or supposed to have been made of the Indians, that the natives complain that there is not a country left to hunt or subsist in.' "

Governor Denny was compelled by pressure of the people to go to the Lancaster conference. At this time, the Cherokees, who were serving in the army at Fort Loudon and Fort Cumberland, were particularly opposed to any peace with the Delawares, and as a consequence, while the conferences were in progress at Lancaster, some Indian outrages occurred within a few miles of that place, so exasperating the people that they brought the mutilated body of a woman, whom the Indians had scalped, and left it on the court house steps as the silent witness, as they said, of the fruits of an Indian peace. All these matters, together with the absence of the great Teedyuscung, made it impossible to accomplish anything definite at Lancaster. George Croghan was anxious that the Western Indians be taken into a treaty of peace at Lancaster, and this question was therefore postponed on account of the absence of Teedyuscung.

While Teedyuscung did not attend the Lancaster treaty, he sent a message complaining bitterly of the Moravians at Bethlehem, as follows:

"Brothers, there is one thing that gives us a great deal of concern, which is our flesh and blood that live among you at Bethlehem and in the Jersies, being kept as if they were prisoners. We formally applied to the minister at Bethlehem [probably meaning Bishop Spangenberg] to let our people come back at times and hunt, which is the chief industry we follow to maintain our families; but that minister has not listened to what we said to him, and it is very hard that our people have not the liberty of coming back to the woods where game is plenty, and to see their friends. They have complained to us that they cannot hunt where they are. If they go to the woods and cut down a tree, they are abused for it, notwithstanding that very land we look upon to be our own; and we hope, brothers, that you will consider this matter and let our people come back into the woods, and visit their friends, and pass and repass, as brothers ought to do."

The Moravian missionaries resented this message of Teedyuscung, claiming that he well knew the sentiments of the Indian converts at Bethlehem, and that they were there of their own free will. The Colonial Government paid no attention, however, to this message. In June, 1757, the Governor received a message from Teedyuscung, asking that four or five horseloads of provisions be sent to Wyoming, not by white people, but by Indians. Said he:

"I desire you to be careful. I have heard and have reason to think it will grieve both you and me to the heart. Though many nations belonging to the French can go round me, and as I have heard and have reason to believe that they know and have understood that I have taken hold of your hand, their aim is to break us apart and to separate us. When I visited the Indians over the Great Swamp and told them my message of peace, they said it was a bait, and that the English would kill us all; but, however, when they saw me come back safe the first time, they dropped their tomahawks and said, 'If the English are true to you they will be true to us.' "

The matter of the fradulent land sales came up at this conference at Lancaster. One of the chiefs of the Six Nations, Little Abraham, spoke as follows concerning the frauds upon the Delawares:

"They lived among you, brothers, but upon some difference between you and them, we [the Six Nations] thought proper to remove them, giving them lands to plant and hunt on at Wyoming and Juniata on Susquehanna. But you, covetous of land, made plantations there and spoiled their hunting grounds. They then complained to us, and we looked over those lands and found the complaints to be true.. . . . . . The French became acquainted with all the causes of complaint that the Delawares had against you; and as your people were daily increasing their settlements, by this means you drove them [the Delawares] back into the arms of the French, and they took the advantage of spiriting them up against you by telling them: 'Children, you see, and we have often told you, how the English, your brethren, did serve; they plant all the country, and drive you back; so that in a little time you will have no land. It is not so with us. Though we built trading houses on your land, we do not plant it. We have our provisions from over the great waters.' "

The Six Nations' chiefs at this conference then advised that part of the lands of the Delawares be given back to them and promised to make both the Delawares and Shawnees return the captives. They further urged that another invitation be sent to Teedyuscung to come and bring some Senecas with him, in order that the land question might be fully settled. Governor Denny followed the suggestion of the chiefs of the Six Nations made at the Lancaster conference, and accordingly arranged for the third council or treaty at Easton, where the complaints of the Delawares might be more fully heard. This treaty we shall discuss in the next chapter.

We close this chapter by calling attention to the following events which took place in the spring of 1757, while Teedyuscung was working for peace:

Atrocities in Monroe County

On March 25th, the Delawares made an incursion into Monroe County, in which Sargeant Leonard Den was killed. This was followed by another on April 20th when Andreas Gundryman, a boy aged seventeen, who had gone to bring some fire wood from the neighborhood of Fort Hamilton to his father's house near the fort, was killed. In the same incursions, Peter Soan and Christian Kline were killed and several others carried into captivity.

Murder of John Spitler and Barnabas Tolon

On May 16th, John Spitler while fixing up a pair of bars on his farm a few miles from Stumpton, was shot and his body cruelly mangled. His body was buried in the graveyard at Hebron, near Lebanon. The following account of his murder and burial is contained in the records of the Hebron church:

"1757, May den 16, wurde Johannes Spitler, Jr., ohnweit von seinem Hause, an der Schwatara von moerderischen Indianern ueberfallen und ermordet. Er war im acht unddreisigsten Jahr seines Alters, und verwichenes Jahr im April, an der Schwatara aufgenommen. Seine uebelzugerichtette Leiche wurde den 17ten May hieher gebracht, und bei einer grossen Menge Leute begleitet auf unsern hiesigen Gottesacker beerdigt."

The following is the translation of the record:

"On the 16th of May, 1757, John Spitler, Jr., was fallen upon and murdered by savage Indians not far from his house on the Swatara. He was in the thirty-eighth year of his age, and had taken up his residence on the Swatara in the preceding April. His badly mangled body was brought here on the 17th of May, accompanied by a large concourse of people, and buried in the graveyard of this place."

On May 22nd, Barnabus Tolon was killed and scalped in

Hanover Township, Lebanon County. "We are," says the editor of the Pennsylvania Gazette, "well informed that 123 persons have been murdered and carried off from that part of Lancaster [Lebanon] County by Indians since the war commenced, and that lately three have been scalped and are yet living."

Massacre on Quitapahilla Creek

"Londonderry Township (Lebanon County) being more towards the interior, was not so much exposed to the depredations of the savages as those on the northern frontiers. Nevertheless, in the more sparsely settled parts they committed various murders. June 19, 1757, nineteen persons were killed in a mill on the Quitapahilla Creek, and on the 9th of September, 1757, one boy and a girl were taken from Donegal Township, a few miles south of Derry. About the same time, one Danner and his son Christian, a lad of twelve years, had gone into the Conewago hills to cut down trees; after felling one, and while the father was cutting a log, he was shot and scalped by an Indian, and Christian, the son, taken captive into Canada, where he remained until the close of the war when he made his escape. Another young lad, named Steger, was surprised by three Indians and taken captive whilst cutting hoop-poles, but, fortunately, after remaining with the Indians some months made his escape."—(Frontier Forts of Pennsylvania).

Murder of Adam Trump

On June 22nd occurred the murder of Adam Trump, in Albany Township, Lancaster Cunty, thus referred to in a letter of James Read, from Reading, on June 25th:

"Last night Jacob Levan, Esq., of Maxatawney, came to see me and showed me a letter of the 22d inst. from Lieutenant Engel, dated in Allemangel, by which he advised Mr. Levan of the murder of one Adam Trump in Allemangel, by Indians, that evening, and that they had taken Trump's wife and his son, a lad nineteen years old, prisoners; but the woman escaped, though upon her flying, she was so closely pursued by one of the Indians, (of which there were seven) that he threw his tomahawk at her, and cut her badly in the neck, but 'tis hoped not dangerously. This murder happened in as great a thunderstorm as has happened for twenty years past; which extended itself over a great part of this and Northampton counties. * * * *

"I had almost forgot to mention (but I am so hurried just

now, 'tis no wonder), that the Indians after scalping Adam Trump left a knife, and a halbert, or a spear, fixed to a pole of four feet, in his body."

News From Fort Duquesne

In the spring of 1757 Lieutenant Baker with five soldiers and fifteen Cherokee Indians made a scouting expedition into the vicinity of Fort Duquesne. His force encountered a party of three French officers and seven men on the headwaters of Turtle Creek, about ten miles from the fort. They killed five of the Frenchmen and took one officer prisoner, who gave the information that Captain Lignery was then commandant of the fort, and that there were six hundred French troops and two hundred Indians at that place. This is the latest definite information received as to the conditions of Fort Duquesne until it was captured in November of the next year by General Forbes.

CHAPTER XXII

Teedyuscung

(Continued)

Teedyuscung at the Third Easton Council

HE third council with Teedyuscung at Easton opened on July 21, 1757, and continued until August 7th. There were almost endless discussions about Teedyuscung's having a secretary of his own, deeds, frauds, and other matters which had come before Indian councils for many years prior to this council. Finally, John Pumpshire was selected by Teedyuscung as his interpreter, and Charles Thomson, master of the Quaker school in Philadelphia, as his clerk. Thomson, in writing of this affair to Samuel Rhodes, says:

"I need not mention the importance of the business we are come about. The welfare of the Province and the lives of thousands depend upon it. That an affair of such weight should be transacted with soberness, all will allow; how, then, must it shock you to hear that pains seem to have been taken to make the King [Teedyuscung] drunk every night since the business began. The first two or three days were spent in deliberating whether the King should be allowed the privilege of a clerk. When he was resolute in asserting his right and would enter into no business without having a secretary of his own, they at last gave it up,. and seem to have fallen on another scheme which is to unfit him to say anything worthy of being inscribed (?) by his secretary. On Saturday, under pretense of rejoicing for the victory gained by the King of Prussia and the arrival of the fleet, a bonfire was ordered to be made and liquor given to the Indians to induce them to dance. For fear they should get sober on Sunday and be fit next day to enter on business, under pretense that the Mohawks had requested it, another bonfire was ordered to be made, and more liquor given them. On Monday night the King was made drunk by Conrad Weiser, on Tuesday by G. Croghan; last night he was very drunk at Vernon's, and Vernon lays the blame on Comin and G. Croghan. He did not go to sleep last night. This morning he lay down under a shed about the break of day and slept a few hours. He is to speak this afternoon. He is to be sure in a fine capacity to do business. But thus we go on. I leave you to make reflections. I for my part wish myself at home."

Teedyuscung Renews Charge of Fraud

Teedyuscung entered this third Easton council with his mind made up not to reiterate the charge of fraud concerning the Walking Purchase, doubtless fearing the Six Nations. His advisors told him that he could afford to wait until peace was fully established, before asserting the Delaware rights to lands drained by the Delaware River. However, Governor Denny was determined to make the great chief deny that any fraud had been practiced upon the Delawares in land purchases. When pressed for the cause of the alienation of the Delawares, Teedyuscung unequivocally asserted that it was the land purchases. Said he:

"The complaint I made last fall I yet continue. I think some lands have been bought by the Proprietors or his agents from Indians who had not a right to sell. . . . . . I think, also, when some lands have been sold to the Proprietors by Indians who had a right to sell to a certain place, whether that purchase was to be measured by miles or hours walk, that the Proprietors have contrary to agreement or bargain, taken in more lands than they ought to have done, and lands that belonged to others. I therefore now desire that you will produce the writings and deeds by which you hold the land, and let them be read in public, and examined, that it may be fully known from what Indians you have bought the lands you hold; and how far your purchases extend; that copies of the whole may be laid before King George, and published to all the Provinces under his Government. What is fairly bought and paid for I make no further demand about. But if any lands have been bought of Indians to whom these lands did not belong, and who had no right to sell them, I expect a satisfaction for those lands; and if the Proprietors have taken in more lands than they bought of true owners, I expect likewise to be paid for that."

Teedyuscung Requests Benefits of Civilization

Said Teedyuscung: "We [the Delawares] intend to settle at Wyoming, and we want to have certain boundaries fixed between you and us, and a certain tract of land fixed which it shall not be lawful for us or our children ever to sell, nor for you or any of your children ever to buy. . . . . . To build different houses from what we have done before, such as may last not only for a little time, but for our children after us; we desire you will assist us in making our settlements, and send us persons to instruct us in building houses and making such necessaries as shall be needed, and that persons be sent to instruct us in the Christian religion, and to instruct our children in reading and writing, and that a fair trade be established between us, and such persons appointed to conduct and manage these affairs as shall be agreeable to us."

Walton's Account of the Council

The remaining matters taken up at this great conference are thus succinctly set forth by J. S. Walton, in his "Conrad Weiser and the Indian Policy of Pennsylvania":

"Teedyuscung then asked that the territory of Wyoming be reserved to the Indians forever. That it might be surveyed and a deed given to the Indians, that they might have something to show when it became necessary to drive the white men away. After these charges were again made the Governor called Croghan and Weiser together to know what was the best thing to do. Each of these men with his large share of experience in Indian affairs agreed in the opinion that some outside influence had induced Teedyuscung to revive these charges. They also united in the opinion that the Indians merely wanted a glimpse of the old deeds, and would be satisfied with a cursory examination of the signatures.

"Upon these assertions the Governor and Council were induced to grant Teedyuscung's request and to show him the deeds of 1636 and 1637 from the Delawares, and of 1749 from the Iroquois. When the Governor applied to Mr. Peters for the papers and deeds they were again refused. Peters declared that he held them as a sacred trust from the Proprietors and would neither surrender them nor permit himself to be placed under oath and give testimony. These two things could only be done, he insisted, in the presence of Sir William Johnson, before whom as a final arbitrator, the Proprietors desired that these charges should be laid. James Logan immediately opposed Richard Peters. He insisted that all deeds relating to lands which the Indians claimed were fraudulently purchased, sould be shown. To refuse this would be unjust to the Indians and dangerous to the cause of peace. Logan explained that the Proprietary instructions should not be too literally construed and obeyed. The Indians were opposed to having their case settled before Sir William Johnson. After an animated discussion in council it was reluctantly agreed that the deeds should be shown. The Council only consented to this after Conrad Weiser had assured them that Teedyuscung did not insist upon seeing all the deeds, but only those pertaining to the back lands. R. Peters again protested, but was overruled. The deeds were laid on the table August 3, 1757.

"Charles Thomson, at Teedyuscung's request, copied these deeds. The chief said he would have preferred to have seen the deeds of confirmation given to Governor Keith in 1718, but the great work of peace was superior to the land dispute, and if the Proprietors would make satisfaction for the lands which had been fraudulently secured, he would return the English prisoners held captive among the Indians. The peace belt was then grasped by the Governor and Teedyuscung, and the two years' struggle for peace was crowned with victory. After much feasting and dancing, drinking and burning of bonfires the treaty closed.

"Teedyuscung promised to fight for the English on condition that his men should not be commanded by white captains. The Governor and his party returned to Philadelphia, deeply worried over the publicity of the Indian charges of fraud which had occurred at the Easton conference. Peace to the Proprietors was dearly purchased, if the people of the Province were confirmed in their belief that the Indian outrages had been caused by fraud in land purchases."

The council ended on Sunday, August 7th. Governor Denny then returned to Philadelphia realizing that two things were imperative. One was to disprove Teedyuscung's charge of fraud, in order to remove from the Proprietaries of the Colony the responsibility for the hostility of the Delawares and Shawnees; the other was to make peace with the Indians of the valleys of the Ohio and Allegheny, in order that the expedition of General Forbes then planned might be a success. The Governor was very apprehensive that, on account of the allegiance of the Western Indians with the French, the proposed expedition of General Forbes would meet with the same fate as the expedition of the ill-fated Braddock in the summer of 1755. Besides, unless the hostile Indians of the Ohio and Allegheny could be persuaded to sever their allegiance with the French, there was little chance of ending the barbarous raids which they were making on the frontier settlements. How these Western Indians were induced by the Moravian missionary, Christian Frederick Post, to sever their allegiance with the French, as General Forbes was marching on Fort Duquesne in the autumn of 1758, has already been told in Chapter XIX.

Atrocities of the Summer of 1757

Indian atrocities still continued as Teedyuscung worked for peace. In August, 1757, incursions were made into Lebanon County. John Andrews' wife and child were captured while going to a neighbor's house. John Winklebach's two sons and Joseph Fischbach were fired upon by fifteen Indians, while bringing in the cows at sunrise. The boys were killed, and Fischbach was badly wounded. At about the same time, Leonard Long's son was killed and scalped while plowing in his father's field, and Isaac Williams' wife was killed. In September, Christian Danner was killed and his son, aged twelve, captured and carried to Canada, where he made his escape after three years, as related in Chapter XXI.

During this summer, incursions were also made into Dauphin County. At the time of one of these incursions, a Mr. Barnett and a Mr. Mackey were at work on the former's farm near Manada Creek, when news reached them that their families were murdered in the block house nearby. They at once started for the scene of horror, but had not gone far until they were ambushed by a party of Indians who killed Mackey and severely wounded Barnett who, nevertheless, was able to escape, owing to the swiftness of his horse. He concealed himself until the Indians left the neighborhood the next day, when he learned that his family was safe with the exception of his son, William, aged nine, whom the Indians had captured, together with Mackey's son about the same age. The Indians proceeded westward with the two little boys. Upon learning that one of the boys was the son of Mackey, whom they had just killed, they forced him to stretch his father's scalp. For a time, the little Mackey boy carried his father's scalp, which he would often stroke with his little hand, and say, "My father's pretty hair."

Mr. Barnett at length recovered from his wound. In the hope of recovering his son, he accompanied George Croghan to Fort Pitt, and attended the council which Crogan, Colonel Hugh Mercer, Captain William Trent, and Captain Thomas McKee held with the Shawnees, Delawares, and other Indians at that place on July 5th, 1759. One day during his stay at the fort, he wished to get a drink of water from Grant's Spring, above the fort, so named from the defeat of Major James Grant at that place in the preceding September. He had proceeded only a short distance, when

something told him to turn back. At the same instant, he heard
the report of a rifle, and looking towards the spring, saw the smoke
of the same and an Indian scalping a soldier, who had gone to the
spring for a drink.

Mr. Barnett returned home without recovering his son, but
Crogan promised to use every endeavor to obtain the child. At
length the boy was brought to Fort Pitt, but so great was his inclination to return to the Indians that it was necessary to guard him
closely until there would be an opportunity to send him to his
father. On one occasion, he jumped into a canoe, and was half
way across the Allegheny River before he was observed. Quick
pursuit followed; but he reached the other side and hid in the
bushes, where it took a search of several hours to find him. Soon
thereafter, he was sent to Carlisle, where the father received him
with tears of joy, and took him home to the arms of the mother.
During his captivity, the Indians frequently broke the ice on
rivers and creeks, and dipped him in "to make him hardy". This
treatment impaired his constitution. He sank into the grave in
early manhood, leaving a wife and daughter. Shortly thereafter,
the mother died. Then Mr. Barnett, the elder, removed to Allegheny County, where he died at the great age of eighty-two years.
His dust reposes in the church yard of Lebanon, Mifflin Township,
Allegheny County.

But, to return to the Mackey boy. The Indians gave this
child to the French, and at the close of the French and Indian War,
he passed into the hands of the English, was taken to England, and
later, became a soldier in the British army, and was sent to America
during the Revolutionary War. He procured a furlough, and
sought out his widowed mother, who had mourned him as dead.
As he stood before her in the strength of robust manhood, she was
unable to see in him any trace of her long lost boy. "If you are
my son," said she, "you have a mark upon your knee that I will
know." He then exposed his knee to her view; whereupon she
threw her arms around his neck in unrestrained joy. He never
returned to the British army, but remained with his mother to the
end of her days, often meeting William Barnett, and recounting
with him their experiences while captives among the Indians.

Teedyuscung's Activities After the Third Easton Council

Two days after the third Easton conference closed, Teedyuscung and his family went to Bethlehem, where he tarried for several days. Reichel, in his "Memorials of the Moravian Church,"
says of this visit:

"Some of these unwelcome visitors halted for a few days, and some proceeded as far as Fort Allen and then returned, undecided as to where to go and what to do. During the month full 200 were counted—men, women and children—among them lawless crowds who annoyed the brethren by depredations, molested the Indians at the Manakasy, and wrangled with each other over their cups at 'The Crown'."

After the third Easton treaty was over, and as Teedyuscung was returning to Tioga, he met three messengers from the Ohio Indians, who stated to him that they were sorry that they had taken up arms against the English, and would do whatever he told them; whereupon, he informed them of the peace that had been established by the treaty at Easton, and that he would give them the tomahawk against the French, and bring them down to Philadelphia for a treaty. He then proceeded to Philadelphia, where he laid this information before the Governor and Provincial Council on August 30th, and advised them that he had sent his son, Amos, and another Delaware back to the Ohio with the three messengers.

Teedyuscung again appeared before the Governor and Provincial Council on September 5th, and asked for a copy of the Delaware deed of release, which Sassoonan and six other chiefs of the Delawares had executed on September 17, 1718, by the terms of which they acknowledged that their ancestors had conveyed to Pennsylvania, in fee, and had then paid for all the land between "the Delaware and the Susquehanna, from Duck Creek to the mountains on this side of Lechay [Lehigh River]". He also asked why the Easton treaty had not been published. Governor Denny explained that it was Sir William Johnson's business to order any publication of the treaty, and that George Croghan had reminded the Governor of this fact. Teedyuscung then declared that Croghan was a rogue, and that he (Teedyuscung) would have nothing to do with either Croghan or Johnson. The Governor then handed over the copy of the deed of 1718, and assured Teedyuscung that the treaty would be published.

Teedyuscung appeared before the Governor and Provincial Council on December 1st to urge that, as winter was coming on, houses should speedily be built for the Indians at Wyoming. He also visited the Governor and Provincial Council on January 17, 1758, in which he advised them that they might be assured that: "I shall use my utmost endeavors to establish the peace so happily concluded at Easton between the people of this Province and their brethren, the Indians."

Teedyuscung Again Asks for Benefits of Civilization

Teedyuscung again came to Philadelphia on March 13, 1758. On this visit he was very spirited and asked for a clerk. The Council having debated for more than an hour whether this request should be granted, Teedyuscung sent a message that he was tired of waiting, was at dinner, and would bring his clerk, or would not speak at all. A public conference was then held in the council chamber of the State House, which many persons of the city attended. He advised the Council that, in compliance with his promise at the third Easton conference, he had given the "Big Peace Halloo", and had secured the alliance of eight nations of the Western Indians, who had taken hold of the peace belt, in addition to the ten for which he had spoken at the Easton treaty. The calumet which these recent allies had sent Teedyuscung in reply to the publication of peace was smoked by himself, the Governor, and members of the Provincial Council and the Assembly.

A week later, when Governor Denny made his reply accepting the alliance of the eight nations and thanking Teedyuscung for his great work in behalf of peace, the great chief repeated the request for the benefits of civilization, which he had made at the third Easton treaty. Said he:

"Brother, you must consider I have a soul as well as another, and I think it proper you should let me have two masters to teach me, that my soul may be instructed and saved at last. Brother, I desire moreover two school masters, for there are a great many Indian children who want school masters. One therefore is not sufficient to teach them all, so that they may be sufficiently instructed in the Christian way. Brother, I have a body as well as a soul. I want two men to instruct me and show me the ways of living, and how to conduct temporal affairs, who may teach me in everything to do as you do yourselves, that I may live as you do, and likewise who may watch over me and take care of my things, that nobody may cheat me. You tell us the Christian religion is good, and we believe it to be so, partly upon the credit of your words, and partly because we see that some of our brother Indians who were wicked before they became Christians live better lives now than they formerly did."

He added that he asked the liberty of choosing the masters and that he wanted two instructors in temporal affairs, so that if one should prove dishonest, the other might prevent him from doing injury to or impose upon the Indians.

Teedyuscung's Appeal Led to Post's Being Sent
on Mission to the Western Indians

During the conferences that attended the above visit of Teedyuscung to the Governor and Provincial Council, the old chief
urged that the Provincial Authorities should not neglect the opportunity to do everything possible to strengthen the alliance with the
eight western nations who had agreed to his peace proposal. He
said: "I have received every encouragement from the Indian
nations. Now, brother, press on with all your might in promoting
the good work we are engaged in. Let us beg the God that made
us to bless our endeavours, and I am sure if you assert yourselves,
God will grant a blessing, and we shall live."

Teedyuscung then urged that a messenger should be sent to his
friends on the Ohio and Allegheny, warning them to sever their
allegiance with the French. Teedyuscung's appeal was the first
move towards the daring mission of Christian Frederick Post to
the Indians of the Ohio in the summer and autumn of 1758, in
which he succeeded in persuading the western tribes not to give
further assistance to the French.

At this same conference, he also requested that a messenger be
sent to stop the Cherokees from coming any further. These Indians
were coming to assist in the expedition of General Forbes against
Fort Duquesne, much to the displeasure of the Delawares and
Shawnees. We have already seen, in Chapter XVII, that it was
the coming of the Cherokees to assist the English that caused
Paxinosa to leave for the Ohio. At the time of which we are writing, there was great danger that the presence of the Cherokees at
Fort Cumberland, Fort Littleton, Carlisle, and other places, with
the English forces, would seriously complicate any proceedings for
peace. Therefore, the Governor and General Forbes later sent
Christian Frederick Post on a mission to Wyoming, for the purpose
of explaining the situation concerning the Cherokees, and to request
the Indians on the Susquehanna to call the friendly Indians east
of the mountains while the General advanced against Fort Duquesne.

Post, accompanied by Charles Thomson and three friendly
Indians, left Philadelphia on June 7th and, reaching Bethlehem
the next day, they employed three others to accompany them.
From that place they went to the Nescopeck Mountain, about
fifteen miles from Wyoming, where they met a party of nine
Indians on their way to Bethlehem, who warned them not to go to

Wyoming, as the woods were full of strange Indians. It was then decided to go back to the east side of the mountain, and to send two messengers forward to invite Teedyuscung to meet them. The next day Teedyuscung came from his new residence at Wyoming. Post complained to him that the path to Wyoming was closed, and it was his (Teedyuscung's) business to keep it open. The Delaware "King" replied that the road had been closed by the Six Nations. He told Post that he expected a great many Mohicans and Wanamis to come during the summer to live with him at Wyoming; and he begged for corn and flour for them, and that arms and ammunition might be sent to Shamokin, whence they might be transported by way of the river to Wyoming. He assured Post that a belt repeating an invitation to the Senecas to join in the English interest would reach their head chief in eight days, and that there must be a great treaty during the summer.

Post got much valuable information from Teedyuscung as to the situation among the Indians of the Allegheny and Ohio. He then returned to Philadelphia on June 16th, and delivered his report to the Governor. On June 20th, a peace message from the Cherokees was delivered to the Governor, who desired to send it at once to Teedyuscung at Wyoming. Post was the messenger selected for this purpose, who set out for Wyoming over the same course that he had recently traveled, at which place he arrived on June 27th, and delivered the message to Teedyuscung. At Wyoming Post met a number of chiefs from the Allegheny, to whom he explained all about the peace measures that were under way. An old sachem, named Katuaikund, upon hearing the good news, "lifting up his hands to heaven wished that God would have mercy upon them, and would help them to bring them and the English together again, and to establish an everlasting ground foundation for peace among them. He wished further that God would move the Governor and the people's hearts toward them in love, peace, and union. . . . He said further that it would be well if the Governor sent somebody with them at their return home, for it would be of great consequence to them who lived above Allegheny to hear from the Governor's mind from their own mouths." At Wyoming, Post learned that the garrison at Fort Duquesne consisted of about eleven hundred French, almost starved, who would have abandoned the fort, had not the Mohawks sent them assistance, and that the commander had recently said that, "if the English come too strong upon me, I will leave." Two of the messengers who had come from the Allegheny with news concern-

ing the situation of the French were Pisquetomen and Keekyuscung.

Post then returned to Fort Allen (Weissport) on June 30th;
and after the Governor heard his report and had talked with
Pisquetomen and Keekyuscung, it was decided to send these two
Indians to the Ohio, in order to gain information as to the situation
among the Indians there, and to advise them of the peace measures.
Post was requested to accompany these messengers, and he agreed
to do so, if Charles Thomson were permitted to go with him. The
Governor replied that "he might take any other person." Post
then left Philadelphia on June 15th, reaching Bethlehem on the
17th, at which place he made preparations for his journey to the
Ohio. On the 19th he reached Fort Allen (Weissport). where
Teedyuscung tried to dissuade him from going on his dangerous
mission. Post says: "He [Teedyuscung] was afraid I should
never return, that the Indians would kill me." Post replied to
Teedyuscung that he was obliged to go, even if he should lose his
life. On the 22nd, when Post again prepared to set out, Teedyuscung again protested saying that he was afraid that the Indians
would kill Post, or that the French would capture him. Post then
made the final reply to Teedyuscung that he would go on this peace
mission to the Ohio, even if he died in the undertaking, and that,
if, unhappily, he should die before completing the mission, he
hoped that his death would be the means of saving many hundreds
of lives. Without further delay, he therefore set forth on his first
mission to the Ohio, accompanied by Pisquetomen and Keekyuscung, as related in Chapter XIX.

Teedyuscung Continues Working for Peace

During all the time between the close of the third council at
Easton, in the summer of 1757, to the opening of the fourth council
at Easton, on October 7, 1758, Teedyuscung worked steadfastly for
peace, and insisted from time to time that a strong fort be
built at Wyoming. However, he was unable to remain neutral,
and he petitioned the Governor for reward on scalps, believing that
if the white man could enjoy the profits of such a bounty, there was
no reason why the Indians friendly to the Province should not
come in for their share. He even sent friendly Indians to protect
the frontiers. When Will Sock, a Conestoga, had been over the
country carrying a French flag, and had murdered Chagrea and a
German in Lancaster County, Teedyuscung took away the flag,

sent it to Philadelphia, and gave him an English flag. In the meantime, also, he kept urging the Provincial Authorities to build houses for the friendly Indians at Wyoming, in accordance with Pennsylvania's promise at the Easton conference of 1757 to enact a law which would settle the Wyoming lands upon him and his people forever.

Mary Jemison, White Woman of Genesee

While Teedyuscung was thus working for peace, two atrocities were committed in Adams County during the month of April, 1758. The first of these was the attack on the home of Thomas Jemison near the confluence of Sharp's Run and Conewago Creek, Adams County, on April 5th, by Indians from the Ohio and Allegheny valleys. On the morning of that day, Jemison's daughter, Mary, aged about fifteen, had returned from an errand to a neighbor's, and a man took her horse to go to his house after a bag of grain. Her father was busy with chores about the house, her mother was getting breakfast, her two older brothers were at the barn, while she, with the smaller children of the family and a neighbor woman, were in the house. Suddenly they were alarmed by the discharge of a number of guns. Opening the door they found the man and the horse lying dead. The Indians then captured Mr. Jemison, his wife, his children, Robert, Matthew, Betsy, and Mary, together with the neighbor woman and her three children, the two brothers in the barn making their escape. The attacking party consisted of six Indians and four Frenchmen. They set out with their prisoners in single file, using a whip when anyone lagged behind. At the end of the second day's march, Mary was separated from her parents. During the night her parents and all the other prisoners, except Mary and a neighbor boy, were cruelly put to death, and their bodies left in the swamps to be devoured by wild beasts. During the next day's march, the unhappy girl had to watch the Indians scrape and dry the scalps of her parents, brothers, sisters, and neighbors. Her mother had an abundance of beautiful, red hair, and she could easily distinguish her scalp from the others,— a sight which remained with her to the end of her days. The neighbor boy was given to the French, and Mary was given to two Shawnee squaws, and carried to the Shawnee towns on the Scioto. Here these squaws adopted her, replacing a brother who had been killed during the French and Indian War.

In the autumn of 1759, she was taken to Fort Pitt, when the

Shawnees and other western tribes went to that place to make peace with the English. She accompanied them with a light heart, as she believed she would soon be restored to her brothers who had made their escape when she was captured. The English at Fort Pitt asked her a number of questions concerning herself, which so alarmed her adopted Indian sisters that they hastily took her down the Ohio in a canoe. Afterwards she learned that some settlers had come to the fort to take her away, but could not find her.

She married two Indian chiefs of renown. The first was a Delaware named Sheninjee, of whom she spoke as "noble, large in stature, elegant in appearance, generous in conduct, courageous in war, a friend of peace, and a great lover of justice." To this husband she bore two children. The first died soon after birth, but the second, who was born in the fourth year of her captivity, she named in memory of her father, Thomas Jemison. Her first husband died while they were enroute with her child to her new home in the Genesee Valley in New York. Several years after the death of her first husband, she married Hiokatoo, also known as Gardow, by whom she had four daughters and two sons. This second husband was a cruel and vindictive warrior.

Two great sorrows came into her life. The first was when her son, John, killed his brother, Thomas, her comforter and namesake of her father. The second was when this same John a few years later killed his other brother, Jesse. Her grief became somewhat assuaged when John was murdered later in a drunken quarrel with two Indians.

Mary Jemison continued to live in the German Flats, New York, and upon the death of her second husband, she became possessed of a large tract of valuable land. She was naturalized April 19, 1817, and received a clear title to her land. In 1823, she sold a major portion of her holdings, reserving a tract two miles long and one mile wide.

This remarkable lady who preserved the sensibilities of a white woman amidst the surroundings of barbaric life, died September 19, 1833, at the age of ninety-one years, and was buried, with Christian rites, in the cemetery of the Seneca Mission on the Buffalo Creek Reservation, in New York. On March 17, 1874, her body was removed to the Indian Council House Grounds at Letchworth Park, where a beautiful bronze statue marks the grave of "The White Woman, The Genesee."

Capture of the Family of Richard Bard

The second atrocity committed by the Indians while Teedyuscung was working for peace, was the attack on the home of Richard Bard, on April 13, 1758. The Bard family resided near a place later known as Marshall's Mills, in Adams County. A little girl, named Hannah McBride, was at the door when the Indians approached. She ran screaming into the house where there were Bard and his wife and six months' old child, an apprentice boy, and a relative of the Bards, Lieutenant Thomas Potter by name, a brother of General James Potter. One of the Indians attacked Lieutenant Potter with a cutlass, but he succeeded in wresting it from the savage. Mr. Bard seized a pistol and snapped it at the breast of one of the Indians, but it failed to fire. As there was no ammunition in the home, the occupants of the house, fearing a slaughter or being burned alive, surrendered, as the Indians promised no harm would be done to them. The savages then went into the field nearby, where they captured Samuel Hunter, Daniel McManiny, and a boy named William White, who was coming to a mill near the Bard home.

The Indians then secured the prisoners, plundered the house, and burned the mill. At a point about seventy rods from the home, contrary to their promises, they killed Lieutenant Potter, and having proceeded over the mountain for several miles, one of them sunk the spear of his tomahawk into the breast of the child, and scalped it. When they had proceeded with their prisoners past the fort into Path Valley, they encamped for the night. The next day they discovered a party of settlers in pursuit. They then hastened the pace of their prisoners under threat of tomahawking them. Reaching the top of Tuscarora Mountain, the party sat down to rest, and one of the Indians, without giving any warning whatever, buried his tomahawk in the head of Samuel Hunter, and scalped him. They then passed over Sidling Hill and the Allegheny Mountains by Blair's Gap, and encamped beyond Stony Creek. Here they painted Bard's head red on one side, indicating that a council had been held; that an equal number were for killing him and for saving his life, and that his fate would be determined in the next council.

Bard then determined to attempt his escape and, while assisting his wife in plucking a turkey, he told her of his intentions. Some of the Indians were asleep, and one was amusing the others by parading around in Mrs. Bard's gown. As this Indian was thus furnishing amusement for the others, Bard was sent to the spring for water, and made his escape. After having made an unsuccessful search for Bard, the party proceeded to Fort Duquesne and then to Kuskuskies, where Mrs. Bard, the two boys and the girl were compelled to run the gauntlet, and were beaten in a most inhuman manner. Here also Daniel McManiny was put to death by being tied to a post, scalped alive, and pierced through the body with a red-hot gun barrel.

Mrs. Bard was separated from the other prisoners, led from one Indian town to another, and finally adopted by two warriors, to take the place of a deceased sister. Finally she was taken to the headwaters of the Susquehanna, and during the journey, suffered greatly from fatigue and illness. She lay for two months, a blanket her only covering and boiled corn her only food. She remained in captivity two years and five months.

Mr. Bard, after having made his escape and after a terrible journey of nine days, during which his only food was a few buds and four snakes, finally reached Fort Littleton, Fulton County. After this, he wandered from place to place throughout the frontier, seeking information concerning his wife. After having made several perilous journeys to Fort Duquesne for the same purpose, and in which he narrowly escaped capture on several occasions, he finally learned that she was at Fort Augusta (Sunbury), where he redeemed her.

During Mrs. Bard's captivity, she was kindly treated by the warriors who had adopted her. Before the Bards left Fort Augusta, Mr. Bard requested one of his wife's adopted brothers to visit them at their home. This he did some time afterwards, when the Bards were living about ten miles from Chambersburg, remaining at the Bard home for some time; but finally he went one day to McDowell's Tavern, where he became intoxicated and got into a quarrel with a rough frontier character by the name of Newgen, who stabbed him dangerously in the neck. Newgen fled from the vicinity in order to escape the wrath of Bard's neighbors. The wounded Indian, however, recovered after being tenderly nursed by his adopted sister, Mrs. Bard. He then returned to his people, who put him to death on the pretext of having, as they claimed, joined the white people.

Other atrocities than the attacks on the Jemison and Bard families, were committed in Eastern Pennsylvania in the month of April, 1758. A man, named Lebenguth, and his wife were killed in the Tulpehocken Valley. Also, at Northkill, Nicholas Geiger's wife and two children and Michael Ditzelar's wife were killed.

Teedyuscung at the Grand Council at Easton

While Christian Frederick Post was on his first mission to the Ohio Indians, Teedyuscung was persuading the Six Nations to send deputies to a fourth grand peace conference at Easton. His purpose was to draw all the Indians into an alliance with the English, and to secure a general and lasting peace. As a preliminary, he had induced the Minisink Indians and a number of Senecas to go to Philadelphia in August and hold a conference with the Governor.

The Grand Council at Easton, known as the Fourth Easton Council, opened on Sunday, October 8, 1758, with more than five hundred Indians in attendance, representing all the tribes of the Six Nations, the Delawares, Conoys, Tuteloes, and Nanticokes. Governor Denny, members of the Provincial Council and Assembly, Governor Bernard, of New Jersey, Commissioners for Indian affairs in New Jersey, Conrad Weiser, George Crogan, and a number of Quakers from Philadelphia, made up the attendance of the whites.

Pennsylvania Deeds Back Albany Purchase of 1754

Three great land disputes came before this council. The first was the Albany purchase of 1754, which, as we have already seen, caused the Delawares of the West Branch of the Susquehanna and the valleys of the Ohio and Allegheny to go over to the French. To the credit of Conrad Weiser, it must be said that he had all along insisted that this was not a just purchase; that the Indians were deceived, and that the running of the lines had been greatly misrepresented. Furthermore, the Six Nations had declared to Sir William Johnson in 1755, that they would never consent to this sale, pointing out that the West Branch of the Susquehanna was held by them simply in trust as a hunting ground for their cousins, the Delawares. The matter was adjusted at this treaty by Governor Denny, on behalf of the Proprietaries, telling the Six Nations that Conrad Weiser and Richard Peters would deed back to them all of the Albany Purchase west of the summits of the Allegheny Mountains, if the Six Nations would confirm the residue of the purchase. This they agreed to, and the mutual releases were executed October 24th.

But before the releases were executed, Christian Frederick Post had succeeded in drawing the Shawnees and Delawares of the Ohio away from the French,—a fact that shows the greatness of his achievement. On his way back from his first mission to the Ohio

Indians, he sent Pisquetomen and John Hickman to Philadelphia to deliver the speech belt which Shingas, Beaver, and other chiefs had given him, while he went on from Harris' Ferry to see General Forbes. Pisquetomen and Hickman then went to the Great Council at Easton, where Pisquetomen delivered the belt.

On the afternoon of October 22nd, just as Pisquetomen and Hickman were leaving Easton, Post arrived at the Council with the news from General Forbes that the General's advance guard, on October 12th, was attacked at Loyal Hanning, later known as Fort Ligonier, at the present town of Ligonier, Westmoreland County, by twelve hundred French and two hundred Indians. Post then left Easton on October 25th on his second mission to the Ohio Indians, to make known to them the results of the Easton Council.

The success of Post's second mission to the Ohio has already been told, as has the fact that, in July, 1759, a great conference was held at Fort Pitt with all the Ohio tribes by George Croghan, Colonel Hugh Mercer, then commander at Fort Pitt, Captain William Trent, and Captain Thomas McKee, which gathered the fruit and glory of the peace missions of this Moravian missionary. King Beaver was the principal speaker of the Indians on this occasion. Guyasuta was also present, and Andrew Montour was the interpreter.

The second land dispute taken up at the Grand Council was the complaint of the Munsee Clan of Delawares (Munseys) that their lands in New Jersey had never been purchased. Governor Bernard, of New Jersey, when asked by the Munseys what he should pay for the New Jersey land, offered them eight hundred dollars, saying that it was a very extraordinary offer. The Munseys then asked the Iroquois deputies for their opinion as to the price. The Iroquois replied that the offer was fair and honorable; that if it were their own case, they would cheerfully accept it; but, as there were a great many of the Munseys to share in the purchase money, they would recommend that the Governor add two hundred dollars more. To this Governor Bernard agreed, and so this second great land dispute was settled.

The third land dispute to come before the Grand Council was the old complaints made by Teedyuscung concerning the Walking Purchase. The Six Nations had not met with the Delawares at any public treaty with Pennsylvania since the treaty of 1742, in which Canassatego, as the spokesman of the Six Nations, ordered the Delawares to remove from the bounds of the Walking Purchase. Three questions called for an answer at the Grand Council:

(1) Was the Walking Purchase just? (2) Had the Six Nations any right to sell lands on the Delaware? (3) Were the Delawares subject to the Iroquois, or were they independent?

Teedyuscung Humbled By Iroquois Chiefs

Before taking up the matter of the Walking Purchase, the Iroquois deputies concluded that the first thing to do was to humble Teedyuscung, and break down his influence and standing. The great Delaware had entered this council more humbly than he did the councils of 1756 and 1757, realizing that his bitter enemy, Nickas, a Mohawk chief, was in attendance.

Nickas began the attack on Teedyuscung, designed to break down his influence. Pointing to Teedyuscung, he spoke with great vigor and bitterness. Conrad Weiser was ordered to interpret Nickas' speech, but declined, and desired that Andrew Montour should do it. Weiser clearly saw that the interpretation of his speech would cause great discord, and he planned to have the interpreation postponed until the anger of the Iroquois had time to cool. He therefore advised that the speech be interpreted at a private conference, which was arranged to take place the next morning, October 14th. The next morning came; but there was no conference. Weiser had succeeded in causing more delay to avert the threatening storm. However, on the morning of the 15th, Nickas, at a private conference, said: "Who made Teedyuscung chief of the nations? If he be such a great man, we desire to know who made him so? Perhaps you have, and if this be the case, tell us so. It may be the French have made him so. We want to inquire and know where his greatness arose."

Nickas was followed by Tagashata, chief of the Senecas, who said: "We do not know who made Teedyuscung this great man over ten nations, and I want to know who made him so." Then Assarandonquas, chief of the Onondagas, said: "I never heard before now that Teedyuscung was such a great man, and much less can I tell who made him so. No such thing was ever said in our towns." Then Thomas King, in behalf of the Oneidas, Cayugas, Tuscaroras, Nanticokes, and Conoys, said: "I now tell you we, none of us, know who has made Teedyuscung such a great man. Perhaps the French have, or perhaps you have, or some among you, as you have different governments and are different people. We for our parts entirely disown that he has any authority over us, and we desire to know from whence he derives his authority."

Under this concerted attack upon his kingly pretensions, Teedyuscung sat like a stoic, never saying a word in reply, and his features betraying no signs of emotion.

The following day, October 16th, after Conrad Weiser had time to advise Governor Denny and Governor Bernard as to the proper reply to make to these speeches of the Iroquois deputies, Governor Denny advised them that he had never made Teedyuscung a great chief. He further told the deputies that, at the former Easton conferences, Teedyuscung had spoken of the Iroquois as his uncles and superiors; and Governor Bernard also denied making Teedyuscung a great chief, or king. Thus, the skillful guidance of Conrad Weiser, in delaying the outburst of Iroquois anger and in framing the proper speeches for the Governors, smoothed matters over, and prevented the cause of peace from suffering a serious setback.

After the apologies of Governor Denny and Governor Bernard, Teedyuscung arose to speak on his land claims. Said he:

"I did let you know formerly what my grievance was. I told you that from Tohiccon, as far as the Delawares owned, the Proprietaries had wronged me. Then you and I agreed that it should be laid before the King of England, and likewise you told me you would let me know as soon as ever he saw it. You would lay the matter before the King, for you said he was our Father, that he might see what was our differences; for as you and I could not decide it, let him do it. Now let us not alter what you and I have agreed. Now, let me know if King George has decided the matter between you and me. I don't pretend to mention any of my uncles' [Iroquois'] lands. I only mention what we, the Delawares, own, as far as the heads of Delaware. All the lands lying on the waters that fall into the Susquehanna belong to our uncles."

He then took another belt and turned to address the Iroquois, but these proud sachems had, during his speech to Governors Denny and Bernard, noiselessly left the room. Teedyuscung then declined to speak further. The next day, October 17th, the Indians spent in private conferences. On October 18th, after Governor Denny had had a private interview with the Six Nations, Teedyuscung came to his headquarters, stating that the Delawares did not claim the land high up on the Delaware, as those belonged to their uncles, the Iroquois, but that the land which he did specifically complain about, was included in the Walking Purchase. Governor Denny avoided giving Teedyuscung a direct reply until he would lay the land dispute before the Six Nations' deputies.

He then explained to the deputies that Pennsylvania had bought land from them which the Delawares claimed, advising that this was a matter which should be settled among themselves. The Six Nations replied that they did not understand the Governor. They said that he had left matters in the dark; that they did not know what lands he meant; that if he meant the lands on the other side of the Blue Mountains, he knew that the Proprietaries had a deed for them (the Purchase of 1749), which ought to be produced and shown to them; that their deeds had their marks, and when they should see them, they would know their marks again. Conrad Weiser then brought the deed. The Iroquois examined it and said: "The land was ours and we can justify it."

Teedyuscung said no more at the Easton conference concerning the Walking Purchase, but he charged the Six Nations with selling his land at Wyoming to the Connecticut interests at the Albany treaty of 1754. In fact, one of the conditions upon which he was willing to make peace was that he and his Delawares be settled at Wyoming, and that a deed be given to them for these lands. Addressing the Iroquois deputies, he said:

"Uncles, you may remember that you placed us at Wyoming and Shamokin, places where Indians have lived before. Now, I hear since that you have sold that land to our brethren, the English, [meaning the Connecticut commissioners]. Let the matter now be cleared up in the presence of our brothers, the English. I sit here as a bird on a bough. I look about and do not know where to go. Let me therefore come down upon the ground and make that my own by a good deed, and I shall then have a home forever; for if you, my uncles, or I, die, our brethren, the English, will say they bought it from you, and so wrong my posterity out of it."

The Grand Council ended on October 26th. Peace was secured, and through the efforts of Post, the Ohio Indians had been drawn away from the French. Thus the good work inaugurated by Canachquasy and furthered by Teedyuscung reached a happy consummation.

The Murder of Dr. John and Family

In February, 1760, a friendly Delaware, named Doctor John, his wife, and two children were massacred near Carlisle. Captain Callender, a member of the inquest, was summoned by the Assembly, and after interrogating him, the Governor offered a reward of one hundred pounds for the apprehension of each person connected with the murder. Great excitement prevailed throughout the Province, on account of the assassination of these friendly Indians; for it was feared that the recently pacified Shawnees and Delawares would retaliate by attacking the settlements on the frontiers. A letter was sent to Christian Frederick Post, the Moravian missionary, desiring him "forthwith to make Teedyuscung and the Indians at Wyoming acquainted with these murders and the issuing of the proclamation, and to assure him that no pains would be spared to discover and punish the authors." Similar messages were sent to the Delawares and Shawnees in the valleys of the Ohio and Allegheny.

Teedyuscung Makes Journey to Western Indians

Christian Frederick Post and John Hays, under instructions from Governor Hamilton, left Easton in May, 1760, for the purpose of making a journey with Teedyuscung up the North Branch of the Susquehanna, thence across to the headwaters of the Allegheny, and thence down this stream to "some principal Indian town over the Ohio", where a great Indian council was to be held. Teedyuscung joined Post and Hays at Wyoming, and the party then went up the Susquehanna as far as Pasigachkunk, on Cowanesque Creek, in Tioga County, where they were stopped by Senecas, and the white men were forced to turn back; "for," said Hays, "there was an old agreement that no white man should pass through their country for fear of spies to see their land." However, Teedyuscung and a few Indian companions, among whom was his son, Amos, kept on, and attended the great council of the western tribes in Ohio.

On September 15th, Teedyuscung appeared before Governor Hamilton and the Provincial Council, and related to them the results of his western mission as follows:

"You may remember that I often promised you to give the halloo through all the Indian nations. I have been a long way back, a great way indeed, beyond the Allegheny, among my friends there. When I got as far as the Salt Lick Town towards the head of Beaver Creek [River], I stopped there and sent messengers to the chiefs of all the Indians in those parts, desiring them to come and hold council. It took three weeks to collect them together; and then, having a large number gathered together, I communicated to them all that had passed between me and this government for four years past, at which they were glad and declared that this was the first time they had a right understanding of these transactions. They said they had heard now and then that we were sitting together about peace, but they were not acquainted till now with the particulars of our several conferences. I concealed nothing from them, and when they had heard all, they were right glad. It gave joy to their very hearts. This is all I have to say at this time. Tomaquior [Tamaque], the Beaver King (who is the head man of the Delawares at the Ohio), did not give me anything in charge to say to the Governor. We were all present at the great council held at Pittsburgh, and heard him [King Beaver] tell the General that he would go to Philadelphia in the summer, and hold a council with this government, in compliance with the several invitations that he had received from it. I told Tamaque that Pittsburgh was no place to hold council as the old fire was there; that Pittsburgh was only a place for warriors to speak in, and that he should do no council business at Pittsburgh. And accordingly Tamaque told the General that he would not say anything to him, but say it at the place where their grandfathers were always used to hold council with the English."

The council referred to by Teedyuscung as being held at Pittsburgh, was the great conference held at Fort Pitt, by General Monckton, with the western tribes on August 12, 1760. The purpose of this conference was to assure the Western Delawares, Shawnees, and other tribes that the English had no design of taking their lands. Reference was made to this conference in Chapter XIX.

In 1761, Teedyuscung wished to leave Wyoming, inasmuch he despaired of securing a title to that region, for his people. Fortunately the Governor was able to persuade him not to do such a rash act, and he continued then to reside at Wyoming until the end of his days.

Teedyuscung is Paid for Withdrawing Charge of Fraud

On April 26, 1762, Teedyuscung attended a conference with Governor Hamilton at Philadelphia, in which he was told that, if he would withdraw his charges against the Proprietors of fraud in the Walking Purchase, he would be given four hundred pounds. Teedyuscung replied that he "never did charge the Proprietors with fraud, but had only said that the French had informed them that the English had cheated them out of their land, that his young men desired him to mention it at the treaty of Easton, and that he did it to please them, and was sorry it had reached their hearts." Governor Hamilton then told him that, if he would acknowledge this in public, he would make him a present, not on account of the lands, which had been bought and paid for, but on account of the chief's needy circumstances. Then, when Teedyuscung made his public acknowledgment, the Governor made him the present of four hundred pounds.

Reference was made, in Chapter XIX, to the fact that a great conference was held at Lancaster beginning August 12, 1762, between the Provincial Authorities and Shingas, King Beaver, and other western chiefs whom Christian Frederick Post had brought from the Muskingum, Tuscarawas, and the Ohio. King Beaver, who was at the head of the Western Indians at this conference, was advised "that about six years ago your brother, Teedyuscung, made a complaint to the Proprietaries wherein he charged them of defrauding the Delawares of a tract of land lying on the River Delaware, between Tohiccon Creek and the Kittatiny Hills. He alleged that this complaint was not made by him on his own account, but on behalf of the owners of the lands, many of whom he said lived on Allegheny. This dispute, brethren, was by mutual consent, referred to our great King George, who ordered Sir William Johnson to inquire fully into the matter, and make his report to him, that justice might be done you, if you had been wronged. Accordingly, Sir William Johnson, about two months ago (June, 1762), came to Easton, whereupon the Proprietaries' commissioners producing and reading sundry writings and papers, Teedyuscung was convinced of his error, and acknowledged that he had been mistaken with regard to the charge of forgery made against the Proprietaries, having been misinformed by his ancestors, and desired that all future disputes about land should be buried under ground, and never heard of more, offering that such of the Indians as were then present should sign a release for the land in question, and that he would endeavour to persuade the rest of his brethren who were concerned to do the same at this treaty at Lancaster. Now, brethren of Allegheny, as we are face to face, be plain and tell whether you are satisfied with and approve of what was done at the last treaty of Easton, and whether you lay any claims to those lands, that there may be no room left for any future dispute about it among our children."

To this King Beaver replied: "As to my own part, I know nothing about the lands upon the River Delaware, but since you

request it I will first speak to my own people about it." Then
King Beaver, having consulted with his counsellors, further
replied: "I must acknowledge I know nothing about lands upon
the Delaware, and I have no concern with lands upon that river.
We know nothing of the Delawares' claim to them. I have no
claim myself nor any of my people. I suppose there may be some
spots or pieces of land in some part of the Province that the Delawares claim, but neither I nor any of my people know anything of
them. As to what you and our brother, Teedyuscung, have done,
if you are both pleased, I am pleased with it. As to my part, I
want to say nothing about land affairs. What I have at heart and
what I came down about, is to confirm our friendship and make a
lasting peace, so that our children and grandchildren may live
together in everlasting peace after we are dead."

Teedyuscung and the Eastern Delawares then conferred together, but what was said by them was not made known. The old
chief then addressed Governor Hamilton as follows: "Before all
these Allegheny Indians here present, I do now assure you that I
am ready and willing to sign a release to all the lands we have been
disputing about, as I told you I would at Easton and desire no
more may be ever said or heard of them hereafter."

Then Teedyuscung was given another present, being two hundred Spanish dollars, and the value of two hundred pounds in
goods,—the last chapter in the history of the charge of fraud, made
by this able Delaware chief to the embarrassment of the Colonial
Authorities.

Teedyuscung was now approaching the end of his earthly career.
He was really a great man. It was but natural that he should, for
a time, have taken up arms against the Province which, by unfair
means, it must be admitted, had gotten possession of the hunting
grounds of his ancestors. In appraising his conduct, all honor
must be given him for his untiring labors in behalf of peace.
Indeed, the prominence that was his, in these labors, caused him
to be the object of the hatred of the Mohawks, who could not brook
the fact that one so much beneath them, a Delaware, should occupy
such an exalted position. This hatred led to Teedyuscung's death.

But this grave and dignified chieftain had a sense of humor.
There is a tradition that, on one occasion, he met, at Stroudsburg,
a blacksmith, named McNabb, a worthless fellow, who thus addressed the great Delaware: "Well, cousin, how do you do?"
"Cousin, cousin", said Teedyuscung, "how do you make that out?"

"Oh, we are all cousins from Adam," said McNabb. "Ah," said Teedyuscung, "then I am glad it is no nearer."

Death of Teedyuscung

This great leader of the Eastern Delawares, the last of their great chiefs, was burned to death on the night of April 16, 1763, as he lay in a drunken debauch on a couch in his house at Wyoming, which was set on fire by some of his Indian enemies, either Senecas or Mohawks. A monument has been erected to this noted chief, in Fairmont Park, Philadelphia, which represents him, bow and spear in hand, a plume of eagle feathers on his brow, as stepping forth on his journey towards the setting sun.

CHAPTER XXIII

Guyasuta

UYASUTA (Kiasutha) has generally been called a Seneca chief, but he was probably of the mongrel Iroquois known as the Mingoes, who inhabited the Allegheny Valley and region to the westward. We have already met him as one of the chiefs who accompanied George Washington from Logstown to Fort LeBouef, when the latter went to that place in November, 1753, carrying the protest of Governor Dinwiddie of Virginia to St. Pierre, the commandant of the French forts. He is referred to in Washington's journal of this trip as the Hunter.

Long years afterward, Washington met Guyasuta near the mouth of the Muskingum, when, in October, 1770, accompanied by his friend, neighbor, and former companion in arms, Dr. Craik, and William Crawford, he journeyed down the Ohio Valley to examine the lands apportioned among the Virginia soldiers. Guyasuta was at his hunting camp when Washington met him. Seventeen years had matured the young ambassador to thoughtful manhood; yet Guyasuta held a perfect recollection of him. With a hunter's hospitality, he gave Washington, Dr. Craik, and Crawford a quarter of a buffalo, just killed. He insisted that they should encamp together for the night, and not wishing to detain Washington, he moved his hunting party to another camp some miles down the Ohio. Here the great Virginian and Guyasuta held long talks around the council-fire that night. During the intervening years, Guyasuta had fought against the English, in the French and Indian War, had helped Pontiac form his great conspiracy, in 1763, and was one of the most vindictive in carrying it into terrible and bloody execution upon the English forts and settlements; while Washington, in both these conflicts, was one of the powerful leaders on the side of the English. We cannot but wonder what were the subjects of conversation of Washington and Guyasuta around that council-fire.

Guyasuta Goes Over to the French

Guyasuta was one of the western chiefs, who went over to the French shortly after Braddock's defeat. At the head of a party

of twenty Senecas, he visited Marquis de Vaudreuil, Governor of
Canada, at Montreal, Joncaire accompanying him as interpreter,
where they were received with much ceremony, so pleasing to the
Indians. Guyasuta, as the chief and orator of the Seneca delegation, addressed the Governor on this occasion. He and his warriors
remained near Montreal during the winter, it being too late in the
year to make the journey back to the Ohio.

Grant's Defeat

The most important service Guyasuta rendered the French
during the French and Indian War was leading the Indians in the
attack on Major James Grant, where the Allegheny County Court
House, in the city of Pittsburgh, now stands, on September 14,
1758. When Forbes' army was advancing on Fort Duquesne in
the autumn of this year, and the advance, under Colonel Bouquet,
had reached the Loyalhanna and Ligonier, Westmoreland County,
Major Grant, with a force of thirty-seven officers and eight hundred and five privates, was sent by Bouquet to reconnoiter the fort
and adjacent country. Grant's instructions were not to approach
too near the fort and not to attack it. The wilderness between
Ligonier and Fort Duquesne was filled with Indians constantly
watching the movements of Grant's little army; yet he succeeded in
coming within sight of the fort without being discovered. Late at
night he drew up his troops on the brow of the fatal hill in the city
of Pittsburgh, which still bears his name, about a quarter of a mile
from the fort.

Not having met with either French or Indians on the march,
and believing from the stillness of the enemy's quarters that the
forces in the fort were small, Grant at once determind to make an
attack. Accordingly, two officers and fifty men were directed to
approach the fort and fall upon the French and Indians that might
be outside. They saw none and were not challenged by the sentinels; and as they returned, they set fire to a large storehouse, but
the fire was extinguished. At the break of day, September 14th,
Grant sent Major Lewis with two hundred regulars and Virginia
volunteers to take a position about a half mile back, and lie in
ambush where they had left their baggage. Four hundred men
were posted along the hill facing the fort, while Captain Mc-
Donald's company, with drums beating and bagpipes playing,
marched toward the fort in order to draw out the garrison. The
music of the drums and bagpipes aroused the garrison from their

slumber, and both the French and Indians sallied out in great numbers, the latter led by Guyasuta.

The French and Indians separated into three divisions. The first two were sent under the cover of the banks of the Mononga-hela and Allegheny to surround the main body of Grant's troops, while the third was delayed awhile to give the others time, and then lined up before the fort as if exhibiting the whole strength of the garrison. This plan worked admirably. Captain McDonald was obliged to fall back on the main body, and at the same time, Grant found himself flanked by the detachments on both sides. A desperate struggle ensued. The highlanders, exposed to the enemy's fire without cover, fell in great numbers. The provin-cials, concealing themselves among the trees, made a good defense for a while, but not being supported and being overpowered by numbers, were compelled to fall back. The result was that Grant's forces were overwhelmingly and ingloriously defeated. Many of his brave troops were driven into the Allegheny River and drown-ed. The total loss was two hundred and seventy killed, forty-two wounded, and several taken prisoners. Among the latter was Major Grant himself.

Grant's expedition was a monstrous blunder. General Forbes, with the main body of the army was as far in the rear as Bedford, and neither he nor Colonel Bouquet had any definite knowledge of the strength of the French and Indians at Fort Duquesne. In view of these facts, it seems strange, indeed, that Colonel Bouquet per-mitted Grant to advance into a death trap. Grant himself showed utter lack of judgment in playing the bagpipes and beating the drums at daylight, which had only the effect of telling the enemy of his advance. Neither the French nor the Indians knew of Grant's presence until the music broke the stillness of the autumn morning. How Grant's conduct impressed the Indians was expressed by one of their chiefs in a conversation with James Smith, at that time a captive among them. This chief told Smith that the Indians be-lieved that Grant "had made too free with spiritous liquors during the night, and had become intoxicated about daylight."

French and Indians Attack the Camp on the Loyalhanna

Emboldened by the defeat of Major Grant, Captain DeLignery, then commander of Fort Duquesne, sent about one thousand French and two hundred Indians, the latter most likely led by Guyasuta, against the English camp on the Loyalhanna, at

Ligonier, hoping to compel them to retreat as did Dunbar after the defeat of Braddock. They attacked the camp on October 12th, but were repulsed by Colonel James Burd, who was then in command of the camp, the English loss being twelve killed, eighteen wounded, and thirty-one missing. Colonel Bouquet was not at the camp at the time of the engagement, being at Stony Creek with seven hundred men and a detachment of artillery.

Before Forbes' army left Ligonier, a thrilling event in the life of George Washington took place. He was a colonel in the army, and, on November 12th, was out with a scouting party which attacked a number of the enemy about three miles from the camp, killing one and taking three pisoners, an Indian man and woman, and an Englishman, named Johnson, who had been captured by the Indians several years before, in Lancaster County. Captain Mercer, hearing the firing, was sent with a party of Virginians to the assistance of Washington. The two parties approaching each other in the dusk of the evening, each mistook the other for the enemy, and fired upon each other, killing several Virginians and wounding about a dozen others. Washington, upon recognizing the terrible mistake, rushed between the two parties, and knocked up the presented muskets with his sword.

Washington's skirmish, on November 12th, was the last clash of arms between the French and Indians on the one side and the English on the other, in the Ohio Valley during the French and Indian War. It will be remembered that Washington was a leading figure in the opening conflict in this war, the attack on Jumonville, May 28th, 1754.

The Englishman, Johnson, gave Forbes the information relative to the conditions at Fort Duquesne that caused the General to decide to press forward against the fort at once, instead of going into winter quarters on the Loyalhanna. His army accordingly left the Loyalhanna on November 17th, finding the way to the fort strewed with the bodies of Major Grant's soldiers who had died on the retreat. On the 24th, the French set fire to Fort Duquesne and fled, and on the 25th, Forbes, army took possession of its smouldering ruins. Says Bancroft: "As the banners of England floated over the waters, the place, at the suggestion of Forbes, was with one voice called Pittsburg(h). It is the most enduring monument to William Pitt. America raised to his name statues that have been wrongfully broken, and granite piles of which not one stone remains upon another; but, long as the Monongahela and the Allegheny shall flow to form the Ohio, long as the English tongue shall be the language of freedom in the boundless valley which their waters traverse, his name shall stand inscribed on the gateway of the West."

Forbes' troops found many of the dead of Grant's defeat within a quarter of a mile of the fort. They also found a number of stakes driven into the ground on which were stuck the heads and kilts of the Highlanders, captured on that fateful September morning. Detachments then buried Grant's dead and the bones of those who were slain at Braddock's defeat over three years before.

Guyasuta at Council of July, 1759

Guyasuta's next act of importance was to attend the council held at Fort Pitt, July 5, 1759, mentioned in Chapters XIX, XX, and XXII, between George Croghan, Colonel Hugh Mercer, Captain William Trent, and Captain Thomas McKee, on the one hand, and the representatives of the Six Nations, Delawares, Shawnees, and Wyandots, on the other, at which the terms of the Easton treaty of October, 1758, were confirmed, and the Western Indians promised to surrender the prisoners taken in the French and Indian War.

Guyasuta in Pontiac's War

The fall of Quebec, in the autumn of 1759, practically ended the French and Indian War. Then the English came to take possession of the surrendered French forts. The Indians soon found that their new masters had a very different attitude towards them than had the French. While the French had lavished presents upon them, the English now doled out blankets, ammunition, and guns with a sparing hand. The proud-spirited western tribes were exasperated at the patronizing air of the English, and their indignation was encouraged by the Frenchmen among them.

A few years of discontent, and then Pontiac, the great chief of the Ottawas, formed a conspiracy, bold in its design and masterful in its execution, to drive the English into the sea. In this plan and in its execution, he was ably assisted by Guyasuta. The Delawares, Shawnees, and, in fact almost all the tribes of the great Algonquin family, and one tribe of the Six Nations, the Senecas, joined in this uprising, known as Pontiac's Conspiracy, also as the Pontiac and Guyasuta War.

In carrying the Pontiac and Guyasuta Conspiracy into execution, these chiefs were ably assisted by Custaloga or Kustaloga, a chief of the Munsee or Wolf Clan of Delawares. Custaloga was living at Venango when John Frazer, the English trader, was driven from that place by the French late in the summer of 1753, and when Washington stopped there in November of that year on his way to St. Pierre, at Fort LeBoueff. However, Custaloga's principal seat was Custaloga's Town, located about twelve miles above the mouth of French Creek and near the mouth of Deer Creek, in French Creek Township, Mercer County. He also ruled over the Delawares at the town of Cussewago, or Cassewago, on the site of the present town of Meadville, the county seat of Crawford County. He was one of the chiefs with whom Colonel Bouquet dealt when he made his expedition to the Muskingum in the autumn of 1764. His successor was Captain Pipe of the Wolf Clan of Delawares.

In May, 1763, the dogs of war were once more let loose on the English forts and settlements. Almost every fort along the Great Lakes and the Ohio was instantly attacked. Those that did not fall under the first onslaught were resolutely besieged. On June 15th, Fort Presqu' Isle (Erie), commanded by Ensign Price, was attacked, and all of the garrison who were not killed, were taken to Detroit, except Benjamin Gray, who escaped to Fort Pitt and gave the news. On June 18th, Fort LeBouef (Waterford, Erie County) was captured; and at about the same time, Fort Venango Franklin, commanded by Lieutenant Gordon, was burned and the entire garrison put to death. Lieutenant Gordon was tortured over a slow fire for several successive nights.

Fort Pitt was attacked on June 22nd, and later the siege of the place was commenced. On the 26th of July a party of Indians approached the gate, displaying a flag of truce, among whom were Shingas and Turtle Heart. They were admitted, and Captain Simeon Ecuyer, the commandant, held a parley with them. The Indian delegation complained that the English were the cause of the war, saying that they had marched their armies into the country and built forts against the repeated protests of the Indians. Said the Indian speaker: "My brothers, this land is ours, and not yours." Captain Ecuyer refused to leave the place, and told the Indians if they would not abandon the siege, he would "throw bomb shells, which will burst and blow you to atoms, and fire cannon among you loaded with a whole bag full of bullets."

Says Parkman: "Disappointed of gaining a bloodless possession of the fort, the Indians now, for the first time, began a general attack. On the night succeeding the conference, they

---

Inadvertantly it was stated in above paragraph that Ensign Price was in command of Fort Prequ' Isle. He was in command of Fort LeBeouf, and Ensign Christie was in command at Fort Presqu' Isle.

approached in great multitudes, under cover of the darkness and completely surrounded it; many of them crawling beneath the banks of the two rivers, which ran close to the rampart, and, with incredible perseverance, digging, with their knives, holes in which they were completely sheltered from the fire of the fort. On one side, the whole bank was lined with these burrows, from each of which a bullet or an arrow was shot out whenever a soldier chanced to expose his head. At daybreak, a general fire was opened from every side, and continued without intermission until night, and through several succeeding days. Meanwhile, the women and children were pent up in the crowded barracks, terror-stricken at the horrible din of the assailants, and watching the fire-arrows as they came sailing over the parapet, and lodging against the roofs and sides of the buildings. In every instance, the fire they kindled was extinguished. One of the garrison was killed, and seven wounded. Among the latter was Captain Ecuyer, who, freely exposing himself, received an arrow in the leg. At length, an event hereafter to be described put an end to the attack, and drew off the assailants from the neighborhood of the fort, to the unspeakable relief of the harassed soldiers, exhausted as they were by several days of unintermitted vigilance."

Fort Bedford, commanded by Captain Wendell Ourry (Uhrig) was also attacked as was Fort Ligonier, commanded by Lieutenant Archibald Blane. Indeed, terror reigned on the whole Pennsylvania frontier. From many fertile valleys rose the smoke of burning settlements. The mutilated bodies of slain settlers were torn and devoured by hogs and wild beasts. Hundreds of families fled over the mountains to the extreme eastern settlements.

Battle of Bushy Run

Then Colonel Bouquet was sent with an army to the relief of Fort Pitt, composed of five hundred regulars, lately returned from the West Indies, and two hundred rangers from Lancaster and Cumberland Counties. On his way to Fort Pitt, Bouquet fought the terrible battle of Bushy Run, about a mile east of Harrison City, Westmoreland County, August 5th and 6th, 1763. Inasmuch as it is almost a certainty that Guyasuta commanded the Indians at this bitterly contested engagement, we give the following description of Bouquet's advance and of the battle, from the classic pen of Francis Parkman, the great authority on Pontiac's Conspiracy:

"Orders were therefore sent to Colonel Bouquet, who commanded at Philadelphia, to assemble as large a force as possible, and cross the Alleghenies with a convoy of provision and ammunition. With every effort, no more than five hundred men could be collected for this service. They consisted chiefly of Highlanders of the 42nd Regiment, which had suffered less than most of the other corps, from West Indian exposure. Having sent agents to the frontier to collect horses, wagons, and supplies, Bouquet soon after followed with the troops, and reached Carlisle about the first of July. He found the whole country in a panic. Every building in the fort, every house, barn, and hovel in the little town, was crowded with the families of settlers, driven from their homes by the terror of the Indian tomahawk. None of the enemy, however, had yet appeared in the neighborhood, and the people flattered themselves that their ravages would be confined to the other side of the mountains. Whoever ventured to predict the contrary drew upon himself the indignation of the whole community.

"On Sunday, the third of July, an incident occurred which redoubled the alarm. A soldier, riding express from Fort Pitt, galloped into the town, and alighted to water his horse at the well in the centre of the place. A crowd of countrymen were instantly about him, eager to hear the news. 'Presqu'Isle, Le Boeuf, and Venango are taken, and the Indians will be here soon.' Such was the substance of the man's reply, as, remounting in haste, he rode on to make his report at the camp of Bouquet. All was now consternation and excitement. Messengers hastened out to spread the tidings, and every road and pathway leading into Carlisle was beset with the flying settlers, flocking thither for refuge. Soon rumors were heard that the Indians were come. Some of the fugitives had seen the smoke of burning houses rising from the valleys, and these reports were fearfully confirmed by the appearance of miserable wretches, who half frantic with grief and dismay, had fled from the sight of blazing dwellings and slaughtered families. A party of the inhabitants armed themselves and went out, to warn the living and bury the dead. Reaching Shearman's Valley, they found fields laid waste, stacked wheat on fire, and the houses yet in flames, and they grew sick with horror, at seeing a group of hogs tearing and devouring the bodies of the dead. As they advanced up the valley, everything betokened the recent presence of the enemy, while columns of smoke, rising among the surrounding mountains, showed how general was the work of destruction.

"On the previous day, six men, assembled for reaping the harvest, had been seated at dinner at the house of Campbell, a settler on the Juniata. Four or five Indians suddenly burst the door, fired among them, and then beat down the survivors with the butts of their rifles. One young man leaped from his seat, snatched a gun which stood in a corner, discharged it into the breast of the warrior who was rushing upon him, and, leaping through an open window, made his escape. He fled through the forest to a settlement at some distance, where he related his story. Upon this, twelve young men volunteered to cross the mountain, and warn the inhabitants of the neighboring Tuscarora Valley. On entering it, they found that the enemy had been there before them. Some of the houses were on fire, while others were still standing, with no tenants but the dead. Under the shed of a farmer, the Indians had been feasting on the flesh of the cattle they had killed, and the meat had not yet grown cold. Pursuing their course, the white men found the spot where several detached parties of the enemy had united almost immediately before, and they boldly resolved to follow, in order to ascertain what direction the marauders had taken. The trail led them up a deep and woody pass of the Tuscarora. Here the yell of the war-whoop and the din of firearms suddenly greeted them, and five of their number were shot down. Thirty warriors rose from their ambuscade, and rushed upon them. They gave one discharge, scattered, and ran for their lives. One of them, a boy named Charles Eliot, as he fled, plunging through the thickets, heard an Indian tearing the boughs behind him, in furious pursuit. He seized his powder-horn, poured the contents at random down the muzzle of his gun, threw in a bullet after them, without using the ramrod, and, wheeling about, discharged the piece into the breast of his pursuer. He saw the Indian shrink back and roll over into the bushes. He continued his flight; but a moment after, a voice earnestly called his name. Turning to the spot, he saw one of his comrades stretched helpless upon the ground. This man had been mortally wounded at the first fire, but had fled a few rods from the scene of blood, before his strength gave out. Eliot approached him. 'Take my gun,' said the dying frontiersman. 'Whenever you see an Indian, kill him with it, and then I shall be satisfied.' Eliot, with several others of the party, escaped, and finally reached Carlisle, where his story excited a spirit of uncontrollable wrath and vengeance among the fierce backwoodsmen. Several parties went out, and one of them, commanded by the sheriff of the place, encountered a band of Indians, routed them after a sharp fight, and brought in several scalps.

"The surrounding country was by this time completely abandoned by the settlers, many of whom, not content with seeking refuge at Carlisle, continued their flight to the eastward, and headed by the clergyman of that place, pushed on to Lancaster, and even to Philadelphia. Carlisle presented a most deplorable spectacle. A multitude of the refugees, unable to find shelter in the town, had encamped in the woods or on the adjacent fields, erecting huts of branches and bark, and living on such charity as the slender means of the townspeople could supply. Passing among them, one would have witnessed every form of human misery. In these wretched encampments were men, women, and children, bereft at one stroke of friends, of home, and the means of supporting life. Some stood aghast and bewildered at the sudden and fatal blow; others were sunk in the apathy of despair; others were weeping and moaning with irrepressible anguish. With not a few, the craven passion of fear drowned all other emotion, and day and night they were haunted with visions of the bloody knife and the reeking scalp; while in others, every faculty was absorbed by the burning thirst for vengeance, and mortal hatred against the whole Indian race.

"The route of the army lay along the beautiful Cumberland Valley. Passing here and there a few scattered cabins, deserted or burnt to the ground, they reached the hamlet of Shippensburg, somewhat more than twenty miles from their point of departure. Here, as at Carlisle, was congregated a starving multitude, who had fled from the knife and the tomahawk.

"By the last advices from the westward, it appeared that Fort Ligonier, situated beyond the Alleghenies, was in imminent danger of falling into the enemy's hands before the army could come up; for its defences were slight, its garrison was feeble, and the Indians had assailed it with repeated attacks. The magazine which the place contained made it of such importance that Bouquet resolved at all hazards to send a party to its relief. Thirty of the best men were accordingly chosen, and ordered to push forward with the utmost speed, by unfrequented routes through the forests and over the mountains, carefully avoiding the road, which would doubtless be infested by the enemy. The party set out on their critical errand, guided by frontier hunters, and observing a strict silence. Using every precaution, and advancing by forced marches, day after day, they came in sight of the fort without being discovered. It was beset by Indians, and, as the party made for the gate, they were seen and fired upon; but they threw themselves into the place without the loss of a man, and Ligonier was for the time secure. ·

"In the meantime, the army, advancing with slower progress, entered a country where as yet scarcely an English settler had built his cabin. Reaching Fort Loudon, on the declivities of Cove Mountain, they ascended the wood-encumbered defiles beyond. Far on their right stretched the green ridges of the Tuscarora, while, in front, mountain beyond mountain rose high against the horizon. Climbing heights and descending into valleys, passing the two solitary posts of Littleton and the Juniata, both abandoned by their garrisons, they came in sight of Fort Bedford, hemmed in by encircling mountains. Their arrival gave infinite relief to the garrison, who had long been beleaguered and endangered by a swarm of Indians, while many of the settlers in the neighborhood had been killed, and the rest driven for refuge into the fort. Captain Ourry, the commanding officer, reported that, for several weeks, nothing had been heard from the westward, every messenger having been killed, and the communication completely cut off. By the last intelligence, Fort Pitt had been surrounded by Indians, and daily threatened with a general attack.

"Having remained encamped, for three days, on the fields near the fort, Bouquet resumed his march on the twenty-eighth of July, and soon passed beyond the farthest verge of civilized habitation. The whole country lay buried in foliage. Except the rocks which crowned the mountains, and the streams which rippled along the valleys, the unbroken forest, like a vast garment, invested the whole. The road was channelled through its depths, while, on each side, the brown trunks and tangled undergrowth formed a wall so dense as almost to bar the sight. Through a country thus formed by nature for ambuscades, not a step was free from danger, and no precaution was neglected to guard against surprise. In advance of the marching column moved the provincial rangers, closely followed by the pioneers. The wagons and cattle were in the centre, guarded in front, flank, and rear by the regulars, while a rear-guard of rangers closed the line of march. Keen-eyed riflemen of the frontier, acting as scouts, scoured the woods far in front and on either flank, so that surprise was impossible. In this order the little army toiled heavily on, over a road beset with all the obstructions of the forest, until the main ridge of the Alleganies, like a mighty wall of green, rose up before them, and they began their zigzag progress up the woody heights, amid the sweltering heat of July. The tongues of the panting oxen hung lolling from their jaws, while the pine trees, scorching in the hot sun, diffused their resinous odors through the sultry air. At length, from the windy summit the Highland soldiers could gaze around upon a boundless panorama of forest-covered mountains, wild as their own native hills. Descending from the Alleganies, they entered upon a country less rugged and formidable in itself, but beset with constantly increasing dangers. On the second of August, they reached Fort Ligonier, about fifty miles from Bedford, and a hundred and fifty from Carlisle. The Indians who were about the place vanished at their approach; but the garrison could furnish no intelligence of the motions and designs of the enemy, having been completely blockaded for weeks. In this uncertainty, Bouquet resolved to leave behind the oxen and wagons, which formed the most cumbrous part of the convoy, since this would enable him to advance with greater celerity, and oppose a better resistance in case of attack. Thus relieved, the army resumed its march on the fourth, taking with them three hundred and fifty pack horses and a few cattle, and at nightfall encamped at no great distance from Ligonier. Within less than a day's march in advance, lay the dangerous defiles of Turtle Creek, a stream flowing at the bottom of a deep hollow, flanked by steep declivities, along the foot of which the road at that time ran for some distance. Fearing that the enemy would lie in ambuscade at this place, Bouquet resolved to march on the following day as far as a small stream called Bushy Run, to rest here until night, and then, by a forced march, to cross Turtle Creek under cover of the darkness.

"On the morning of the fifth, the tents were struck at an early hour, and the troops began their march through a country broken with hills and deep hollows, everywhere covered with the tall, dense forest, which spread for countless leagues around. By one o'clock, they had avanced seventeen miles, and the guides assured them that they were within half a mile of Bushy Run, their proposed resting place. The tired soldiers were pressing forward with renewed alacrity, when suddenly the report of rifles from the front sent a thrill along the ranks; and, as they listened, the firing thickened into a fierce, sharp rattle, while shouts and whoops, deadened by the intervening forest, showed that the advanced guard was hotly engaged. The two foremost companies were at once ordered forward to support it; but far from abating, the fire grew so rapid and furious as to argue the presence of an enemy at once numerous and resolute. At this, the convoy was halted, the troops formed into line, and a general charge was ordered. Bearing down through the forest with fixed bayonets, they drove the yelping assailants before them, and swept the ground clear. But at the very moment of success, a fresh burst of whoops and firing was heard from either flank, while a confused noise from the rear showed that the convoy was attacked. It was necessary instantly to fall back for its support. Driving off the assailants, the troops formed in a circle around the crowded and terrified horses. Though they were new to the work, and though the numbers and movements of the enemy, whose yelling resounded on every side, were concealed by the thick forest, yet no man lost his composure; and all displayed a steadiness which nothing but implicit confidence in their commander could have inspired. And now ensued a combat of a nature most harassing and discouraging. Again and again, now on this side and now on that, a crowd of Indians rushed up, pouring in a heavy fire, and striving, with furious outcries, to break into the circle. A well-dircted volley met them, followed by a steady charge of the bayonet. They never waited an instant to receive the attack, but, leaping backwards from tree to tree, soon vanished from sight, only to renew their attack with unabated ferocity in another quarter. Such was their activity that very few of them were hurt, while the English, less expert in bush fighting, suffered severely. Thus the fight went on, without intermission, for seven hours, until the forest grew dark with approaching night. Upon this, the Indians gradually slackened their fire, and the exhausted soldiers found time to rest.

"It was impossible to change their ground in the enemy's presence, and the troops were obliged to encamp upon the hill where the combat had taken place, though not a drop of water was to be found there. Fearing a night attack, Bouquet stationed numerous sentinels and outposts to guard against it, while the men lay down upon their arms, preserving the order they had maintained during the fight. Having completed the necessary arrangements, Bouquet, doubtful of surviving the battle of the morrow, wrote to Sir Jeffrey Amherst, in a few clear, concise words, an account of the day's events. His letter concludes as follows: 'Whatever our fate may be, I thought it necessary to give your excellency this early information, that you may, at all events, take such measures as you will think proper with the provinces, for their own safety, and the effectual relief of Fort Pitt; as, in case of another engagement, I fear insurmountable difficulties in protecting and transporting our provisions, being already so much weakened by the losses of this day, in men and horses, besides the additional necessity of carrying the wounded, whose situation is truly deplorable.'

"The condition of these unhappy men might well awaken sympathy. About sixty soldiers, besides several officers, had been killed or disabled. A space in the centre of the camp was prepared for the reception of the wounded, and surrounded by a wall of flour-bags from the convoy, affording some protection against the bullets which flew from all sides during the fight. Here they lay upon the ground, enduring agonies of thirst, and waiting, passive and helpless, the issue of the battle. Deprived of the animating thought that their lives and safety depended on their own exertions; surrounded by a wilderness, and by scenes to the horror of which no degree of familiarity could render the imagination callous, they must have endured mental sufferings, compared to which the pain of their wounds was slight. In the probable event of defeat, a fate inexpressibly horrible awaited them; while even victory would by no means insure their safety, since any great increase in their numbers would render it impossible for their comrades to transport them. Nor was the condition of those who had hitherto escaped an enviable one. Though they were about equal in numbers to their assailants, yet the dexterity and alertness of the Indians, joined to the nature of the country, gave all the advantages of a greatly superior force. The enemy were, moreover, exulting in the fullest confidence of success; for it was in these very forests that, eight years before, they had well-nigh destroyed twice their number of the best British troops. Throughout the earlier part of the night, they kept up a dropping fire upon the camp, while, at short intervals, a wild whoop from the thick surrounding gloom told with what fierce eagerness they waited to glut their vengeance on the morrow. The camp remained in darkness, for it would have been highly dangerous to build fires within its precincts, which would have served to direct the aim of the lurking marksmen. Surrounded by such terrors, the men snatched a disturbed and broken sleep, recruiting their exhausted strength for the renewed struggle of the morning.

"With the earliest dawn of day, and while the damp, cool forest was still involved in twilight, there rose around the camp a general burst of those horrible cries which form the ordinary prelude of an Indian battle. Instantly from every side at once, the enemy opened their fire, approaching under cover of the trees and bushes, and levelling with a close and deadly aim. Often, as on the previous day, they would rush up with furious impetuosity, striving to break into the ring of troops. They were repulsed at every point; but the English, though constantly victorious, were beset with undiminished perils, while the violence of the enemy seemed every moment on the increase. True to their favorite tactics, they would never stand their ground when attacked, but vanish at the first gleam of the levelled bayonet, only to appear again the moment the danger was past. The troops, fatigued by the long march and equally long battle of the previous day, were maddened by the torments of thirst, more intolerable, says their commander, than the fire of the enemy. They were fully conscious of the peril in which they stood, of wasting away by slow degrees beneath the shot of assailants at once so daring, so cautious, and so active, and upon whom it was impossible to inflict any decisive injury. The Indians saw their distress, and pressed them closer and closer, redoubling their yells and howlings, while some of them sheltered behind trees, assailed the troops, in bad English, with abuse and derision.

"Meanwhile the interior of the camp was a scene of confusion. The horses, secured in a crowd near the intrenchment which covered the wounded, were often struck by the bullets, and wrought to the height of terror by the mingled din of whoops, shrieks, and firing. They would break away by half scores at a time, burst through the ring of troops and the outer circle of assailants, and scour madly up and down the hillsides; while many of the drivers, overcome by the terrors of a scene in which they could bear no active part, hid themselves among the bushes and could neither hear nor obey orders.

"It was now about ten o'clock. Oppressed with heat, fatigue, and thirst, the distressed troops still maintained a weary and wavering defence, encircling the convoy in a yet unbroken ring. They were fast falling in their ranks, and the strength and spirits of the survivors had begun to flag. If the fortunes of the day were to be retrieved, the effort must be made at once; and happily the mind of the commander was equal to the emergency. In the midst of the confusion he conceived a stratagem alike novel and masterly. Could the Indians be brought together in a body, and made to stand their ground when attacked, there could be little doubt of the result; and to effect this object, Bouquet determined to increase their confidence, which had already mounted to an audacious pitch. Two companies of infantry, forming a part of the ring which had been exposed to the hottest fire, were ordered to fall back into the interior of the camp, while the troops on either hand joined their files across the vacant space, as if to cover the retreat of their comrades. These orders given at a favorable moment, were executed with great promptness. The thin line of troops who took possession of the deserted part of the circle, were, from their small numbers, brought closer in towards the centre. The Indians mistook these movements for a retreat. Confident that their time was come, they leaped up on all sides, from behind the trees and bushes, and, with infernal screeches, rushed headlong toward the spot, pouring in a most heavy and galling fire. The shock was too violent to be long endured. The men struggled to maintain their posts, but the Indians seemed on the point of breaking into the heart of the camp, when the aspect of affairs was suddenly revers- ed. The two companies, who had apparently abandoned their position, were in fact destined to begin the attack; and they now sallied out from the circle at a point where a depression in the ground, joined to the thick growth of trees, concealed them from the eyes of the Indians. Making a short detour through the woods, they came round upon the flank of the furious assailants, and dis- charged a deadly volley into their very midst. Numbers were seen to fall; yet though completely surprised, and utterly at a loss to understand the nature of the attack, the Indians faced about with the greatest intrepidity, and boldy returned the fire. But the Highlanders, with yells as wild as their own, fell on them with the bayonet. The shock was irresistible, and they fled before the charging ranks in a tumultuous throng. Orders had been given to two other companies, occupying a contiguous part of the circle, to support the attack whenever a favorable moment should occur; and they had therefore advanced a little from their position, and lay close crouched in ambush. The fugitive multitude, pressed by the Highland bayonets, passed directly across their front, upon which they rose and poured among them a second volley, no less destructive than the former. This completed the rout. The four companies, uniting, drove the flying savages through the woods, giving them no time to rally or reload their empty rifles, killing many, and scattering the rest in hopeless confusion.

"While this took place at one part of the circle, the troops and the savages had still maintained their respective positions at the other; but when the latter perceived the total rout of their comrades, and saw the troops advancing to assail them, they also lost heart, and fled. The discordant outcries which had so long deafened the ears of the English soon ceased altogether, and not a living Indian remained near the spot. About sixty corpses lay scattered over the ground. Among them were found those of several prominent chiefs, while the blood which stained the leaves of the bushes showed that numbers had fled severely wounded from the field. The soldiers took but one prisoner, whom they shot to death like a captive wolf. The loss of the English in the two battles surpassed that of the enemy, amounting to eight officers and one hundred and fifteen men.

"Having been for some time detained by the necessity of making litters for the wounded, and destroying the stores which the flight of most of the horses made it impossible to transport, the army moved on, in the afternoon, to Bushy Run. Here they had scarcely formed their camp, when they were again fired upon by a body of Indians, who, however, were soon repulsed. On the next day, they resumed their progress towards Fort Pitt, distant about twenty-five miles, and though frequently annoyed on the march by petty attacks, they reached their destination, on the tenth, without serious loss. It was a joyful moment, both to the troops and to the garrison. The latter, it will be remembered, were left surrounded and hotly pressed by the Indians, who had beleaguered the place from the twenty-eighth of July to the first of August, when, hearing of Bouquet's approach, they had abandoned the siege, and marched to attack him. From this time, the garrison had seen nothing of them until the morning of the tenth, when, shortly before the army appeared, they had passed the fort in a body, raising the scalp-yell, and displaying their disgusting trophies to the view of the English.

"The battle of Bushy Run was one of the best contested actions ever fought between white men and Indians. If there were any disparity of numbers, the advantage was on the side of the troops, and the Indians had displayed throughout a fierceness and intrepidity matched only by the steady valor with which they were met. In the provinces, the victory excited equal joy and admiration, more especially among those who knew the incalculable difficulties of an Indian campaign. The assembly of Pennsylvania passed a vote expressing their high sense of the merits of Bouquet, and of the important service which he had rendered to the province. He soon after received the additional honor of the formal thanks of the king.

"In many an Indian village, the women cut away their hair, gashed their limbs with knives, and uttered their dismal howlings of lamentation for the fallen. Yet though surprised and dispirited, the rage of the Indians was too deep to be quenched, even by so signal a reverse, and their outrages upon the frontier were resumed

with unabated ferocity. Fort Pitt, however, was effectually relieved, while the moral effect of the victory enabled the frontier
settlers to encounter the enemy with a spirit which would have been
wanting, had Bouquet sustained a defeat."

Andrew Byerly

In this connection, we call attention to the fact that Andrew
Byerly, at the head of a detachment of eighteen of the Royal
Americans, was in the advance of Bouquet's army when the battle
of Bushy Run commenced. Also, during the terrible night of
August 5th, he, at great risk, brought several hatfuls of water from
a neighboring spring to allay the thirst of Bouquet's wounded.
This noted man of the Westmoreland frontier had settled in the
Brush Creek Valley along the Forbes road, in 1759. In the latter
part of May, 1763, the Indians had warned Byerly to leave this
settlement. Captain Ecuyer, in a letter written to Colonel
Bouquet, on May 29th, refers to this fact as follows:

"Just as I had finished my letter three men came in from
Clapham's [Colonel William Clapham, who lived near West
Newton, Westmoreland County] with the melancholy news that
yesterday, at three o'clock in the afternoon, the Indians murdered
Clapham and everybody in his house. These three men were out at
work, and had escaped through the woods. I immediately armed
them and sent them to assist our people at Bushy Run. The
Indians have told Byerly to leave his place in four days, or he and
his family would all be murdered."

Later, Mr. Byerly and his family escaped to Fort Ligonier,
as thus related in Cort's "Colonel Henry Bouquet":

"As Ecuyer states, Byerly had received warning; but his
family was in no condition to be moved. Mrs. Byerly had just
been confined and the departure was delayed as long as possible,
indeed until certain death was imminent, if the flight should be
any longer postponed. Byerly had gone with a small party [per-
haps Clapham's men referred to above] to bury some persons who
had been killed at some distance from his station. A friendly
Indian who had often received a bowl of milk and bread from Mrs.
Byerly came to the house after dark, and informed the family that
they would all be killed, if they did not make their escape before
daylight. Mrs. Byerly got up from her sick couch and wrote the
tidings on the door of the house for the information of her husband when he should return. A horse was saddled on which the

mother with her tender babe three days old in her arms, was placed, and a child not two years old was fastened behind her. "Michael Byerly was a good sized lad, but Jacob was only three years old and had a painful stone bruise on one of his feet. With the aid of his older brother who held him by the hand and sometimes carried him on his back, the little fellow, however, managed to make good time through the wilderness to Fort Ligonier, about thirty miles distant. But although he reached his ninety-ninth year, he never forgot that race for life in his childhood, nor did he feel like giving quarter to hostile Indians, one of whom he killed on an island in the Allegheny in a fight under Lieutenant Hardin in 1779, although the savage begged for quarter.

"Milk cows were highly prized by frontier families in those days, and the Byerly family made a desperate effort to coax and drive their small herd along to Fort Ligonier. But the howling savages got so close that they were obliged to leave the cattle in the woods to be destroyed by the Indians. Byerly in some way eluded the Indians and joined his family in the retreat. They barely escaped with their lives. The first night they spent in the stockade, and in the morning the bullets of the pursurers struck the gates as the family pressed into the fort."

Attempt to Inoculate Indians with Small-pox

When Colonel Bouquet was preparing to lead his army over the mountains to the relief of forts Bedford, Ligonier, and Pitt, General Sir Jefferey Amherst, then in command of all the English troops in the colonies, wrote him as follows: "I wish to hear of no prisoners, should any of the villians be met with in arms. . . . Could it not be contrived to send the small-pox among those disaffected tribes of Indians?" To this Bouquet replied: "I will try to inoculate them with some blankets, and take care not to get the disease myself. As it is a pity to expose good men against them, I wish we could use the Spanish method, to hunt them with English dogs who would, I think, effectually extirpate or remove that vermin." Then Amherst replied: "You will do well to try to inoculate the Indians by means of blankets, as well as to try every other method that can serve to extirpate this exorable race."

Parkman calls attention to the fact that, while there is no direct evidence that Bouquet carried into effect the shameful plan of infecting the Indians with small-pox, yet a few months after Amherst's suggestion, this disease made havoc among the tribes of the Ohio. Also, on June 24th, Captain Ecuyer, the commandant at Fort Pitt, after narrating the fact that he and Alexander McKee held a short parley that day with Turtle Heart and another Delaware chief who had come to the fort for the purpose of terrifying the garrison by reports of great numbers of Indians marching against the place, noted the following in his journal: "Out of our regard to them [Turtle Heart and his companion], we gave them two blankets and a handkerchief out of the Small-pox Hospital. I hope it will have the desired effect."

Murder of Colonel William Clapham

In closing the account of Bouquet's expedition to the relief of forts Ligonier, Bedford, and Pitt, we call attention to the fact that Colonel William Clapham, mentioned above, had taken his family to the frontier near the present town of West Newton, in the early spring of 1763. On May 28th, the Indians rushed into his house, killed and scalped his wife and three children, and another woman. The two women were treated with shocking indecency. At the time of the murders, three men who were working at some distance from the Clapham house, hastened to Fort Pitt, and carried the news to the garrison. Two soldiers who were in Clapham's detail of scouts, who were stationed at a saw-mill near the fort, were also killed and scalped by the same party. It would appear that others were slain in this same massacre, for Colonel Burd entered in his journal on June 5th that, "John Harris gave me an account of Colonel Clapham and twelve men being killed near Pittsburgh and two Royal Americans being killed at the saw-mill." Thus it is seen that the Indians visited terrible retribution upon Colonel Clapham for the expedition which he sent against them in the summer of 1756, as related in Chapter XVIII.

Guyasuta Confers with Bradstreet and Bouquet

Guyasuta, in August, 1764, attended a conference with Colonel Bradstreet, near Erie, in which Bradstreet concluded a peace with the Delawares and Shawnees. However, Colonel Bouquet, upon learning of this fact, while at Fort Loudon, Franklin County, and perceiving that the Delawares and Shawnees were not sincere in their intentions, as they continued their depredations, refused to ratify the treaty, and pushed on with his army to the Muskingum, as referred to in Chapter XIX, where he compelled Guyasuta and the other chiefs of the western tribes to surrender the prisoners captured during Pontiac's War, as well as many captured during the French and Indian War. Bouquet dealt sternly with the chiefs, and they were glad to make peace.

More than two hundred prisoners were yielded up to Bouquet by Guyasuta and his associate chiefs. Some of the captives had been among the Indians since the early days of the French and Indian War, and in many cases, it was with extreme reluctance that they consented to accompany Bouquet's army back to the Pennsylvania settlements. Indeed, in some cases it was found necessary to deliver the captives bound to Bouquet. The Indians had become greatly attached to these captives, and had adopted them into their families. They shed torrents of tears when they were compelled to deliver them up.

However, Colonel Bouquet, on account of the lateness of the season, was obliged to return to Pennsylvania without having secured all the prisoners held by the Shawnees. On November 12th, he held a conference with a number of their chiefs, among whom were Nimwha and Red Hawk. At this conference, he took hostages from the Shawnees, and laid them under the strongest obligation for the delivery of the rest of the prisoners at Fort Pitt in the ensuing spring. These hostages escaped soon afterwards, thus giving reason to doubt the sincerity of the intentions of the Shawnees with respect to performance of their promises. But to the credit of the Shawnees it must be said that they punctually fulfilled all their promises. Ten of their chiefs, with about fifty of their warriors, met George Croghan, then deputy agent to Sir William Johnson, at Fort Pitt, on May 9, 1765, and delivered the remainder of their prisoners, "brightened the chain of friendship, and gave every assurance of their firm intentions to preserve the peace inviolable forever."

CHAPTER XXIV

Guyasuta

(Continued)

OTHER EVENTS OF THE PONTIAC-GUYASUTA WAR IN PENNSYLVANIA

Maiden Foot and Miss Means

URING the spring of 1763 Lieutenant Blane, in command of Fort Ligonier, was visited by several parties of friendly Indians, among whom was a young brave named Maiden Foot. When Maiden Foot was at the fort on one of these occasions, a settler named Means with his wife and little daughter, Mary, aged eleven, were there also. Maiden Foot seemed much pleased with the girl. The Means' home was about a mile south of the fort. On leaving the fort, Maiden Foot gave Mary Means a string of beads. He seemed sad and heartbroken at the time.

In the latter part of May or early in June, after the Pontiac and Guyasuta War had started, Mrs. Means and Mary started for the fort on hearing a rumor that the Indians had become hostile. On their way to the fort, they were captured by two Indians, who took them into the woods and tied them to saplings. Soon they heard the report of rifles, which was the first Indian assault on the fort. Later in the afternoon, Maiden Foot appeared before Mrs. Means and her daughter, no doubt being the Indian selected to scalp them. He recognized them, cut the bands which bound them to the tree, and conducted them by a roundabout way to their home, where Mr. Means met them. Maiden Foot then told the family to flee to the mountains, and pointed to a ravine in which they could hide until after the Indian band left the neighborhood. On leaving them Maiden Foot took the little girl's handkerchief, on which was worked in black silken thread her name "Mary Means".

Some years afterwards the Means family moved to a point near Cincinnati, Ohio, where the parents died; and the girl having grown to womanhood, married an officer named Kearney, who commanded a company under Wayne at the battle of the Fallen

Timbers, August 20, 1794. After this battle, Kearney and some companions found an elderly Indian sitting on a log on the battlefield and waving a white handkerchief. On their approaching him, the Indian said that he had been a warrior all his life; that he had fought at Ligonier, at Bushy Run, the Wabash against St. Clair, and at the recent battle against Wayne. He then explained that he had enough of war, and desired henceforth to live in peace with all mankind. Searching in his pouch he brought forth the handkerchief of Mary Means. Officer Kearney had often heard his wife tell the story of Maiden Foot. He took the old Indian home with him. Mrs. Kearney and the Indian immediately recognized each other, although thirty-one years had elapsed since they parted near Fort Ligonier. Maiden Foot now explained that shortly before he met Mary Means, he had lost a sister about her age and size, and that the giving of the string of beads to her was in effect the adopting of her as his sister. He was taken into the Kearney family, according to Boucher's "History of Westmoreland County", and upon his death four years later, was buried in a graveyard at Cincinnati, where a tablet was erected at his grave bearing the following inscription:

"In memory of Maiden Foot, an Indian Chief of the
Eighteenth Century, who died a Civilian and a Christian."

Expedition Against Great Island

At the time of Colonel Bouquet's expedition for the relief of Fort Pitt, the Delawares, Shawnees, and other tribes composing Pontiac and Guyasuta's confederation, planned to attack the interior settlements of Pennsylvania as far as Tulpehocken, their main object being to capture Fort Augusta, at Sunbury. Reports reaching Carlisle, Paxtang, and other places that Fort Augusta would be attacked by a great force of Indians, Colonel John Armstrong, with about three hundred volunteers from Cumberland and Bedford counties marched from Carlisle to destroy the Indian town at Great Island, [Lock Haven.] At Jersey Shore, Lycoming County, Armstrong's force advanced so suddenly upon the Indian village located there, that the Indians were scarcely able to escape, leaving their food, hot upon their bark tables, which they had prepared for dinner. Arriving at Great Island, Armstrong found the place had been deserted a few days before. His army then destroyed the village at Great Island together with a large quantity of grain and provisions.

As part of Armstrong's army was returning down the West

Branch of the Susquehanna, on August 26th, 1763, they encountered a force of Indians at Muncy Creek Hill, Lycoming County. A
hot skirmish followed in which four of Armstrong's men were
killed and four wounded; while the Indians suffered as severely,
and carried away their dead and wounded.

Captains Patterson, Sharp, Bedford, Laughlin, and Crawford,
with seventy-six of their comrades arrived at Fort Augusta the
next day, and other stragglers came in that night and the following
day. These soldiers reported the details of the battle at Muncey
Creek Hill and also that, after the battle, a party of twelve Indians
returning to Great Island from a mission to Bethlehem, were
attacked by them on a hill north of the present town of Northumberland, and, they believed, all were killed.

Attacks on Friendly Indians

In September and October, 1763, Indian outrages were committed as far into the heart of the settled parts of the Province as
the neighborhood of Reading and Bethlehem; and many of the
settlers believed that the Moravian Indians were secretly giving
assistance to their brethren at war against the Province. A party
of rangers murdered a number of the Moravian Indians as they
were found asleep in a barn. Among these were an Indian woman
named Zippora, who was thrown down upon the threshing floor
and killed, and an Indian man named Zachari, his wife and little
child, who were put to the sword, although the mother begged
upon her knees that the life of her child might be spared.

About the middle of October a party of rangers marched
against the Moravian Indians at Wichetunk, in what is now Polk
Township, Monroe County, intending to surprise them by night,
but their plans were frustrated by a violent storm in the evening.
The Moravian missionary, Bernard Adam Grube, then led these
Indians to Nazareth, but Governor Penn suggested that, in order
to watch their behavior, it would be better to disarm them and
bring them into the interior parts of the Province. They were
accordingly taken to Province Island on the Delaware by the
Moravian missionary, John Roth.

Among the troops under the command of Captain Jacob
Wetterhold, stationed at Fort Allen during the summer and
autumn of 1763, was Lieutenant Jonathan Dodge, "a most precious
scoundrel", who committed many atrocious acts against his fellow
soldiers, and particularly against friendly Indians. One of the
wrongs he committed against the Indians, is thus described in a

letter which he wrote to Timothy Horsfield, on August 4th, 1763:
"Yesterday there were four Indians came to Ensign Kern's. . . . .
I took four rifles and fourteen deer skins from them, weighed them,
and there were thirty-one pounds." After these Indians had left,
Dodge continues: "I took twenty men and pursued them; then I
ordered my men to fire, upon which I fired a volley on them; could
find none dead or alive." These were friendly Indians, who were
on their way from Shamokin (Sunbury) to the Moravian mission
at Bethlehem.

In the "Frontier Forts of Pennsylvania", we read of another
attack made by Dodge upon friendly Indians:

"Jacob Warner, a soldier in Nicholas Wetterholt's company
made the following statement September 9th: 'That he and
Dodge were searching for a lost gun, when, about two miles above
Fort Allen, they saw three Indians painted black. Dodge fired
upon them and killed one; Warner also fired upon them, and
thinks he wounded another; but two escaped; the Indians had not
fired at them. The Indian was scalped, and, on the 24th, Dodge
sent Warner with the scalp to a person in Philadelphia, who gave
him eight dollars for it. These were also friendly Indians."

The Killing of Captain Jacob Wetterholt

Determined to avenge themselves on account of the atrocious
acts of Dodge, the Delawares attacked Captain Jacob Wetterholt
on October 8th, as thus described in Egle's "History of Pennsylvania":

"Before daybreak in the morning of the 8th of October, some
Delawares attacked the house of John Stenton, in Allen Township,
(Northampton County), on the main road from Bethlehem to Fort
Allen, eight miles northwest from the former place, where Captain
Jacob Wetterhold, of the Province service, with a squad of men,
was lodging for the night. Meeting with Jean, the wife of James
Horner, who was on her way to a neighbors for coals to light her
morning fire, the Indians, fearing lest she should betray them or
raise an alarm, dispatched her with their tomahawks. Thereupon
they surrounded Stenton's house. No sooner had Captain Wetterhold's servant stepped out of the house (he had been sent to saddle
the captain's horse) than he was shot down. The report of the
Indian's piece brought his master to the door, who, on opening it,
received a mortal wound. Sergeant Lawrence McGuire, in his
attempt to draw him in, was also dangerously wounded and fell,
whereupon the lieutenant advanced. He was confronted by an

Indian, who, leaping upon the bodies of the fallen men, presented a pistol, which the lieutenant thrust aside as it was being discharged, thus escaping with his life, and succeeding also in repelling the savage. The Indians now took a position at a window, and there shot Stenton as he was in the act of rising from bed. Rushing from the house, the wounded man ran for a mile, and dropped down a corpse. His wife and two children had meanwhile secreted themselves in the cellar, where they were fired upon three times, but without being struck. Captain Wetterhold, despite his sufferings, dragged himself to a window, through which he shot one of the savages while in the act of applying a torch to the house. Hereupon, taking up the dead body of their comrade, the besiegers withdrew. Having on their retreat plundered the house of James Allen, they attacked Andrew Hazlitt's, where they shot and scalped a man, shot Hazlitt after a brave defence, and then tomahawked his fugitive wife and two children in a barbarous manner. Finally they set fire to his house, and then to that of Philip Kratzer, and crossing the Lehigh above Siegfried's bridge, passed into Whitehall Township.

"In this maraud twenty-three persons were killed, and many dangerously wounded. The settlers were thrown into the utmost distress, fleeing from their plantations with hardly a sufficiency of clothes to cover themselves, and coming into the town of Northampton (now Allentown), where, we read, there were but four guns at the time, 'and three of them unfit for use, with the enemy four miles from the place.' At the same time, Yost's mill, about eleven miles from Bethlehem, was destroyed, and all the people at the place, excepting a young man, cut off.

"This was the last invasion of the present Northampton County by a savage foe. Old Northampton, and especially that part of it which was erected into Monroe, by act of Legislature, in April, 1836, suffered subsequently, at intervals, from the Indians as late as 1765."

The Murder of the Conestogas

One of the events of the Pontiac and Guyasuta War, which, as Dr. Geo. P. Donehoo remarks, "attracted wide attention and has been a source of discussion ever since," was the murder of six members of the Conestoga tribe at the town of Conestoga, Lancaster County, on December 14, 1763, by a band of Scotch-Irish settlers, "The Paxton Boys", from the neighborhood of Paxtang church not far from Harrisburg. Edward Shippen, in a letter to Governor Penn, dated at Lancaster December 14th, gives the following account of this event: "One, Robert Edgar, a hired man to Captain Thomas McKee, living near the Borough acquainted me today that a Company of People from the Frontier had killed and scalped most of the Indians at the Conestoga Town early this morning; he said he had his information from an Indian boy who made his escape; Mr. Slough has been to the place and held a Coroner's inquest on the corpses, being Six in number; Bill Sawk and some other Indians were gone towards Smith's Iron Works to sell brooms; but where they are now we can't understand. . . . . . Warrants are issued for the apprehending of the murderers, said to be upwards of fifty men, well armed and mounted."

Great excitement was caused in Philadelphia by the murder of these Indians. Just a short time before, on November 30th, they sent a letter to John Penn, in which they congratulated him on his arrival in the Province and asked his favor and protection. The Quakers especially were loud in their denunciation of this atrocity, seemingly unmindful of the fact that John Harris and Colonel John Elder, pastor of the Presbyterian Church at Paxtang, had frequently appealed to the Colonial Authorities to remove the Conestogas to a place of safety, owing to the excitement prevailing in the Paxtang region on account of the many raids of the hostile Indians.

Furthermore, during October, Captain Bull, the son of the great Teedyuscung, had led a band of one hundred thirty-five Delawares from the Ohio and Allegheny, with whom he had lived for ten years, into the Wyoming Valley. They committed many atrocities. Many of the Paxton Boys had just returned from an expedition against Captain Bull's band and, as Rev. Elder said, in a letter written on October 25th, had seen "the mangled carcasses of these unhappy people", which "presented to our troops a melancholy scene, which had been acted not above two days before their arrival." The Paxton Boys were therefore in a state of excitement and rage against all Indians, especially when they discovered that some of the Indians who were committing outrages along the Susquehanna had been traced to Conestoga. Likewise, it must be said to the credit of Rev. Elder that, when he learned that a large number of the Paxtang settlers were assembling to march against the Conestogas, he sent a messenger to them urging them to desist.

Governor Penn issued a proclamation on December 22nd, calling upon judges, justices, sheriffs, and other civil and military officers, to make diligent search for the perpetrators of this crime, and to place them in the public jails of the Province, the remaining Conestogas, fourteen in number, in the meantime having been placed in the Lancaster workhouse for protection. How the Paxton Boys replied to this proclamation of the governor is thus set forth in a letter of Edward Shippen to Governor John Penn written from Lancaster on December 27th: "I am to acquaint your Honor that between two and three of the clock this afternoon, upwards of a hundred armed men from the westward rode very fast into town, turned their horses into Mr. Slough's (an In-keeper) yard, and proceeded with the greatest precipitation to the work house, stove open the door and killed all the Indians, and took to their horses and rode off. All their business was done, and they were returning to their horses before I could get half way down to the Work House."

The details of the massacre of these unarmed and defenseless Conestogas are most shocking and revolting. Protesting their innocence and their love for the English, they prostrated themselves with their children before their infuriated murderers, and plead for their lives. Their appeal was answered by the rifle, hatchet, and scalping knife. Some had their brains blown out, others their legs chopped off, and others their hands cut off. Bill Sawk (Sock) and his wife, Mollie, with their two children, had their heads split open, and were scalped. The mangled bodies of these Indians, who had never been at war with the whites and had always been claimed as friendly Indians, were buried at Lancaster.

Thus perished the last remnant of the once mighty tribe of Susquehannas. The excitement on the frontier at the time, and the laxity on the part of the Colonial Assembly in providing for the defense, may, in a measure, explain why the harassed frontiersmen committed such a horrid and notorious act; but the historian searches the records of the time in vain for any justification for this atrocity, which is a black spot on the pages of the history of Pennsylvania.

Not content with the butchery of the Conestogas, the Paxton Boys threatened to go to Philadelphia and kill the Moravian Indians on Province Island. These Indians were then lodged in the barracks in Philadelphia. A report reached the city that the Paxton Boys were on the march. Cannon were then planted around the barracks, volunteers were called into service, and alarm bells were rung. About two hundred of the Paxton Boys actually crossed the Schuylkill at Swedsford, and advanced to Germantown, when hearing of the preparations which had been made, they wisely proceeded no further.

Pennsylvania Offers Bounty For Scalps

On July 7th, 1764, Pennsylvania offered a bounty for Indian scalps, even the scalps of children, "for the better carrying on of offensive operations against our Indian enemies", as follows:

"For every male Indian enemy above ten years old, who shall be taken prisoner and delivered at any forts garrisoned by the troops in the pay of this Province, or at any of the county towns, to the keeper of the common gaols there, the sum of one hundred & fifty Spanish dollars, or pieces of eight; for every female Indian enemy taken prisoner and brought in as aforesaid, and for every male Indian enemy ten years old, or under, taken prisoner, and delivered as aforesaid, the sum of one hundred and thirty pieces of eight; for the scalp of every male Indian enemy above the age of ten years, produced as evidence of their being killed, the sum of one hundred and thirty-four pieces of eight; and for the scalp of every female Indian enemy above the age of ten years, produced as evidence of their being killed, the sum of fifty pieces of eight; and that there shall be paid to every officer, or officers, soldier, or soldiers, as are or shall be in the pay of this Province, who shall take, bring in, and produce any Indian enemy prisoner, or scalp, as aforesaid, one half of the said several and respective premiums & bounties."

As a result of the scalp bounties, "secret expeditions", say the Pennsylvania Archives, "were set on foot by the inhabitants which were more effectual than any sort of defensive operations."

Murder of Schoolmaster Brown and His Pupils

One of the most terrible atrocities committed within the bounds of Pennsylvania by the Delawares during the Pontiac-Guyasuta War is thus described in "Colonel Henry Bouquet and His Campaigns", by Cort:

"In 1764, July 26, three miles northwest of Greencastle, Franklin County, was perpetrated what Parkman, the great historian of Colonial times, pronounces 'an outrage unmatched in fiend-like atrocity through all the annals of the war.' This was the massacre of Enoch Brown, a kindhearted exemplary Christian schoolmaster, and ten scholars, eight boys and two girls. Ruth Hart and Ruth Hale were the names of the girls. Among the boys were Eben Taylor, George Dustan and Archie McCullough. All were knocked down like so many beeves, and scalped by the merciless savages. Mourning and desolation came to many homes in the valley, for each of the slaughtered innocents belonged to a dif-

ferent family. The last named boy, indeed, survived the effects
of the scalping knife, but in somewhat demented condition. The
teacher offered his life and scalp in a spirit of self-sacrificing devotion, if the savages would only spare the lives of the little ones
under his charge and care. But no! the tender mercies of the
heathen are cruel, and so a perfect holocaust was made to the
Moloch of war by the relentless fiends in human form. . . . . . It
is some relief to know that this diabolical deed, whose recital
makes us shudder even at this late date, was disapproved by the
old warriors, when the marauding party of young Indians came
back with their horrid trophies. Neephaughwhese, or Night
Walker, an old chief or half-king, denounced them as a pack of
cowards for killing and scalping so many children. . . . . Who
can describe the horror of the scene in that lonely log school house,
when one of the settlers chanced to look in at the door to ascertain
the cause of the unusual quietness? In the center lay the faithful
Brown, scalped and lifeless, with a Bible clasped in his hand.
Around the room were strewn the dead and mangled bodies of
seven boys and two girls, while little Archie, stunned, scalped and
bleeding, was creeping around among his dead companions, rub-
bing his hands over their faces and trying to gain some token of
recognition. A few days later the innocent victims of savage
atrocity received a common sepulchre. All were buried in one
large rough box at the border of the ravine, a few rods from the
school house where they had been so ruthlessly slaughtered. Side
by side, with head and feet alternately, the little ones were laid
with their master, just as they were clad at the time of the massacre."

John McCollough, a cousin of Archie, had been captured in
the same neighborhood just nine year previously, and was living
among the Delawares at Muskingum when the young warriors returned with the scalps of the schoolmaster and his pupils. He was
among the prisoners surrendered to Bouquet, and is the authority
for the statement concerning the indignation expressed by old
Night Walker.

During the same incursion in which Schoolmaster Brown and
his pupils were killed, Susan King Cunningham, who lived in the
same neighborhood, was brutally murdered while on her way
through the woods to call on a neighbor. As she did not return
when expected, a search was made, and her body was found near
her home. Not content with murdering and scalping the poor
woman, the fiends performed a Caesarian operation, and placed
her child on the ground beside her.

Guyasuta at the Council at Fort Pitt

But to return to Guyasuta. His next act of importance was to attend the great council at Fort Pitt which opened on May 10th, 1765, relative to resuming trade relations between Pennsylvania and the Western Indians after Pontiac's War. He was one of the principal speakers on this occasion, and represented the Senecas. The Delawares were represented by New Comer, King Beaver, Wingenund, Turtle Heart, White Wolf, Sun Fish, Thomas Hickman, and many others. George Croghan, as deputy agent of Indian affairs, had arrived at the fort on February 28th, accompanied by Lieutenant Alexander Frazer. At the council Guyasuta made the following speech:

"When you first came to drive the French from this place, the Governor of Pennsylvania sent us a Message that we should withdraw from the French, & that when the English was settled here, we should want for nothing. It's true, you did supply us very well, but it was only while the War was doubtful, & as soon as you conquer'd the French you did not care how you treated us, as you did not then think us worth your Notice; we request you may not treat us again in this manner, but now open the Trade and do not put us off with telling us you must first hear from your great man before it can be done. If you have but little goods, let us have them for our skins, and let us have a part of your rum, or we cannot put dependence on what you tell us for the future."

To the above speech of Guyasuta and the speeches of the other chiefs, Croghan faithfully promised that trade relations would be opened without delay.

When Croghan set out from Philadelphia for Fort Pitt, he gave a pass for a large number of wagons and pack horses belonging to Boynton and Wharton of Philadelphia, loaded with guns, knives, blankets, and other goods intended as presents for the Indians at Fort Pitt. However, the people of Cumberland County and the valley of the Conococheague, upon whom such terrible atrocities had been so recently committed by the Indians, determined to prevent these war-like supplies being carried to the Indians. Accordingly, on March 6th, when the pack train had reached Sidling Hill, about seventeen miles beyond Fort Loudon, sixty-three horse loads were either burned or pillaged by the force of infuriated settlers, since known as the "Sidling Hill Volunteers", led by Colonel James Smith, who, it will be remembered, was a captive at Fort Duquesne at the time of Braddock's defeat. This action of Smith and his followers obstructed communication with Fort Pitt for some time.

Guyasuta Attends Council at Fort Pitt, April and May, 1768

Guyasuta also attended the great conference held at Fort Pitt from April 26th to May 9th, 1768, for the purpose of adjusting the difficulties due to the fact that many settlements had been made in the valleys of the Youghiogheny and the Monongahela on land not purchased from the Indians. This conference led to the purchase at Fort Stanwix (Rome, New York), November 5th, 1768, more particularly described in Chapter XX, and needing no additional reference at this point, except to point out that, shortly after the treaty and purchase of Fort Stanwix, marauds were made into Western Pennsylvania. On February 26, 1769, eighteen persons were either killed or taken prisoner in the Brush Creek settlement, in Westmoreland County. Whether Guyasuta had anything to do with these outrages is not known.

Guyasuta Arouses Anger of White Eyes

In May, 1774, Guyasuta attended a conference with George Croghan at Ligonier. On October 27th, 1775, he was the principal speaker at the treaty held at Fort Pitt between the Commissioners of the Continental Congress and a few of the chiefs of the Senecas, Delawares, Shawnees, and Wyandots, in an effort to secure their neutrality during the Revolutionary War. He represented the Iroquois, or Mingoes, in the Allegheny Valley and Ohio. As an Iroquois, he assumed to speak for all the western tribes, and thereby aroused the anger of White Eyes, the great Delaware chief, who thereupon declared the absolute indpendence of the Delawares. This council was far from harmonious, but the chiefs declared their intention to remain neutral; and Guyasuta promised to use his influence at the Great Council of the Iroquois in New York, to obtain a decision in favor of peace.

Guyasuta in the Revolutionary War

In May, 1776, Sir Guy Johnson and Colonel John Butler held a great council with the Iroquois chiefs at Fort Niagara, New York, when the overwhelming majority of the sachems voted to accept the war hatchet against the Americans. Guyasuta then came from his home near Sharpsburg, Allegheny County, to a council at Fort Pitt on July 6th of that year, and declared that neither the English nor the Americans should be permitted to pass through the territory of the Six Nations. This was a conference between Majors Trent and Ward, and Captain Neville, on the one hand, and Guyasuta, Captain Pipe, a Delaware chief, Shade, a

Shawnee chief, and other Western Indians. The object of the conference seems to have been to enable Guyasuta, as the outstanding representative of the Six Nations in the Ohio and Allegheny valleys, to define his position in the struggle between England and her American Colonies.

"I am appointed," said Guyasuta, "by the Six Nations to take care of this country, that is of the nations on the other side of the Ohio [meaning the present Allegheny River], and I desire you will not think of an expedition against Detroit, for, I repeat, we will not suffer an army to pass through our country." Captain Neville replied that the Americans would not invade Guyasuta's domain, unless the British should try to come through the same towards Fort Pitt. Detroit was then in the possession of the British, and, no doubt, as an actual ally of the British, it was the task assigned Guyasuta to prevent an advance against this post by the Americans.

At any rate soon thereafter this great chief of the Senecas took up arms against the Americans, and led many a bloody expedition against the settlements of Western Pennsylvania. During the summers of 1778 and 1779, he was especially active against the settlements of New York and Pennsylvania, and decorated the Seneca towns of the upper Allegheny with the scalps of hundreds of settlers.

Broadhead's Expedition Against Guyasuta's Warriors

In order to put a stop to the raids of Guyasuta's warriors Colonel Broadhead, who was in command of Fort Pitt during the summer of 1779, begged General Washington for permission to lead an expedition into the Seneca country. Early in the same summer, Washington directed General John Sullivan to invade the territory of the Iroquois from the East; and about the middle of July, Broadhead received permission from Washington to undertake a co-operating movement up the Allegheny. With sixty boats, two hundred pack horses and six hundred and five soldiers, he left Fort Pitt on August 11th. Small garrisons were placed at Fort McIntosh (Beaver), Fort Crawford (New Kensington, Westmoreland County), and Fort Armstrong (Kittanning, Armstrong County). A band of friendly Delawares, under Captain Samuel Brady and Lieut. John Hardin, accompanied the expedition as scouts. Broadhead's small army ascended the beautiful Allegheny, whose banks were now clothed in the verdure of midsummer.

> *Majestic stood the river hills,*
> *Clothed in living green,*
> *While Allegheny gently rolled*
> *Its winding way between.*

Reaching the mouth of the Mahoning, Broadhead left the river and followed the Indian trail running almost due north through the wilderness of what is now Clarion County, and reached the Allegheny near the mouth of Tionesta Creek, Forest County. A few miles below the mouth of Brokenstraw Creek, Warren County, Broadhead's force encountered a party of thirty Seneca's, under Guyasuta, descending the Allegheny on their way to raid the frontier settlements. Both sides discovered each other at about the same time, took position behind trees and rocks, and a sharp fight commenced, which lasted but a few minutes, when a party of Broadhead's scouts, moving over the river hill, attacked the Senecas on the flank. The Indians then took to flight, leaving five of their number dead on the field. It has been said that Cornplanter was the commander of the Indians at this engagement, but it is clear that he was at this time in the Genesee country endeavoring to oppose the advance of Sullivan's army. Broadhead then marched up the river, destroyed the Seneca towns, and burned one hundred thirty of their houses, some of them large enough for three or four families. They also destroyed five hundred acres of corn, of which Broadhead said: "I never saw finer corn, although it was planted much thicker than is common with our farmers."

Guyasuta Burns Hannastown

The hardest blow dealt by the Indians during the Revolutionary War, within the limits of Western Pennsylvania, was the burning of Hannastown, the county seat of Westmoreland, by Guyasuta, on Saturday, July 13th, 1782. This historic frontier village was located about three miles north of Greensburg. The town grew up around the tavern of Robert Hanna, on the old Forbes Road, before the Revolutionary War.

At the time of its destruction, Hannastown contained thirty log houses, and, at the northern end, was a stockade fort of logs set upright, and erected in 1773. In the centre was a spring whose waters still gush forth to quench the thirst of the lover of Pennsylvania history, who makes a pilgrimage to the spot where the frontier village stood.

Guyasuta, with a band of one hundred Seneca warriors and sixty Canadian rangers, left Lake Chautauqua, New York, descended the Allegheny River to a point a short distance above

Kittanning, and leaving the canoes on the bank of the river, marched overland into the settlements of Westmoreland. While the expedition was making its visitation of death and destruction, many of these canoes broke loose from their moorings, and floated down the river to Fort Pitt, where some of them were picked up by the garrison.

On this midsummer day when Guyasuta's warriors destroyed the historic town, one of the harvesters, who were cutting wheat on the farm of Michael Huffnagle, the county clerk, about a mile north of the village, discovered a band of Indians, in war paint, creeping through the woods. He informed his companions, and all fled unseen to the stockade. The alarm was spread throughout the Hannastown settlement by Sheriff Matthew Jack. About sixty persons were in the village, and they took refuge within the fort. Huffnagle carried most of the county records safely into the fort.

Four young men were sent out to scout. Coming upon the Indians creeping through the thick woods in the valley of Crabtree Creek, they narrowly escaped death, and fled back to the fort, followed closely by the Indians. It seems that Guyasuta intended to take the fort by storm; for his warriors did not shoot or yell until they rushed into the village. One man was wounded before he reached the fort.

The Indians then drove into the woods all the horses found in the pasture lots and stables, killed one hundred cattle, and plundered the deserted houses. From the shleter of the houses, they opened a hot rifle fire upon the stockade, defended by twenty men with seventeen rifles, only nine of which were fit for use. With these, the frontiersmen took turns at the loopholes, and succeeded in preventing the Indians from assaulting and battering down the gates. At least two of the savages were killed, and others wounded; while only one person inside the stockade was wounded, a maiden of sixteen summers named Margaret Shaw, who received a bullet in her breast while exposed before a hole in one of the gates, as she was rescuing a child, who had toddled into danger. The young lady died from the effects of her wound about two weeks later. Her dust reposes in the soil of "Old Westmoreland", a short distance north of Mt. Pleasant.

The attack on the fort continued until night, when the Indians set fire to the village, and danced in the glare of the flames. The county jail and all the other buildings, except the court house and one dwelling, were reduced to ashes. These two had been set on fire, but the fire went out; and, as they stood near the fort, the unerring rifles of the frontiersmen frustrated an attempt to set fire to them again. Happily, the wind blew strongly from the north, carrying the flames and burning embers away from the fort. After the buildings were burned, the Indians and their white allies retired to the valley of Crabtree Creek, and reveled and feasted until late at night.

The attack was not renewed in the morning, and Guyasuta and his forces made good their escape. It was not until Monday morning that a force of sixty frontiersmen took up the pursuit, following them to the crossing of the Kiskiminetas.

Other places in the neighborhood of Hannastown were also attacked with deadly effect. A wedding had taken place, on July 12th, at the home of Andrew Cruikshank at Miller's Station, two miles south of Hannastown; and on July 13th, many friends of the happy couple were gathered at the Cruikshank home for the wedding party, when Guyasuta's warriors fell upon them, killing several and making prisoners of fifteen. Among the latter were Lieutenant Joseph Brownlee, his wife and several children, Mrs. Robert Hanna and her daughter, Jennie, and a Mrs. White and two of her children. As these prisoners were being taken through the woods, Mrs. Hanna addressed Lieutenant Brownlee as "Captain"; whereupon the Indians killed him, his little son whom he was carrying, and nine other captives. The others were taken to Canada.

Also, on Sunday morning, some of Guyasuta's force attacked the Freeman settlement on Loyalhanna Creek, a few miles northeast of Hannastown, killing one of Freeman's sons and capturing two of his daughters. On the same day, an attack was made on the Brush Creek settlement west of Hannastown, where many farm animals were killed, and several farm buildings burned. This attack was promptly reported to General William Irvine, then the commander at Fort Pitt, by Michael Huffnagle, the defender of the Hannastown fort.

Hannastown never arose from its ashes. Court was held there for a few sessions after the burning of the village. Then a new road was laid out from Bedford to Pittsburgh, following the course of the present Lincoln Highway; and, in January, 1787, the Westmoreland Court began its sessions in the town of Greensburg, on the new road, the present county seat of the historic county of Westmoreland.

It appears that there was a previous attack on Hannastown.

Boucher, in his "History of Westmoreland County," refers to this former attack, as follows:

"Eve Oury was granted a special pension of forty dollars per year by Act of April 1, 1846. The act itself recites that it was granted for heroic bravery and risking her life in defense of the garrison of Hannastown Fort in 1778, when it was attacked by a large number of Indians, and that by her fortitude, she performed efficient service in driving away the Indians, and thus saved the inmates from a horrid butchery by the merciless and savage foe."

Eve Oury (Uhrig) was the daughter of Francis Oury. She died at Shieldsburg, Westmoreland County, in 1848, and is buried at Congruity, in the same county.

Reference has been made to the fact that the Six Nations, owing principally to the influence of Sir Guy Johnson, Colonel John Butler, and other British sympathizers and agents, were overwhelmingly on the side of the British during the Revolutionary War. The British offered the Iroquois great plunder and bounties for American scalps, as an inducement for them to attack the Americans. To be specific, the League of the Iroquois voted to take no part in the great conflict, but allow each tribe to decide for itself. A large part of the Tuscaroras and nearly all the Oneidas, owing to the influence of Rev. Samuel Kirkland, remained neutral; but the other four tribes of the historic confederation went over to the British, and brought desolation and death upon the frontiers of New York and Pennsylvania. Witness Cherry Valley, in New York, and Wyoming and Hannastown, in Pennsylvania.

Guyasuta's tribe, the Senecas, were the most numerous and warlike of the Six Nations. A recital of the bloody outrages committed by them upon the Americans struggling for liberty during the American Revolution would fill many pages. While it is not to be wondered at that Guyasuta sided along with his nation in the American Revolution, it is sincerely to be regretted that one of the most noted chiefs that ever trod the soil of Pennsylvania took the side of the British in this conflict Terrible was the retribution visited upon the Senecas and their allies by General Sullivan—a retribution that led to the final extinction of the Iroquois Confederation. No wonder that the old chief's declining years were embittered.

Last Days of Guyasuta

After the Revolutionary War, Guyasuta lived in the vicinity of Fort Pitt. As old age crept upon him, he became virtually destitute. In 1790, he sent a pathetic message to the Quakers of Philadelphia, addressing them as the sons of his beloved "Brother Onas" and imploring their assistance. Said he: "When I was young and strong, our country was full of game which the good Spirit sent for us to live upon. The lands which belonged to us were extended far beyond where we hunted. Hunting was then not tiresome; it was diversion; it was pleasure. When your fathers asked land from my nation, we gave it to them, for we had more than enough. Guyasuta was among the first people to say, 'give land to our brother Onas for he wants it; and he has always been a friend to Onas and his children. But you are too far off to see him. Now he is grown old. He is very old and he wonders at his own shadow; it has become so little. He has no children to take care of him and the game is driven away by the white people. . . . I have no other friends but you, the children of our beloved Brother Onas."

From December, 1792, to the middle of April, 1793, General Anthony Wayne trained the Legion of the United States at that place on the Ohio River, twenty miles below Pittsburgh, since known as Legionville. Before leading the Legion from that place against the Western Indians, he was visited by Guyasuta.

In May, 1793, Captain Samuel Brady was tried at Pittsburgh for the murder of certain Indians near the mouth of the Beaver, in the spring of 1791. Due at least in part to the testimony given in his behalf by Guyasuta, he was acquitted. Guyasuta's testimony was so strongly in favor of the defendant that even Brady's counsel, James Ross, Esq., was abashed. At the close of the trial, Mr. Ross spoke to Guyasuta, expressing his surprise at the decided tone of his testimony. The aged chief then clapped his hand upon his breast, and said: "Am I not the friend of Brady?"

General James O'Hara bought Guyasuta's interest in the large tract of land on the west side of the Allegheny near Sharpsburg, Allegheny County, and gave the old chief a home on the plantation during his declining years. Here he died some time in the closing years of the eighteenth century, and his body was placed in the old Indian mound on the estate by General O'Hara. Guyasuta station on the Pennsylvania Railroad nearby bears the name of this noted chieftain.

The claim has been made, however, that Guyasuta died at Custaloga's Town on French Creek about twelve miles above its mouth and near the mouth of Deer Creek in French Creek Township, Mercer County, and was buried at that place. (See Frontier Forts of Pennsylvania, Volume Two, pages 322, 323).

CHAPTER XXV

New Comer, White Eyes and Killbuck

NEW COMER

NEW COMER, or Nettawatwees, was a chief of the Turtle Clan of Delawares, his authority being limited, it seems, to that Clan alone, though he was the nominal head of the Delaware nation. His first appearance in history is when he was a witness to the deed which Sassoonan and six other chiefs gave to William Penn, on September 17th, 1718, by the terms of which they released all the land "between the Delaware and the Susquehanna from Duck Creek to the Mountains [the South Mountain] on this side of Lechay [the Lehigh River]", mentioned more particularly in Chapter VII.

New Comer was one of the chiefs who met George Croghan at Logstown in January, 1754, and joined with Scarouady, Tanacharison, Shingas, and Delaware George, in requesting both Pennsylvania and Virginia to build forts near the Forks of the Ohio as a place of security for the Indians of that region in case of war with the French. He went to the Muskingum and Tuscarawas near the close of the French and Indian War, from which place he joined with King Beaver and Shingas in sending White Eyes and Wingenund to Philadelphia in May, 1761, to advise the Governor that a large delegation of chiefs from Ohio proposed coming to meet him in order to cement the bond of peace.

When Colonel Bouquet led his expedition to the Muskingum and Tuscarawas in the summer and autumn of 1764, to quell Pontiac's uprising and to force the Western Indians to deliver up the prisoners which they had captured, New Comer, as chief of the Turtle Clan was nominally the head of the Delaware nation at that time. Bouquet deposed him on this occasion for refusing to attend the conference between this resolute soldier and the chiefs of the hostile tribes. The deposition, however, was never accepted by the Delawares.

New Comer attended the conference at Fort Pitt, beginning May 10th, 1765, relative to resuming trade relations with the western tribes after the close of Pontiac's War; also the great coun-

cil at the same place, April 26th to May 9th, 1768, relative to the
settlements made at Redstone and other places in the valleys of the
Monongahela and Youghiogheny, on land not purchased from the
Indians—the council which led to the Great Congress at Fort
Stanwix, (Rome, New York,) in October of that year, at which
Pennsylvania purchased from the Six Nations that part of the
state known as the "Purchase of 1768", the counties included in
which were set forth in Chapter XX.

In his latter years, New Comer came under the influence of
the Moravian missionaries, and granted them lands on the Tuscarawas, in 1772. He was especially friendly to Bishop Zeisberger
of the Moravian Church. He was much perplexed, however, on
account of the lack of unity among Christians. He could not
understand why there were so many different denominations; and,
in the latter part of 1772, he advised the Governor of Pennsylvania that he intended to go to England to consult the King on
this matter which was disturbing his heart, a journey which he did
not take, however.

Last Days of New Comer

When William Wilson, as the ambassador of George Morgan,
then in charge of Indian affairs at Fort Pitt, was sent in the summer of 1776 on a mission to invite the Delawares, Shawnees, and
Wyandots of Ohio to a conference to be held at Fort Pitt in
October of that year, he was greatly befriended by New Comer at
the Delaware town of Coshocton, located on the site of the present
town of that name, in Coshocton County, Ohio. Wilson, in spite
of the interference of Hamilton, commander of the British fort at
Detroit, succeeded in persuading a number of the chiefs of the
western tribes to attend the conference at Fort Pitt in October
Among these chiefs was the venerable New Comer. Unusual
solemnity was given to the conference by the fact that he breathed
his last at Fort Pitt before the treaty was concluded.

WHITE EYES

White Eyes, also sometimes Grey Eyes, became the ruler of
the Turkey Clan of Delawares upon the death of King Beaver.
During the winter of 1776-1777, he was elected chief sachem of the
Delaware nation, following the death of the aged New Comer in
Pittsburgh in the autumn of 1776. His Delaware name was
Coquetakeghton.

While White Eyes met Post on the latter's first mission to the

Ohio in the summer of 1758, his first appearance of importance in
Pennsylvania history is when he and the Delaware chief, Wingenund, as the ambassadors of King Beaver and New Comer, met
Governor Hamilton in council at Philadelphia, on   May 22nd,
1761, and delivered the promise of these "chief men at Allegheny"
to meet the Provincial Authorities in the near future further to
confirm the peace "that was begun at Easton" [Treaty of Easton,
October, 1758], "a peace", said White Eyes, "that has a good face,
and seems to be as well established as that made by William
Penn. . . . . at the first settlement of the Province." Andrew
Montour was the interpreter.   The Governor received White
Eyes and Wingenund very cordially, and requested them to advise
their superior chiefs to make arrangements for the delivery of the
white prisoners taken in the French and Indian War, a request,
which, as was seen in Chapter XIX, was carried out by King
Beaver and Shingas, at the Lancaster conference of August, 1762.

Nothing definite is known as to the part taken by White Eyes
in Pontiac's War. But in Lord Dunmore's War, in the autumn
of 1774, we find him an earnest advocate of peace. Many of his
people reviled him and accused him of ingratiating himself with
the Virginians in his efforts to persuade the Shawnees to make
peace with Dunmore; but the great chieftain's purpose was to save
the Shawnees from destruction. Taunts and abuse did not swerve
him. He was Lord Dunmore's advisor; and, when peace was
concluded between the Virginians and the Shawnees, at Camp
Charlotte, near Circleville, Ohio, in October, Lord Dunmore took
occasion to extol White Eyes and his people, saying that they had
been the unflinching advocates of peace, and telling the Shawnees
that only out of regard for them, the Delawares, as "grandfathers"
of the Shawnees, had he made the terms of peace so lenient. Both
the Shawnees and the Virginians had suffered severe losses at the
battle of Point Pleasant, West Virginia, described in the sketch of
Cornstalk, Chapter XXVII.

Reference was made, in Chapter XXIV, to the fact that White
Eyes attended the treaty held at Fort Pitt on October 27th, 1775,
in an effort to secure the friendship of the western tribes in the
Revolutionary War, at which he resented Guyasuta's claim to
represent the Delawares. White Eyes' sympathy for the Americans gave offense to Guyasuta, who reminded him that the Delawares were "women".

"Women!" was the scornful reply of White Eyes. "Yes, you
say that you conquered me, that you cut off my legs, put a petti-

coat on me, and gave me a hoe and cornpounder in my hands.
. . . . . Look at my legs. If, as you assert, you cut them off,
they have grown again to their proper size. The petticoat I have
thrown away; the corn-hoe and pounder I have exchanged for
these firearms; and I declare that I am a man. Yes, all the
country on the other side of that river"—waving his hand in the
direction of the Allegheny—"is mine."

White Eyes Accompanies William Wilson to Detroit

In the sketch of New Comer, reference was made to the fact
that, in the summer of 1776, William Wilson, as agent of George
Morgan, made a journey among the Indians of Ohio, to invite
them to a treaty at Fort Pitt in October, and that he was befriended
by New Comer at Coshocton. On this occasion, New Comer, believing it unsafe for Wilson to proceed to the Wyandots at Sandusky, sent Killbuck to carry his message to them. Killbuck returned in eleven days with word from the Wyandot chiefs that
they wanted to see Wilson and hear his message from his own
mouth. Wilson then decided to go to see them, and New Comer
directed Killbuck to accompany him. Scarcely had the journey
begun when Killbuck became ill, and his place was taken by White
Eyes. Proceeding, Wilson and White Eyes learned that the
Wyandot chiefs had gone to Detroit. Wilson then boldly pressed
on to the neighborhood of the British post, where he and White
Eyes met the Wyandots. Both he and White Eyes addressed them
urging them to attend the treaty. The Wyandot chiefs betrayed
Wilson's presence to the British commander, Colonel Henry Hamilton, Lieutenant Governor, to whom Wilson frankly told the object of his mission. Though greatly angered, Hamilton respected
Wilson's character as an ambassador, and gave him a safe conduct through the Indian country to Fort Pitt; but scathingly denounced White Eyes, and ordered him to leave Detroit within
twenty-four hours, if he valued his life.

White Eyes Makes Alliance With the Americans

The Delawares on the Tuscarawas and Muskingum, owing
principally to the influence of White Eyes, having maintained
neutrality between the Americans and the British, during the early
years of the Revolutionary War, and this remarkable chieftain
having shown an intelligent sympathy with the American cause and
expressed the hope that the Delaware Nation might form the four-

teenth state in the American union, Congress, in June, 1778, ordered a treaty to be held at Fort Pitt, on July 23rd, for the purpose of forming an alliance with these Indians, and requested Virginia to choose two commissioners and Pennsylvania, one, for this purpose. Pennsylvania neglected to choose a commissioner; but Virginia appointed General Andrew Lewis, the conqueror of Cornstalk, at Point Pleasant, and his brother, Thomas Lewis, a civilian. The time of the treaty was postponed to September, owing to the inability of the American troops to reach Fort Pitt in July.

Messengers had been sent to the Shawnees, inviting them to come with the Delawares to the treaty, but they declined, except a small band under Nimwha, who lived with the Delawares at Coshocton.

The conference began on September 12th, and the treaty was signed on the 17th. Besides White Eyes, the Delawares were represented by Killbuck, successor to New Comer of the Turtle Clan, Captain Pipe, successor to Custaloga, of the Wolf Clan, and Wingenund, the Delaware "wise man." These three chiefs appeared at the councils, in all their gaudy attire, painted, feathered, and beaded; while General McIntosh and his staff officers attended in new uniforms. The interpreter was Job Chilloway, a Delaware from the Susquehanna, who had learned the English language from having lived for a number of years among the white people.

General Lewis advised the Delaware chiefs of his intention to send an army against the British at Detroit, and asked the permission of the Delawares for the army to pass through the territory over which they claimed control, bounded on the east by the Ohio and Allegheny, and on the west by the Hocking and Sandusky.

By the terms of the treaty as finally concluded, all offenses were mutually forgiven; a perpetual friendship was pledged; each party agreed to assist the other in any just war; the Delawares gave permission for an American army to pass through their territory, and agreed to furnish meat, corn, warriors and guides for the army. The United States agreed to erect and garrison a fort, within the Delaware country, for the protection of the old men, women, and children; and each party agreed to punish offenses committed by citizens of the other, according to a system to be arranged later. The United States promised the establishment of fair and honest trade relations; and lastly, the United States guaranteed the integrity of the Delaware nation, and promised to admit it as a state of the American Union, "provided nothing contained in this article be considered as conclusive until it meets the approbation of congress." With reference to the promise to admit the Delaware nation as a state of the Union, the commissioners must have known that this was an impossibility.

But the guileless White Eyes never suspected that he and his people were being imposed upon. Said he: "Brothers, we are become one people. We [the Delawares], are at a loss to express our thoughts, but we hope soon to convince you by our actions of the sincerity of our hearts. We now inform you that as many of our warriors as can possibly be spared will join you and go with you."

The great courage of White Eyes in forming this alliance of the Delawares with the Americans is seen when it is recalled that all the other western tribes were on the side of the English, and, for some time, had been endeavoring, by solicitation and threats, to draw the Delawares into a British alliance. Governor Hamilton, at Detroit, who had charge of the operations of the British against the frontiers, had been ordered, on October 6th, 1776, to enlist the various western tribes and have them ready for a campaign against the frontier the next spring. Hamilton gave the savages fifty dollars for each American scalp taken by them. The Americans held him in abhorrence, and called him the "hair-buyer" general. For more than two years before White Eyes allied his people with the Americans, the other western tribes, instigated by the British and induced by the scalp bounty, were desolating the Pennsylvania frontier. The terrible situation of the settlers in this region is shown by the following letter written to President Wharton, in November, 1777, by Archibald Lochry, County Lieutenant of Westmoreland:

"The distressed situation of our country is such, that we have no prospect but desolation and destruction. The whole country on the north side of the road [Forbes Road] from the Allegheny Mountains to the river is all kept close in forts; and can get no subsistance from their plantations; they have made application to us requesting to be put under pay, and receive rations. . . . . . As we could see no other way to keep these people from flying and letting the country be evacuated, we were obliged to adopt these measures."

Then, on March 28th, 1778, the Pittsburgh Tories, Captain Alexander McKee, Matthew Elliott, Robert Surphlit, and Simon Girty, deserted the American force at Fort Pitt, and went over to the British. McKee was a man of education, and had long been in secret correspondence with British officers in Canada. General

Hand, the commandant at Fort Pitt, had received a hint of Mc-Kee's intention, early in the evening, and he ordered a squad of soldiers to go to the deserter's house the next morning, and remove him to the fort. When the troops arrived the next morning, they found that the renegades had escaped from McKee's house during the night. For a number of years, Captain McKee had lived on a plantation of fourteen hundred acres, at the mouth of Chartiers Creek, granted to him by Colonel Bouquet, in 1764, the site of the town of McKees Rocks, on the left bank of the Ohio, in Allegheny County. It was from the house on this plantation that he made his escape.

He and his companions made their way to the chief town of the Delawares, Coshocton, Ohio, where they endeavored to arouse this tribe against the Americans. A great debate took place in the Delaware council between Captain Pipe, who advocated that the Delawares give McKee's request favorable consideration, and White Eyes, who, by his oratory thwarted the plans of the renegades.

The renegades then went to the Shawnees on the Scioto, where they were welcomed. James Girty, a brother of Simon, was there with the Shawnees, having been sent by the commandant of Fort Pitt on a peace embassy. This natural savage at once joined his brother and the other tories. Then Governor Hamilton, learning that McKee and his companions were among the Shawnees, sent Edward Hazle to the Scioto, who conducted them safely to Detroit, where Hamilton gave them commissions in the British service, and they became the merciless scourgers of the frontiers.

Thus, it is seen that White Eyes, in daring to form an alliance with the Americans, exposed the Delawares to destruction by the British and their savage allies. But he had the courage to do what he believed to be right.

White Eyes' Grand Plan

At this treaty, White Eyes avowed that his people had embraced Christianity. During the few years prior to this treaty, the Moravian missionaries made good progress in Christianizing the Delawares, under White Eyes, in their villages on the Tuscarawas. White Eyes told the Moravians, in 1774, that he sincerely believed the Gospel. He then unfolded to Bishop Zeisberger this grand plan: Christianity should be the national religion. He would go to England and lay before the king the differences between the Delawares and the white people, tell the king of the rapid westward march of the whites, and induce him to guarantee to the Delawares the country they then possessed, which should be their home to all generations. There the Delawares would live as a civilized and Christian people. To bring about this happy result should be the work of the Moravian missions. Then White Eyes journied to Philadelphia and requested the Continental Congress to send the Delawares teachers and clergymen of the Episcopal Church. Lord Dunmore had promised this remarkable chief his assistance; but later, on account of the disturbed condition of the colonies, persuaded him to give up his projected visit to England.

The noble aspirations of the great chieftain command our admiration. Behold the contrast between the plans of Pontiac and those of White Eyes. Pontiac desired the Indian to remain for all time a warrior and hunter; and, in an attempt to carry his plans into execution, and drive the English into the sea, he drenched the frontiers with the blood of the settlers. White Eyes, on the other hand, deeming the plow a blessing and all the implements of industry good, hoped, by statesman-like negotiations, to secure for his people a home, where they might enjoy the benefits of civilization.

Plot Against Friendly Delawares

Due to the alliance between the Delawares and the United States, Colonel Broadhead, then commandant at Fort Pitt, in the autumn of 1780 received the aid of more than forty friendly Delawares, who had come to assist him in his operations against the hostile tribes. In a letter to President Reed, dated November 2nd, 1780, he says: "I believe I could have called out near an hundred. But as upwards of forty men from the neighborhood of Hannastown have attempted to destroy them whilst they consider themselves under our protection, it may not be an easy matter to call them out again, notwithstanding they [the Hannastown settlers] were prevented from executing their unmanly intention, by a guard of regular soldiers posted for the Indians' protection. I was not a little surprised to find that the late Captains Irwin and Jack, Lieutenant Brownlee, and Ensign Guthrie concerned in this base attempt. I suppose the women and children were to suffer an equal carnage with the men."

It was very fortunate for Colonel Broadhead that he was able to save the lives of these friendly Delawares. Provisions at Fort Pitt had become very scarce, and Colonel Broadhead had sent

Captain Samuel Brady through the Chartier's Creek settlement for the purpose of procuring cattle and sheep for the hungry garrison. The Scotch-Irish settlers of this region greatly resented Brady's activities, and his mission was a failure. Then Colonel Broadhead sent many of the friendly Delawares, whose lives he had saved, to the Great Kanawha to spend the winter there hunting buffaloes, and to bring the meat to Fort Pitt.

White Eyes and Heckewelder

White Eyes was a very warm friend of the Moravian missionary, Heckewelder. They first met when Heckewelder visited him at his home near the mouth of the Beaver, when the missionary was on his way to the Tuscarawas in the spring of 1762. Heckewelder relates the following incidents in the life of this noted chieftain:

"In the year 1777, while the Revolutionary War was raging, and several Indian tribes had enlisted on the British side, and were spreading murder and devastation along our unprotected frontier, I rather rashly determined to take a journey into the country on a visit to my friends. Captain White Eyes, the Indian hero, whose character I have already described, resided at that time at the distance of seventeen miles from the place where I lived. Hearing of my determination, he immdiately hurried up to me, with his friend Captain Wingenund, whom I shall presently have occasion further to mention, and some of his young men, for the purpose of escorting me to Pittsburgh, saying, 'that he would not suffer me to go, while the Sandusky warriors were out on war excursions, without a proper escort and himself at my side.' He insisted on accompanying me, and we set out together. One day, as we were proceeding along, our spies discovered a suspicious track. White Eyes, who was riding before me, inquired whether I felt afraid. I answered that while he was with me, I entertained no fear. On this he immediately replied: 'You are right; for until I am laid prostrate at your feet, no one shall hurt you.' 'And even not then,' added Wingenund, who was riding behind me; 'before this happens, I must be also overcome, and lay by the side of our friend Koguethagechton [the Indian name of White Eyes].' I believed them, and I believe at this day that these great men were sincere, and that, if they had been put to the test, they would have shown it, as did another Indian friend by whom my life was saved in the spring of the year 1781. From behind a log in the bushes where he was concealed, he espied a hostile Indian at the very moment he was leveling his piece at me. Quick as lightning he jumped between us, and exposed his person to the musket shot just about to be fired, when fortunately the aggressor desisted, from fear of hitting the Indian whose body thus effectually protected me, at the imminent risk of his own life. Captain White Eyes, in the year 1774, saved in the same manner the life of David Duncan, the peace messenger, whom he was escorting. He rushed, regardless of his own life, up to an inimical Shawanese, who was aiming at our ambassador from behind a bush, and forced him to desist."

Death of White Eyes

Immediately after the forming of the alliance with the Delawares, General McIntosh, then in command at Fort Pitt, prepared to lead an expedition against the British at Detroit. With an army of thirteen hundred troops, he moved down the Ohio to the mouth of the Beaver early in October, 1778. Here he built Fort McIntosh on the high bluff overlooking the Ohio, on the western side of the Beaver. Four weeks were consumed in erecting the fort, and the sixty Delaware warriors who accompanied the army, could not understand why so much time was spent in erecting a fortification that would not be needed when Detroit was taken. However, on November 5th, the army began its march through the wilderness towards Detroit. In accordance with the provisions of the treaty with the Delawares, General McIntosh intended to erect a fort for the protection of their women and children at the Delaware capital of Coshocton at the junction of the Tuscarawas and the Walhonding. On the march to the Tuscarawas, White Eyes was treacherously put to death, it is believed by a Virginia militiaman, causing dismay among the warriors, most of whom returned to Coshocton. Such is the account of his death, given by most authorities. However, DeSchweinitz, in his "Life of David Zeisberger", says that this greatest and best of the later Delaware chiefs died of small-pox on November 10th, in the camp on the Tuscarawas. But whatever the manner of his death, whether by the hand of an assassin or by small-pox, the sudden ending of his earthly career had the effect of causing General McIntosh to abandon the attempt to take Detroit that winter.

Says DeSchweinitz: "Where his [White Eyes'] remains are resting, no man knows; the plowshare has often furrowed his grave. But his name lives; and the Christian may hope that in the resurrection of the just, he, too will be found among the great multitude redeemed out of every kindred, and tongue, and people, and nation."

KILLBUCK

Upon the death of White Eyes, Killbuck, the firm friend of the Americans, was elected as his successor. However, he soon found himself in the minority, and Captain Pipe, the head of the war faction among the Delawares, influenced the great Delaware council at Coshocton, as will be seen in Chapter XXVI, in February, 1781, to join the hostile tribes in alliance with the British. Killbuck was absent at Fort Pitt when this action was taken, and on account of threats against his life, was afraid to return to Coshocton. He went to Salem, located on the Tuscarawas about fourteen miles below New Philadelphia. Here, on February 26th, he wrote a long letter by the hand of Missionary Heckewelder, to Colonel Broadhead, advising him of the action taken by the Delaware council. Then, as will be seen in Chapter XXVI, Broadhead determined to punish the Delawares for their perfidy, and in April, 1781, led an expedition against the Delaware capital of Coshocton. As Broadhead's troops were on their way back from the attack at Coshocton and while resting at New Comer's Town, Killbuck appeared in the camp and threw at Broadhead's feet the scalp of "one of the greatest villians" among the hostile Delawares.

After Broadhead's expedition against Coshocton, the hostile Delawares, under their leader, Captain Pipe, went to the headwaters of the Sandusky, while those friendly to the United States moved, with Killbuck, to Smoky Island (also known as Killbuck's Island) within sight of Fort Pitt. Here Killbuck remained until after the Revolutionary War.

Killbuck's Indian name was Gelelemend (i. e. a leader). He was a grandson of the great New Comer. In consequence of his friendship for the United States during the Revolutionary War, he incurred the hatred of the war faction among the Delawares, which continued even after the general peace concluded between the Delawares and the United States by the treaty of Greenville, August 3rd, 1795. Most authorities say he was born near the Lehigh Water Gap, Carbon County, Pennsylvania, in 1737. In the summer of 1788, he united with the Moravian Indians at Salem, on the Petquotting, in Tuscarawas County, Ohio, being given, in baptism, the name ,William Henry, after Judge William Henry of Lancaster, Pennsylvania. Here he died in the early winter of 1811. Says DeSchweinitz: "The vices of the generation, which he had lived to see, caused him deep sorrow, and he protested, even with his dying breath, against their degeneracy."

CHAPTER XXVI

Captain Pipe and Glikkikan

CAPTAIN PIPE

APTAIN PIPE was a chief of the Wolf Clan of Delawares, and succeeded Custaloga. He was "a very artful and designing man, and a chief of considerable ability and influence." He was very active in Pontiac's War; and when Colonel Bouquet left Fort Pitt, in the summer of 1764, on his way to bring the western tribes into subjection, and compel them to surrender the prisoners taken in that memorable uprising, he had this chief detained at the fort as a hostage.

Shortly after the treaty held at Fort Pitt on October 27, 1775, at which White Eyes, replying to the taunts of Guyasuta, boldly asserted the independence of the Delawares, Captain Pipe seceded from the tribe with a number of his followers. His ostensible reason for this action was that he feared that the speech of White Eyes would arouse the anger and vengeance of the Iroquois; but his real reason seems to have been that he was not in sympathy with the friendly attitude of the Delawares towards the American cause; for later on he boldly declared against the Americans.

When the renegades, McKee, Elliott, and Girty, came to the Delaware capital of Coshocton in the spring of 1778, they reported that the American armies on the Atlantic Seaboard had been overwhelmed by the English. This false report encouraged Captain Pipe to renew vigorously his attempts to have the Delawares take up arms against the Americans. It has already been related how he was opposed in the Delaware council by White Eyes, whose oratory prevailed. The Moravian missionary, Rev. John Heckewelder, left Bethlehem, Pa., on March 23, 1778, to visit the Moravian missions in Ohio. Arriving at Fort Pitt, he found the garrison much disturbed over the flight of the tories, McKee, Elliott, and Girty, and hastened to the Ohio Delawares as fast as his horse could carry him. Upon his arrival, he gave the Delaware council the true state of affairs as to military operations in the East, advising them of the recent capture of General Burgoyne and his army. Captain Pipe then left the council in chagrin and went back to his village.

On the death of White Eyes, Captain Pipe continued as head of the war faction among the Delawares; and so great was his influence that he succeeded in persuading the majority of the tribe, in violation of the alliance which they had made with the Americans, to go over to the British. The Delaware council at Coshocton took this action in February, 1781, during the absence of Killbuck at Fort Pitt. Colonel Broadhead, then in command at Fort Pitt, determined to attack the Delaware town of Coshocton, and punish them for their perfidy. He proceeded to Wheeling with his little army of three hundred troops, from which place he took up the march toward the Delaware capital, on April 10th. On April 20th, Broadhead's advance having come upon three Delawares about a mile from Coshocton, captured one, but the other two escaped and gave the alarm. Broadhead's force then dashed into the Delaware capital, where they found but fifteen warriors, every one of whom was put to death in the resistless rush of the American troops; but no harm was done to the old men, women and children. Broadhead's troops then set fire to the town after having "taken great quantities of peltry and other stores", and destroyed about forty head of cattle. The reason that Broadhead found so few warriors in Coshocton was that a band of forty who had just returned from a raid on the settlements, laden with scalps and prisoners, had crossed to the farther side of the river, a few miles above the town, to enjoy a drunken revel. On account of the swollen condition of the stream and the fact that the war parties had taken their canoes with them, the troops were unable to cross to the farther side. Broadhead wished to send a detail to the Moravian towns farther up the river, for the purpose of procuring boats; but the volunteer soldiers protested, saying that they had done enough, suffered severely from the weather, had almost worn out their horses, and proposed to return to fort Pitt. The Colonel, finding that he could not help himself, inasmuch as the troops were not subject to strict military discipline, consented to their proposal.

On the return march, Broadhead followed the Tuscarawas to New Comer's Town, at which place he found about thirty friendly Delawares who had withdrawn from Coshocton when the Delaware council voted to espouse the British cause. "The troops," said Broadhead in his report of the expedition, "experienced great kindness from the Moravian Indians and those at New Comer's Town, and obtained a sufficient supply of meat and corn to subsist the men and horses to the Ohio River."

Captain Pipe Befriends the Moravian Missionaries

When the Delaware council at Coshocton voted to take up arms against the United States, the Moravian converts renounced all fellowship with them. The British, believing that the converts were being instigated by the Moravian missionaries to take an active part on the American side, set on foot measures to punish them. A treaty with the Iroquois took place at Niagara, at which the renegade, McKee, as agent of Indian affairs, proposed, by authority of the commandant of Detroit, an expedition against the Moravian towns. The Six Nations were not willing themselves to take part in the expedition, but sent a message to the Chippewas and Ottawas, saying: "We give you the believing Indians and their teachers to make broth of." These tribes declined, and then the same message was sent to the Wyandots, whose chief accepted it, but, as he protested, merely in order to save the lives of the Christian Indians. The expedition was then planned at a great feast among the Shawnees on the Scioto "in the presence and by the help of British officers and under the folds of the British flag. Wyandots, Mingoes, and Delawares, together with a few Shawnees, formed the troop. To the captains only was the real object of the expedition made known. They received secret instructions to drive the Christian Indians from their seats, to seize their teachers, and either convey them as prisoners to Detroit, or put them to death and bring their scalps."

The result of the expedition was that the Moravian missions were broken up, the Christian Delawares taken to the north bank of the Sandusky, in Wyandot County, Ohio, and the Moravian missionaries taken to Detroit for trial, on the charge that they had rendered assistance to the Americans. The exodus from the missions began in September, 1781; and the trial took place in November, before Major De Pyster, who had succeeded to the command of Detroit after the capture of Hamilton, the "hair buyer", by George Rogers Clark, in February, 1779. De Pyster opened the council by rehearsing the charges against the missionaries, and then addressing Captain Pipe, asked him whether the accusations were correct and founded in fact, and especially whether the missionaries had corresponded with the Americans.

"There may be some truth in the accusations," said Captain Pipe. "I am not prepared to say that all that you have heard is false. But now nothing more of that sort will occur. The teachers are here." De Pyster replied: "I infer, therefore, that these men have corresponded with the rebels, and sent letters to Fort Pitt. From your answer this seems to be evident. Tell me, is it so?"

Captain Pipe then sprang to his feet and exclaimed: "Father, I have said that there may be some truth in the reports that have reached you; but now I will tell you exactly what has occurred. These teachers are innocent. On their own account they never wrote letters; they had to do it. I [striking upon his breast] and the chiefs at Goshachgunk are responsible. We induced these teachers to write letters to Pittsburgh, even at such times when they at first declined. But this will no more occur, as I have said, because they are now here."

Major De Pyster then acquitted the missionaries, explaining that he was not opposed to the preaching of the Gospel among the Indians and cautioned the missionaries not to meddle with the war. He gave them permission to return to their converts as soon as they pleased.

Andrew Poe's Fight with Big Foot

"A striking incident in the history of Washington County was connected with the removal of the Moravians [to Sandusky, just related]. While the exiles were being conducted up the Walhonding, seven Wyandot warriors left the company and went on a raid across the Ohio River. Among the seven were three sons of Duquat, the half-king, and the eldest son, Scotosh, was the leader of the party. They crossed the Ohio on a raft, which they hid in the mouth of Tomlinson's run. They visited the farm of Philip Jackson, on Harman's creek, and captured Jackson in his flax field. The prisoner was a carpenter, about 60 years old, and his trade made him valuable to the Indians, as he could build houses for them. The savages did not return directly to their raft, but traveled by devious ways to the river, to baffle pursuit. The taking of the carpenter was seen by his son, who ran nine miles to Ft. Cherry, on Little Raccoon Creek, and gave the alarm. Pursuit the same evening was prevented by a heavy rain, but the next morning seventeen stout young men, all mounted, gathered at Jackson's farm. Most of the borderers decided to follow the crooked and half obliterated trail, but John Jack, a professional scout, declared that he believed he knew where the Indians had hidden their raft, and called for followers. Six men joined him, John Cherry, Andrew Poe, Adam Poe, William Castleman,

William Rankin, and James Whitacre, and they rode on a gallop directly for the mouth of Tomlinson's run.

"Jack's surmise was a shrewd one, based on a thorough knowledge of the Ohio River and the habits of the Indians. At the top of the river hill, the borderers tied their horses in a grove and descended cautiously to the river bank. At the mouth of the run were five Indians, with their prisoner, preparing to shove off their raft. John Cherry fired the first shot, killed an Indian, and was himself killed by the return fire. Four of the five Indians were slain, Philip Jackson was rescued without injury, and Scotosh escaped up the river with a wound in his right hand.

"Andrew Poe, in approaching the river, had gone aside to follow a trail that deviated to the left. Peering over a little bluff, he saw two of the sons of the half-king sitting by the stream. The sound of the firing at the mouth of the run alarmed them, and they arose. Poe's gun missed fire, and he jumped directly upon the two savages, throwing them to the ground. A fierce wrestling contest took place. Andrew Poe was six feet tall, of unusual strength, and almost a match for the two brothers. One of them wounded him in the wrist with a tomahawk, but he got possession of the only rifle that was in working order and loaded, and fatally shot the one who had cut him. Poe and the other savage [His English name was Big Foot. He was a large and powerful Indian] contested for the mastery, awhile on the shore, and then in the water, where Andrew attempted to drown his antagonist. The Indian escaped, reached land and began to load his gun, when Andrew struck out for the opposite shore, shouting for his brother Adam. At the opportune moment, Adam appeared and shot the Indian through the body, but before he expired the savage rolled into the water and his corpse was carried away down the stream. One of the borderers, mistaking Andrew in the stream for an Indian, fired at him and wounded him in the shoulder. The triumphant return of the party to Ft. Cherry was saddened by the death of John Cherry, who was a man of great popularity and a natural leader on the frontier.

"Scotosh, the only survivor of the raiding band, succeeded in swimming the Ohio and hid over night in the woods. In the morning he made a small raft, recrossed the stream, recovered the body of his brother lying on the beach, conveyed it to the Indian side of the river and buried it in the woods. He then made his way to Upper Sandusky, with a sad message for his father and the tribe."
—(Hassler's "Old Westmoreland").

Moravian Delawares Murdered—Crawford Burned

The most dastardly act of Captain Pipe's career was the burning of Colonel William Crawford, the friend of Washington, at the stake, near Sandusky, Ohio, in June, 1782. But, before giving the details of this atrocious act, attention is called to the following facts which led to the same:

In the spring of 1781 Killbuck, after the destruction of Coshocton by Colonel Broadhead, removed with Nanowland and a few other friendly Delawares with their relatives to the vicinity of Fort Pitt, taking up their residence on a small island at the mouth of the Allegheny, known as Killbuck Island, later Smoky Island, and gave active assistance to the American cause. Killbuck became a colonel in the army, and some of his men received commissions as captains.

In the autumn of 1781, the Scotch-Irish settlers of Western Pennsylvania, believed that the Moravian converts on the Tuscarawas, even if they did not join the war parties, were giving food and shelter to the hostile Indians. David Williamson of Washington County, gathered up a force of about one hundred men, and marched to the Tuscarawas, in November, to compel the Moravians either to remove to Fort Pitt, or to migrate farther into the hostile country. Williamson was unaware that the missions had already been broken up, the converts taken to Sandusky, and the missionaries to Detroit. He found only a few Christian Indians who had wandered back to gather corn. These he conducted to Fort Pitt.

The spring of 1782 opened early, mild weather beginning about the first of February. This caused Indian raids in Southwestern Pennsylvania to begin as early as February 8th, greatly alarming and perplexing the settlers, as they could not believe that the Indians had come from a point farther away than the Moravian missions on the Tuscarawas. Among the outrages committed at this time were the murder of John Fink, on February 8th, near Buchanan's Fort on the upper Monongahela; the murder of Mrs. Robert Wallace, and the capture of her three children on February 10th, on Raccoon Creek, near Vance's Fort, Washington County; and the capture of John Carpenter, on February 15th, on the Dutch Fork of Buffalo Creek, in Washington County. Four of the Indians who captured Carpenter were Wyandots, but two others, who spoke German, informed Carpenter that they were Moravians. After his captors had taken him across the Ohio, Carpenter made his escape. Coming to Fort Pitt, he told Colonel Gibson the story of his capture, and then returned to his home on Buffalo Creek, where he told his story to the settlers.

Accordingly, the settlers of Washington County turned out to the number of one hundred sixty, under the command of Colonel Williamson, and crossing the Ohio at Mingo Bottom, a few miles below Steubenville, marched against the Moravian villages. On the evening of March 6th, they were within striking distance of the Moravian town of Gnadenhuetten, when their scouts brought the intelligence to the camp at night that the town was full of Indians. Williamson and his force believed that the occupants of the town were the savages who had been making the raids, but as a matter of fact they were Moravian converts who, after being compelled to go to Sandusky in the preceding autumn, had come back to their old homes to gather their corn.

Williamson attacked the town the next morning. The presence of women and children was plain notice to the frontiersmen that the town was not occupied by a war party. Furthermore, no resistance was made and there was no show of hostile action. Holding a council with a few of the converts who could speak English, Williamson advised them that they must go to Fort Pitt instead of returning to Sandusky. To this they agreed, and at his suggestion, sent messengers down the river to Salem to tell the converts of that place to come to Gnadenhuetten. While the Indians were being assembled and conducted to the church at Gnadenhuetten, an Indian woman was found to be wearing the dress of the wife of Robert Wallace, who, as we have seen, had been killed on February 10th on Raccoon Creek, Washington County, and three of her children captured by some hostile Indians. The Indian men were then examined, one at a time, but none of them acknowledged guilt. It developed, however, that some Wyandot warriors who had journeyed with the converts from Sandusky halted a short period at Gnadenhuetten, and then proceeded on their way to pillage the frontier settlements.

The frontiersmen then began to clamor for the execution of the whole band of Delawares, and Williamson put the question to vote whether they should be taken to Fort Pitt or put to death on the spot. All but eighteen voted to slay all the Indians in the morning.

Bishop Loskiel, in his "History of the Missions of the United Brethren", says that the converts were informed that evening of the fate which awaited them, and that they spent the night in praying, singing hymns, and exhorting one another to die with the fortitude of Christians.

Accordingly, on the morning of Friday, March 8th, 1782, the terrible decree was carried into execution. The Indian men were led two by two to the cooper shop, where they were beaten to death with mallets and hatchets. Many of them died with prayers on their lips, while others met their death chanting songs. Altogether eighty men, twenty women, and thirty-four children were inhumanly butchered. Only two escaped. One was a boy who hid himself in the cellar under the house in which the women and children were butchered, and crept forth during the night. The other was a boy who was scalped among the men, but later revived and crawled into the woods in the night time.

Before Williamson's troops left for home, they burned every building in Gnadenhuetten, "including the two slaughter houses with their heaped-up corpses." The neighboring Moravian villages of Schoenbrun and Salem were also reduced to ashes.

About two weeks after Williamson's forces reached home, the militiamen living in the valley of Chartier's Creek assembled again, and marched against the friendly Delawares on Killbuck Island. The attack was made on Sunday morning, March 24th The United States soldiers on the island were made prisoners, and several of the friendly Indians were shot down, among them being Nanowland, the friend of Captain Samuel Brady. Chief Killbuck, however, and most of his band, succeeded in making their escape to Fort Pitt, where Colonel Gibson, then in temporary command, protected them. Two warriors fled through the woods to Sandusky, one being Chief Big Cat, who ever afterward was the bitter foe of the Americans. Before the militiamen returned to their homes, they sent word to Colonel Gibson that they would kill and scalp him at the first opportunity, for no other reason than that he had protected the friendly Indians and saved them from a fate like that which befell the Christian Delawares at Gnadenhuetten.

Although many of the Western Pennsylvania frontiersmen approved Colonel Williamson's butchery of the Indian women and children at Gnadenhuetten, they felt that, after all it was not a glorious exploit. It was not long until there was a general desire throughout Washington County especially, for a campaign against the Western Indians, especially the Wyandot and Delaware towns on the Sandusky River. A general call then went out for volunteers to strike the stronghold of these Indians. The general muster was fixed for Monday, May 20th, at Mingo Bottom; and a few days later, four hundred and eighty horsemen assembled at that place, and elected Colonel William Crawford as leader of the expedition, he, through the influence of General Irvine, then in command at Fort Pitt, receiving five votes over Colonel David Williamson. General Irvine had been requested to lead the expedition, but declined. When he was pressed to give the expedition assistance, he agreed to furnish some gun flints and powder, on condition that the expedition would conform to military laws and regulations. He also detailed Surgeon John Knight and Lieutenant Rose to serve in the expedition.

While preparations were being made for this expedition, the Ohio Indians, aroused to greater hostility by the butchery at Gnadenhuetten, made many incursions into Washington and Westmoreland counties. "Thomas Edgerton was captured on Harman's Creek and John Stevenson near West Liberty. Five soldiers were ambushed in the woods near Fort McIntosh; two were killed and the three others were taken to Lower Sandusky, where they successfully ran the gauntlet. Two men were killed on the border of Washington County; at Walthour's Block House, near Brush Creek in Westmoreland, a man of name of Willard was killed and his daughter carried away and murdered in the woods. On Sunday, May 12th, Rev. John Corbly and his family, while walking to their meeting house on Muddy Creek, in what is now Green County, were attacked by the savages. The preacher alone escaped without injury. The wife and three children were killed and scalped. Two daughters were scalped, but survived to endure their suffering."—(Hassler's "Old Westmoreland").

On May 25th, the expedition left Mingo Bottom, and marched towards Sandusky. On the 28th, the troops turned aside to visit the ruins of the Moravian town at Shoenbrun, where they fed their horses on the standing corn. On the evening of June 13th, the troops reached the upper Indian town on the Sandusky finding the place deserted, the Indians having had warning of Colonel Crawford's approach. Crawford then advised a retirement, but was overruled in council. The next morning the command began the march toward the principal Wyandot town, proceeding through the beautiful plain on the west side of the Sandusky River.

In the afternoon, as the troops neared a large grove, they were fired upon by British and Indians in the grove. The Americans, however, charged, and driving out the enemy, occupied the grove themselves. Dismounting and forming a line along the northern side of the grove, they for several hours exchanged a brisk rifle fire with the British and Indians lying in the bushes. In this combat, five of Crawford's men were killed and nineteen wounded, while the enemy lost six killed, and eleven wounded, among the wounded being the British commander, Captain Caldwell.

During the night, Crawford's men were unable to get much rest owing to the hideous yells of the savages, and when the day dawned, the battle was resumed in long-range fighting. In the afternoon, a band of one hundred and forty Shawnees joined the other Indians. The Americans observed their arrival, and believing that they were greatly outnumbered by the savages, held a council of war in which it was decided to retreat during the night. As a matter of fact, however, the Indian forces, even when augmented by the arrival of the Shawnees, did not exceed the number of Crawford's forces.

No sooner had Crawford's men begun to retreat during the night, than a strange panic seized them. Many fired their guns into the darkness, and others leaving the ranks fled like maniacs across the prairie. Meanwhile, the savages were slaying and scalping the straggling fugitives. A few of the troops, exhausted by the long fighting, had fallen asleep in the grove and awoke to find themselves deserted. These were almost all overtaken and scalped

In the expedition were Crawford's only son, John, his nephew, William Crawford, and his son-in-law, William Harrison. In the wild retreat, the Colonel was unable to find them. Standing by the trail as the fugitives rushed by, he called for his son, and receiving no answer, fell to the rear and became lost. He then met with Dr. Knight, the surgeon, and nine other men; and together they wandered about for two days, when they were captured by a band of Delawares. Captain Pipe ordered them to be burned at the stake. In the meantime, Colonel Williamson had made good his escape, and with 300 soldiers, arrived at Mingo Bottom, on June 12th.

In the hope of escaping such a dreadful fate, Colonel Crawford asked that his old friend, the Delaware chief, Wingenund, might be sent for. Wingenund appeared before the Colonel, who entreated him to save his life, calling his attention to the fact that they had always been friends. Wingenund reluctantly advised the Colonel that it was beyond his power to save him. He told him that the Delawares and other tribes making up the Indian forces, were determined to avenge Colonel Williamson's butchery of the helpless women and children at Gnadenhuetten during the preceding March. He told Crawford that if Colonel Williamson had not been with Crawford's forces, it might be possible to save Crawford's life; that the Indians had their spies watching Crawford's march from the very beginning; and that these spies saw him turn aside from the line of march and visit the ruins at Shoenbrun. These things, said Wingenund, convinced the Indians that Crawford's expedition was simply seeking an opportunity to commit an outrage similar to the atrocity committed by Williamson's troops, especially since Williamson hastened to retreat. Failing to capture the hated Williamson, they determined that Crawford must pay the penalty. Then Wingenund burst into tears, and turned aside that he might not witness the torture of his friend.

The place of Crawford's torture was in the valley of Tymoochee Creek, about five miles west of upper Sandusky. He was tied by a long rope to a pole; his body was shot full of gun powder; his ears were cut off; burning fagots were pressed against his skin, and he was horribly gashed with knives. The unfortunate man endured this terrible agony for four hours in the presence of Dr. Knight and the renegades, Simon Girty and Matthew Elliott. He appealed to Girty to shoot him and end his misery, but in vain. Falling unconscious, his scalp was torn off, and burning embers were poured upon his bleeding head. The excruciating pain revived him; he rose to his feet and started once more to walk around the pole, then groaned and fell dead. The indians then burned his body to ashes.

Thus perished this prominent man of the Western Pennsylvania frontier, the friend and land agent of George Washington. His residence was, for some years prior to his tragic death, at Connellsville, Fayette County. Crawford County bears his name.

The other prisoners were divided among the several Indian villages, and tortured to death. So far as is known, only two escaped, Dr. Knight, the surgeon, and John Slover, one of the guides.

Captain Pipe Rebukes the Shawnees

During the summer of 1793, commissioners representing the United States endeavored to establish peace between the Western Indians and the United States Government after the defeats of General Harmar and General St. Clair. In the latter part of July, these commissioners were met at the mouth of the Detroit River by about thirty chiefs of the Western Indians, who came to inquire whether the United States would consent to the Ohio River as the boundary line of the Indian territory. The commissioners replied that this was impossible, and offered large presents if the Indians would confirm the limits as agreed upon by the treaties of Fort McIntosh and Fort Harmar. This reply was reported to a grand council of the western tribes on the Maumee. Then a violent debate took place; some of the Indians were in favor of peace on these terms, and others advocated that the war go on. Among the latter were the Shawnees who were under the influence of Simon Girty and other British emissaries. Among those who were in favor of peace was Captain Pipe. Addressing Captain Henry, chief of the Mohawks, Pipe delivered the following sarcastic speech referring to the circumstances under which the Shawnees came to Pennsylvania in the early days of the history of the Province: "See the Shawnees. You brought him to me when he was a little boy; you gave him to me, saying, 'Have mercy on this child; receive him that he may live; you are old, and he may help you, fetch you a drink of water occasionally, and shoot you a squirrel!' Moved with pity, I consented; received the Shawnees; adopted him as my grandson, because, without a single friend in the world, he went about forsaken and forlorn. I kept him with me; I instructed him in that which is good; I educated him; he was always about me. But no sooner had he reached manhood than he became disobedient. I admonished him; I punished him; but he grew more wicked continually. And now he listens neither to me nor to any one else, but does evil only. Therefore I am of the opinion that the Great Spirit did not create the Shawnees, but that the devil created him."

Last Days of Captain Pipe

Little is recorded concerning Captain Pipe's activities from the time of the torture of Colonel Crawford. He remained friendly to the Moravian missionaries, and expressed regret that he had been a party to causing the removal of the Christian Delawares from the Tuscarawas to Sandusky, in the autumn of 1781. When Washington became first president of the United States, in 1789, the old chief urged the western tribes to maintain peaceful relations with the young republic. He ended his days shortly before the overwhelming defeat of these Indians by General Wayne, at the Battle of the Fallen Timbers, on the 20th day of August, 1794.

GLIKKIKAN

Among the Christian Delawares who were killed at the Gnadenhuetten massacre was Glikkikan. He had formerly lived in the

Kuskuskies region, in Lawrence County, and was the principal counsellor of the Delaware chief, Packanke, whose capital was New Kas-
kaskunk, which some authorities say stood on or near the site of
New Castle, and others on or near the site of Edenburg, Lawrence
County. In the summer of 1769, Glikkikan made a journey to
the Moravian mission at Lawunakhannek, located on the east
bank of the Allegheny, a short distance above Tionesta, Forest
County, for the purpose of refuting the doctrines of Christianity.
On his way to that place, he held a successful disputation with the
French Jesuits at Venango, and was very confident that he could
put the Moravian missionaries to confusion. Zeisberger, the head
of the mission, was absent when Glikkikan arrived, but Anthony,
a native convert and assistant, made such an impressive speech to
Glikkikan, setting forth the doctrines of Christianity, as to
astonish the chieftain. Zeisberger arrived shortly afterwards and
confirmed Anthony's speech with the result that Glikkikan, instead
of delivering the elaborate speech which he had prepared against
Christianity, replied: "I have nothing to say. I believe your
word." When he returned to his home, instead of boasting of a
victory over the Moravians, he advised his associate warriors to
go and hear the Gospel preached by the Moravians.

Soon afterwards he made another visit to the mission, informed the Moravians that he desired to embrace Christianity, and
invited them in the name of his chief, Packanke, to come and settle
on a tract of land on the Beaver near Kaskaskung, which he offered
for the use of the mission. The Moravians accepted his invitation,
and moved to the valley of the Beaver, in April, 1770, settling
where the town of Moravia, Lawrence County, now stands. Soon
thereafter Glikkikan became a devout Christian, and so continued
until his death.

The conversion of this bravest warrior and most eloquent
counsellor of Packanke exasperated this chief, and he reproached
Glikkikan, and denounced the Moravians. He taunted Glikkikan
with deserting him with his council, and with having a desire to
turn white. To these reproaches Glikkikan replied: "I have
joined the Brethren. Where they go I will go; where they lodge,
I will lodge; their people shall be my people and their God my
God." A few days later Packanke was so affected by the preaching of the Moravians that he sobbed aloud. Said Zeisberger: "A
haughty warrior captain weeps publicly in the presence of his
former associates. It is marvelous!" In the spring of 1773, the
mission at Moravia removed to the Muskingum.

CHAPTER XXVII

Cornstalk

ORNSTALK was one of the greatest chiefs of the Shawnees, and was born at least as early as 1720. Some authorities have identified him with the Shawnee chief Tamenebuck, or Taming Buck.. Assuming the identity of these two chiefs, the first important appearance of Cornstalk in the history of Pennsylvania is when he attended a conference or treaty at Philadelphia, July 27th to August 1st, 1739, along with Neucheconneh, then living at Chartier's Old Town, Kakowatcheky, then living at Wyoming, and Kishacoquillas, then living at the mouth of the creek of the same name, on the Juniata, in Mifflin County. Cornstalk was no doubt living at Chartier's Old Town, on the Allegheny, at this time. Also, assuming the identity of these two chiefs, Cornstalk was one of the Shawnee chiefs who accompanied Peter Chartier when the latter deserted to the French in 1744, and as was seen, in Chapter VIII, he was one of the Shawnee chiefs who met the Pennsylvania commissioners in council at Lancaster, July 21st, 1748, when these chiefs asked the forgiveness of the Pennsylvania authorities for having been in Chartier's band. On this occasion, he made a speech imploring forgiveness, as was also seen in Chapter VIII.

Cornstalk Commands Shawnees at Battle of Point Pleasant

In the latter years of his life, Cornstalk was the head chief of the Shawnees who had settled in the valley of the Scioto. In July, 1773, the Iroquois sold to Virginia a large tract of land south of the Kanawha. The sale greatly incensed the Shawnees, as they claimed that the land did not belong to the Iroquois Confederation. Presently settlers came in great numbers, in many cases erecting their cabins close to the wigwams of the Indians. Consequently, the indignation of the Shawnees was increased. Murders on both sides followed, bringing on that great conflict between Virginia, on the one hand, and the Shawnees and their allies, on the other, known as Lord Dunmore's War,—a war whose coming was hastened by the wanton murder of the family of Logan, chief of the Mingoes, on April 30th, 1774.

Governor Dunmore raised an army of about three thousand troops to check the Indian uprising. General Andrew Lewis commanded one division and Dunmore the other. Lewis' division of eleven hundred troops marched down the Kanawha River to Point Pleasant, West Virginia, where they were attacked on the morning of October 10th, 1774, by one thousand Indians under the command of Cornstalk. Cornstalk had opposed the entrance of his tribe into war with Virginia, but the rest of the chiefs overruled him. It is claimed that on the evening before the battle he made another attempt to bring about peace, and was again overruled.

The battle raged throughout the entire day, and above its noise and din could be heard the voice of Cornstalk as he encouraged his warriors, and shouted, "Be Strong! Be Strong!" He displayed masterly generalship, so maneuvering the Indians that the Virginians were forced into a triangle whose sides were the Ohio and Great Kanawha rivers, and whose base was the Indian forces. His tactics won the admiration of General Lewis and his officers.

At nightfall Cornstalk's forces withdrew, crossed the Ohio, and headed for the Shawnee villages. What his losses were was never ascertained, but during the battle, the Shawnees were observed to throw many of their slain into the Ohio. As for the Virginians, seventy-five of their force lay dead on the field, and one hundred and forty were wounded. A council of the chiefs was held, and although Cornstalk was bitterly opposed by many of the chiefs, he was able to persuade them to seek a peace with the Virginians.

Accordingly, in November, Cornstalk entered into a treaty of peace with Lord Dunmore, at Chillicothe, Ohio. On this occasion, he made a very impressive speech, boldly charging the whites as being the cause of the war, and dwelling at length upon the atrocious murder of the family of Logan, chief of the Mingoes. It is said that his powerful, clarion voice could be heard distinctly over the whole camp of twelve acres. Among those present was Colonel Benjamin Wilson, who speaks thus of Cornstalk's address:

"When he arose he was in nowise confused or daunted, but spoke in a distinct and audible voice without stammering or repetition and with peculiar emphasis. His looks while addressing Dunmore were truly grand and majestic; yet graceful and attractive. I have heard the first orators in Virginia, Patrick Henry and Richard Henry Lee, but never have I heard one whose powers of delivery surpassed those of Cornstalk on that occasion."

Death of Cornstalk

After making the treaty of peace with Lord Dunmore, Cornstalk remained at peace with the whites. During the spring of
1777, when most of the Ohio tribes were going over to the English,
the old chief came to the Moravian missionaries, and warned them
that the Shawnees, except those in his own tribe, were going over
to the British; that he was powerless to prevent them, and that
ammunition was being sent them from Detroit, to be used against
the Americans. On a previous visit to the Moravians with more
than one hundred of his warriors, he adopted missionary Schmick
and his wife, making Schmick his brother and Mrs. Schmick his
sister.

Seeing that there was danger of a general Indian uprising,
Cornstalk late in the summer of 1777, taking with him a young
chief named Red Hawk, went to Point Pleasant to warn Captain
Matthew Arbuckle of the threatened uprising. He and Red
Hawk were then arrested and detained as hostages. While thus
held, one afternoon his son, Ellinipisco, came to visit his father.
Unhappily, on that same day two soldiers who were out hunting
on the opposite side of the river, were attacked by two Indians,
who killed and scalped one of them. A company of men brought
the body of the dead soldier to the fort, and then the cry went up:
"Let us go and kill the Indians." The company, under the command of Captain Hall, went to the house where Cornstalk was
detained. Captain Arbuckle endeavored to restrain them, but was
threatened with death, if he interfered. Cornstalk's son was
blamed with having brought the hostile Indians with him, but this
he strenuously denied. Turning to his son, Cornstalk said: "My
son, the Great Spirit has seen fit that we should die together, and
has sent you here to that end. It is His will and let us submit;
it is all for the best." The old chief then arose and with great
dignity advanced to meet the soldiers, receiving seven bullets in his
body, and sinking in death without a groan. Ellinipisco was then
instantly killed, and Red Hawk, who had hidden himself in the
chimney, was dragged out and hacked to pieces.

Thus, one of the bravest and noblest of the Indian race, while
a hostage and on a mission of mercy, was barbarously murdered
by those whom he sought to befriend. His exalted virtues and his
most unhappy fate "plead like angels, trumpet-tongued, against
the deep damnation of his taking off", arousing the vindictive
spirit of the Shawnees, never broken, until General Wayne defeated

the western tribes at the battle of the Fallen Timbers, on the 20th day of August, 1794, and compelled them to sign the treaty of Greenville, by the terms of which they gave up possession to 25,000 square miles of territory north of the Ohio.

It seems that Cornstalk had a presentiment of approaching death. On the day before he was murdered, he was admitted to a council held at the fort, where he said: "When I was young and went to war, I often thought each might be my last adventure, and I should return no more. I still live. Now I am in the midst of you, and if you choose, may kill me. I can die but once. It is alike to me whether now or hereafter."

In 1896, a monument was erected in the Court House yard at Point Pleasant to the memory of this brave and energetic warrior, skillful general, and able orator. Here he fought courageously; here he died heroically. May his well deserved fame be as enduring as the granite of his monument—as enduring as the hills and mountains of the land he loved.

CHAPTER XXVIII

Logan, Chief of the Mingoes

LOGAN was the second son of Shikellamy, the vice-gerent of the Six Nations. His Indian name was Tah-gah-jute, which means, "His eyelashes stick out and above as if looking through or over something—hence spying." He was born at the Indian village of Osco, or Wasko, now Auburn, New York, in about 1725, where a large monument has been erected to his memory. When he was about three years old, his parents took up their residence at Shikellamy's Town, a short distance below Milton, Pennsylvania, upon Shikellamy's appointment by the Onondaga Council as the vice-gerent of the Six Nations over the Shawnees and other tribes of the Susquehanna Valley. Later, Shikellamy removed to Shamokin (Sunbury), where the son grew to manhood. The father re-named him James Logan after James Logan, Secretary of the Provincial Council of Pennsylvania, for whom he had a high regard.

Logan's mother was a Cayuga and he, too, married a Cayuga, who, after bearing him several children of whose after life nothing definite is known, died of fever at Shamokin, in October, 1747. Later, Logan married a second wife, a Shawnee, who survived him, but bore him no children.

During the French and Indian War, as well as during the uprising of Pontiac, Logan remained at peace with Pennsylvania, and rendered considerable service to the Colony. He was a close friend of Conrad Weiser, Scarouady, and Andrew Montour.

Logan Removes to the Juniata Valley

Early in the summer of 1765 Logan removed to the beautiful valley of the Juniata, building his cabin near Reedsville, Mifflin County. Nearby the cabin was a limestone spring, which is known to this day as "Logan's Spring". Here in the heart of the mountains he lived for the next five years, making an honest living by hunting and selling dressed deer skins to the traders, and much esteemed by his white neighbors. On one occasion during his sojourn at this place, he was cheated by a tailor, who traded him some spoiled wheat for good deer skins. Logan at once made complaint, and when Judge Brown decided in his favor, he said, "Law good, makes rogues pay."

The following letter written by Hon, R. P. Maclay of the state senate of Pennsylvania to George Darsie of the same body, revealing Logan's high sense of honor, was printed in the "Pittsburgh Daily American" of March 21, 1842:

"Allow me to correct a few inaccuracies as to place and names in the anecdote of Logan, the celebrated Mingo chief, as published in the 'Pittsburgh Daily American' of March seventeenth, to which you call my attention. The person surprised at the spring, now called Big Spring, and about four miles west of Logan's Spring, was William Brown—the first actual settler in Kishacoquillas Valley and one of the associate judges of Mifflin County from its organization till his death at the age of ninety-one or two, and not Samuel Maclay as stated by Dr. Hildreth. I will give you the anecdote as I heard it related by Judge Brown himself while on a visit to my brother, who then owned and occupied the Big Spring farm, four miles west of Reedsville:—

" 'The first time I ever saw the spring,' said the old gentleman 'my brother, James Reed, and myself had wandered out of the valley in search of land and finding it very good, we were looking for a spring. About a mile from this we started a bear and separated to get a shot at him. I was traveling along looking about on the rising ground for the bear, when I came suddenly on the spring; and being dry and more rejoiced to find so fine a spring than to have killed a dozen bears, I set my rifle against a bush and rushed down the bank and lay down to drink. Upon putting my head down, I saw reflected in the water on the opposite side the shadow of a tall Indian. I sprang to my rifle, when the Indian gave a yell whether for peace or war I was not just sufficiently master of my faculties to determine; but upon my seizing my rifle and facing him, he knocked up the pan of his gun, threw out the priming and extended his open palm toward me in token of friendship. After putting down our guns we again met at the spring and shook hands. This was Logan, the best specimen of humanity I ever met with, either white or red. He could speak a little English and told me there was another white hunter a little way down the stream and offered to guide me to his camp. There I first met your father.

"We visited Logan at his camp at Logan's Spring, and your father and he shot at a mark for a dollar a shot. Logan lost four or five rounds and acknowledged himself beaten. When we were about to leave him, he went into his hut and brought out as many deer skins as he had lost dollars and handed them to Mr. Maclay, who refused to take them, alleging that we had been his guests and did not come to rob him—that the shooting had been only a trial of skill and the bet merely nominal. Logan drew himself up with great dignity and said: 'Me bet to make you shoot your best; me gentleman and me take your dollar if me beat.' So he was obliged to take the skins or affront a friend whose sense of honor would not permit him to receive even a horn of powder in return.

" 'The next year,' said the old gentleman, 'I brought my wife up and camped under a big walnut tree on the bank of Tea Creek until I had built a cabin near where the mill now stands and have lived in the valley ever since. Poor Logan (and the big tears coursed each other down his cheeks) soon went to the Allegheny and I never saw him again."

Logan is said to have carved on a giant oak tree at Standing Stone, now Huntingdon, Pennsylvania, a full-length figure of an Indian brandishing a tomahawk. This was probably done while he made a visit to that place from his home near Reedsville.

Logan Moves to the Ohio

In 1770 Logan moved to the Ohio, taking up his residence at the mouth of the Beaver. Here he was visited by the Moravian missionary, John Heckewelder, in 1772. Logan.had been accepted by that part of the Iroquois living in the Ohio Valley, and known as the Mingoes, as their chief; and he explained to Heckewelder on this visit that he had difficulty in holding his young men in check from making bloody reprisals upon the whites under the influence of liquor. He confessed to the missionary his own fondness for rum—a weakness which his father, the great Shikellamy, never indulged, because, as he said, he did not wish to be a fool. While living at the mouth of the Beaver, he was also visited, in 1773, by the missionary, McClure, who found him under the influence of rum and painted as a warrior. While living at this place Logan made many trips to Fort Pitt to trade, and no doubt visited Guyasuta at his village near Sharpsburg. He also frequently visited the traders at Venango, and was a visitor at Custaloga's Town on French Creek, in Mercer County.

After residing at the mouth of the Beaver for three years, Logan moved his family down the Ohio, and took up his residence on the north bank of this stream at the mouth of Yellow Creek, a few miles below where Wellsville, Ohio, now stands. The town of Mingo Junction, twenty miles farther down the river, perpetuates the name of his tribe and his memory on the strength of Logan's having resided at that place for a short time, at least.

The Murder of Logan's Family

On April 29, 1774, while Logan was away from his home at the mouth of Yellow Creek on a hunting trip, some of his men were trying to capture horses tethered on their ground in the neighborhood, and two were shot down by a man named Meyers, a Virginia land-grabber. It is said that Logan's camp planned revenge, and that a squaw, either Logan's sister or sister-in-law, informed Meyers' band of outlaws of the intention of Logan's followers. Meyers' band were lodged on the south side of the Ohio, under the command of Daniel Greathouse.

Greathouse then invited Logan's men across the river to be his guests at Baker's tavern for the next day. The invitation was accepted, and the band crossed the river and went to the tavern, leaving their guns in their tents, as it was to be a friendly visit. Upon their arrival, they were treated freely to rum and three of them became greatly intoxicated, the others refusing to drink, as it was a general custom among the Indians for at least one of the party to remain sober in order to take care of their intoxicated companions. The sober Indians, among whom was Logan's brother, John Petty, were challenged to shoot at a mark. The Indians shot first, and as soon as they had emptied their guns, Greathouse's band shot down the three sober Indians in cold blood. One of the party, a sister-in-law of Logan, endeavored to escape by flight, but was also shot down. She lived long enough to implore the murderers to spare the life of her little babe two months old, explaining to them that it was one of their kin; and its life was spared on that account. The whites then set upon the drunken Indians with tomahawks and butchered them all. Altogether ten Indians were killed by these white fiends, among whom were the mother, sister, and brother of Logan. As stated in Chapter XXVI, this cold-blooded murder of Logan's family was one of the prime causes of Lord Dunmore's War, which took place during the summer and autumn of 1774.

There has been lack of agreement among historians as to the exact date of this atrocity, but most authorities say that it was on the 30th of April; and this date must be correct, as on May 3rd,

Valentine Crawford, a brother of Colonel William Crawford, on writing from his home on Jacob's Creek, near Connellsville, says: "On Saturday last, about twelve o'clock, one Greathouse and about twenty men fell on a party of Indians at the mouth of Yellow Creek, and killed ten of them. They brought away one child a prisoner, which is not at my brother, William Crawford's." Also Colonel William Crawford, in a letter written to George Washington on May 8th, says: "Daniel Greathouse and some others fell on some Indians at the mouth of Yellow Creek and killed and scalped ten, and took one child about two months old, which is at my house. I have taken the child from a woman that it had been given to."

What eventually became of this Indian babe, nephew of Logan, and the grandson of the famous Shikellamy, is not known. Historians agree that it was the son of Colonel John Gibson who, as we shall presently see, translated Logan's great speech.

When Logan returned from his hunting trip and learned of the murder of his family and friends, he determined to avenge their death. Said he later, "Logan thought only of revenge; Logan will not weep." Like his famous father, he had always been a friend of the whites; and only a few days before the murder of his family a council of Mingo chiefs assembled, many of whom were in favor of war, but his counsel prevailed, and the chiefs decided not to take up the hatchet on this occasion. Logan said, "I admit that you have just cause of complaint. But you must remember that you, too, have sometimes done wrong. By war you can only harass and distress the frontier settlements for a time; and then the Virginians will come like the trees in the woods in number and drive you from the good lands you possess, from the hunting grounds so dear to you." Also when Heckewelder visited him in 1772 he said that while Logan complained "against the English for imposing liquor upon the Indians; yet he otherwise admired their ingenuity; spoke of gentlemen, but observed that the Indians unfortunately had but few of them as their neighbors."

Logan Takes Revenge

Therefore, from the friend of the whites and an advocate of peace, Logan changed into a fearless and terrible foe of the race that was gradually driving the Indian from his hunting grounds. He at once led a band of warriors against the traders at Canoe Bottom, on the Hockhocking River, but the Delaware chief, White

Eyes, foiled this attempt. On the 19th of May, he set out once more with a band of eight chosen warriors, who were later joined by four more, and went to the neighborhood of Ten Mile, Dunkard and Muddy creeks, in Southwestern Pennsylvania, where, after waiting and watching for two weeks, he and his band killed a settler named Spicer, together with his wife and six children, taking prisoner two of the children, William, aged nine, and Betsy, aged eleven.* Betsy was afterwards released, but William grew to manhood among the Indians. Two days later Logan's band killed two men on the site of the fort on Dunbar Creek. On the 22nd of June, he returned to the Indian town of Wakatomica, now Dresden, Ohio, with sixteen scalps and two prisoners.

Several days later Logan started on the war-path the third time, leading a party of seven warriors to the Monongahela region where he thought the murderers of his family lurked. On the 12th of July his band came upon William Robinson, Thomas Hellen, and Colman Brown, pulling flax in the field opposite to Simpson Creek. Brown was killed on the spot and Robinson and Hellen started to run, but Logan succeeded in capturing both. Logan made himself known to Robinson, and told him that he would have to run the gauntlet, but gave him "such complete instruction and directions as they traveled together that Robinson ran the gauntlet safely and reached the stake without harm." The warriors then determined to burn Robinson at the stake; but Logan made three attempts, the last one successful, to prevent this atrocity. He loosed the cords which bound the unfortunate man, placed a belt of wampum around his neck as a mark of adoption, introduced him to a young warrior, and said: "This is your cousin; you are to go home with him and he will take care of you." Robinson afterwards said that so fervent was Logan's impassioned eloquence on his behalf, that the saliva foamed at his mouth when he addressed the assembled warriors. Hellen, after being un· mercifully beaten while running the gauntlet, was adopted into an Indian family.

Logan believed that Captain Michael Cresap was the leader of the outlaws who murdered his family; and three days after Robinson had been adopted, he dictated to him (Robinson) the following note to Cresap, dated July 21, 1774, which was written with suggestive ink made of gun-powder mixed with water:

"To Captain Cresap:

What did you kill my people on Yellow Creek for?
The White People killed my kin at Conestoga a great
while ago and I thought nothing of that; but you killed
my kin again on Yellow Creek and took my cousin prisoner. Then I thought I must kill too; and I have been
three times to war since; but the Indians are not angry,
only myself."

The "cousin" that Logan refers to in the above note was the
child of his sister. It is usual for the Indians to refer to relatives
generally as cousins.

Once more Logan went on the war-path, this time setting out
with a few chosen braves to the Holston and Clinch rivers in
Southwestern Virginia, where he had been informed Captain Cresap
made his home. He and his warriors reached the neighborhood in
the middle of September, where on Reedy Creek, a branch of the
Holston, they killed the whole family of John Robertson except
one young boy, whom they carried off captive. At least all the
circumstances point to this murder as having been committed by
Logan, inasmuch as the note which Logan addressed to Captain
Cresap was found tied to a club in the house of the unfortunate
settler, where, on the floor, were found the dead bodies of the
family.

About the middle of October, Logan's party came to Old
Chillicothe, Ohio, where a number of Delawares, who had taken
part in Lord Dunmore's War, were now located among the Shawnees, after having been driven from the Muskingum by the Virginia troops. The party brought with them five scalps and
Robertson's little boy, as well two other prisoners. It is said that
during these incursions, Logan had taken thirty scalps and prisoners. His thirst for revenge· was now satisfied. He "sat still",
and refused to lead or accompany any more war parties.

Logan's Famous Speech

Logan arrived from the Holston raid at the time when Cornstalk's defeated warriors had returned from the terrible battle of
Point Pleasant (October 10th), and the chiefs were assembled in
council. Both Logan and Cornstalk argued for peace, and the
council decided not to continue the war. A deputation of chiefs
was then sent to Lord Dunmore to sue for peace. Dunmore
agreed to a conference, whereupon runners were sent out to invite

all the chiefs to assemble at Camp Charlotte, the place of the conference.

Logan refused to attend the conference. Then Lord Dunmore sent Colonel John Gibson, the alleged father of the infant of Logan's sister, whose life was spared when the rest of Logan's family was murdered, as a special messenger to invite and bring the great chieftain to the conference. Logan refused again to attend the conference, and proposed that he and Colonel Gibson take a walk into the woods to talk matters over. At length they sat down on a log under a large elm, still standing on the Pickaway plains, about six miles south of Circleville, Pickaway County, Ohio, and known to this day as Logan's Elm.

Here, with Colonel Gibson as his only auditor, and with tears rolling down his face, Logan delivered his famous speech, one of the finest specimens of eloquence in the English language, as follows:

"I appeal to any white man to say if ever he entered Logan's cabin hungry, and I gave him not meat; if ever he came cold or naked, and I gave him not clothing.

"During the course of the last long and bloody war, Logan remained in his tent, an advocate for peace. Nay, such was my love for the whites, that those of my own country pointed at me as they passed, and said, 'Logan is the friend of white men.' I had even thought to live with you, but for the injuries of one man. Colonel Cresap the last spring, in cold blood, and unprovoked, cut off all the relatives of Logan; not sparing even my women and children. There runs not a drop of my blood in the veins of any human creature. This called on me for revenge. I have sought it. I have killed many. I have fully glutted my vengeance. For my country, I rejoice at the beams of peace. Yet, do not harbor the thought that mine is the joy of fear. Logan never felt fear. He will not turn on his heel to save his life. Who is there to mourn for Logan? Not one."

Gibson wrote down the speech, and read it the next day at the conference at Camp Charlotte. Thomas Jefferson, in his "Notes on Virginia", published in 1781 and 1782, gave "Logan's Lament", as he called it, world-wide publicity. Colonel John Gibson, on April 4, 1800, made an affidavit before J. Barker, of Pittsburgh, as to the authorship of the great speech, and the accuracy of his translation of the same. Logan spoke in Delaware. Says Heckewelder, "For my part I am convinced that it was delivered precisely as it was related to us, with only this difference, that it possessed a force and expression in the Indian language which it is impossible to transmit to our own."

Thomas Jefferson challenges Cicero, Demosthenes, and both European and American statesmen to surpass this speech—the cry of the wrongs of the Indian race that came up from the breaking heart of Logan, and made his name immortal. It is at once bold, lofty, and sublime; and yet it is permeated with a note of sadness. It has been recited in the schools throughout the United States for more than a hundred years. It was copied in England, and has been translated in French, German, and other modern languages as a specimen of classic oratory. The Ohio Archaeological and Historical Society has erected a monument near Logan's Elm bearing the following inscription:

> "Under the spreading branches of a magnificent elm
> tree nearby is where Logan, a Mingo chief, made his
> celebrated speech."

Death of Logan

After the treaty with Lord Dunmore, Logan returned to his cabin at Old Chillicothe, now Westfall, on the banks of the Scioto. Before long he left there and took up his residence at Pluggy's Town, eighteen miles north of Columbus, Ohio. Here, on July 25, 1775, he was instrumental in saving the life of Captain Wood while on his way to invite the western tribes to the conference held in Pittsburgh in October of that year.

During the latter years of his life, he wandered from tribe to tribe, a broken man. He drank freely and suffered much from despondency. Often he was heard to say that it would have been better if he had never been born. There is a tradition that he wandered back to the Wyoming Valley on the Susquehanna. Here, according to the tradition, he arrived on July 2nd, 1778, just the day before the Wyoming massacre, and in time to give the alarm to a number of his friends among the whites. Campbell refers to this tradition in his poem, "Gertrude of Wyoming", in which the character Outalissi represents the great chief of the Mingoes.

In the autumn of 1778 he saved the life of Simon Kenton, the scout, and companion of Daniel Boone, who had been caught stealing horses of the Indians and was condemned to die at the stake. Kenton was lodged with Logan for safe keeping until the torture should commence. Logan addressed him and said: "Be strong,

I am a great chief. They talk of taking you to Sandusky and burning you there. I will send messengers to speak good for you." He then sent two runners to Sandusky, in the meantime holding the angry Indians in check, and with great difficulty got Kenton released.

Heckewelder says that during the year 1779, Logan adopted a white woman into his family as his sister to take the place of the sister who was killed at Yellow Creek five years before. During the remaining year he lived among the Mingoes on the Sandusky River, spending much of his time, however, roving from place to place. In 1780, he went over to the British side and joined the force of volunteers, regulars, and Indians, which Captain Henry Bird led to Kentucky and destroyed the settlements at Ruddell's and Martin's stations. As Captain Bird was conveying the prisoners to Detroit, Logan became very friendly with some of them, especially John Duncan to whom he said: "I know that I have two souls—the one good, the other bad. When the good has the ascendency I am kind and humane. When the bad soul rules, I am perfectly savage and delight in nothing but blood and carnage."

After he returned from this raid, he went to a council of chiefs at Detroit in the autumn. While the conference was in session Logan, crazed by drink, struck his wife such a terrible blow that it was thought he had killed her. He then fled towards his home on the Sandusky, but was pursued by a band of Indians, among whom were his wife's relatives and his own nephew, Tod-kah-dohs, Logan was overtaken at a camping place near Brownsville, Ohio. Suspecting that they had pursued him for the purpose of punishing him for striking his wife, he threatened to scalp the whole party. His nephew knowing his alertness and that the only way of escape was to strike first, shot the famous chief as he was leaping from his horse. The next morning his body was buried by a band of Wyandots.

The above is the account usually given of Logan's death. Another account is that he was killed on the way, while making this same journey from Detroit to Sandusky; that he had a quarrel with his nephew, Tod-kah-dohs, and that, while he was sitting by the camp fire with his face between his hands, in deep meditation, Tod-kah-dohs stole up behind him, and buried his tomahawk in his brain.

We close this sketch of the immortal Logan with the following lines composed for the occasion of the dedicating of the monument to his memory, erected near Logan's Elm:

"Logan, to thy memory here
White men do this tablet rear;
On its front we grave thy name,
In our hearts shall live thy fame.
While Niagara's thunders roar,
Or Erie's surges lash the shore;
While onward broad Ohio glides
And seaward roll her Indian tides,
So long their memory, who did give
These floods their sounding names shall live.
While time in kindness burries
The gory axe and warrior's bow.
O justice, faithful to thy trust,
Record the virtues of the just."

Murder of Joseph Wipey

As we have seen, it was in the spring of 1774 that the family of Logan was killed. During this same spring, occurred the murder of another friendly Indian, Joseph Wipey. The exact location of the murder is hard to determine; but it seems to have been near the mouth of Hinckston's Run, which flows southward through Cambria County, and empties into the Conemaugh at Johnstown, although some authorities say that the murder occurred in the southeastern part of Indiana County.

When, after the purchase at Fort Stanwix, in October, 1768, the Delawares left their towns on the Kittanning Trail, and the region of the purchase began to be rapidly settled by the white people, this elderly Delaware remained on the hunting grounds of his forefathers, and built his cabin by a stream north of the Conemaugh. He was an inoffensive, harmless old hunter and fisher, and had given many evidences of his friendship for the whites. At peace with all mankind, he was gently gliding down the stream of life, awaiting his summons to the Happy Hunting Grounds. John Hinckston and James Cooper wantonly murdered him, some time in May of this year, while he was fishing from his canoe. Arthur St. Clair, writing from Ligonier to Governor John Penn, on May 29th, concerning this murder, says: "It is the most astonishing thing in the world—the disposition of the common people of this country. Actuated by the most savage cruelty, they wantonly perpetrate crimes that are a disgrace to humanity, and seem, at the same time, to be under a kind of religious enthusiasm, whilst they want the daring spirit that usually inspires."

The murder of Logan's family had much to do with bringing on Lord Dunmore's War. And now, St. Clair feared that the wanton murder of Wipey would bring on a Delaware war that would devastate the western settlements. He advised Governor Penn that this atrocity gave him "much trouble and vexation." Happily, though, the Delawares did not again take up arms against the Province until the latter years of the Revolutionary War.

CHAPTER XXIX.

Bald Eagle

BALD EAGLE was a chief of the Wolf Clan of Delawares. Bald Eagle Township, in Clinton County, Bald Eagle Mountain, and Bald Eagle Valley, in Clinton and Center counties, are named for him. Early in the Revolutionary War, this chief espoused the British cause, and his war parties brought death and desolation to the settlements on the West Branch of the Susquehanna.

Bald Eagle Kills James Brady

One of the bloody deed of Bald Eagle was the fatal wounding of James Brady, son of Captain John Brady, and youngest brother of the famous Captain Samuel Brady, near Williamsport, Lycoming County, on August 8, 1778, an account of which is given in Menginess' "History of the West Branch Valley", as follows:

"A Corporal and four men, belonging to Colonel Hartley's regiment, and three militiamen, were ordered about two miles above Loyalsock, on the 8th of August, 1778, to protect fourteen reapers and cradlers, who went to assist Peter Smith, the unfortunate man that had his wife and four children murdered about a month previous, to cut his crop. Smith's farm was on Turkey Run, not far from Williamsport, on the opposite side of the river.

"James Brady, son of Captain John, the younger brother of Captain Sam Brady of the Rangers, was with the party. According to custom in those days, when no commissioned officer was present, the company generally selected a leader, whom they styled 'Captain', and obeyed him as such. Young James Brady was selected Captain of this little band of about twenty men.

"On arriving at the field, they placed two sentinels at the opposite ends, the sides having clear land around. The day being Friday, they cut the greater part of the grain, and intended to complete it the next morning. Four of the reapers improperly left that night, and returned to the fort. A strict watch was kept all night, but nothing unusual occurred. In the morning they all went to work; the cradlers, four in number, by themselves, near the house; the reapers in another part of the field. The reapers, except young Brady, placed their guns round a tree. He thought this was wrong, and placed his some distance from the rest. The morning proved to be very foggy, and about an hour after sunrise, the sentinels and reapers were surprised by a number of Indians, under cover of the fog, quietly approaching them. The sentinels fired and ran towards the reapers, when they all ran, with the exception of young Brady. He made towards his rifle, pursued by three Indians, and when within a few yards of it, was fired upon by a white man with a pistol, probably a tory, but falling over a sheaf of grain, the shot missed him. He rose again, and when almost within reach of the rifle, was wounded by a shot from an Indian. Here another sentinel fired his gun, but was immediately, with a militiaman, shot down. Brady succeeded in getting his rifle, however, and shot the first Indian dead. He caught up another gun, and brought down a second savage, when they closed around him in numbers, but being a stout active man, he struggled with them for some time. At length one of them struck a tomahawk into his head, when he fell, and was wounded with a spear in the hands of another. He was so stunned with the blow of the tomahawk, that he remained powerless, but strange as it may seem, retained his senses. They ruthlessly tore the scalp from his head as he lay in apparent death; and it was a glorious trophy for them, for he had long and remarkably red hair.

"The cradlers, who it appears were in a low spot, in a distant part of the field, on hearing the alarm, ascended an eminence and partly beheld this unhappy affair. The Indians, as soon as they accomplished their bloody work, left instantly, probably fearing an attack from the whites.

"The Corporal and three men, with the cradlers, proposed to make a stand; but the others thought it imprudent, and they all immediately left. The cradlers being acquainted with the country, took the nearest way to Wallis'; the Corporal and his three men pushed right down the road. At Loyalsock they were fired upon by a party of Indians, probably the same that killed Brady. They returned the fire, when the Indians fled; and they retook three horses from them, and brought them to the fort in safety.

"After Brady was scalped, he related that a little Indian was called and made to strike the tomahawk into his head, in four separate places. He was probably taking lessons in the art of butchery.

"After coming to himself, he attempted, between walking and creeping, to reach the cabin, where an old man named Jerome

Vaness, had been employed to cook for them. On hearing the report of the guns, he had hid himself; but when he saw Brady return, he came to him. James begged the old man to fly to the fort, saying, 'The Indians will soon be back and will kill you.' The worthy man positively refused to leave him alone, but stayed and endeavored to dress his frightful wounds. Brady requested to be assisted down the river, where he drank large quantities of water, when he still insisted on the old man leaving him and trying to save himself; but he would not do it. He then directed his faithful old friend to load the gun that was in the cabin, which was done, and put into his hands, when he lay down and appeared to sleep.

"As soon as the sad intelligence reached the fort, [Fort Muncy], Captain Walker mustered a party of men and proceeded to the spot. When they came to the river bank, Brady heard the noise, and supposing it was Indians, jumped to his feet and cocked his gun. But it was friends. They made a bier and placed him on it, and brought him away. He requested to be taken to Sunbury to his mother. His request was granted, and a party started with him, amongst whom was Robert Covenhoven. He became very feverish by the way, and drank large quantities of water, and became partly delirious. It was late at night when they arrived at Sunbury, and did not intend to arouse his mother; but it seemed she had a presentiment of something that was to happen, and being awake to alarms, met them at the river and assisted to convey her wounded son to the house. He presented a frightful spectacle, and the meeting of mother and son is described to have been heart-rending. Her heart was wrung with the keenest anguish, and her lamentations were terrible to be heard.

"The young Captain lived five days. The first four he was delirious, on the fifth his reason returned, and he described the whole scene he had passed through very vividly, and with great minuteness. He said the Indians were of the Seneca tribe, and amongst them were two chiefs; one of whom was a very large man, and from the description was supposed to be Cornplanter; the other he personally knew to be the celebrated chief Bald Eagle, who had his nest near where Milesburg, Center County, now stands.

"On the evening of the fifth day, the young Captain died, deeply regretted by all who knew him; for he was a noble and promising young man. Vengeance, 'not loud, but deep,' was breathed against the Bald Eagle, but he laughed it to scorn, till the fatal day at Brady's Bend on the Allegheny.''

Samuel Brady's Vow

Lieutenant (later Captain) Samuel Brady, was at Carlisle accompanying his regiment, the Eighth Pennsylvania, to Fort Pitt, when he received word of the scalping of his brother. He had parted from him about a week before. Samuel now hastened to Sunbury, but arrived too late to find James alive.

Samuel Brady's rage over the murder of his beloved brother stirred the depths of his soul. He made a solemn vow that he would never make peace with the Indians of any tribe.

Captain John Brady Killed

Lieutenant Samuel Brady arrived at Fort Pitt on September 10th, 1778, accompanying his regiment. Here he was destined to achieve fame as an Indian fighter, but not before he received another crushing blow. On April 11, 1779, his father, Captain John Brady, was conveying supplies from Fort Wallis to Fort Muncy, when three Iroquois Indians, secreted in a thicket, shot him dead from his horse.

The body of Captain John Brady was buried in an old graveyard near Halls, Lycoming County, where a heavy granite marker was erected at his grave, bearing the following inscription:

Captain John Brady
Fell in Defense of Our Forefathers
At Wolf Run, April 11, 1779
Aged Forty-six Years

One hundred years after his death, funds were raised for the erection of a large monument to his memory in the cemetery at Muncy, the shaft being unveiled on October 15, 1879.

Bald Eagle Killed By Samuel Brady

Samuel Brady received the news of the murder of his father at about the time he was chosen by Colonel Broadhead as a forest ranger, at Fort Pitt. In his frenzy of grief, it is said that he renewed the vow taken after the murder of his brother, raising his hand on high and saying:

"Aided by Him Who formed yonder sun and heavens, I will avenge the murder of my father; nor while I live, will I ever be at peace with the Indians of any tribe."

Samuel Brady did not have long to wait for an opportunity to avenge the death of his brother. In June, 1779, a band of the

Wolf Clan of Delawares and probably some Senecas, came down the Allegheny River and made a raid into Westmoreland County, killing a soldier between Fort Hand (near Apollo) and Fort Crawford (Parnassus), attacking the settlement at James Perry's Mill on Big Sewickley Creek, killing a woman and four children and carrying off two children, the latter possibly being the children of Frederick Heinrich (Henry), near Greensburg.

The attack on the home of Frederick Henry is thus described in Rev. W. A. Zundel's "History of Old Zion Church":

"Frederick Henry (Heinrich), of Northampton, Burlington County, New Jersey, settled, shortly after 1770, in the Herold settlement [in Hempfield Township, Westmoreland County]. In time, the new settlers cleared some land and erected a house and stables. Four children cheered this lonely settlement. During the spring of 1779, when the husband, Frederick Henry, was compelled to leave home to take some grist to a distant mill, a band of Indians, perhaps Senecas, descended upon the helpless home.

"As was their custom, the Indians sneaked up to the house to ascertain if the men were home and on guard. Now, the Henry's had a large cock that frequently came to the door of the home to be fed. Mrs. Henry, seeing some feathers moving near the door, sent one of the children to shoo away the big rooster; whereupon the Indians, decked out in the feathers of their war headgear, burst in upon the helpless family. Mrs. Henry bravely attempted to defend her little ones; whereupon she was tomahawked and scalped in the presence of her small children.

"One child, seeing the Indians coming at the door, fled into the corn field and hid among the corn, and thus escaped, the Indians being in a hurry, fearing the wrath of the settlers. The Indians now took the three children captive, and after firing the buildings, started on their journey toward the Indian country. It soon developed that the youngest child, a mere infant, would be too much bother to the Indians, so when it began to cry, a big Indian took it by its feet, and dashed its brains out against a maple tree on the Solomon Bender farm, now owned by William Henry. This tree was held sacred by the pioneers and it stood until recent times (about 1900). The other children were carried away.

"Immediately upon the return of Henry, a posse of settlers started out in pursuit of the Indians. One account relates that the Indians were in their camp above Pittsburgh on the Allegheny, and after a lively skirmish, the children were recaptured, and the murderer of the wife and child identified, tied to a tree, and dispatched by the daughter, Anna Margaret, then about nine years old. Another account agrees with the report of Colonel Broadhead, that Captain Brady, with twenty white men and a Delaware chief, effected the capture."

The news of this raid reaching Fort Pitt, two parties were sent out against these Indians, one marching into the Sewickley settlement and attempting to follow the Indian trail, and the other consisting of twenty men under Captain Samuel Brady, ascending the Allegheny River.

Brady's forces were painted and dressed like Indians. He had with him his "pet Indian", the unfortunate Nanowland, who, as we have seen, was killed at Killbuck Island, near Fort Pitt, in the spring of 1782, by the Scotch-Irish settlers living on Chartier's Creek. Brady's reason for going up the Allegheny was that he was satisfied that the Indians came from the north and would return that direction to get possession of their canoes, which they had no doubt hidden along the river bank when they had left the stream. Brady came upon the canoes of these Indians drawn up within the mouth of one of the creeks entering the Allegheny from the east. There is lack of agreement among historians as to the identity of this creek. Some say that it was the Big Mahoning; but Colonel Broadhead, in his report to General Washington, written on June 24th, says that the scene was "about fifteen miles above Kittanning", which agrees with the location of Red Bank Creek, not far from the beautiful bend on the Allegheny, which bears the name of Brady.

The Indians were in camp in the woods north of the creek and were preparing supper when Brady discovered them. They had hobbled the horses which they had stolen, and turned them loose to graze on the meadow near the creek. On account of the swollen condition of the creek, Brady's men were compelled to ascend it two miles before they were able to cross. Waiting until after nightfall, Brady and his men descended the northern side of the creek to a point near the camp, and then lay in the tall grass.

Laying aside their arms, Brady and Nanowland crept on their stomachs to within a few yards of the Indian camp, in order to count the number of the Indians and learn the position of the captives taken. As Brady and his faithful Delaware were lying in the grass, one of the warriors arose from his position near the fire, stepped forth to a few feet from where Brady lay, stood there for a while and then returned to his companions, and lay down to sleep. Then Brady and Nanowland crept back to their companions and prepared to attack the Indians at daybreak. As the first streaks of dawn floated over the verdant hills of the Allegheny, one of the Indians awoke and aroused his companions. The whole band then stood about the fire, when suddenly a sheet of flame blazed from the rifles of Brady and his men, and the chief of the seven Indians fell dead, while the others fled into the surrounding forest, two of them severely wounded. It was Brady's own rifle that brought down the chief, who was none other than Bald Eagle. With a shout of triumph, Brady leaped upon the fallen chieftain and scalped him. Thus, on the banks of the Allegheny, far from the harvest field near the banks of the Susquehanna, where Bald Eagle killed young James Brady, during the preceding summer, Captain Samuel Brady avenged the death of his youngest and favorite brother.

The children captured by Bald Eagle's band were recovered unharmed and returned to Fort Pitt. The death of Bald Eagle had a good effect in that the Indians made no more raids into Westmoreland during that summer. Three weeks later, Captain Brady returned to the neighborhood of the attack on Bald Eagle's band. Observing a flock of crows hovering above the thicket, he made a search and found the partially devoured body of one of the Indians that died of his wounds.

There seems, however, to have been another chief by the name of Bald Eagle. Withers, in his Chronicles of Border Warfare, says that this latter was an Indian of notoriety, not only among his own nation, but also the inhabitants of the northwestern frontier of West Virginia, with whom he was in the habit of associating and hunting. Says Withers: "In one of his visits among them he was discovered alone by Jacob Scott, William Hacker and Eliza Runner who, reckless of the consequences, murdered him solely to gratify a most wanton thirst for Indian blood. After the commission of this most outrageous enormity, they seated him in the stern of a canoe and with a piece of journey-cake thrust into his mouth, set him afloat on the Monongahela. In this situation he was seen descending the river by several who supposed him to be, as usual, returning from a friendly hunt with the whites in the friendly settlements, and who expressed some astonishment that he did not stop to see them. The canoe floated near to the shore below the mouth of George's Creek [in southwestern Fayette County, Pennsylvania], and was observed by Mrs. Province, who had it brought to the bank, and the friendly but unfortunate old Indian decently buried." The murder of this friendly Indian took place near New Geneva, Fayette County, in 1773.

Captain Samuel Brady

We close this chapter with a few additional references to Captain Samuel Brady. He was the most noted scout connected with Fort Pitt during the Revolutionary War; and his exploits would fill many pages. On one occasion he started from Pittsburgh with a few picked men on a scout toward the Sandusky villages. While they were on their return trip they were pursued by Indians and all killed except Brady, who succeeded in getting as far towards Fort Pitt as the hill named for him near Beaver. He was not wounded, but almost dead from fatigue. He well realized that he was being tracked by the Indians, and that if he did not resort to some trick to elude them, he would be lost. Having selected a large tree, lately been blown down having a leafy top, he walked back carefully in his tracks a few hundred yards, and then turned about and walked in his old steps as far as the tree. This was done in the hope and belief that the Indians would be sure to follow him thither. He then walked along the trunk of the tree, and hid himself in its leafy top. He believed that the Indians would track him to the tree, and finding no further trace of him, would sit on the trunk or log of the same for con- ' sultation. He had not long to wait. Presently three Indians with their eyes bent to the earth followed his tracks, came to the tree, which they closely examined for the trail beyond, but not finding any, sat down on the trunk to consult together just as Brady had anticipated. Quickly and silently Brady raised his rifle and shot the foremost Indian dead. The bullet passed through his body and wounded the other two. Springing upon these with clubbed rifle, Brady soon dispatched them both.

On another occasion, as this noted scout was returning to Fort Pitt, he realized that he was being tracked by an Indian with a dog. Occasionally he had seen the Indian in the distance passing from tree to tree and advancing on his trail. For his ambush he selected a large chestnut tree which had been blown out of root. He walked from the top of the tree along its trunk, and sat down in the hole made by the uprooting of the tree. In a short time he saw a small dog mount the log at the other end and with nose to the trunk approach him, closely followed by a plumed warrior. Brady had to make a choice between the dog and the Indian. He preferred shooting the former, which he did. As the dog rolled off the log dead, the Indian with a loud whoop ran into the forest and disappeared.

One of the well known stories concerning Brady is that of his famous leap. Historians are not in accord as to the exact location of this exploit. Some have placed it on Slippery Rock Creek, in Butler County, but there seems to be very little doubt that it took place in Portage County, Ohio. On this occasion he was hotly pursued by Indians, and coming to a stream with a high bank, summoning all his powers, leaped across the same, although the distance was more than twenty-five feet. His Indian pursuers stopped on the bank.

Brady's scouting covered a vast extent of territory, to the headwaters of the Allegheny, to Sandusky on the west, and to the West Branch of the Susquehanna, on the east. In "Meginness' History of the West Branch Valley", is an account of an "Indian hunt" which Brady and Peter Grove made, most likely in 1780, through the counties of Huntingdon, Clearfield, Center, Lycoming, Clinton, and Union. They would creep up on Indian camps, fire into the same, each killing an Indian, and then bound off through the woods like antelopes. They were matchless sprinters, and the Indians were never able to overtake them. In this "hunt", they killed many Indians, among them being Black-snake, the Panther, the Greatshot, and Wamp. It is a terrible story of butchery. Grove says that his heart was wrung to tears with the cries of Wamp's squaw. Some time after they had shot the Panther and the Blacksnake, they returned to the camp where the massacre occurred. Says Grove: "We found the Panther dead, but the Blacksnake was yet alive, and vomiting blood. We made all dead shots that day."

After the Revolutionary War, Brady left Fort Pitt and the Chartier's settlement nearby, where he had spent much of his time, and went to West Liberty, West Virginia, where he died.

Cornplanter

CORNPLANTER, whose Indian name was Garganwahgah, or Gyantwachias, meaning "The Planter", was a noted chief of the Senecas, also known as John O'Bail, supposed to have been born at Ganawagus on the Genesee River, in New York, some time between 1732 and 1740. His father was a white trader named John O'Bail, or O'Beel, said by some historians to have been an Englishman, while others say that he was a Dutchman. Cornplanter's mother was a full-blood Seneca.

In a letter written by Cornplanter to the Governor of Pennsylvania, he gives the following facts of his early youth: "When I was a child, I played with the butterfly, the grasshopper, and the frogs; and as I grew up, I began to pay some attention and play with the Indian boys in the neighborhood, and they took notice of my skin being of a different color from theirs, and spoke about it. I inquired from my mother the cause, and she told me my father was a resident of Albany. I still ate my victuals out of a bark dish. I grew up to be a young man and married a wife, and I had no kettle or gun. I then knew where my father lived, and went to see him, and found he was a white man and spoke the English language. He gave me victuals while I was at his house, but when I started to return home, he gave me no provisions to eat on the way. He gave me neither kettle nor gun."

By some authorities he is said to have been among the Indians at Braddock's defeat, but this statement has been doubted. During the Revolutionary War, he went over with his tribe to the English side. Being a chief of high rank and in the full vigor of manhood, he no doubt participated in the principal engagements of the Senecas against the United States in that conflict. Some authorities have said that he was present at the massacres at Cherry Valley and Wyoming, in which the Seneca tribe took a prominent part. We saw in Chapter XXIX, that he was probably with Bald Eagle when young James Brady was killed, in August, 1778. Some authorities have said, too, that he was with Guyasuta when Colonel Broadhead defeated the forces of the latter at the mouth of the Broken Straw, in the summer of 1779. This can very well be doubted, inasmuch as it is clear that, at this time, Cornplanter was actively engaged in the Genesee country in New York in opposing the campaign of General Sullivan.

In 1780, under Brandt and Johnson, Cornplanter led the Senecas in their raids against the settlers in the valleys of the Schoharie and Mohawk. On one of these raids, his father fell into his hands as a prisoner. The father did not recognize the son, and after marching for some miles, Cornplanter stepped before him and addressed him as follows:

"My name is John O'Bail, commonly called Cornplanter. I am your son. You are my father. You are now my prisoner, and subject to the custom of Indian warfare; but you shall not be harmed. You need not fear. I am a warrior. Many are the scalps which I have taken. Many prisoners have I tortured to death. I am your son. I was anxious to see you and greet you in friendship. I went to your cabin and took you by force; but your life shall be spared. Indians love their friends and their kindred, and treat them with kindness. If you now choose to follow the fortunes of your yellow son and to live with our people, I will cherish your old age with plenty of venison, and you shall live easy. But if it is your choice to return to your fields and live with your white children, I will send a party of trusty young men to conduct you back in safety. I respect you, my father. You have been friendly to Indians, and they are your friends." The father preferred his white children, and chose to return to them.

Cornplanter at the Treaty of Fort Stanwix (Rome, N. Y.), in October, 1784

Notwithstanding the fact that Cornplanter was a bitter enemy of the United States during the Revolutionary War, he became a firm friend of the young Republic upon the conclusion of peace. He comprehended the growing power of America, and was incensed with the ingratitude which Great Britain showed to the Senecas for their fidelity during the American Revolution. He attended the treaty at Fort Stanwix (Rome, N. Y.), in October, 1784, between the Six Nations and the "Thirteen Fires", as the Indians called the United States, where he used all the energies of his brilliant intellect in favor of peace. At this treaty the Six Nations, on October 23rd, ceded to Pennsylvania that part of the state northwest of the boundary of the purchase of 1768, the description in the deed being set forth as follows:

"Beginning on the south side of the river Ohio, where the western boundary of the State of Pennsylvania crosses the said river, near Shingo's old town, at the mouth of Beaver Creek, and thence by a due north line to the end of the forty-second and the beginning of the forty-third degrees of north latitude; thence by a due east line separating the forty-second and the forty-third degree of north latitude, to the east side of the east branch of the Susquehanna River; thence by the bounds of the late purchase made at Fort Stanwix, the fifth day of November, Anno Domini one thousand seven hundred and sixty-eight, as follows: Down the said east branch of Susquehanna, on the east side thereof, till it comes opposite to the mouth of a creek called by the Indians Awandac, and across the river, and up the said creek on the south side thereof, all along the range of hills called Burnet's Hills by the English, and by the Indians ...., on the north side of them, to the head of a creek which runs into the west branch of Susquehanna, which creek is by the Indians called Tyadaghton, but by the Pennsylvanians Pine Creek, and down the said creek on the south side thereof to the said west branch of Susquehanna; thence crossing the said river, and running up the south side thereof, the several courses thereof to the forks of the same river, which lies nearest to a place on the river Ohio called Kittanning, and from the fork by a straight line to Kittanning aforesaid; and thence down the said river Ohio by the several courses thereof to where said State of Pennsylvania crosses the same river, at the place of beginning."

It will be noticed in the above deed of the Purchase of 1784, that the line was to run along the south bank of the West Branch of the Susquehanna; thence "crossing the said river, and running up the south side thereof, the several courses and distances thereof to the forks of the same river, which lies nearest to a place on the river Ohio called Kittanning, and from the fork by a straight line to Kittanning aforesaid." The name "Canoe Place" is given in the old maps of the state to designate the point on the West Branch of the Susquehanna from which the purchase line ran to Kittanning. The point also designated the head of navigation on the West Branch. A survey of that line was made by Robert Galbraith, in 1786, and a cherry tree, standing on the west branch of the river was marked by him as the beginning of his survey. The same cherry tree was also marked by William P. Brady as the southeast corner of a tract surveyed by him "at Canoe Place", in 1794, on a grant in the name of John Nicholson, Esq. The town of Cherry Tree, Indiana County, now covers a part of this ground. The historic cherry tree disappeared many years ago. The Legislature of Pennsylvania, in 1893, granted an appropriation of fifteen hundred dollars for marking the historic site, and a substantial granite monument now stands where the tree stood.

Purchase at Fort McIntosh

The deed given at Fort Stanwix extinguished the Iroquois title to this region, but it became necessary to appease the Wyandots, Delawares and other western tribes, who likewise claimed title to the same lands. Therefore, the same commissioners who were at the treaty at Fort Stanwix, were sent to Fort McIntosh, the site of the present town of Beaver, Beaver County, where, on January 21, 1785, Pennsylvania received a deed from these Indians for the same land. The Fort Stanwix deed and the Fort McIntosh deed are identical as to boundaries, but the consideration in the former was five thousand dollars, and in the latter two thousand dollars. "Thus," says Meginness, "in a period of about one hundred and two years was the whole right of the Indians to the soil of Pennsylvania extinguished."

These deeds included all of the counties of Lawrence, Mercer, Crawford, Butler, Venango, Forest, Warren, Clarion, Jefferson, Elk, Kane, Cameron, Potter, and a part of Beaver, Allegheny, Armstrong, Erie, Indiana, Clearfield, Clinton, Tioga, and Bradford. That part of Erie County, called "the triangle," was ceded to Pennsylvania by the United States, in 1792.

Cornplanter Attends Other Treaties,
and Appeals to Washington

Cornplanter also attended the treaty at Fort Harmar in 1789, in which extensive territory was conveyed to the United States in the present state of Ohio. However, his name does not appear among the signers of the treaty. He also attended the treaties of September 15, 1797, and of July 30, 1802. These acts rendered him unpopular with the Senecas, and for a time his life was in danger. The chief, Red Jacket, seized upon these matters as a means of promoting his own popularity at the expense of Cornplanter.

In 1790, Cornplanter, accompanied by his half-brother, the Seneca chief, Half-Town, visited Philadelphia to lay before President Washington certain complaints of the Senecas against Colonel John Gibson.

In a speech to Cornplanter on this occasion, Washington said:
"When you return to your country, tell your people that it is my desire to promote their prosperity by teaching them the use of domestic animals, and the manner in which the white people plow and raise so much corn; and, if upon consideration, it would be agreeable to the nation at large to learn those arts, I will find some means of teaching them at such places within their country as shall be agreed upon."

In 1792, Pennsylvania granted Cornplanter a tract of 500 acres of land on the Allegheny, at the mouth of Oil Creek, where Oil City, Venango County, now stands. This he sold in 1818.

"For his many valuables services to the whites", Pennsylvania again granted him a large tract of land on the Allegheny, in Warren County, on March 16, 1796. On the 8th of this same month, he appeared before the representatives of the United States Government appointed to meet him, at Franklin, where he spoke as follows:

"I thank the Almighty for giving us luck to meet together at this time, and in this place as brethren, and hope my brothers will assist me in writing to Congress what I have now to say.

"I thank the Almighty that I am speaking this good day. I have been through all Nations of America, and am sorry to see the folly of many of the people. What makes me sorry is they all tell lies, and I never found truth amongst them. All the western Nations of Indians, as well as white people, have told me lies. Even in Council I have been deceived, and been told things which I have told to my chiefs and young men, which I have found not to be so, which makes me tell lies by not being able to make good my word; but I hope they will all see their folly and repent. The Almighty has not made us to lie, but to tell the truth one to another; for when two people meet together, if they lie one to the other, the people cannot be at peace, and so it is with nations, and that is the cause of so much war.

"General Washington, the father of us all, hear what I have now to say, and take pity on us poor people. The Almighty has blest you, and not us. He has given you education, which enables you to do many things that we cannot do. You can travel by sea as well as by land, and know what is doing in any other country, which we poor people know nothing about. Therefore you ought to pity us. When the Almighty first put us on this land, He gave it to us to live on. And when the white people first came to it, they were very poor, and we helped them all in our power; did not kill them, but received them as brothers. And now it appears to me as though they were going to leave us in distress."

Sometime prior to 1795, Cornplanter and a few of his tribe resided for a while at the mouth of Cornplanter's Run which flows into Buffalo Creek, in South Buffalo Township, Armstrong County, near the present village of Boggsville. His village seems to have been on both sides of the creek. On the top of a wooded hill, about a mile to the west, the traces of the burial ground of the village can still be seen. Smith, in his excellent "History of Armstrong County", says that when Charles Sipe, Sr., great-great grandfather of the present author, and his sons hunted along Buffalo Creek and Cornplanter's Run, in 1794 and 1795, the corn fields of the village were still distinguishable. These were on the flats on both sides of the creek.

Day's "Historical Collections" Quoted

The following facts concerning this noted chieftain are quoted from Day's "Historical Collections":

"Having buried the hatchet, Cornplanter sought to make his talents useful to his people by conciliating the good-will of the whites, and securing from further encroachment the little remnant of his national domain. On more than one occasion, when some reckless and blood-thirsty whites on the frontier had massacred unoffending Indians in cold blood, did Cornplanter interfere to restrain the vengeance of his people. During all the Indian wars from 1791 to 1794, which terminated with Wayne's treaty, Cornplanter pledged himself that the Senecas should remain friendly to the United States. He often gave notice to the garrison at Fort Franklin of intended attacks from hostile parties, and even hazarded his life on a mediatorial mission to the western tribes. He ever entertained a high respect and personal friendship for General Washington, 'the great councillor of the Thirteen Fires,' and often visited him, during his presidency, on the business of his tribe. His speeches on these occasions exhibit both his talent in composition and his adroitness in diplomacy. Washington fully reciprocated his respect and friendship. . . . . . . When Washington was about retiring from the presidency, Cornplanter made a special visit to Philadelphia to take an affectionate leave of the great benefactor of the white man and the red.

"After peace was permanently established between the Indians and the United States, Cornplanter retired from public life, and devoted his labors to his own people. He deplored the evils of intemperance, and exerted himself to suppress it. The benevolent efforts of missionaries among his tribe always received his encouragement, and at one time, his own heart seemed to be softened by the words of truth; yet he preserved, in his later years, many of the peculiar notions of the Indian faith."

Colonel Thomas Proctor Meets Cornplanter

In the spring of 1791, Colonel Thomas Proctor was sent on a mission to the Indians of the Northwest. During his journey, when he had reached the "Great Bend" on the upper Allegheny on April 6th, he met four Indian runners going with belts from Cornplanter to the Indians at the headwaters of the Allegheny, to inform them that several Delawares had recently been killed near Fort Pitt by some white people, said to be a party of Virginians. The Indians who had escaped being killed turned against the whites and killed and scalped seventeen of them some miles above Pittsburgh. The Indians who thus fell upon the settlers were pursued by a band of militia which overtook them, and compelled the Seneca chief, Newarle, to accompany them to Fort Pitt. Newarle and the commander at Fort Venango (Franklin) were taking a boatload of supplies for Cornplanter's Indians at the time when he was overtaken by the militia, and these supplies were likewise taken by the militia to Fort Pitt, although they had been purchased by Cornplanter.

Colonel Proctor, after holding a conference with the four Indian runners, descended the Allegheny to Fort Venango, where he met Cornplanter and accompanied him up the Allegheny to his town in Warren County. Here Proctor was entertained by the great Seneca, with a feast in true Indian hospitality.

Cornplanter and General Irvine

Cornplanter entertained a high regard for General William Irvine who, for several years subsequent to 1792, was engaged in superintending the surveys of land northwest of the Allegheny. Indeed, an affectionate intimacy subsisted between the two, and reciprocal visits were often made by them. Cornplanter said that General Irvine was one of the few white men who spoke the truth. On one occasion, when some Delawares of the Wolf Clan had threatened the life of the General, Cornplanter sent some of his own Indians to watch their movements. General Irvine at this time took up large tracts of land on Brokenstraw Creek in Warren County, some miles below Cornplanter's Reservation.

Cornplanter Visits General Wayne

When General Anthony Wayne was drilling the Legion of the United States at that place, since known at Legionville, on the north bank of the Ohio, about twenty miles below Pittsburgh, preparatory to leading it against the Western Indians, in 1794, he was visited by both Cornplanter and Guyasuta. Afterwards Cornplanter went on a peace mission among the hostile western tribes, but in vain. He found them too much elated by the overwhelming and inglorious defeats which they had administered to the armies of Generals Harmar and St. Clair, and too much under the influence of British traders. While Cornplanter was on his peace mission, three of his people were basely attacked near the Genesee by some whites, who killed one and severely wounded another. On hearing this news, Cornplanter said: "It is hard when I and my people are trying to make peace with the whites that we should receive such a reward."

Cornplanter's Letter to Major Isaac Craig

In the early winter of 1795, Major Thomas Butler, then in command at Fort Franklin, informed Major Isaac Craig of Pittsburgh, that Cornplanter had at his saw mill a large quantity of boards. Craig immediately dispatched Marcus Hulings, an experienced waterman, with three bags of money and some other articles up the Allegheny to Cornplanter's town to purchase this lumber. Hearing the next day that some private persons had gone on the same errand, Major Craig dispatched James Beard on horseback with a letter, informing the great Seneca of Hulings' object. Mr. Beard arrived in time and secured the lumber. The following is the letter of Cornplanter to Major Craig in reply to the latter's letter:

"Genesadego, 3d December, 1795.

"I thank the States for making me such kind ofers. We have made peace with the United States as long as watter runs, which was the reason that I built a mill in order to suport my family by it. More so, because I am geting old and not able to hunt. I also thank the States for the pleashure I now feel in meeting them again in friendship, you have sent a man to make a bargain with me for a sertain time which I do not like to do. But as long as my mill makes boards, the United States shall always have them in preference to any other, at the market price, and when you want no more boards I can't make blankets of them. As for the money you have sent, if I have not boards to the amount, leave it and I will pay it in boards in the Spring.

"I thank you kindly for the things you have sent me. I would thank Major Craig or Col. Butler to let Col. Pickering and Gen. Washington know that there is a grate deal of damage done in this country by Liquor; Capt. Brant has kiled his son and other chiefs has done the same, and when the drink was gone and they began to think of the horid crime they had comited, they resigned their command in the Nation; two Chiefs has been kiled, the one at Fort Franklin the other at Genesee. I have sent a speech to the States conserning the Chief killed at Franklin, and has been waiting all summer to receive pay for him, but can see no sign of its coming. I am by myself to bear all the burden of the people. Now father take pitty on me and send me 40 dollars worth of black Wampum and 10 of white; and I expect to see it in two months and an half, as I must make new Chiefs with it again that time, to help me. I wish to hear from my son and what progress he is making in his learning, and as soon as he is learned enough I want him at home to manage my business for me. I will leave it all to my father, Gen. Washington, to judge when he is learned enough. My compliments to my father and the United States, and I wish it was possible for me to live forever in the United States.

his

CAPT. X. O. BEAL.

mark"

It will be noted that, in the above letter, Cornplanter asks what progress his son "is making in his learning". This was his favorite son, Henry O'Bail, who was carefully educated, but later became a drunkard, and caused much sorrow to his aged father.

Cornplanter Offers to Assist Americans in War of 1812

Reference has been made to the fact that Cornplanter was a firm friend of the United States. He gave additional proof of this friendship when, in 1812, he came from the retirement of his sylvan retreat on the banks of the Allegheny, and offered himself and two hundred warriors to Colonel Dale, at Franklin, for a regiment which the Colonel was forming in Crawford and Venango counties to go to the defense of Erie. He was much disappointed when he learned that his services could not be accepted. However, a number of the Senecas did take an active part in the War of 1812. Among them were Cornplanter's son, Major Henry O'Bail, and his half-brother, Half-Town. Both of these were conspicuous in several engagements on the Niagara frontier.

Reverend Timothy Alden Visits Cornplanter

Reverend Timothy Alden, then president of Allegheny College, visited Cornplanter at his village on the Allegheny, in Warren County, in 1816, and thus describes the chief and his village:

"Jennesedaga, Cornplanter's village, is on a handsome piece of bottom land, and comprises about a dozen buildings. It was grateful to notice the agricultural habits of the place, and the numerous enclosures of buckwheat, corn, and oats. We also saw a number of oxen, cows, and horses, and many logs designed for the saw mill and the Pittsburgh market. Last year, 1815, the Western Missionary Society established a school in the village, under Mr. Samuel Oldham. Cornplanter, as soon as apprised of our arrival, came over to see us, and took charge of our horses. Though having many around him to obey his commands, yet, in the ancient patriarchal style, he chose to serve us himself, and actually went into the fields, cut the oats, and fed our beasts. He appears to be about 68 years of age, and 5 feet 10 inches in height. His countenance is strongly marked with intelligence and reflection. Contrary to the aboriginal custom, his chin is covered with a beard three or four inches in length. His house is of princely dimensions compared with most Indian huts, and has a piazza in front. He is owner of 1,300 acres of excellent land, 600 of which encircle the ground-plot of his little town. He receives an annual stipend from the United States of $250.00. Cornplanter's brother, lately deceased, called the prophet, was known by the high-sounding name Guskukewanna Konnediu, or Large Beautiful Lake. Kinjuquade, the name of another chief, signified the place of many fishes;—hence probably the name of Kinjua."

Day's "Historical Recollections" Again Quoted

Once more we quote from Day's "Historical Collections":

"In 1821-22 the commissioners of Warren County assumed the right to tax the private property of Cornplanter, and proceeded to enforce its collection. The old chief resisted it, conceiving it not only unlawful, but a personal indignity. The

sheriff again appeared with a small posse of armed men. Cornplanter took the deputation to a room around which were ranged
about a hundred rifles, and with the sententious brevity of an Indian, intimated that for each rifle a warrior would appear at his call.
The sheriff and his men speedily withdrew, determined, however,
to call out the militia. Several prudent citizens, fearing a sanguin-
ary collision, sent for the old chief in a friendly way to come to
Warren and compromise the matter. He came, and after some
persuasion, gave his note for the tax, amounting to $43.79. He
addressed, however, a remonstrance to the Governor of Pennsylvania, soliciting a return of the note, and an exemption from such
demands against land which the state itself had presented to him.
[Cornplanter's note was never paid. The state exempted his
lands from taxes]. He met them at the court house in Warren,
on which occasion he delivered the following speech, eminently
characteristic of himself and his race:

" 'Brothers: Yesterday was appointed for us all to meet here.
The talk which the governor sent us pleased us very much. I
think that the Great Spirit is very much pleased that the white
people have been induced so to assist the Indians as they have
done, and that He is pleased also to see the great men of this state
and of the United States so friendly to us. We are much pleased
with what has been done.'

" 'The Great Spirit first made the world, and next the flying
animals, and found all things good and prosperous. He is immortal and everlasting. After finishing the flying animals, He
came down on earth and there stood. Then He made different
kinds of trees, and weeds of all sorts, and people of every kind.
He made the spring and other seasons, and the weather suitable
for planting. These He did make. But stills to make whiskey
to be given to Indians He did not make. The Great Spirit bids
me tell the white people not to give Indians this kind of liquor.
When the Great Spirit had made the earth and its animals, He
went into the great lakes, where He breathed as easily as anywhere
else, and then made all the different kinds of fish. The Great Spirit
looked back on all that He had made. The different kinds He
made to be separate, and not to mix with and disturb each other.
But the white people have broken His command by mixing their
color with the Indians. The Indians have done better by not
doing so. The Great Spirit wishes that all wars and fighting
should cease.

" 'He next told us that there were three things for our people to attend to. First, we ought to take care of our wives and children. Secondly, the white people ought to attend to their farms and cattle. Thirdly, the Great Spirit has given the bears and deer to the Indians. He is the cause of all things that exist, and it is very wicked to go against His will. The Great Spirit wishes me to inform the people that they should quit drinking intoxicating drink, as being the cause of disease and death. He told us not to sell any more of our lands, for He never sold lands to any one. Some of us now keep the seventh day; but I wish to quit it, for the Great Spirit made it for others, but not for the Indians, who ought every day to attend to their business. He has ordered me to quit drinking any intoxicating drink, and not to lust after any woman but my own, and informs me that by doing so I should live the longer. He made known to me that it is very wicked to tell lies. Let no one suppose this I have said now is not true.

"I have now to thank the Governor for what he has done. I have informed him what the Great Spirit has ordered me to cease from, and I wish the Governor to inform others of what I have communicated. This is all I have at present to say.'

"The old chief appears, after this, again to have fallen into seclusion, taking no part even in the politics of his people.

"Notwithstanding his profession of Christianity, Cornplanter was very superstitious. 'Not long since,' says Mr. Foote, of Chautauqua County, 'he said the Good Spirit had told him not to have any thing to do with the white people, or even to preserve any mementoes or relics that had been given to him, from time to time, by the pale-faces, whereupon, among other things, he burnt up his belt, and broke his elegant sword.' "

Cornplanter Visits the Steamboat, Allegheny

In the "Pittsburgh Gazette" of May 28, 1830, we read an account of a trip of the steamboat, the "Allegheny", as follows:

"She left Pittsburgh on her third trip on the 14th of May, 1830, with sixty-four passengers and twenty-five or thirty tons of freight, and arrived at Warren at nine o'clock on the 19th,—three and one-half days' running time,—and on the same evening she departed from Warren for Olean. At nine o'clock the next day she arrived opposite the Indian village of Cornplanter. Here a deputation of gentlemen waited on this ancient and well-known Seneca chief, and invited him on board this new and, to him, wonderful visitor, a steamboat. He was in all his native simplicity of dress and manner of living, lying on his couch, made of rough pine boards, and covered with deer skins and blankets. His habitation, a two-story log house, was in a state of decay, without furniture, except a few benches, and wooden bowls and spoons to eat out of. He was a smart, active man, seemingly possessed of all his strength of mind and perfect health. He, with his son, Charles, sixty years of age, and his son-in-law, came on board and remained until she passed six miles up, and then returned in their own canoe, after expressing great pleasure.

Last Days of Cornplanter

Concerning the last days of this great leader of the Senecas, a gentleman wrote the following in "The Democratic Arch", a newspaper of Venango County:

"I once saw the aged and venerable chief, and had an interesting interview with him, about a year and a half before his death. I thought of many things when seated near him, beneath the widspreading shade of an old sycamore, on the banks of the Allegheny —many things to ask him—the scenes of the Revolution, the generals that fought its battles and conquered, the Indians, his tribe, the Six Nations, and himself. He was constitutionally sedate,—was never observed to smile, much less to indulge in the 'luxury of a laugh.' When I saw him, he estimated his age to be over 100 years. I think 103 was about his reckoning of it. This would make him near 105 years old at the time of his decease. His person was much stooped, and his stature was far short of what it once had been—not being over 5 feet 6 inches at the time I speak of. Mr. John Struthers, of Ohio, told me, some years since, that he had seen him near 50 years ago, and at that period, he was about his height—viz., 6 feet 1 inch. Time and hardship had made dreadful impressions upon that ancient form. The chest was sunken, and his shoulders were drawn forward, making the upper part of his body resemble a trough. His limbs had lost their size and become crooked. His feet, too, (for he had taken off his moccasins,) were deformed and haggard by injury. I would say that most of the fingers on one hand were useless; the sinews had been severed by a blow of the tomahawk or scalping knife. How I longed to ask him what scene of blood and strife had thus stamped the enduring evidence of its existence upon his person! But to have done so would, in all probability, have put an end to all further conversation on any subject,—the information desired would certainly not have been received,—and I had to forgo my curiosity.

"He had but one eye, and even the socket of the lost organ was hid by the overhanging brow resting upon the high cheek bone. His remaining eye was one of the brightest and blackest hue. Never have I seen one, in young or old, that equalled it in brilliancy. Perhaps it had borrowed lustre from the eternal darkness that rested on its neighboring orbit. His ears had been dressed in the Indian mode; all but the outside ring had been cut away. On the one ear this ring had been torn asunder near the top, and hung down his neck like a useless rag. He had a full head of hair, white as the 'diven snow', which covered a head of ample dimensions and admirable shape. His face was not swarthy; but this may be accounted for from the fact, also, that he was but half Indian.

"He told me that he had been at Franklin more than 80 years before the period of our conversation, on his passage down the Ohio and Mississippi, with the warriors of his tribe, on some expedition against the Creeks or Osages. He had long been a man of peace, and I believe his great characteristics were humanity and truth. It is said that Brant and the Cornplanter were never friends after the massacre of Cherry Valley. Some have alleged, because the Wyoming massacre was perpetrated by the Senecas, that the Cornplanter was there. Of the justice of this suspicion there are many reasons for doubt. It is certain that he was not the chief of the Senecas at that time; the name of the chief in that expedition was Ge-en-quah-toh, or He-goes-in-the-smoke.

"As he stood before me—the ancient chief in ruins—how forcibly was I struck with the truth of the beautiful figure of the old aboriginal chieftain, who, in describing himself, said he was 'like an aged hemlock, dead at the top, and whose branches alone were green.' After more than one hundred years of most varied life —of strife, of danger, of peace—he at last slumbers in deep repose, on the banks of his own beloved Allegheny."

Death of Cornplanter

This great leader of the Senecas died at Cornplanter Town, Warren County, on the banks of his long-loved Allegheny, on February 18th, 1836,—the passing of the last great Indian chief of Pennsylvania. "Whether at the time of his death he expected to go to the fair Hunting Grounds of his own people or to the Heaven of the Christians, is not known." It was his wish that his grave should remain unmarked. However, the State of Pennsylvania erected a monument at his grave, in 1866, the first monument erected by any state of the Union to an Indian chief, bearing the following inscription:

"Gy-ant-wa-chia, The Cornplanter,
JOHN O'BAIL, ALIAS CORNPLANTER,
DIED
At Cornplanter Town, Feb. 18, A. D. 1836,
Aged About 100 Years.

"Chief of the Seneca tribe, and a principal chief of the Six Nations from the period of the Revolutionary War to the time of his death. Distinguished for talent, courage, eloquence, sobriety, and love for tribe and race, to whose welfare he devoted his time, his energy, and his means during a long and eventful life."

Three of Cornplanter's children were present at the dedication of his monument, the last of whom died in 1874, aged about one hundred years. Other descendants still reside on the Cornplanter Reservation, in Warren County, cherishing the memory of "one of the bravest, noblest and truest specimens of the aboriginal race."

CHAPTER XXXI

Other Indian Events in Pennsylvania During the Revolutionary War

HOUGH not directly connected with any of the outstanding Indian chiefs of Pennsylvania whose biographies we have just concluded, we devote this chapter and the next to a narration of additional Indian events in Pennsylvania during the Revolutionary War—a story of outrages and terrible atrocities.

In weighing the conduct of an individual, of a group of individuals, or of a nation, we should take into consideration their mental endowment, moral standard, social aptitude, and the kind of temptations they meet or that may have been thrust upon them. And so, in reading the account of the Indian atrocities during the Revolutionary War, we should not lose sight of the fact that, as was pointed out in former chapters, the British, early in this struggle, stirred up the Indians against the Americans, offering them rewards for American scalps, well knowing that Indian warfare meant suffering and death to the innocent and the helpless. The aged father, whose form was bent by a life of toil and hardship on the frontier; the aged mother, whose hair was silvered by child-birth pain and a life full of care and rich in service; the widow, lingering by the grave of her buried love; the matron, devoted and ministering to her children; the young man of talent, promise, and joyous parental hope; the boy just opening into adolescence; the maiden in the loveliness of grace, beauty, and virtue; the child, angel-eyed and silken haired, prattling at its parent's knee; the tender and helpless babe on its mother's breast— the merciless Indian dashed out the brains of all these, tore off their reeking scalps, carried them to British agents, and received the British scalp bounty for their dreadful work.

As pointed out in former chapters, the British general, Henry Hamilton, who was in command at Detroit, was directed, on October 6th, 1776, to enlist the Indians in the British service, and have them ready for operations against the western frontier the next spring. Hamilton incited many Indian incursions against the frontier, and gave the Indians $50.00 for each scalp. About

June 1st, 1777, he began to enlist and send out war parties against the frontiers of Kentucky, Virginia, and Pennsylvania. About the end of July of that year, he reported to his superior commander at Quebec, that he had sent out fifteen war parties, consisting of 30 white men and 289 Indians, an average of 21 in each band. These Indians were chiefly Wyandots and Miamis, of Northwestern Ohio, and Shawnees of Southern Ohio. The Americans held Hamilton in abhorrence, and nick-named him the "hairbuyer" general. He continued his dreadful work until his capture by Colonel George Rodgers Clark, at Vincennes, Indiana, February 25th, 1779, who sent him to Richmond as a prisoner where he was confined in irons.

The British agents in New York were no better than Hamilton They sent the Senecas and various other tribes of the Six Nations in alliance with them, against the frontiers of New York and both Eastern and Western Pennsylvania. As will presently be seen, they gave their Indian allies ten dollars each for the two hundred and twenty-seven scalps of principally old men, women and children, killed at the Wyoming cassacre of July 3rd, 1778.

Franklin, in his list of twenty-six British atrocities, gives the 10th and 14th as follows:

"10th. The King of England, giving audience to his Secretary of War, who presents him a schedule entitled 'Account of Scalps'; which he receives very graciously.

"14th. The commanding officer at Niagara, sitting in state, a table before him, his soldiers and savages bring him scalps of the Wyoming families and presenting them. Money on the table with which he pays for them."

Who stands with the greater condemnation before the judgment seat of Almighty God? Is it the untutored Red Man with passions wild as the storms of his native mountains? Or, is it the anointed children of education and civilization, who were the instigators of his deeds of blood and death?

Attack on the Campbell Family

Robert Campbell lived with his parents near Pleasant Grove Church in Cook Township, Westmoreland County. In July, 1775, he and his brothers, William and Thomas, were working in the harvest field when they were captured by a band of Senecas. After capturing the boys, the Indians went to the Campbell home, where they killed and scalped the mother and her infant. Their bodies were found the next day. They also captured the girls, Polly, Isabella, and Sarah. The youngest girl, who had difficulty in riding a horse upon which the Indians placed her, was killed about a mile from the home, and her body was found a few days later. The three boys and two girls were then taken across the Kiskiminetas below the mouth of the Loyalhanna, and carried to New York. After four years, the two girls were released, and returned to their father. Robert escaped in 1782, and succeeded in returning to his home. At the close of the Revolutionary War, William was exchanged, and also returned home. Thomas never returned. What became of him is unknown.

The Easton Conference of January 27, 1777

Prior to entering into the treaty with the Delawares, an account of which was given in Chapter XXV, the Continental Congress as early as January, 1777, received information "that certain tribes of Indians living in the back parts of the country near the waters of the Susquehanna within the Confederacy and under the protection of the Six Nations, the friends and allies of the United States", intended coming to Easton to hold a conference with the Continental and Colonial Authorities. Thereupon, the Continental Congress appointed a commission, consisting of George Taylor, George Walton, and others, to purchase suitable presents and to conduct a treaty with these Indians; while the Assembly of Pennsylvania named Colonels Lowry and Cunningham as their commissioners, and the Council of Safety sent Colonels Dean and Bull. Thomas Paine was appointed to act as secretary of the commission.

Some of the Indians reached Wilkes-Barre on January 7th, and announced the coming of the larger delegation, which reached the same place on January 15th. They then proceeded to Easton, where the conference was opened on January 27th, in the German Reformed Church. It is claimed that, before proceeding to business, the members of the commission and the Indians shook hands with one another, and drank to the health of the Continental Congress and the Six Nations, as the notes of the organ filled the auditorium. There were seventy men and one hundred women and children in the Indian delegation; and among the chiefs were the following: Taasquah, or "King Charles", of the Cayuga; Tawanah, or "The Big Tree", of the Seneca; Mytakawha, or "Walking on Foot", and Kaknah, or "Standing by a Tree", of the Munsee; Amatincka, or "Raising Anything Up" of the Nanti-coke; Wilakinko, or "King Last Night" of the Conoy, and Thomas Green, whose wife was a Mohawk, as interpreter.

The conference did not proceed far until it became evident that the British, through the influence of Colonel John Butler, then at Niagara, were having great success in turning the Six Nations against the Americans. The results of this conference are thus set forth in the report of the treaty, made to the Supreme Executive Council of Pennsylvania: "The Indians seem to be inclined to act the wise part with respect to the present dispute. If they are to be relied upon, they mean to be neuter. We have already learned their good intentions." But, as has been seen, the overwhelming majority of the warriors of the Six Nations took the British side in the Revolutionary War.

Capture of Andrew McFarlane

In the autumn of 1774, Andrew McFarlane, with his brother, James, had started a trading post at Kittanning. The Revolutionary War having come on, the Continental Congress, in July, 1776, ordered the raising of a regiment of seven companies from Westmoreland, and one from Bedford, to erect and garrison forts at Kittanning, LeBoueff, and Erie, to protect the Allegheny Valley from the incursions of Tories and Iroquois. This regiment, under the command of Colonel Aeneas Mackey, with George Wilson as Lieutenant-Colonel, and Richard Butler, for whom Butler County is named, as Major, rendezvoused at Kittanning late in the fall, built Fort Armstrong at that place, and prepared to advance up the Allegheny to erect the other forts, when a call was received for the regiment to march eastward across the state, and join the army of General Washington near the Delaware. In spite of a storm of protest on the western frontier this regiment, afterwards known as the Eighth Pennsylvania, began its long and terrible march in January, 1777, to join Washington's army. After the regiment left Kittanning, McFarlane was deserted by all his neighbors except two clerks. In the meantime he had, without success, requested the Westmoreland commissioners to send some militia to guard the stores that Colonel Mackey left at Kittanning; and he and Samuel Moorehead, who lived at Black Lick Creek, Indiana County, undertook to raise a force of volunteer rangers, McFarlane being his lieutenant.

On February 25th, two British subalterns, two Chippewa, and

two Iroquois Indians, sent by the British commandant at Fort Niagara to descend the Allegheny, arrived on the west side of the Allegheny opposite McFarlane's trading post at Kittanning, and shouted toward the other shore, calling for a canoe. McFarlane, thinking that the Indians had come to trade or possibly to bring some important news, crossed in a boat to the western shore. Upon stepping from his boat, he was seized by the Indians and told that he was a prisoner, his capture being witnessed by his wife "and some men at the settlement". His captors carried him to Quebec where, through the efforts of his brother, James, then a lieutenant in the First Pennsylvania Regiment, he was exchanged, in the autumn of 1780, and rejoined his wife, Margaret Lynn Lewis, at Staunton, Virginia. Soon thereafter he opened another trading house on Chartier's Creek, Allegheny County, where he lived for many years.

Upon the capture of her husband, Mrs. McFarlane with her infant in her arms fled through the wilderness to Carnahan's block house, more than twenty miles distant, and located in Bell Township, Westmoreland County, about two miles from the Kiskiminetas River.

Andrew McFarlane's brother, James, as the leader of a band of insurrectionists during the Whiskey Rebellion, lost his life in July, 1794, in an attack upon the house of General Neville, Revenue Collector, near Bower Hill, Allegheny County. His dust reposes in the Old Mingo Creek Cemetery near Monongahela City, Washington County.

Indian Massacre Near Standing Stone

On June 19th, 1777, occurred the massacre at what was known as the Big Spring several miles west of the fort at Standing Stone, now Huntingdon, Pennsylvania. The Indians destroyed the plantations in the neighborhood, and the inhabitants fled to the fort. Felix Donnelly, his son, Francis, Bartholomew Maguire, and his daughter, Jane, residing near the mouth of Shaver's Creek, placed their effects upon horses, and with a cow started for the fort, when the Indians entered the neighborhood. Jane Maguire proceeded on ahead driving the cow, while her father and the Donnellys followed in the rear on horseback. When they had reached a point about opposite the Big Spring, an Indian fired from ambush and killed the younger Donnelly. His father who was close beside him, caught him as he was falling from his horse;

whereupon, Maguire rode to his side, and the two held the dead body of the boy upon the horse. The Indians then rushed from their hiding places and fired upon the party, one bullet striking Donnelly and another grazing Maguire's ear. Donnelly fell to the ground as did the body of his dead son. The Indians scalped the boy and pursued Jane Maguire, who succeeded in escaping after she had lost her dress in freeing herself from an Indian who attempted to capture her. Some men on the opposite side of Shaver's Creek hearing the firing, rushed to the scene, and the Indians then retreated into the woods, not knowing the strength of the party. Maguire and his daughter reached the fort and alarmed the garrison, which started in pursuit of the Indians, but failed to overtake them. The dead body of young Francis Donnelly was then buried at a spot now within the limits of the town of Huntingdon.

Outrages in Westmoreland County in 1777

During October and November, 1777, when General Edward Hand, who was then in command of Fort Pitt, was endeavoring to recruit his army for an invasion of the Indian country, many raids were made into Westmoreland County, principally by the Senecas. These raids were no doubt instigated by Guyasuta, and possibly some of them were led by him. An incursion was made into the Ligonier Valley about the middle of October, and eleven men were killed and scalped near Palmer's Fort, located in Fairfield Township, midway between the Chestnut Ridge and Laurel Hill Mountain. A few days later four children were killed within site of this fort; and three men were killed and a number captured within a few miles of Ligonier.

On November 1st, Lieutenant Samuel Craig, who lived near Shield's Fort, located near the town of New Alexandria, Westmoreland County, was riding toward Ligonier for salt, when he was waylaid and either killed or captured at the western base of Chestnut Ridge. Rangers found his mare lying dead near the trail with eight bullets in her body, but no trace of Craig was ever discovered.

At about the same time a band of Senecas led by a Canadian, attacked Fort Wallace, about a mile south of Blairsville, but their leader was killed and they were repulsed. At about the same time, also, Major James Wilson, hearing the firing of guns at the cabin of his neighbor while at work on his farm, got his rifle and

went to investigate.   He found the neighbor killed, the head being
severed from his body.   Wilson then hurriedly took his wife and
children to Fort Barr, located on a tributary of the Loyalhanna,
about five and one-half miles southeast of Fort Wallace.

On November 2nd, 1777, William Richardson was killed and
scalped about three miles from Fort Ligonier.   At the same time,
two men were killed and a woman captured not far from the place
where Richardson met his death.

Among the prisoners taken by the Indians during these incursions, were Major Charles Campbell and Randall Laughlin, who
were carried to Quebec, where they were exchanged in the fall of
1778.   The band of Indians perpetrating these outrages, was pursued by a party of rangers led by the celebrated Colonel James
Smith, Captain John Hinkston, and Robert Barr.   Smith and his
rangers overtook the Indians on the east bank of the Allegheny
River, near Kittanning, killed five of them, and returned in
triumph to the settlements with the scalps of these Indians and
with the horses which they had stolen.

The Squaw Campaign

General Hand, aroused by the above depredations, and learning that the British had built a magazine where Cleveland, Ohio,
now stands, and had stored it with arms, ammunition, and clothing
for use of the Indian incursions proposed to be made the next
spring, determined to lead an expedition for the destruction of
these supplies.   His expedition left Fort Pitt in February, 1778,
descending the Ohio to the mouth of the Beaver and then ascending the Beaver to the mouth of the Mahoning.   By the time the
Mahoning was reached that stream was almost impassable, and
Hand was so disheartened that he was about to give up the expedition and return, when the footprints of some Indians were discovered on the high ground.   These tracks led to a small Indian
village, where Edinburg, Lawrence County, now stands.   Hand's
forces attacked the village, but found that it contained only one
old man, and some squaws and children, the warriors being away
on a hunt.   The Indians escaped except the old man and one
squaw, who were both shot, and another squaw, who was taken
prisoner.   This woman captive informed Hand that ten Delawares of the Wolf Clan were making salt ten miles farther up the
Mahoning.   Hand then dispatched a detachment after these
Indians, who proved to be four squaws and a boy.   The soldiers

killed three of the squaws and the boy, and the other squaw was taken prisoner.

The condition of the weather making further progress impossible, General Hand led his army back to Fort Pitt with the two squaw captives. His formidable force of five hundred horsemen had slain one old man, four women, one boy, and captured two women. On Hand's arrival at Fort Pitt, the frontiersmen derided his recent exploits and dubbed the expedition the "Squaw Campaign." Discouraged and humiliated, he asked General Washington to relieve him, and on May 2nd, Congress voted his recall, and commissioned General Lachlan McIntosh to succeed him.

The Tories of Sinking Spring Valley

While the Tory plotting leading to the flight of the Tories, Captain Alexander McKee, Matthew Elliott, Robert Surphlit, and Simon Girty from Fort Pitt, during the winter of 1777 and 1778, as related in Chapter XXV, was going on, British agents from Niagara and Detroit visited several isolated settlements in the mountains of Pennsylvania, in an effort to persuade the mountaineers to espouse the British cause. One of these agents succeeded in deluding a number of frontiersmen in what is now Blair County, promising that any man who deserted the American cause should have two hundred acres of land on the conclusion of peace. He told these settlers that, if they would join a force of British and Indians coming down the Allegheny in the spring of 1778, they would be permitted to join in a general incursion against the frontier settlements, and receive their share of the pillage.

The frontiersmen who yielded to the persuasions of the British agent, held meetings in the isolated Sinking Spring Valley, in Blair County, in February and March, 1778, their leader being John Weston. In the meantime, after fully enlisting Weston, the British agent returned up the Allegheny, promising to come to Kittanning about the middle of April with a force of three hundred Indians and Tories to meet Weston's followers, and then attack Fort Pitt and the frontier settlements. By about the first of April, Weston had increased his band to thirty, and was joined about that time by a man named McKee, who came from Carlisle. At Carlisle, McKee had been in communication with a British officer who had been held at that place as a prisoner of war, who gave McKee a letter addressed to all British officers, vouching for the loyalty of McKee and his associates. This letter was to be used in securing the protection of the plotters of the Sinking Spring Valley, when they would meet the force of British and Indians at Kittanning.

Presently word reached the plotters that a force of Indians had gathered at Kittanning, and occupied the fort at that place, which had been deserted by the Americans the year before. Then Weston and his associates set out in their march over the mountains to Kittanning, crossing the main range of the Alleghenies at Kittanning Point, and following the Kittanning Indian Trail. On the afternoon of the second day, they encountered a band of one hundred Iroquois who were on a plundering raid of their own, and believed Weston and his men to be enemies. Weston ran forward waving his hand and shouting: "Friends! Friends!" The Iroquois being ignorant of the conspiracy, killed and scalped Weston, and then darted into the thickets. McKee waving in one hand the letter he had received from the British prisoner at Carlisle and in the other a white handkerchief, called out to the Indians: "Brothers! Brothers!" The Indians did not respond, but vanished into the forest.

Weston was buried where he fell, and his companions decided to proceed no further. Many perished from hunger in the wilderness. Some, after great suffering, reached British posts in the southern colonies. Five returned to their homes, and were later lodged in jail at Bedford. The leader of these, Richard Weston, brother of the dead plotter, was caught in the Sinking Spring Valley by a party of Americans, and lodged in jail at Carlisle to await trial, but later made his escape. Those who had fled were charged with treason, and their estates were forfeited. After the Revolutionary War was over, a few returned to Pennsylvania, succeeded in procuring the removal of the attainder, and got back their land.

Outrages in Westmoreland County in 1778

In April, 1778, the Senecas crossed the Kiskiminetas and Conemaugh, and once more entered Westmoreland County. On the 28th of that month about twenty rangers, commanded by Captain Hopkins who had gone out from Fort Wallace, were surprised by a larger force of Indians, and defeated. Nine of the rangers lay dead in the forest and their bodies were left behind, while Captain Hopkins was slightly wounded. Four of the Indians were killed in the engagement.

Hassler, in his "Old Westmoreland" suggests that this was probably the combat referred to by Dr. Joseph Smith in his "Old Redstone", in which Ebenezer Finley, son of the pioneer preacher, James Finley, took part. According to Smith, a horseman dashed into the fort with the word that he had seen two men and a woman fleeing through the woods from Indians. About twenty of the militia at Fort Wallace then sallied forth, and at about a mile and a half from the fort were ambushed. Presently, the militia retreated toward the fort, in the meantime many being shot down or tomahawked. Ebenezer Finley having fallen behind his companions while trying to prime his gun, exerted himself tremendously to prevent his being overtaken. In this effort he succeeded in passing a comrade by striking him on the shoulder with his elbow. At almost the same instant his comrade was brained with a tomahawk. Says Hassler: "Thus young Finley saved himself by sacrificing the life of another, and the pious author [Dr. Joseph Smith] would have it that Finley escaped by the interposition of Providence."

Hassler, in his "Old Westmoreland" describes another event which tradition says took place near Fort Wallace possibly in the summer of 1778, as follows:

"The story goes that signs of Indians were seen near Fort Barr, and the settlers throughout the southern part of Derry took refuge there. They were preparing to withstand an attack, when brisk firing was heard in the direction of Fort Wallace. Major James Wilson, at the head of about forty men, promptly set out from Barr's to the relief of the other post. They arrived within sight of Fort Wallace, which they found heavily besieged; but as soon as Wilson's company appeared, the savages turned upon it and assailed it in overwhelming force. The principal conflict took place on a bridge over a deep gully, about 500 yards from the fort. Several Indians were there slain and others were thrown over the bridge; but Wilson's party was forced to retreat and fought desperately all the way back to Fort Barr. During this retreat two of Robert Barr's sons, Alexander and Robert, were killed, but their bodies were saved from the scalping knife. All others gained the stockade in safety, and the Indians soon afterward disappeared from the settlement."

In 1778, a settler named Reed lived not far from Fort Ligonier. When Indian troubles threatened the settlement, Reed and his family moved to the fort, where his oldest daughter, Rebecca, distinguished herself in running foot races with various

athletes of the garrison.   Some time during the summer, Rebecca
and her brother, George, a young man named Means, and his
sister Sarah, left the fort to gather berries in a clearing about two
miles away.   On their way, the young men, who were walking
ahead, met Major McDowell coming toward the fort.   At that
instant the party were fired upon by Indians.   McDowell's rifle
was splintered by a bullet, and young Reed was mortally wounded.
Young Means ran back to protect the girls, and was captured.
The girls started to run toward the fort, but the Indians soon
caught Miss Means.   Miss Reed, however, outdistanced her pursuers as she fled toward the fort.

The garrison hearing the firing, a relief party headed by a
young man named Shannon, proceeded in the direction of the firing.
These met Miss Reed a short distance from the fort, and Shannon
conducted her to safety, while the others proceeded to the scene of
the firing, where they found the lifeless bodies of young Reed and
Miss Means.   Three years later young Means returned from his
captivity and reported that the warrior who had chased Miss Reed
was renowned as an athlete among the Indians, but had lost his
prestige on account of his failure to catch the "white squaw."
Later young Shannon married Rebecca Reed, and they spent a
long and happy life in the Ligonier Valley.

The Ulery family lived about two miles south of Ligonier.
In the month of July, most likely in the year 1778, the three girls,
Julian, aged twenty, Elizabeth, aged eighteen, and Abigail, aged
sixteen, were raking hay a short distance from their home, when
they were attacked by Indians.   The girls ran toward the house
with their pursuers close on their heels.   Abigail was unable to
keep up with her sisters, and when the latter got into the house,
they immediately closed and barred the door, thinking that Abigail
had been captured.   The father then shot through the door,
wounding one of the Indians.   In the meantime, Abigail ran into
the woods above the house, and hid herself among leaves and weeds
in a depression made by the uprooting of a tree.   The Indians
came near where she lay concealed; but the wounded member of
the band was moaning so piteously that his companions, without
making further search for Abigail, carried him away, and soon
disappeared over the brow of the hill above the Ulery home.   No
doubt this Indian died, for shortly afterwards a newly made grave
was found at that place, and many years later the grave was opened and human bones exhumed by Isaac Slater.

The following day, Julian and Elizabeth went to work in the

same field, when Indians, evidently the same band that made the attack the day before, got between the girls and the house, and succeeded in capturing them. Julian and Elizabeth struggled desperately with their captors. Then, in the hope of making the girls reconciled to going along with them, the Indians gave them new moccasins. The captives still struggled, and were dragged along to the rivulet near Brant's school house, when the Indians became desperate and told them to make a choice between captivity and death. The girls struggled all the harder, and were then tomahawked and scalped on the spot. The Indians then hurried on, but presently returned to remove the moccasins from the girls, when they found Elizabeth partly recovered, and sitting up against a tree. An Indian then sunk his tomahawk into her brain. Julian was conscious but lay still, and the Indians thought her dead. She recovered but was never strong, and her scalp never healed. She spent her days on the homestead with her sister Abigail.

The Harman family lived in 1777 near Williams' block house about midway between Stahlstown and Donegal, Westmoreland County. Some time during the summer of this year, Mr. Harman and three of his neighbors were returning from some gathering in the neighborhood, when they were fired upon by Indians from ambush, and all killed except one, who, throwing his arms about his horse's neck, rode beyond the reach of the Indians. His body was found the next day with his horse standing by its side.

Mrs. Harman and her sons, Andrew, John, and Philip, spent the next winter at the block house, and then returned to the farm on Four Mile Run. One morning in the spring of 1778, Mrs. Harman sent John and Andrew to chase some horses of a neighbor out of a field of growing grain. A band of Senecas who were watching, captured the boys, and carried them to the headwaters of the Allegheny. A member of this Indian band had the tobacco pouch of Mr. Harman, which the boys recognized, and he was no doubt a member of the band who killed the father during the preceding summer. Both John and Andrew were adopted by the Senecas. John died among them about a year after his capture, but Andrew after two years was sold to a British officer for a bottle of rum, who took him to London where he was kept for another two years as a servant. At the end of the Revolutionary War, he was exchanged and sent to New York, from which place he immediately went to his old home in the Ligonier Valley, where he found his mother overjoyed to meet him. Andrew had many thrilling experiences during his captivity.   He was among the Senecas when Colonel Broadhead marched against them in the summer of 1779.

Massacre on Lycoming Creek

On June 10th, 1778, occurred the terrible massacre at Lycoming Creek, within the limits of the present town of Williamsport, Lycoming County. On this day, Peter Smith, his wife and six children, William King's wife and his two daughters, Ruth and Sarah, Michael Smith, Michael Campbell, and David Chambers, and two men named Snodgrass and Hammond, were going to Lycoming in wagons; and when they arrived at Loyalsock Creek, John Harris met them, told them that he heard firing up the creek, and advised them to return to Fort Muncy. Smith said that the firing would not stop him; and he and his party continued up the West Branch of the Susquehanna, while Harris proceeded to Fort Muncy and told the garrison of the firing which he had heard. A detail of fifteen soldiers then started from the fort in the direction of the firing.

When Smith and his party were within half a mile of Lycoming Creek, they were ambushed by Indians, and Snodgrass fell dead with a bullet through his forehead at the first fire.   The Indians then rushed toward the wagons, and the white men hurried toward the shelter of some trees, while two of the children, a boy and girl, escaped to the woods.   The Indians then endeavored to surround the party, and their movements being discovered, the other men fled leaving Campbell, who was fighting at too close quarters to join in the flight.   Campbell was killed and scalped on the spot.   Before the men were out of sight of the wagons, they saw the Indians attacking the women and children with their toma-hawks. This attack occurred just before sundown.   The boy who had escaped, fled to the stockade on Lycoming Creek, and inform-ed the garrison what had happened. In the meantime the detail of fifteen soldiers from Fort Muncy, under Captain William Hep-burn, arrived at the scene of this massacree and found the bodies of Snodgrass and Campbell. It was then too dark to pursue the Indians, but they pressed on toward Lycoming and met the party going out from that place.

On the following morning they returned to the scene of the massacre, and found the body of Peter Smith's wife. She had been shot, stabbed, and scalped. A little girl and a boy had also been killed and scalped. The body of Snodgrass was also found, shot through the head and scalped. The boy who had made his escape insisted that Mrs. King must be somewhere in the thicket, as he heard her scream and say that she would not go along with the Indians when they were dragging her away. The party then made another search and found the body of Mrs. King near the stream, to which she had dragged herself. She had been tomahawked and scalped, but was not dead. When her husband approached her she arose to a sitting position, greeted him, and then expired, not living long enough to relate the details of the massacre.

Broken-hearted, William King returned to Northumberland, and many years later, learning that his daughters were still alive, he started on foot for Niagara, accompanied by a faithful old Indian. He soon found his daughter Sarah and later, after much suffering and hardship, succeeded in finding the other daughter, Ruth. The three then returned to their home near Milton, Northumberland County.

Among those taken captive were Peter Wyckoff, his son, Cornelius, Thomas Covenhoven, and a negro, the latter of whom was burned at the stake in the presence of the other prisoners. Wyckoff and his son remained among the Indians for two years, when they were given their freedom.

A boulder bearing a bronze tablet has been erected in the town of Williamsport telling of this melancholy event.

Outrages on the North Branch of the Susquehanna

We have just seen how outrages were committed on the West Branch of the Susquehanna during the month of June. During this same month the North Branch of the Susquehanna was also devastated. On the 12th of the month, William Crooks and Asa Budd went up the river to a point several miles above Tunkhannock. Crooks was fired upon by some hostile Indians and killed. On the 17th, a party of six went up the river in canoes to observe the movements of the Indians. About six miles below Tunkhannock, those in the forward canoe landed and ascended the bank, when they saw an armed force of Indians and Tories advancing against them. Giving the alarm, they returned to their boats, and endeavored to get behind an island to escape the fire of the Indians. In this canoe were Mina Robbins, Joel Phelps, and Stephen Jenkins. Robbins was killed and Phelps wounded, while Jenkins escaped unharmed. Captain Jewett went up the river with a scouting party on the 26th, returning on the 30th with the news that the Indians and Tories were assembling in great force up the river. On the same day, June 30th, Benjamin Harding, Stuckely Harding, James Hadsall, and his sons, James and John, Daniel Weller, John Gardner, and Daniel Carr, went up the river into Exeter to their labor in the fields. Late in the afternoon they were attacked by Indians. Weller, Gardner and Carr were taken prisoners. Benjamin Harding, Stuckely Harding, James Hadsall, and his son James were killed. On July 1st, Colonel Nathan Denison and Lieutenant-Colonel George Dorrance with a small force marched from Forty Fort to Exeter, eleven miles distant, where the murders of the preceding day had been committed, and buried the dead.

The Wyoming Massacre

On July 3rd, 1778, occurred the terrible massacre of Wyoming. Late in June Colonel John Butler with his Tory rangers, a detachment of Sir John Johnson's Royal Greens, and a large body of Indians, chiefly Senecas, altogether a force numbering about four hundred British and Tories and seven hundred Indians, descended the North Branch of the Susquehanna, and entered the charming valley of the Wyoming, in Luzerne County. On July 2nd, Fort Jenkins, located within the present limits of the town of West Pittson, was attacked by these invaders, and capitulated after four of its defenders were killed and three taken prisoners. On the same day Wintermoot's fort, about a mile below Fort Jenkins, threw open its gates and here the British and Tories assembled.

There were several small stockades at Wyoming, but no cannon; and none of the forts was able to hold out against such a large force. Moreover most of the able-bodied men of Wyoming were in the American army. Colonel Zebulon Butler of the Continental army, happened to be at home at Wyoming at the time, and assumed command of the settlers, most of them being old men and boys who organized and formed themselves into companies to garrison the forts.

On July 3rd, Colonel Zebulon Butler's forces marched out to meet the invaders, Butler assisted by Major Garret, commanding the right wing, and Colonel Denison assisted by Lieutenant-Colonel George Dorrance, commanding the left. The engagement began between four and five o'clock in the afternoon. The enemy outnumbering the gallant defenders nearly three to one, were able to outflank them, especially on the left, where a swamp well suited

Indian warfare. The men of Wyoming fell in great numbers, and it soon becoming impossible to maintain their position, Colonel Dorrance gave an order to fall back, so as to present a better front to the enemy. His command, however, was mistaken as a signal for retreat. The defenders becoming demoralized, were slaughtered without mercy. Even those who surrendered as prisoners of war, were subjected to the most cruel torture. Sixteen Americans were arranged around a large stone, since known as the Bloody Rock, or Queen Esther's Rock, where Queen Esther Montour, a granddaughter of Madam Montour, dashed out their brains with a tomahawk as she passed around the circle. By a desperate effort three men, named Hammond, Evans, and Joseph Elliott, escaped her fury. In another similar ring nine persons were butchered in the same manner. Many were shot swimming the Susquehanna, and others were hunted out and killed in their hiding places. Only sixty of those who had marched out to give battle survived. The stockades were filled with widows and orphans. It has been said that one hundred and fifty widows and six orphans were the result of this battle, and that about two-thirds of the defenders were slaughtered. The Indians secured 227 scalps, for which the British afterwards paid ten dollars each. A monument has been erected marking the site of this, the most dreadful massacre in the annals of Pennsylvania.

At Forty Fort, located within the limits of the town of that name, the firing at Wyoming was distinctly heard, and the spirits of the defenders of that place were high until they learned the dreadful news of Wyoming, when the first fugitives reached there in the evening. Many other fugitives came to Forty Fort during the night, among them being Colonel Dennison, who rallied the little band for defense, and succeeded the next day in entering into terms of capitulation with the Tory leader, Colonel John Butler. The enemy marched into Forty Fort six abreast, the British and Tories at the northern gate, and the Indians at the southern. In violation of the terms of capitulation the Indians began immediately to rob, plunder, and destroy. Tory Butler did nothing to stop it. When night came on the blaze of burning dwellings lighted up the valley, and the terrified survivors of the massacre fled to the Pocono Mountains beyond Stroudsburg. Many of them however, perished in the dreadful wilderness on the way, and these places are still called "Shades of Death". In a few days Colonel John Butler led the first part of his force away, but the Indians continued their work of burning and plundering until almost every building in the beautiful valley was consumed.

Queen Esther, the fury in form of woman, was the most infamous of all the Montours. She became the wife of Eghohowen, a chief of the Wolf Clan of Delawares, at Asinsam, above Tioga, in 1760. After the death of her husband, she ruled as chieftainess of his tribe. At the time of the Wyoming massacre, she had her residence at Queen Esther's Town, opposite the western shore of Tioga Point, Bradford County. In the fall of that same year, Colonel Thomas Hartley led a force that destroyed her village, and she afterwards settled near the head of Cayuga Lake, New York, where she died.

The Great Runaway

The massacre of Wyoming was followed by the "Great Runaway" of the settlers on the West Branch of the Susquehanna, when they learned the fate of the settlers at Wyoming. Within two days following the massacre news had penetrated the entire North Branch Valley, and as far up the West Branch as Fort Antes, now Jersey Shore, Lycoming County. On July 12th, Colonel Matthew Smith wrote from Paxtang that he had just arrived at Harris' Ferry and beheld the greatest scenes of distress that he had ever seen, the place being crowded with settlers who had come down the river, leaving everything. Also William McClay, later the first United States senator from Pennsylvania, wrote from Paxtang on the same day as follows: "I left Sunbury and almost my whole property on Wednesday last. I will not trouble you with a recital of the inconveniences I suffered while I brought my family by water to this place. I never in my life saw such scenes of distress. The river and roads leading down it were covered with men, women and children, flying for their lives. In short. Northumberland County is broken up." At the same time, Robert Covenhoven wrote concerning the flight of the settlers: "I took my own family safely to Sunbury and came back in the keel boat to secure my furniture. Just as I rounded a point above Derrstown [now Lewisburg, Union County], I met the whole convoy from all the forts above. Such a sight I never saw in all my life. Boats, canoes, hog-troughs, rafts, hastily made of dry sticks, every sort of floating article had been put into requisition and was crowded with women, children, and plunder. Whenever an obstruction occurred at any shoal or ripple, the women would leap out into the water and put their shoulders to the boat or raft and launch it again into deep water. The men of the settlement came down in single file on each side of the river to guard the women and children. The whole convoy arrived safely at Sunbury, leaving the entire range of farms along the West Branch to the ravages of the Indians."

It is a remarkable fact that but few persons were killed by the Indians during this wild and precipitate flight of the settlers.

In answer to Colonel Hunter's appeal, Colonel Daniel Broadhead with the Eighth Pennsylvania Regiment, then on its march to Fort Pitt, was ordered to the West Branch, arriving at Fort Muncy on July 24th. Also Colonel Thomas Hartley with a small regiment arrived at Fort Augusta on August 1st and marched to the relief of Colonel Broadhead at Fort Muncy. After Colonel Hartley's expedition, which we shall now describe, some of the more venturesome settlers returned to their habitations.

Colonel Hartley's Expedition

Reference has already been made to Colonel Thomas Hartley's expedition in the autumn of 1778. Leaving Samuel Wallis' at Muncy on September 21, he led a force of two hundred men through swamps, over mountains, twenty times crossing the Lycoming River; and on the 26th, his advance party of nineteen fired upon an equal number of Indians, killed their leader, and put the rest to flight. This engagement caused the alarm to be given to the main body of the Indians against whom his expedition was aimed; and a few miles further he found where seventy warriors had slept the preceding night, from which place they had turned back. Furthermore, one of his men who had deserted him, had warned the Indians, as was learned when the expedition reached Sheshecununk, Bradford County, where fifteen Indians were taken prisoner.

From Sheshecununk, Hartley advanced to Tioga, destroyed the town, and captured a prisoner. Butler, the Tory leader, had been there with a force of three hundred Tories and Indians only a few hours before Hartley reached that place. Ascertaining at Tioga that a force of five hundred was fortifying itself at Chemung, only twelve miles distant, Hartley retreated to Sheshecununk, at which place he crossed the North Branch of the Susquehanna, and proceeded to the Indian town of Wyalusing, Bradford County. There with the supply of provisions exhausted, his force spent the night of September 28th, and devoted the next morning to killing and cooking beef. Seventy of his force left for home in canoes, and the remainder were attacked three times below Wyalusing, with the loss of four killed and wounded. At Wyoming three men going out looking for potatoes, were scalped, and Hartley left half of his detachment as a garrison at that place. He then returned to Sunbury and, the term of his militiamen having expired, he appealed to Congress and the Provincial Council for more troops. His expedition had marched three hundred miles in two weeks, devastating the country of Queen Esther, and destroying her town, as well as Tioga, Sheshecununk, and Wyalusing. In the forests and groves he found where the Indians had dressed and dried the scalps of the frontier victims.

About the 1st of November, the Indians came down the North Branch of the Susquehanna, destroying the settlements as far as the mouth of the Nescopeck, and investing Wyoming. Colonel Hartley then advanced from Fort Jenkins, (which was situated on the north shore of the North Branch of the Susquehanna about midway between Berwick and Bloomsburg, in Columbia County), with its garrison to the relief of Wyoming, clearing the country of the enemy.

Frances Slocum, the Lost Sister of Wyoming

On November 2nd, 1778, Jonathan Slocum and his sons, William and Benjamin, were at work harvesting their corn near Wyoming. At the Slocum home were the other members of the family and a Mrs. Nathan Kingsley and her two sons. About noon, the Kingsley boys, who were sharpening a knife on the grindstone in the front yard, were attacked by Indians. Mrs. Slocum hastened to the door and was horrified to see the lifeless body of the elder Kingsley boy lying on the ground, and the Indian who had killed him, preparing to scalp him with the knife that the boys were sharpening. Snatching her infant from the cradle and calling to the others to run for their lives, she fled out of the rear door of the house over a log fence into a swamp beyond, where she hid herself and her baby. In the meantime, the younger Kingsley boy and Frances Slocum, a girl five and a half years old, hid themselves under a staircase, and Judith Slocum with her three year old brother, Isaac, also fled toward the swamp, while little Mary Slocum, a girl nine years of age, started to flee in the direction of the fort at Wyoming, carrying her baby brother, one and one-half years old, in her arms. Ebenezer Slocum, a boy thirteen years old, was a cripple, and was unable to flee.

While the Slocums were fleeing from their home, the Indians

made their way into the house, dragging forth young Kingsley, Frances Slocum, and Ebenezer Slocum. Mrs. Slocum then, leaving her baby behind, rushed among the Indians and implored them to release the child. She pointed to the crippled feet of Ebenezer, and exclaimed: "The child is lame, he can do thee no good." The Indians then released Ebenezer, but in spite of the piteous pleadings of the mother, they refused to release little Frances. The leader of the Indians, throwing Frances athwart his shoulder, and another of the band doing likewise with young Kingsley, they dashed into the woods. Little Frances looked toward her mother and stretched out her little arms in a pitiful appeal. This was the last sight that the mother ever had of her little daughter,—a picture that was in her memory every waking moment until death.

Long years afterwards it was learned from Frances Slocum that she and the Kingsley boy were carried to a cave, where the Indians kept them that night. Setting out at sunrise the next morning, they traveled for many days before arriving at the Indian village to which the captors belonged. When they arrived at this village, the Kingsley boy was taken away, which was the last she ever saw or heard of him.

The chief who took Frances gave her to an aged Delaware couple, who adopted her, giving her the name of Weletawash, which was the name of the couple's youngest child, who had lately died. This Indian couple was living in Ontario, Canada, when the Revolution ended. They then moved to the site of the present city of Fort Wayne, Indiana, where Frances grew to womanhood, and in 1790 married the Delaware, Little Turtle. In 1794 her husband deserted her and went west. Later she married a chief of the Miamis called Shepoconnah, and in 1801 they, with their two sons and daughter removed to the Osage village about one mile from the confluence of the Mississineva and Wabash rivers in the state of Indiana. Here Shepoconnah was made a war chief of the Miamis and Frances was admitted into the Miami tribe, and given the name of Maconaquah, signifying "A Young Bear." Shepoconnah died in 1832.

After the capture of Frances her father was killed. Many efforts were made to obtain clues as to her whereabouts, but to no avail. Also, after peace was declared ending the Revolutionary War, her brothers made a journey to Fort Niagara, where they offered one hundred guineas for her recovery. The brothers never gave up the search for their sister. They visited many Indian villages and traveled thousands of miles, even enlisting the United

States Government in the search. They also attended every gathering of Indians where white children captives were given up.

Finally, in 1835, Colonel George W. Ewing, an Indian trader, was quartered in the home of Maconoquah, as Frances Slocum was now called, where she related the story of her life to him. Marveling at its mystery, Colonel Ewing wrote the postmaster at Lancaster, Pennsylvania, a letter containing the narrative of Maconoquah. No one however, was interested; but two years later John W. Forney, publisher of the Lancaster Intelligencer, ran across this letter and published it in July, 1837. Immediately the narrative was read by those who knew the story of the lost sister of Wyoming. A short time afterward Joseph Slocum journeyed to the home of Maconoquah, where he positively identified her as his long lost sister. She acknowledged him as her brother, but declined to leave her wigwam to enjoy the comforts of her brother's home in Wilkes-Barre. Said she: "No, I cannot. I have always lived with the Indians; they have always used me kindly; I am used to them. The Great Spirit has always allowed me to live with them, and I wish to live and die with them." The brother then returned to his home, and correspondence was kept up between the lost sister of Wyoming and her relatives until her death, which occurred March 9, 1847.

The Fatal Voyage of David Rodgers

In the spring of 1778, Governor Henry of Virginia, directed Captain David Rodgers, also a Virginian, then living at Redstone (Brownsville, Fayette County), to organize an expedition to bring powder from New Orleans by way of the Ohio River. Rodgers at once gathered up a force of forty settlers in the vicinity of Redstone, proceeded to Fort Pitt, and constructed two large flat boats. Among his force, was Basil Brown, one of the founders of Brownsville. Leaving Fort Pitt in June, Rodgers' force floated down to the mouth of the Arkansas River. At a Spanish fort near this place, he learned that the powder had been sent up the Mississippi to St. Louis. Leaving his boats and most of his men at the post, he, with six companions, floated in a canoe down to the Spanish capital of Louisiana, obtained there the proper papers, and then returned to St. Louis and secured the powder.

The voyage up the Ohio was uneventful until the mouth of the Licking was reached. Here, on an October afternoon, several Indians were seen crossing the Ohio to the Kentucky shore, about a mile up stream. Rodgers believed that the Indians did not see his boats, and decided to halt and attack them. Pulling his boats on the beach in the mouth of the Licking, he penetrated the forest, where a strong force of Indians, led by Simon Girty and Matthew Elliott, outnumbering Rodgers' party two to one, surrounded the voyagers and killed the entire party except thirteen. The Indians who had been seen crossing the Ohio were only decoys. Captain Rodgers was fatally wounded but, by the help of John Knotts, was able to hide in a dark ravine, where Knotts left the dying man in the morning, and returned through the wilderness to Redstone. Afterwards an unsuccessful search was made for the body of Rodgers, which had probably been devoured by wolves.

Robert Benham, commissary of the expedition, was wounded in both legs, but crawled into a tree-top. Here, on the afternoon of the second day, suffering greatly from hunger, he shot a raccoon which came within range of his rifle At the sound of his gun, he heard a voice which he believed to be the shout of an Indian, and at once re-loaded his rifle. Footsteps were heard approaching, and a white man covered with blood came out of the thicket. This was Basil Brown. He was wounded in the right arm and left shoulder, both arms being helpless. Benham pointed out the dead raccoon, and Brown kicked it to where Benham reclined, who built a fire, dressed and cooked the animal, and fed both Brown and himself. Benham then placed his folded hat between Brown's teeth, and the latter, wading into the Licking, dipped the hat into the water, and carried it full to his thirsty companion. During the days which followed, Brown would drive rabbits, wild turkey, and other game, within the range of Benham's rifle, and when the latter had shot them, Brown kicked them to the fire, and Benham dressed and cooked the game. Thus, these two men lived in the wilderness for nineteen days, when a flat boat descending the Ohio, rescued them, and took them to what is now Louisville, Kentucky. Brown returned to the Redstone settlement; but Benham, when the war was over, settled at the place which was the scene of Rodgers' disaster, the site of Newport, Kentucky.

CHAPTER XXXII

Other Indian Events in Pennsylvania During the Revolutionary War

(Continued)

The Prowess of Mrs. Experience Bozarth

BOUT the middle of March, 1779, several families who were afraid to stay at home, gathered at the house of Mrs. Experience Bozarth on Dunkard Creek, Greene County. About April 1st, a band of Indians made an attack upon the house, when all the men except two were absent. Some of the children, who were playing near the house, came running in great haste, saying that "there were ugly red men". One of the men in the house stepped to the door, receiving a bullet in his side, causing him to fall back into the house. The Indian who shot him came in over his prostrate body, and engaged the other man in the house. This man tossed the Indian on a bed, and called for a knife to kill him. Mrs. Bozarth not finding a knife, took up an axe that lay nearby, and with it knocked out the brains of this Indian. At the same instant, a second Indian entered the door, and shot the man dead who was struggling with the Indian on the bed. Mrs. Bozart immediately attacked this second Indian with her axe, giving him several large gashes which let his entrails appear. He bawled with pain. Then one of several other Indians who had been engaged in killing the children out of doors, rushed to the relief of the wounded Indian, and Mrs. Bozarth split his head open with her axe as he came through the door. Another Indian dragged the wounded and bellowing savage out of doors; whereupon Mrs. Bozarth with the assistance of the man who had been shot, but by this time was a little recovered, shut the door and fastened it. The inmates of the house kept garrison for several days until a relief party arrived. In the meantime, the dead white man and the dead Indian were both in the house with them.

Capture of Assemblyman James McKnight

On April 26th, 1779, James McKnight was captured by the Indians at Fort Freeland, located about four miles east of Watson-

town, Northumberland County.   He was a member of the general
Assembly of Pennsylvania, having been elected to that office in
1778.   The following letter written by Colonel Samuel Hunter
from Fort Augusta (Sunbury), on April 27th, 1779, gives an
account of this event and other outrages on the frontier:

"I am really sorry to inform you of our present disturbances;
not a day, but there is some of the enemy makes their appearances
on our frontiers.   On Sunday last, there was a party of savages
attacked the inhabitants that lived near Fort Jenkins, and had
taken two or three familys prisoners, but the garrison being
appris'd of it, about thirty men turned out of the fort and rescued
the prisoners; the Indians collecting themselves in a body drove
our men under cover of the fort, with the loss of three men kill'd
and four badly wounded; they burned several houses near the fort,
kill'd cattle, and drove off a number of horses.

"Yesterday there was another party of Indians, about thirty
or forty, kill'd and took seven of our militia, that was stationed at
a little Fort near Muncy Hill, call'd Fort Freeland; there was two
or three of the inhabitants taken prisoners; among the latter is
James McKnight, Esqr., one of our Assemblymen; the same day
a party of thirteen of the inhabitants that went to hunt their
horses, about four or five miles from Fort Muncy was fired upon
by a large party of Indians, and all taken or kill'd except one man.
Captain Walker, of the Continental Troops, who commands at
that post, turned out with thirty-four men to the place he heard
the firing, and found four men kill'd and scalped and supposes
they captured ye remaind'r.

"This is the way our frontiers is harrassed by a cruel savage
enemy, so that they cannot get any spring crops in to induce them
to stay in the county.   I am afraid in a very short time we shall
have no inhabitants above this place unless when General Hand
arrives here, he may order some of the troops at Wyoming down
on our frontiers; all Col. Hartley's Regiment, our two months'
men, and what militia we can turn out, is very inadequate to guard
our country.

"I am certain everything is doing for our relief, but afraid it
will be too late for this county, as it's impossible to prevail on the
inhabitants to make a stand, upon account of their women and
childer.

"Our case is really deplorable and alarming, and our county
on ye eve of breaking up, as I am informed at the time I am writing this by two or three expresses that there is nothing to be seen

but desolation, fire and smoke; as the inhabitants is collected at particular places, the enemy burns all their houses that they have evacuated."

The family of James McKnight had other terrible experiences with the Indians. In the autumn of 1778 Mrs. James McKnight and Mrs. Margaret Wilson Durham, each with an infant in her arms, started on horseback from Fort Freeland to go to Northumberland when, near the mouth of Warrior Run, about two miles from the fort, they were fired upon by a band of Indians and ambushed. Mrs. Durham's child was killed in her arms, and an Indian rushed out of the bushes and scalped her. Alexander Guffy, Peter Williams, and Ellis Williams hastened to the scene of the shooting, and were greatly surprised to find Mrs. Durham alive and piteously calling for water. These men bound up her head as best they could and conveyed her in a canoe down the river to Sunbury, where Colonel William Plunkett, who was also a physician, dressed her wounded head. She recovered and lived to the mature age of seventy-four years, dying in 1829.

Mrs. McKnight was not injured. Her horse became frightened at the shooting, and ran back to the fort. As the horse wheeled, Mrs. McKnight's child fell from her arms; but she caught it by the foot, and thus held it until the fort was reached. Two of Mrs. McKnight's sons, who were accompanying her and Mrs. Durham on foot, were captured, as was Mr. Durham. The father and the two boys were taken to Canada, and returned home after the close of the Revolutionary War.

Outrages in Westmoreland County in 1779

Early in the spring of 1779, the inhabitants of Westmoreland County suffered terribly from Indian raids. In the latter part of April, a band of Senecas entered the Ligonier Valley, killed one man, and carried two families into captivity. On April 26th, Fort Hand, garrisoned by seventeen men under Captain Samuel Moorhead and Lieutenant William Jack, was attacked, possibly by the same band, estimated to be one hundred strong. At one o'clock in the afternoon, the Indians fired upon two ploughmen, who escaped to the fort. Then the fort was attacked, several women within making bullets while the riflemen fired at the Indians. The firing was kept up until nightfall. In the meantime, three of the garrison were wounded, one of them fatally. This was Sergeant Philip McGray, who occupied a sentry box. He died in a few days.

After McGraw had been shot and removed, a man named McCauley, who took his place, was also wounded.

During the night, the Indians shot at the fort, and mimicked the sentinel's cry, "All's well." At midnight, they set fire to John McKibbon's barn near the fort, and the tories among them cried: "Is all well now?" During the night, a messenger was sent to Fort Pitt for aid. The Indians gave up the siege the next forenoon, and forty soldiers who were hurried from Fort Pitt, arrived too late to intercept them.

The dreadful situation of the Westmoreland settlers during that spring is seen in the following statement in a letter sent to President Reed by Archibald Lochry, from Hannastown, on May 1st: "The savages are continually making depredations among us. Not less than forty people have been killed, wounded, or captured this spring, and the enemy have killed our creatures within three hundred yards of this town."

Charles Clifford lived on Mill Creek, about two and one-half miles northward from Ligonier. On April 22nd, 1779, he and his two sons went to work in the field. Leaving his sons to continue the work, he went in search of his horses. After searching for some time without success, he reached the Forbes Road leading to the stockade near Laughlintown, when five Indians who lay concealed behind a log, shot at him. One bullet splintered his gun and cut his face, which bled freely, but otherwise he was unharmed. The Indians believed that Clifford was protected by the Great Spirit. They approached him, wiped the blood from his face, and told him that they were glad that they had not killed him. They then took him along with them, and when they had reached a point near Fairfield, Westmoreland County, they met fifty-two others proceeding northward, having with them a prisoner named Peter Maharg. The chief of this band wore many silver trinkets on his head and arms. After a while the two bands separated, Clifford going with one, and Maharg with the other. Clifford was carried to the Seneca region on the headwaters of the Allegheny, and after six weeks, was delivered to the British at Montreal. He was well liked by the British officers, and from one he secured a compass, which he gave to James Flock, who with it made his way back to his home in Westmoreland, where he had been captured sometime before. After two and one-half years, Clifford was exchanged and returned to his home in the Ligonier Valley.

This was not the only experience that the Clifford family had with the Indians. On the 18th of October, 1777, Clifford's son,

James, shot an Indian while hunting with a dog near Bunger's spring about a quarter of a mile from the fort at Ligonier. The Indian was not killed outright, and a party of militia immediately turned out from the fort to search for him. They traced him by blood on the path for about forty rods, at which point the Indian seems to have stopped the wound with leaves. They were unable to find him.

Atrocities in Union County

After the Great Runaway of July, 1778, a few of the most venturesome of the inhabitants returned to the valley of the West Branch of the Susquehanna. The following year, in May, the Indians entered Union County, and killed John Sample and his wife on White Deer Creek. There were about twenty Indians in this band. Christian VanGundy and Henry Vandyke, with a small force of settlers, hastened to the scene to bring away those who had survived the massacre. While quartered in the Sample home, Indians made an attack during the night, endeavoring to break down the door with a log, and setting fire to the roof. Those inside fired upon them wounding two, whom the other Indians carried off. VanGunday was wounded in the leg while extinguishing the fire, and one of his companions was shot in the face. At daybreak, they decided to leave the house and seek safety in flight. On opening the door, they found the leader of the Indian band lying dead in front of it. VanGundy took his rifle and Vandyke his powder horn. The other Indians then came from ambush. VanGundy, with his two rifles, hastened to a ravine, and endeavored to get the others to follow him. They refused to follow, and then the Indians killed and scaiped the old people of the place. Colonel John Kelly led a party which came upon five of these Indians sitting upon a log. Four were killed at one volley, and the fifth escaped. On July 8th, Indians again entered this neighborhood, destroying the mill of the widow of Peter Smith, near the mouth of White Deer Creek, and killing one man in the attack. This was a famous grist, saw and boring mill. Here many gun barrels were bored for the Continental army.

The Battle of Minisink

One of the most hotly contested engagements of the Revolutionary War was the battle of Minisink, which was fought July 22nd, 1779. The place of the battle was what is now Port Jervis,

New York, just across the Delaware River from the town of Lackawaxon, Pike County, Pennsylvania. Early in July the Mohawk chief, Joseph Brant, with four hundred of his warriors, left the Susquehanna and approached the settlements on the Delaware. On the 19th of July the Tories who were with Brant's forces, disguised as Indians, came to the village of Minisink, now Port Jervis, and set fire to the town. The fort, the mill, and twelve houses and barns were burned, and several persons were killed. Most of the inhabitants fled to the mountains for safety. The Tories then took their prisoners and booty to Grassy Brook, where Brant had left the main body of his Indians.

In the meantime, a force of one hundred and fifty volunteers had assembled to pursue the invaders. Colonel Tuesten, fearing the craftiness and treachery of Brant, opposed pursuit, but was overruled. Then Major Meeker mounted his horse and shouted: "Let the brave follow me; cowards may stay behind."

On July 22nd, the pursuers came upon the Indian encampment of the previous night at Halfway Brook. The smouldering fires gave plain evidence that the savages were in great force, and the two colonels very prudently advised against further pursuit, but were overruled. A captain was then sent forward with a scouting party, but being discovered, was slain. The volunteers eagerly pressed forward, and at nine o'clock, saw the enemy marching in the direction of the fording place on the Delaware. In the meantime, Brant had deposited much of his plunder in Pike County. The commander of the volunteer troops then decided to intercept Brant's forces at the fording place, but the wily chieftain, comprehending the designs of the Americans, wheeled his columns and, by skillful movement, brought his whole force in the rear of the volunteers. Indeed, he had formed an ambuscade and deliberately selected a battle ground suitable for his purpose.

The Americans surprised and disappointed at not finding Brant's forces where they expected them, were marching back, when they encountered the Indians. Brant's forces greatly outnumbered the Americans and, to make matters worse, the ammunition of the latter was limited, making it necessary for them to fire, not at random, but to make every shot count. The engagement began at eleven o'clock, and when night fell it was still undecided. By that time, the ammunition of the Americans was almost expended, and their line was broken. The Americans then began a retreat. Dr. Tuesten, who was dressing the wounds of seventeen who were injured, was fallen upon, and he and the entire seventeen were killed.   Many were shot while swimming the river. Some escaped under the cover of darkness.   A few succeeded in reaching the wilds of Pike County.   Only thirty of the force of one hundred and fifty that went out to battle, returned to tell the story of the engagement.   "The massacre of the wounded Americans", says Frederic A. Godcharles, "is one of the darkest stains upon the memory of Brant whose honor and humanity were often more conspicious than that of his Tory allies."

Capture of Fort Freeland

As related presently, General John Sullivan was sent by General Washington, in the summer of 1779, with an army to invade the territory of the Six Nations, in New York.   No sooner had General Sullivan started on his march from Easton than the Indians learned of his plan and, assisted by the Tories, took measures to defeat the expedition.   Captain John MacDonald, a Tory in command of a force of British and three hundred Senecas, marched from the vicinity of Wyalusing, Bradford County, and attacked the garrison at Fort Freeland on July 28th, where many settlers had gathered for protection.   The firing on the fort could be distinctly heard at Fort Boone, located about a mile above the town of Milton, Northumberland County; whereupon, Captain Hawkins Boone, a cousin of the famous Daniel Boone, hastened from the fort with a detail of thirty-two soldiers to the relief of the defenders at Fort Freeland.   However, in a few hours Fort Freeland was a mass of ruins, and its gallant defenders were either tomahawked or taken prisoners.   It is said that the resistance was so stubborn that the articles of capitulation were not accepted until Captain MacDonald had made the third proposal, and not even then, until all the ammunition in the fort was exhausted, the women even melting the pewter into bullets while the men fired them at the British and Indians.

Upon the surrender of the fort, the British and Indians gathered together the provisions and proceeded to the creek, where they made preparations for a feast.   While they were feasting Captain Boone's party arrived on the opposite bank of the creek and fired a volley into the midst of the revelers, killing about thirty of them. However, the British and Indians soon rallied and surrounded Boone's forces, killing thirteen of them, among whom was Captain Boone himself.   As a result of the capture of Fort Freeland, one hundred and eight settlers were killed or taken prisoner.   The enemy then ravaged the country in the vicinity, advancing as far as Milton, and burning everything before them.

Fifty-two women and children, and four old men were permitted by the British commander to go to Fort Augusta. The captives were taken to Niagara. The few who survived the hardships of the terrible march through the wilderness and the sufferings of long imprisonment, returned to the surviving members of their families after the close of the Revolutionary War.

The capture of Fort Freeland and the ravaging of the country in the vicinity was not strictly an Indian incursion. The Senecas under Hickatoo, the husband of Mary Jemison, White Woman of Genesee, were simply allies of the British detachment commanded by Captain John MacDonald.

General Sullivan's Expedition Against the Six Nations

General Washington, exasperated at the continued outrages of the Six Nations, determined that the power of that great Confederacy should be broken. Accordingly, in the summer of 1779, he sent General John Sullivan into the Iroquois country in Northeastern Pennsylvania and Southern New York with an army of five thousand men. Sullivan rendezvoused at Easton May 26th. His line of march passed through Wyoming, Tunkhannock, Wyalusing, Sheshecununk, Tioga, and Chemung. At Newtown on the present site of Elmira, New York, the Indians, fifteen hundred strong, under Joe Brant and Captain John McDonald, and the British and Tories, under Colonel John Butler and the two Johnsons, made a determined stand, on August 29th, but were overwhelmingly defeated. Sullivan then marched through the heart of the territory of the Six Nations, burning their houses, destroying their corn, killing their cattle, and felling their orchards which had been growing for generations. Terrible was the retribution which he visited upon them for siding with the British and devastating the American frontier.

We quote the following account of Sullivan's Expedition from Headley's "Washington and His Generals":

"Our Revolution called forth every variety of talent, and tried it in every mode of warfare. Perhaps there never was a war into which such various elements entered. We had not only to organize a government and army, with which to meet a powerful antagonist, and also quench the flames of civil war in our own land, but were compelled to meet a cloud of savages on their own field of battle—the impenetrable forest—and in their own way. The English enlisted them against us by promises of plunder, and appealing to their revenge; while their own bitter hatred prompted them to take advantage of the defenseless state of our frontiers, to fall on our settlements and massacre our people.

"The tragedies which were enacted at Cherry Valley and Wyoming, with all the heart-sickening details and bloody passages, finally aroused our government to a vigorous effort. Washington, being directed to adopt measures to punish these atrocities and secure our frontiers, ordered Sullivan to take an army and invade the Indian territories. The Six Nations, lying along the Susquehanna and around our inland lakes, extending to the Genesee flats, were to be the objects of this attack. His orders were to burn their villages, destroy their grain, and lay waste their land.

"A partisan warfare had been long carried on between the border inhabitants and the Indians, in which there had been an exhibition of bravery, hardihood, and spirit of adventure never surpassed. The pages of romance furnish no such thrilling narrative, examples of female heroism, and patient suffering, and such touching incidents as the history of our border war. For personal prowess, manly courage, and adventure, nothing can exceed it. Yet it had hitherto been a sort of hand-to-hand fighting, a measuring of the Indian's agility and cunning against the white man's strength and boldness; but now a large army, with a skillful commander at its head, was to sweep down everything in its passage.

"The plan adopted was for the main army to rendezvous at Wyoming, and from thence ascend into the enemy's country, while General James Clinton, advancing with one brigade along the Mohawk west, was to form a junction with it, wherever Sullivan should direct. The first of May, 1779, the troops commenced their march, but did not arrive at Wyoming till the middle of June. It was a slow and toilsome business for an army to cut roads, bridge marshes, and transport artillery and baggage through the wide expanse of forest between the Delaware and Susquehanna. At length, however, the whole force assembled at Wyoming; and on the thirty-first of July took their final departure.

"So imposing a spectacle those solitudes never before witnessed. An army of three thousand men slowly wound along the picturesque banks of the Susquehanna—now their variegated uniforms sprinkling the open fields with gay colors, and anon their glittering bayonets fringing the dark forest with light; while by their side floated a hundred and fifty boats, laden with cannon and stores—slowly stemming the sluggish stream. Officers dashing along in their uniforms, and small bodies of horse between the columns, completed the scene—while exciting strains of marital music rose and fell in prolonged cadences on the summer air, and swept, dying away, into the deep solitudes. The gay song of the oarsman, as he bent to his toil, mingled in the hoarse words of command; and like some wizard creation of the American wilderness, the mighty pageant passed slowly along. The hawk flew screaming from his eyrie at the sight; and the Indian gazed with wonder and affright, as he watched it from the mountain-top, winding miles and miles through the sweet valley, or caught from afar the deafening roll of the drums and shrill blast of the bugle. At night the boats were moored to the shore, and the army encamped beside them—the innumerable watchfires stretching for miles along the river. As the morning sun rose over the green forest, the drums beat the reveille throughout the camp, and again the pageant of the day before commenced. Everything was in the freshness of summer vegetation, and the great forest rolled its sea of foliage over their heads, affording a welcome shelter from the heat of an August sun.

"Thus, day after day, this host toiled forward, and on the twelfth from the date of their march, reached Tioga. Here they entered on the Indian settlements and the work of devastation commenced. Here also Clinton, coming down the Susquehanna, joined them with his brigade—and when the head of his column came in sight of the main army, and the boats floated into view, there went up such a shout as never before shook that wilderness.

"Sullivan, in the meantime, had destroyed the village of Chemung; and Clinton, on his passage, had laid waste the settlement of the Onondagas. The whole army, now amounting to nearly five thousand men, marched on the 26th of August up the Tioga River, destroying as it went. At Newtown the Indians made a stand. From the river to a ridge of hills, they had thrown up a breastwork a mile in extent, and thus defended, boldly withstood for two hours a heavy fire of artillery; but being at length attacked in flank by General Poor, they broke and fled. The village was immediately set on fire, and the rich fields of corn cut down and trodden under foot.

"On the first of September the army left the river, and struck across the wilderness, to Catherine's Town. Night overtook them in the middle of a swamp, nine miles wide; and the rear guard, without packs or baggage, were compelled to pass the whole night on the marshy ground. This town also was burned, and the fields ravaged. Having reached Seneca Lake, they followed its shores northward, to Kendaia, a beautiful Indian village, with painted houses, and monuments for the dead, and richly cultivated fields. It smiled like an oasis there in the wilderness; but the smoke of the conflagration soon wrapped it, and when the sun again shone upon it, a smoldering heap alone remained—the waving corn had disappeared with the dwellings, and the cattle lay slaughtered around.

"Our troops moved like an awful, resistless scourge through this rich country—open and fruitful fields and smiling villages were before them—behind them a ruinous waste. Now and then, detachments sent off from the main body were attacked, and on one occasion seven slain; and once or twice the Indians threatened to make a stand for their homes, but soon fled in despair, and the army had it all their own way. The capital of the Senecas, a town consisting of sixty houses, surrounded with beautiful cornfields and orchards, was burned to the ground, and the harvest destroyed. Canandaigua fell next, and then the army stretched away for the Genesee flats. The fourth day it reached this beautiful region, then almost wholly unknown to the white man. The valley, twenty miles long and four broad, had scarce a forest tree in it, and presented one of the most beautiful contrasts to the surrounding wilderness that could well be conceived.

"As the weary columns slowly emerged from the dark forest, and filed off into this open space, their admiration and astonishment knew no bounds. They seemed suddenly to have been transported into an Eden. The tall, ripe grass bent before the wind—cornfield on cornfield, as far as the eye could reach, waved in the sunlight—orchards that had been growing for generations, were weighed down under the profusion of fruit—cattle grazed on the banks of the river, and all was luxuriance and beauty. In the midst of this garden of nature, where the gifts of Heaven had been lavished with such prodigality, were scattered a hundred and twenty-eight houses—not miserable huts, huddled together, but large, airy buildings, situated in the most pleasant spots, surrounded with fruit trees, and exhibiting a civilization on the part of the Indians never before witnessed.

"Into this scene of surpassing loveliness the sword of war had now entered, and the approach of Sullivan's vast army, accompanied with the loud beat of the drum and shrill fife, sent consternation through the hearts of the inhabitants. At first they seemed resolved to defend their homes; but soon, as all the rest had done, turned and fled in affright. Not a soul remained behind; and Sullivan marched into a deserted, silent village. His heart relented at the sight of so much beauty; but his commands were peremptory. The soldiers thought, too, of Wyoming and Cherry Valley, and the thousand massacres that had made our borders flow in blood, and their hearts were steeled against pity. An enemy who felt no obligations, and kept no faith, must be placed beyond the reach of inflicting injury.

"At evening, that army of five thousand men encamped in the village; and just as the sun went down behind the limitless forest, a group of officers might be seen, flooded by its farewell beams, gazing on the scene. While they thus stood conversing, suddenly there rolled by a dull and heavy sound, which startled them into an attitude of the deepest attention. There was no mistaking that report—it was the thunder of cannon—and for a moment they looked on each other with anxious countenances. That solitary roar, slowly traversing the mighty solitudes that hemmed them in, might well awaken the deepest solicitude. But it was not repeated; and night fell on the valley of Genesee, and the tired army slept. The next morning, as the sun rose over the wilderness, that heavy echo again shook the ground. It was then discovered to be the morning and evening gun of the British at Niagara; and its lonely thunder there made the solitude more fearful.

"Soon after sunrise, immense columns of smoke began to rise the length and breadth of the valley, and in a short time the whole settlement was wrapt in flame from limit to limit; and before night those hundred and twenty-eight houses were a heap of ashes. The grain had been gathered into them, and thus both were destroyed together. The orchards were cut down, the cornfields uprooted, and the cattle butchered and left to rot on the plain. A scene of desolation took the place of that scene of beauty, and the army encamped at night in a desert.

"The next day, having accomplished the object of his mission, Sullivan commenced his homeward march. Ah! who can tell the famine, and disease, and suffering of those homeless Indians during the next winter? A few built huts amid the ashes of their former dwellings, but the greater part passed the winter around Fort Niagara.

"On the fifteenth of October, after having been absent since the first of May, or five months and a half, the army again reached Easton. Two hundred and eighty miles had been traversed over mountains, through forests, across swamps and rivers, and amid hostile Indians. The thanks of Congress were presented to Sullivan and his army for the manner they had fulfilled their arduous task."

The great Confederacy of the Six Nations never recovered from the terrible blow dealt them by General Sullivan. The following winter is known as "the winter of the deep snow", and was perhaps the severest winter in the history of the United States. In January, New York harbor was frozen over so solidly that the British drove laden wagons on the ice from the city to Staten Island. One heavy snowstorm followed another, and by February first, the snow lay four feet deep in the woods and mountains of Pennsylvania and New York. Their food supplies destroyed by Sullivan's army, great numbers of the Iroquois starved and froze to death during this terrible winter.

Lieutenant Samuel Brady Rescues Mrs. Jennie Stoops

The spring of 1780 had scarcely opened when the Indians began their incursions into the Western Pennsylvania settlements. On Sunday morning, March 12th, a party of Wyandots, falling upon five men and six children at a sugar camp on Raccoon Creek, in southern Beaver County, killed the men, and captured the children, three boys and three girls. Near the end of this month, a band of the Munsee Clan of Delawares, led by Washnash, captured a flatboat going down the Ohio River to Kentucky, killing three men and making prisoners of twenty-one men, women, and children.

Early in May, Colonel Broadhead, then in command at Fort Pitt, sent Godfrey Lanctot, a Frenchman, who spoke several Indian languages, to visit the Shawnees, Wyandots, and Delawares of the Munsee Clan in Ohio, in an effort to make peace; but his efforts were fruitless. During the same month the Senecas coming down the Allegheny invaded Westmoreland County, where they killed and captured five prisoners near Ligonier, burned Laughlin's Mill, killed two men on Bushy Run, and two on Braddock's Road near Turtle Creek.

Colonel Broadhead then received a report that an army of British and Indians was assembling on the Sandusky River in Ohio, intending to attack Fort Pitt. Accordingly, he directed Lieutenant (later Captain) Samuel Brady to go to Sandusky with a few scouts, in order to learn the plans of the proposed expedition against Fort Pitt. Late in May, Brady set out for Sandusky with five white companions and two Delawares, the whole company being dressed and painted like Indians. When Brady's company approached the Wyandot country, they traveled only by night, hiding in the forests by day. One of the Delawares became faint-hearted and returned to Fort Pitt.

When Brady and his remaining companions drew near the Wyandot capital near upper Sandusky, he and one Delaware companion waded to a wooded island opposite the Indian town, where they lay all the next day watching the Indians enjoy a horse race near the bank of the river. They found the town full of warriors. The indications were that the savages were preparing for the warpath. During the night Brady and his companion rejoined the others, and started toward Fort Pitt. When they had reached a point about two miles from Sandusky, they captured two Indian maidens at a camp, and took them along, believing that they might divulge valuable information. At the end of six days, one of these squaws escaped. The food supply of Brady and his men was now exhausted, and for an entire week they had nothing to eat but berries. Brady succeeded in shooting an otter; but even these hungry frontiersmen could not eat the rank flesh.

When Brady and his companions reached a point near the old Indian town of Kuskuskies, at the junction of the Mahoning and Shenango rivers, in Lawrence County, Brady saw a deer and attempted to shoot it; but his gun flashed in the pan. He was preparing again to fire, when he heard the voices of Indians. Concealing himself, he saw an Indian captain riding a grey horse followed by six warriors on foot, coming along the Indian trail. On the same horse with the Indian captain, were a captive white woman and her child, the woman riding behind the Indian, who held her child in his arms. Brady at once recognized the woman as Mrs. Jennie Stoops, who had been captured some time before on Chartier's Creek, at a point near the present town of Crafton, Allegheny County. Taking careful aim Brady shot the Indian captain through the head. The savage fell from his horse, dragging the woman and child with him. Brady then dashed forward shouting for his men to come on. The hostile Indians being surprised at the sudden death of their leader, fired a few shots, and then fled. Being dressed like an Indian, Mrs. Stoops did not recognize Lieutenant Brady, but thought him an Indian. "Why did you shoot your brother?" she asked. Brady took the child in his arms, saying, "Jennie Stoops, I am Captain Brady; follow me, and I will secure you and your child." Taking Mrs. Stoops by the hand and the child in his arms, Brady hastened into the thicket, where he found his companions cowering in fear, who had let the other Indian squaw escape.

After going a few miles further along the trail toward Fort McIntosh (now Beaver), Brady and his scouts met a band of settlers from the Chartier's Valley, pursuing the captors of Mrs. Stoops and her child. Mrs. Stoops and her infant were then restored unharmed to the husband and father; and Brady returned to the scene of the adventure, where he found and scalped the Wyandot captain.

Outrages in the Wyoming Valley in 1780

Terrible as was the retribution which General Sullivan visited upon the Six Nations in the summer of 1779, it did not prevent their entering the Wyoming Valley the next spring, and bringing terrible suffering to the settlers of Luzerne County. This incursion is thus described in Miner's "History of Wyoming":

"In the latter part of March an alarm was given that Indians were in the valley. On the 27th, Thomas Bennett and his son, a lad, in a field not far from their house, in Kingston, were seized and made prisoners by six Indians. Lebbeus Hammond, who had been captured a few hours before, they found tied as they entered a gorge of the mountain. Hammond had been in the battle, [the Wyoming Massacre of July 3rd, 1778] and was then taken prisoner, but had escaped from the fatal ring at bloody rock, where Queen Esther was pursuing her murderous rounds as previously related. He was a prize of more than ordinary value. No doubt could exist but that he was destined a victim to the cruelest barbarity. The night of the 27th they took up their quarters about twelve miles north from the valley. The next day, having crossed the river near the three islands, they pushed on toward Meshoppen with all the speed in their power. While on their march they met two parties of Indians and Tories, descending for murder and pillage upon the settlement. A man by the name of Moses Mount, whom they knew, was particular in his inquiries into the state of the garrison and the situation of the inhabitants. On the evening of the 28th they built a fire, with the aid of Mr. Bennett, who being an old man, was least feared, and permitted to go unbound. To a request from Mr. Bennett, of the Chief, to lend him an awl to put on a button, the savage, with a significant look replied, 'No want button for one night,' and refused his request. The purpose of the Indians could not be mistaken. Whispering to Hammond, while the Indians went to a spring near by, to drink, it was resolved to make an effort to escape. To stay was certain death; they could but die. Tired with their heavy march, after a supper of venison, the Indians lay around the fire, Hammond and the boy tied between them, except an old Indian who was set to keep the first watch. His spear lay by his side, while he picked the meat from the head of a deer, as half sleeping and nodding, he sat over the fire. Bennett was allowed to sit near him, and seemingly in a careless manner, took the spear, and rolled it playfully on his thigh. Watching his opportunity when least on his guard, he thrust the spear through the Indian's side, who fell with a startling groan upon the burning logs. There was not a moment to be lost. Age forgot its decrepitude. In an instant Hammond and young Bennet were cut loose, the arms seized, three of the remaining savages tomahawked, and slain as they slept, and another wounded. One only escaped unhurt. On the evening of the 30th the captive victors came in with five rifles, a silver mounted hanger, and several spears and blankets, as trophies of their brilliant exploit.

"Another band of ten Indians, on the same day that Bennett and Hammond were taken, shot Asa Upson in Hanover, (near where the bridge crosses the canal below Carey-Town). On the 28th, two men were making sugar about eight miles below Wilkesbarre, one was killed, the other taken prisoner. On the 29th, Jonah Rogers, a lad of fourteen or fifteen, was taken prisoner from the lower part of the valley. The Indians then pushed down the river to Fishing Creek, where, on the 30th they surprised the family of the Van Campens. Moses Van Campen was taken prisoner after they had murdered and scalped his father, his brother, and his uncle, and captured a boy named Pence. Directing their course northeast, the savages passed through Huntington, where they were met by a scout of four men under the orders of Capt. Franklin. Shots were exchanged, and two of his men wounded. Too few to cope with the Indian party, Capt. Franklin took up a position in an old log house; but the enemy preferred to pursue their course, and the same evening came to a camp where Abraham Pike, with his wife, were making sugar. Pike, who was a British deserter, was a most desirable acquisition. The wife and her child they painted, and sent into the settlements. The party now bent their way to the lake country, crossed the Susquehanna at the little Tunkhannock, and pursued their course up the east branch of the river.

"Lieut. Van Campen, a man of true courage, brave and enterprising, formed a plan, with Pike, Rogers, and Pence, to rise on the ten Indians, and effect their liberation, or die in the attempt. It was a bold and hazardous enterprise. The party had ascended to within fifteen miles of Tioga Point, where they encamped on the night of the 3rd of April. The Indians, beyond the probability of pursuit, all lay down to sleep, five on each side of the prisoners, who were carefully bound. Van Campen had observed that a knife, used by one of the Indians, fell near him, and placing his foot on it, secured the inestimable prize. About midnight, finding the enemy buried in profound sleep, Van Campen cut himself loose, and with noiseless celerity liberated the hands of his companions. Springing to their feet, placing the guns in a secure place, tomahawks were used with the utmost vigour. The Indians made a desperate, but unavailing effort for the mastery, but were overpowered, and several of the ten killed, two others wounded, and two or three escaped unhurt. After scalping the dead, recovering the scalps of those of our people whom the Indians had slain, making a hasty raft, the party, taking the guns, tomahawks, spears, and blankets of the foe, descended the Susquehanna, and on the evening of the 5th of April arrived with their spoils in triumph at Wyoming.

"No nobler deed was performed during the Revolutionary war. In a narrative of his life and services, written in 1837, and presented as a memorial to Congress, asking for a pension, Lieut. Van Campen represents his companions in this affair, except Pence, as terrified and inactive, thus impairing his own credit, and marring the beauty of a most chivalrous achievement. There was honour enough for all; there could be no motive but excessive self-glorification, for representing Pike and Rogers as cowards. But when that narrative was written Van Campen was an old man, Pike and Rogers were both dead, and he may have supposed no one remained to rescue their names from the odium. The writer of this knew Abraham Pike and Jonah Rogers well. Mr. Rogers was a highly respectable citizen, and was well understood, though quite a youth, to have performed his duty like a man. That he was collected and cool is evident from his observing that Pike struck his first blow with the head of his axe, then turned it and gave the edge. The former he has often heard recount the daring exploit, and until this recent statement of Van Campen, never heard a doubt of Pike's courage expressed. Familiarly he was called 'Serjeant Pike, the Indian killer,' and as such was every where welcome. An Irishman! A regularly disciplined soldier! The presumption would be strong against the charge of cowardice. 'But death was certain if taken to Niagara; even cowardice itself would have stimulated a man, so situated, to fight. That Van Campen's memory had become impaired, is apparent from the fact that he claimed to have killed nine of the ten Indians. Col. Jenkins, in a memorandum made at the time says: 'Pike and two men from Fishing Creek, and two boys that were taken by the Indians, made their escape by rising on the guard, killed three, and the rest took to the woods, and left the prisoners with twelve guns,' &c. No! without detracting from the bravery and good conduct of Van Campen, we cannot but conclude, that he had told the story of his own prowess, heightening the colouring in his own favour, as he found it gave him consideration with his wondering listeners, until, perhaps, he believed himself the sole hero of the victory.

"On the 30th of March, three persons, named Avery, Lyons, and Jones, were taken prisoners by the Indians, from Capouse.

"The unfortunate, or fortunate Hammond, who, twice in such fearful jeopardy, had twice escaped, had now the pleasure of appearing at Head-Quarters, having been sent on the 3rd of April, by Col. Butler, express, with despatches for his Excellency.

"In the course of these predatory excursions, the savages set fire to the simple log buildings which the settlers had erected for their temporary residence."

Capture of the Gilbert Family

On April 25th, 1780, occurred the capture of the family of Benjamin Gilbert, in what is now Carbon County. The following account of this event is quoted from Egle's, "History of Pennsylvania":

"As late as 1780 the Gilbert family, living on Mahoning Creek, five or six miles from Fort Allen, were carried into a bitterly painful captivity by a party of Indians, who took them to Canada, and there separated them. At the time of its occurrence, this event caused intense excitement throughout the State, and from an interesting narrative published shortly after their release from captivity, we append the following synopsis:

"Benjamin Gilbert, a Quaker from Byberry, near Philadelphia, in 1775, removed with his family to a farm on Mahoning creek, five or six miles from Fort Allen. His second wife was a widow Peart. They were comfortably situated, with a good log dwelling-house, barn, and saw and grist mill. For five years this peaceable family went on industriously and prosperously; but on the 25th of April, 1780, the very year after Sullivan's expedition, they were surprised about sunrise by a party of eleven Indians, who took them all prisoners. At the Gilbert farm they made captives of Benjamin Gilbert, Sr., aged 69 years; Elizabeth, his wife, 55; Joseph Gilbert, his son, 41; Jesse Gilbert; another son, 19; Sarah Gilbert, wife to Jesse, 19; Rebecca Gilbert, a daughter, 16; Abner Gilbert, a son, 14; Elizabeth Gilbert, a daughter, 12; Thomas Peart, son to Benjamin Gilbert's wife, 23; Benjamin Gilbert, a son of John Gilbert of Philadelphia, 11; Andrew Harrigar, of German descent, 26; a hireling of Benjamin Gilbert's; and Abigail Dodson, 14, a daughter of Samuel Dodson, who lived on a farm about one mile from Gilbert's mill. The whole number taken at Gilbert's was twelve. The Indians then proceeded about half a mile to Benjamin Peart's dwelling, and there captured himself, aged 27; Elizabeth, his wife, 20, and their child, nine months old.

"The last look the poor captives had of their once comfortable home was to see the flames and falling in of the roofs, from Summer Hill. The Indians led their captives on a toilsome road over Mauch Chunk and Broad mountains into the Nescopec path, and then across Quakake creek and the Moravian pine swamp to Mahoning Mountain where they lodged the first night. On their way they had prepared moccasins for some of the children. Indians generally secure their prisoners by cutting down a sapling as large as a man's thigh, and therein cut notches in which they fix their legs, and over this they place a pole, crossing it with stakes drove in the ground, and on the crotches of the stakes they place other poles or riders, effectually confining the prisoners on their backs; and besides all this they put a strap round their necks, which they fasten to a tree. In this manner the night passed with the Gilbert family. Their beds were hemlock branches strewed on the ground, and blankets for a covering. Andrew Montour was the leader of the Indian party. [Not the son of Madam Montour].

"The forlorn band were dragged on over the wild and rugged region between the Lehigh and the Chemung branch of the Susquehanna. They were often ready to faint by the way, but the cruel threat of immediate death urged them again to the march. The old man, Benjamin Gilbert, indeed, had begun to fail, and had been painted black—a fatal omen among the Indians; but when his cruel captors had put a rope around his neck, and appeared about to kill him, the intercessions of his wife softened their hearts, and he was saved. Subsequently, in Canada, the old man, conversing with the chief, observed that he might say what none of the other Indians could, 'that he had brought in the oldest man and the youngest child.' The chief's reply was impressive: 'It was not I, but the great God, who brought you through; for we were determined to kill you, but were prevented.'

"On the fifty-fourth day of their captivity, the Gilbert family had to encounter the fearful ordeal of the gauntlet. 'The prisoners,' says the author of the narrative, 'were released from the heavy loads they had heretofore been compelled to carry, and were it not for the treatment they expected on their approaching the Indian towns, and the hardship of separation, their situation would have been tolerable; but the horror of their minds, arising from the dreadful yells of the Indians as they approached the hamlets, is easier conceived than described—for they were no strangers to the customary cruelty exercised upon the captives on entering their towns. The Indians—men, women, and children—collected together, bringing clubs and stones in order to beat them, which they usually do with great severity, by way of revenge for their relations who have been slain. This is performed immediately upon their entering the village where the warriors reside, and cannot be avoided; the blows, however cruel, must be borne without complaint. The prisoners are sorely beaten until their enemies are weary with the cruel sport. Their sufferings were in this case very great; they received several wounds, and two of the women who were on horseback were much bruised by falling from their horses, which were frightened by the Indians. Elizabeth, the mother, took shelter by the side of one of them (a warrior), but upon his observing that she met with some favor upon his account, he sent her away; she then received several violent blows, so that she was almost disabled. The blood trickled from their heads in a stream, their hair being cropped close, and the clothes they had on in rags, made their situation truly piteous. Whilst the Indians were inflicting this revenge upon the captives, the chief came and put a stop to any further cruelty by telling them 'it was sufficient,' which they immediately attended to.

"Soon after this a severer trial awaited them. They were separated from each other. Some were given over to Indians to be adopted, others were hired out by their Indian owners to service in white families, and others were sent down the lake to Montreal. Among the latter was the old patriarch, Benjamin Gilbert. But the old man, accustomed to the comforts of civilized life, broken in body and mind from such unexpected calamities, sunk under the complication of woe and hardship. His remains were interred at the foot of an oak near the old fort of Coeur du Lac, on the St. Lawrence, below Ogdensburg. Some of the family met with kind treatment from the hands of British officers at Montreal, who were interested in their story, and exerted themselves to release them from captivity.

"Sarah Gilbert, the wife of Jesse, becoming a mother, Elizabeth left the service she was engaged in—Jesse having taken a house—that she might give her daughter ever necessary attendance. In order to make their situation as comfortable as possible, they took a child to nurse, which added a little to their income. After this, Elizabeth Gilbert hired herself to iron a day for Adam Scott. While she was at her work, a little girl belonging to the house acquainted her that there were some who wanted to see her, and upon entering the room, she found six of her children. The joy and surprise she felt on this occasion were beyond what we shall attempt to describe. A messenger was sent to inform Jesse and his wife that Joseph Gilbert, Benjamin Peart, Elizabeth his wife, and their young child, and Abner and Elizabeth Gilbert the younger, were with their mother.

"Among the customs, or indeed common laws, of the Indian tribes, one of the most remarkable and interesting was adoption of prisoners. This right belonged more particularly to the females than to the warriors, and well was it for the prisoners that the election depended rather upon the voice of the mother than on that of the father, as innumerable lives were thus spared whom the warriors would have immolated. When once adopted, if the captives assume a cheerful aspect, entered into their modes of life, learned their language, and, in brief, acted as if they actually felt themselves adopted, all hardship was removed not incident to Indian modes of life. But, if this change of relation operated as amelioration of condition in the life of the prisoner, it rendered ransom extremely difficult in all cases, and in some instances precluded it altogether. These difficulties were exemplified in a striking manner in the person of Elizabeth Gilbert the younger. This girl, only twelve years of age when captured, was adopted by an Indian family, but afterwards permitted to reside in a white family of the name of Secord, by whom she was treated as a child indeed, and to whom she became so much attached as to call Mrs. Secord by the endearing title of mamma. Her residence, however, in a white family, was a favor granted to the Secords by the Indian parents of Elizabeth, who regarded and claimed her as their child. Mr. Secord having business at Niagara, took Betsy, as she was called, with him; and there after long separation, she had the happiness to meet with six of her relations, most of whom had been already released and were preparing to set out for Montreal, lingering and yearning for those they seemed destined to leave behind, perhaps for ever. The sight of their beloved little sister roused every energy to effect her release, which desire was generously seconded by John Secord and Colonel Butler, who, soon after her visit to Niagara, sent for the Indian who claimed Elizabeth, and made overtures for her ransom. At first he declared that he 'would not sell his own flesh and blood;' but, attacked through his interest, or in other words, his necessities, the negotiations succeeded, and, as we have already seen, her youngest child was among the treasures first restored to the mother at Montreal.

Eventually they were all redeemed and collected at Montreal on the 22nd of August, 1782, when they took leave of their kind friends there, and returned to Byberry, after a captivity of two years and five months."

Pennsylvania Again Offers Bounties for Scalps

In Chapter XVI, we saw that Pennsylvania offered bounties for Indian scalps during the French and Indian War, the proclamation being made on April 14th, 1756. Also, in Chapter XXV, we saw that the Province offered similar bounties during the Pontiac and Guyasuta War, this proclamation being made on July 7th, 1764. Likewise, we saw in Chapters XXV and XXXI, that the British General, Henry Hamilton, "the hair buyer", who was in charge of operations against the American frontier during the Revolutionary War, gave his Indian allies fifty dollars for each American scalp they were able to get. Now, when the Indians in alliance with the British, urged on by the substantial bounties which the British and Tory commanders at Detroit and in New York were giving for American scalps, even the scalps of babes, were making the soil of the land of Penn red with the blood of its inhabitants, combatants and non-combatants alike, and torturing many of them to death in the Indian villages, Pennsylvania again offered bounties for Indian scalps. Colonel Samuel Hunter and Colonel Jacob Stroud were authorized to offer these rewards.

On April 7th, 1780, President Reed wrote Colonel Hunter as follows: "The council would and do for this purpose authorize you to offer the following premiums for every male prisoner whether white or Indian, if the former is acting with the latter, Fifteen Hundred Dollars, and One Thousand Dollars for every Indian scalp". And on April 11, 1780, he wrote to Colonel Jacob Stroud, "We have therefore authorized Lieutenant of the county (Northampton) to offer Fifteen Hundred Dollars for every Indian or Tory prisoner taken in arms against us, and One Thousand Dollars for every Indian scalp."

On June 27th, 1780, Colonel Hunter wrote to President Reed from Sunbury, stating that several small parties have "made attempts to get scalps or prisoners agreeable to the proclamation, but have returned without success in that way." President Reed then replied with a letter of "condolence", in which he said: "We are sorry to hear the attempts which have been made to get scalps and prisoners have been so unsuccessful and hope perseverance will in time produce better effects". "Better effects" were presently "produced". Many scalping parties were organized, which were quite successful. On one occasion thirteen scalps were sent to Fort Pitt in one package. Moreover, the scalp bounty law was brought into disrepute by the killing of friendly Indians to sell their scalps.

Captain Samuel Brady was a recipient of scalp bounties. In the minutes of a meeting of the Provincial Council on February 19th, 1781, we find an order to Colonel Lochry, Lieutenant of Westmoreland County, "for the sum of twelve pounds, ten shillings, state money, to be paid to Captain Samuel Brady as a reward for an Indian's scalp, agreeable to a late proclamation of this board."

Finally, when General Sir Guy Carleton, in the autumn of 1782, shocked by the cruel burning of Colonel William Crawford and other American prisoners, put an end to the British alliance with the Indians, Pennsylvania no longer gave money for the scalps of the Indians.

Outrages in Allegheny and Washington Counties

On September 4th, 1780, two settlers were killed near Robinson's Run, in Allegheny County, and on the same day, two men descending the Ohio in a canoe, were fired upon, and one of them was wounded. About the middle of September, the Wyandots killed and captured ten settlers on Ten Mile Creek, Washington County.

Attack on Stock Family

One of the principal Indian outrages of the Revolutionary War was the attack on the Stock, or Stuck, family near Selinsgrove, Snyder County, in 1781. Three of the sons of Mr. Stock were at work in a field when a band of thirty Indians appeared. The Indians did not attack these three, but found another son ploughing in the field, whom they killed. They then entered the Stock home, occupied at the time by Mrs. Stock and her daughter-in-law. Mrs. Stock defended herself with a canoe pole, in the meantime retreating toward the field where Mr. Stock was working. The Indians overtook her, however, and sank a tomahawk into her brain. Then, after plundering the house, they carried the daughter-in-law into the woods, and killed and scalped her.

When Mr. Stock returned and found the mutilated bodies of his wife, son, and daughter-in-law, he gave the alarm. Then Michael Grove, John Stroh, and Peter Pence pursued the enemy, coming upon them encamped on the North Branch of the Susquehanna on the side of the hill covered with fern. Grove crept close enough to the Indian band to discover that their rifles were stacked around a tree, and that all but three of the Indians were asleep. One was telling his companions in great glee how poor Mrs. Stock defended herself with the canoe pole. Lying quiet until all the Indians were asleep, Grove then returned to Stroh and Pence. The three frontiersmen then decided to attack, and creeping close to the camp, they dashed among the sleeping Indians, Grove applying his deadly tomahawk, while Stroh and Pence seized the rifles and fired among the sleeping warriors. After several Indians were killed the others, believing that they were attacked by a large force, fled into the forest. A captive white boy was liberated on this occasion, and the frontiersmen returned with the scalps of the slain Indians and their best rifles.

Colonel Lochry's Unfortunate Expedition

In the summer of 1781, the militia officers of Westmoreland County directed Colonel Archibald Lochry to raise three hundred men to assist in the western campaign of George Rogers Clark; but owing to the fact that the many Indian raids into Westmoreland had caused scores of families to seek safety east of the mountains, Colonel Lochry was able to muster less than one hundred men. These began to assemble at Carnahan's block house on August 1st, where the muster was held the next day. On August

---

Massacre of Settlers at Philip Klingensmith's

Just before Lochry's expedition, twenty men, women, and children were massacred at Philip Klingensmith's, in the Brush Creek Settlement, Westmoreland County, July 2nd, 1781, by a band of seventeen Indians, probably Senecas, or Munsee Clan of Delawares, or both. Only three settlers escaped. About the same time, the Indians killed two women in the Ligonier Valley.—Penna. Archives, Vol. IX, page 240.

3rd, the little band of eighty-three militiamen began its march to join Clark at Wheeling. Crossing the Youghiogheny at West Newton and the Monongahela at Monongahela City, Lochry's force went overland by the settlements on the headwaters of Chartiers and Raccoon creeks, Washington County, and reached the Ohio River at Wheeling, West Virginia, on August 8th, just a few hours after Clark's force left that place. Descending the Ohio in boats, the little flotilla on the forenoon of August 24th, approached a level spot at the mouth of the creek since known as Lochry's Run, and being the dividing line between Ohio and Dearborn counties, Indiana, Colonel Lochry at once ordered a landing; the boats were beached, and the men and horses were soon on the shore.

No sooner had they landed than half a hundred rifles blazed from the woods that flanked the level ground near the shore. Many of Lochry's men were killed and others wounded. Others hastened to the boats and pushed for the Kentucky shore. Says Hassler, in his "Old Westmoreland: "Painted savages then appeared, shrieking and firing, and a fleet of canoes filled with other savages shot out from the Kentucky shore, completely cutting off the escape of Lochry's men. The volunteers returned the fire for a few moments, but were entrapped, and Colonel Lochry offered to surrender. The fight ceased, the boats poled back to shore and the force landed the second time. Human blood was now mingled with that of the buffalo in the languidly flowing river. [The troops had shot a buffalo at the water's edge just before the attack.] . . . . . . The Westmoreland men found themselves the prisoners of Joseph Brant, the famous war chief of the Mohawks, with a large band of Iroquois, Shawnees, and Wyandots. George Girty, a brother of Simon, was in command of some of the Indians. The fierce Shawnees could not be controlled and began at once to kill their share of the prisoners. While Lochry sat on a log, a Shawnee warrior stepped behind him and sunk a tomahawk into the Colonel's skull, tearing off the scalp before life was gone. It was with great difficulty that Brant prevented the massacre of the men assigned to the Mohawks and Wyandots."

In this ill-fated expedition, forty of Lochry's force were slain, most of them after the surrender. The prisoners who were not butchered by the savages, were taken to Detroit and from there to Montreal, at which place a few escaped, and the remainder were released after the treaty of peace ending the Revolutionary War. Among the few who returned to Westmoreland County, were

Captain Robert Orr and Lieut. Samuel Craig, Jr., the latter a son of Lieut. Samuel Craig who, as we have seen, was either killed or captured at the base of the Chestnut Ridge on November 1st, 1777.

Murder of the Frantz Family

The murder of the Frantz family, who lived on the farm which is now the home of the Greensburg Country Club, occurred, most authorities assert, some time before the attack on Hannastown. This event is thus described in Boucher's "History of Westmoreland County":

"The murder of the Francis [Frantz] family was one of the most inhuman and barbarous incidents in border warfare. The family resided two miles or more east of Brush Creek. There had been no special alarm on account of the Indians for some months, and their usual vigilance was somewhat relaxed. On the day of the murder, they did not have their cabin door barricaded, and a party of Indians, therefore, very easily gained access. Two of the family were killed at once and the remaining members were taken prisoners. One was a young girl who lived to return to the settlement, where she married and has left descendants in Hempfield Township. Her brothers and sisters were divided among several tribes represented among the captors. Those who were killed were scalped, and their bodies were found near the ruins of the cabin the day following. They were buried in the garden, a custom then prevalent among the pioneers and which lasted till regular cemeteries or graveyards, as they were called, were established."

A tradition in the Frantz family is as follows:

"That Mr. Frantz was at work in a field when his horses gave warning of the approaching of the Indians, becoming excited, tearing themselves from the harness, and starting to run. Mr. Frantz then ran to the house, quickly entered it, and seizing a musket, killed his closest pursuer. His wife and little daughter, Emma, then seven years of age, were captured, after several other occupants of the home had been killed. The Indians then started carrying Mr. and Mrs. Frantz and Emma with them; but when they had gotten as far as the boundary line of the farm, Mr. and Mrs. Frantz refused to go further, whereupon, they were killed. Little Emma made her escape from the Indians several years afterwards, when a trader from Pittsburgh, who occasionally made trips to the Seneca country in Northwestern Pennsylvania, found her among the Indians, secreted her among some furs in his boat, and brought her to Pittsburgh."

Attack on Walthour's Station—The Lame Indian

Some time in April, 1782, the Indians invaded the Brush Creek settlement and attacked the stockade of Christopher Walthour, about a mile and a half east of Irwin, Westmoreland County. On this occasion six men were working in a field near the stockade, among them being Walthour's son-in-law, named Willard. The Indians killed Willard, and captured his daughter, aged sixteen, who was carrying water for the men at work. An Indian rushed forward to scalp Willard; but just as he was in the act, a bullet fired from the stockade wounded him in the leg. Uttering a howl of pain, he ran away into the thicket, leaving his gun behind him.

As soon as possible, a body of frontiersmen started in pursuit of the Indians. They followed their trail to the Allegheny River, but were unable to pursue them farther. About two months afterwards, some hunters found the body of Willard's daughter not far from Negley's Run. She had been tomahawked and scalped.

On the evening of the thirty-eighth day after the attack on Walthour's Station, a lame Indian limped into the village of Pittsburgh, almost starved, a living skeleton in appearance. Feebly asking a young woman for a drink, she gave him a cup of milk and other nourishment; and, after he had eaten ravenously, he told her that he had received the wound on his leg in a quarrel with a Mingo Indian on the Beaver River. The Indian was then taken to the fort, where he was recognized as Davy, a Delaware sub-chief. The surgeon of the fort upon examining Davy's wound, found that it was an old one; and the officers therefore entirely discredited his story about the quarrel with a Mingo. Later, Davy confessed to the officers at Fort Pitt that he was the Indian who had killed Willard, and had been wounded when he was in the act of scalping him. He said that, owing to the bone in his leg having been broken by the bullet from the stockade, he was unable to keep up with his companions; that he had lived on nothing but berries and roots for more than five weeks; that, crawling toward the Allegheny River, he lay for several days on a hill above a small stockade on Turtle Creek, meditating surrender, but finding that the garrison of this stockade were militiamen, and not regulars, he knew that surrender meant death.

Davy was confined in the guard house at Fort Pitt and presently the news of his capture reached the settlement of Brush Creek. Then Mrs. Mary Willard, wife of the man whom Davy had killed, came to Fort Pitt and asked General Irvine to give up the prisoner into the hands of the Brush Creek settlers. At that time, Mrs. Willard was not aware that her daughter had been killed. Mrs. Willard was finally persuaded to let Davy remain at Fort Pitt, in the hope that an arrangement might be made for trading him for her daughter. Shortly after Mrs. Willard's visit, the body of the daughter was found; and then a mass meeting was held of the Brush Creek settlement, and a committee composed of Joseph Studebaker, Jacob Byerly, Francis Byerly, Jack Rutdorf, Henry Willard, and Frederick Willard were chosen to go to Fort Pitt and ask for the surrender of Davy. On July 21st, General Irvine delivered Davy to this committee, enjoining them that they were not to punish him without first giving him a trial by two Justices of the Peace and reputable citizens.

The committee forthwith took Davy back to the Brush Creek settlement and made preparations for burning him at the stake on the very spot where he had killed Willard. Word was sent throughout the settlements for the assembling of the magistrates. Davy was confined in a log block house for several days. On the night before he was to be burned, the young men who were guarding the block-house, fell asleep, and when they awoke in the morning, found that Davy had made his escape by crawling through the narrow space between the roof and the top of the wall. For two days the angry settlers searched for the Indian. On the third day, a boy who had gone into the forest after some horses, ran breathless to Walthour's stockade and said that he had seen a crippled Indian mount a horse from a large log, and beating it with a stick, dash off in the direction of the Allegheny River. The settlers at once took up the pursuit, following the trail with considerable difficulty, as the Indian had ridden the horse along the bed of streams, so as not to leave a track. Finally, when they reached a point near the mouth of the Kiskiminetas River, they found the horse covered with foam eating grass near the water's edge. Although the river bank was searched for miles, Davy was never found. Possibly he had drowned while endeavoring to swim the river, or had died of starvation in the wilderness.

Attack on Rice's Fort

On September 13th, 1782, a band of about seventy Indians attacked the block house of Abraham Rice, on Buffalo Creek, in what is now Donegal Township, Washington County. The attack continued from two o'clock in the afternoon until two o'clock the following morning. Although the little fort was defended by only six men, yet the Indians were not able to capture it. One of the defenders, George Felebaum, was shot through the brain while peering through a loop-hole, and four of the Indians were killed. As the Indian band was returning to the Ohio River, they met two settlers who were on their way to the relief of Rice's stockade, and killed them. The attack on Rice's fort was the last invasion of Western Pennsylvania by a large body of Indians.

End of the Revolutionary War

Cornwallis surrendered his army of more than eight thousand men to Washington at Yorktown, on October 19th, 1781. However, as we have seen, warfare continued on the frontier throughout the following year. Finally, on April 19th, 1783, exactly eight years after the battle of Lexington, Washington proclaimed that the war was at an end, and discharged the patriot army. The Angel of Peace then descended on the war-scarred, desolated country to plume her ruffled pinions, and to bring the blessings of Heaven in her train.

CHAPTER XXXIII

Last of Indian Outrages in Pennsylvania

PON the close of the Revolutionary War, enterprising men turned their attention to the settlement of the vast and fertile region west of the Alleghenies; and Congress, in 1787, formed the Northwest Territory out of which the states of Ohio, Indiana, Illinois, Michigan, and Wisconsin have been formed. General Arthur St. Clair was appointed governor of the Northwest Territory, and, early in 1789, held a treaty at Fort Harmar, at the mouth of the Muskingum River, with representatives of the Six Nations, Wyandots, Delawares, Ottawas and other Western Indians, by the terms of which they ceded large tracts of land to the United States. However, the great majority of these Indians refused to acknowledge the validity of the treaty, and shortly thereafter, instigated by British traders, went on the warpath, sending many of their war parties into the valleys of the Ohio and Allegheny.

General Harmar's Defeat

General Harmar was then sent with an army against these western tribes, leaving Fort Washington, (Cincinnati, Ohio), on September 30th, 1790. His force consisted of about fourteen hundred militia and regulars. After a march of seventeen days, he came within striking distance of the enemy, and on October 21st, his army went down to inglorious and overwhelming defeat. The Miami chief, Little Turtle, and the Seneca chief, Blue Jacket, commanded the Indian forces.

Attack on the Home of James Kirkpatrick and Capture of John and Nancy Sloan

Following the defeat of General Harmar, many bloody incursions were made upon the Western Pennsylvania frontier. One of these was the attack on the fortified home of James Kirkpatrick, in South Bend Township, Armstrong County, on April 28th, 1791. Mr. Kirkpatrick's family had just completed morning worship, when George Miller, who was at the home at that time, went to the

door and found three savages with their rifles cocked and tomahawks ready for attack. They rushed forward to enter the house,
but Miller succeeded in closing it before them. The Indians then
fired through the door and wounded Mr. Miller in the wrist, and
killed Kirkpatrick's child lying in its cradle. Mr. Kirkpatrick
then went to the loft, made an incision in the wall, and began to
fire on the Indians, killing one of them on the spot. In the meantime, Mrs. Kirkpatrick remained below busily employed in making
bullets, while her husband and his companion were defending the
house.

The above is the account given by most historians; but attention is called to the fact that, on Page 555 of Volume Four of the
Second Series of the Pennsylvania Archives, William Findley, in
a letter written to A. Dallas, Secretary of the Commonwealth, on
April 29th, 1791, states that there were six militia in Kirkpatrick's
house at the time of the attack. Also Andrew Gregg, in a letter
written to Colonel Samuel Bryson, and recorded in the same
volume of the Pennsylvania Archives, Page 559, states that two
men were killed in this attack and one wounded, in addition to the
killing of the babe. Smith, in his "History of Armstrong
County", describes this attack and the capture of John and Nancy
Sloan, about the same time, as follows:

"The early settlers were subject to the attacks of the Indians.
A blockhouse was built on the land then owned by William Clark,
but which is now (1883) owned by S. E. Jones. There was another house with port holes—not built, perhaps, expressly for a
blockhouse, but used as a place of refuge and defense from those
attacks—on the road now leading from Elderton to the old
Crooked Creek salt works, on the farm heretofore known as the
Down's farm. It was attacked one morning by the Indians.
George Miller and James Kirkpatrick were then in charge of it;
the Indians fired upon them, killed a child in the cradle, and
wounded an adult person in the building. The women made
bullets while the men were defending them and their children. One
Indian, while putting a charge of powder in his gun, was shot
through the hand and body, and was killed, and some of the other
Indians were wounded. George Miller escaped from the rear of
the building, mounted a horse and started for Clark's blockhouse.
In his absence the Indians fled, carrying with them the dead and
wounded.

"Two children, John Sloan and his sister Nancy, were captured about the time of that affair on the farm near the present

Lutheran and Reformed church, formerly in Plum Creek, but now in South Bend Township [Armstrong County], and about sixty rods northwest from the present residence of William Heintzel-man. They were working in the cornfield at the time. Having been retained by the Indians several years, they were exchanged near Cincinnati or Sandusky, Ohio. They returned home the same year that Samuel Sloan, still living (1883), was born. Their relatives and some other settlers soon after their capture, followed the trail of the Indians to the point where they crossed the Alle-gheny River above Kittanning. The writer's informant, Ex-Sheriff Joseph Clark, also said he had seen bullet holes in the door of the above mentioned house on the Down's farm, and that his aunt, Mrs. Joseph Clark, had told him that she used to stand with rifle in hand, and guard her husband while at work on the farm now occupied by William T. Clark in Plum Creek Township."

Murder of Mrs. Mitchell

The Mitchell family lived in Derry Township, Westmoreland County, on the Loyalhanna, about two miles east of Latrobe. In 1791 the family consisted of the mother and two children, Charles, aged seventeen, and Susan, aged fifteen, the father having died a few years before. During this year, four Indians approachd the home while Charles and Susan were in the stable attending to the work of feeding the stock. Charles tried to escape by running towards the Loyalhanna, but was captured. Susan hid under a trough for feeding horses, and the Indians were unable to discover her. They then captured the mother, and started north with her and Charles. They soon found that Mrs. Mitchell was too old to travel. Then two Indians pushed on ahead with Charles, while the other two loitered behind with Mrs. Mitchell. After a while those conducting Charles stopped to build a fire, when the two who had charge of Mrs. Mitchell joined them with her bleeding scalp. They stretched and dried it in the presence of her son. The band then crossed the Kiskiminetas into Armstrong County where they came upon the tracks of two white men, which Charles recognized as those of Captain John Sloan and Harry Hill. There was snow on the ground, and Captain Sloan's exceedingly large feet made such large marks as to astonish the Indians. One of them took the ramrod of his rifle and measured Sloan's tracks. Charles told him that Sloan was a well-known Indian fighter; whereupon the Indians decided not to follow Sloan and Hill, and immediately pushed on northward, taking Charles to the Senecas on the headwaters of the Allegheny River. Here he escaped three years later, and returned to the Ligonier Valley.

Captain John Sloan was a prominent figure in the early history of Westmoreland County. In 1795, he and his nephew, John Wallace, and two neighbors named Hunt and Knott left Derry Township, Westmoreland County, for a trip to the valley of the Big Maumee. Here they were attacked by Indians. Knott was killed, Sloan wounded, and Hunt captured, never to be heard of again. Sloan and Wallace then went to Fort Hamilton, which had been erected four years before by General St. Clair. In an attack upon this fort by the Indians the day after Sloan and Wallace arrived there, Sloan killed and scalped an Indian. Returning to his home on the Loyalhanna, Sloan brought the Indian's scalp with him, and displayed it on a number of public occasions for many years thereafter. He was elected sheriff of Westmoreland County, serving from 1804 to 1807.

Capture of Jacob Nicely

One of the outrages committed by the Senecas was the capture of little Jacob Nicely, aged five years, the son of Adam Nicely, who lived on Four Mile Run, in Westmoreland County, about two miles from its junction with the Loyalhanna. Authorities differ as to the time of the capture, some stating that it was during the summer of 1790, and others during the summer of 1791.

Little Jacob and his brothers and sisters were picking blackberries. Jacob returned to the house where his mother, who was baking, gave him a cake and told him to rejoin his brothers and sisters. He then started to return to the other children, when a band of Senecas, who were concealed in the woods, captured him. The father with some companions followed the captors as far as the Kiskiminetas, where their trail was lost in the forest.

Years came and went, and no trace of the captured child was found. Finally, in 1828, a man from Westmoreland County, who was trading among the Senecas in Warren County, recognized Jacob, and brought back this information to the mother, who was then an old lady past seventy years of age. In the meantime the father had died. A brother then traveled on horseback to the Seneca reservation, and found the long-lost Jacob. The brothers recognized each other. Jacob had been adopted by the Indians, had a family, and considerable possessions. A tradition in the

Nicely family says that some time prior to 1828, Jacob had made a journey to Westmoreland County, in an effort to locate his relatives, but being unable to speak English and mispronouncing the family name, had returned to his Indian family without finding his mother, brothers, and sisters.

Jacob accompanied his brother part way on the latter's return to Westmoreland County, and presented him with a rifle and other implements. He promised to return the following summer to visit the aged mother. However, he did not return as he had promised, perhaps having died. It is said that the father was unable to converse on the subject of the capture of "Jakey" without shedding tears. The aged mother went to her grave with the vivid recollection of her child captured so many years before.

Attack on Mead's Settlement

In the spring of 1791 occurred the attack on Mead's settlement, where the town of Meadville, the county seat of Crawford County, now stands, thus described by Hon. William Reynolds in the "Centennial History of Crawford County":

"During 1789 the little colony known as "Mead's settlement" was reinforced by the arrival of the family of Darius Mead, Frederick Baum, and Robert Ritz Randolph and their families, Frederick Haymaker, William Gregg, Samuel Lord and John Wentworth. On April 1st, 1791, the settlers were warned by Flying Cloud—a son of the Chief Connedaughta—of threatened danger from the hostile western tribes, and on the same day eleven strange Indians were seen a few miles northwest of the settlement. The women and children of the colony were gathered within the Mead house and cellar and on the next day sent in canoes to Fort Franklin. The Indian chief, Half Town—who was a half-brother to Cornplanter—was encamped here at the time with twenty-seven of his braves. Twelve of these he sent to guard the canoe, six on each side of the creek, and with his remaining warriors he joined the settlers in a fruitless search for the hostiles seen by Gregg. On the following day all the men departed for Franklin with their horses, cattle and moveable effects.

"On May 3rd, Cornelius VanHorne, William Gregg and Thomas Ray returned to plant the spring crops. Stopping for the night at Gregg's cabin, they shelled a bag of corn, part of which they ground the next morning at the Mead house. Arriving at the corn field, VanHorne laid his gun on the bag of seed corn and ploughed while Gregg and Ray planted. At noon Gregg and Ray returned to the Mead house for dinner and fresh horses. While ploughing, VanHorne saw two Indians emerge from the woods. The one dropping his bow and the other his gun, they rushed to the attack with their tomahawks. VanHorne grasped the uplifted arm of the first savage and entered on a struggle for life. By his superior strength and agility he shielded himself from the attack of his more formidable foe with the body of his weaker antagonist, calling loudly for help. After a time the Indians promised his life on condition of surrender. Mounting the horses, VanHorne between them, they crossed the Cussewago, and entering a ravine on the hillside they met two other Indians. They tied the arms of their prisoner and three returned to the corn field. Van Horne and the Indian rode the horses to Conneaut Lake and crossed the out-let. Here they dismounted and VanHorne was tied by the ends of the rope which secured his arms to a tree while his captors left in search of game. With a knife he had secreted he succeeded in cutting the rope and made his escape to the settlement where by good fortune he found thirty soldiers under Ensign Jeffers, on their return from Erie to Fort Franklin.

"Gregg and Ray returning with the horses discovered the three Indians and fled, crossing the Cussewago near its mouth. Gregg, after reaching the opposite bank, was wounded, and seating himself on a log he was shot by his pursuers through the head with his own gun. Ray was captured and carried to Detroit, then occupied by a British garrison. Here he was recognized by an old school-fellow of his boyhood in Scotland, Captain White, who purchased him from his captors for two gallons of whiskey, furnished him money and sent him on a vessel to Buffalo, from whence he was piloted to Franklin by Stripe Neck—an old Mohawk chief, who lived after the early settlement on the west side of French Creek near the site of the present tannery in Kerrtown. Ray made his settlement and ended his days in the northwest corner of Mead Township.

"In the summer of the same year Darius Mead, the father of David and John, was captured near Franklin. His body was found side by side with that of one of his captors, Captain Bull, a Delaware chief. The duel had been to the death and they were buried side by side where found, near the Shenango Creek in Mercer County."

General St. Clair's Defeat

President Washington chose General Arthur St. Clair to lead an army against the Western Indians. "Beware of a surprise," said Washington, as St. Clair left Philadelphia to take charge of the army. With eighteen hundred men, he marched from Fort Washington, in October, 1791, and proceeded against the Miami villages. As he advanced into the Indian country, his force became weakened by desertions and mutiny. On November 4th, his forces were ambushed on a branch of the Wabash, and defeated with great slaughter. Nearly half of their number lay dead or wounded on the field, while the remainder fled precipitately through the forest. Among the slain was General Richard Butler, second in command, for whom Butler County is named.

This was one of the most crushing and disastrous defeats in the Indian annals of America. The country was shocked, humiliated, and disheartened; and the Indians were much emboldened. Washington was extremely agitated on hearing of St. Clair's misfortune, and gave way to passionate invective, but recovering himself said: "General St. Clair shall have justice. I will receive him without displeasure; I will hear him without prejudice; he shall have full justice." His investigation into St. Clair's conduct resulted in the General's honorable acquittal.

St. Clair had fought courageously against the Indian hordes led by Blue Jacket, Little Turtle, and Simon Girty, the renegade; but he never rose again in public estimation. Upon his removal as Governor of the Northwest Territory, in 1802, he retired to his mansion, which in the days of his affluence, he had built about two miles northwest of Ligonier, in the Ligonier Valley. Financial reverses soon came upon him, and his beautiful home and all his other property were sold. He then removed to a log house on the summit of the Chestnut Ridge, where his son had purchased a small farm for him. Here the old soldier spent the remainder of his days in poverty, eking out a miserable existence by keeping tavern and selling supplies to teamsters. He made frequent appeals to the Legislature of Pennsylvania and to Congress for aid in his declining years. His claim against the Government was based upon the fact that he personally stood good for the supplying of much provisions and equipment for the army which he led against the Ohio Indians, on the promise of the Secretary of the Treasury to reimburse him. In 1813 Pennsylvania gave him an annuity of four hundred dollars; and shortly before his death, Congress voted him the sum of two thousand dollars in settlement of his claims against the Government, and a pension of sixty dollars per month, dated back one year. Not a dollar of the settlement gave any relief to the aged man, as it was all seized by his creditors.

On August 30th, 1918, while driving down the Chestnut Ridge with a pony hitched to an old wagon, he fell from the jolting vehicle upon the rough road, where Susan Steinbarger found him lying unconscious as she was going out to gather berries. The pony was standing nearby. The General was then taken to his humble home, but never regained consciousness, dying the next day at the great age of eighty-four years. He is buried in the old Presbyterian cemetery at Greensburg, where the Masons have erected a monument at his grave containing the statement that it is "erected to supply the place of a nobler one due from his country."

Capture of Massa Harbison

Massa Harbison, whose terrible sufferings at the hands of the Indians have been given wide publicity in Western Pennsylvania, was born in Amwell Township, Somerset County, New Jersey, March 18th, 1770, the daughter of Edward White, a soldier in the Revolutionary War. As a child she witnessed the battles of Long Island, Trenton, and Monmouth. In 1773 her father settled in Brownsville, Fayette County, where she married John Harbison, in 1787.

Her husband was a soldier in St. Clair's army. Being wounded at the defeat of St. Clair, he was given lighter duty as a scout, serving along the Allegheny frontier. On March 18th, 1792, Indians attacked the home of Thomas Dick below the mouth of Deer Creek, Allegheny County, and captured the entire family. On the 22nd of March of the same year, seven Indians attacked the house of Abraham Roose, about two miles above the mouth of Bull Creek in the same county, and massacred his entire family. The news of these massacres alarmed Mrs. Harbison, and with a small child in her arms and another tied on the horse behind her, she traveled seven miles from her home to James Paul's at Pine Run, at which place about seventy women and children were collected and from there taken to a place on the east side of the Allegheny River, called Reed's block house, or Reed's station, about two miles below the mouth of the Kiskiminetas.

Here Mrs. Harbison was captured within gunshot of the block house on May 22nd, 1792, by a band of Munsees and other

Indians, the account of which is thus related in Smith's authoritative "History of Armstrong County":

"John Harbison was a soldier in St. Clair's army. Having been wounded, he was, after his recovery, employed as a spy to watch the movements of the savages. In the spring of 1792, his family resided in a house near Reed's station. While he was absent on duty, his house, about 200 yards distant from the block house, was entered by Indians on the morning of May 22nd, and his wife and children were captured. Before proceeding with the account of their capture, the reader's attention is directed to what William Findley wrote to A. J. Dallas, Secretary of the Commonwealth, June 1: 'I was but a few days at home until the Indians broke into the settlement by Reed's station. It was garrisoned by rangers under Cooper. They had never scouted any. They had been drinking and were surprised, in want of ammunition, and the officer was absent from the station. However, the Indans fired only a few rounds upon the blockhouse, with which they killed one man and wounded another, and went away without any exertions being made by the rangers. They then killed and took Harbison's family in sight of the station. Harbison was one of the spies, and was reported as having relaxed a little in his duty. Indeed, the duties of the spies in this county is (are) too hard, and they are not assisted by the troops as was designed at laying the plan. The alarm was quickly spread; indeed, they themselves (the Indians) promoted the news of their coming by burning some of the first houses they came to. This occasioned the country to fly before them with the greatest rapidity, and being about forty in number took the country before them, keeping nearly the course of the Kiskiminetas, going in small parties from five to seven, as far as has been observed.'

"Two spies, Davis and Sutton, having lodged at Harbison's house, left the next morning, Sunday, May 22nd, when the horn at the blockhouse was blown, leaving the door open. Several Indians soon afterward entered, and drew Mrs. Massey (corrupted from Mera) Harbison and her two eldest children by their feet from their beds, the third or youngest one, about a year old, being in bed with her. While these dusky burglars were rummaging the house and scrambling to secure whatever each one could of her clothing and other articles, she went outdoors and hallooed to the men in the blockhouse. One Indian then ran up and stopped her mouth; another rushed toward her with his raised tomahawk, which a third one seized, calling her his squaw and claiming her as his own. Fifteen Indians then advanced toward and fired upon both the blockhouse and the storehouse, killing one and wounding another of the soldiers, one of whom, by the name of Wolf, was returning from the spring and the other either coming or looking out of the storehouse. When Mrs. Harbison told the Indians who remained with her that there were forty men in the blockhouse, each having two guns, those who were firing were brought back. Then they began to drive her and the children away. Because one of her boys, three years old, was unwilling to leave and was crying, they seized him by his feet, dashed his brains out against the threshold of the door, and then stabbed and scalped him. Her heart rent with agony, almost bereft of sight and all her other senses, still keeping her infant in her arms, she gave a terrific scream, and for that one of her savage captors dealt a heavy blow on her head and face, which restored her to consciousness.

"She and her two surviving children were then taken to the top of a hill, where they all stopped, and while the Indians were tying up their booty, she counted them, their number being thirty-two, among whom were two white men painted like Indians. Those were probably the 'treacherous persons among us' mentioned in another part of Findley's letter to Secretary Dallas. Several of those Indians could speak English. Mrs. Harbison knew three or four of them very well; two were Senecas and two were Munsees, whose guns her husband had repaired almost two years before. Two Indians were detailed to guard her, and the rest then went toward Puckety. When she, her children and their guards had advanced about 200 yards, the latter caught two of her uncle John Currie's horses, and then placing her and the youngest child on one and one of the guards and the remaining child on the other, proceeded toward the Kiskiminetas to a point opposite the upper end of Todd's island, where in descending the steep river hill, the Indian's horse fell and rolled more than once. The boy fell over the horse's back, receiving a slight injury, and was taken up by one of the Indians. On reaching the shore the horses could not be made to swim, so the Indians took the captives across to the head of that island in bark canoes. [The Island in the Allegheny, opposite Freeport, Armstrong County.]

"After landing, the elder boy, five years old, complaining of the injury he had received from his fall and still lamenting the death of his brother, one of the guards tomahawked and then scalped him, the other guard having first ordered the mother to move on ahead of them, actuated, perhaps, by a slight assertion of humanity, to save her the pain of witnessing the murder of another of her children. When she beheld that second massacre of her offspring, she fell senseless to the ground with her infant in her arms beneath her with its little hands about her head. She knew not how long she remained in that insensible condition. The first thing she remembered on recovering her consciousness, was raising her head from the ground and being overcome by an extreme, uncontrollable drowsiness, and beholding as she looked around, the bloody scalp of her boy in the hand of one of these savages. She then involuntarily sank again to the earth upon her infant. The first thing which she remembered after that, was the severe castigation that her cruel guards were inflicting upon her, after which they aided her in rising and supported her when on her feet. Why they did not massacre her she attributed to the interposition of Divine Providence in her behalf. There must have still been a little streak of humanity lingering in their ferocious breasts, for they concealed the scalp of her boy from her sight. Having restored her dormant senses by leading her knee-deep into the river, all proceeded to a shoal near the head of the island, between it and the mainland or 'Indian side of the country,' where her guards forced her before them into and through the water breast deep, she holding her child above the surface, and by their assistance she with her child safely reached the opposite shore.

"They all moved thence as fast as they could across the forks to the Big Buffalo, which, being a very rapid stream, her guards were obliged to aid her in crossing. Thence they took a straight course 'to the Connoquenessing Creek, the very place where Butler now stands.' (The narrator probably wrote or the compositor printed 'to' for 'toward'.) Thence they advanced along the Indian trail, heretofore mentioned, to the Little Buffalo, which they crossed at the very place where B. Sarver's mill stood when her narrative was written, and there ascended the hill. Having become weary of life, she fully determined to make these savages kill her, to end her fatigue and the prospective miseries and cruelties which she conceived awaited her. They were then moving in single file, one guard before and the other behind her. She stopped, withdrew from her shoulder a large powderhorn which, besides her child, they compelled her to carry, and threw it to the ground, closing her eyes momentarily expecting to feel their deadly tomahawks. But, contrary to her expectations, they replaced it on her shoulder. She threw it off a second time, expecting death. But they, indignant and frightful, again replaced it. She threw

it down a third time as far as she could over the rocks. While the
one that had been engaged in that little contest was recovering it,
the other one who had claimed her as his squaw and who had witnessed the affair, approached and said: 'Well done; you did right
and are a good squaw, and he is a lazy son of a b—h; he may
carry it himself.' That would-be husband of hers had evidently
a penchant for at least some of the polite language which he had
heard some of the white men use. The guards having changed
their positions, the latter taking the rear probably to prevent the
other from injuring her, they proceeded until they reached, shortly
before dark, without refreshment during the day, the Salt Lick on
the Connoquenessing, nearly two miles above the present site of
Butler, where there was an Indian camp made of stakes driven into
the ground sloping, covered with chestnut bark, long enough for
fifty men, appeared to have been occupied for some time, was very
much beaten, and from which large beaten paths extended in
different directions.

"Mrs. Harbison was taken that night from that camp into a
large dark bottom, about 300 rods up a run, where they cut away
the brush in a thicket, placed a blanket on the ground and permitted her to sit down with her child, which it was difficult for her
to manage, as they had pinioned her arms so that she had but
slight freedom of their use. There, without refreshment, thus
pinioned, with those two savages who had that day massacred in
her presence two of her boys, one of those guards on each side of
her, she passed the first night of her captivity.

"The next morning one of the guards left to watch the trail
they had traveled, and ascertain whether any of the white people
were in pursuit. During his absence the other, being the one who
claimed her as his squaw, and who had that day killed her second
boy, remained with her and took from his bosom the scalp which he
had so humanely concealed from her sight on the island, and stretched it upon a hoop. She then meditated revenge, attempting to take
the tomahawk which hung by his side, and deal a fatal blow, but
was, alas! detected. Her dusky wooer turned, cursed her, and
called her a Yankee, thus intimating that he understood her intention, and to prevent a repetition of her attempt, faced her. The
feigned reason that she gave for handling his tomahawk was, that
her child wanted to play with its handle. The guard that had
been out, returned from his lookout about noon, and reported that
he had not discovered any pursuers, and remained on guard while
the other went out for the same purpose. The one then guarding

her, after questioning her respecting the whites, the strength of their armies, and boasting of the achievements of the Indians in St. Clair's defeat, examined the plunder which he had brought from her house, among which he found her pocketbook, containing $10 in silver and a half-guinea in gold. All the food that she received from her guards on that Sunday and Monday was a piece of dried venison, about the size of an egg, each day, for herself and her child, but by reason of the blows which they had inflicted upon her jaws she could not eat any of it, and broke it up and gave it to her child. The guard who had been on the lookout in the afternoon returned about dark. Having been removed to another station in the valley of that run, that evening, she was again pinioned, guarded, and kept without either fire or refreshment, the second night of her captivity, just as she had been during the first one. She, however, fell asleep occasionally and dreamed several times of her arrival at Pittsburgh.

"Her ears were regaled the next morning by the singing of a flock of mocking-birds and robins that hovered over her irksome camp. To her imagination they seemed to sing, 'Get up and go off!' One of the guards having left at daybreak to watch the trail, the remaining one appeared to be sleeping, on observing which, she began to snore and feigned to be asleep. When she was satisfied that he had really fallen asleep, she concluded it was her time to escape. She would then have slain or disabled him, but for the crying of her child when out of her arms, which would of course awaken him and jeopardize her own life. She, therefore, was content to take a short gown, handkerchief, and child's frock from the pillow case containing the articles which the Indians had brought from her house, and escape, about half an hour after sunrise. Guided by those birds, and wisely taking a direction from instead of toward her home, in order to mislead her captors she passed over the hill, reached the Connoquenessing, about two miles from the point at which she and they had crossed it, and descended it through thorns and briers, and over rocks and precipices, with bare feet and legs. Having discovered by the sun and the course of the stream that she was advancing too far in her course from her home, she changed it, ascended the hill, sat down till sunset, determined her direction for the morrow by the evening star, gathered leaves for her bed, without food, her feet painful from the thorns that were in them, reclined and slept.

"About daybreak the next morning, she was awakened by that flock of birds which seemed to her to be attending and guiding her through the wilderness. When light enough to find her way, she started on her fourth days' trial of hunger and fatigue, advancing, according to her knowledge of courses and distances, toward the Allegheny River. Nothing unusual occurred during the day. It having commenced raining moderately about sunset, she prepared to make her bed of leaves, but was prevented by the crying of her child when she set him down. Listening she distinctly heard the footsteps of a man following her. Such was the condition of the soil that her footprints might be discerned. Fearing that she was thus exposed to a second captivity, she looked for a place of concealment and providentially discovered a large fallen tree, into whose thick foliage she crept with her child in her arms, where, aided by the darkness, she avoided detection by the Indian, whose footsteps she had heard. He having heard the child's cry, came to the spot whence the sound proceeded, halted, put down his gun, and was then so near to her that she distinctly heard the wiping-stick strike against his gun. Fortunately the child, pressed to her bosom, became warm and lay quiet during the continuance of their imminent peril. That Indian in the meantime, amidst that unbroken stillness, stood for nearly two hours with listening ears to again catch the sound of the child's cry; and so profound was that stillness that the beating of her own heart was all she heard, and which seemed to her to be so loud that she feared her dusky pursuer would hear it. Finally, answering the sound of a bell and a cry like a night-owl's, signals which his companions had given, and giving a horrid, soul-harrowing yell, he departed.

"Deeming it imprudent to remain there until morning, lest her tracks might be discovered in daylight, she endeavored, but found it difficult, by reason of her exhaustion, to remove; but compelled by a stern necessity and her love of life, she threw her coat around the child, with one end between her teeth, thus carrying the child with her teeth and one arm; with the other, she groped her way among the trees a mile or two, and there sat in the damp, cold air till morning.

"At daylight the next morning, wet, hungry, exhausted, wretched, she advanced across the headwaters of Pine Creek, not knowing what they were, and became alarmed by two freshly indented moccasin tracks of men traveling in the same direction that she was. As they were ahead of her, she concluded that she could see them as soon as they could see her. So she proceeded about three miles to a hunter's camp at 'the confluence of another branch of the creek, at which those who preceded her had kindled a fire, breakfasted, and leaving the fire burning, had departed. She afterward learned that they were spies, viz: James Anderson and John Thompson. Having become still more alarmed, she left that path, ascended a hill, struck another path, and while meditating there what to do, saw three deer advancing toward her at full speed. They turned to look and she, too, looked intently at their pursuers, and saw the flash and heard the instantaneous report of a gun. Seeing some dogs start after the deer, she crouched behind a large log for shelter, but fortunately not close to it; for, as she placed her hand on the ground to raise herself up, that she might see the hunters, she saw a large mass of rattlesnakes, her face being very near the top one, which lay coiled ready to strike its deadly fangs into her. With a supreme effort she left that dangerous spot, bearing to the left, reached the headwaters of Squaw Run, which through rain, she followed the rest of the day, her limbs so cold and shivering that she could not help giving an occasional involuntary groan. Though her jaws had sufficiently recovered from the pain caused by the blows inflicted upon her by the Indians, she suffered from hunger, procuring grapevines whenever she could and chewing them for what little sustenance they afforded. Having arrived at eveningtide within a mile of the Allegheny River, though she did not know it, at the root of a tree, holding her child in her lap and her head against the tree to shelter him from that night's drenching rain, she lodged that fifth night since her capture.

"She was unable for a considerable time the next morning to raise herself from the ground. Having, with a hard struggle, gained her feet, with nature so nearly exhausted and her spirits so completely depressed as they were, her progress was very slow and discouraging. After proceeding a short distance, she struck a path over which cattle had passed, following which for about a mile, she reached an uninhabited cabin on the river bottom. Not knowing where she was, and overcome with despair, she went to its threshold, having resolved to enter it and then lie down and die. But the thought of the suffering to be endured in that event, nerved her to another desperate effort to live. Hearing the sound of a cowbell, which awakened a gleam of hope in her extreme despondency, she followed that sound until she reached a point opposite the fort at Six-Mile Island, where, with feelings which can be more readily imagined than expressed, she beheld three men on the left bank of the river. They appeared to be unwilling to come for her when she called to them, and requested her to inform them who she was. When she told them that she was the one who had been taken prisoner up the Allegheny on the morning of the 22nd—in the narrative, it is Tuesday morning—and had escaped, they requested her to walk up the bank of the river for awhile, that they might see whether or not the Indians were making a decoy of her. When she told them her feet were so sore that she could not walk, James Closier came over for her in a canoe, while the other two stood on the river bank with cocked rifles, ready to fire in case she proved to be a decoy. When Closier approached the shore and saw her haggard and dejected appearance, he exclaimed: 'Who in the name of God, are you?' So great was the change wrought by her six days' sufferings that he, one of her nearest neighbors, did not recognize either her face or voice.

"When she arrived on the other side of the river, she was unable to move or to help herself in any way. The people at the fort ran to see her. Some of them took her child and others took her from the canoe to Mr. Carter's house. Then, all danger being passed, she enjoyed for the first time since her capture, the relief which comes from a copious flow of tears. Coming too suddenly to the fire and the smell of the victuals, she fainted. Those hospitable people might have killed her with their exuberant kindness, had not Maj. McCulley, who then commanded the line along the Allegheny River, fortunately arrived. When he saw her situation and the bountiful provision those good people were making for her, he immediately ordered her out of the house, away from the heat of the fire and the smell of the victuals which were being cooked, and prohibited her from taking anything but the whey of buttermilk, in very small quantities, which he himself administered. By that judicious treatment, she was gradually restored to health and strength of mind and body. Sarah Carter and Mary Ann Crozier—whether single or married is not stated—then began to extract the thorns from her feet and legs, to the number of 150, as counted by Felix Negley, who watched the operation, and who afterward resided at the mouth of Bull Creek (Tarentum). Many more were extracted the next evening. Some of the thorns went through and came out on the top of her feet. The skin and flesh were excruciatingly mangled, and hung in shreds to her feet and legs. So much exposure of her naked body to rain by night and heat of the sun by day, and carrying her child so long in her arms without relief, caused so much of her skin to come off that nearly her whole body was raw, and for two weeks her feet were not sufficiently healed to enable her to put them to the ground to walk.

"The news of her escape spread rapidly in various directions, reaching Pittsburgh the same evening of her arrival at the fort at Six-Mile Island. Two spies proceeded that evening to Coe's— now Tarentum—and the next morning to Reed's station, bearing the intelligence to her husband. A young man employed by the magistrates at Pittsburgh came for her to go thither for the purpose of making before one of them her affidavit of the facts connected with her captivity and escape, as was customary in early times, for publication. Being unable either to walk or ride on horseback, she was carried by some of the men into a canoe. After arriving at Pittsburgh she was borne in their arms to the office of John Wilkins, a justice of the peace and a son of the late Judge Wilkins of the United States Court, before whom she made her affidavit, May 28, 1792. The facts which she thus stated being circulated, caused a lively sensation in and for twenty miles around Pittsburgh. Her husband arrived there that evening, and the next morning she was conveyed to Coe's station. That evening she gave to those about her an account of the murder of her boy on Todd's Island, whither a scout went the next morning, found and buried the corpse, which had lain there unburied nine days.

"From her above-mentioned affidavit and her subsequent and more elaborate narrative, prepared from her statement by John Winter, the writer has condensed the foregoing facts, credited by the early settlers who were her neighbors, and which were made during those six terrible days of her life.

"She resided during several subsequent years at Salt Lick, a mile and a half north of Butler, on the Connoquenessing, at or near the site of the Indian camp mentioned in her affidavit and narrative. The last years of her life were passed in a cabin on the lot on the northeastern corner of Fourth Street and Mulberry Alley, Freeport, opposite the Methodist Episcopal Church, being the same lot now occupied by William Murphy, where she died on Saturday, December 9th, 1837."

Concerning her husband, John Harbison, Smith's "History of Armstrong County" relates the following incident:

"On a certain occasion Craig [Captain John Craig, commander of the blockhouse at Freeport], ordered a scouting party to make a tour of observation as far up the country as the mouth of Red Bank. They went, and on their return reported that they had not discovered any Indians. One of them, however, while on his death-bed, many years afterward, sent for Craig and confessed to him that, while on that tour, he and his comrades had captured an Indian, and after obtaining all the information possible from him, and not wishing to have the trouble of taking him as a prisoner to the blockhouse, they concluded to keep his capture a secret, and to dispatch him by tying him to a tree and each one shooting him, so that, all being equally guilty, there would be no danger of anyone disclosing their dread secret. Others of that scouting party, having been questioned about that affair, acknowledged to finding the Indian, but averred that John Harbison, who had just cause for a deadly hate toward all Indians, tomahawked him while he was conversing with another one of the party who understood the Indian language, and that they all agreed to keep that deed secret on Harbison's account."

Massa, however, in her narrative says that the killing of this Indian occurred on Puckety Creek, Westmoreland County.

The capture of Massa Harbison was the most memorable of any on the Allegheny frontier; yet no tablet has been erected on the site of the home from which she and her children were dragged by the ruthless savages, and on whose threshold her little son was killed. Her dust with that of many others of the pioneers, was removed to the new cemetery at Freeport some years ago, where a marble monument has been erected at her grave, bearing the following inscription:

Massa, Wife of John Harbison,
1770—1837
Captured By Indians May 22,
and Escaped May 27, 1792.

Murder on Fort Run Near Kittanning

In 1791 or 1792, an outrage occurred on Fort Run, near Kittanning, thus described in Smith's "History of Armstrong County":

"George Cook, who was born about 1764, was a soldier, a scout, and resided in the Manor [Manor Township] from either his boyhood or his early manhood until he was nearly four score, used to narrate to his neighbors, among whom was William McKellog, of 'Glentworth Park,' from whom the writer obtained a statement of these tragical facts: While Cook was a member of a scouting party who occupied a fort or blockhouse near Fort Run, so called from Fort Armstrong, some Indians made a small cord from the inner bark of a linden tree, with which they anchored a duck in a hole or pool in that run, formed by the action of the water about the roots of a sugar maple tree on its brink. Three of the scouting party, while out on a tour of duty, noticed the duck which must have appeared to them to be floating on the water. They set their guns up against a buttonwood tree, which with the sugar maple tree, was cut down after that land came into the possession of Richard Bailey. While they were stooping to catch the duck, as it was presumed they did, they were shot by Indians, probably three, because three reports of guns were heard. They fell dead into the run, whose water was colored with their blood. Hence that stream also bears the name of Bloody Run. The bodies of those three men were buried on a knoll opposite where they were shot, eight or ten rods higher up the river. The Indians were probably concealed among the weeds, which were then quite rank and abundant."

"Several of the men who were in the fort or blockhouse, on hearing the gun shots, came out, saw what had occurred, and discovered the Indians' trail, which, on that or the next day, they followed to the mouth of Pine Creek, and were about to give up the pursuit, when, looking up the hill, they saw a smoke on its face. After dark, they crossed the mouth of the creek, and ascertained the exact position in which the Indians were. The next morning they crawled as carefully and quickly as possible through the weeds and willows, until they thought they were within sure gunshot of the murderers of their comrades. They saw one of them mending his moccasin. The other two were, they thought, cooking meat for breakfast. They shot and killed two of the Indians, and captured the other. Having brought him past the mouth of that creek, on their return, and having reached 'an open grove,' they told him that they would give him a start of some distance ahead of them, and if he would beat them in running a race, he should be released. He accepted the offer, started, but was overtaken, fatally shot, and his body was left where he fell."

The Attack on the Party of Captain Sharp

In May, 1794, the Indians again made their appearance on the Allegheny and attacked a canoe going up the river to Franklin, killing John Carter and wounding William Cousins and Peter Kinner. They were unable to get any scalps on this occasion, as the other occupants paddled it out of their reach.

Major Denny mentions the above attack in his journal under June 1, 1794, stating that this band of Indians then "crossed to the Kiskiminetas and unfortunately fell in with a Kentucky boat full of women and children, with but four men, lying to, feeding their cattle." This was the attack on Captain Sharp, which is thus described in Smith's "History of Armstrong County":

"Among the pioneers in the Plum Creek region was Captain Andrew Sharp, who had been an officer in the Revolutionary service, under Washington. He, with his wife and infant child, emigrated to this region in 1784, and purchased, settled upon, and improved the tract of land, consisting of several hundred acres, on which are Shelocta and the United Presbyterian Church, near the county line.

"Captain Sharp, after residing about ten years on his farm, revisited his kindred in Cumberland County, procured a supply of school books and Bibles for his children, and returned to his home in the wilderness. Determined that his children should have facilities for education which did not exist there, he traded his farm there for one in Kentucky. In the spring of 1794, he removed with his family to Black Lick Creek, where he either built or purchased a flatboat, in which he, his wife and six children, a Mr. Connor, wife and five children, a Mr. Taylor, wife and one child, and Messrs. McCoy and Connor, single men, twenty in all, with their baggage and household effects, embarked on the proposed passage down the Kiskiminetas and Allegheny rivers to Pittsburgh, and thence on to Kentucky. Low water in the Black Lick rendered their descent down it difficult. They glided down the Conemaugh and Kiskiminetas to a point two miles below the falls of the latter, at the mouth of Two Mile Run, below the present site of Apollo. Capt. Sharp tied the boat there, and went back for the canoe which had been detached while crossing the falls. When he returned the children were gathering berries and playing on the bank; the women were preparing supper, and the men who led the horses had arrived. It was about an hour and a half before sunset. A man then came along and reported that the Indians were near. The women and children were called into the boat, and the men having charge of the horses tied them on shore.

"It was then thought best that the party should go to the home of David Hall, who was the father of David Hall, of North Buffalo Township, this county, and the grandfather of Rev. David Hall D. D., the present (1883) pastor of the Presbyterian Church at Indiana, Pennsylvania, to spend the night. While the men were tying the horses, seven Indians concealed behind a large fallen tree, on the other side of which the children had been playing half-an-hour before, fired on the party in the boat. Capt. Sharp's right eyebrow was shot off by the first firing. Taylor is said to have mounted one of his horses and fled to the woods, leaving his wife and child to the care and protection of others. While Capt. Sharp was cutting one end of the boat loose, he received a bullet wound in his left side, and, while cutting the other end loose, received another wound in his right side. Nevertheless, he succeeded in removing the boat from its fastenings before the Indians could enter it, and, discovering an Indian in the woods, and calling for his gun, which his wife handed to him, shot and killed the Indian. While the boat was in the whirlpool, it whirled around for two and a half hours. When the open side of the boat, that is, the side on which the baggage was not piled up for a breastwork, was toward the land, the Indians fired into it. They followed it twelve miles down the river, and bade those in it to disembark, else they would fire into them again. Mrs. Connor and her eldest son—a young man—wished to land. The latter requested the Indians to come to the boat, informing them that all the men had been shot. Capt. Sharp ordered him to desist, saying that he would shoot him, if he did not. Just then young Connor was shot by one of the Indians, and fell dead across Mrs. Sharp's feet. McCoy was killed. All the women and children escaped injury. Mr. Connor was severely wounded. After the Indians ceased following, Capt. Sharp became so much exhausted by his exertions and loss of blood, that his wife was obliged to manage the boat all night. At daylight the next morning they were within nine miles of Pittsburgh. Some men on shore, having been signaled, came to their assistance. One of them preceded the party in a canoe, so that when they reached Pittsburgh, a physician was ready to attend upon them. Other preparations had been made for their comfort and hospitable reception, by the good people of that place.

"Capt. Sharp, having suffered severely from his wounds, died July 8, 1794, forty days after he was wounded, with the roar of cannon, so to speak, reverberating in his ears, which he had heard celebrating the eighteenth anniversary of our national independence, which he, under Washington, had helped achieve. Two of his daughters were the only members of his family that could follow his remains to the grave. He was buried with the honors of war, in the presence of a large concourse of people. His youngest child was then only eleven days old. As soon as his widow had sufficiently recovered, she was conducted by her eldest daughter, Hannah, to his grave.

"Col. Charles Campbell, in his letter to Gov. Mifflin, June 5th, 1794, respecting the stopping of the draft of the support of the Presque Isle station, stated: 'The Indians, on the evening of May 30th, fired on a boat that left my place to go to Kentucky, about two miles below the Falls of the Kiskiminetas, killed three persons and wounded one, who were all the men in the boat, which drifted down to about twelve miles above Pittsburgh, whence they were aided by some persons on their way to Pittsburgh.'

"Mrs. Sharp—her maiden name was Ann Wood—and her children were removed to their kindred in Cumberland County, Pennsylvania. Having remained there three years, they returned to the farm near Crooked Creek, of which they had been repossessed, where the family remained together for a long time.

"Mrs. Sharp's death occurred fifteen years after her husband's. Their daughter Agnes is said to have been the first white child born this side, or west, of Crooked Creek, in this section of Pennsylvania. She was born on that farm February 21, 1785; married to David Ralston in 1803, and, after his death, to James Mitchell in 1810, and died August 2, 1862, and was buried in the Crooked Creek cemetery."

The attack on Capt. Sharp and his party was the last Indian outrage in Pennsylvania, except the murder of the Wigton family, in Butler County, June 30th, 1843, by Samuel Mohawk, while returning to his home on the upper Allegheny, from Pittsburgh, to which place he had assisted in floating a raft of lumber down the Allegheny. This outrage, however, does not belong to the period of Indian occupation.

CHAPTER XXXIV.

Wayne's Victory and Final Peace

HE uprising of the Western Indians and the raids upon the Western Pennsylvania frontier continuing, as we have seen, the country, burning under the disgrace of Harmar's and St. Clair's defeats, called loudly for a third expedition. Then President Washington chose General Wayne, "Mad Anthony", the hero of Stony Point, to lead the expedition. He was a strict disciplinarian, and determined to avoid the faults which brought overwhelming and inglorious defeat upon his predecessors. He arrived in Pittsburgh in June, 1792, having been furnished with instructions from Washington in which it was stated "that another defeat would be irredeemably ruinous to the reputation of the Government." His force was to consist of five thousand men, carefully drilled, and to be called "The Legion of the United States."

In December, 1792, his legion was taken to the beautiful plain overlooking the Ohio, about twenty miles below Pittsburgh, where sham battles were fought and daily drills held. The place of this winter camp is known as Legionville to this day. While here, he was visited by the old Indian chiefs, Guyasuta and Cornplanter, then friends of the United States.

Breaking camp on April 13th, 1793, Wayne led his forces to Cincinnati, where they were reinforced by regulars and mounted militia from Kentucky. It was so late in the season before all his forces were collected and supplies procured, that the offensive movement was delayed until the next spring. During the winter, Wayne remained at a fort which he had built on a western fork of the Little Miami, swept the country between this place and the Miami villages, and took possession of the ground upon which St. Clair was defeated, erecting a fort there which he called Fort Recovery. His force now consisted of thirty-six hundred troops.

In the meantime, in the spring of 1793, commissioners representing the United States met the western tribes in council, and proposed that, in consideration of the lands ceded by the treaty at Fort Harmar, the United States should pay the Indians "a large sum of money, or goods, besides a full yearly supply of such articles as they needed." The chiefs replied that money was of no value to them. Said they: "You talk to us about concessions. It appears strange that you should expect any from us, who have only been defending our just rights against your invasions. We want peace. Restore to us our country, and we shall be enemies no longer."

In the summer of 1794, Wayne was joined by General Charles Scott, with sixteen hundred mounted volunteers from Kentucky. He then moved forward, skirmishing with bands of lurking Indians as he advanced. Arriving at the site of the present village of Defiance, Ohio, Wayne erected Fort Defiance, and made proposals of peace with the Indians. These were rejected contrary to the advice of Little Turtle, and in accordance with the advice of Blue Jacket. Said Little Turtle: "We have beaten the enemy twice under separate commanders. We cannot expect the same good fortune always to attend us. The Americans are now led by a chief who never sleeps. The night and the day are alike to him, and during all the time that he has been marching upon our villages, notwithstanding the watchfulness of our young men, we have never been able to surprise him." Indeed, so stealthy had been Wayne's advance that the Indians nicknamed him "the Blacksnake".

On the morning of August 20th, Wayne advanced ahd had proceeded about five miles, when his advance guard was fired upon heavily by Indians in concealment, and fell back. He then formed his men in two lines where a tornado had blown down a number of trees in the woods—a circumstance which gave the engagement the name of the "Battle of the Fallen Timbers." The fallen trees made cavalry operations difficult, and afforded a shelter for the two thousand Indians and Canadians who were posted among them in three lines. Wayne's militia charged impetuously with the bayonet, leaping over the logs and delivering a well-directed fire, while General Scott with his mounted volunteers, turned the right flank of the enemy by a circuitous movement, and Colonel Campbell, with his legionary cavalry, turned the enemy's left flank. The Indians were driven for more than two miles through the forest, and decisively beaten. Nine of their chiefs lay dead on the field.

The Indians were driven under the guns of the British fort in the neighborhood, and so strong was the resentment of Wayne's men against the English, that it was with difficulty that they could be restrained from storming the fort. Indeed, many of the Kentucky troops advanced within gunshot of the fort and hurled a volley of curses against the garrison. Captain Campbell, the British commandant, sent a message to Wayne, complaining of this insult and demanding by what authority Wayne's troops trespassed upon the precincts of the British garrison. Mad Anthony replied in terms little less polite than those of the Kentucky troops, informing Captain Campbell that his only chance of safety was silence and civility. Then Wayne's troops destroyed the Indian cornfields, orchards, trading-houses, and stores. In addition to breaking forever the power of the western tribes, one of the results of the battle of the Fallen Timbers was the surrender to the United States of Niagara, Detroit, Mackinac, Miami, and other posts hitherto held by the British, from which bases they had assisted and encouraged the Indians in their hostility against the Americans.

Finally, on August 3rd, 1795, the conquered tribes signed the Treaty of Greenville, Darke County, Ohio, by the terms of which they ceded to the United States 25,000 square miles of territory north of the Ohio River, about two-thirds of the present state of Ohio. That part of Pennsylvania west of the Allegheny River and hitherto known as "the Indian country", henceforth was free from Indian raids. Settlers rapidly took up their abode in the fertile region, felling the forest, cultivating the virgin soil, and laying the foundation of the material prosperity which there abounds today. Meanwhile the Indian continued his march toward the untrodden West before the great tide of white immigration that was pressing him away from the lands he and his forefathers considered their own, as the gift of the Great Spirit, Who had stocked the forests with game and the streams with fish for His Red Children.

CONCLUSION

The first overt act of war committed by the Indians of Pennsylvania against the Province was the attack on the German settlers on Penn's Creek, October 16th, 1755. Less than forty years elapsed between that event and the Treaty of Greenville. Before this latter event took place, all the Indians of Pennsylvania had removed from her borders, except the few hundred Senecas on Cornplanter's Reservation in Warren County, and a few families here and there who fondly lingered on choice hunting grounds in the western counties. The recital of the terrible atrocities committed by the Pennsylvania Indians, during these forty years, is a shocking and appalling story; but over against these, must be placed the atrocities committed upon the untutored Indian by the anointed children of education and civilization—the massacre of the Conestogas by the "Paxton Boys", the murder of ten Indians by Frederick Stump, the murder of the family of Logan, chief of the Mingoes, the murder of Cornstalk and his son, the murder of the friendly old Delaware, Joseph Wipey, the murder of the Delaware, Dr. John, and his family, and the butchering of the Moravian Indians by the settlers of Washington County.

There were many frontiersmen who, actuated by unrelenting hatred for the whole Indian race, made no distinction between good Indians and bad Indians. They were simply Indian hunters and killers at all times, whether in peace or in war, and without regard to age or sex. A good example of these was Tom Quick, "the Indian killer", who is said to have claimed on his death bed, in 1795, that he had killed ninety-nine Indians, and begged that an old Indian who lived near might be brought to him, in order that he might kill him, and thus bring his record to an even hundred.

Nor should we lose sight of the fact that hundreds of atrocities perpetrated by the Indians on the settlers of Pennsylvania, during the Revolutionary War, were committed at the instigation of the British and British agents, who paid the Indians substantial rewards for American scalps. Furthermore, we should remember, as pointed out in former chapters, that Pennsylvania gave rewards for Indian scalps, not exempting Indian boys and girls over the age of ten years. Think of offering a reward for the scalp of a ten year old Indian girl!

In weighing the conduct and estimating the character of the Pennsylvania Indians, we must not lose sight of degradation of character wrought among them by the abuses of the rum traffic. Rum was the curse of the Red Man, and their leading chiefs recognized it as such. Hence, from the very beginning of this traffic among them, we find a series of protests by their chiefs to the Pennsylvania Authorities. The great Shikellamy, it will be remembered, shortly after taking up his residence on the Susquehanna, notified the Colonial Authorities that, if the soul destroying traffic were not better regulated, friendly relations between the Six Nations and the Province would cease. "The rum ruins us", said Scarouady at the Carlisle Conference of October, 1753. And Conrad Weiser, than whom no one was better qualified to speak, in writing to the Provincial Council, November 28th, 1747, characterized the havoc wrought among the Indians by the rum traffic as "an abomination before God and man."

Unhappily, too, the Pennsylvania Indians came into direct and frequent contact with the worst element among the whites—

the English traders, who, taking advantage of the Indians' inordinate appetite for rum, cheated them out of their skins and furs, and debauched their women. The Pennsylvania Assembly, in a message to Governor Hamilton, February 27th, 1754, characterized the traders as "the vilest of our own inhabitants and convicts imported from Great Britain and Ireland." The traders of the other colonies, many of whom entered Pennsylvania, were no better. Said Governor Dinwiddie of Virginia, in a letter to Governor Hamilton of Pennsylvania, May 21st, 1753: "The Indian traders, in general, appear to me to be a set of abandoned wretches." In a word, the English traders, with few exceptions, were a vile and infamous horde, who, instead of contributing to the betterment of the Indian, corrupted and debauched him.

And what shall we say of the land frauds, especially the Walking Purchase of 1737 and the Albany Purchase of 1754? The least that we can say is that they had much to do with alienating the Delawares and Shawnees and causing them to bring upon Pennsylvania the bloodiest Indian invasion in American history.

Furthermore, the settling of the whites on lands not purchased from the Indians, especially in the valleys of the Juniata, Monongahela, and Youghiogheny, greatly aggravated the Red Man. The white man's inordinate greed for land aroused the wild passions of the children of the forest.

The Pennsylvania Indians loved the hills, the mountains, the valleys, and the streams of this great state. They exulted in the fact that they were the first owners of this vast region which they were fighting and dying to protect. They were proud spirits who were born free, and loved freedom more than life itself. They were a proud race that abhorred the thought of extinction. Now that they have yielded their pleasant land to the stronger hand of the white man, and live only in the songs and chronicles of the race that pressed them away from their loved hunting grounds, may these chronicles be faithful to their rude virtues as men. They were children of nature. They had no background of centuries of Christian civilization—no knowledge of the God of Revelation. Down the perspective of history comes the impartial verdict that the fate forced upon them by a more highly favored race was galling and unjust. And it shall be more tolerable for them, in the Judgment than their conquerors, the children of the God of Revelation.

THE END

Chronological Table of Some Leading Events in the Indian History of Pennsylvania

INDEX